. . . And So the Snake Spoke

. . . And So the Snake Spoke

Geoffrey Dixon

Node A Publishing

Paperback Edition January 2021
ISBN 978-3-96749-006-0
Node A Publishing is an imprint of Node A Consulting GmbH
82031 Grünwald, Germany - Registered: AG München HR B 174 685
Contact: publishing@node-a.com

'Book One' was first published under the title
'The Wolf Cataclysm' in August 2019 - © Geoffrey Dixon, 2019.
Printed and bound by Amazon Media EU S.à r.l., Luxembourg
Bibliographic information by the *Deutsche Nationalbibliothek* is available via http://dnb.d-nb.de.

To Tom, Roze and Carla, forever my loving source of brilliant inspiration...

...and to Ann for encouraging me to finally finish the story, and continue with the sequel

...and last but not least, I also dedicate this literary journey to David Taylor (DLT), who forged and crafted my mathematical thinking long ago.

Preface

We all want to know what happens in the end. Why were the pyramids built? What do they represent? Why is the World covered in dolmens, stone circles, and other complex megalithic structures and hundreds of similar friezes of ancient geometrical cave art?

If you have been trying to build a time machine to find out, you can stop. This book saves you the trouble.... I only hope you are brave enough to face the harsh reality and consequences of your desire to know the truth.

GD

Contents

Book One

Book Two

Annex

Book One

1 Cairo: some lost hieroglyphs, trouble at the museum, then a warning

Cairo, Egypt.

Suddenly the movie screen paused, and the captain's announcement cut through the in-flight entertainment.

'Good Morning ladies and gentlemen, this is the captain. I hope you enjoyed the flight and our in-flight service. We will be landing in about 30 minutes. I have just received the latest weather reports from Cairo. It's a beautiful day. It's already 26 degrees Celsius, that's 78 degrees Fahrenheit in old money. We'll be approaching the airport from the Mediterranean across the Nile Delta. We're not expecting any delays. If there is any change, I'll get back to you.' Then the broadcast abruptly ended.

Whatever the film had been about, Chad actually didn't care anymore, and he took off his headset and peered out through the window. Below him he could see the shimmering blue of the Mediterranean, and then Egypt's coast and the spectacular Nile delta. In fact, the early morning descent into Cairo International Airport was now a relief after the 17-hour journey from New York. The stopovers in Detroit and Amsterdam had been bearable and Chad had got a decent amount of sleep. It had certainly been worth paying that extra for premium economy.

Some half hour later, the aircraft reached the gate and Chad joined other premium economy passengers for priority disembarkation. Another perk, he thought. In the main corridor, he was soon stuck behind a slowly moving hoard of passengers from another flight, but he was now eager to get outside. With some deft side steps, he quickly manoeuvred past the less keen and was early reaching the kiosk to buy a tourist visa. Twenty-five good American dollars later, visa in hand, he was ready for passport control. Finally, he was at the head of the queue and he handed his passport and papers to the impassive looking official. The elderly immigration officer barely gave Chad even a cursory glance before keying in his passport and 30-day tourist visa details. He stamped the papers, stapling one in Chad's passport before handing everything back. 'Thanks,' said Chad. The official mildly smiled and lightly nodded his head in reply.

Chad Walker, a geologist with a keen interest in Egyptology, had now officially arrived in Egypt. He only needed his basic luggage to enable his few extra days' vacation to begin. Chad strolled optimistically towards the baggage-reclaim area.

Grabbing his scuffed leather bag from Cairo airport's clattering luggage conveyor, he breathed a sigh of relief. Despite having persuaded the New York check-in staff at La Guardia that his single bag was compact and had material he needed to work through on the flight, he had failed to convince the KLM boarding gate personnel, who had relieved him of his 12kg bag just before boarding. No worries, he was now reunited with essential clothes and papers — enough to tide him over for three days until his wife Jeanette and 12-year-old daughter Chloe arrived on Thursday. Why they had gone up to Toronto to visit her mother, was not worth arguing about. He could have argued, but she was going anyway. This way, he could at least spend a few extra days before they continued down to Sydney on Saturday for his older brother Tom's fiftieth.

Like many North African airports, Cairo was teeming with travellers. Chad needed to change some money and he headed over to the ATMs. After waiting in line for what seemed an age, he was finally in front of a machine. Despite the very confusing user interface, his mood was quickly lifted when he eventually managed to withdraw $500 in Egyptian pounds. Now he could escape the airport and see the sights.

What first? The hotel. Chad headed outside into the heat of the day towards the taxi rank. Moving slowly along with the dragging crowd of unsteady passengers, he needed to remain vigilant to avoid incumbents who were struggling to steer unwieldy trolleys of oversized suitcases.

'Welcome to Cairo — the City of a Thousand Minarets', the signs declared, while Chad slowly shuffled forward in the taxi queue. The air was quite unpleasant. It was hot and humid and stank like an open sewer. The endless cacophony of car horns and shouting, all combined with the stench of diesel exhaust fumes, which succeeded to reduce any feeling of good karma. Almost there now. He had been warned that Cairo was one of the most densely populated cities in the world, and there was

already every reason to believe that. Taxis were battling to get in and out, while unlicensed drivers, heavily laden with passengers and luggage, continually tried to stop directly in front of the doors. An angry altercation broke out between one taxi driver, who was attempting to pull away, and another driver, who had stopped his vehicle dead in front of the other taxi to unload. A middle-aged woman dressed in brightly coloured drapes, in the back of the departing taxi, was shouting and gesticulating angrily as the driver of the car ahead opened the boot and proceeded to unload.

Finally, it was Chad's turn, and pretty soon, a slightly rusting, black and yellow taxi with shiny green leather seats, drew up alongside. The opportunity to escape all this chaos was a welcome relief. He threw his bag onto the back seat and climbed in, closing the door behind him. There was even air-conditioning in this old wreck, and the pipe music from the Arabic radio station was already helping to cut out the stress of the bustle. 'Where are you going?' the driver asked.

'Inter-Continental Hotel please, er, somewhere near Tahrir Square?'

'OK, you mean the Inter-Continental in Corniche al Nil,' the driver answered, as he slowly swung the taxi out into the traffic and pulled away. 'You American?'

'Yeah, from Boston.'

'Oh. I have a granddaughter studying in America.'

'Where is she studying?' Chad asked.

'California, at UCLA. She is studying medicine.'

'That's a good University, but quite a challenge to fund,' Chad added.

The driver nodded. 'She's doing OK, but I do send her a little money from time to time.'

Outside, the day was on, and Chad was preparing to embrace it; it was already 10 a.m. and getting hotter. Maybe he should have taken that later flight. Arriving in Cairo mid-morning was something to avoid.

Looking through the window, Chad observed a yellow haze of pollution hanging over the city skyline, and the traffic was diabolical. Within half a mile of the airport, their progress had slowed to barely walking pace as they edged forward through a sea of cars and trucks. The taxi driver was constantly shifting lane, wherever he felt they could gain those few extra ten metres or so. Eager street vendors were wandering between the slowly moving traffic jam, offering fruit and newspapers and bottled water. Chad's driver remained calm yet focused, somewhat unphased by the vendors. He seemed to be a bit of a veteran.

'So how long have you been a taxi driver?' Chad asked.

'I started after I came out of the army in 1984,' the taxi driver replied.

'More than thirty years! Wow! How long have you had this car?'

'This car? I bought it new, the day I started. It still runs fine. My son has a garage repair shop. He keeps it running. You know, in the old days, I drove people everywhere. I even took tourists down to Luxor and back. That's more than six hundred miles round trip. I was often away several days at a time. I don't do that anymore. Driving at night can be dangerous. I prefer to drive only during the day. What are your plans? Are you on holiday or is it business?'

'A short holiday. Just enough time to see the sights, visit the pyramids,' Chad replied. 'Is it safe for me here? No trouble for American tourists?'

'Cairo is safe now. We've had a lot of support from America over the years. We had some trouble down in the Nile Valley in the eighties and nineties - rising tension with Islamic fundamentalists who were targeting the tourist industry. Then there was the Arab Spring and the Muslim Brotherhood. America soon became our friend again. President Obama's *at-a-distance* détente was appreciated. Some stories about tourist safety are sometimes distorted by the media, but I would still be a little careful to avoid *Minia, Asyout* and *Sohag*.'

'Ah, so the tombs at *Bani Hassan* in Minia and the *Temple of Abydos* in Sohag are off limits?' Chad asked, somewhat concerned.

'You can get police escort, if you want to go it alone, but I recommend joining an official tour. So, you are interested in Egyptian history?'

'Yes, I have done quite a bit of reading, although this is my first trip to Egypt. I'm really interested in the pyramids. I'd like to spend some time at Giza. There seem to be a lot of unanswered questions.'

'Yes, many. Who built them and when and why? I can take you to Giza. When do you want to go? I can give you my mobile number. Just call me.'

'Well, how long does it take to get there?' Chad asked tentatively.

'Around 30 minutes, depending on the traffic. My sister lives nearby. If you like, I can take you to Giza, and I can spend time with her until you call me. Then I can take you back to your hotel. If you want to go today, that's also possible.'

Chad was only thinking as far as the hotel, and this driver wasn't pushy, just throwing up some options. Now Giza was already a possibility for the day.

'Well, I was planning a few trips. Today is possible. Best not waste the day. I just need to check in at the hotel.'

'No problem,' the driver replied.

Chad sat back in the taxi and looked out at Cairo, drinking in this very different and exciting culture. The raw and vivid expression of the Egyptian people was very different from life back in New England. This was very refreshing. They soon cleared the traffic jams and the journey from the airport took around 35 minutes.

'That's the Inter-Continental Hotel over there,' the taxi driver explained. 'I'll drop you off, then you can call me on this number.'

He handed Chad his business card. *'Tau Taxi'* was embossed in silver lettering on a shiny green card with a mobile number and some address in Cairo.

'My nickname is Tau. It means lion,' he added with a smile.

The taxi pulled up at the front of the Inter-Continental Hotel.

'How much do I pay you now?' Chad asked.

'You can pay me at the end. If I'm taking you to Giza and back, then it's easier that way.'

'OK, I'm good with that. I guess this may take 15 minutes or so. Shall I send you a text?'

'No, just call me. I won't answer it. I will then pick you up from there,' Tau said pointing. 'Just type in my number and call me now to be sure, then I will have your number also.'

Chad carefully typed Tau's number into his cell phone, adding the +20 prefix for Egypt. Tau's old Nokia phone rang, and he cut the call. 'OK, see you soon,' he said.

This was good. Chad now had a plan. Rather than just waste the day in and around the hotel, his sightseeing holiday would start right away. The Inter-Continental Hotel was also only a short walk from the Egyptian Museum, and he was intending to pass many hours there. A brilliant jewel in Cairo's crown, the Egyptian Museum housed the finest collection of Egyptian antiquities anywhere in the world.

The hotel looked impressive. Chad had thoughtfully chosen the Inter-Continental for Jeanette because it overlooked the Nile. He had even managed to book a room high up on the 15th floor at the southern end of the building. From the balcony, there was a spectacular view both westward over the Nile and eastward over Cairo's sprawling Metropolis. He had imagined a few romantic evenings of he and Jeanette toasting one another from that vantage point. Chad was sure his wife and daughter would be happy here for a few days. He walked up to the check-in desk.

'Yes sir? Good Morning. You have a reservation?' the girl at the hotel front desk asked warmly.

'Good Morning. Yes, under Walker, Chad.'

'One moment sir.'

After some typing, the hotel receptionist then looked up. 'Mr Chad? We have no reservation under that name sir. I will just check with our manager.'

'No, no, it's Chad *Walker*, family name Walker. I have the reservation paper somewhere here.'

Chad unlocked the small padlock on his old leather bag, releasing the zip and took out a travel pouch, stuffed with various papers. He selected one, 'Here you are.'

'Of course! Yes, we have your reservation Dr Walker. You are booked into room 1515. That is on the fifteenth floor. I see a note here with your reservation that your wife and daughter are arriving in three days on Thursday. There is a door connecting the adjoining room 1516 for your daughter. Breakfast is from seven o'clock. In your room you will find a list of all the hotel services. I will just need to take your credit card details.'

Chad handed her his Amex card, 'Here'.

'Thank you, Dr Walker. Would you like a newspaper in the morning? I can offer you the *Herald and Tribune*.'

'That would be great.'

'Thank you, Dr Walker, and please enjoy your stay.'

'Thanks.'

Chad took the lift up to his room, took a very quick shower and changed into a fresh set of clothes then called Tau's mobile number. It rang twice and then he cut the call. He took a small grey canvas rucksack out of his leather bag, put in two bottles of water, which were standing on a side table, and added a packet of peanuts from the mini bar. Grabbing his money belt and key card, he left his room then took the lift back down to the lobby. Walking out of the lift, he could see Tau's taxi through the revolving door. He quickly walked outside and climbed in the back.

'Hello again,' Tau said, with a smile.

'Hi, good to see you! Let's go to Giza. I'm quite excited about seeing the pyramids. Are you still OK to bring me back?'

'Well, I just called my sister, and she's actually very happy for me to visit. Whenever I drive out to Giza, I try to call in. Her husband died last year. He worked at the Egyptian Museum for more than forty years. He was one of the most senior curators of ancient artefacts. He was a very interesting man and very knowledgeable. I really recommend that you do visit the museum.'

'Yes, I certainly intend to do that,' Chad replied.

They were soon on the ring road heading south. It was approaching 11 a.m. and the day was getting even hotter.

'I'm going to drop you close to one of the main entrances, which is where I will pick you up. It takes around ten minutes to drive from my sister's place so please be patient. The traffic can be really bad.'

'OK. That's great. I'm happy to pay you when we get to Giza.'

'No, don't worry. You can pay me when we arrive back at the hotel,' Tau said reassuringly.

'Your brother-in-law, did he have a special area of interest?'

'Yes, he was interested in deciphering hieroglyphs. He even had a small private collection, which he had put together over many years. He gave many to the museum I believe. He died of cancer. It was only last year, in fact just before he died, that he told me he had found many artefacts on his own allotment patch. Can you believe that? He was certain they were significant. I thought he was joking of course. Why on earth would there be artefacts on an allotment? I have taken over that allotment now. I always wondered what he was on about. According to my sister, he did make some notes about them, but he rarely spoke of them, even with her.'

'I'm actually quite interested in hieroglyphs myself,' Chad added.

'Well, I'm happy to show you his collection of old stones at the allotment if you want. I doubt if you will find it as interesting as the pyramids.'

'I have several days. My wife and daughter are arriving on Thursday. They wouldn't be at all interested. It all sounds pretty mysterious.'

Chad felt quite inspired. Nevertheless, this did start to sound quite surreal. A taxi driver with a family member who had worked at the Egyptian Museum as curator, and one who had found artefacts on his own allotment patch, and now an option, to see them first hand.

'It's actually very close now. If you look left you can see those cultivated strips over there,' Tau said pointing. 'This is the Mariotia Road. My brother-in-law grew up nearby in Taha Bogdaia. His family owned those allotments for quite a long time.'

'So, do we know what the significance is? Or are there artefacts all over the city?'

'I don't think so. My brother-in-law was adamant. He was collecting for years and he said the allotments seemed to be unique. You sound interested already. Do you really want to see them? It's very close. I'm happy to make a detour.'

'OK. Yeah, let's do it, I'm intrigued.'

'OK. I need to get off this ring road then double back. We can stop, and you can take as long as you like. Don't worry. You won't be on the meter. I only charge when we are driving. I can even pick up some lettuces and tomatoes for my sister. She will like that.'

As the main motorway turned west, Tau took a turnoff north and then doubled back, eventually passing under the motorway. After a few more turns through built up areas, the taxi eventually came to the allotments. They looked pretty typical: neat rows of seedlings and various other plants, all in verdant abundance thanks to copious watering no doubt. Above them, the traffic on the ring road roared by unceasingly.

'Here we are. As I said, it's only an allotment but I can show you the collection. They are in a wooden chest in the shed.'

Tau parked the taxi along the dried-out verge and Chad followed him along a small path towards a rickety wooden structure at the end of the allotment.

Tau undid the padlock on the shed door, slid back the bolt and dragged the door open. It was stiflingly hot inside. He opened a skylight in the roof to let the hot stale air out. Within moments the inside of the shed was just about bearable. Under rolls of well-used, rusted chicken wire was a large object obscured by an old tattered purple blanket. Lifting the old blanket revealed a well-varnished chest of drawers. Tau reached up to a plant pot on a high shelf, took out a key, unlocked the chest and pulled open the top drawer. Inside, under a sheet of surprisingly clean, clear glass was an arrangement of stone fragments, bearing hieroglyphs, all resting on a sheet of polystyrene, as good as anything you might see in a museum.

'Wow,' murmured Chad. 'They're amazing! Can I examine them?'

'Of course, the glass opens here,' Tau explained, and lifted up the glass. 'You take your time, I'm going gardening.' With that, Tau disappeared off into the neat rows of vegetables.

Chad's eyes immediately fell upon a large, flat rock carved with hieroglyphs and a pattern of five parallel lines. He then recognised immediately the hieroglyph for the Nile: a feather next to a hemisphere over a lens beside a bird and three wavy lines. Why had he kept this one? Could it be significant? Five lines seemed to break off at the edge, as if the inscription continued. He looked out through the grimy window and could see Tau pulling up lettuces and onions for his sister.

The other stone fragments were equally interesting. If Tau's brother-in-law had presented many to the museum, what was it about these artefacts, which were worth keeping? A serious expert in the field and artefact collector would have had a hunch about something. What could it have been and what clues did this collection have?

Chad pushed back the top drawer and opened the one below. This contained similar fragments and a piece of what looked like carved ivory — again covered in hieroglyphs. Two others had the same five parallel lines with additional symbols. One showed an inverted 'v' above the five lines.

Chad went through all five drawers. Together they contained perhaps more than a hundred fragments. Outside, Chad could see Tau bundling up some lettuces and other vegetables and laying them in old wooden seed trays. He seemed almost ready to leave. Other fragments had a five-pointed star under a semi-circle beside a stretched isosceles triangle. That had to be Sopdet, which the ancient Egyptian astronomers associated with Sirius, the Dog-Star, Chad thought. In fact, quite a few fragments seemed to combine Sopdet with the Nile and the partial connecting hieroglyph of five horizontal lines. Surely these sequences were pretty common. The artefacts all bore hieroglyphs. There was no *demotic script* like on the Rosetta stone, which suggested that they were very old. According to the conventional interpretation of the Rosetta Stone, Demotic script would have dated them to 650BC at the earliest.

Sopdet in Boat

Chad heard a noise behind him and he turned to see Tau at the door. 'What do you think? Anything special?' he asked.

'Yes, they seem very interesting. The big question is: What hunch did your brother-in-law have about them?' Chad remarked. 'Do you know what kind of things he gave to the museum?'

'Well, they did name a collection after him. There is one display case with the artefacts he donated,' Tau added.

'My phone camera isn't working, and I left my proper camera back in the hotel. It would have been great to have had the opportunity to compare the ones in the museum with these two at least,' Chad reasoned.

'You are welcome to take a few with you if you like, but I would want them back afterwards. You know, the ones he gave to the museum? He never admitted where he'd found them. They all come from here, every one of them, including a few, I guess, from his neighbouring gardeners! He just didn't want a whole team of archaeologists digging over his allotment. He kept the Department of Antiquities wondering for years. He claimed to have found them way out in the Western Desert. They even sent out an archaeological team once to one of his dreamed-up locations. They were out there for weeks. When they returned with some valuable shards of pottery, discovered purely by chance, he was congratulated!'

'Well, may I borrow just these two?'

'Of course.' Tau then closed up the chest, locked it and replaced the purple blanket and heaped over the chicken wire, recreating the image of an uninteresting pile of old junk. After putting the key back in the pot on the shelf, he closed the skylight and closed and locked the shed padlock. 'Look, I will place the key under this brick. If you want to come back to replace those two artefacts and I can't bring you, at least you can gain access.'

'Tau, thanks. I promise to return them.'

'So, what do you want to do now?' Are we still going to Giza or are you now inspired to go straight to the Egyptian Museum?'

'Well these artefacts are very interesting. I am more interested to go to the museum. Can I take you up on your offer of back to the city?'

'I would still like to call in at my sister's place if you don't mind. I'll just charge you the current meter reading and drive you back to the hotel for free.'

'Of course,' Chad replied. 'That would be great.'

Chad helped carry the seed trays of onions, lettuces and tomatoes back to the taxi. As they pulled away Tau switched off the meter and they drove off through the back streets. It was already after noon. Time had raced by.

'My sister has three children. They are all grown up and living elsewhere. One daughter is married to an Englishman,' Tau explained. 'My sister will be happy to meet an American. She speaks English better than me. She studied English literature in England herself.'

'What is your sister's name?'

'Maria,' Tau replied.

The day was very hot now; the *mad dogs and Englishmen* midday Sun was full on, and a shimmering heat haze was rising off the road. The streets seemed very empty. The residents of these suburbs were sensibly inside. There were still a few ardent street traders, wheeling barrows of produce along the sides of the roads. Many were walking barefoot. A few thin, straggly dogs were running along the pavements, scavenging for the odd scraps among discarded rubbish.

The taxi pulled up alongside a whitish picket fence, definitely in need of a new coat of paint. 'Here we are,' Tau remarked.

With the seed trays of produce from the boot, they walked up an uneven concrete path round to the back door. 'Maria, I have a visitor,' Tau called.

The door opened and out stepped a late middle-aged lady, dressed in brightly coloured drapes and a headscarf, similar in style to that lady in the taxi at the airport. She exchanged several phrases in Arabic with Tau and then turned to Chad.

'Good afternoon! I am pleased to meet you,' she said holding out her hand.

'Good afternoon ma'am. Chad Walker,' Chad said with a smile, shaking her hand softly.

'So, you are an American who is interested in Egyptian artefacts and hieroglyphs. Please come in. Perhaps I should thank you for bringing my brother here. I haven't seen Tau in quite a while. You even managed to get him to bring over some fresh produce from the family allotment. I thank you for that. Please, come this way.'

Chad and Tau entered through the kitchen. It was remarkably cool inside. The house's thick, whitewashed walls were working well keeping out the heat of the day, while overhead, a large ceiling fan was clattering noisily.

Several flowering plants stood in pots along the tiled windowsill. Through the kitchen window, Chad could see a back garden of scrub with several olive trees. In the corner of the yard, an old dog was resting in the shade of a large acacia tree. The kitchen smelled of home cooking and exotic spices.

'Please stay for a cup of tea. There is no milk, so I hope you are happy to drink it Egyptian style. Tau tells me that your wife and daughter are arriving in a few days,' Maria added.

'Yes, on Thursday. My wife Jeanette has taken our daughter Chloe up to Canada to visit her mother for a few days to break up the journey. I am particularly interested in spending time at the Egyptian Museum. That will just be a chore for them. Their idea of a holiday is beach and pool and a sun tan.'

'So, you are not staying long in Egypt?' Maria concluded.

'No, this is just a break in the journey, and one of the important places to visit, at least once in a lifetime. The pyramids are very special. We are all leaving for Sydney Australia on Saturday for my brother Tom's fiftieth birthday, but may I say that it is a real privilege to meet you and Tau and to be here. I'm already quite excited about your late husband's work. I am already wondering what he was thinking. I'm actually a geologist myself, and only an amateur Egyptologist, but very attracted to a puzzle.'

'You are very welcome.' Maria started collecting together cups and saucers while the kettle started to murmur on the gas.

'My late husband Mustapha was very sure he had discovered something important about the pyramids, in particular what they were built for. He believed he had discovered some new sequences of hieroglyphs, which were apparently missing from the monuments. He also suggested that there was a clear mistranslation in the *Pyramid Texts* which revealed their true significance. To be honest, although he was very excited about it, I never really took the time to discuss it with him in depth. It is almost as if he took the secret to his grave. He was a lovely man and a good husband.'

Maria went over to a cedar wood desk. 'Somewhere here I have some notes he made. I'm afraid they are mostly in Arabic. He did have contact for many years with someone at the British Museum in London. Here we are.'

Maria handed Chad a folder of cuttings and a hardback notebook. Inside the book were hand drawings of various hieroglyphic sequences, with short paragraphs in Arabic. Several had short annotations in English.

'You are welcome to borrow that, if you want to read through it,' Maria offered.

'Ah, many of the comments are in English,' Chad said with some relief in his voice. 'I think I recognise some of the hieroglyph drawings here.

They are of some of the artefacts I saw earlier. Tau said I might borrow two. I borrowed this one from the allotment,' he said, pointing at the page. Chad reached into his pocket and lifted out the large flat stone with the Nile sequence carved into it. The edge of the artefact had the sequence of five lines. In the notes, there was a ring around the five lines and several sentences in Arabic. Chad could make out the word *'important'* beside a sequence of letters and numbers.

'Mustapha's colleague, John Mann, from the British Museum was here several times. Well, he's also dead now. He didn't speak Arabic, and Mustapha prepared those additional notes for him. John died more than four summers ago. It was so sad for Mustapha. I think John had become the friend he could confide in. For personal reasons, I think Mustapha began to feel he could not trust the director at the Egyptian Museum,' Maria explained.

She poured the tea and handed a cup to Chad. 'Thank you,' he replied. 'Do you think these numbers and letters are a reference?'

'No, I think that is just Mustapha's paranoia,' Maria said with a sigh. 'That's a coded entry. I'm not sure whether he even told John Mann to what they referred. It's likely that part of the mystery will only become clear if you can make any sense out of the coded entries. Look here,' said Maria, as she turned a few extra pages to reveal several pages of coded writing. 'This has to be quite an explanation. I believe the original text for this bit is in English. Mustapha was writing an overview for John.'

Chad stared at the sequences of alphanumeric characters, interspersed with superscripts and asterisks. Beside them was a photo of an ancient Egyptian figure holding some kind of rod beside three triple-bumped hieroglyphs. A red ring had been penned above the top of the head where the stone carving was missing. Beside it stood the ominous words *'Sopdu, a god of the sky: surface seems scraped flat - clear intentional damage!'*.

'There's another mystery here apparently,' Chad remarked.

Today had already been quite remarkable. From learning about a unique location where hieroglyphs had been found, the story had now evolved into a dedicated man's life work of detailed coded notes explaining a mystery of the pyramids. Suddenly, Chad's cell phone in his pocket gave a sharp buzz. Apologising, he drew it out to see a text message from Jeanette. *'Arrived OK, how about you? Love you J + Ch x'*.

Sopdu

'Oh, a message from my wife,' Chad said. 'Excuse me a moment.' '*Everything OK here, call later, love C*', he wrote, then hit send. After that he switched his mobile phone off.

Tau stood up. 'Chad, I think we need to be on our way. We also need to agree with Maria how long you can borrow those papers.'

'Of course,' Chad replied.

'Well, why not keep them for a few days at least,' Maria said. 'You know you would be welcome to come for a meal. I know, why not come on Friday and bring your wife and daughter.'

'That is really kind. Hopefully I will have solved part of the mystery by then.'

Maria smiled.

Chad opened his rucksack and carefully slid the notebook, papers and hieroglyph artefacts inside.

Maria and Tau exchanged a few more phrases in Arabic and then Chad and Tau made their way back to the car. It was approaching 5 p.m. Somehow the excitement of the adventure had been keeping Chad wide-awake. For the first time, he suddenly felt quite tired. Maybe it was because he was hungry. He hadn't eaten since the plane. He took the two bottles of water and the peanuts from his rucksack. 'Here, would you like a bottle of water?' he asked, offering one to Tau.

'Thank you, yes,' Tau replied, opening it and taking a sip.

The journey back to the Hotel InterContinental went in a flash. Chad's mind was racing. He opened the bag of peanuts and poured a handful of nuts into his hand. Tau turned on his old radio, which was now playing some Arabic music.

'Tau, until what time is the Egyptian Museum open today?'

'Today? I think it is open until quarter to seven. But you need at least two hours. Each visit will cost one hundred and twenty Egyptian Pounds — that's about seven US.'

'I was just thinking of finding your brother-in-law's donated collection. Your sister mentioned that there was a display case with his name. Would that be easy to find?'

'I will write something for you in Arabic and you can show that at the desk. Everyone speaks English there, but it may help if I add something in Arabic. I think Mustapha was well-respected and a very important man at the museum, and many of the senior staff still working there knew him well.'

Tau drove through the back streets rather than take the ring road again. The streets were now busier as the early evening started to become alive. As the taxi pulled up in front of the Hotel, Chad noticed the meter had stopped earlier on 260. He handed Tau three hundred-pound notes. 'For you, keep the change.'

'Thank you,' said Tau, putting the money in an old leather wallet, already stuffed with banknotes. 'I will just write you a short note.' He then took a notepad from the dashboard and a pencil and started to write, occasionally looking up and pondering between the phrases. He handed it to Chad. 'This should help at the museum.'

'Thanks. Tau, I am already thinking of going to the pyramids tomorrow early. Can you pick me up here tomorrow morning, say at eight?'

'8 a.m. is fine. I will see you then. I can't wait in front of the hotel. Just call me as before and I will drive up to the hotel. I will need to wait in a side street.'

Chad went up to his room, had a two-minute shower to freshen up, took another tee shirt from his bag, and then took the papers from his rucksack and placed them into the wall safe. What should he do about the hieroglyph stones? Should he take them? Probably against his better judgment, he put them back in his bag, went down to the lobby and stepped out into the street. The museum was only a five-minute walk from the hotel.

The Egyptian Museum looked very impressive in the light of the setting Sun. Its pinkish terracotta walls with its arched windows and grand white archway entrance seemed radiant. There were still dozens of people milling around outside in front of the building. As he approached the museum, the Meret Basha road on the right, one of Cairo's main transport thoroughfares, already had three lanes of slowly moving traffic. The acrid smell of their diesel fumes was distinctly noticeable, but a light breeze gave some respite. Chad walked past a carved granite sphinx, towards the main entrance. The sphinx was standing alongside a sleepy rectangular pool, abundant with lilac flowering water lilies. A stone island stood in the middle, bearing a fertile clump of bamboo. Seven bucks, even for this first short visit, would certainly be worth it.

'No cameras in here, no photography. You can keep your mobile phone if there is no camera,' the serious looking official asserted. Chad placed his rucksack onto the X-Ray scanner belt while a soldier used a metal detector on his body. He was waved on and went to pick up his bag. The woman studying the screen was talking to a colleague and pointing. Chad could see the solid shapes of the two hieroglyph stones.

'Oh, I'm a geologist. They're just rock samples,' he called.

'Please, show me,' insisted the man with the black, peaked cap.

Somewhat nonchalantly, Chad opened his bag and pointed to the two stones. 'They are just samples.' He certainly did not want to draw attention to them.

'May I?' he asked. Chad nodded. The official put his hand into the bag and took one out. He immediately saw the hieroglyphs. 'Interesting. Where did you get these from?' he asked curiously.

'They belong to a friend. I was just going to compare them with artefacts on display here,' Chad said, hoping to sound casual.

'They are remarkable samples. Not exactly just rock samples, are they?' the official said, giving Chad an inquiring look. 'All the museum artefacts are locked up, or too heavy to carry. So, you can keep them with you but the museum's director Dr Al-Facqui might be interested to see them. Which hotel are you staying at in Cairo?'

'The Inter-Continental. I would be happy to meet your director. I am in Cairo for several days. I am actually interested to see one of the collections.' Chad handed the official the note written by Tau. The official read the note then looked up.

'Oh, so you are acquainted with the family of the museum's old curator, Mustapha Hamoun. Interesting. Well, his collection is in a display case on the upper floor. It is in gallery nineteen near the north-east stairs.'

'Thank you,' Chad said and zipped up his rucksack and walked away. As he threw the rucksack over his shoulder, a coin fell from his side pocket and he stooped down to pick it up. At that moment, he just happened to notice the official at the bag scanner now talking on the phone and apparently looking directly at him. Obviously, something was causing questions to be asked. It could have been nothing. Or was the name of Maria's brother, in association with an American bringing hieroglyph samples into the museum, already cause for some concern?

The vast main gallery, with its collection of carved stone sarcophagi and statues, was thronging with tourists. The cool air and the reverberating echo of many footsteps on the cold stone floors, and voices in many languages, made the experience vibrant and alive. But while many visitors were probably just wandering around, drinking in some of the greatest pieces of art from one of the Earth's earliest civilizations, Chad was on a mission and he headed straight to the hieroglyph collection. There would be time for a tourist visit later with Jeanette and Chloe.

Chad walked through the main gallery; its ancient treasures of antiquity were truly stunning to behold. Suddenly, he found himself in front of the famous, carved black-basalt pyramidion capstone. He paused momentarily, but there was no time today. He continued to the end of the gallery and walked up the formidable stone spiral northeast staircase and headed to gallery nineteen. At the far end of the gallery was a large glass case of carved artefacts bearing hieroglyphs. Chad was excited. There were several other people in the gallery. He took off his rucksack and secretively pulled out his two stone samples, looked at them intensely, then slid them into his pocket.

Chad then systematically scanned the glass case. The middle section had a wooden plaque with gold lettering saying: *The Mustapha Hamoun Collection*. Underneath was an even smaller text saying: *Curator of the Egyptian Museum 1981 to 2017*.

Several of the artefacts had that symbol for Sopdet, a five-pointed star beneath a closed semicircle, beside a tall isosceles triangle. Others had the hieroglyph sequence for the Nile. Chad was looking for the five-line sequence, but none of the artefacts showed this. What if more recent additions included these hieroglyphs? He scanned the next display case for any clues as to when the artefacts were presented to the museum. Then at the far end he saw an artefact with its broken edge starting with a sequence of five dots beside the hieroglyphs for 'mat' meaning granite. As an amateur Egyptologist, Chad was familiar with this sequence: a sickle above long forceps beside a granite bowl. Next to this was a stretched stepped seat shape above an eye beside a sitting god. That was another form of Osiris. What was the relation between granite and Osiris? Then right at the bottom of the display, Chad spotted an artefact with another symbol he knew: the closed box with a diagonal line meaning journey and the constellation Orion. At the broken jagged edge of the rock were five short lines.

Just at that moment, he heard loud footsteps approaching and he turned around. Two members of the museum staff were approaching. One looked like the official on the bag scanner. The other was a grey-haired man.

'Excuse me sir, I am Dr Al-Facqui, director of the museum,' the grey-haired man said with a polite smile. 'I understood from my colleague here that you are interested in the hieroglyph collection, particularly that of the late Mustapha Hamoun? I am specialised in this area, perhaps I can assist you with your research.'

'Oh, thank you,' Chad replied, somewhat disturbed by the encounter. 'Yes. Did you know Dr Hamoun?'

'Yes, very well. We were colleagues for more than 30 years. He worked as chief curator under me. He headed up the hieroglyph collections and the hieroglyph study program. Did you have any particular questions about the collection?'

'Er, no. I was just interested to see them. I see he has a dedicated display case here. I was just wondering about the significance of these artefacts.'

'They are good examples of hieroglyphs from the Old Kingdom, around 2500BC. Dr Hamoun was very respected here.'

What was it Maria had said? That Mustapha did not trust his boss. Perhaps Chad ought to be careful.

‘I understand that you have brought in some artefacts. I would be very interested to see them. May I?’ Dr Al-Facqui asked.

Chad reluctantly agreed and took the two artefacts out of his pocket and placed them on the top of the glass case. Immediately Chad noticed that one edge of the larger artefact matched the broken edge of the one under glass. They were clearly part of a sequence.

‘Interesting,’ Dr Al-Facqui stated. ‘Do you have any more?’

‘No, only these two. They seem similar to those on display.’

It was apparent that the Director of the Egyptian Museum had also noticed something about the artefacts.

‘You seem very interested in this collection. I would be very happy to talk with you. The museum is closing soon. Please come again tomorrow and meet me after ten o'clock. Does that work? I think I may have an interesting story for you,’ Dr Al-Facqui said.

‘I had planned to go to the pyramids tomorrow in Giza. I would be happy to come on Wednesday morning if that suits?’

‘Alright, Wednesday then, ten o'clock. Call for me at the desk. Good day Dr Walker.’

At that, Dr Al-Facqui said something to the official from the bag scanner in Arabic and then the two of them turned and walked briskly away. Dr Walker? How did they know his name? Oh yes, he had given the name of his hotel. So, they had phoned the hotel, but why? Something about his visit and bringing in artefacts had already set off alarm bells downstairs. What on earth had Tau written on that note?

Chad compared the hieroglyphs with the ones in the case one more time. Laying his artefact above the one with the jagged edge, they seemed to match perfectly. According to Tau, Mustapha had lied about where he had found his hieroglyphs. What if Mustapha had made up a different story for each one? Then he saw it. In the corner of the display case was a key and a map. In Mustapha's collection, each specimen had a code and a corresponding grid reference on the map. According to the key, each specimen had come from different locations all across the Western Desert, and of course, none from anywhere near his allotment patch. Great. It was pretty likely that Dr Al-Facqui had scrutinized the geo-references, dispatched archaeologists and, on the whole, found nothing. No wonder the director of the museum had questions, but Chad had no answers.

Now Chad was anxious about the collection just sitting in a shed on an allotment patch. Maria had insisted that her husband had worked out something. She had also mentioned that he did not trust Dr Al-Facqui. Chad needed to head back to the hotel and look through the papers Maria had given him.

He put the artefacts back into his rucksack, then walked back towards the northeast staircase and down to the main gallery. He would come back on Wednesday, but he would need to get his story right. Perhaps he should ask Tau if he could meet Maria again.

There was no one on the bag scanner as he exited the museum. He walked outside and past the back of the Nile Hilton, then crossed through the busy traffic on the El Tahrir back to the Hotel. He went straight through the lobby to the lifts and up to his room. As he opened the door, he saw the beige paper envelope lying on the carpet just inside. It had obviously been pushed under his door. He opened it and stared somewhat incredulously at the hand-written warning.

2 UC Berkeley: presenting SETI, and the decoding of an extraterrestrial signal

Sibley Auditorium, University of California at Berkeley

It was a hot afternoon in Berkeley. The airy lecture hall in the Engineering Department was filled with senior staff and post-grads from the University. In front, a large overhead display screen was showing various graphs and data. At the top corner was the SETI logo — *Search for Extra Terrestrial Intelligence*. Three people were sitting on a panel in the front of the room. One of them, a middle-aged guy with a neatly cropped beard turned to his colleague momentarily, then tapped the microphone in front of him. Dull thuds emanated from the speakers around the room. The name card in front of him read Dr Carl Rhodes.

'OK people, listen up. Welcome back. You heard the numbers before the break and I hope you had time to generate a few ideas. SETI is costing us too much for us to be making an error of sending out batch files of radio data from the same area of sky for weeks on end. We should be trying to avoid this kind of thing. I don't want the plug pulled on this. Although you may think it's trivial, the *SETI At Home* program is getting fewer new subscribers than ever before, and the existing subscribers seem to be processing less data. As you know, we have been running SETI more than fifteen years now and there's still a lot more sky out there to process.'

He paused for a moment as if to emphasise the point, then continued.

'There have been a few bits of interesting data. For those of you who weren't here earlier, I will just make a short recap. We started off with the SETI progress report for the past twelve months. We followed this with an overview of target objectives for the next year, as well as a marketing strategy to get more overseas subscribers, which we hope to tie in with *Facebook*. We will run several ads. The bottom line is: it's costing us too much, and the project survival is becoming an issue. Before the break we went through a few case studies. The constellation of *Volans* was the biggest excitement last year. Ted Curtis already went through the details of the processing strategy that he and his good team at Caltech used to attack the narrow band signals, which were identified last year in *Volans*. I just want to use this to emphasise the *catch 22* we are always facing. Do we commit limited resources to post process, or do we write off a signal of high potential?

We all know the story of Ohio State and the 72 second 1420MHz signal recorded in Sagittarius back in 1977, . . . never to be heard again. I even recently saw someone wearing a tee-shirt saying *WOW-Equus 6, but where are the horsemen?* after the 6EQUJ5 field strength reading.' There was a murmur of laughter in the auditorium.

'We now believe this was just radio noise from a passing comet, but as always there is much disagreement, particularly from the original Big Ear team at Ohio State.'

He touched a key on his laptop and a star map appeared overhead; he turned and pointed at the screen with his green laser pointer. He leaned forward, closer to the microphone, while making a ring with the pointer.

'This is *Volans* here. As you may know, in his Star Atlas of 1603, the great Bavarian celestial cartographer, Johann Bayer, originally called this constellation *Piscis Volans*, the flying fish. Well, the final analysis of the SETI data suggested that the signals were coming from the faint barred, spiral galaxy NGC2442 about half way between *gamma Volantis*, here, and *epsilon Volantis* here. Moreover, Ted's team's extensive processing concluded that there is a distortion of a pulsar signal by a strong radio source somewhere here . . .'

'Or a new class of stellar object,' Ted interjected.

Carl smiled, 'Or a new class of stellar object, with all the accolades which go with that, which is likely interfering a substantial part of a wider spectrum. So, three hundred thousand dollars of serious work later, we determined that the narrow-band signal in the constellation of *Volans*, the flying fish, was nothing more than a *red herring*.' The auditorium responded with muffled laughter.

'So, funding remains an issue, and one we are going to have to think seriously about. As you know, we have a special guest today, and I now want to hand over to Dr Jacqui Hau from NASA AMES Research Center.

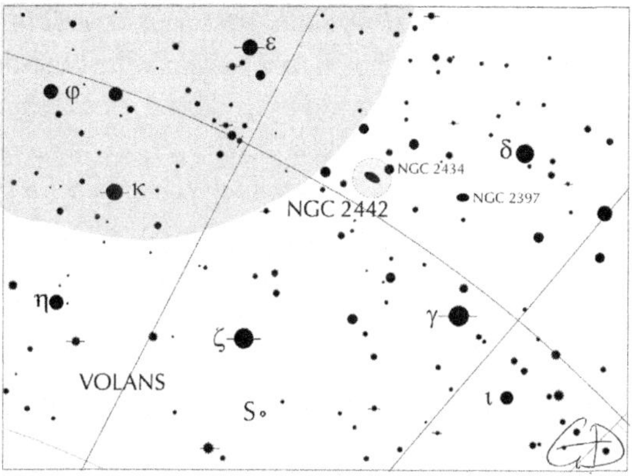

Volans

I'll just say something about AMES. Many people wonder where the name AMES comes from. Jacqui reminded me at the break to say that AMES is named after Joseph Ames, a Professor of physics and past President of Johns Hopkins University in Maryland from 1929-1935. Joseph Ames was also director of the Physics Laboratory and headed an executive committee that evolved into NASA and, for that reason his name is rightly associated with such an honourable institution.' He paused and turned to the young attractive lady on his right and said in a softer voice 'Was that good, Jacqui?'

'Perfect, Dr Rhodes,' she replied with a smile.

He continued. 'You all know that SETI now operates out of the Hat Creek Radio Observatory, some 220 miles north of here, but there is still a huge archive of data being sent to us, which was unofficially captured, intermittently, from the Arecibo Observatory in Puerto Rico. As you know, this site took a hit from *Hurricane Maria* back in September 2017, and although brought back on line, in December 2020 it was finally pushed beyond repair when its instrument platform came crashing down through the dish. In its heyday, Arecibo was of course very famous for several key astrophysics' events. In 1964 *Pettengill's team* determined the true rotation of Mercury. In 1968 the 33-millisecond periodicity of the *Crab Pulsar* was the first solid evidence that neutron stars exist, and then in 1982, *Hulse and Taylor* discovered the first binary pulsar for which they became Nobel laureates. Of course, a very relevant event for today's seminar was the famous, but many would add irresponsible, 1974 Arecibo

Message constructed by *Frank Drake* and *Carl Sagan*, describing what kind of life form we are and where a hostile alien civilization can find us. It was transmitted towards the Messier cluster, some 25,000 light years away, but I don't want to steal Jacqui's thunder, so I will say no more. Dr Hau is here to tell us more about problems which can arise when processing data. For the SETI program, one of the very recent setbacks was caused by a multiple batch file error, which her team cleverly identified at AMES. The data from the radio telescope at Arecibo was good; the only problem for us at SETI was that we ended up gathering thousands of samples from the same patches of sky for weeks on end. We're not blaming anyone, not even Bill Gates this time.'

There was more laughter from the audience. 'As you know, while Arecibo was operational, we were piggybacking on other astronomers' work schedules, which meant that unless we pay, we can't choose where the data comes from. Scheduling radio telescopes is done by approval, years in advance, so that was out of the question. We found in a few cases, we had acquired data for more than 600 hours from the same astronomical coordinates. We have enough data to process, that's not a problem. The problem is when we ask our three million volunteers to process the data, we end up with some serious redundancy. Well, the problem was cracked, and Jacqui is going to tell us how she did it. He turned towards Jacqui with an outstretched arm, 'Dr Jacqui Hau everyone.' The room erupted into a warm applause.

'Hello.' There was some strong feedback from the microphone. Jacqui instinctively stepped back from the microphone. 'OK now?' Jacqui's strong East Asian accent was distinctly clear. A technician off to the right waved and called out 'It's good now.'

'Hello. It's really a pleasure to be here. My name is Jacqui Hau. I have a PhD in Astrophysics from Cornell University in New York. I have been working at NASA since 2004. I am sure you all know that while the radio telescope at Arecibo was probing the cosmos, it was also gathering SETI data for the *SETI At Home* program.'

She touched her laptop and then turned around. A photo of the Arecibo observatory was now showing on the overhead screen. 'OK, we have images too,' she said with a smile.

She continued, 'This is a photo of the radio telescope at Arecibo in Puerto Rico before the accident. Yes, it's in the sunny Caribbean. It was managed for more than 50 years by Cornell University from under a cooperative agreement with the National Science Foundation. Until the end it was operated by the University of Florida, Yang Enterprises and UMET, the Metropolitan University in Puerto Rico. I'll just start with some basic data on the dish.' She touched her keypad again to reveal the next slide.

'The dish was, until 2016, the largest curved focusing dish in the world. That accolade now belongs to the Chinese FAST 500m Aperture Spherical Telescope in Guizhou. So, Arecibo was the *second* largest dish, with a diameter of 305m and it sat in a natural depression in the landscape called a karst sinkhole. For the geologists among you, this is formed from the result of mildly acidic water acting on weakly soluble bedrock such as limestone as we have here. The surface was slowly dissolved over time, along fractures or bedding planes in the limestone bedrock. So, we can thank natural geological processes for forming the ideal site for the Arecibo dish.'

'It was a spherical reflector, not a parabolic reflector, and the radio telescope was aimed by moving the receiver to intercept signals reflected from different directions by the spherical dish surface. For those of you interested in the structural details, I have brought along a pile of handouts with glossy printed colour photographs,' Jacqui patted a pile of papers in front of her. 'All courtesy of NASA.'

There was a teasing but quiet '*whoopee*' from someone in the back-benches followed by some subdued laughter in the audience.

Jacqui Hau looked up and smiled, then continued: 'Just a couple of historical points, the Arecibo observatory was originally built in 1963 under direction of *William Gordon* and *Zachary Sears* of Cornell University to study the ionosphere. Dr Gordon calculated he needed a 305m dish and proposed using the karst sinkhole. Their original design had been a parabolic reflector, which would have greatly limited the telescope's use. Of course, with a spherical reflector, the focus is along a line rather than at a point, as you would get with a parabolic reflector. The antenna reflects radio energy towards these feed lines suspended above the dish.'

She moved the laser pointer over the image.

'The telescope was focused to receive radio data from different parts of the sky by shifting the location and angle of the feeds at the focus of the radio telescope's dish. Originally, the telescope surface was just a wire mesh laid over the catenary shaped hanging cables. Mathematicians among you can prove that a shallow catenary curve approximates a semi-circular arc. In 1974, the old wire mesh surface of the dish was upgraded and replaced with almost forty thousand individually adjustable aluminium panels. For SETI, this upgrade was important; it raised the highest usable frequency from 500MHz to about 5GHz. In 1997, a Gregorian reflector system was added which extended the range up to 10GHz.'

'Now for the data bit, for *SETI At Home*, the Arecibo radio telescope collected radio data over a 2.5MHz band centred on 1420MHz and post-processing creates work units of 10kHz bandwidth each of 107 seconds duration. Some of you know that 1420MHz is the hydrogen line.'

There was a slight pause. Jacqui looked up. 'So, somehow the post-processing collected data from the same area of sky. Firstly, I am here to say that we know what happened and why, and that the likelihood that we would face this kind of problem again is close to absolute zero. Well, deep space has a temperature of around 2.73 Kelvin.' There was some more laughter in the room.

'Jacqui, that's good news,' Carl Rhodes added. 'Well of course if we ever discovered a viable signal, we might one day want to focus on one area, but until then, we want to continue to map as much of the unmapped sky as possible.'

Jacqui continued, 'We discovered the multiple batch file error purely by chance at AMES. We were asked via the National Science Foundation to run some diagnostic checks and look at signal-to-noise ratios. Since my own research at Arecibo was in optimising signal extraction, they asked me.'

'So, it was another holiday in the Caribbean for you, Jacqui?' Carl Rhodes added.

'Ha-ha, sadly no, Dr Rhodes. As you know, even during my research days, I barely left the observatory. I think I went to the beach twice in three years. This time, the task was a purely stay-at-home, data-processing assignment, so not even a flight.'

'I was just defending you,' he interjected, 'and confirming the point that NASA works its employees hard and that there are no free lunches. Just in case there are any would-be journalists here today,' he added with a smile. 'Please continue.'

'OK, I now show a sequence of slides which take us through the signal-to-noise optimization on the Arecibo radio telescope data files. We used the SETI data because it was collected consistently in the same frequency band. We ran several different signal enhancement processes to see if we could get a substantial reduction in noise. Then as a control, we cross-correlated different batch files randomly together. Since the data files were all different we should have got zero results. But in many cases, we did not. This was a crazy result, right? Different radio data collected from different parts of the sky giving enhanced signal to noise ratios? Impossible! Pretty fast we worked out what had happened. I contacted Dr Rhodes and he paid my flight here!'

'Again, no NASA money spent. I paid this out of my own budget,' Dr Rhodes stated reassuringly. 'So, what was the cause Dr Hau and how do we avoid this in future?'

'Right, so what was the cause? Well, when we accessed and processed the telescope control system log, we found it was a combination of baseline resetting of the telescope tracking system and duration testing of focusing, which all occurred during an extensive maintenance period. No one switched off the SETI data gathering system. Each time the maintenance checks were performed, the receivers refocused onto the same celestial coordinates and maintained that focal point to the limit of the telescope geometry on a rotating Earth, which is close to a 40° arc. This created nine focal points every 24 hours and thus nine focal locations on the celestial sphere where extensive data was collected for weeks.'

'And the moral of this tale, Dr Hau?' Carl Rhodes asked.

'The moral Dr Rhodes? The lesson is the same. If you are not using it, remember to switch it off,' she replied.

'Right, *switch it off*,' Carl Rhodes confirmed with a sigh. 'Thanks for that Jacqui. So, going forward, before sending SETI data out, we will check whether the SETI data was collected during genuine scheduled astronomy research and not during maintenance periods. We can't recall the data files and we won't know *what-is-what* until it's all processed and we get it back. So, I think it's best that we conclude there. Thanks Dr Jacqui Hau and please, everyone, show your appreciation.'

The room erupted in applause. As the clapping died down a little, Carl leaned forward to his microphone, 'By the way, don't forget that we have part two of this seminar series, the day after tomorrow in this same auditorium starting at 10 a.m. You can find it advertised on the website and all around the faculty under the name *'SETI, Drake, and the 1420MHz 21cm Hydrogen line.'* It all starts with the big Fermi Paradox question: If we're not alone, why the heck haven't they called by yet?! You're all welcome.'

Jacqui turned to Carl. 'Dr Rhodes, wasn't it your namesake, the late Carl Sagan, who suggested 1420MHz *times pi* as an alternative communication frequency. The 21cm wavelength choice was all based on the likelihood of advanced civilizations mapping out the galaxy using Hydrogen, right?'

'That's true. You're around for a couple more days Jacqui. I know, I arranged your flights. Why not come along?'

'I would love that,' Jacqui replied, with a smile.

'In the meantime, come on, let me buy you some coffee. There's a good Starbucks just the other side of the campus and the walk will do us good.'

3 Accra, Ghana: understanding ancient long distance communication

Galaxy International School, East Legon, Accra, Ghana

It was a hot, humid afternoon at the Galaxy International School in one of the more affluent districts of Accra. A geography teacher, Miss Ubuku, stood at the whiteboard before a class of twenty-eight eleventh-grade students, who were now eager for the last bell to end the day.

'OK class. Today's assignment is communication. We have been looking at how different means of communication enhance development. Ghana is one of Africa's most developed countries and our coastal city and capital, Accra, has benefitted from international interest and development from many European nations for centuries. Historically, the Ghana Empire, after which Ghana is named, was located further to the northwest in what is today south-eastern Mauritania and western Mali. That empire grew rich from the trans-Saharan camel caravans trading in gold and salt. This part of Africa, which became our country, the Republic of Ghana, also flourished from trade, starting with contact with the Portuguese in the 15th century, who built *Elmina Castle* as a fortified trading post.' She tapped a ruler on an image of Elmina Castle.

Elmina Castle

She continued, 'Elmina castle was subsequently seized by the Dutch in 1637 and became part of the Dutch Gold Coast. In fact, more than thirty forts and castles were constructed, to protect the interests of the Portuguese, Dutch, British and Spanish merchants.'

Her students were getting a little agitated. Most were paying attention.

She continued, 'While Ghana was known as the *Gold Coast,* due to its significant Gold resources, Ghana's western neighbour Côte d'Ivoire, or Ivory Coast in English, was so named by the French merchants who were impressed by the ivory trinkets worn by its coastal inhabitants. To the east, our neighbour Togo became known as the Slave Coast due to the numbers of coastal persons who were victimized by the slave trade. So, we see that names get assigned to places based upon what travellers learned about those places.'

'Historically, the Dutch controlled this part of the world until 1871 when this territory became part of the British Empire.'

'Of course, no one wants to be ruled by a colonial power and throughout the major part of the 19th century, the Ashanti people opposed British rule. This desire for self-determination continued throughout the first half of the 20th century. Some of us here, have grandparents who remember the struggle for independence from Britain until we gained our autonomy in 1958.'

'So, we have seen how international interest, driven by the opportunities to trade, was the foundation of modern Ghana. So now we understand this sequence of steps in our history, I want each of you to identify some factors, which were most influential in the making of our great nation.' She looked at one of her brightest students sitting in the front row. 'Manu Umbezi, please start us off. Give me a factor that attracted others to make contact with us.'

Manu had been distracted. His mobile phone had just buzzed, alerting him to an incoming text and he was trying to read it under the table. His older brother Kofi had left by train several weeks earlier and now he had finally made contact. Manu was intending to join him a hundred miles north in Kumasi later that week after the summer term ended.

Noticing his slightly bewildered look, 'Is that a mobile phone?' Miss Ubuku asked.

'Yes Miss, sorry Miss. I have been trying to hear news from my brother for several days now,' Manu replied. 'He went north to Kumasi to get a summer job.'

There was immediate laughter from some members in the class. 'You're in big trouble now boy!' someone shouted out. There was more laughter.

'Quieten down,' Miss Ubuku continued. 'So, Manu, in answer to my earlier question, in other words you are saying that *curiosity about a place and information about any profitable opportunities* is one factor which influences our desire to make contact?' she said with a smile, exploiting the situation.

'Yes Miss,' Manu replied quietly, somewhat embarrassed.

She continued, 'We make choices to go to places based upon the knowledge of what we can expect. Kojo Enam, what do you think? What are the dangers of just going somewhere on the basis of what someone tells us?'

'The story may not be true Miss.'

'Right. The story may not be true,' she reiterated.

'. . . Or out of date or out of context Miss,' Kojo continued.

'So, you think that Manu's brother here could be sending him false information. Why would a person send someone else false information? Anyone? Yes, Mensah?'

'To make out he's having a better time than he is Miss,' Mensah answered. The class roared with laughter again.

'Thank you. Another reason?' she urged the class.

'To lure someone into a situation, or to attempt to dissuade that person from coming to that place,' a girl from the back of the class added.

'Yes, thank you Serwa. Spreading disinformation is a method to attempt to influence another person's interest to come to a place. There is evidence of this happening in the development of our own nation. Give me some evidence for this.'

'Well Miss, many white men died in this part of the world due to diseases such as malaria. If they had been fully informed about the consequences, they might not have come so willingly in the first place,' Serwa added.

'Well yes, although the causes of malaria were not fully understood.

Not that. Something else was going on. In particular, several European countries had self-interests at heart for several centuries and they fought for control of this part of the coast,' Miss Ubuku clarified. 'I was looking more for reasons why early settlers would want to keep others away. Why did more people come to colonise what is now Ghana and build forts and castles here rather than elsewhere? What did they find here?'

'Gold, Miss,' another student concluded.

'Yes Morowa, gold. Not only did colonial powers want to establish trade and access to resources, they wanted to protect the management and transfer of those resources back to their own countries. For this they needed forts and castles.'

'Of course, communication in those pioneering days of the 16th and 17th century was difficult and slow. Information travelled only by ship — possibly taking months before that information arrived back in Bristol or Lisbon. As time passed, the coastline became transformed by the building of the forts and castles and the coastline appeared more developed, more affluent. How would this have affected passing merchants?' Several hands went up eagerly. 'No, someone who hasn't contributed yet. Kwesi?'

'They would have seen the castles and would have deduced that local markets were probably more developed and the opportunities for trade would be easier,' Kwesi suggested.

'Why would this attract them to come to this section of coast then?' Miss Ubuku asked. Mensah?'

'These early merchants were exchanging European manufactured goods for gold, ivory and slaves. The building of coastal forts was an indication of the rate of development of that region and the extent to which communities there were prospering.'

'Right. Yes, thank you Mensah. Just think how merchants passing in their ships some way off, might be influenced by an indication of prosperity. Prosperity suggests places where trade is flourishing.'

Suddenly, the continuous ringing of the end-of-lesson bell loudly interrupted the momentary calm of the lesson. Miss Ubuku held up her hand. 'OK, wait, wait a moment. For your holiday assignment which you can hand in next term, I want you to describe an example of successful long-distance communication and where you have been influenced by the exchange of data with someone a long distance away. Thank-you class.

Have a good break and see you next term.'

A huge commotion immediately erupted as everyone stood up, sliding chairs back and grabbing papers and bags. Some students quickly took out their mobile phones checking text messages. A hubbub of chattering started. The school day was over, the holiday was about to begin.

****

It was only 3 p.m. in the afternoon and there would be a good three hours of daylight left. Manu looked down at the message from his brother *'Yo bro I got me a job as a tour guide — camping and fishing too! Gt ur rs over ASAP nxt wknd! Bus to Kumasi, then text me. Stay cool, Kofi'*. Manu smiled.

Manu went over to the bike shed, unlocked his bike and cycled left out of the school gates. He headed along the Osu Badu Crescent Loop for three blocks and then took a right passing the swimming pool, before going under the motorway and then left towards Odum Street.

Manu felt privileged to be at Galaxy. His father was working in the cocoa industry for one of the principal growers and the company had subsidised Manu's place at the school. It had always seemed a coincidence that the school bore the name of a well-known chocolate bar.

It had rained for most of the morning and steam was now rising up from the road in the strong afternoon sun. After a few minutes, he was home. They had a fine house at the end of Odum Street. He left his bike up against the sidewall and headed into the house by the back door. His mother was already home. He could see her softly rocking from side-to-side in a hammock in the shade of two palm trees at the end of the garden. The message from his brother deserved an equally provocative answer but it could wait.

He took the stairs up to his room and threw his bag down on the bed. His computer was still on. He touched the mouse and in a few seconds the screen came to life. His SETI client had been working away. He had been subscribed for nearly a year now, inspired by an Australian *Facebook* buddy who he had met via a friend of a friend. The moving red spectral images of the Fourier transform calculation were still busy. The work unit was 98% complete but something was very different here. 'Wo!' he murmured softly. Typically, the processed data showed a random 3D representation of hundreds of 107-second spectral slices of randomly spaced peaks and troughs. This was indeed very different. Manu stared at the red, pink and blue graphic. It had to be wrong. In the centre of the 3D spectral map was a single peak and the rest of the spectra were virtually flat, signifying the extreme difference in amplitude between the signal and the noise. This was potentially mind blowing. Was this the real deal? Instead of random spectral noise, was this a signal from beyond? That had to be impossible. It had to be a bad file. Could it really be a signal?

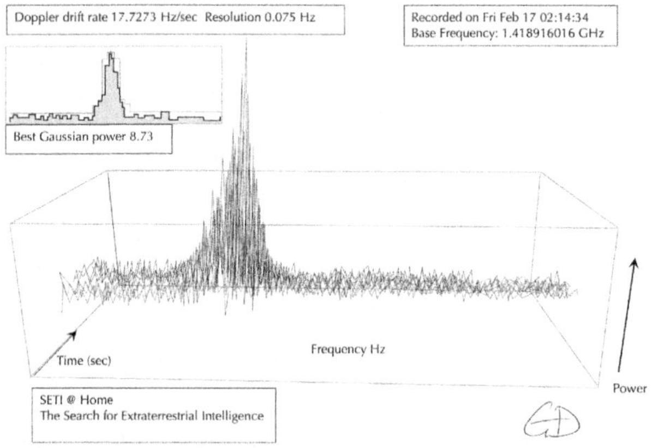

SETI Plot

With new vigour and feeling inspired, he checked his *Facebook* page and then posted a note on Patrick Walker's wall, adding a jpeg of the SETI spectrum. *'Is this an error or have I finally found something?'* Patrick might still be awake.

Within moments, Manu saw the reply, *'You too? Check this out!'* and a link to Patrick's last SETI spectrum. The two spectra were identical. It had to be an error, some extreme terrestrial signal, which had overwhelmed the radio dish receiver. What a pity! Manu looked again, the signal-location data descriptors seemed to be the same; they had been sent the same data file to process. How on earth had that happened?

Funny situation. Miss Ubuku had asked him to write about long distance communication and here he was talking to Patrick in Australia via *Facebook* and they were both exchanging SETI data files — potentially from a distant world. What if the data file was real? Why had they both received the same data file? That wasn't how SETI worked.

4 Cairo: missing Egyptian artefacts and unexplained enigmas

Inter-Continental Hotel Cairo, room 1515

Chad stared at the message; it was from Tau. Above the note was scribbled '*6:15 p.m*'. He glanced at his watch; it was now 6:25 p.m. He had only just missed him. The note read '*Chad, I hope you are safe. Maria got a strange call from the museum around 6 p.m. Please text me as soon as you read this. I can pick you up from the hotel. I am a little concerned for you and for Maria. Tau.*'

Chad took his iPhone from his bag; it was still switched off. He switched it on and after a while it came to life and then he saw the missed call. Tau had called him at 6:02 p.m. Tau must have come to the hotel after realising his phone was off. He quickly typed a reply: '*Tau, got your note. I can meet you. What time is good for you? Regards Chad*'.

Chad hit the send button and waited. Within a minute came the reply. '*I will pick you up at 7 p.m. Be careful. Tau*'.

Chad switched on the TV to catch the latest CNN news, but his mind was elsewhere. He took out the artefacts and looked closely at the hieroglyphs. What was so important about these inscriptions? He took the papers Maria had given him from his wall safe and started to leaf through them. Suddenly there was a knock at his door. He went quietly to the door and looked through the peephole, there were two young men outside. He didn't recognise either of them and decided it would be wiser to keep the door closed. After a few moments, they turned and walked away.

It was probably just paranoia. They could have just been hotel staff, but neither was wearing a badge nor a hotel uniform. Maybe it would be better to leave the hotel and wait for Tau outside; a rash decision maybe, but it seemed the better option. What would he do with Maria's documents and the artefacts? He still wanted to hang on to them for the time being.

The room safe was not anchored to the wall but free standing on the side. It didn't seem secure enough for anything valuable. According to his own paranoid counter-logic, Chad squeezed the notebook and papers behind the bed headboard and put the two artefacts under the tissues at the bottom of the tissue dispenser in the bathroom. Next, he took his rucksack, money belt, phone and room-key then quietly opened the door of his room, carefully looking right and left to check all was clear. He had half an hour to kill. He decided he would walk a few blocks in the area.

He took the stairs down to the foyer and once there, made his way to the main door. A man in a peaked cap standing at the concierge desk smiled and wished him *'Good Evening'* as he passed. It was already getting dark outside, and the air temperature was falling. Cars were passing quite quickly and, at times, Chad was blinded by their poorly dipped, bright white headlights. He set off to the left and started to retrace his journey back towards the museum. He estimated that he could walk about four blocks and then return to arrive back just before 7 p.m.

Almost immediately after he set out, he was startled by the screech of tyres as a car cut across the busy traffic. It braked heavily and came to a stop some distance behind him. He heard a car door being slammed shut. He looked around. About thirty metres away a man was getting out of the car, shouting in his direction. The figure started to walk quickly towards him while the car waited with the engine running. What was going on? This was very worrying. Chad's phone rang in his pocket. He took it out.

It was Tau. 'Hello, Tau?' he answered. 'Chad, I see you. Wait. I am here with my son. We are not in the taxi,' Tau said. 'Do you see me?' Tau flashed his lights.

'Tau, OK. I am coming,' Chad replied, sounding a little agitated. He cut the call and put his phone back in his pocket.

Chad looked at the figure walking towards him, who was much closer now. The man was quite smartly dressed, probably in his mid-forties. Within a few moments the man had reached him. 'Chad, I am Rami, my father is in the car. He recognised you walking by. We passed you then doubled back.'

Somewhat relieved that there was no threat, Chad took a deep breath. 'Hello Rami, I'm Chad,' he said holding out his hand. They shook hands and walked back to the car and Chad climbed in the back.

'Tau, hello. It's good to see you again. Some strange people came to my hotel room. I felt it better to leave the hotel.'

Tau swung out into the evening traffic. 'Chad, I am glad to see you're safe. Maria has been phoned by the museum. They now want to talk with her about you bringing in those two artefacts. I have told Rami here what is going on. One of Rami's friends, Hafiz, works at the museum. I think it is best that we meet him.'

'I called Hafiz,' Rami added. 'I told him about what happened. It's not normal that the director from the museum calls someone. He is a powerful man in Cairo and you don't want to be on the wrong side of him.'

'What? The director of the museum called Maria? How is she?' Chad asked.

'She is fine,' Tau said reassuringly. 'She has done nothing wrong. Something about those artefacts that you brought to the museum has upset Dr Al-Facqui. I didn't anticipate this reaction.'

'I wondered what you had written in the note, Tau? As soon as the man at security read it, he was on the phone to someone. Almost as soon as I arrived in gallery nineteen, where the Mustapha Hamoun collection is displayed, the museum director Dr Al-Facqui turned up with the security guy.'

'I only wrote *'a friend of Mustapha Hamoun's family has come to view the artefacts he donated. Please assist him'*. From what I understand from Maria, they discovered you bringing in artefacts at security.'

'Yes, sorry for that, and I was comparing them with those in the display when Al-Facqui turned up. One of the artefacts clearly matched the broken edge of another in the display. Al-Facqui said he wanted to meet me on Wednesday. I said I would meet him.'

A police car screamed past them going in the other direction. Tau and Hafiz muttered a few words in Arabic to each other. 'Exciting stuff,' Tau exclaimed, '. . . if it weren't so serious.'

Now, at night, the streets of Cairo had become a fast-moving sea of vehicles, and drivers were showing quite an aggressive mood. Those fed up after a day's work and eager to get home were now battling with those setting out for their evening appointments. Tau, an experienced taxi driver, drove calmly on, unphased as ever.

He continued, 'You said you had visitors to your room Chad. Who were they? What did they want?'

'I didn't answer the door. I had just read your note. I just looked at them through the peephole and decided I would wait for them to go, and then leave the hotel.'

'What did they look like?' Rami asked.

'They were in their late twenties. Neither had any hotel badge nor uniform.'

'Could have been nothing,' Tau added. They were approaching a busy traffic intersection. Tau started to slow down. 'Rami, it's a left turn here, right?'

'Yes, here. Take a right at the second block, by that restaurant over there,' Rami confirmed, pointing. 'Chad, we're going to meet Hafiz at that restaurant.'

Bright green lights and plants in pots outside the front door set the place apart from anything in the street. This was a more run-down part of the city. Tau parked the car behind a refuse skip, which seemed precariously overfilled with a heap of building debris from an adjacent construction. The sides of the street were cluttered with stacks of breezeblocks, and huge piles of scaffolding poles covered the pavements.

'A new development area,' Rami added, smiling. 'The future tenants already have a great local place to eat.'

They walked into the restaurant. It was almost empty. Two men were sitting by the window, eating a goulash or something. It smelled quite spicy. Soft Arabic pipe music was playing in the background. A rotund man, squeezed into a dark blue suit, approached them speaking Arabic. Chad could only make out the words *Rami* and *Hafiz* in the short dialogue which followed. The man ushered them to a table at the back of the restaurant where someone else was sitting at a wooden table, talking on a mobile phone and drinking coffee. In the centre of the table a large candle was burning. The man was smartly dressed in a dark jacket. He was just finishing his call and looked up as they approached. 'Chad, this is my good friend Hafiz.'

'Hello, I'm Chad.'

'Hafiz,' he said, holding out his hand. 'Pleased to meet you. From what I hear from Rami, it sounds as if you have stepped into some hot water at the museum. By the way, my Uncle runs this restaurant and for the sake of friendships, new and old, you are all invited for a meal.'

'Thank you,' Chad replied sincerely.

'Thank your uncle from me and Rami also,' Tau added. He continued, 'Chad here, is in a situation. Hafiz, you probably remember that my sister's husband, Mustapha Hamoun was curator at the museum, in charge of artefacts bearing hieroglyphs dating to the Old Kingdom.'

'Yes, yes. I worked with him for several years. He was an interesting old man, very clever. He always seemed to have a new angle on things.'

'Well, I met Chad at the airport today. It was just a standard trip downtown and then we got talking. During our conversation, it turned out Chad is interested in hieroglyphs and I ended up taking him to the family allotment, where Mustapha had discovered quite a large number of artefacts. I lent him a couple. I then took him to meet my sister. Later, he went to the museum and Dr Al-Facqui ran into him and found him comparing the artefacts with some in the display.'

'OK. OK. Starts to sound bad. Dr Al-Facqui is quite a dangerous man. He is very well connected. So, he saw you with artefacts?' Hafiz remarked, looking at Chad, raising his eyebrows.

'I was only interested to compare them. Maria, Tau's sister, mentioned there was a mystery: why Mustapha had kept his own collection and given others to the museum.'

'I remember Mustapha. I also spoke with him about his collection,' Hafiz added.

'We are all friends here Chad. You can be open with Hafiz,' Tau reassured.

'What did Mustapha say about the collection?' Chad asked.

At that moment, a waiter came to the table bringing a bottle of mineral water. Hafiz said something in Arabic to the waiter then turned to Chad. 'I have ordered a spicy lamb dish for us all,' he said. Hafiz then filled the four glasses on the table with water from the bottle.

'The bottom line is that Mustapha was building an artefact collection and selective about what he gave to the museum. Several people including Al-Facqui started to suspect that,' Hafiz explained.

'He was always being asked to come to Al-Facqui's office to explain why very few other artefacts were ever found in the locations where Mustapha had claimed his samples had come from. I don't think this whole affair was just about artefacts. Only a few months ago I overheard Al-Facqui saying to another colleague that he had found a serious mistranslation in the *Pyramid Texts* which changes its meaning dramatically. It may even lead back to the Rosetta Stone. Apparently there are still questions as to the accuracy of that translation in the 19th century, and why they are, as yet, still unable to translate the walls of hieroglyphs in the tombs of the Valley of the Kings. Maybe both Mustapha and Al-Facqui were working on the same puzzle. Don't get me wrong; I liked Mustapha and I was very loyal to him. He also took me a few times to his allotment to see his hieroglyph collection. I never told anyone.'

'So, you think the director of the museum was also trying to decipher a sequence of hieroglyphs, maybe for several years, trying to crack a code. Maybe he had a similar hunch to Mustapha?' Chad asked. 'That is possible, isn't it? Could it not just be competition between two academics, each trying to solve the same problem?'

'If it were just that, no one would have contacted Maria,' Tau replied. 'Whatever Dr Al-Facqui has determined from the sequence, he must be pretty close and just missing some essential part of the story. Given the serious interest, you can be sure there is big money somewhere.'

'That guy is bad news,' Hafiz added. 'You don't want to get on the wrong side of Al-Facqui. There are CCTV cameras everywhere in the museum. You can be sure that he took images of you and probably those artefacts. He has linked you to Mustapha Hamoun and now he is turning up the heat on Tau's sister.'

'What did Maria tell you, Tau?' Chad asked.

At that moment, the waiter appeared with four plates of food.

'Please, enjoy. With complements from my Uncle,' Hafiz declared.

'Thanks,' Chad replied. The spicy lamb and green bean stew was very aromatic and tasted great. This was Chad's first meal of the day.

'Maria is very wise,' Tau replied. 'She told the museum that she knew nothing and could not help them. It's a pity I wrote that note. I apologized to her. I did not see the harm at the time.'

'All roads lead to Rome,' Hafiz added.

'So, do we now go to the allotment and move the collection?' Tau asked. 'I don't want Maria to be coerced into declaring where Mustapha's collection is hidden. If they find it, they will dig up all kinds of old laws about concealing artefacts from the State.'

'OK. If we go now, where shall we take them? If we just remove the drawers of artefacts, we can take them in the back of my pick-up,' Rami suggested. 'I have some space in an old cellar in my garage workshop. Then they are at least out of the way.'

'What about the notes and hardback book Maria lent me, and the two artefacts? They are still in my room at the hotel?'

'You can keep hold of them for the time being,' Tau confirmed.

The four men enjoyed the lamb stew and after around 30 minutes were finished. Tau stood up. 'OK, no time to lose, let's go,' he said. 'Chad, you come with me. Hafiz will follow with Rami.'

They stood up and Hafiz said something to the waiter at the door. They crossed the street. Chad and Tau walked towards Tau's old saloon, while Rami headed off with Hafiz.

'They know the way,' Tau said. 'We'll meet them there in about twenty minutes.'

Tau unlocked the car, they got in and Tau started the engine. Within moments they had turned around and were heading through dimly-lit backstreets towards the allotments.

'This seems crazy. Why is the director of the museum so interested in getting hold of a few extra artefacts? There must be hundreds of others not on display in the archives,' Chad reasoned.

'As I said in the restaurant, there is big money somewhere and it seems to have something to do with deciphering hieroglyphs.'

Within a short while they had arrived at the allotment. There was still quite some traffic passing overhead, on the main motorway. Another car, a pick-up, suddenly emerged from a side road and parked up. 'That's Rami and Hafiz,' Tau remarked.

Together, all four of them headed with torches towards the allotment shed. Tau found the key, unlocked the shed and went inside. 'Come in and help me pass the drawers out to the boys,' he said to Chad. After removing the chicken wire and blanket from the chest, Tau reached up and took the key to unlock it. With his small torch in his mouth, one by one, he removed each of the five drawers of artefacts and handed each one to Chad who passed them out to Rami and Hafiz waiting at the door.

Just as Tau was pulling out the last drawer, his torch caught the edge of a large brown envelope underneath the bottom drawer.

'Tau, look. There is something,' Chad exclaimed. Tau handed the last drawer to Chad and reached down to pick up the envelope, thick with papers.

'Another clue, possibly. We are probably quite lucky to find this at all. Who on earth would ever have taken the drawers out?' Tau added.

Taking two drawers each, Rami and Hafiz headed to the pick-up. With one hand also gripping a torch to light the pathway, Chad followed them to the car and handed them his drawer, then went back to find Tau. Tau was locking up the shed. He tried the door then handed Chad the envelope. 'Maybe I don't even want to know what's in this,' he said. Tau unlocked the car, opened the door and as the interior light came on, he looked at his watch. 'It's only nine o'clock. I think it would be friendly just to call on my sister, to check she is OK.'

'Of course,' Chad replied.

There was a slam of a car door. Tau looked up and could see Rami walking back towards them. Tau wound down the window and they exchanged a few words in Arabic.

Rami turned towards Chad, 'Enjoy your trip to the pyramids tomorrow, and stay safe.'

'Thanks. I will,' Chad replied. Tau shouted something in Arabic after Rami, as he walked away, and then he started the engine and they drove off.

This trip to Egypt had become vividly surreal. It was full on, as if everything had been pre-planned. The reality was that Chad had only arrived that morning for a few extra days' sightseeing and he was now caught up in some major plot of intrigue.

'Don't worry for the time being,' Tau reassured him. 'The artefact collection is safe, and you are welcome to see them again.'

Looking out of the window, Chad thought he recognised the suburb near to Maria's house. Tau took another right turn then parked the car under an old white streetlamp. 'It's over there. It certainly looks quite different at night, doesn't it?' Tau said. They stepped out of the car.

'I hope Maria is not upset by my visit, and problems I caused at the museum for her,' Chad said.

'Don't worry. I am sure it will be fine.'

Instead of going to the door, Tau took out his mobile and called Maria. After a few words he hung up and they noticed a curtain move and then a face in one of the downstairs windows. Then there was a sound at the backdoor and Maria stepped outside. 'Hello again Chad. Come inside. Don't worry, nothing has happened to me. I am safe,' Maria said with a smile.

Back inside the house, Chad and Tau followed Maria to the kitchen where they sat down around the kitchen table. 'I was just making tea,' she said, pouring two more cups. 'So, the artefacts are safe and away from the allotments?'

'Chad, Rami, Hafiz and I have loaded them into Hafiz' truck and they have been taken to a safe place,' Tau said. 'We did find something new though, this envelope. It was under the bottom drawer. It may contain additional clues but of course it may be personal, so I thought it best that you opened it.'

Maria murmured something in Arabic and then looked a tiny bit disapprovingly at Tau. Shaking her head, 'We had no secrets. If you found it in the chest, you can be sure it is most likely another part of Mustapha's research. You open it Tau.'

Tau undid the metal tie on the back of the envelope and pulled out a heap of documents and newspaper cuttings. Chad immediately noticed an article torn from The Times, from four years earlier *'Senior Egyptologist dies in unexplained accident'* with a photo of someone. Maria also saw it. 'That's John Mann,' she exclaimed. 'Mustapha never accepted that his death was an accident.'

Tau leafed through the other documents. Several had sequences of hieroglyphs with annotations. There were also many photographs and maps. Tau opened one out, which showed a detailed layout entitled *The Serapeum* at Saqqara.

'There's something,' Chad said, pointing at the image. '*The Serapeum* is supposedly a temple dedicated to the sacred Apis bull. It's an underground complex of at least 24 granite boxes, each set inside its own niche. Together with their lids, each box weighs around 100 tons. The mystery is that the boxes seem to be machine cut to an incredible tolerance, with perfectly flat sides. The *Serapeum* was rediscovered in 1850 by August Mariette who excavated the site and found all the box lids opened, apart from one which he blasted open. There were reportedly a few bones inside. How the huge massive granite boxes got there is a huge mystery.'

'It seems certainly likely that Mustapha was attempting to make sense of ancient Egyptian antiquities in the context of an original new theory,' Maria explained. 'He did mention to me that the official story about the construction date and method of construction of the pyramids, particularly Khufu, is highly questionable. That thinking is indeed very controversial, because so many others claim that thousands of men dragged the carved stones, some weighing seventy tons or more, up ramps using ropes. It has always seemed quite intriguing, how millions of extremely heavy stones were not only carved so perfectly but also positioned so accurately, and for what? There are no ornate inscriptions inside Khufu. What was its true purpose, and how old is it really? There are some at the Egyptian museum, who will not be too happy if real evidence surfaces which disproves the official story.'

'I do not believe that alone could explain Chad's experience at the museum today,' Tau remarked. 'I always remember Mustapha as a person who was very interested in hidden knowledge.'

Tau continued to leaf through the pile of documents from the envelope. 'Chad, is there anything special about these?' Tau asked, holding up some photos of huge carved stone monoliths.

'That's yet another mystery,' Chad replied. 'Those photos are of the *Colossi of Memnon* near Luxor. They are carved quartzite monolithic statues first described by Napoleon, and weighing more than 1000 tons each. Quartzite is incredibly hard and there is simply no explanation of how the quartzite was carved. Even Pharaoh Amenhotep III, dating back to 1350BC, described the carvings as *stones obtained after a miracle*. That could be another potential candidate on the Mustapha hunch list.'

'The *Colossi of Memnon* also look terribly damaged,' Chad added, looking closer at the photos. 'That dark colouring suggests that they were exposed to intense heat.'

'What if Mustapha were close to solving the same puzzle?' Maria suggested. 'What if he were close to explaining how the quartzite was carved? He mentioned that copper chisels and hand rock-hammers simply cannot achieve the quality and perfection of the early carvings. Nevertheless, that still doesn't explain why Dr Al-Facqui would be so determined to chase Mustapha out of his grave just for a couple of artefacts.'

'Unless he had a hunch that there were many more and Al-Facqui was close to solving his own mystery,' Chad reasoned. 'Hafiz mentioned something about overhearing Al-Facqui deciphering a sequence of hieroglyphs which changed the meaning and significance of the *Pyramid Texts* substantially. As far as I understand, the current translation of the *Pyramid Texts* comprises a list of ancient Egyptian spells, describing the pharaoh's journey to ascend to the stars. Could Mustapha have discovered the same mistranslation?'

'You could be right, Chad,' Maria said.

Her dog was now in the kitchen under the table. It was alert now for some reason. 'He wants some food. I hope he doesn't bother you.'

'I have a dog, a husky, back home in Boston. Dogs always seem to know that whenever there's a good conversation in the room, we are more willing to feed them. Your dog seems just the same.'

Maria gave her dog a friendly pat on the head. Tau smiled and spoke to the dog in Arabic.

'Chad, Maria is safe. We should be planning to leave soon. One last thing, Maria, you did not say what you agreed with the museum?'

'They seemed to have a load of questions, which is why I called you. As far as I am concerned, I know nothing about any artefacts and Mustapha never discussed his work with me. Hopefully they will not bother me anymore. Chad, please take these papers, they are more interesting for you right now,' Maria said, offering the pile to Chad.

'Maria, thank you,' Chad said warmly, carefully placing them in his rucksack.

'We have all had quite a day. Chad, I will give you a ride back to the hotel.'

Leaving Maria's house, Maria called after them, 'You are still invited for Friday. I hope to meet your wife and daughter then.'

'Of course. Thank you. Hopefully you will not be disturbed again by the museum,' Chad replied.

Tau and Chad made their way back to the car. Pausing just for a moment, Chad looked at Tau, 'Tau, I've just had a thought. Several of Mustapha's artefacts are also carved from quartzite. An odd choice of material, unnecessarily difficult to carve.'

5 | Sydney: a celebration and a new SETI paradox

Nick's Seafood Seafood Restaurant, Cockle Bay Wharf, Sydney Australia

In the early evening, a large gathering had fully booked the landmark seafood restaurant. The tables were buzzing with good conversation and the odd scream of laughter. There was a warm party mood in the room and copious white wine and champagne were flowing. The chink of wine glasses and the aroma of fish and clams and freshly baked bread filled the air. Then, a stylishly-dressed lady of around forty-five years old stood up and started tapping a wine glass with a spoon.

'OK everyone. I know this is not the main event,' she announced, 'But because Tom turned fifty today, we have come out for this surprise meal. I just want us all to raise our glasses. Everybody, to Tom, Happy Birthday!'

Glasses were held up and everybody called out *'Happy Birthday'*. After a few moments, a few started singing Happy Birthday and then the whole party joined in, ending with clapping and *'speech, speech, come on!'*.

A more serious-looking man in his early fifties then called out quite loudly. 'Tom, it ain't so bad mate. They say at fifty while you're old enough to know better, you're still young enough to keep doing it!'

The room erupted with laughter and cheers.

Tom stood up. Tom was an astrophysicist working at UTS, *University of Technology Sydney*. Slightly balding, he still had a good physique from his fitness regime and looked a lot younger than fifty. He was wearing a bright blue tee shirt which read *Wolf-Rayet Stars ... a flash of light to signal your present is en route ... but will be arriving later!*

'Thank you everyone,' he started. 'About three hours ago, my wife Mary-Anne asked me to assist her with some purchases. She lied of course and drove me here. That's why I'm still sporting my new astrophysics department shirt. What a lovely surprise this evening has turned out to be. I know nothing about the *big party* or who is coming. You probably all do, and I am looking forward to finding out. So, to my lovely wife Mary-Anne who is still happy to live here, miles from our dearly beloved family and friends back in New England. To Mary-Anne.'

'To Mary-Anne,' the room replied.

Mary-Anne's phone buzzed once in her bag under the table. She reached down and took it out. It was a message from their son Patrick.

'Tom, it's Patrick, there's evidently a power cut at the Homestead. He says it's not the fuse box. All the lights are out in the street.'

'Tell him to light a candle,' somebody called out. 'Or get a pretty Sheila in,' someone else shouted. More laughter ensued.

'I will ignore that last comment,' Mary-Anne remarked. 'He's only 15. Tom, can't he switch to the battery storage system connected to the solar PV?'

'Yeah, that should work. Just tell him to pull the main switch down on the front panel. I guess he wants to get back on line with his mates on *Facebook*. By the way, did he tell you about his SETI data? He got a high amplitude signal. He was really excited, until some other *Facebook* mate of his in Ghana got the same result. There's probably something wrong with the data.'

'OK, maybe we'd better call him back. Will you please just speak to him for a moment?' Mary-Anne asked. Tom nodded, 'Sure.'

She dialled the number and then handed the phone to Tom. Tom stood up and stepped outside to escape the noise of the restaurant. Moments later he returned. 'I told him we would not be staying too long. For your information, he had already lit a few candles and indeed the girl from next door, whose name *is* Shelly, is already round.'

'He takes after his old man. He never misses a trick. He probably fused the system himself!' Everyone laughed.

Tom continued, 'Patrick has successfully brought the battery back-up online and now they have the only TV on in the street. He suggested that if we want a seat in the front room, we'd better get back soon.'

'OK everyone,' Mary-Anne concluded. 'Thanks for coming tonight. This has been great. I have already paid, so please continue to drink up the wine. Tom and I had better go back now, ... and we'll all see you at *you-know-where* very soon.'

'Tom mate, you've had quite a few beers mate. I hope you're not driving,' a friendly looking guy at the end of the table called out.

'Peter, *I* am driving,' Mary-Anne reassured him. 'I've had only one glass of white wine, and that was two hours ago.'

'No worries then! See you later!'

Tom and Mary-Anne left the restaurant and walked around the corner where their family saloon was parked. It was ten o'clock.

'Thanks for this lovely evening,' Tom said softly.

'You are welcome. I really hope next week goes well. Some special friends will be coming,' Mary-Anne added. 'Not everyone could make it, but everyone who couldn't come has promised to visit us this year.'

There was no moon, and the night sky was clear. When they reached the edge of the suburbs and the Pacific Highway north to *Wahroonga*, the starry skies opened up before them. 'Could be a good night for the telescope,' Tom said softly, 'Particularly if there's a power outage.'

'Well you can have your fun. Just remember that I'm not putting our house back in darkness. I need to work on my archaeology paper that I submitted to the editor of *Science Advances*. He wants me to respond to the peer reviewed comments,' Mary-Anne explained.

'That's no problem. For us astrophysicists, it's the back-scattered light from the street lighting, which reduces deep space visibility. When it's as black as this, there's a real opportunity to do some time travel, and take a good look back in time at the more distant stellar objects.'

'I am happy if you are. Why not show Patrick. He doesn't have much to do, now that school has broken up for the winter break,' Mary-Anne reasoned.

They crossed the Sydney-Newcastle Freeway and soon arrived at Waitara. Mary-Anne took a left down Yardley Avenue. The whole road was in complete darkness. Mary-Anne pulled into the drive. Through the front windows she could see some house lights on. It seemed a bit of a light oasis in the gloom, while every other house just had a faint glow from candles.

'We probably have the least romantic house in the street,' she whispered. 'At least you can give me a kiss before we are officially home.'

Tom gave her a hug and kissed her. 'The lights may all be back soon honey. So please forgive me for escaping to the observatory.' Tom unlocked the front door. 'Hello. Patrick, we're home,' he called.

Shelly and Patrick emerged from the living room.

'Hello Dr Walker, I hope you don't mind. My parents are out this evening and I came round to see Patrick and then there was a power cut.'

'You are always welcome, Shelly. Listen, I am going to do some stargazing. Patrick, you are welcome to join me, but I don't want to distract you, if you and Shelly are in the middle of watching a film or something,' Tom explained.

'What do you think Shelly? Fancy seeing some amazing stuff through the telescope? Could be good in the darkness,' Patrick said.

'Sure, that sounds fun,' Shelly replied.

They followed Tom through the house and right down the garden towards the observatory, which was raised up on a landscaped mound. Tom unlocked the front door of the observatory then ducked through the opening. Next, he slid back the roof cover revealing the Meade 10-inch LX200 on its steel pillar. Tom powered up the control electronics then selected the library function. 'It's a good night to see M8 the *Lagoon Emission Nebula* up in the eastern sky,' he said, searching for the entry data. 'It's quite impressive. It's in the constellation Sagittarius. The *Lagoon Emission Nebula* is interwoven with a cluster of stars. It gets its name from the dark curved line running through the centre of the nebula.'

'How far away is it?' Patrick asked.

'Five thousand two hundred light years, so we're travelling back in time to around the official date of the building of the Pyramids,' Tom replied, as he continued to enter data into the tracking control. The telescope suddenly whirred into life, increasing its azimuth angle and rotating towards the eastern sky. After it stopped, Tom stepped forward and looked into the eyepiece.

'Now, that's impressive,' he murmured. 'I never saw it this good. Take a look Shelly.'

Shelly moved cautiously towards the eyepiece. Taking care not to touch the telescope, she looked into it. 'Wow, that's beautiful!' she gasped.

'Yes, it looks grey but if you take a photo of it, it will be red in colour due to the large amount of hydrogen. The *Lagoon Emission Nebula* is actually a stellar nursery where large volumes of gas are condensing to form young stars,' Tom added.

'So why don't we see it as red then?' Patrick asked, as he looked into the eyepiece. 'That is incredible!'

'Well, it's all to do with our eyes and the low levels of light here, which are simply not high enough to trigger the colour-sensitive cone cells in our eyes. As you know, we see in *black and white* in the dark. Modern CCD cameras can take long exposures and are capable of recording the actual colours.'

A voice called out from across the garden. 'Shelly, your Dad is here! What shall I tell him?' It was Mary-Anne.

'Tell Bill to stay for a drink. It's still my birthday for . . . at least another twenty minutes,' Tom called back, checking the time on his watch, as he held it near to the display light on the telescope display panel. 'I'll be right there!'

'Patrick, are you kids happy to keep looking through the telescope? You can show Shelly M17, the *Omega Nebula*, first discovered in 1745. It's quite close by. You know how to input the tracking coordinates, don't you Patrick?'

'Sure Dad. Would you like to see some more Shelly?'

Shelly continued to look through the eyepiece. 'I think my Dad would like to see this also.'

'Listen, I will pour Bill and myself a drink and return shortly to see how you are progressing. There's some homemade lemonade if you want. Just help yourself,' Tom added smiling.

'Thanks Dad. OK let's try to find the *Omega Nebula*,' Patrick remarked, as Tom wandered back towards the house. Tom walked into the kitchen and found Mary Anne and Bill chatting.

'Hi Bill, how are things? Just so you know, Patrick has kidnapped your daughter and is holding her hostage in the telescope observatory.'

'Finally, some drama in the street,' Bill replied. 'First a power cut and now a kidnapping. I hear it's your birthday, but you don't look a day over sixty, you old goat! What's your secret mate?' Bill said with a grin, giving Tom a firm slap on the back.

'You old bastard Bill, good to see you too! Fancy a scotch, or a shot of rat poison?' Tom chuckled.

'You should know that too much scotch will kill rats mate. So, I guess it's the rat poison for me, and make it a large one.'

Tom poured out two glasses of *Talisker*. 'Maybe Mary-Anne will join us.' Turning to his wife he asked, 'Honey, would you like to join me and Bill for a drink?'

'I'll just have a taste,' Mary-Anne replied, taking a quick sip. 'You know I need to keep my head clear to continue my latest rewrite about that 11,000-year old archaeological site at *Göbekli Tepe* in Turkey. The site was completely buried and there is no agreed explanation for that. I now see the editor is requesting that I write more about the strange animal carvings in the T-shaped pillar stones, which I suggested are clearly *constellation imagery*.'

'How very intuitive of you my darling,' Tom replied with a smile and a wink. 'I was very impressed when you suggested that.'

'You made very persuasive arguments. I still thank you. You know I wanted to make you a co-author, but Professor Cayman didn't want an astrophysicist on the paper. You know how protective they are.'

On the kitchen table in front of them was the print out of Patrick's SETI chart. 'Oh, Bill look here, this is Patrick's latest SETI plot, his search for extra-terrestrial intelligence.'

'Looks like a clear signal to me mate. So, we're not alone then?' Bill remarked, taking a sip of the fine single malt. 'Are the green men coming tonight?'

'That's what it seemed for a good two hours until he got a posting on *Facebook* from a SETI buddy in Ghana. His mate also got the same identical spike. Something has obviously corrupted the SETI data.' Tom turned to Mary-Anne. 'Mary-Anne, did Patrick print out that other SETI plot?'

'Yes, it's over there on top of the fridge. I must leave you now. Goodnight Bill and love to Rachel,' she replied, as she hurried out of the kitchen and up the stairs to her study.

'Goodnight Mary-Anne,' Bill called after her.

'Yeah, look at this,' Tom said placing the two SETI plots side by side. 'Look, here,' he said pointing, 'they have the same sky coordinates. Strangely, SETI sent them both the same data to process. It's probably some heavily interfered data. Still, it gave him a buzz for a few hours.'

'So, what do these two time-stamps mean?' Bill asked, pointing at the data. 'They're different, in fact more than three hours apart,' Bill exclaimed, trying to make sense of the two plots.

Tom looked at the time stamps. This was much more mysterious now: a high-powered signal in the same patch of sky more than three hours apart? At that moment, Patrick and Shelly walked in from the darkness.

'Hi Dad,' she said. 'Do you want to take a look through the telescope? It's really cool.'

'My sweet daughter, I will do that just before we leave. Did Patrick show you his SETI data plots?'

'Sure. It seems like an error. Patrick thinks it's noise on the data and they both got the same file to process.'

'Yes, Mr Hughes,' Patrick added, 'I have never heard of anyone getting any extra-terrestrial signal before, and the same day, a SETI friend of mine based in Ghana processed the same data from the same patch of sky. It looks like some interference.'

'Well Patrick, we may have a surprise for you. Look at the time stamp information, they're both different,' Tom replied, handing him the two printouts.

Patrick stared at the two plots. His brow became wrinkled as he tried to make sense of it. 'Uh? That's strange. They're three hours and four minutes apart. How can that be?' Patrick exclaimed. 'The Arecibo radio telescope would not have had an undetectable noise signal for almost three hours without others noticing it. I will have to message Manu.'

'Worth further investigation, as they say in science. Did you offer Shelly a drink? There's cold lemonade in the fridge,' Tom asked.

'OK, Shelly, would you like a drink?'

'That would be nice,' she replied.

After pouring two glasses, Patrick added ice and a slice of lemon, then handed one to Shelly. 'Happy Birthday Dr Walker!' she said, raising her glass.

'Yes, Happy Birthday Dad,' Patrick added. 'One minute and then you're over fifty.'

'*Fifty? You're only fifty mate?*', Bill said grinning. 'Well here's to you Tom, Happy Birthday!'

'Thanks everyone. Listen, I'm taking Bill outside for some late stargazing, do you two want to come?' Tom asked.

'Actually, I think I should go home,' Shelly replied. 'Is Mum still up, Dad?'

'Yes, my sweet, and looking forward to seeing her daughter emerge safe-and-sound from the darkness,' her father replied.

'Goodbye Patrick,' Shelly said, 'It was great fun. Dr Walker, thanks for showing me the nebula, it was fabulous.'

'You are welcome, Shelly. Do come again. We'll make a scientist of you yet,' Tom replied.

'Bye Shelly,' Patrick called just as the front door closed.

Just at that moment there was a loud click as the mains power reversed the battery supply. Moments later everything went dark again just leaving a solitary candle flickering on the windowsill.

'That was quick. Must be another power cut,' Bill remarked.

'Maybe not, wait a moment. It may take a few attempts,' Tom replied. Then there was another click and the lights all came on again. Outside, the bright white street lamps were on.

'I think that's it,' Tom replied. 'Come on Bill, let me show you some stellar objects. Behind the house we're not too affected by the street lights.'

They downed the last sip of whisky and headed back outside into the garden.

Patrick raced upstairs and went back online. He needed to tell Manu that there was definitely something odd about their SETI plots. He opened his email then immediately saw a mail from Manu containing two other SETI plots. Both were also from the same sky coordinates on the same day but at different times showing just noise. Below the plots he had written:

Something very strange here. Processed these too. Look, they are all from the same day. All the same sky coordinates but only 2 with data. What causes 2 signals 3 hours, 4 minutes and 32 seconds apart but not at the other times? Patrick, I'm away for 2 weeks but you can reach me via email. Manu

6 Breakfast in Cairo, then on to examine the secrets of the Khufu pyramid

Cairo, Inter-Continental Hotel beside the Nile

It was approaching midnight now as Chad walked in through the revolving doors of the InterContinental Hotel. The clerk at the front desk looked up as he passed, *'Goodnight Sir.'*

'Goodnight,' Chad replied, his voice sounding distinctly weary. He took the lift up to the fifteenth floor. He walked back along the carpeted corridor to room 1515. It was time to get some rest.

As he approached his room he saw a lady with a catering trolley talking with a senior looking hotel official and a man in blue overalls. Then he realised they were outside his room. The door was open and as he looked in he could see an open black tool case on the floor.

'Excuse me, is there a problem?' Chad asked, looking very concerned now.

'Is this your room sir?' the senior hotel official asked.

'Yes, what's going on?' Chad walked slowly into his room. There were towels on the carpet under the radiator and the wardrobe against the wall had been moved out revealing some pipe system connections. There was an acrid smell of stale water in the air.

'There was a problem with the radiator sir. The circulation was blocked in your room. We had to replace the radiator. You can now move your bags to the room next-door, room 1514. This room will need to be thoroughly cleaned. I am very sorry for the inconvenience.'

'OK, I will move my things,' Chad replied, too tired to argue.

'Of course, sir. Your new room key is in that envelope on the table. Take your time and when you are happy that you have taken everything, please have a good night in room 1514. There will be no charge for tonight.

Goodnight sir.'

'Goodnight and thank you,' Chad replied.

The hotel official then walked away with the man in blue overalls with the hotel-catering lady following behind.

'This is unreal,' Chad murmured to himself. First, he checked his brown leather bag. It was still locked. Unlocking it, he saw his passport and wallet were still inside. He then moved the bed headboard and was relieved to see that the notebook and papers that Maria had given him, were still hidden there. It didn't look as if they had been moved. In the bathroom, the two artefacts were still wedged under the tissues in the dispenser. He carefully put everything into his rucksack.

Chad suddenly caught a glimpse of his face in the mirror and smiled. What a day! Grabbing his leather bag and rucksack, he checked one last time that he had left nothing behind, then took the key-card envelope from the table and unlocked the room next door.

Room 1514 looked identical and was very clean inside. It even smelled good. He switched his mobile back on. Within a few moments two text messages came in. One was from Jeanette *'Toronto warm and sunny. Chloe found a new dress for the party. See you Thursday, love J + Ch xx'*. The other was from Tau *'Try to get some rest tonight. Earlier pick up from the Hotel to avoid the traffic. Be ready around 7am, Tau'*.

Chad ambled over to the window, pulled back the net curtain and looked out at the flickering lights of the city at night. Cairo was still alive with life. The sound of passing traffic would continue on through the night. Down on the Nile he could see lights of barges and other river craft still plying the waters. The shock surprise of the room night-maintenance, and the need for sudden relocation had really woken him up in spite of the day's events. A lot had already happened today. Still, something didn't seem quite right about being moved next door, but he hadn't yet worked out what.

He went over to the room safe, which in this room was firmly bolted to the wall, and locked his money and passport in. This time he decided to place the two artefacts in as well. He took the notebook and the envelope, pulled out the papers and newspaper cuttings and leafed through them again. Maria's husband had clearly been building a case for something but what on earth was it?

Chad sat on his bed trying to make sense of the artefact images. He looked again at the photo of Sopdu with its red-penned ring and glaring comment. Surely there was a real puzzle to be solved here. Other cryptic paragraphs seemed to be directed to the five horizontal lines on some of the artefacts and their illegible annotations were obviously key to the mystery. He laid his head on the pillow in deep contemplation, and then fell sound asleep.

****

The next thing he heard was his phone buzzing. He opened his eyes. It was already light. He looked at his phone. It was Tau. He looked at the clock. It was 7 a.m. What about breakfast? Tau had sent a message. He blinked at it. *'Waiting downstairs and ready for Giza. I invite you for breakfast. Tau'*

Chad sent a quick reply. *'OK, 5 minutes - see you soon, Chad'.* In virtually no time, Chad took a lightning wake-up shower, managed to find his last clean tee-shirt, put the notebook and envelope in the safe, took out his passport and money, grabbed his rucksack and the two *welcome* bottles of water from the side table and left his room. He ran along the corridor towards the lift. He was down in the foyer at 7:06. As he walked out of the hotel, Tau's taxi pulled up alongside. He climbed in the back. 'Good Morning Tau. How are you? I'm almost awake.'

'Good Morning. Good to see you,' Tau declared, stretching out a hand. 'Certainly, an eventful day yesterday.'

'Well, I don't know if this is only a minor adventure or something more sinister,' Chad replied, still trying to embrace the new day.

'I propose we go first for breakfast. I know a good place downtown in *Khan el-Khalili*, the Bazaar District, where you can get a great *shakshouka*. It's like spicy scrambled egg in chili and tomatoes, a true taste of North Africa. Are you up for that?'

'Yes, sounds great. Let's do it.'

Tau turned northwards along the Nile then turned east on the *El Tahrir* towards the old city.

'The Bazaar District has been a centre of trade right back to the middle ages. Throughout the Arab world we call this kind of commercial quarter a *souq*,' Tau explained.

'Was this then the centre of the old city of Cairo?'

'Over time it became Cairo's main market. Traditionally, *souqs* were outside cities and were places for caravans loaded with goods to stop where merchants could display their goods for sale. The famous Khan el-Khalili was originally a *caravanserai* on the famous Silk Road and dates back to 1382. The bazaar grew up around it,' Tau continued. 'One of the sights to see in Cairo. I am sure your wife and daughter will find it interesting.'

'If it involves an opportunity for spending money, you can be sure they will find it interesting.'

The traffic was already heavy, and they had almost slowed to a stop as they turned north on to the *Mohammed Farid.*

'It's getting bad already. The back streets would probably have been better now,' Tau murmured. As they approached the *Qasr Al Nil* roundabout, the traffic was at a total standstill. Ahead, two police cars with flashing lights were blocking both lanes as a huge telescopic mobile crane was slowly reversing out into the road. Several policemen were waving and shouting, trying to direct the crane from different angles. Many drivers were becoming irritated and started hooting their car horns. Tau turned on the radio. There was some discussion in Arabic. Shortly afterwards he turned it off again.

'So how far is the Bazaar?' Chad asked.

'The *Khan el-Khalili Bazaar* is in the Islamic District of Cairo. We are about one kilometre away,' Tau replied. There was suddenly a loud crash as the rear of the crane collided with a water hydrant and a jet of water shot up in the air.

'No time to wait for that,' Tau remarked. 'We'll go via the backstreets.'

Before other motorists had taken in the implications of the collision, Tau had already performed a wide U-turn in the road to head south. After a few blocks he turned east again. In the narrower backstreets, driving took on a greater need for care and attention to avoid any mishaps. There were many street traders wheeling heavy barrows laden with olive oil and fruit, while ambling groups of tourists, seemingly unaware of moving traffic, were frequently stepping off the pavement into the road.

Sitting on a wide stone doorstep, two neighbours were chatting and playing backgammon while drinking coffee, apparently oblivious to the bustle of pedestrians passing them.

'See that Chad,' Tau said pointing as they drove by. 'They're playing the game of Pharaohs.'

'I didn't know backgammon was that old.'

'Well, the game as played today may have different rules, but they believe it's a direct descendent of the Old Dynasty *Senet* board game found in Tutankhamun's tomb.'

Tau continued on until he reached a taxi-waiting zone, directly in front of a street filled with trader stalls.

'This is the start of the Khan Bazaar. We'll leave the car here. We taxi drivers can get away with a few things from time to time. Wait here a moment!' Tau said as he stepped out of the car. 'I won't be long. I just need to speak to someone.'

Chad watched as Tau walked across the road and went into a small shop opposite. A few moments later he emerged, talking together with a man dressed in a white-hooded *thobe* and black headband who was waving his arms towards the bazaar. Tau had a serious look on his face and seemed to be listening intently. Tau then smiled, shook the man by the hand and then came back to the taxi.

He opened the rear taxi door. 'Come on,' he said. 'Breakfast is waiting. That was Moshe, a friend of mine. He says the best *shakshouka* is now found near the spice market. It's a short way up through here. By the way, there's been another development we need to discuss.'

'Don't tell me, it relates to Egyptian antiquities,' Chad remarked.

'Well everything in Cairo relates to Egyptian antiquities in some way or other. I got a call early this morning from my son Rami. We can discuss it over breakfast,' Tau confirmed as they walked along.

The Khan el-Khalili street market was bustling with shoppers. Competing merchants, with their fresh and enticing vegetable displays, were persistently calling out to the passing Egyptian women, as they walked by wearing their brightly-coloured headscarves.

Gradually the air became strongly fragrant with the scent of ginger, turmeric and ground nutmeg. Large baskets of dates and nuts lined the street.

'This way Chad, down here,' Tau said.

Tau then turned down a long-covered passageway leading to a sunlit courtyard beyond. There was neither a sign out front, nor indeed any indication that food was sold there at all. Emerging into the courtyard, Chad could see two white metal tables, each with several matching metal chairs. Flowering climbing plants set in terracotta pots adorned a white-painted brick wall; the flowers, with their vivid shades of pink and purple, looked quite magnificent.

Tau called out something in Arabic and moments later, a man walked outside from what seemed to be a kind of kitchen area. Upon seeing Tau, he grinned then shook his hand. The two spoke for a little while in Arabic, and then Tau gestured towards Chad. 'Chad, this is Youssef. He's from Tunisia, the birthplace of *shakshouka*.'

'Hello Mr Chad, and welcome to my café,' Youssef said warmly. 'Please sit here,' he said, quickly wiping the surface of the table with a dishcloth. 'So, you want to taste *shakshouka*. This is the delicacy of the Berber people. Can I get you real *Arabica* coffee as well?'

'That would be great. Thanks!' Chad replied.

Youssef disappeared back into the kitchen. Sunlight somehow cascaded in, down through the opening in the buildings above, and it felt warm on Chad's face. Tau sat down at the table and beckoned Chad to join him. 'Chad, I told you there was another development. I don't want to worry you, but early this morning when Hafiz went to work he was called in to an impromptu meeting at the Egyptian Museum. There was an announcement that an operation was underway to raid several addresses across Cairo to attempt to recover lost artefacts. He quickly called Rami who called me as I was driving to your hotel.'

'It must be Maria's address,' Chad said with some concern in his voice. 'No one knew that we were removing the artefacts from the shed to take them to your son's garage. I am sorry Tau. I have caused this problem,'

'No Chad, the situation could easily have been pre-empted by any number of events in the past. Mustapha was under suspicion from the museum for a long time. His house was always a potential target for the special operations group linked to the museum. The announcement was clearly that several addresses would be visited.'

'Tau, when I came back to my hotel room last night, they were repairing the central heating radiator. The door was open, and I was moved next door,' Chad declared.

'Central heating repairs in mid-summer? Does that sound normal? I think your hotel room may have been on the list. Did you check that you had not lost anything? What about the notebook and papers, and the artefacts?'

'All recovered from hidden locations in the room, all safe and locked away now,' Chad replied. 'What about Maria? Have you told her?'

'As soon as Rami called me, I called Maria and warned her. She told me she would put together a bag of essentials and leave immediately and go stay with her sister-in-law, Habibah, for a few days. She already had a long-standing invitation. The dog is being looked after by the neighbour.'

'Does she have to go far?'

'No, just a few streets away. Oh, and she said that you and your wife and daughter are still invited, but now to Habibah's place. I know the address and I'm happy to be your driver,' Tau replied reassuringly.

At that moment, Youssef suddenly emerged from the kitchen carrying a tray bearing two plates of steaming fragrant food and a bowl of bread and two glasses of water. 'Here you are, real Tunisian *shakshouka*,' he announced. 'The coffee will be ready shortly.'

'*Shukran* Youssef,' Tau replied. 'Chad, this is very special. Just right to start a day in Cairo.'

'Thank you, it looks and smells delightful.'

'There are some extra chillies in this small bowl here,' Youssef said pointing, as he placed the plates on the table. Enjoy your meal or as we say here, *Bilhanā wa ashshifā*.'

'*Shukran* Youssef, *Shukran*,' Tau replied.

'*Il'afw* Tau, you are both welcome,' Youssef added.

Breakfast was delicious. The combination of chilies and tomatoes with scrambled egg, carried a rich mélange of flavours, complimented by the freshly baked bread and aromatic Arabica coffee. Chad took out his wallet and put 300 Egyptian pounds on the table. 'I'd like to pay for this. Is this about right?'

'Two hundred is generous. Youssef will be very grateful, and you can bring your wife and daughter here next time.'

'That's good. I will certainly bring them here, that is, if I can ever find it again!' Chad answered with a smile.

'Come on Chad, time to go to Giza. The pyramids await you, and with any luck we will arrive by 8:30 before the tourists do,' Tau said as he stood up. Youssef came outside again.

'*Shukran* Youssef,' Chad said, attempting some Arabic.

'*Il'afw* Mr Chad,' Youssef replied, with a smile, nodding his head slightly.

Tau and Chad made their way back up the passage towards the bustling spice market and then back to the taxi. Tau unlocked the door and Chad climbed in the back. Within minutes they reached the *Kobri Al Azhar* and travelled east for a short distance before turning south onto the *Salah Salem*. Unlike the backstreets, this road was a main thoroughfare, heading due west across the city and soon they reached the *Abbas Bridge* linking Old Cairo with Giza. Below them, the Nile flowed wide and blue, sparkling in the bright mid-morning light. All manner of brightly coloured sailboats, tourist river cruisers, and transport barges filled the busy waters.

'We're leaving Old Cairo behind us now and entering Giza. Giza is a separate city forming part of the Greater Cairo Metropolis. The pyramids are located in the Giza Plateau. It's about fifteen minutes from here, depending on the traffic.'

'So, Maria doesn't live in Cairo, but in Giza.'

'Yes, and so does Habibah, her sister-in-law. Nevertheless, the authoritarian powers of the Egyptian Museum and the Supreme Council of Antiquities are wide reaching. They could already be paying a visit to her house right now.'

'Do you want to drive past, to see. . . ,' Chad suggested.

'To see if anyone recognises you in the back of my taxi?' Tau interrupted, with a surprised tone in his voice. 'No, certainly not! I'm driving you to the Pyramids in Giza. After that, I'm heading to visit my sister and Habibah. I also have another surprise for you. I have arranged a guide, and trust me, you do not want to be a sole tourist wandering around. Without a guide, you may be hassled the whole time.'

'Oh, I didn't think of that. Is it that bad?'

'It can be very intimidating. An ex-army buddy of mine has a son Ahmed, who was a boxer. I called him last night. He has agreed to show you around. With Ahmed as your guide, any persistent camel owners and sellers shouldn't bother you too much. Many people, just like you, have looked forward for years to come and visit the pyramids and wander quietly around them. They come unprepared and then experience extra tension from this harassment the whole time. You won't have this problem today.'

'Tau, you're really looking after me. Thanks.'

As they sped now southwest down the *Al Ahram*, the pyramids came ever clearer into view, rising up from the granite plateau. Chad was awestruck. Their mottled, yellow-white sandstone blocks glinted brightly in the morning light. No words could adequately convey their magical and austere beauty. They stood majestically, beckoning all to gaze upon them. As Tau approached the Giza Plateau, he turned left towards the main ticket office.

'OK Chad, I'm going to drop you here. There is the north entrance gate to the Giza Plateau over there,' he said pointing. 'Ahmed is waiting somewhere here for you. He's working on some engineering project and has access to everything that you will want to see. You won't even need to buy a ticket.'

'That's really great! Thanks Tau.'

Tau stopped the car then turned to Chad in the back seat, 'Look, it's coming up to 8:45. I guess you'll want to spend a few hours here. Just call me when you're ready to be picked up. As I said, it will take me about twenty minutes to drive from Habibah's. I agreed with Ahmed, I will pick you up outside the other entrance below the Sphinx.' Tau took out his mobile phone. 'I'll just give Ahmed a call.'

Within moments Tau got through to Ahmed. After a short dialog in Arabic, Tau opened his door and stepped out of the taxi, looking towards the ticket office, shading his eyes with one hand while holding the mobile close to his ear with the other. He then held his left arm straight up and a figure leaning against a wall, in a red tee shirt, white baseball cap and mirror sunglasses lifted his arm in return.

'There's Ahmed,' Tau declared.

'Thanks Tau. I'll call you in a few hours.'

'You're welcome. Have a great visit. See you later.'

Chad climbed out of the taxi and walked towards the figure standing by the entrance gate. He took out his sunglasses and put on his own baseball hat to protect himself from the Sun. 'Ahmed?' Chad called as he approached.

'Hi Chad, hello. I'm Ahmed. How are you doing?'

'Hi Ahmed, I'm good. How are you?' Chad replied warmly. Ahmed nodded, 'Good thanks.'

Ahmed was solidly built, and his firm handshake sent a small spasm up Chad's arm. 'Thanks for agreeing to show me around. Tau mentioned you were a boxer.'

'OK yeah, in the old days, when I was young. Sixty-eight fights, fifty-two wins and three knockouts, but I don't box any more, just work out,' Ahmed added quietly. 'Tau is a close friend of my father and I'm happy to help a friend of his. You won't have any trouble from the hustlers. Where would you like to go first?'

'Ahmed, first things first, what do I owe you for the tickets?'

'Nothing. This is work. I am managing a project in the Khufu pyramid. The inside of the pyramid is actually closed to tourists for the next week. You are coming in with me. I have a pass for you. Here, put this on.' Ahmed handed Chad a plastic badge on a cord and Chad put it around his neck.

'Ahmed, I am very grateful for you showing me around. If I give you five hundred, will that cover today? Please, take your wife or girlfriend out for a meal,' Chad added, not wanting to offend.

'Yeah, my wife and my girlfriend don't get on. So, I guess it will be one or the other, but which?' Ahmed remarked with a quite serious expression. Moments later he smiled then gave Chad a hearty pat on the back. 'Just a joke! I'm married with three children. Chad, that is generous.'

'One moment, it's already quite hot. Have some water,' Chad insisted, taking the two bottles from his rucksack, handing one to Ahmed. Ahmed nodded gratefully, twisted open the plastic top and took a swig.

Ahmed and Chad walked the short distance towards the Khufu pyramid. The sky was a perfect blue and there was no breeze at all. The air was very hot. Directly ahead of them was *Khufu*, the Great Pyramid. To its left stood *Khafre*, seeming identical in size, with several hundred casing blocks still hanging to its apex, and left of that, stood the smaller pyramid *Menkaure*.

The huge crowds of tourists had yet to arrive, although there were a few already. They walked past a group of camels sitting on the ground, with their bright, red and green carpet-covered saddles. Ahmed nodded to the camel drivers as they passed. The Giza Plateau looked truly vast. Several men with camels were approaching lonely tourists who were pausing to take photos.

'It's a pity for those tourists, but here, most local people have nothing and need to feed their families,' Ahmed remarked.

'Tell me about your work here.' Ahmed seemed very educated.

'OK. I'm an engineer. I studied at Cairo University, did my PhD in Berlin and I now work for a company doing work for the Supreme Council of Antiquities. The humidity inside the pyramid gets very high due to the number of tourists and a layer of salt has been building up on the surface of the stones lining the interior passageways. Periodically, we need to monitor the dehumidifying system and that is why the pyramids are closed. Only persons working on the project have access. Today that includes you.'

'Ahmed that's sounds incredible. So, we get to go inside Khufu. Access all areas?'

'Access all areas and beyond. I also have some detailed plans of the pyramid internal structures and there are a number of ladders inside for you to get a very close view of anything you may want to see. Tau mentioned that you are a geologist, right?' Chad nodded. 'That is very interesting,' Ahmed murmured.

They walked up to the entrance gate and Ahmed spoke to the official on duty in Arabic. The man then suddenly stepped towards Chad and shook him firmly by the hand then let them pass through.

'What did you say to him,' Chad asked, somewhat surprised.

'Only that an American geologist has just flown in from the US and come to advise us for free,' Ahmed replied with a smile.

'You are kind, thanks Ahmed. But are there specific things you need to do for the project today? I hope I'm not interfering with your work plan.'

'No, no, in fact the project is on hold today. We are waiting for some more humidity control sensors. They won't be arriving until later today, or tomorrow. Come over to the office,' Ahmed said pointing towards a porta-cabin positioned close to the pyramid entrance. 'I can at least show you the pyramid internal layout.'

They passed by a large group of disappointed-looking tourists, lingering in front of the Khufu pyramid entrance. There was now a manned barricade in front of it and several officials preventing access. Quite clearly, their journey of a lifetime had not anticipated being prevented from entering. An argument was going on between their tour guide and one of the officials.

Ahmed commented, 'It's a pity for them. The dehumidifier system went down two weeks ago, and we were immediately asked to fix it. This wasn't a case of scheduled works being planned months in advance. There was nothing we could do to let the tourists know, and some of them must have planned this trip, years in advance. Come, let's get out of the heat.'

Ahmed led Chad up the sandy steps of the grimy porta-cabin and unlocked the door. The refreshing shock of the cool, air-conditioned room was exhilarating. A pile of papers covered the table and various charts of the pyramid were pinned up on the back wall. Chad peered out through the tinted glass at the tourists baking in the heat outside.

'We don't advertise how cool it is in here, or there would probably be a stampede trying to push the door down.'

Ahmed opened out a detailed map of the pyramid on the table.

'Before we go outside, let me give you an overview of the structure. Take a look here. This is the layout of the Khufu pyramid. As you can see, there are three chambers. The main entrance here, leads down 100 metres at an angle of around 26° to an unfinished subterranean chamber. However, after about 30 metres from the main entrance there is this ascending passage going upwards at 26°, which after 10 metres opens up into the 8-metre high Grand Gallery. I need to warn you that the ascending passage is a bit of a cramped scramble. At the very start of the Grand Gallery, a horizontal passage, here, continues to the Queen's Chamber, which has these two diagonal shafts going up towards the surface of the pyramid, but they stop somewhere inside the pyramid. At the top end of the Grand Gallery, this horizontal passage continues into the King's Chamber, which has two diagonal airshafts. These shafts actually do reach the surface of the pyramid.'

'It looks pretty complicated inside,' Chad remarked. 'What's this other curving passage going almost straight down from the bottom of the Grand Gallery down to almost the subterranean chamber?'

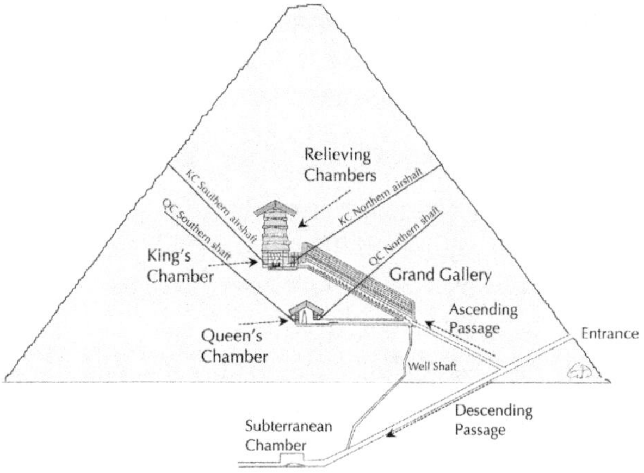

Khufu Pyramid Layout

'That is the well-shaft. There are of course many theories as to the purpose of the resulting multi-chamber and shaft configuration. They vary from a clever plan of deception to disguise the main burial chamber from grave robbers, to the idea that the pyramid construction was changed during construction. This would account for the Queen's Chamber being centrally aligned and the first set of airshafts no longer reaching the surface, while the King's Chamber is off-axis.'

'Interesting. So, a kind of redesign midway through construction?' Chad commented.

'It's just a theory, and we may never know for sure,' Ahmed reiterated. 'The work done in the early 1990s by the Cairo-based German Archaeology Institute sent up a robotic crawler with a camera to examine the shafts. They reached a stone blocking the passage, which had two curved metal inserts in the stone. All kinds of theories evolved around that, from battery terminals to a temporary sealing block, which was left in place during construction. I have copies of the images somewhere.' Ahmed opened the bottom drawer of a filing cabinet and pulled out a glossy photo. 'Here.'

'Wow, that's pretty remarkable. So, do we have any better idea today about how long it took to build?'

'Well, the official story is around 20 years, but that of course doesn't make sense. There are 2.3 million blocks, each weighing around two tonnes. That would mean that teams working twelve hours a day for twenty years needed to quarry, carve, transport and place a block precisely in position, every two and half minutes! Bear in mind also that the blocks are so perfectly placed that you cannot get a piece of paper in between them. The detailed survey done by the famous *Sir Flanders Petrie* in 1882, also identified that the placement error of the four base corners is less than 58mm!' Ahmed continued. 'There are certainly many remarkable construction details which need detailed clarification.'

'Aren't there particular mathematical and astronomical data points associated with the Giza pyramids? Something about the *golden ratio* or *golden number*, and the particular alignment and pyramid dimensions?'

'That's right,' Ahmed replied. 'Like many structures throughout the ancient World, the dimensions were chosen to echo the natural golden ratio. This has been shown to be found throughout nature, such as the twist angle ratio that a new leaf on a plant turns through, relative to the previous one, to maximise exposure to sunlight, and the spiral packing of sunflower seeds in the seed head. The ratio of pyramid height to angled slope length approximates the golden ratio.'

'That must be why it looks so beautiful, and pleasing to the eye,' Chad added.

'Of course. The builders strived to capture that aspect. One additional aspect is the total base length of the four sides. There seems to be some reason for the dimensions. If you multiply that distance by a particular number, 43,200, you get the equatorial radius of the Earth to within 0.5 of one minute of arc.'

'That's a coincidence, right?' Chad urged.

'Well, any other number might be, but it's as if the pyramid is a scale model of the Earth. Also, 43,200 is also half the number of seconds in the 24-hour day.'

'But they didn't have our measure of time, the second. That isn't possible,' Chad reasoned.

'You would think that, but they did have two units of measurement, the Egyptian Royal Cubit and the pyramid inch. It turns out, the base perimeter is 36,524.2 pyramid inches, which is exactly 100 times the number of solar days in a tropical year. Also, if you consider a pendulum, for a pendulum swinging along an arc length of one Egyptian Royal Cubit, and at any angle within an arc of 30°, the half period to swing one way, is exactly one second. The Egyptian world is made up of distinct differences between day and night, and each period of twelve hours has a duration of 43,200 seconds,' Ahmed continued.

'OK, what about the location and the alignment of being close to 1/20 of a degree off perfect due north?'

'Well, there are many publications about it being aligned to the 4 cardinal directions and questions asking why it is 1/20 of a degree off. Many fail to acknowledge that the Earth has *polar motion*: a physical change in the Earth's real spin axis due to melting of ice sheets and tectonic activity. Current measurements show that the spin axis is physically moving by around a third of an arc-second every hundred years.'

'That must mean the Earth latitudes are changing also, right?'

'Precisely, and if polar motion would be linear, which it is not, a third of an arc-second every century would translate to a 1/20 degree, or a 180 arc-second change over 50,000 years, but polar motion is not linear. A substantial rise in temperature and melting of the ice sheets could cause a phenomenal rate of change of the spin axis *within* the Earth. I'm not convinced the pyramid was built 1/20 of a degree off. For me they did an incredible job, and I think the pyramid was probably perfectly aligned when it was completed, or it was deliberately built 1/20 of a degree off.'

'. . . and the spin axis changes direction anyway. That almost 26,000-year precession cycle, where the spin axis slowly rotates, gives the Earth a changing axial direction, currently towards the Pole star,' Chad added. 'Moving about one degree every 72 years.'

'OK, that's different. You're talking about the *precession of the equinoxes* where the spin axis of the Earth slowly changes direction. So, over a long period of time, the star that the northern spin axis points towards, changes. Many writers think it is constant, that is wrong, it is not, and its change is also not linear. The cycle is significantly influenced by the Moon, which is slowly drifting outwards, and that is slowly increasing the cycle length. The current value determined by satellites is 25,774 years. We know that ancient cultures built structures to identify the *vernal*, or spring equinox. Records show that they were indeed aware that there was a variation in the background stars at the time of the vernal equinox. It doesn't make much sense to try to prove the ancient builders of the pyramid knew of the precession cycle duration, if that number is not constant and is increasing over time.'

'OK, what about the location?'

'Well, some say that the latitude is extremely significant, but that again is also based on a non-scientific evaluation. We know the Sumerians developed a mathematical system using a full angle of rotation of 360 degrees. The Egyptians adopted this. It turns out that the Khufu pyramid is at 29.97 degrees north. Some say that it was chosen to demonstrate that the builders knew the speed of light, which is 299,792,458 metres per second. For me that is a bit of a stretch. Add to that an unknown amount of polar motion, which changes latitudes anyway. That makes it even less sense to seek meaning in an absolute value of the current latitude of the pyramid's location.'

'Come, let me now take you on your official tour inside the Great Pyramid. You'll need some kit, though. Here, take this headlamp and put on these flexible boots. You look a size 42, right? They will give more grip on the smooth stones. You might also want these kneepads for the scramble up the narrow passage to the Grand Gallery. You can leave your rucksack here. I'll lock everything up.'

Ahmed picked up a rolled-up map and two powerful hand torches and put them in a rucksack. Chad put on the boots and grabbed his camera from his rucksack.

'Brace yourself for the heat again Chad!' Ahmed reminded, as they stepped outside. Ahmed turned and locked the door behind them, then led the way towards the officials manning a wooden barricade in front of the entrance. In front of them, an Italian tour guide was pleading to be allowed just to take a look in, but the guards had their orders. As Ahmed approached, one of them opened the barricade. 'I'll just explain that we have a guest today. Show your pass.'

Ahmed said something to one of the officials, which made him laugh, and Ahmed patted him on the back. Within moments, Ahmed and Chad were standing right at the base of the last of the wonders of the ancient world.

'Take a look up there, Ahmed! Isn't she beautiful? See how the morning light casts those lines of shadows on the limestone blocks.'

'This pyramid is stunning,' Chad murmured, as he peered upwards, with his hand shielding his eyes from the bright light. 'What an unimaginable amount of work this must have been. Oh, why are there two entrances up there?'

'Well, the upper one is believed to be the true entrance, but that was rediscovered much later. The lower entrance, called the Robbers' Entrance, was supposedly dug by Caliph al-Ma'mun in 820 AD. Let me take you first up to the original entrance. There are some interesting features to see.'

They clambered up ten courses of limestone blocks until they reached a hollowed-out section of the front face. Pausing to take a breath and a swig of water, Chad stared in wonder at the two enormous corbels. 'Why is it hollowed out?'

'The original casing stones and masonry were removed from here long ago,' Ahmed explained, 'and this is believed to be the main entrance. An early writing dating back to 24 B.C. by a Greek geographer, *Strabo*, describes the pyramid having an entrance with a moveable stone, which when lifted, revealed a descending passage. These two giant corbels either side of this entrance may have carried this tilting door. Through that entrance is the start of the descending passage.'

'A tilting door? Incredible! Hey, what is that double bump symbol carved under those diagonal keystones?' Chad asked, his hand pointing upwards. 'Is that a hieroglyph?'

'Interesting question. To date there has been no general agreement on that. Some say it is related to the hieroglyph for horizon while others say it is the name of the pyramid. The hieroglyph for horizon is a rounded valley between two peaks which we don't really see there: just two bumps with a lower and raised level either side. It may yet prove to be more significant than we think. There is another mystery here. Take a look at this,' Ahmed urged, pointing at a sequence of four strange symbols. As if they came from a different alphabet, the symbols seemed to be a mathematical representation of some equality: $V0 \equiv \Phi$.

'Very interesting,' Chad replied. 'It's also mind-boggling to wonder how these giant corbel stones were set in place. Their weight must be tens of tons each. Why would anyone go to the unimaginable effort to design and build such a structure to carry a moveable door, and so high up, if it was always intended to hide a tomb? Are we going in through this upper entrance?'

'No, we will use al-Ma'mun's tunnel. We have some sensitive sensor equipment set up to analyse airflow in the upper section of the descending passage. We're going in lower down.'

Chad and Ahmed started clambering down towards the opening of the Robbers' Tunnel. Ahmed continued his story.

'Until a recent publication, it always struck me as quite illogical that al-Ma'mun just reasoned a place to start digging: direct centre on the North face, seven courses up. After only 27 metres using copper tools, vinegar and fire and water, he made a left turn and conveniently encountered the Descending Passage just at the junction of the Ascending Passage.'

'What did the publication say?'

'Well, again it's just a theory, but it sounds credible. There is a granite coffer in the King's Chamber. The well-published theory is that it was Pharaoh Khufu's burial coffer, although there are absolutely no lavish hieroglyphs or painted images anywhere inside the pyramid, which kind of challenges the idea that the pyramid was a burial structure at all. The coffer seems to be missing its lid. The publication suggested if it did have a lid, it could not have been removed from the pyramid because the lid would have been too large to turn at the bottom of the Ascending Passage, and that is just where al-Ma'mun's tunnel happens to start.'

'So, what was the conclusion?'

'That al-Ma'mun's tunnel was actually dug from the *inside* outwards, using the shortest path to allow them to run off with the coffer lid. Getting at least something for their trouble. There is of course another story which says they found the *Ark of the Covenant* inside, and there are reasons to believe that there was indeed something inside, which I will show you.'

'The other non-credible detail from the inward-dug tunnel theory is that while hammering, al-Ma'mun's men apparently heard a sound through metres of limestone and changed direction. Their tunnel then broke through just below an out-of-place granite stone above them, which they dug round and discovered the three granite plugs and the start of the Ascending Passage. We know grave robbers are part of Egyptian history. Surely, the granite plugs were found earlier by earlier tunnelers and I can hardly hear my noisy neighbours through a brick wall, so how could they possibly hear through metres of limestone?'

'Here, take this.' Ahmed took out the two hand lamps from his bag and gave one to Chad. 'The battery will last about two hours, so should be sufficient for this trip.'

'So, this is the Robbers' Tunnel. For me, there is no indication as to which direction it was dug. Besides, these huge blocks have been smoothed by thousands of tourists.'

'This is all limestone,' Chad remarked as they walked into the tunnel, 'Certainly of the same type found directly outside in the Giza plateau.'

'From here, the tunnel starts to curve to the left, and brings us conveniently right to the granite blocks plugging the Ascending Passage. Look! We can climb these steps and pass the granite plugs. The Ascending Passage is narrower here and so these three blocks have jammed into the lower end. It makes no sense to think they were slid into place after a burial.'

'What is that gate down there?' Chad asked, shining his torch down towards a locked gate.

'That's where the Descending Passage continues down to the Subterranean Chamber. That's officially totally off-limits these days, and to be honest there's nothing of much interest down there. I was intending on focusing more on all the other stuff today. I have detailed plans and photographs which I can give you later.'

'That is totally OK. I am grateful for the tour. By the way, I read somewhere about some *Trial Passages* or something. What are they?'

'Yes, that's right, just east of the pyramid base. The Trial Passages were rediscovered by the great archaeologist Petrie back in 1881. It's a carbon copy of this junction between the Ascending and Descending passages. If it wasn't built as a test-bed, it was certainly a good map of what to look for inside. For a test-bed, there are no test granite plugs jammed inside.'

'OK. So, you're saying it's a roadmap for future explorers, or maybe even a test-bed to create the original granite plugs,' Chad commented, looking up at the plug stones in front of him. 'These granite blocks definitely look out of place. Any would-be grave robber would have been very curious to get behind them. Looking at the geometry here, I'm getting more convinced about the story that the tunnel was dug outwards to remove a coffer lid.'

'Well, the three granite plugs were originally hidden behind a limestone plug, which blended perfectly with these rocks of the Descending Passage. It is very possible that the Trial Passages gave all the clues where to start digging. By the way, just look at this perfectly carved tunnel, straight to within a few millimetres.'

'It's incredible!' Chad remarked.

'We are now going up the Ascending Passage towards the chambers. It's a bit of a scramble on this ridged boarding but it's well lit. It's about 38 metres long and climbs up at 26°,' Ahmed explained. 'Come on!'

'So originally, this was just a slippery slope.'

'Precisely! This was never meant for people to walk up,' Ahmed confirmed.

Chad and Ahmed carefully scrambled upwards along the narrow, low passage on the wooden-slatted walking boards, up to the start of the Grand Gallery.

Emerging out of the claustrophobic tunnel, Chad stared upwards at the magnificent Grand Gallery, which opened up above them. 'Wow, this is very impressive. How high is this?'

'Well the Ascending Passage we've just been through was only just a metre wide and around 1.2 metres high. The Grand Gallery rises to almost nine metres and is around 47 metres long. You can see how these seven layers of polished limestone step inwards towards the ceiling. Officially it's called corbelling. It's around two metres wide here where we're standing, and just over a metre wide where the stones close the structure.'

'What is the latest theory on this structure,' Chad enquired, shining his torch up the walls. 'There's certainly a lovely hollow echo sound!' he remarked.

'The most logical theory, published recently by Houdin, suggests that it was for a counterweight system to raise up the 70-ton blocks of stone, which form the relieving chambers above the King's Chamber. You may have read that Houdin proposed an internal spiral ramp structure, which obviates the need for an external ramp. That internal ramp has yet to be discovered, although a team of Swiss geophysicists did find some hollow zones, which match his theory,' Ahmed continued. 'There are other wild theories about the Grand Gallery construction and its intended purpose as a resonant acoustic chamber, but geometrical structures like these will always have resonances at a number of frequencies. As for a pharaoh's burial tomb, there just simply aren't any decorative hieroglyphs.'

'What about those ceiling blocks? No secrets there?' Chad asked, pausing to shine his torch upwards.

'Yes, it could be another possible chamber location. The ceiling blocks are rather wide. Maybe they will drill through and put a camera through one day.'

'I should add that in 2017, a group discovered a new 30-metre long chamber above the Grand Gallery using differential cosmic particle absorption. Muons, which are like heavy electrons and are found in cosmic particle streams, get absorbed as a function of rock thickness. They set up muon detectors all around the pyramid outside. By comparing how the background muon count changed, passing through different thicknesses of stone in different directions, the *Big Void*, as it is now called, was discovered.'

'This of course further confounds the Egyptologists.'

'Is that your kit up there?' Chad asked, shining his torch at the sensor system.

'Yes, we are using a wireless humidity detector and surface chemical analysers. As I said, the build-up of salt from tourists is a real problem. Each visitor breathes out approximately twenty grams of water, which evaporates, leaving salt on the limestone. This salt leeches into the stone and slowly eats it away. Back in 1993, it was Rudolf Gantenbrink, who sent his first robot crawler up the airshafts to investigate the possibility of using them to house ventilation equipment.'

'What are those notches in the walls?'

'Again, the jury is still out on that one. Logic suggests that the notches could form part of the support structure for Houdin's counterweight system. We can examine them closer shortly, but first let me take you into the Queen's Chamber, which is down that passageway, straight ahead in front of us. It's a narrow entrance but the room is spacious inside. The centre of the gallery rises up above this tunnel. The Khufu tomb protagonists will have you believe that this was the makeshift tomb while the King's Chamber was still in construction.'

'The floor is all pink granite,' Chad observed, as he crawled towards the light coming from the chamber.

'Hey Chad, the passage floor drops about half a metre as you approach the end,' Ahmed called out behind him. 'Take care!'

'No worries. I see the floor is now limestone beyond the step.'

'Yes, they think the pink granite covered the whole floor and was removed by robbers in the past. It would have come from quite a distance away, from some 500 miles away, down in Aswan.'

Ahmed and Chad stepped into the smooth-walled Queen's Chamber. Chad stood in front of a deep-set niche in the end wall.

'That's the corbelled niche, but no one knows what it was for. It may have contained a statue according to the Egyptologists, or something else to others,' Ahmed added. 'Some think the increasing vertical step dimensions relate to an energy wavelength tuning device, and that the ancient Egyptians had knowledge of this. Personally, I find it interesting that the corbelled niche suggests the form of the hieroglyph, which means *ascend*.'

'How big is this chamber?'

'It's almost a cubic volume, measuring about 5 metres by 5 metres on the floor, with the walls rising to just more than 4.5 metres. The angled ceiling slabs rise to around 6.5 metres in the centre.'

'Are these the airshafts you mentioned,' Chad asked, shining his torch up an opening in the wall.

'Yes, they were discovered in 1872 by an enterprising explorer called Dixon. He decided there had to be shafts here also, after finding two in the King's Chamber. They were fully concealed in the wall, not intending to be found. They were covered by about ten centimetres of masonry. After sticking a wire into a crack in the wall, he found a void and then employed a carpenter to cut through the wall.'

'Did they find anything inside?'

'Yes, a stone ball, a bronze hook and a piece of wood. These are now believed to form part of an early surveying tool. The two airshafts in the King's Chamber had been known since 1610, so Dixon reasoned after finding *one*, there should be another one opposite and that's how he found the *second*. Since then, nothing much happened until Gantenbrink's recent robot explorations of both airshafts in the 1990s, when he discovered each airshaft closed off by a polished slab of light limestone.'

'The two shafts terminate some distance from the edge of the pyramid, right?' Chad asserted. 'There was something about them pointing at certain stars.'

'Yes, they both terminate around six metres from the edge of the pyramid. The popular held view is that the airshafts enable the Pharaoh's soul to ascend to the stars. Funerary texts describe the Pharaoh's soul encountering a series of doors before passing to the afterlife, which seemed to explain to some, why the shafts were closed off. I brought a couple of photos to show you the slabs.' Ahmed pulled out two photos from his wallet. 'Look, each has two central copper fittings, almost like ornate handles. Are they doors, or are they just closed off for some other reason... who knows? Gantenbrink was allowed to drill into one slab to see what was behind it. He only found a closed cubic chamber. Interestingly, there was some hieroglyphic text on the floor.'

'It seems strange to me,' Chad remarked. 'Why create two airshafts then close them off at both ends? What angles are they rising at?'

'The latest estimates for the Queen's Chamber suggest the southern shaft is rising at around 32.5 degrees. Unlike the northern shaft, it is straight. That runs horizontal for around 2 metres then rises at around 45 degrees. Both shafts rise above the level of the King's Chamber so the story of the Queen's Chamber not serving any function is challenged. If the pyramid was completed layer-by-layer, even after the King's Chamber was completed, masons were still cutting complicated shaft sections for the Queen's Chamber through limestone,' Ahmed replied. 'I personally have a hunch that something changed during the construction of the pyramid, which caused them to abandon the Queen's Chamber shafts.'

'That sounds intriguing. Well, what stars are the shafts supposedly pointing at?'

'There are many candidates. Everyone wants there to be a single star but that of course makes no sense. Some say the Queen's Chamber northern shaft is directed towards Kochab, officially called Ursa Minoris Beta ... the brightest star in the bowl of the Little Dipper. The southern shaft seems to be aligned with Sirius. Of course, the Earth is rotating about its axis, so each of the shafts points to a *ring* of stars as the Earth rotates and any alignment of the shafts is only momentary. Others say that the alignment must only be considered at precise times and dates.'

'What is your hunch about the shafts?'

'Well, I have been considering the angular difference between the two sets of shafts. The Queen's Chamber shafts are at 32.5° and 45° for the north and south respectively, while both the north and south King's

Chamber shafts rise at around 39°. If you consider the angular difference between each set of shafts, to within half a degree, it is almost exactly 102°. It's as if the Earth's spin axis changed during construction…'

'Due to *polar motion*, for example, a shift in the Earth's spin axis direction due to sudden melting of the ice sheets,' Chad interrupted. 'Greenland ice cores show a substantial global temperature rise took place at the end of the *Younger Dryas*, some 11,770 years ago.'

'Precisely, …and then the King's Chamber shafts provide the new corrected orientation,' Ahmed continued. 'Giza is 30° N, so an elevation of around 39° means the possible candidate stars for the northern shaft are found in a ring some 9° off the Earth's spin axis direction. To make any sense of that, we would also need to consider what the night sky looked like when the Khufu pyramid was built. As I said, the Earth is slowly precessing, which is changing the direction of the Earth's spin axis quite substantially. The southern shaft stars point to a ring at an altitude of 39° above the horizon.'

'As to the copper hooks on the undersides of the blocks in the Queen's Chamber shafts, which Gantenbrink's robot found. These might only be handles to which ropes were attached to pull the stone blocks in place to close them off.'

'Come on, let's get up to the King's Chamber,' Ahmed urged. 'There are more interesting things to see in there.'

They made their way out of the Queen's Chamber and back along the passage leading to the bottom of the Grand Gallery.

'This is an impressive structure,' Chad exclaimed, gazing upwards at the smoothly polished walls. 'These notches and bevelled edges …and the corbelling, all were extremely precisely made. Are we ever likely to know their exact purpose?'

'I am convinced that this pyramid is definitely a technical machine. It was very carefully constructed for a particular purpose. Whether we will ever discover that, is hard to say.'

Chad shone his torch upwards at the roof of the Grand Gallery. 'This is really very impressive,' he murmured.

Chad and Ahmed carefully made their way upwards through the Grand Gallery, along the wooden walkway towards the narrow passage to the King's Chamber.

'Be careful here, we are going to clamber through this opening to the King's Chamber,' Ahmed cautioned. 'Take a good look at the portcullis-type arrangement of the entrance tunnel blocks. The design is a feat of engineering.'

'Quite astonishing,' Chad remarked, momentarily out of breath.

'This is the antechamber. This suspended stone slab is called the Granite Leaf,' Ahmed added, shining his torch. 'It's around 45cm thick and fitted into grooves either side in the wall. Duck down!'

Directly past the suspended slab, three pairs of wide grooves were cut either side in the walls.

'Do we know if portcullis stones existed here?'

'Well, there is a broken portcullis stone just outside the main entrance. It most likely came from here.'

'Aha, I see that the soft limestone has suddenly changed to hard red granite,' Chad remarked. 'A much stronger stone. They must have done that for a reason.'

Two and a half metres later, the antechamber tunnel opened out into the King's Chamber.

'Welcome to the King's Chamber. You made it into the heart of the Khufu pyramid mystery.'

Ahmed took out a tuning fork and tapped it against the stone wall. 'Listen to this!'

The empty chamber became resonant with sound and echoes.

'What are the dimensions?' Chad asked, shining his torch all around.

'The chamber is around ten metres by five, and almost six metres high,' Ahmed explained. 'And this is the only artefact left, this coffer.'

'The coffer without a lid, if it ever had one,' Chad murmured.

'Well, this ridge on the inside is a pretty good suggestion that it did,' Ahmed remarked, running his finger along the inside ledge. 'This also rings like a bell!' he said, giving the coffer a hard tap.

'This has been carved from a single block of this chocolate coloured granite, and I am told it is even harder than the granite walls of this chamber.'

'From a geological perspective, this colour suggests that the granite has undergone significant heating,' Chad explained. 'I wonder what caused that.'

'And look at this corner, it has been smashed away. This is what I was talking about. I think that when al-Ma'mun's men found the coffer with a lid, they managed to break into the coffer. As soon as they saw that something was inside they were eager to break it open.'

'Look over here. This is one of the air shafts. The other is across there,' Ahmed added shining his torch. 'They are around 21cm square and extend around 60 metres to the outside.'

'Have they always been open?'

'Well, Colonel Vyse discovered them on an expedition in 1834 and helped clean them to let air through. Vyse is also the person who linked the pyramid with the pharaoh Khufu, although there is much controversy about that,' Ahmed continued.

'So, no other doorways have been discovered to this room?'

'Well, new theories are emerging. Look at this lower block adjacent to the coffer. That guy Houdin demonstrated that this lowest block is not load-bearing, due to the arrangement of the blocks above it. So, the block was not so tightly jammed in. There are rumours of some investigations by the Egyptian authorities, but any discoveries remain secret and unpublished. It may indeed lead to another antechamber.'

Chad gazed in wonder at the remarkably smooth granite walls of blocks.

'Chad, come with me, let me take you up above into the chambers above the King's Chamber.'

They crawled back out through the antechamber to the Grand Gallery. A ladder stood up against the end wall. At the top of the ladder was a narrow opening with a rope hanging out. Ahmed went first, grabbing the rope and pulling himself into the opening of the passage. Chad followed. After a short crawl they entered the first of the relieving chambers.

'So, this is *Davison's Chamber,* discovered in 1763 by the British Consul Nathaniel Davison. He apparently noticed that his voice echoed in a strange way while in the Grand Gallery, which led him to discover the small rectangular access hole. Each of these nine rough granite slabs weigh as much as 70 tons, so quite a feat getting them up here. Above us we see the same type of ceiling as seen from the King's Chamber. It was

Colonel Vyse who blasted his way to discover the other four chambers. He claimed to have finally made the connection with Khufu by discovering Khufu's cartouche painted on the ceiling. Let's head there now.'

Chad and Ahmed clambered upwards through the narrow, carved tunnel and finally reached the upper chamber. The ceiling was now a vaulted granite roof, covered in the most diverse graffiti.

'We can see that the chamber ceilings comprise flattened blocks on the underside and very roughly hewn surfaces on the top. Some have suggested that this is to tune the blocks to resonate in a particular way,' Ahmed explained. 'Look, here is the Khufu cartouche.'

'Is this the proof then?' Chad asked, shining his torch at the dull red ochre image.

'That is the dilemma and controversy. That cartouche does not actually read Khufu. We believe that Vyse most likely had a copy of the cartouche translations with him, but that book had the same Khufu cartouche error. It actually reads *Ra-ufu*.'

'Does that mean anything?' Chad enquired.

'Sure, it does. *Ra* is the sun God of course and *ufu* means horizon. So, we could understand Ra-ufu as meaning the setting or rising point of the Sun. It can also be that Ra-ufu was a king of the 4th Dynasty.'

'So, what is the proper hieroglyphic script for Khufu.'

'It's a sun followed by a bird, then a snake followed by a bird. I don't know why a sun and snake would be symbolic for Khufu. By the way, I am happy to let you have my thoughts privately, but I am careful what I say publicly. I do value my job here!'

'So, the Khufu connection is still up for review?'

'Indeed!' Ahmed replied with a smile. 'Come on, it's time to clamber down out of here and back to the world of the living.'

Chad felt very privileged to have seen first-hand the inside of the great Pyramid of Khufu or Ra-ufu. It did seem to have been well and truly damaged over the years. It seemed less and less likely that it was a burial tomb. But if not, why had it been built and what could it possibly do? Was it some kind of machine? The air shafts seemed very strange, and if they pointed towards any stars then they did this only momentarily as the Earth spun on its axis.

After a steep descent down the Grand gallery and Ascending Passage, they walked out through al-Ma'mun's tunnel and they were back outside in the hot Egyptian sunshine. The bright sunlight was momentarily blinding, after spending so long in the dimly lit passageways, but it was quite refreshing to be out in the fresh air at last. Ahmed continued his story.

'One more comment about Vyse. Not only did he seriously damage the internal structure above the King's Chamber, he also caused the loss of the coffer that was found in the small Menkaure pyramid.'

'How did he manage that?'

'Well, he was the person who rediscovered the passageway leading to the inner chamber of Menkaure, where he found the apparently highly ornate, blue granite coffer, also without a lid. A year later, in 1839, British officials arranged for it to be dragged out and sent by sea to Liverpool. It never arrived. The ship carrying it, sank off the Spanish port of Cartagena. There are plans to try to locate it and return it to Egypt.'

'That would be good, if they can relocate it.'

Ahmed's mobile suddenly buzzed. 'I am reachable now I guess,' he murmured, checking the incoming message. 'Uh oh, I have a delivery coming today in around an hour. Listen Chad, I really need to meet my delivery today. I propose we head back to the cabin, you drop off this gear and pick up your rucksack. I will then call Tau and get him to come to the south gate below the Sphinx, and we can wander down there together. My delivery will be arriving there.'

'Ahmed, that sounds great.'

They walked back to the cabin and Chad put his trainers back on, and left the torch and knee pads. He grabbed his rucksack and Ahmed then called Tau. 'He's there in 30 minutes.'

'Perfect,' Chad replied.

They walked back outside and Ahmed locked up the cabin. 'Come let's head to the south gate.'

'By the way, Ahmed, before I forget, what happened to all the Great Pyramid casing stones? Surely people didn't climb all the way up and remove them from the top down,' Chad asked, pointing up the pyramid slope.

'That would be impossible. There are records of an earthquake in 1303 which caused them to tumble down. They were gathered and carted off and used for various buildings. It would have looked fantastic with the white casing stones in place. There are also many questions as to how the ancient Egyptians carved the casing stones so flat. We can see these few still in place at the base here.'

'So, what about the apparent machine cuts and wide bore holes that are reported in several places across the Giza plateau?'

'That again is very controversial and there are no adequate explanations. If you look down, we are walking across the foundation of the pyramids. This was constructed before the pyramids were even started.'

'Wow, some of these blocks are enormous!' Chad remarked.

'Yes, and this is a three-dimensional jigsaw. Under this surface is a complex layer of giant blocks into which the top layer of limestone rocks fits. Huge efforts were made in creating this flat foundation. We can absolutely describe it as *bedrock engineering*. Some of these weigh up to 100 tons,' Ahmed explained.

'The reality is that we cannot use science to date the pyramids of course. Only organic matter can be carbon dated. What if the pyramids are truly ancient, even 15 thousand years old?' Chad asked. 'I was just thinking, what if there was a cataclysm at any time in the distant past. Much of the evidence of any lost civilization on the surface of the Earth might have been truly destroyed, leaving only the giant megalithic structures, such as the pyramids, for future civilizations to discover.'

'OK, before you come up with a new theory on that, I would be interested to hear your thoughts as a geologist on the Sphinx,' Ahmed replied with a smile.

It was close to midday. The Sun was very hot. As they walked down across the plateau, with its tumbled down blocks, strewn everywhere, the head of the Sphinx slowly rose up into view.

They walked to the edge of the excavated courtyard. The graceful mysterious Sphinx was also truly awesome to behold. Chad looked at the head. It did seem somewhat disproportionately small for its lion-like body.

'So, I have a question for you Chad. You are the geologist. What do you make of the weathering on the Sphinx and on the courtyard walls? I should add that this entire courtyard was excavated to produce limestone blocks for a nearby temple. The Sphinx was only fully rediscovered in 1936 after being partially buried in the sand for aeons.'

Chad paused a while and then answered.

'OK, well there are two types of weathering. The horizontal weathering is all due to wind and sand, where the extent of the erosion is due to the density of the different limestone layers. This is all sedimentary rock. The vertical weathering is due to water. The extent of that depends upon how acidic the water is. It hasn't rained in the Sahara for thousands of years. We may be talking 10,000 years plus!'

'Ahmed added. 'So, extensive acid rain could make it happen fast? Are there any cataclysmic events that can produce acid rain?'

'If we are talking extra-terrestrial, I would need to ask my brother Tom. He's the astrophysicist.'

'They say that the head was re-carved at least once from a lion's head, or even a jackal's head. That explains the disproportionate size. There are also tunnels and chambers underneath which may contain the sought-after *Hall of records*. Nearby, under the causeway is the *Osiris Shaft*. It is closed off today so we can't get access, but it comprises a series of vertical shafts going down some 30 metres or more, in several levels, via long rusty ladders. There are a number of large granite boxes down there, each having a lid, weighing a hundred tons or more. One of them strangely is made of a strange stone *dacite*, which can only have come from Romania, or even Mexico! That is really strange!'

'Wow, that's interesting!' Chad replied. 'Are they similar to the granite boxes in the Serapeum at Saqqara?'

'I hadn't thought of that, but yes they are quite similar to the Serapeum sarcophagus boxes. Each one finely produced, as if machine cut out of a single block of granite, using some lost ancient technology, then placed in their virtually inaccessible locations underground. Something that we simply cannot achieve today.'

'What if they are not sarcophagi?'

'Are you still thinking about your cataclysmic event?'

'I am! I need to think a lot about the different things you told me. There is something about the pyramids which starts to convince me more and more, that they describe something greater than themselves. They seem to form part of a larger structure. Maybe the great pyramid is indeed some kind of machine, but what is it and what can it do? The realisation that so much effort was taken to build the foundation, suggests the builders intended that it would last a phenomenal amount of time, even perhaps tens of thousands of years. The structures must be very old.'

'We were also talking about the *Pyramid Texts* earlier. You know that they are found written inside several of the other pyramids, as if the texts needed to be protected also,' Ahmed remarked. 'Unless they were added later, of course.'

Looking down still at the Sphinx, reclining inside its eroding enclosure, Chad started to wonder if it had any connection with the Pyramids at all. It would all depend upon the age of the two constructions, something that seemed pure conjecture. He had read that records described how Khufu had made repairs to the Sphinx. He was therefore clearly not the builder and there was no evidence or records which described how the pyramids were built. This suggested that they possibly predated the Egyptian dynasties by a significant amount of time.

It was a short walk down past the Sphinx, lying serenely in the Sun. They walked out onto the road, and Tau's taxi was just coming towards them.

'Well, I hope you've had a great time. I've really enjoyed spending the time with you. You ask difficult questions!'

'Ahmed, thanks very much. This has been great!'

'Chad, do let me know what your brother says. I want to know if it is a random cataclysmic event, or one which could occur again.'

'Of course. I will.'

Tau pulled up beside them. He got out.

'So, did you have a good time? Make any discoveries?'

'I think so. This has been great!'

Tau chatted for a short while with Ahmed, then they shook hands and it was time to leave.

'Ahmed, goodbye! I'll get a message to Tau if my brother has any knowledge of a cataclysm.'

'Great! See you!' he replied.

Chad had had the day of his life. He was becoming truly immersed in this whole pyramid mystery. He also started to think about the *double bump* carving above the main pyramid doorway. That was something no one had yet been able to explain. The carving above the main entrance surely had some significance.

'Welcome back from your Giza experience,' Tau said, as he pulled away. 'I have to say, you look pretty affected by what you've seen and heard.'

'Tau, I am. I am actually quite shocked. I did not think this would be so awe-inspiring. Thank you so much for this.'

'You are welcome. Has the trip inspired any further plans for the afternoon. I can drive you to Saqqara if you want. It is only 27km away. Or do you want to head back to the hotel, or the museum?'

'Is Saqqara so close? Even just a short visit there would be awesome, from what I've heard.'

'Of course. Saqqara and the Serapeum it is. We should be there in around 40 minutes. You will be happy to know that one of Ahmed's friends works there as a guide. I'll call him,' Tau said, reaching for his phone. After a short call, he added, 'All set!'

'Great!' Chad replied, and he sat back to enjoy the comfortable leather seat as they headed off.

7 California: a new perspective on SETI, Drake and the Fermi Paradox

Campus Starbucks, University of California at Berkeley

Ted Curtis, Jacqui Hau and Carl Rhodes were sitting around a coffee table with a group of other researchers. An astrophysics journal was open on the table and there was some excitement in the air. Carl was making a point.

'OK you say thousands Ted. It says 3500 exoplanets *potentially* discovered, but we're not talking *Goldilocks zone*, where planets are rocky and terrestrial-like, and warm enough to have liquid water. Only around a thousand have been confirmed, and that number includes the Hot Jupiters, and many of the unconfirmed exoplanets are orbiting very old stars.'

'*Hot Jupiters*, Dr Rhodes?' Jacqui asked. 'I thought gas giants were cold.'

'Most are . . . but some of them became very hot. Gas giants only form far from a star where it's cold enough for water, methane and ammonia to condense into solid ice grains. So, you want to know how they ended up so close to the star?' Carl continued.

'OK how?' Jacqui nodded.

'Well, *migration theory* suggests terrestrial-like planets and Gas Giants can end up with very close-in orbits with periods of only a few Earth days. If terrestrial-like planets form while the protoplanetary disk is still present, they interact with it and lose momentum, causing them to spiral inwards. Gas giants can clear a path but can also lose momentum and move inwards . . .'

'Or get flung inwards by gravitational scattering from a close encounter with another large planet,' a researcher interjected.

'So why don't the atmospheres of these Hot Jupiters just vaporize under the intense heat of the star?' Jacqui asked.

'They do to a certain extent. Stellar heating causes *hydrodynamic escape*, i.e. the loss of atmosphere, stellar gravity causes *tidal disruption*, which can alter the orbit leading to atmosphere loss, and extreme ultra-violet radiation causes *photo-evaporation* of light molecules in their atmospheres. In spite of all that, the massive *Hot Jupiters* can pretty much hold on to their atmospheres for the ten-billion-year typical lifetime of their host star. It's the much less massive, very closely orbiting *Hot Neptunes* who don't make it. At a certain point they hit the *catastrophe signature* and lose their entire atmosphere, resulting in a rocky core, much resembling a terrestrial planet,' Carl explained. 'Some people are asking is that what Earth is? Are we sitting on the core of a *Hot Neptune* somewhat shifted back out by cometary impact or Gas Giant displacement?

'So how many Earth-like planets have they found?' Jacqui asked.

'Thousands of exoplanets so far, but not many Earth-like planets. More importantly, we're interested in finding *terrestrial* planets in the *habitable* zone. That generally means rocky planets orbiting at a particular distance from their star, having an atmosphere where liquid water can exist on the surface. *Life as we know it* is based on carbon and needs water,' Carl replied.

'There are Klingons on the starboard bow, Jim,' another researcher added.

'And that's not a true *Trekkie* quote either, that's from the song,' Carl retorted. *''It's life, Jim, but not as we know it'*, is *also* a misquote from the original series.'

Jacqui smiled.

'That's why they call it the *Goldilocks zone*,' Ted interjected bringing the serious discussion back on track, 'Not too hot, not too cold.'

'Can we detect these planets just through a telescope, even if they are so far away?' Jacqui asked.

'Not exactly. The resolving power of telescopes just isn't good enough to observe the planets directly, particularly close to a very bright star. We can however determine their presence indirectly. There are three methods. We can observe the drop in intensity, of a star as a planet transits in front of it, provided it's along our line of sight,' Carl explained. 'I need a prop to help explain this.'

Grabbing a glass saltshaker from the table, Carl moved a pen across the front of the shaker with the other. 'For larger planets, orbiting close to a distant star, we can measure the *drop in stellar intensity* for the duration of the transit.'

'We really need something as good as the Hubble telescope for that,' the researcher added.

'Yeah, Hubble was key for exoplanet detection. You will remember from your fourth-grade physics that *Kepler's third law* equates period squared to semi-major axis cubed — that's approximately the orbital radius — so we get . .'

'For *Sun*-like stars,' the researcher added.

'I'm keeping this simple Chris,' Carl added politely, 'But we know enough about stellar magnitudes and their distances to adapt Kepler's third law. But it means we can determine the orbital radius and maybe even the planetary radius from the drop, in intensity.'

Putting his pen down, Carl started to move the shaker in a small circular motion. 'The second method involves detecting the movement of a star caused by a planet. The presence of a large planet near to a star will cause that star to wobble like this, as they both orbit around a common centre of mass, and we can detect that wobble against the background fixed stars. The period of the wobble is the period of the orbit, and knowing the mass of the star, we can work out the mass of the planet.'

'I'm impressed,' Jacqui replied.

'The challenge with this method is that the wobble is so small that this *astrometry* method requires really high-resolution imaging. I think NASA has a program. Ted, is the NASA SIM Lite satellite back on schedule?' Carl asked, turning to his colleague.

'Carl, they *postponed it indefinitely* back in 2010,' Ted replied. 'Some serious scientific lobbying is still required.'

'OK, but there is a third method which is bearing fruit. The spectra of these wobbling stars are getting Doppler-shifted back and forth as the planet orbits the star. This gives a fluctuating radial velocity of the star, equivalent to the radial velocity of the planet. The *Doppler shift* is really small, but most home telescope equipment is sensitive enough to detect it. By measuring these spectroscopic frequency shifts back and forth, we can indirectly determine the planet's orbital period, and thus from Kepler's third law, the orbital radius, and even the degree of elliptical eccentricity. From a good estimate of the stellar mass, from its magnitude, we can even determine the exoplanet's mass,' Carl continued.

'. . . and that's how we know whether the exoplanet is an Earth-like terrestrial planet and in the star's habitable *Goldilocks zone*,' Ted interjected.

'Thank-you guys. What a succinct explanation,' Jacqui replied with a smile.

'There's also the *gravitational microlensing* method which sometimes shows the presence of an exoplanet orbiting the lensing star, as a pulse in the spectrum as it crosses the path of the vastly distant star,' the researcher added excitedly.

'Chris, you're right, but wait, wait . . . that's *General Relativity* . . . ,' Carl exclaimed.

'Uh oh, yep, you got him Carl, and that's a forfeit! Probably worth a doughnut each . . . ,' Ted confirmed.

'. . . and I remember that the Faculty staff banned discussions of *curved space-time* in Starbucks, subject to a forfeit. We all signed up to it last Fall,' Carl continued in a serious tone.

'Really? But I never mentioned the *G word*,' Chris remarked, somewhat disbelievingly.

'. . . and particularly if there are guests,' Ted added. 'Hey guys, look at the time, we should really think about making a move for the SETI seminar. Carl, you're chairing it.'

'Registration and coffee happening until 10:30 at least. But yes, it's time to go. Chris, don't think we're letting you off. Those doughnuts certainly look very good from here.'

'A forfeit for discussing *General Relativity* in Starbucks?' Jacqui inquired, wide-eyed. 'Really? Surely not?'

'Absolutely,' Carl replied.

'They're just too quick. They've been angling to get me for some time, ever since I got a letter-to-the-editor in *Nature* published.'

'Slam dunk,' Carl added with a smile.

'What did you write?' Jacqui asked.

'I'm a co-author with a colleague, Tom Walker, from Sydney. It's a summary review about dark matter with a new cosmological consideration that extremely curved space-time is equivalent to mass. The whole basis for the dark matter hypothesis was the need for missing mass to flatten out the galactic rotation curves. The famous quote is: *matter tells space how to curve, curved space tells matter how to move*. Compressed spacetime could be this missing mass'

'Right, right,' Jacqui interjected. 'Classical gravitation theory requires orbital velocities to drop off as a function of one over the root of the orbital radius, but at about fifteen kiloparsecs from our Galactic centre supermassive black hole, the orbital velocities just flatten off and all have the same magnitude.'

'Right, so conventional thinking says there has to be nine times more mass outside our galaxy to explain the rotation curves,' Chris continued. 'No one considered that compressed space-time, produced by our own supermassive black hole — for example from a Kerr spin-pulsing behaviour — could extend throughout our galaxy, forming concentric zones of a so-called compressed-spacetime equivalent-mass . . . just like standing gravitational waves. If this exists, logic suggests that further out, stars are confined between multiple concentric shells of equivalent-mass compressed space-time, thereby stabilizing their velocities to a single value at higher radius.'

'I like it. I like it. That sounds really compelling!' Jacqui replied.

' . . . and what if these standing waves extend well beyond our galaxy before they fade away. We see dark matter influencing *gravitational lensing* well beyond galaxies. Also, if we consider our central supermassive blackhole to be precessing, this could be the cause of the spiral arms,' Chris continued.

'That sounds very radical,' Jacqui remarked.

'Yes, but a precessing supermassive black hole would also explain why the spiral galaxy NGC 4622 in *Centaurus* is spinning backwards,' Chris added persuasively. 'Hubble discovered that spiral arm galaxy some 111 million light years away back in 2002. No one has been able to explain that!'

'Jacqui, I told Chris that this isn't what we true academics do,' Carl interjected. 'We all travel the same journey. We reinforce the works of others by not making radical suggestions, which may take years to substantiate. I know a professor at Oxford. He keeps a file of students' ideas about new models of gravity and cosmology. They are buried in a bottom drawer and will never see the light of day. Where would he or I get research funding for detecting dark matter if some bright spark proves that dark matter is just a further dimension of *General Relativity?*'

'In fairness Chris, although I jest, I'm secretly impressed with you. You could also be right that gravitational waves have proved so difficult to detect because they pass through concentric spherical shells of compressed space-time. The problem here is that Chris may well have the last laugh. The jury's still out on dark matter and the *weakly interacting massive particles*, or WIMPs, are yet to be detected. Just think of the millions being spent on those research areas. The question for me is about the moving nature of gravitational waves, and the self-generating space-time distortion of Chris's hypothesis. If Chris would just do the math and prove how compressed space-time can have a standing wave behaviour, which leaves an imprint on galactic models, then we can all move on. Until then it's dark matter funding for all!'

'Carl, I didn't know you cared.'

'Chris, seriously, do the math! The world waits, you could be absolutely right,' Carl replied with a shrug and a smile.

They walked into the main amphitheatre. Carl headed off towards the stage to join the speakers' panel. The others sat down in the reserved seats at the front of the theatre. A lectern stood off to the right. Carl bent down to say a few words to a friendly looking guy with grey hair sitting at the end of the panel, who suddenly burst out laughing. He then walked over to the lectern and took the microphone in his hand.

'Hello everyone, a lovely day for a campus walk in the Sun. Welcome to this seminar, part two of our *SETI, Drake, and the 1420MHz 21cm Hydrogen line*. Two days ago, we talked about the status of the SETI program and our involvement. Today we talk about the famous *Drake equation* and the implications of Enrico Fermi's *Fermi Paradox*. I want to keep this pretty informal, so please just interrupt if you have any questions. This is just a short seminar where we will cover the two questions, then we break for some lunch, which is a nutritious buffet in the room next door, or so I am informed. After that we will divide into groups for a break-out session and attack this whole list of SETI issues,' Carl explained, holding up a sheet of A4.

'So, many of you know it was *Frank Drake* who devised a scientific estimate to ascertain the number of detectable intelligent civilizations out there in our Galaxy.'

'Is he still alive?' a voice called out, quietly.

'What? Yes, I do believe so. I saw him speak at Cornell back in 2017,' Carl replied. 'Indeed. By the way, don't be shy. Just shout out your comments and questions. Let's keep the room alive.'

Carl turned towards the full screen behind him and saw the first Drake slide was up with the full equation.

$$N = R_* \cdot f_P \cdot n_e \cdot f_l \cdot f_i \cdot f_c \cdot L$$

The Drake Equation

'OK. Here we go. I know this equation looks very formidable, but it's pretty straight forward and we can take it one bite at a time. It was *Frank Drake* who dared first to pose the question, way back in the 1960s, when he was at Cornell. He is considered the father of SETI and creator of the famous, or *infamous, Arecibo Message* with help from Carl Sagan. That message was transmitted towards some potentially hostile civilization in a globular cluster of some hundred thousand stars, some 25,000 light years away in the constellation of *Hercules*. Hopefully we won't hear from them any time soon!'

'OK, so today, with help from data captured by the *Kepler Telescope*, which like Frank, is well retired now, and the *Hubble Telescope*, we have been able to come up with some good estimates on the number of intelligent civilizations out there trying to communicate.'

'So, we are talking only about our galaxy. The equation does not consider any other galaxy. Our closest galaxy *Andromeda* is more than 2.5 million light years away. Since interstellar communication is difficult enough, we don't consider intergalactic communication, given the distances involved. I take a slightly different approach to Drake, I don't consider the rate of star formation per year, but just start by considering the total number of stars in our galaxy, and then reduce that number to an estimate of rocky planets and moons which could support life.'

'So, if we take the number of stars in the Milky Way, the mid-range estimate is pretty much accepted as 400 billion. We then multiply that

400 billion by the *fraction of stars which are actually suitable to host planets with life*, and here we need to exclude many stellar environments hostile to life, like variable stars and binary stars etc. We think that's around half of them. That gives us 200 billion potential candidates. We then multiply by *the number of locations which can support life*, and that includes both planets *and moons*. In our solar system the number of locations that can support life is around 5-15, where we are additionally considering all moons where the precursor of life, water, is present.'

The grey-haired man at the end of the panel called out something towards Carl. 'What is that Jack?' Carl urged.

'*Europa*? Precisely. In the past, people have always talked just in terms of planets, but Jupiter's moon, Europa, is a promising candidate for life in our own solar system. Sure, it's completely covered in ice, and far away from the Sun, but during its elliptical orbit around the gas giant Jupiter, it gets squeezed and stretched, generating a lot of heat under that ice. It's highly likely that under that ice, is a vast ocean of water, and in that ocean, there is likely to be life. Sure, the lifeforms may be primitive, but Europa is worth a trip.'

'The *mantis shrimp* civilization!' someone called out from the audience. The room erupted with laughter.

'Indeed,' Carl responded with a smile.

'OK, for those of you who were not in a bizarre lecture last week, someone proposed that the remarkable, highly developed eye of the mantis shrimp, proved it had survived a cataclysm, and was from a different *tree of life* than our own. It's quite an extraordinary creature with an eye having 16 different colour cones, capable of detecting 16 different hues. Personally, I don't believe they came from the moon Europa.' There was more laughter in the room. 'It is of course possible that they are survivors of a cataclysm, but there is no evidence for that yet. Nevertheless, excellent comment. We continue.'

'So, if we take the low figure of 5 locations per star system, this gives us a first total estimate of 1000 billion potential Milky Way real-estate locations, where the accepted conditions for life to originate and flourish, in some form, are found. Now if we determine *the fraction of locations where life actually occurs* . . . and we assume that if the *Goldilocks Zone* conditions last long enough, why shouldn't life arise? . . . then that is *in all 100 % of them*, right? So, we multiply by one. Now we come to the more controversial estimates. Of these planets and moons in a *Goldilocks Zone*, where life has developed, *what fraction of these will develop intelligent life?,*' Carl was interrupted again.

'How do we define intelligence?' someone called out.

'Good point, but let us assume that it is more than poking a seed out of a hole with a stick, as one *YouTuber* defined it.'

'Fundamentally, we think that nature and evolution complexity is heading forward. We don't see species becoming less intelligent, so we believe that all these planets can evolve intelligent life. Again, we multiply by one. But we want to know the *fraction of locations in our galaxy where intelligent life can evolve and build interstellar communications systems*, and additionally, *who want to communicate and be detectable*. In general, the solutions to difficult questions are not obvious. We just can't assume that technology evolution will progress at the same rate on different planets. Just consider the tenuous path we have walked, where great minds have made substantial contributions to our global knowledge through rare insights and skills.'

'In astrophysics, we only need think of the unsung academic, Henrietta Leavitt, and the huge contribution she made in determining how far away the nearby dwarf galaxies are. She was a Harvard graduate, yet worked for next-to-nothing as a *computer* ... yes, that was her official title ... in the early part of the 20th century. She meticulously analysed thousands of photographic plates for decades and deduced the relation between the pulsing rate of the Cepheid variable stars and their absolute luminosity or brightness. That discovery enabled Hubble to determine that the nebulae were actually galaxies outside our own.'

'What about Schwarzschild?' a voice called.

'And Friedmann?' another called.

'Exactly, thank you, and the point made there is that Einstein discovered and defined the field equations of general relativity, but he never solved them. It was Schwarzschild who provided the first proof, but he was dead within a year of providing this proof. And Friedmann created his famous equations which enabled us to understand cosmology, yet he was dead within a year after publication of his ground-breaking paper. So many significant breakthroughs in science have been made by academics who barely managed to publish before their great minds were lost.'

'OK, so, according to our calculation so far, we now have 1000 billion locations in our galaxy where intelligent life has the capability to evolve.

'Now we consider the fraction which developed interstellar communication equipment, in a way we can detect. We are assuming that intelligent life would use radio telecommunications.'

'*We* probe the galaxy to look for hydrogen clouds by listening on 1420 Megahertz, so we assume other intelligent civilizations out there will do the same, hence SETI includes that frequency. Actually, the SETI band covers the entire *water hole* frequency range from 1420-1720 Megahertz, including both the *hydrogen atom* and the *hydroxyl molecule*, which combine together to form water. I think it is reasonable to think that developing radio telecommunications may be extremely rare, so let us estimate *0.1% of them do*. We also need to ask: *do they want to use that technology?* I estimate that maybe again, only one in a thousand want to do so. So, our current estimate of the Drake Equation gives us *one million* detectable intelligent civilizations out there.'

'So why haven't they visited us yet?' a voice called out.

Carl peered towards the person in the front row who called out the question. It was Jacqui Hau. He smiled.

'Excellent prompt Jacqui, you lead me right on to the *Fermi Paradox*.'

'Yes, why haven't we been visited yet? Enrico Fermi postulated his famous paradox way back in 1950 while at Los Alamos. I can see that I have overrun on time a little, so I will try to keep this to the point. Then we can break for lunch in about ten minutes or so, as I promised. We can continue in much more detail at the start of the afternoon session.'

'I'm starving,' someone called, then added in a sweet voice, 'but I can wait.'

'Excellent, OK, the question is, are we all alone in an empty Universe, or are there really other civilizations out there? Well I started off with Drake to make the case for there being at least a million intelligent civilizations out there in our galaxy, trying to communicate, but where are they?'

'In the Fermi Paradox we think in terms of the hypothetical *Great Filter*, through which, planets potentially harbouring life, must pass. In analysing the consequences of the paradox, the *Great Filter* ends all life on the planet, be it through climatic catastrophe, by self-destruction such as thermonuclear war, or caused by some astrophysical cataclysm. If the *Great Filter* is behind us, we have survived, and the good times are ahead. That also implies that few civilizations may pass the *Great Filter* and that intelligent life may be extremely rare.'

'If the *Great Filter* is still ahead, then I'm afraid things look very bad for us and we may represent the end game of intelligent life, before we also all will die.'

A voice called out from the audience, 'Have we not survived a cataclysm? The asteroid which wiped out the dinosaurs 66 million years ago was clearly extinction level.'

'Indeed, and maybe we wouldn't even be here if it hadn't hit. The dinosaurs would still be the ones in charge. For me, we need to be aware how fragile life is. The stellar environment is really hostile. We are lucky to be well away from the galactic centre, or star forming regions. Life cannot evolve there because of the radiation levels. It is a good question, have we survived a cataclysm? The problem is that it is impossible to plan for. How would we ever get a warning? Maybe we might see an asteroid or comet heading in, but I can't think of how we would get an advanced warning.'

'There are many suggestions for the Fermi Paradox. Are we the first to evolve to this level? That is unlikely. Have other civilizations on distant planets not reached sufficient level of technology? That is also unlikely, given that some may be millions of years older than us. It may be that managing the social aspects of intelligent civilizations and avoiding self-destruction may be extremely difficult. Look at the endless conflicts on our own planet. It may also be that intelligent civilizations are too far apart for communication to be possible. Maybe we are not listening carefully enough.'

'What if they have been here and even set up the right kind of communication equipment?' a girl with very blonde hair, sitting two rows back, asked.

'If we were hunter gatherers at the time, how would we possibly have understood what the equipment was?' someone else added.

'Good points. The extra-terrestrials land, find people living in mud huts and wonder whether it's worth building the transmitter. If they do, they also need to leave the instructions, which future generations can then decode, hopefully. I guess they could explain the whole machine by carving instructions in pictographic form, into a cliff face, like the ancient Egyptian hieroglyphs. Or maybe they would give up, write us off, and head on to the next planetary system.'

'Listen up. We are going to end it here and meet back after lunch. We can then look at different *civilization classes*, and also explore the reasons why intelligent life may *not* want to communicate, remaining hidden somewhere out there in stealth mode, keeping their affairs private. Thanks.'

The amphitheatre erupted with a round of applause, and everyone headed to the door.

8 Kumasi, Central Ghana: a visit to lake Bosumtwi & plans to go north to Dogon country

Kumasi, central Ghana

The pastel skies of sunset were already fading into the starry heavens as the bus headed into downtown Kumasi. Somewhere in the centre, Manu's brother was waiting for him. They were late. Despite the six-hour journey, he was growing quite excited, anticipating meeting Kofi again after almost a month. This VIP bus trip up from Accra had been quite an adventure to say the least. Initially, he had considered himself fortunate to get a seat on the early morning service, but it had not left until well after midday. Despite polite requests from many of the passengers, the bus driver maintained that it was company policy not to leave until each and every seat was filled. It had proven to be a portent of things to come.

Manu had not been far inland before; in fact, not further north than his grandmother's house at Dodowa, just outside Accra's city limits. After setting off, as the miles passed, the rich verdant interior of the country slowly opened up before his eyes. Leaving the coastal plains, the countryside became ever more vivid and inviting as the undulating low hills started to climb towards the forested plateau of the sandstone Ashanti uplands. Gone were the noisy, crowded, city roads as the long and straight, dusty tarmac headed ever northwards through lush and fertile grasslands, dotted with palm and spiky-bark silk cotton trees. He passed the time sending text messages and finishing his food and drinks. He could not stop thinking about his and Patrick's SETI plots. He had brought printed copies for his brother to see.

Kofi had started texting a few hours ago asking where he was, and Manu had tried to keep him up to date with the increasing delays. According to the schedule, it had indeed been intended that the bus make a short stop at the designated halfway town of Nkawkaw. All the passengers had been more than happy to get out and stretch their legs for 20 minutes. Manu spent his time wandering along the bric-a-brac stalls of a local street market. High above the town, to the east, the impressive sandstone escarpment of the edge of the Kwahu plateau cut a sharp skyline.

Looking back, perhaps it had been that rest stop in Nkawkaw, which had sparked the driver's growing discontent. For the rest of the journey he was irritable and his driving style more erratic. The misunderstanding between the driver and the elderly gentleman from neighbouring Togo had not helped. According to the driver, the man from Togo no longer wanted to get off, had changed his plans and wanted to continue to Kumasi. There must have been a language problem; Manu had tried to help. The man's handwritten ticket said Kumasi via Nkawkaw. The driver was having none of it, already complaining that if the old man had made his mind up earlier, he could have avoided Nkawkaw, taken the bypass and saved more than an hour.

Instead, the traffic jam out of Nkawkaw back to the main highway then only made matters worse. The cause was only discovered some hour or so later: a logging truck had shed its load of mahogany logs right across the road. Once clear of the obstruction, the route to Kumasi was clear. Right now, as they were finally driving into Kumasi they were more than 2 hours behind schedule.

He now sent a text to Kofi: *'VIP Bus arriving in Market Street, 10 minutes'.*

Within moments he got the reply: *'You came VIP? I'm at the tro-tro stop!'*

There was no way Manu would ever have taken a *tro-tro* minibus. They stopped at every village and homestead along the way, sometimes taking eight hours or more for the trip. In stifling summer heat, the journey would have been an unbearable ordeal. At least VIP had air-conditioning.

Manu stepped down from the bus and the gleaming white smile of Kofi was there to greet him. 'Hey Manu, welcome to Kumasi. A VIP tour bus! Wow, you lucky man. I guess our mum paid. Well, I'm your official tour guide. Check out my official cap, and I have one for you,' Kofi said, pulling a cap over Manu's head. 'You just got promoted. You are working with me tomorrow. After that I have a few days off!'

'Hey that's cool bro,' Manu replied. Manu pulled the hat off for a moment and studied the badge *Ghana Tours* then replaced it with a smile.

'OK.'

'Yeah, and you can sleep on my floor at the hotel. I got you another mattress,' Kofi added. 'Let's go get some food. I wanna hear about that SETI stuff.'

'I brought some printouts of what we found. Take a look at these. Something's not right. My Facebook buddy in Australia got the same results.'

'Food first, with something cool to drink, then we talk the heavy science stuff. OK?'

'OK,' Manu nodded.

They wandered over to a street stand. 'I recommend this street sausage and avocado and some yam balls and sauce. D'ya wanna beer?' He was looking at the bottles in buckets of ice water.

'I'll have a cold Pepsi, Kofi.'

'... and one Stone Strong and a cold Pepsi,' Kofi told the vendor.

When they had finished, Manu took out the SETI plots. 'Hey Manu, you remember, I was doing this SETI stuff for years before you took over.'

'I'm using the old computer. I didn't even change the account.'

'So that's what *I* found then?' Kofi replied with a grin. 'Hey, this looks very different from what I remember. That signal is very strong. What did SETI say? Did they confirm it? Surely, it's noise. That signal is way too strong.'

'If this is real ... and I believe it is ... then it's hot! Look, we both got the same results.'

'Your buddy got the same result? But why did you both get the same SETI batch file to process? Oh no, right, the time stamps are different,' Kofi reasoned.

'Yes, they are 3 hours 4 minutes apart.'

'So maybe it's just terrestrial noise then, which was just saturating the receiver for a long time.'

'No, because we processed other batch files from the same celestial coordinates at times in between and there are no signal peaks, just noise. SETI don't know anything yet. Patrick and I haven't sent back the processed files.'

'Wow, sounds pretty cool. You keep me posted bro. Come on, you've had a long journey and we're getting up at 6 a.m. tomorrow.'

'Why so early? What's happening?'

'You and I be the *official guides* for some travellers, taking them to the meteor crater and sacred *Lake Bosumtwi*. It will be a long day, so let's get some sleep bro.'

Manu and Kofi headed back across town to the hotel and walked in the front entrance. They were just walking past the reception when a low voice called out behind Manu, 'Hello kind sir.'

Manu turned; it was the old man from the bus, the traveller from Togo. He smiled and shook the man's outstretched hand.

'Good evening to you sir, are you staying here? This is my brother Kofi.'

'Yes, and by the look of those caps, we are on the same trip tomorrow to Lake Bosumtwi. Pleased to meet you Kofi. My name is Claude. I am a historian and archaeologist. Your brother was very courteous to me on the bus today.'

'Yes sir, we are on the same trip tomorrow. I am happy that my brother was polite to you. Actually, I am your tour guide tomorrow. Manu will be assisting me. I have been working here for three weeks now.'

'That is nice. I have planned this journey for several years. I am researching the expansion of the old Ghana Empire up into Mali and their contact with the Dogon people,' Claude explained. 'I will see you tomorrow. Good Night!'

'Good Night sir,' Manu replied.

'Good Night sir. We leave at 6:30 a.m. tomorrow. The reception will call everyone in time,' Kofi added.

****

There was quite a bustle in the hotel lobby in the early morning. Claude was standing talking to a young couple from New Zealand. Manu and Kofi were chatting to the girl at reception when their driver appeared.

'Ready to leave? I have already picked up our other guests from the Luxus Hotel. Is this your brother Kofi?' The driver grinned at Manu showing a bright gold front tooth. 'Welcome. You two boys are sitting up front with me. Please, this way. I am sure you have all had a good breakfast. Nevertheless, there is water and a packed lunch for everyone on the seats.'

Everyone followed the driver outside to the bus. Kumasi was already coming alive. A street market opposite the hotel was thronging with tourists and local residents. Soon everyone was on board and the bus headed south.

Kofi picked up the microphone to greet the passengers. 'Good morning everyone! This is the *Ghana Tours* trip to lake *Bosumtwi*. My name is Kofi. This morning's journey is only around 35km and we expect to be there within an hour. Please sit back and enjoy the trip. As many of you know, lake *Bosumtwi* is an ancient meteorite crater and is estimated to be around one million years old. It is around eight kilometres across and eighty metres deep at its deepest point. There are some important sacred traditions associated with the lake. The local Ashanti people never let iron touch the lake water, which is why no modern boats are seen on the water. There is a market today where you can buy souvenirs. I wish you a happy day. If you have any questions, please do not hesitate to ask me, or my new assistant Manu. We are both wearing these Ghana Tours caps,' Kofi said, turning towards the back of the bus holding up his hat.

Claude, the gentleman from Togo, was sitting two rows away. He momentarily looked up from being deeply engrossed in a book.

When the bus eventually pulled off the main road and headed into rich rainforest, the mood in the bus was quite buoyant. The road was covered with potholes from the frequent downpours. This was the wet season.

Lake Bosumtwi then came into view. Clinging on to a support bar to stabilize himself against the heaving and lurching of the bus, Kofi stood up and turned to address the passengers.

'OK everyone, we are almost there. For those of you who have signed up for the rainforest trail walk make your way to the northern end of the market where a park ranger is waiting. North is that way,' he said, pointing a finger. 'For everyone else, enjoy the market and the lakeside walk. The bus will leave around 3 o'clock this afternoon from where we stop. Please try to be back on time. Have a great day.'

The bus continued along the lake. Low white clouds were clinging to the peaks and valleys of the forested hills on the far side. Grasses were growing right down to the sandy shoreline, where fishermen were upturning their shallow teak rafts, about to set out over the choppy waters, towards plastic water bottles marking their submerged fishing nets.

The bus pulled up outside a large café and everyone got off. Directly opposite was a market where local people were buying fish and fruit and vegetables. Closer to the water was a line of market stalls, filled with carvings and artefacts of the region. Claude made his way directly there.

The air was filled with the sound of a different *Ashanti* dialect. Kofi and Manu wandered slowly towards the lake shore. After skimming a few stones, Kofi headed to the café to pick up some Coca-Cola and Manu headed towards the market where he found Claude examining a carved stone object.

'Is that something special?' Manu asked.

'Yes, and it's authentic. It's Dogon, and very early, I believe,' Claude replied, running his finger over the image.

The carving showed an abstract ring around a cross.

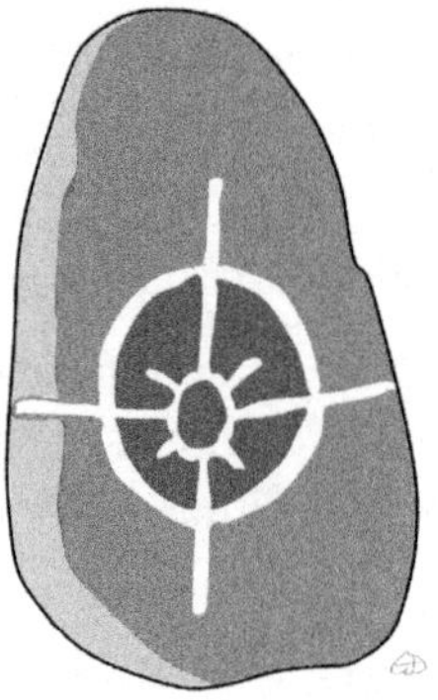

Dogon Artefact

'This shows a representation of ancient knowledge of the Dogon tribe who live in present day Mali,' Claude explained. 'Their culture and traditions make strong references to the star Sirius, which you may know was also important to the ancient Egyptians. This carving shows Sirius as a triple star system having a planet.'

'We only know this because back in the 1930s, anthropologists, Marcel Griaule and Germain Dieterlen lived with the Dogon, winning the trust of the high priests who eventually shared the secrets of their tradition.

They were shown artefacts dating back hundreds of years showing Sirius as a triple star system. The Dogon traditional dances and ceremonies include the orbital periods of the stars which we know from astronomers today are remarkably accurate. Interestingly, the Dogon share a cultural heritage with ancient Egypt and the Dogon people may have migrated west from Egypt long ago,' Claude continued.

'The enigma is that western astronomers only discovered Sirius B in 1862, while a possible third star in the system, Sirius C was only first suggested in literature in 1994. Scientists have argued that the Dogon acquired knowledge of Sirius B from travellers passing through their land, but they are a remote people and that doesn't seem possible.'

'Wait, how could the Dogon have knowledge of Sirius as a triple star system if Sirius C wasn't discovered until 1994?' Manu asked. 'They surely don't have telescopes.'

'Well, the jury is still out on whether Sirius C actually exists, but where they got the knowledge about Sirius B is certainly a mystery. They live in primitive mud and clay-brick houses, yet their cultural ceremonies incorporate significant details of the Sirius system. Sirius A is the brightest star in the night sky and can be seen with the naked eye. It is around 9 light years away, 8.6 to be exact. That means it takes light 8.6 years to reach us here, so we are looking at Sirius as it was 8.6 years ago. Sirius A is not so important to the Dogons as the really small Sirius B star which orbits it, which is invisible to all but the largest telescopes. The Dogon ceremonies describe the 50-year orbital period of Sirius B around Sirius A, which astronomers have confirmed is accurate.'

'Wow, that sounds amazing,' Manu replied. 'Is it possible that there are planets orbiting any of these stars?'

'Well, this artefact shows the three stars and a planet orbiting the unconfirmed star Sirius C. The Dogon also describe Sirius B as a very small and very dense star, which it is. It's a white dwarf, the extremely dense, massive remnant of a star similar to the size of our Sun, at the end of its life,' Claude added.

'What else do the Dogon say?' Manu asked. 'Why is Sirius so important?'

'That is the most interesting part. The Dogon tradition describes them being visited long ago by the *Nommo*, some kind of extra-terrestrial fish-beings, who claimed to be from this planet orbiting Sirius C. They claim the Nommo gave the Dogon their knowledge. Of course, this story has been ridiculed from every possible angle, even arguing that the Sirius star system is only, at most, 300 million years old, and thus life could not have evolved within that time. But that misses the key aspect of the Fermi Paradox, that the Nommo colonised the planet as they travelled around the Galaxy.'

'What's the Fermi Paradox?' Manu asked.

Claude turned to Manu and spoke quite sincerely. 'That is the fundamental question about whether life is unique to planet Earth or whether there is any other life out there. If there is, then why haven't they visited us? There are many Sun-like stars harbouring Earth-like planets, and some may be billions of years older than us, and thus vastly more advanced than us. If intelligent life has evolved on those planets, their interest in obtaining resources should surely have led them to develop interstellar travel to colonise nearby star systems. Current estimates are that it should only take around two million years for an advanced civilization to colonise the whole galaxy. So why haven't they visited us?'

Manu was amazed. 'Very interesting!' That quiet old man on the bus was turning out to be an extremely interesting person. He gazed out over lake Bosumtwi watching the many Ashanti fishermen sitting astride their plank boards, casting and emptying their nets into round baskets.

'Claude, what is your plan after today?' Manu asked.

'Well tomorrow I meet my old Mali archaeologist friend, Ebu Jande, who is a qualified pilot. He will fly me north over Burkina Faso to Mali,' Claude replied. 'He speaks the Dogon language *Tombo* and shares my interest in the Dogon.'

'That sounds amazing! If you need anyone to carry your bags, I am always available,' Manu replied, joking of course.

Claude smiled, 'Absolutely. You and your brother are both welcome to come along if you wish. There are extra seats on the plane.'

'Are you serious? That would be incredible!' Manu remarked sounding quite shocked. He felt thrilled. It would be utterly incredible to fly to Mali and visit the Dogon. Kofi was returning with two bottles of coke in his hand. 'What do you think Kofi? Do you want to come with Claude and me to Mali?'

'Wow, that sounds fantastic! It would be an unforgettable experience.

I am owed a few days holiday already. Claude, when might you be coming back?' Kofi asked.

'I have a fixed schedule and it will be a fast turn-around trip, staying there only one night, coming back the next day,' Claude replied. 'If we leave early Friday, then we are back Saturday evening.'

Manu smiled. What an incredible adventure this trip had become.

Manu and Kofi continued to wander around the stalls, sipping their cold drinks, and then they went to sit by the lake. Several hours later, they were back on the bus, heading back to Kumasi.

Kofi got off the bus first, wishing all the passengers a pleasant evening.

Claude spoke to Manu, 'Our pilot, my good friend Ebu Jande will pick us up at 5 a.m. to bring us to the airport. Please arrange a wake-up call and make sure you have packed whatever you need for 48 hours into one very small bag each. There's not much space on the plane for luggage.'

'Of course,' Manu replied with a smile. 'Thank you so much! See you at 5 a.m. tomorrow morning!'

9 | The Saqqara mystery, south of the Giza plateau

Approaching Saqqara, south of Giza

Chad's mind was racing. The whole Giza Plateau seemed to be an enigma. The official story of the pyramids' construction and use as burial chambers, in virtually every guidebook, just didn't seem right. Every structure on the Giza Plateau seemed very ancient, but almost all of them looked badly damaged, not just old, indeed, as if a cataclysm had hit the whole area. The ground was scorched and barren, but why? Each of the pyramids was surely not built in a short timescale of 20 or so years. Why was the Great Pyramid of Khufu, so complex inside? Why did it have airshafts from the King's chamber, and unfinished shafts at a different angle from the Queen's chamber. What did that double bump hieroglyph mean above the original entrance? There had to be an obvious explanation, but what was it?

Tau was quiet. The radio was playing some Arabic station. He was leaving Chad with his thoughts.

Chad looked back towards the pyramids. There was all this evidence in plain sight. Hundreds of creative people had suggested countless explanations over centuries, while others in more influential positions, had unimaginatively filtered, concluded and dictated a preferred history, which was to be the official narrative. Later that evening, he would try to call his brother. This trip to the Serapeum would hopefully evoke more food for thought.

'We are here!' Tau announced as he swung off the main road and pulled up to the main entrance. He looked down at his phone. 'Hassan has sent a text. I'll give him a call. I'll park here and come in with you and say hello. Do you have 200 pounds? To be discrete, I propose that I pay him.'

'Of course,' Chad replied, handing Tau the money.

Tau took his phone and called. They continued to walk towards the ticket office. A door opened, and a man walked out from a side office. 'Tau?' he said.

'Hassan,' Tau replied and held his hand out. 'This is Chad. Thanks for agreeing to show him around. I know you are the most informed guide here. Chad is a geologist from the US and I know he would love to hear your views on the Serapeum. He has just spent the morning with Ahmed.' Tau subtly pressed the money into Hassan's hand.

Hassan gave Tau a knowing look and a nod. He turned to Chad, 'Chad, good to meet you.'

'Hassan, thanks,' Chad replied sincerely, shaking his hand.

'So, you met Ahmed?' Hassan continued. 'Ahmed is a real scientist. I have worked with him on several conservation projects here.'

'Yes, Ahmed took me right inside Khufu at Giza. It's a remarkably complex structure. The official story seems to be lacking a convincing explanation.'

'Tell me about it.'

'Listen guys, I will leave you now, and Chad, I'll be back in around two hours. Hassan, is that about the right amount of time needed for a tour?'

'Sure, two hours is perfect.'

'Great. See you later Chad.'

'See you later,' Chad replied.

'So, you want the official tour and textbook explanation, or do you want the totally unofficial and very controversial tour?' Hassan asked, giving Chad a deep look, raising his eyebrows

'I guess, I want your honest opinion, rather than some official line. From what I have seen, there seems to be so much, which isn't adequately explained.'

'OK. You'll get my honest opinion. What I will tell you is totally off the record, and hopefully it will make more sense. Come, welcome to the Serapeum.' He handed Chad an ID badge. 'Put this on. Tau suggested we should go with the same US geologist story.'

'Thanks, I will.'

'Before we go inside the Serapeum, and to put everything into some kind of context, I will just tell you a little about the whole Saqqara site. During our tour I will tell the official story and then pose some difficult questions to challenge that. This will help you figure out your own conclusions.'

'Sounds good. Please continue.'

'OK, so we are at Saqqara, in Memphis, which is officially the necropolis of ancient Egypt. At the northern side of the plateau we find evidence of burials of First Dynasty nobles, going back to around 3000 B.C.. In addition to being a royal burial ground, in recent years, a vast number of mummified animals have also been discovered here. The famous Djoser step-pyramid and funerary complex which you can see over there, dates from 2700BC, and is described as one of the earliest stone pyramids in Egypt. It is very primitive in its construction, when compared to the Giza pyramids.'

'In different parts of the site, there are large sunken shafts going into the ground. These have been repaired in later times, but the original shafts are perfectly cut down through the bedrock. The purpose of these shafts is unknown, and where the shafts lead to, also remains a mystery.'

He led Chad towards the ticket inspector at the gate, and as before, they were waved through. The ticket inspector patting Chad on his back as he passed.

'They are so grateful that you are here!' Hassan said, with a chuckle.

'What can I say?' Chad replied. 'But I don't want to give the impression that I am unwilling to pay. Is there a contribution box? I can at least donate the equivalent of the entry fee.'

'There is one of course. Don't worry, I will show you at the end of the tour.'

They eventually reached the long passageway leading to the underground complex. As they walked down the walkway cut into the bedrock, Chad noticed the surface discolouration in the surface rocks. 'The surface has clearly suffered intense heat damage. It has penetrated into the ground more than a metre!'

'This part we are walking down, was originally all covered, and part of the Serapeum. It collapsed in the distant past, and the rubble was all removed.'

At the bottom of the long steps, they turned to the left. They were inside a long straight corridor, with a curved roof, cut perfectly into the limestone bedrock. Alcoves went off to the left and right. White painted, curved archways lined the passageway every five or so metres, giving a very pleasing aesthetic. The yellow mood-lighting further enhanced the experience. A huge block of grey granite stood immediately in front of them.

'This is only one of the *lids* of the boxes.'

'Just the lid!' Chad exclaimed, running his hand over the smooth surface.

'No one has moved it since it was left here.'

'So, something suddenly stopped all activity. You wouldn't go to all that trouble in making the lid, and not put it in place. But how on earth did they move these stone lids, they must weigh ten tons or more?' Chad replied.

'You haven't seen the boxes yet! There are 24 stone boxes with lids; each box and lid is perfectly crafted from a single piece of granite. Some of the boxes are, I believe, from diorite, and likely quarried from Aswan, some 500 miles away.'

'This is a remarkable subterranean environment. The temperature must be, what 20°C? I bet the overlying rock can keep the temperature very stable down here. It was quite warm in the Kings Chamber inside Khufu, but this is pleasant.'

'Yes, the temperature is stable all the year round.'

They soon came to the first alcove with a granite box in, the lid slightly pushed open. 'My God!' Chad remarked. 'It's enormous! I didn't expect this. It's immaculately cut. The sides and angles are perfectly right-angled!'

'Yes, it always gives everyone that *shock and awe* feeling.'

'So, what is the official story? What were they supposedly for and who discovered them?'

'Well, the official story is that this is an extensive necropolis for the Apis Bull. The ancient Egyptians considered the Apis Bull to be the incarnation of the god of Memphis, who they called Ptah. As you can see, the boxes are clearly at least four times the size needed for a bull. The whole complex was rediscovered by a French archaeologist called August Mariette, who was tasked by the French government in 1850, to seek out and purchase the best early manuscripts for the Louvre. We are talking Coptic, Arabic etc. His search led him eventually to Saqqara and he was so intrigued by the site, he decided to excavate, and eventually he discovered the whole complex.'

They walked along the softly lit tunnelway. Towards the far end there were six alcoves on each side. The massive dark grey, granite boxes each had their ten-ton lids slightly slid back. The alcoves were barely bigger than the boxes themselves. They couldn't have been cut from stone *in situ*. There simply was just not enough room to be able to work around them. The curved alcove ceilings were also cut from the rock. Clearly, shafts had not been cut vertically down through the rock above. No, these 70-ton stone boxes had been moved along the tunnel and swung round and pushed into their own alcove. Halfway along the passageway, the way was almost completely blocked by one box without a lid. They needed to squeeze past along one side. Again, it seemed as if workers had simply downed tools, never to return to complete the task. Chad was totally perplexed, but how on earth had they moved them?

'You seem shocked Chad,' Hassan said with a smile.

'I just don't understand how they moved them.'

'Also, just look at the quality of the work in each case. We are talking almost as if the stone boxes were machine cut. Getting this result surely was not possible with copper chisels and rock hammers. Also, look here, on the underside of the lid. See this darkening. It seems to be some coating on the stone. It is as if a liquid has run down under the edge of the lid. It's the same on each end face proving that this box was closed at one time.'

'The boxes have an unbelievably shiny finish,' Chad murmured. He ran his finger along the outside corner edge. 'And this is remarkably sharp and cut perfectly at 90°.'

'Again, the official story is that the surfaces were polished using sand and water, but that cannot explain this change in colour. Come, we can get inside one box.'

He led Chad towards a box which was missing its end.

'When the French guy Mariette found this one, it was the only one with the lid still on, so he blasted it open with gunpowder. He said there were only a few bones inside, although the official story is that he found a mummified bull. It is difficult to verify the truth.'

They climbed inside. Hassan pointed out the beautiful flat surface and the obviously machined 90° corners.

Chad ran his hand over the absolutely flat polished surfaces. 'What on earth were these made for?' he murmured to himself.

'The boxes were all cut from a single piece of stone. Just think of the complexity of doing that. Also ask yourself why they wanted to build such a complicated underground maze of tunnels, with barely enough space to move the boxes. Why didn't they cut vertical shafts and lower them down?'

This just didn't make any sense at all to Chad. Here at Saqqara there was clear evidence for heat damage again, on the surface. Now he was thinking there had to be a very significant reason to create this Serapeum complex. Was this again evidence for a cataclysm, but you can't plan for a cataclysm? Sure, you can work out that a volcano might erupt, but you can't be sure, and you wouldn't spend years preparing. Was Saqqara linked to a cataclysm?

'Chad, look here at this box. Just like the others, it has a highly polished surface. Look at the quality of the hieroglyphs. The workers clearly didn't show the same rock-cutting skills as the box makers. The hieroglyphs have been crudely etched in.'

'What if these hieroglyphs are a final quick message to describe the contents in time, as if written by one of the last workers before they left?' Chad replied. He couldn't believe he was now thinking that this related to preparations for a cataclysm. He needed to talk to his brother Tom. He would definitely call him tonight.

'What did you say Chad?'

'I agree with you. The writings surely don't have the same quality.'

They spent the next hour exploring the side tunnels and dark chambers. Hassan had a powerful torch and was able to show the extent of the workings. In one corner, a pile of rocks seemed to block another tunnel. He pulled a few rocks away and remarked, 'The underground complex clearly extends way beyond here. I look forward to more extensive excavations, to explore what's in here at least.'

Chad noticed a donation box, took out his wallet and pushed in 500 pounds. Hassan noticed and smiled. 'This was really great Hassan.'

They walked back outside, and Chad sent a message to Tau. Almost immediately he got a response.

'Tau is only 5 minutes away! Thank you so much Hassan. I've had a truly inspiring experience.'

'You are welcome, and if you ever want to come back and have another tour, I will be most happy to be your guide.'

'Thanks.' They shook hands and Chad walked out towards the parking area. Tau was just arriving. Tau pulled up his car alongside Chad and wound the window down.

'You look quite shocked,' Tau remarked. 'More than after this morning.'

Chad climbed in the back. 'Tau, I am becoming more and more convinced that this area was hit by a cataclysm, but something doesn't make sense. You can't plan for a cataclysm.'

'That's true. Where do you want to go? Back to the hotel?'

'Back to the hotel please,' Chad replied, now feeling extremely tired after a remarkably long day.

Tau leaned forward, turned his radio up a little and drove Chad all the way back to his hotel.

Chad hardly noticed the city or the traffic or the boats down on the Nile as they passed by. His thoughts were totally absorbed in this huge conundrum. What on earth had happened here?

Back at the hotel, he paid Tau a thousand Egyptian pounds. 'Tau, this is for everything, please,' he said, noticing Tau's reluctance to take it all.

'Call me if you need me again, whenever. When your wife and daughter arrive, remember we have a meal planned with Maria at Habibah's place on Friday.'

'Of course, I am looking forward to that. I will keep you updated if any plans change,' Chad replied reassuringly.

Chad climbed out of the taxi and watched and waved as Tau drove away. He walked into the hotel and nodded to the concierge as he passed and then went straight to his room. He slumped down on his bed and took out the envelope of papers Mustapha had collected together. Was there another clue in Mustapha's notes?

****

Chad must have drifted off, because when he awoke it was close to 2 a.m. It was time to call his brother Tom, it would be late morning in Sydney. He grabbed his phone.

10 Sydney Australia: attempting to solve the great pyramid paradox

Wahroonga, Sydney Australia

Patrick was sitting with his Dad in the kitchen, trying to make sense of the SETI data plots. The big question was whether this was just noise or really a signal from beyond.

Breakfast was over. The pinewood table was cluttered with empty plates and bowls. Patrick sipped a tall glass of freshly squeezed orange juice. Mary-Anne was in the adjoining utility room.

'Guys, I'm putting on a load of washing. If you have anything you need me to do, tell me now. I'll be upstairs in my study working on my paper for the rest of the day. I need to finish my rewrite and send it off by 6 p.m. so you may not see me much. Patrick? Tom?'

'Mom, I threw it all in the basket,' Patrick replied.

'I'm good. Mine is there too,' Tom called.

'What about that tee shirt? The one you wore yesterday,' she added.

'It was brand new yesterday. It will be my favourite blue tee shirt from now on. It will surely last one more day,' Tom replied.

'Help yourself to lunch later. There's enough food in the fridge to make a Greek salad with olives, cucumber, feta and tomatoes. I think there's half a bag of rocket. There's fresh bread . . .'

'Mom, we'll be fine,' Patrick confirmed.

'Your Dad can make an excellent Greek salad.' The washing machine emanated a beep and then the sound of water rushing in could be heard. 'Guys, have a great day.' Mary-Anne came back through the kitchen, pausing a moment to lean forward to give Tom a sweet kiss on his cheek.

'Success, honey!' Tom called, as she walked off.

Tom stood up and walked over to the coffee machine and switched it on. *Empty drip tray* it read on the display. He dragged out the plastic tray and poured the water away in the sink then pushed the tray back. *Please refill water tank*, the display now read. He sighed and filled the tank. *Urgent cleaning of brewing unit required* it now read.

'You are kidding! What is going on?' he complained. 'I'm in charge here *Mr Coffee Machine*. I don't need to take instructions from you.'

'Just ignore it Dad. You can always get one more cup out of it. Do it next time. I'm sure it won't be a problem,' Patrick reasoned.

'Yeah, and your Mom will be pretty disappointed with me if the darn thing now locks itself, which is what it is threatening. She will need her coffee all day today! I've been cancelling the darn *clean request* a few times now. I'll do it! You'll get your clean now. Just asking for attention when me and my son are about to have an important discussion,' he said, slapping the machine on the top. 'You know, this is the first step proving that machines are taking over our lives.'

'Not really Dad. You want a cup of coffee and the machine is pre-programmed to enhance your life by reminding you of what to do,' Patrick replied.

'OK then, let's hit *start*,' Tom murmured. *Open side panel and follow written instructions* the display now read. 'We can keep talking, I'll just rinse this.' He removed the brewing unit, walked over to the sink, and turned on the water.

'That looks genuinely clogged Dad! I think the machine did you a favour.'

'Yeah, you're right,' he sighed. 'Look, it even shows in symbols and words what I need to remove on the front here.'

'Provided you understand English and how to decode those messages.'

'These symbols are a common language. Well OK, if you are from this planet,' he said, replacing the brewing unit. 'Coffee time again!' he exclaimed, as the machine murmured into life. 'No last message mate?' he said tauntingly. 'Too late! I'm having coffee now,' and he placed his warmed mug on the plate and hit the start button, and the grinder suddenly roared into life.

'Dad, talking about interpreting communications, I would really like your honest opinion about those SETI plots. What do you think they mean? I just got two more from Manu. Two have data, and two don't, but they all come from the same sky coordinates, only at different times.'

'They definitely suggest a signal at two times and then no signal at the other times. As I said, it's more likely that it's local interference, but sometimes it's good to dream. Let's break it down into a thought experiment. If I were an extra-terrestrial, how would I send you signals?'

'Well, I don't think you would be sending signals from some kind of spacecraft. The craft just wouldn't have the power unless you were very close by. Also, from a spacecraft, you wouldn't be transmitting from the same place in the sky.'

'OK. That's a good start. So, I would have built something to transmit from my home planet, . . . or the planet I just colonised. Now you need to anticipate what my signals would look like.'

'What do you mean?'

'Well, you need to predict the signal structure, or you won't know what to look out for, right? Start to think how my planet's motion might affect the signal transmission.'

'Well, I can assume your planet is rotating, and also moving around a star,' Patrick continued.

'Maybe the orbit around the star won't influence the signal you receive over a few hours from a very long distance away, but a spinning planet might,' Tom added. 'So, explain to me what the signal will look like.'

'OK, so won't it flash as the planet spins? A spinning planet should generate a beam which grows in amplitude as it comes into alignment with my distant receiver, then fades as the alignment slowly recedes.'

'Yes, that's true, but just think about how powerful my beam needs to be if it is a flashing beacon. My signal will only be pointing in your direction for a very short time. Isn't it more likely that I will align the beam north-south with the spin axis, then I am permanently transmitting, with a continuous beam?'

Patrick looked very pensive. 'So, if your beam is aligned with the spin axis, say pointing north or south . . . ,' he reasoned.

' . . . or *beams* pointing *both north and south*.'

Freshly ground coffee permeated the air. 'Finally.' He took a sip, and closed his eyes. 'Ah,' he sighed.

'. . . or *beams* pointing both north and south,' Patrick continued. 'Then there would be two beams, each going in different directions. But if the beams are aligned north and south and at some elevation angle, won't the angle of the beams have an effect?'

'What effect is that?' Tom urged. 'Think in terms of how that beam might now move. A beam coming from the north pole would just be shining straight up along the spin axis. But what would an angled beam, say at the Equator, give, . . . shining towards the north?'

Patrick held his right elbow with his left hand and moved it in a circle. 'OK, then the angle of the beam would create a ring of light moving around the spin axis,' he replied with excitement.

'Precisely, and that ring of light would be detectable on a number of planets which cross through that ring of light,' Tom continued. 'At a long distance away, the beam would look virtually continuous because it will spread, unless you can collimate it into a narrow beam. Obviously, if I am trying to communicate with you, then I will design my angled beam to shine towards you. Do you see another challenge with this set up?'

'Well, what if the spin axis of your planet does not point towards me? Then, I couldn't see you,' Patrick suggested.

'Well, I could change the angle of my beam to form any ring, north or south. A steeper angle would give a larger ring. But, a larger ring would also spread the transmitted power in the beam, reducing the signal strength. But ideally, I would want my spin axis to be pointing as close as possible towards you,' Tom explained. 'So, can you imagine now why you might first get a signal, then no signal?'

'Is it to do with some slight off-axis alignment of your spin axis pointing towards me?' Patrick suggested.

'Precisely. You can't change that. At an off-axis angle, you will receive a beacon beam signal for part of the rotation of my planet, then nothing for the rest of the rotation. That repeats. You have just deduced quite a valid explanation for these SETI plots . . . if they are indeed transmissions from a distant World. Well done!'

'So, can we imagine what the transmitter looks like? What is it? What does it comprise?' Patrick asked.

'OK, so the transmitter would need to have a very powerful energy source driving it, which couples with an antenna or waveguide. If we are talking SETI microwave frequencies, then it would need to be of the dimensions of the wavelength. A waveguide is ideal.'

'What do you mean by a waveguide?'

'OK. Imagine a square-, or rectangular-section hollow metal pipe pointing up to the sky at some desired angle. By the way, the waveguide does not need to be absolutely straight, it can also be curved. A microwave signal remains trapped within the waveguide as it propagates along it. It is the end of the waveguide which needs to be pointed in some particular direction.'

'What are they made of?'

'They need to be made of a material which helps propagate the radio signal within it. Copper is ideal for waveguide material. You would only need to copper-plate the inside of a rigid tube for it to become a waveguide. The tube itself can be made of anything you like: plastic, wood, ... even stone, although I wouldn't know why someone would want to use stone unless they wanted the transmitter to last an unbelievably long time.'

'So, you are saying that the only requirement for the transmitter frequency is the dimension of the waveguide?'

'No, you need to generate the frequency, then couple it to your waveguide. The dimensions of the waveguide determine the wavelength of the signal being propagated along it.

For SETI, which is looking for 1420MHz signals and remember from your physics, $c = f\lambda$ ... or speed of light c, equals frequency f, times wavelength λ, so the wavelength turns out to be 21cm, so a waveguide of dimension 21cm across would be ideal.'

'... and so I could construct a massive stone structure with 21cm shafts pointing up to the sky at some predetermined angle, which only need to be internally coated with copper, and I have the basis for a transmitter to another world ... letting them know where I am. All I need is to build those shafts, so they couple to a transmitter with an energy source?' Patrick continued.

'Well, you would surely need to know, or guess, that there are planets in the direction of your transmissions. Also, unless a visiting extraterrestrial visitor has already told you, you would need to be quite advanced in astronomy to work out, where in the night sky, the closest planets to Earth are to be found. That means you have developed telescopes and satellites for exoplanet detection. Another thing you should consider is whether your signals are just beacons, or do they contain data?'

'What do you mean?'

'Well, you have gone to the phenomenal trouble of building some massive stone structure with an internal energy source and 21cm shafts pointing up to the night sky at precise angles, just to send me a beacon of 21cm wavelength microwave energy? Don't you also want to send me some data? If you are trying to tell me that you are an intelligent civilization, a dumb beacon signal may not convince me.'

'Of course I do, but how can I do that? What will make my signals intelligent?'

'You need to add some information to your signals. You need to modulate the beam in some way, just like radio, so the signal when received and analysed, decodes with some information,' Tom explained.

'OK, what do you recommend?'

The sound of footsteps interrupted their conversation. 'I can smell *fresh coffee!*' Mary-Anne exclaimed with a smile, as she entered the kitchen. 'Hard at work guys?'

'How's it going honey?'

'All organised and on track. Later on, I would be really grateful if you might direct me towards material on ancient civilizations and their depiction of animals relating to groups of stars,' she replied. 'We know that different cultures made similar constellation structures. I found the star map of Ptolemy, and the Egyptian zodiac on the ceiling of *Hathor's Temple* in Dendera. There are lots of common themes.'

'I have a good book in my study, it's a large A3 hardback, *Ancient Constellations of the Heavens* I think it's called.'

'I know it! Great. Thanks honey. Bye guys!' she replied, taking her coffee and quickly walking away.

'Bye Mom!' Patrick called after her. 'Where were we?'

'I was asking you, how you were going to change some dumb beacon transmissions, which I might receive and ignore, into something which I would decode into a message of intelligence.'

'Well, I have built some massive stone structure which I guess is pretty much self-contained. It probably has a very dangerous, high energy source, so once set off, it will probably continue until the power supply runs out. Any intelligence would need to be in what was transmitted. Maybe I could interrupt the beam in a periodic way,' Patrick reasoned.

'Maybe, but given the distances to even the nearby planets, and you not knowing how evolved any life forms on them are, you will have chosen to build a transmitter which lasts for hundreds, even thousands of years. Moving parts are definitely a no-no. Something could break, with no-one to fix it. Everyone who remembers building your hi-tech stone-age communication device is long gone! No, you need to come up with a way to design a signal, which looks very unnatural, such that it must have been sent by some intelligent life form.'

'I know, what if I send a second transmission with the first? At least it will have a combined component,' Patrick suggested.

'Is it a second radio signal? That would work. You would need a second transmitter of some kind.'

'Can I use the same waveguide?'

'Sure, you can send many frequencies along the same waveguide, as long as they are above the waveguide *cut-off frequency*.'

'OK, I will do that, then at least it will decode to something else,' Patrick confirmed.

'Carl Sagan, a famous astrophysicist, suggested using *pi times* 1420MHz as an intelligent signal. Maybe you could add that as well,' Tom added. 'Sounds like you are all set! Build the structure, install the transmitter, fuel up, seal off the structure, and start communicating!'

'Hopefully you made wise choices about to whom you will be transmitting. You will have chosen planets orbiting stars of five or six billion years old, which are in the *Goldilocks* zone. . . ,' Tom continued.

'*Not too hot and not too cold . . .* ,' Patrick added.

'Right, so the planets have liquid water at the surface, allowing life to evolve in the same way we believe it did here. Knowing the age of the host star is very important. There has been life on Earth for more than 3.5 billion years. You won't get much response from some phytoplankton!'

'Or the *stromatolites* in Shark Bay, Western Australia,' Patrick added. 'They are even older.'

'Excellent answer! You know your stuff! Yeah, I think the phytoplankton have been around for 500 million years, while the *stromatolites* have been here since *Goldilocks* took her first walk across the beach, some 3.7 billion years ago!'

'Also, the candidate planets should be chosen from those as close as possible, since it will take the signals one year to travel each light year in distance they are away,' Patrick remarked. 'Radio signals will take 4.24 years to reach our nearest neighbour *proxima Centauri*.'

'Indeed. You're all set now!'

'What about the SETI program? From what I read, the choice to use the 1420MHz band is based on the likelihood that any intelligent lifeforms are using that frequency to map out the hydrogen clouds in the Milky Way galaxy. That is what we on Earth are using to probe the galaxy, isn't that right?'

'Sure, that's why we're listening on a frequency of 1420MHz - the 21cm wavelength band. But why are you transmitting? You don't know anyone is out there, and your transmitter is pretty directional, sending out these beams of energy. That may be a pretty energy-intensive power plant you have, transmitting day and night, 24-7. What do you know that makes you so sure that someone is out there? We don't transmit highly directional 1420MHz signals in the microwave band, 24-7, towards distant Worlds. That aspect of *directional* is probably very important because it is about transmitting a concentrated beam in a particular direction.'

'Maybe I know something? Do I know you are there? How could I know?' Patrick slowly replied, questioningly. 'Isn't there another question here? Where did I get the technology from?'

'OK, that's original. Are you suggesting that you did not develop the transmitter? So, where did you get it from?'

'What if higher intelligence extra-terrestrials visited my planet, and built the transmitter?' Patrick replied, his eyes lighting up.

'How could you operate it? How would you know how it worked? You may be just a primitive civilization living in mud huts?'

'OK, I don't know how to operate the transmitter. I don't know how it works. What if the extra-terrestrials built the transmitter, and left enough clues scattered among different primitive tribes. As the civilization developed, becoming increasingly advanced over thousands of years, they eventually worked out how to operate it . . . ,' Patrick continued. 'They could have carved symbols in rocks, hoping I could decipher them one day.'

'Well, there is always the danger that after evolving, you found the symbols, and then just adopted them, using them in your own way, each having a totally different meaning,' Tom reasoned.

'Widespread use of the new meaning would erase any meaning in the original messages. There is always that danger. Also, just imagine that you found the stone-age transmitter, not knowing what it was or how it worked, and just smashed your way in out of curiosity, totally destroying its capability, rendering it useless for ever! OK, but continuing your reasoning, . . . your evolved civilization somehow fails to destroy it, works out how to operate it, switches it on, and signals back to the precisely aligned distant planet, that their civilization hadn't destroyed itself through wars, but was now advanced technologically. Hopefully, the signals arrive before the visitors' own planet expired or suffered a cataclysm. You may be interested to know that there are several stars within 20 light years of us, which have exoplanets orbiting in the *Goldilocks zone*.'

'Is it only possible to get a signal from a planet orbiting an ancient host star?' Patrick asked. 'What about colonization?'

'You are right. If we consider an advanced civilisation colonizing the galaxy, they are passing through, so their presence is not limited by the age of planetary systems. However, their decision to trek across light years of space will be influenced by the age of the star system they are heading towards. They can determine the age of a star system, and they will target the oldest planetary systems where life has had a chance to develop. They will take pretty big decisions if it takes several generations on board to arrive at the chosen destination. But you are right, there may be very intelligent life on relatively young star systems, which have planets in the habitable zone, if that is where the colonizers have landed. Water might be another consideration. If they can identify water on an exoplanet in a younger star system, that might be the basis for establishing a colony there.'

'This sounds pretty convincing Dad. What do you think? Could these SETI signals be from a transmitter built by extra-terrestrials, which has now been activated because their own civilization has finally evolved to a technological state, that they have worked out how to switch it on?' Patrick asked excitedly.

'Or it is nothing, just periodic noise in the SETI receiver. Occam's razor, the most obvious answer is the most likely!'

'OK then, if we can find a transmitter left on our own planet, that might be a first level of proof. We then need to identify and visit scattered primitive tribes to see if they have any retained knowledge in their cultural heritage,' Patrick suggested. 'We then gather all their data and see if there is any suggestion of a visitation or knowledge of how to operate an ancient transmitter.'

'So, you are suggesting that we need to find a very massive old structure with stone waveguides ready for coating with copper, and an internal structure which can generate a powerful energy source to power the transmitter,' Tom exclaimed.

'That sounds very exciting and compelling. Maybe we can start with the Australian indigenous peoples?' Patrick reasoned. 'They live quite close by.'

'Sounds good. There will be quite a lot of stuff online. We may find other tribes with well-documented cultural history data,' Tom replied.

'By the way, I meant to ask. What did that UTS astrophysics slogan mean, on your new tee-shirt? Something about Wolf rays? What are they?'

'Oh, you mean my UTS *Wolf-Rayet* tee-shirt!' Tom said with a laugh. 'That's my current area of interest. A Wolf-Rayet star is potentially something very dangerous for us here on Earth. We haven't found too many of them and they are quite unstable. They are extremely hot massive stars which are off the *main sequence* . . .'

'That's where most stars are, just fusing hydrogen into helium for most of their existence, right?'

'Right, and the Wolf-Rayet stars are off the main sequence and are now burning heavier elements in their cores, like helium into carbon. We can identify them from their spectra. My tee shirt slogan actually reads *Wolf-Rayet Stars . . . a flash of light to signal your present is en route . . . but will be arriving later!*.'

'Yeah, but what does that mean?'

'It's the *Doomsday star*. The type was named after Wolf and Rayet who discovered it in 1867. Just imagine a seriously massive star with a surface temperature up to six times that of the Sun. Like all stars, they end their life by a total core collapse, but these Wolf-Rayet stars are spinning at a very high rate, flinging off material as they spin. When they run out of fuel and undergo a total core collapse, they go out with the most massive bang! The amount of energy they release in a few seconds, can be equivalent to all the energy released by the Sun over its ten-billion-year lifetime. The supernova, or even hypernova, which is ten to a hundred times more powerful, is brighter than the entire galaxy. Just prior to the supernova, the collapsing core sends out a burst of gamma rays in a beam along its spin axis, in both directions. As long as this happens far away, we are safe. To date, we have only observed them in other galaxies. More importantly, we do not want to be directly on the receiving end of the gamma ray burst.'

'Is that why it's called the *Doomsday star*?'

'Unfortunately, it gets a lot worse. In many cases the GRB, or Gamma Ray Burst, is accompanied by the beam of highly energetic particles which caused the GRB, known as a *relativistic jet*, moving at around a quarter of the speed of light. That is the really bad news. If the Wolf-Rayet star is 1000 light years away and you are aligned to receive the gamma ray burst, it is almost guaranteed that you will receive the deadly relativistic jet, some 3000 years later,' Tom explained with a frown.

'Why not 4000 years? It's moving at a quarter the speed of light? Oh, of course, it has travelled a quarter of the distance after 1000 years when the gamma ray burst arrives,' Patrick concluded

'Well reasoned.'

'But I thought *gamma rays themselves* are deadly.'

'Sure, and the gamma ray burst is accompanied by a long afterglow from X-Rays to radio waves. The whole gamma ray burst from this kind of event lasts around 100 seconds, and we have an atmosphere, which can absorb gamma rays to a certain extent, but a Wolf Rayet star core collapsing so close at only 1000 light years away, will generate such a high intensity of gamma radiation, that serious long-lasting damage will be done to our planet. That, however, is nothing compared to the environmental catastrophe that is to follow, if the gamma ray burst is accompanied by the relativistic jet.'

'Why, if we see the gamma ray burst, is it certain that we will also get the relativistic jet?'

'The gamma ray burst is caused by the relativistic jet impacting the gas and dust around the dying star during the final seconds of the core collapse. They are travelling along the same path, in a very tight beam, but as I said, in many cases we have observed the jet travelling at a quarter of the speed of light. At only around 1000 light years away, studies show that intense levels of gamma radiation would seriously destroy the ozone level in our atmosphere, which protects us from harmful ultra violet radiation.'

'Well, isn't ozone a greenhouse gas? So, the planet would then cool down?'

'You are right, but high intensity gamma radiation will produce vast amounts of nitrogen oxide, greenhouse gases up to 300 times as effective as carbon dioxide, which will cause an immediate rise in temperature. Eventually a cooling period will occur due to a photochemical smog, greatly reducing the surface temperature of the planet. There will be all manner of mutations due to the high influx of ultra violet and there will be nitric acid rain dissolving away limestone monuments and the like. Just the gamma ray burst will have a serious effect on life at the surface, while the polar caps will then start to increase as the global temperatures plummet.'

'So, what happens next? Does everyone need to do everything they possibly can to prepare themselves for the ultimate catastrophe, when the relativistic jet eventually arrives.'

'Sure they do, and if they are a civilized race with advanced technology, the date can be computed very precisely. All you can do is start to prepare for your fate, a direct impact with the jet is unsurvivable. The extent of the miss and the duration of the transit would determine the extent by which the Earth, and life on it, is affected. The only things remaining effectively undamaged would be permanent megalithic structures, or whatever is buried well under ground. In extreme cases, all trace of any previous civilizations might be substantially erased from the surface of the planet,' Tom replied soberly.

'Are you suggesting that even cities and technologies would be erased?'

'A relativistic jet transiting close enough to the Solar System would seriously impact life on the surface, and the environmental impact would be substantial and devastating.'

'Unless the life is underground or under water,' Patrick suggested.

'Well, the atmosphere would be extremely turbulent, and a substantial amount of the polar ice caps would vanish, again depending upon the transit duration. Very deep-sea life forms and life away from the surface might survive,' Tom confirmed. 'But the duration of the relativistic jet transit is the key factor.'

'So, we don't have a chance? There's nothing we can do?' Patrick asked, his eyes quite wide with concern.

'Well, future generations can hope that the environmental impact will be much less. Some 3000 years later, the Sun would have continued its orbit further along around the Milky Way's supermassive black hole, and we would have moved a bit further, but the collimated beam may still be hundreds if not thousands of solar systems wide in diameter. One plan might be to spend the 3000 years building a series of monuments which carry an encoded message to future generations telling what happened in the past. Perhaps vast numbers of seeds could be collected and stored underground in protected chambers. Now we go back to our first discussion about your SETI signals. Even if no signals had been received from other extra-terrestrial civilizations in recorded history, maybe I would still build a structure to at least let our possible nearest neighbours know, along the lines you suggested: a massive stone structure with an internal energy supply to power a beacon, to let any possible civilizations know who are living on the nearest exoplanets that we once were here.'

'Wow, Dad! You now know what I am wondering. Is there anything in the climate record which suggests that this may already have happened?'

'Now you're talking! Come on, let's get online and check the last 20,000 years. We're looking for a signature of a sharp temperature rise, followed by a long period of cooling, then a sharp temperature rise, . . . and then *a civilization emerging with amnesia*.'

Tom grabbed his laptop. Within moments he had logged into the UTS online database. Quickly he accessed Greenland ice core plots of global temperature rises for the past 20,000 years.

'OK, I think we might have something,' he murmured. 'Look at this graph. At the end of the *Pleistocene*, almost 15,000 years ago, we've got a very rapid global temperature rise of around 12°C. This is followed by the onset of some serious cooling and a drop of 12°C, over a 3000-year period. This is described as the *Bølling-Allerød* and *Younger Dryas* epochs. Then at the end of the *Younger Dryas*, about 12,000 years ago, there is another 12°C rise in a very short time. This is unbelievable. This is just the signature of our imagined Wolf-Rayet gamma ray burst and relativistic jet impact!'

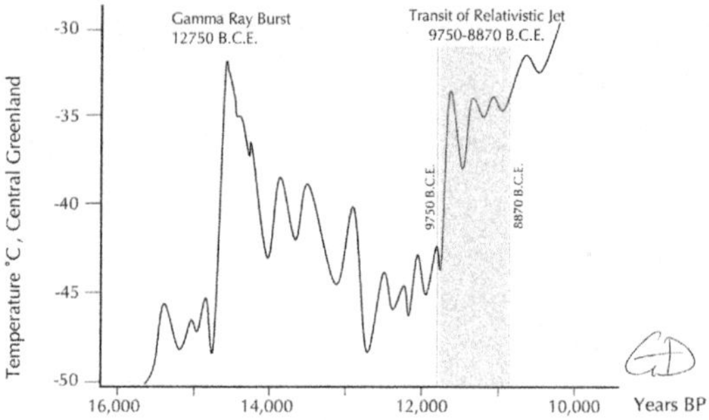

Climate Graph

'Doesn't that mean there must have indeed been a Wolf-Rayet star around 1000 light years away, that underwent core collapse?'

'I'll launch *Stellarium*. I have a few candidates in mind. Wolf-Rayet stars tend to form in clusters.'

He booted up his Stellarium program. 'This free program is awesome. You can investigate the night sky from anywhere on the Earth, and travel back in time 100,000 years.'

'Here we go, *gamma Velorum*, a multiple star system in the constellation Vela. It's one of the brightest stars in the night sky and contains the closest and brightest Wolf-Rayet star. The Wolf-Rayet star has the traditional name *Suhail al Muhlif* but is now known by the more popular name *Regor*. OK, so this star is 1116.97 light years away, if it had a nearby Wolf-Rayet companion, which went into core collapse, which emitted a relativistic jet moving at around a quarter of the speed of light, . . . get that calculator Patrick.'

'What did you say? The gamma ray burst arrived after 1116.97 years, and travelling at a quarter of the speed of light *c*, the relativistic jet would have taken four times as long to make the same trip, so 4467.88 years. But it left at the same time, so we take off 1116.97 . . . ,' Patrick reasoned as he typed.

'Spot on. What do you get mate?' Tom asked, with an Australian lilt.

'3350 years. What is the time between those two global heating spikes on that graph?' Patrick said excitedly.

'Well, looking closer at the graph, the Bølling-Allerød starts around 14,800 years ago, that could be the gamma ray burst, and the end of the Younger Dryas is around 11,800 years ago. That is a 3000 year interval. We can't know the relativistic jet speed exactly, and allowing for errors in the ice core data, this looks spot on!'

'And, of course, we have the megalithic structures,' Patrick retorted.

'What do you mean?'

'The pyramids of Giza!'

'Oh my God!' Tom murmured.

Just then Tom's mobile started ringing on his desk. He looked at the screen. It was his brother Chad, calling on Skype.

'It's my brother Chad calling. He's actually in Egypt right now!' Tom exclaimed.

'Chad! How are you doing? It's amazing that you're calling right now. You're still in Egypt, right? Listen, I'm with Patrick here.'

'Hi Patrick, ... Tom. I'm good. How are you guys doing? I'm on my way to see you guys, for a special event Tom, as you know. Just a little diverted in Egypt so to speak.'

'Are Jeanette and Chloe with you?'

'No, they join me, hopefully, tomorrow evening. They arrive from Canada. Jeanette went to visit her Mom. Listen, I need to ask you something about astrophysics.'

'OK, but Chad, what time is it there?'

'It's after 2 a.m. I just woke up. An astrophysics question keeps buzzing round my head. It's probably nothing.'

'*No worries mate*, but good timing! We also need to ask you something about Egypt and the pyramids. It's a very long and complex story. We'll tell you more when you arrive,' Tom explained. 'What's your question? Hope we can help.'

'OK. I've been having the most surreal experiences here in Egypt. You know I'm really into Egyptology and hieroglyphs and the pyramids?'

'Sure'

'Listen, no one has any real proof when they were built or why. I've been spending time with some very interesting people, who have quite original ideas. Today I was wandering around the Giza Plateau for hours. There are loads of buildings. They say things have just fallen down but, in truth, the landscape around the Giza Plateau looks like a wasteland, almost as if has been violently struck by some cataclysm. The many structures there are all surrounded by piles of rubble. It's like the place was devastated by something, and from a geologist perspective, the rocks have clear signs of high temperature heat damage, and I mean burned ...'

'What did you say Uncle Chad?' Patrick retorted. 'Burned?'

'Yes, and at Tanis, a site up near the Nile delta, they say there are clear indications that many of the finely carved quartzite statues have suffered both high intensity heating and even melting. I was inside the great pyramid Khufu with a private guide and there are shafts pointing up to the stars from the Kings Chamber. One to the north and one to the south.'

'Wait, this is so weird! Patrick and I have just been talking about those things here. Do you have the exit angles of those shafts from the Kings Chamber?'

'Sure, wait I wrote it down. Both north and south shafts rise at 39°.'

'OK, listen, I have my Stellarium astronomy program running right now. I can easily check what is seen at 39° to the south and north. I am setting the location as Giza Plateau. Now let's see what we have, if we go back in time to *a certain date* ... and I'll tell you more about that date in a moment ... passing through the 39° elevation to the north, the closest stars to Earth I see are Vega at 25.04 light years, and then only η Draconis at 92.08 light years. There doesn't seem to be anything obvious, there's *Rastaban* and *Eltanin*, but they are both more than 150 light years away.'

'What kind of stars are they? Do they have exoplanets?' Chad enquired.

'OK, Vega is a pulsating variable star, so may not have suitable exoplanets for life, unless the exoplanets are tidally locked, showing the same face to the star, having one rotation per orbit. Life could evolve close to the far side.'

'And to the south, Tom. Anything interesting?'

'To the south, at that special date, passing through the 39° elevation, we have... oh wait for it, you won't believe this ... *proxima Centauri*, our closest neighbour!'

'Dad, surely this confirms it. There had been no extra-terrestrial contact. They were alone. It was a cry for help, to the closest possible planets.'

'What are you saying guys? What date is that?

'First, what was your astrophysics question Chad?'

'OK. I was just wondering if any kind of astrophysical event could have caused a cataclysm which could have struck the Earth from outer space. Something that could have caused the burning of and melting of rock?'

'It is so amazing that you are calling right now. Patrick and I have only just figured this all out. Indeed, there is a unique event which we believe explains everything.'

'Go on, I'm all ears now.'

'Well, there is a very unique star called a Wolf-Rayet star. It's a fast spinning, absolutely super-massive highly-energetic star which, when it runs out of fuel, it undergoes instantaneous core collapse, and super-novas, generating as much energy in a few seconds as the Sun radiates in its ten-billion-year lifetime.'

'Go on. Sounds really intriguing!'

'Yeah, so this Wolf-Rayet star undergoes core collapse, and generates this incredible energy. This can happen in different ways. In one extreme core-collapse, the star doesn't supernova, but goes into a *hypernova*, re-leasing so much energy that a relativistic jet is emitted along each of its axes. This jet impacts the surrounding dust and gas and generates the long gamma ray burst. So the result is both the transmission of a gamma ray burst travelling at light speed, combined with a high-energy relativistic jet, in a highly collimated beam, travelling at around quarter the speed of light, both heading in the same direction.'

'Oh God, I get it. If you see the event and get blasted by a gamma ray burst, which I guess is already pretty bad, you know you are just waiting for the devastating relativistic jet to arrive.'

'You're right. Now I tell you the amazing thing. This Wolf-Rayet star has a unique effect on a planet's climate. We would expect a sharp rise in temperature from the gamma ray burst, then consistent deep cooling until the relativistic jet arrives. An impact would totally destroy the planet, so we are talking *transit.* It is this transit which will cause substantial heating through the jet's interaction with the Sun, causing the whole planet to heat up again.'

'You found the climate signature? It happened?'

'Indeed, and we believe we've found the candidate. Wolf-Rayet stars tend to form in clusters and there is a cluster at 1116 light years away.'

'Well I guess you are entering my field now guys. Are we possibly talking *Bølling-Allerød,* and the end of the *Younger Dryas*?'

'Exactly,' Tom confirmed.

'From memory, those two dates were somewhere around 12,780 and 9750 B.C.E..'

'So, after surviving the aftermath of the devastation of the gamma ray burst, an advanced civilization with detailed knowledge of astronomy, could predict exactly when that jet would arrive and transit our part of the Galaxy, and possibly, or most probably, cause a *near extinction level event.* Since all stars have slightly different orbits around the galaxy, just maybe they could hope that there would be some drift out of alignment, but they would have needed to plan for the worst. They would have known exactly how much time they had to make preparations, to protect as many people as possible, and we are talking generations planning and developing a survival strategy. Life on this planet was at stake. The whole planet must have worked together in harmony, utterly dependent upon each other. That time must have been remarkable.'

'Or not. It may have been anarchistic. It's a sobering thought Tom.'

'Dad, let's check where that Wolf star cluster was on the date the jet transit started.'

'OK, *Regor* ... what was that? Around 11770 years ago? ... *Regor* was ... oh my God, look! Chad, you're not going to believe this. It's a total confirmation of everything.'

'Where was it?'

'11770 years ago, *Regor* was exactly ... 0.000 degrees elevation above the horizon, perfectly due south from the Giza plateau. That is totally unbelievable. That's pretty statistically significant.'

'How is that possible Dad?' Patrick asked, sounding very alarmed.

'It can only mean one thing, that the pyramid complex is a monument marking the moment a previous civilization of Earth had acknowledged it would most likely be completely wiped out.'

'And us, who are we and where are we from, if the population of the Earth was wiped out?' Chad asked.

'Unless, despite the terrible cataclysm, there were survivors in remote places, and those people are our true ancestors,' Tom remarked.

'So, they had around 3000 years to design and build the pyramids,' Chad replied, as if listening to his own words. '3000 years to determine what the pyramids would signify and where they would be located. Every detail would have been planned meticulously. They would have reasoned what symbolism would be added, anticipating that perhaps the Earth would be cast back to some kind of primitive stone age era, maybe for aeons. From basic survival, to hunting and gathering, then farming all over again. Everything would need to be relearned, rediscovered and reinvented. The monument would need to survive the cataclysm, and endure the time needed for a new civilization to emerge, which could then reason out the message it carried. It all makes sense. A significant part of the Earth's surface might possibly have suffered intense burning, scouring much evidence of an earlier advanced civilization, leaving only megalithic monuments, many in ruins, all over the World.'

'And that's what we see today,' Tom confirmed. 'All around the World. There are mysterious megalithic structures in Tiwanaku in western Bolivia, Teotihuacan in Mexico ...'

'And the Giza Plateau, I would hazard to guess,' Chad added.

'What if the message got through? What if the pyramid was sending some kind of transmission out at 39° elevation towards *proxima Centauri?* Extra-terrestrials may have come and resurrected our planet, bringing us back from the abyss,' Patrick suggested.

'It's certainly a possibility. I must say, it's quite mind-blowing what we've hypothesised,' Tom remarked quietly. 'Chad, do you think you might be able to find anything more, which can further confirm this? Photos of burnt rocks? A possible direction of the transit relative to the Earth's orbit? Our hypothesis certainly suggests a relativistic jet transit coming from the south, which might suggest corresponding burn marks on the southern sides of monoliths.'

'This is quite sobering and shocking, Tom and Patrick. Not sure if I will easily sleep now! I will change my plans now and head to Tanis in the Nile Delta tomorrow. As I said, there's supposed to be many heavily burnt and melted rocks there. You know, earlier today, I saw 24 massive stone boxes in alcoves under the ground in Saqqara, each weighing in excess of 100 tons. They had perfect flat sides and were polished to a glass finish. For me, this just had to have been done by machine. How they were moved hundreds of metres underground is unimaginable for us, even today. I am starting to think that they are part of this. What if they were some kind of storage system for seeds, to enable survivors to re-plant after the cataclysm?'

'I think you may just have solved another famous enigma. There are so many ancient stories of Noah and his Ark. In fact, the *flood myth* has been found among the cultural traditions of peoples all around the World, extending back to the Neolithic. The written record is key. The most ancient version of the story is found in the Babylonian *Epic of Gilgamesh*. I know this because Mary-Anne published a paper about the flood myth traditions last year. An ancient clay cuneiform tablet appeared in 1872, which when correctly translated, described how *Enki*, the Sumerian god of water, tasked their Noah, a guy they called *Utnapishtim*, to build an Ark . . . *as a box*! Since this disagreed with later versions of the Noah and his Ark story, which appeared thousands of years later, it was strangely decided that the earlier version must have been a cuneiform misprint, so they decided to correct the earlier translation to mean boat! What if the Ark comprised both boats *and boxes*?'

'What about the waters covering the Earth? Do we now have an explanation of that?' Chad asked.

'Of course! When the relativistic jet passed by the Solar System, . . . and I am trying to work out how far away it might have been . . . it would have likely caused *significant sea-level rise from the melting of the icecaps*, leading to phenomenal floods all around the World, possibly covering parts of continents maybe more than ten or more metres deep. There would have been vast movement of sediments. Other sites could have been completely buried, as if they were purposely filled in.'

'Are we talking Göbekli Tepe?' Chad asked.

'Possibly. Maybe we should tell Mary-Anne!'

'So, we did survive?' Patrick suggested.

'It would seem that way. Those stone boxes under Saqqara could be another important aspect of the Noah's Ark story as described in the Babylonian epic,' Tom added.

'There is another paradox,' Chad replied. 'In a deep shaft under the Giza Plateau, there are other 100-ton stone boxes. One is made from *dacite* and the closest rock formations to source that, are either Greece or Zambia. That suggests that other people were possibly building their own boxes and then maybe filling them with their own seed varieties then delivering them to a safe underground complex.'

'So how did they come to the conclusion to put animals onto boats? Why did they not just leave them on land?' Patrick asked.

'Well, they might have been unsure about the extent of the flooding when the jet transit started. Alternatively, they may have predicted significant sea-level rise, and extensive rainfall and flooding as well. Moreover, this ancient civilization might even have had recorded history of this having happened in an earlier epoch. Perhaps a relativistic jet transit had happened before, and they half knew what to expect. Consequently, both components of the Noah's Ark story are likely true,' Tom replied. 'At this point, we have only just reached the bare outlines of a new hypothesis. This all needs some careful and deep thinking. *Cities underground* also comes to mind, something like *Derinkuyu* in Turkey. They believe up to 20,000 people could have lived there. If they had 3000 years to plan. I always wondered why they needed those massive stone doors to block the entrances. One commentator had suggested that the huge millstone-like doors could be rolled to close off the passage for privacy, or for stopping dogs running in and out, but that didn't seem to make any sense. To protect against a cataclysm, sounds much more convincing.'

'There are pyramids all around the World!' Patrick exclaimed. 'Could they all be part of this?'

'Possibly. My goodness, what a shocking revelation. It seems likely that the Earth may have likely survived the most horrific cataclysm. A previous advanced civilization was possibly almost completely wiped out, yet strangely, and fortuitously, they had 3000 years to plan for it,' Chad added. 'One hundred generations working towards a single goal!'

'Wow!' Patrick sighed.

There was a very long pause of silence, then Chad spoke. 'Guys, that was quite a conversation! It's very late here. I now need to crash. I'll message you if I discover anything else, otherwise we meet next week.'

'Chad, this was great that you called! It's also extremely useful that we have a *man on location*. Good luck with your search, and look forward to meeting up next week.'

'Thanks. Patrick, Tom, great to talk! See you next week. We should really keep this story completely quiet until we've worked everything out!'

'Of course, our secret. See you next week, safe flight!'

'Bye guys.'

'Bye Chad,' Tom replied, then he cut the Skype call.

Patrick and Tom just looked at one another in disbelief.

Mary-Anne suddenly walked into the kitchen. 'You haven't moved! I'm struggling to rewrite a really complicated paper, which is seriously challenging. You haven't even cleared up the breakfast things!'

'Mom, we've just worked out that the pyramids may have taken up to 3000 years to build,' Patrick replied, excitedly.

'What? Please guys, come on! The kitchen needs to be cleared. I'd really appreciate a little support, and Tom, I really think it would be helpful if you would cut the grass. We have visitors coming tomorrow and the weather is good for mowing right now!' Mary-Anne retorted.

'Of course, honey,' Tom replied, smiling at Patrick and giving him a wink.

Patrick was totally frozen, his hands open, and his mouth wide open in astonishment.

'Later Patrick,' Tom whispered, giving him a knowing look. 'We're cool. We're cool. I'd love to cut the grass honey. Patrick and I will clear up here?'

'Great, guys!' Mary-Anne exclaimed. 'You gave the right response.'

'How's it going honey?' Tom asked.

'It's so difficult adding a totally new section, and then getting it to flow. I need some more coffee,' she sighed, sounding very irritated. She pushed the button on the machine, the bean grinder started, the coffee slowly filled her cup. Taking her coffee, she murmured, 'Back to work.'

'Good luck, honey' Tom called sweetly, as she walked away.

11 From Ghana to Mali to confront the Dogon's Sirius Mystery

Kumasi, central Ghana

'Mr Kofi, Mr Kofi, it's quarter to five! You asked for a wake up!' a voice called from the corridor. The person was also softly tapping on the bedroom door.

'Thanks!' Kofi called back. He was already awake. 'Manu! Manu! It's time to get up. We have a plane to catch.'

Manu suddenly opened his eyes. There was barely time to get dressed and down the stairs and out onto the street. He still felt very heavy with sleep. 'OK,' he murmured.

They both got dressed. Kofi had two large bottles of mineral water. 'Let's take these,' he said, packing a change of clothing and his wallet and phone into a small rucksack.

'Good idea. 'I have a spare tee-shirt and shorts over there,' he said pointing. Is there room?' Kofi nodded and packed them.

Manu then realised he would likely be totally *incommunicado* for two days. He quickly sent a Messenger message to Patrick, his SETI buddy. *Heading off-grid —— back Sunday.*

Manu and Kofi raced down the stairs and wandered out in front of the hotel. Claude was standing by the entrance. 'Good morning! Good to see you both!' he said. His small brown leather suitcase stood on the steps beside him. He was wearing a white cotton suit and holding a walking cane, with an intricately carved wooden handle.

Within moments an old open-top khaki green Jeep pulled up in front of them. It was covered in a fine coating of red dust. The driver had a beaming smile. 'Hello Claude!' he said loudly, in a very deep voice.

'Ebu Jande! So good to see you at last, my old friend. Please, I want to introduce my two new friends, Manu and Kofi. They will be accompanying us on our round trip to Mali.'

'Of course! Welcome!' Ebu Jande replied, climbing out of the Jeep. Ebu Jande took Claude's suitcase, strapping it down onto a rack over the trunk. 'It will be a fine flight to Mali. Our plane has passed the pre-flight. We're all fuelled up and ready to go. The airport is six kilometres from here. Our slot is 6:15 a.m. Come!'

Claude climbed into the front, and Manu and Kofi climbed into the back seats. Ebu Jande started the engine and drove the car in a wide arc heading back the way he had come.

Manu was feeling really excited, but naturally a little apprehensive. Neither he nor Kofi had flown before.

'You boys ever flown before?' Ebu Jande asked.

'No sir,' Manu replied.

'You call me Ebu Jande!' he corrected in his deep voice. 'We're on first name terms now.'

'Of course,' Manu replied.

The loud roar of the Jeep's engine, and the air rushing past as they drove, made conversation difficult. Kumasi was already awake. There were hundreds of people on the sandy streets. The honks of *tro-tro* mini buses were all around. It seemed as if the whole city was on the move.

'Ebu Jande, I must tell you about my two new friends Manu and Kofi here. I met Manu on the bus up from Accra and they were my guides visiting *Bosumtwi*. They both share our fascination in ancient artefacts and adventure!'

Claude turned to the boys in the back seat. 'As I told you, Ebu Jande here is our pilot to Mali. We have visited many archaeological sites together. I have known Ebu Jande a long time. What is it now? Eighteen years?'

'Too long!' Ebu Jande shouted, with his beaming smile. 'Way too long!'

Everybody laughed.

'You boys have a bag?' Ebu Jande shouted, looking up at them in the mirror.

'Sure, this rucksack, enough for two days,' Manu replied.

'Just to confirm,' Claude continued, 'I checked yesterday. I have booked you in to my hotel in Mopti. You boys are my guests.'

'Claude, thank you,' Manu replied.

'Yes, thank you,' Kofi added.

Claude turned again to the boys in the back seat. 'So, the plan is, we take off from Kumasi, head almost due north over Burkina Faso, and touch down some 500km later at some remote airstrip near Bandiagara, the heart of Dogon country. Ebu Jande speaks fluent Tombo. Is that our flight plan Ebu Jande?'

'Yes Claude. Our plane is a Twin Otter with extra fuel tanks. We will have fine views of Burkina Faso's southern forests and then the wide, open savannah in the north,' Ebu Jande explained. 'The landing in Mali is on a dirt strip, above the Bandiagara cliffs. It's the rainy season now, but weather reports today are good, only light winds, and we'll be between two weather systems. Hopefully no turbulence.'

Ebu Jande turned into the airport. He parked the car in a reserved area. 'Everybody set? Our journey to Mali begins! First, I just need to sign both you boys in, to update the flight plan.'

'Ebu Jande, I don't have a passport,' Manu confessed.

'You know, where we are going, we'll be lucky if there is even a herd of goats to greet us! I promise you, it won't be a problem!'

'Great!' Manu replied, heaving a sigh of relief.

'I'll just be a moment,' Ebu Jande said, and disappeared inside the main building.

He emerged shortly. 'We're ready. Let's get into the air.'

They walked out across the airfield to where the aircraft was parked. Two mechanics were walking around it with a checklist, tapping the fuselage and moving the ailerons.

'Ebu Jande!' one of them called out, seeing them approach.

'David, everything OK? I did a pre-flight but wanted a confirmation. I have important guests today.'

'Everything is perfect. I put 4 food packages in, as you asked, and there is coffee, coca cola and water . . . ,' David explained.

'No *iced* coffee?' Ebu Jande exclaimed with a pretend disappointed lilt.

'... and 4 cans of iced coffee, although in about half an hour, they won't be iced anymore,' David continued.

'Good man! Thank you so much. Listen, if everything goes to plan, we are back tomorrow afternoon. Gentlemen, we are boarding now. Who is joining me up front? Claude?'

'Yes, I will join you, we can always swap during the flight.'

'I will take the right-hand seat Claude. You are on the left. Old habits die hard!'

'Of course'

Manu, Kofi and Claude carefully climbed aboard and took their seats, and belted up. Claude squeezed into the front, left-hand seat. Manu and Kofi sat either side of the aisle. Manu was amazed at the huge array of buttons, switches, and dials in the cockpit.

Outside, Ebu Jande was signing the bottom of a paper that David had on his clip board. He then climbed into the aircraft and pulled up the steps, locking the hatch behind him. He walked forward and sat up front next to Claude. He put on his headphones and started the two engines, first one, then the other.

Ebu Jande turned round and shouted, 'Boys, put on those noise-cancelling headphones! Then we can all talk to each other.'

Manu and Kofi put the headphones on and suddenly the engine noise was much quieter. Ebu Jande's voice sounded very electronic but was clear. 'You can all listen to the inflight communications. I will switch you off when I am speaking. Welcome to Dogon Airways!'

Ebu Jande did a few more stationary checks. He took the engines to full throttle for ten seconds then throttled back. He checked the movement of all the ailerons then gave a thumbs-up towards David. He then spoke into the intercom: *'Kumasi Ground. Twin Otter X-ray Victor Charlie, at Romeo 1, with information Zulu, taxi for take-off?'*

Within moments came the reply, *'Twin Otter X-ray Victor Charlie, at Romeo 1, Kumasi Ground. Taxi to runway one eight left.'*

'X-ray Victor Charlie, to one eight left', Ebu Jande confirmed.

Ebu Jande then slowly increased the throttle, and the twin propeller aircraft suddenly started to move forward. He then taxied the aircraft towards the runway and waited, with engines throttled back. *'Kumasi*

Tower. X-Ray Victor Charlie. Ready for departure one eight left. Request left downwind departure, wind cleared.'

'*X-ray Victor Charlie, Kumasi Tower. Hold short, runway one eight left, landing traffic,*' came the response.

'*Kumasi Tower. X-Ray Victor Charlie, hold short, runway one eight left.*'

Ebu Jande flicked the intercom switch. 'We have landing traffic, so we'll need to wait a moment,' he said, then flicked back the intercom.

'*X-Ray Victor Charlie. Kumasi Tower, Runway one eight left. Take position and hold,*' the air-traffic controller said.

'*X-Ray Victor Charlie. Position and hold, one eight left,*' Ebu Jande repeated slowly.

Shortly, a large, bright yellow DHL transport came into view, touching down some 200m away. It raced past in front of them. They watched as it headed off down the runway, slowing down. Then, at the far end, it turned around and taxied off to a holding area.

Almost immediately, the controller's voice came over the intercom, '*X-Ray Victor Charlie. Runway one eight left. Cleared for take-off.*'

'*X-Ray Victor Charlie. Cleared for take-off, runway one eight left.*' He slowly increased the throttle to full, and the Twin Otter roared into life and headed off along the runway. Within a short time, the aircraft picked up speed and lifted off the ground. They were airborne!

The light aircraft quickly climbed high over the city of Kumasi. It seemed to dance a little as it rose through the turbulent air. Ebu Jande then slowly banked the aircraft, turning it in a 180° arc and levelled out, heading north.

'Welcome everyone, I think we'll arrive in Mali under two hours from now. The time is 06:50 now, so let's say . . . around 08:45. That's my estimate.'

Manu was amazed. They were flying in the sky above Ghana. Kofi was equally excited. Below them, Manu could see a line of trucks heading north. It was incredible how small they seemed.

'Just help yourself to anything to eat or drink. We can all speak now, I have switched over the intercom.' Ebu Jande pulled the ring on his can of iced coffee. It was still ice cold.

Claude turned to them. 'Well, what do you think Manu, Kofi? Quite exciting isn't it?'

'Thanks Claude. This is just unbelievable,' Manu replied.

Away to the west, dark ominous clouds were rolling in. It was the rainy season. 'If you look left, there are rain clouds coming, but at our speed we should be avoiding that weather system. Maybe there'll be a little turbulence, but still with some blue sky here and there.'

Manu and Kofi chatted together, pointing out various landmarks and guessing the names of the towns below them from a handheld map.

'Ebu Jande, do we cross into Ivory Coast?' Manu asked.

'Good question, but no. We'll be keeping east of the border until we cross north into Burkina Faso. We should be crossing into Burkina Faso around 5 minutes from now. I will shortly report in to Burkina Faso Air Traffic Control to let them know who we are. I already filed a flight plan, so they should be expecting us.'

Ebu Jande switched over the radio frequency and made the call. '*Burkina Faso Air Traffic Control, Twin Otter X-ray Victor Charlie, inbound from Kumasi Ghana, two nine hundred, heading three four zero Bandiagara Mali over.*'

Within moments, a lady air traffic controller came back. '*X-Ray Victor Charlie, Burkina Faso Air Traffic Control, two nine hundred, heading three four zero Bandiagara Mali, clear to proceed.*'

'*Burkina Faso Air Traffic Control, X-Ray Victor Charlie, Bandiagara Mali, clear to proceed.* OK, we are identified on their radar. Everything is on track.'

Manu and Kofi were drinking in the stunning views as they crossed the border. Up front, in the cockpit, Claude and Ebu Jande were discussing their various past trips.

'Claude, do you remember that journey we made to Mauritania? In search of Atlantis, the *Eye of Africa?*'

'Indeed, that flight over the *Richat Structure* was something I will remember forever. For you two boys in the back, in central west Mauritania there is a bizarre, multiple-ring rock formation, almost mimicking the description of Atlantis by *Plato*.'

'Yeah, we flew over it and I saw this landing strip. So, we thought we would land. Remember, this is very remote country, almost in the middle of the Sahara Desert! Then, just as we were making our final approach, I just happened to notice, far in the distance, way to the north, the sky was *wall-to-wall orange*, a mile high! It was a massive sand storm! We couldn't land, we had to get out of there as quick as we could. I sharply banked the aircraft to turn a full 180° arc, and then we flew like the wind. We only just made it. It was pretty exciting stuff. No way was I risking the aircraft on the ground, covered in sand. It was a two-hour flight back to lush Senegal,' Ebu Jande explained, with a wide smile, laughing off the experience.

'We made it by the skin of our teeth!' Claude added. 'That was seat-of-your-pants stuff!'

'Indeed. No such excitement today. A standard flight to a remote airstrip in the middle of the *back of beyond*.'

'Will the aircraft be safe?' Manu asked. 'I mean if there is no one to guard it.'

'No worries. The aircraft will be locked and covered with a canvas. It'll be fine.'

Soon the landscape was changing below them. Green savannah was changing to the yellows and browns of arid semi-desert. They were getting much closer to Mali.

'This is still Burkina Faso below us here. We're crossing the border soon. Now I need to report to Mali airspace on their frequency and tell them who we are.' He switched the intercom and rotated the frequency dial. '*Mali Air Traffic Control, Twin Otter X-ray Victor Charlie, inbound from Kumasi Ghana, two eight hundred, heading three four zero Bandiagara over.*'

There was some static and a really long pause, then the Mali controller came back. '*X-Ray Victor Charlie, Mali Air Traffic Control, two eight hundred, heading three four zero Bandiagara, clear to proceed.*'

'*Mali Air Traffic Control, X-Ray Victor Charlie, Bandiagara, clear to proceed.*'

'We're all sorted now. We are now legally in Mali and heading for Bandiagara. Only a few minutes now.'

Soon, the settlement of Bandiagara was coming into view. As they got closer, a long, red sandy strip, south of the town was clearly visible, running east-west. The aircraft banked and descended, and the red landing strip loomed in front of them, getting bigger and bigger. They quickly lost altitude and within a short time, the wheels touched the ground, and the aircraft bumped along the sandy runway.

Ebu Jande brought the aircraft to the far end of the landing strip, then turned off to a holding area and cut the throttle. There was no one about. The only sound was the wind. There was no endless cacophony of crickets; there was absolutely no vegetation at all. Even though it was only just before 9 a.m., the temperature was already 30°C. The ground was parched.

'Welcome to Bandiagara. Remember to bring that food with you boys. Don't leave it in the aircraft.'

'Claude, and Ebu Jande, I must say again how grateful we are to be on this trip with you,' Manu insisted.

'You are very welcome,' Claude replied with a smile.

Ebu Jande switched off several systems and then took out the key. He squeezed out of his seat, then unlocked and opened the door and lowered the steps. They all then stepped down from the aircraft. Ebu Jande then unlocked the luggage compartment. 'Come, help over here,' he said.

Together they all helped unload all the bags, several boxes, and a bundled-up canvas sheet. Ebu Jande then locked the aircraft door, and dragged the canvas sheet away from the aircraft.

'Boys, I need some help,' he called. 'We need to protect the aircraft from the Sun, sand and birds.'

'Of course!' Together they hauled the canvas sheet over the airframe, and lashed it down with straps. '

From the far end of the air strip, an old rusty Peugeot van was approaching.

Manu watched it. It seemed to be *completely rusty*. Did it have any paint on it at all?

Ebu Jande looked up. 'Ah, it must be Ousmane.'

'Just on time,' Claude said. 'Manu, Kofi, our adventure continues. We have transport. I propose we just head out to a village below the cliffs. Everyone can just help themselves to food and water as they need it. I estimate it will take about 2 hours.'

'Time to speak *Tombo* now,' Ebu Jande announced.

The van pulled up. Ebu Jande walked over to Ousmane, who was stepping down from the van. They shook hands and laughed together. Ebu Jande handed him a bag of various things, and Ousmane peered into the bag, smiling and nodding, and looked quite grateful.

Ebu Jande turned to Claude and the boys, 'Ousmane welcomes you.'

'Please give our greetings back,' Claude replied.

Ebu Jande smiled and they all climbed in, and headed off.

'I should tell you that the Dogon country is a very under-developed part of the World,' Claude explained. 'The Dogon people live a very different life from the one that you and I experience. Some say it as if we are almost visiting a *stone age* culture. I say that they possess a rare and rich tradition, greatly coloured by their belief that they were visited long ago by the *Nommo*, a fish-like being from another World. Yesterday, at *Bosumtwi*, we were talking about their knowledge of Sirius, as potentially a triple star system. Something that scientists in the West did not have any evidence for until the 1990s. That remains still unproven. Please keep an open mind and let us enjoy the richness of their vivid tradition.'

Ebu Jande was in the front, sitting next to Ousmane, chatting away in Tombo. Then Ebu Jande turned around. 'OK, Ousmane just told me the route. The road runs about ten kilometres along the top of the escarpment, then we descend, and drive in front of the Bandiagara Cliffs. This sandstone escarpment extends some 200km, and rises in height up to 600m in places. All along these cliffs, there are several hundred Dogon villages, each having 500 or so inhabitants. Ousmane just explained that there is one village, in particular, where they are holding a special festival now, which I know Claude is interested to see.'

'Excellent,' Claude replied.

The rusty van had no air-conditioning, and apart from the two-pane front wind shield, it had empty open windows, with no glass at all.

Manu just had to ask. 'Does the intense Sun completely remove a vehicle's paint here?' he said.

'No, it's mainly the sand storms when combined with strong winds. For that reason, many vehicles you see here are just *rust* coloured.'

'Don't you also need water to get rust?' Manu continued.

'Of course,' Ebu Jande replied. 'At night, the temperature can fall really low such that condensation forms on the bare metal. That's why they get so rusty.'

'Of course,' Manu replied.

Kofi turned to Claude. 'What time does the festival start?'

'Well, when we talk of Dogon festivals, they can last many days and months! The most important festival, *Sigui*, happens every 60 years and that one lasts several years! The next *Sigui* isn't until 2027, however.'

'That's right,' Ebu Jande explained. 'We do not need to arrive at a certain time today, it will be going on all day and into the night. As far as I understand, the festival at the village we are going to, is a dance festival to honour and recognise the Dogon's first ancestors. You will see men dancing and jumping wearing the most elaborate, brightly coloured, carved masks.'

'It sounds quite inspiring,' Manu remarked.

'My real interest is to get confirmation first hand, of credible stories and to see credible artefacts, like the one I found at *Bosumtwi*. The Dogon's strong belief that their ancestors came from a planet orbiting one of the stars in the Sirius triple star system remains perplexing,' Claude added.

Soon Ousmane had turned onto a winding sandy track which led them below the *Bandiagara* escarpment. The road had all but vanished. Suddenly, Ousmane was pointing and shouting excitedly. In the distance, Manu could see a man hanging perhaps 40 metres up in the air, holding onto a rope. 'Wow, what is he doing?' Manu asked.

'That takes great strength and expertise,' Ebu Jande explained. 'The rope is made from the bark of the *baobab* tree. The Dogon collect pigeon guano and, also unfortunately, artefacts left in the cliffs by the indigenous *Tellem* people, who lived here hundreds of years ago. They sell the guano as much needed fertiliser, but the artefacts can make a fortune if sold to private collectors. The Mali government is working hard to try to keep the artefacts in the country.'

Manu strained his neck to look directly upwards at the man, as they passed virtually underneath him.

Ousmane started explaining something to Ebu Jande in Tombo.

'OK. We are almost here,' Ebu Jande announced. 'It's not permitted to drive any closer while the dance festival is on.'

They parked the rusty Peugeot, and walked towards the village. Up above them, bizarre, cuboid, and tubular-shaped huts clung to the rocky cliffs. In a clearing, a crowd of villagers surrounded two men with masks, who were jumping and screaming. The masks extended some two metres above their heads into the air, comprising some kind of wooden, banded blade.

Three orange, hairy-coated figures suddenly appeared, dancing and screaming, while a man tapped a goatskin drum. Then the villagers started to join in the dance, as if intoxicated by the rhythm. Half of them were wearing special costumes; their heads completely hidden behind elaborate masks of extended bands of white beads, or made of brightly coloured hair. Two purple-masked men on stilts then became the focus of the festival.

'This is the very important *Dama Mask Dance*,' Claude quietly explained. 'The Dogon believe it creates a bridge into the supernatural world. Those men dancing with the short, geometric wooden extensions on their masks, are wearing *Kanaga* masks. They represent the first human beings.'

The cyclic drumming rhythms and chanting, created a vibrant atmosphere. Ousmane was pointing things out to Ebu Jande, who then turned to Claude and the boys. 'The man over there is the *Hogon*, or village spiritual leader.'

A really strange hemispherical house with a dark orange roof, and multiple vertical sculpture-posts, stood to the edge of the dancing men. Ebu Jande continued, 'That is the *House of Words*. Every village has one. It is the male social centre. Notice also that no women are dancing.'

After some time, Ousmane led them away from the dance towards a group of old Dogon men sitting in a clay brick doorway. On the ground, a variety of carved stones and pots and wooden masks were laid out before them. Ousmane started talking through the artefacts with Ebu Jande, occasionally asking comments from the old Dogon men. Ebu Jande showed them Claude's recent acquisition from *Bosumtwi* market.

After a slow puzzling interchange of Tombo, Ebu Jande turned to Claude. 'Claude, this is indeed a representation of the Sirius star system. It is very old and possibly comes from the western end of the escarpment. Some details on the carving are very unique to those villages.'

'Very interesting. So, what do they actually say about how long they have had this knowledge of Sirius being a triple star system?' Claude asked.

After a long conversation, with help from Ousmane, Ebu Jande attempted to articulate a response. 'So, from astronomical observations, we know that Sirius A has a binary companion Sirius B which is a dense white dwarf star, which is the remnant of a collapsed burnt out star. A *white dwarf* has around half the mass of the Sun, but a diameter of 10km. The Dogon call Sirius B *Po Tolo*. *Po* means smallest seed, which corresponds to the plant *Digitaria*, and *tolo* means star. They say it is white and is extremely heavy, which matches the scientific description of a white dwarf. They also say that Sirius B takes 50 years to orbit around Sirius A, which of course scientists have now confirmed. Strangely, they claim to have had this knowledge for hundreds of years. As you know, we only had Sirius B confirmed through a telescope in 1862.'

'It just seems so unlikely that these primitive people, living in isolation, would have heard such an obscure fact from travellers passing through,' Claude replied. 'Their languages isolate them phenomenally. Only 70 years later, they disclosed the complexity of their secret tradition to French anthropologists who won their trust. It is clear that the large number of really old masks and carvings used to celebrate the Sirius tradition, clearly predate this period by hundreds of years.'

Ebu Jande continued, 'They also believe there is indeed another star, Sirius C, a dark cool star known as a red dwarf, making it a *triple* star system, and around Sirius C, they claim that a watery planet is orbiting. They claim that it is from this planet orbiting Sirius C that the amphibious *Nommo* beings came to Earth.'

'And that is the significant dilemma. I am so happy to now have it confirmed directly from these people. We are lucky that Ousmane is so respected in this village by the elders here, that they share their knowledge with him,' Claude added.

The buildings were built carefully against the cliffs. Somehow the Sun didn't strike them full on, so the Sun's scorching rays didn't quite reach them. It was clear that the village buildings were hundreds of years old.

Claude realised that the artefact he had bought might be very important to these men. 'Ask them if they want it? A present for their kindness,' he said, holding it out to the old men.

Ebu Jande translated Claude's words into Tombo. The old men seemed excited, as they handled the artefact. One of the elders then lifted up a newly-carved mask, discussing it with Ousmane and Ebu Jande.

'Claude, he is saying they are very grateful for your gift, and you are welcome to have this representation of a Dama dance mask in return,' Ebu Jande explained.

'A *Kanaga* mask! That is very kind, and I accept most graciously. Please thank them. You know I have been planning this trip for a really long time. I just wanted the opportunity to meet the Dogon in their own land, and observe and hear first-hand what they say about Sirius, and their belief that the *Nommo* indeed spoke to their ancestors. I have to say, I am convinced they hold this conviction and everything I see, suggests it predates when Sirius B was first observed in the 19th century.'

Dogon Kanaga Mask

The festival continued and several other dances with different rhythmical chants followed. The men on stilts reappeared and beckoned to some of the men in the crowd, taunting them. This was a pure and sincere artistic expression of a vivid cultural belief.

Sometime later, Claude, Ebu Jande, Manu, Kofi, and Ousmane walked back to the rusty old Peugeot and climbed in.

'To be honest, I didn't expect we would see so much, or have such an interaction with these people,' Claude declared. 'I feel that the purpose of my visit has truly been fulfilled.'

'So, we are left with the possibility that there has indeed been some kind of extra-terrestrial contact with people on this planet,' Ebu Jande replied.

'You said that the Dogon migrated from Egypt, which also had a Sirius culture,' Manu added.

'Yes, that is what the migration patterns suggest. The Dogon have this culture with strong ties to extra-terrestrial amphibious beings, the *Nommo*, yet there is no association between Egypt and an amphibious culture. In ancient *Babylonian*, *Akkadian*, and *Sumerian* cultures, all from Mesopotamia, we find myths describing similar amphibious beings from outer space. Did the *Nommo* come, and if they did, why did they not speak with the people of Egypt? Surely Egypt existed then as another centre of civilization,' Claude reasoned. 'In short, there is an enigma here. Why do several ancient cultures describe being assisted, even educated, by extra-terrestrial amphibious beings, while the Egyptian culture does not?'

'Good point,' Ebu Jande replied. 'Moreover, by the look of the sophistication of the Egyptian culture, we would have expected clear signs of such a contact there, more than anywhere. Unless, of course everything has been totally misinterpreted. Perhaps there is an even more obvious explanation staring us right in the face.'

Ousmane started the engine and turned the van around. They travelled back in front of the Bandiagara cliffs. To the south were the vast, empty and arid *Bongo plains*. After an hour, they were climbing back up the escarpment towards Bandiagara.

At the top of the escarpment, the air was noticeably three or four degrees cooler. They then continued on the *Route Nationale 15* all the way to Mopti, some 75 kilometres away.

It was pretty hot in the van. Even the endless rush of wind through the vehicle didn't give much respite from the 40°C air temperature. It was like being in a hairdryer. 'At least we have a wind screen!' Ebu Jande remarked at one point.

Eventually they reached Mopti and the banks of the Niger river, with its sand flats disrupting the channel. Ousmane then turned along the river front until the Hotel Kanaga. It was already late afternoon, close to 5p.m. and everyone was very weary after a very long day.

'At last,' Claude remarked. 'It is surely air-conditioned inside. Let's have dinner and a cold drink. We're all pretty exhausted!'

Ousmane helped them unload everything and then spoke with Ebu Jande.

'He will be back tomorrow around 10 o'clock in the morning. Then we will head back to the plane,' Ebu Jande explained.

'It's like a palace!' Manu said, as they walked through the gate, under a carved red stone-column structure. 'There's a pool too!'

'You boys can enjoy a dip after we've checked in,' Ebu Jande confirmed.

Shortly, they were all signed in, and Manu and Kofi then headed to their very rectangular block room, while Claude and Ebu Jande headed out to the terrace to have iced coffee.

There was even *Internet*! Manu switched on his phone and logged in. There was a message from Patrick '*After a long discussion with my Dad, I am starting to think that our SETI signals might even be from another planet*'.

Manu quickly replied: *I am north in Mali . . . a long story . . . there is a tribe here, the Dogon, who claim they were visited by extra-terrestrials, thousands of years ago, who brought them knowledge and education*.

After Manu and Kofi had had a swim in the pool, they all met up for a great meal in the restaurant. At only 8 p.m. everyone said goodnight and headed off to sleep.

****

The next morning, after breakfast, Ousmane arrived. They checked out of the hotel and travelled back to Bandiagara. The bleak, almost lifeless, rocky landscape seemed very unwelcoming. 'Did the Nommo really choose this place to seek out the Dogon people?' Manu wondered to himself. 'No one would have expected to find any life here. Surely their story must have been brought from somewhere else and from a very long time ago.'

An hour later, they had arrived back at the plane. They removed and stowed the canvas, loaded up and climbed aboard.

As the aircraft lifted off the red sandy strip to head back to Kumasi, Manu wondered if he had uncovered an important part of the SETI puzzle.

The flight back was equally as wonderful as the journey down. The views across Burkina Faso and then Ghana were absolutely divine.

Manu and Kofi had a great time together. Ebu Jande and Claude were deep in conversation for the whole trip.

They touched down in Kumasi, some two hours later. Ebu Jande completed various checks on the aircraft, then went inside to do some paperwork. After that, he drove them all back to the hotel in the Jeep.

Manu took his phone and decided to send Patrick another message: *I am left here with an enigma. Are the suggestions of extra-terrestrial contact just a distortion and reinterpretation of obscure events half-remembered from long ago? There does not seem to be a logical reason why the Dogons would hold such a unique belief of having had contact unless it were true. Is this the evidence for some kind of extra-terrestrial contact? What do you think? Any more thoughts about our SETI signals? Regards Manu*

Manu's phone then buzzed: *Manu, good point! It is also possible that our SETI signals may be proof of another civilization seeking to make contact with Earth. If they are directional they might have been intended for us! Hopefully they are friendly ;) Patrick.*

12 Evicted from Egypt carrying unpublished secret knowledge

Inter-Continental Hotel Cairo, beside the Nile

Suddenly, there was a heavy pounding on Chad's bedroom door and he was abruptly awoken from a very deep sleep. He looked at his watch it was only just after 8 a.m. He walked over and peered through the peephole. This looked very serious. He opened the door. There were several people outside.

'We are from the Ancient Antiquities Department Police,' a man said, wearing a uniform. 'You are to come with us immediately. Take all your possessions. There are serious questions as to your motives and activities here in Egypt. Your visa has been revoked, and you will be leaving Egypt today. Because you are an American citizen, there will be no charges at this time. Enquiries show that you are travelling on to Sydney Australia, business class. Your flights have been changed. You depart within three hours.'

Chad froze. 'I have done nothing wrong,' he pleaded. 'My wife and daughter are arriving this evening. We are on a family trip to Sydney Australia via Egypt.'

'We know, Dr Walker. I suggest that you get in touch with them and either encourage them to fly directly to Sydney, or at least change their flights. You are leaving today,' the official declared.

What on earth had they decided he had been doing? He was only trying to formulate a coherent single explanation of everything he had seen and heard. Surely that wasn't a crime? He quickly realised that maybe many people's ego's might be damaged. A lot was at stake. Perhaps he was getting too close to a hidden truth. Chad gathered his things together, packing everything into his leather bag. There wasn't time for anything else other than leave. 'What about my hotel bill and checking out?' he asked.

'Consider yourself fortunate. Everything has been paid for by the Department of Ancient Antiquities. We want you out of the country as soon as possible,' the man confirmed.

Chad was numbed by the shock of this event. Taking his leather bag, he was led down in the lift to a chauffeur-driven car.

He stepped inside. The driver, clearly oblivious to what had just transpired, smiled and said, 'We have police motorcycle escort to accompany our drive to the airport sir. I hope you have enjoyed your stay here.'

'I have thanks,' Chad replied, shaking his head slowly.

He took his phone and sent a text to Jeanette: *Hi Honey, I need to be very frank now. For some odd reason, I am being evicted from Egypt. Please try to rearrange your flights from Toronto to Sydney. I will message you as soon as I get to the airport. I love you, C xxx*

Within thirty seconds, Chad's phone buzzed: *Sorry to hear Honey. We also got a visit today from an official here in Canada. We have just been offered business class flights direct from Toronto to Sydney today. Chloe is thrilled! This whole thing sounds bizarre, but we are so happy to travel business class direct. We are leaving for the airport in twenty minutes. Love you! See you in Sydney. You can tell us the whole story then. Love J and Ch xxxx.*

Next, Chad sent a long message to Tau, explaining as much as he could and thanking him for all his help and kindness. Chad also offered to leave Mustapha's notes and artefacts at the airport. Almost immediately, Chad got a reply: *It has been my pleasure Chad. Please keep everything. Maria already told me she wanted you to have Mustapha's notes. Sorry we don't get to meet again on Friday. Safe flight. Tau*

Chad's limousine and police escort soon arrived at the airport, where an official was ready to meet him. Chad was led into the building and past the immigration officials. 'Your passport has been pre-processed, I will just take the inserted immigration paper,' the man said.

Chad took out his passport and the man tore out the paper stapled inside. 'I think you may also have something that belongs here, Dr Walker,' the official said, with a knowing look.

Chad realised the official meant the two carved stones from Mustapha's collection. He opened his leather bag and pulled out the two quartzite artefacts and handed them over.

'Thank you, Dr Walker,' he replied in a dry voice. 'Have a good trip. Here are your flight details.' He handed Chad a piece of paper. 'The business class lounge is in terminal three.'

Chad was soon past security. He headed straight for the business class lounge. He had two hours to wait before his Sydney flight. He was certain that a large *gin and tonic* awaited him there.

When he arrived at the Egyptair lounge, he handed over his passport with the paper that the man had handed him. The lady at the reception desk was wearing a name badge, *Maria*. He immediately thought of Maria and Tau and the talks they'd had. He hadn't even been in Egypt for three days, and now he was leaving. It seemed totally surreal.

'Welcome Dr Walker,' the lady at the reception replied with a smile. 'Your Egyptair Qantas flight will be boarding in around two hours. Please listen for the announcement. Enjoy your stay.'

Chad walked through into the lounge, and dumped his old scuffed leather bag onto a chair next to the window, then walked over to help himself from the buffet. The food looked very fresh and appealing. He took some smoked salmon and some potato salad with capers, and poured a glass of cold white wine. The gin and tonic would have to wait.

He walked back to his chair and pulled out the large envelope of papers that Mustapha had hidden in the bottom of the chest of drawers. I mean, you just couldn't even make this stuff up. It was a modern Sherlock Holmes, *Who Dunnit?* Mustapha's hidden papers surely held some more clues.

Leafing through the papers, he found a map of Cairo. He unfolded it and a small piece of paper fell out. It was the constellation of Orion with Sirius marked on it as well. There were some notes in Arabic, but he wouldn't be asking anyone else for a translation. He looked down on the map and saw a red ring had been drawn around the three Giza pyramids. Another ring had been drawn around another location on the map of Cairo. He quickly realised that it was Mustapha's allotment patch. So, Mustapha had correlated the location of the pyramids and the allotment patch with Orion's belt and Sirius. But there was something more! An arrow on his hand-drawn constellation of Orion, was pointing beyond Sirius, about the same distance but further below it. Chad looked on the map again. Sure enough, there were two red marks close together, one right in the middle of the Nile, the other over the words *West Cairo Power*

Station. That one had a line through it. He wondered whether Mustapha might have been worried that the power station was burying something important, or whether it had been adequately excavated before it had been constructed. Somehow, Mustapha had concluded that, whatever it was, had been consigned to the bottom of the river Nile at that location.

What had Tom said? The cataclysm was caused by the core collapse of a Wolf-Rayet star. It was in the vicinity of another Wolf-Rayet star. What was it called again? Right, *gamma Velorum*. Was that mark on the map, the position of *a gamma Velorum companion* relative to Orion and Sirius? The more Chad thought about it, perhaps a huge river would remain following its exact course after a cataclysm. It just could be that something was buried in the river at that point, and that might even be a candidate for *crowd funding* one day if enough people were interested.

Chad started to think more about the artefacts Mustapha had collected from his allotment, as if the whole Sirius story was directing the argument towards discovering the cataclysmic event, but what on earth did Sirius have to do with the cataclysm? The sequences of hieroglyphs describing the Nile were most likely alluding to *the gamma Velorum companion*. Could there be something buried in the riverbed sands of the Nile at that location? If so, what could it be?

Clearly, Mustapha had worked the whole thing out. His boss had been on the same trail. No wonder there was so much animosity. Was it about being the first to publish, or was his boss trying to prevent disclosure? A whole industry revolved around the pyramids being built in only 20 years. In fact, every Egyptian site had been described exclusively from the context of the Egyptian pharaoh dynasties. No one had entertained that these structures vastly predated them. Saqqara was described in every text book as a vast necropolis dedicated to the burial of the Apis Bull, but it was growing increasingly obvious to Chad that this was an important additional part of the story of the *Ark*, as described in the *Epic of Gilgamesh*, built to protect seeds for replanting after an expected cataclysm had passed.

Chad took the last bite of smoked salmon, then swallowed the rest of his white wine. He gave a long sigh, then wearily stood up and walked over to get that gin and tonic.

The ice clinked loudly as it fell into his glass. He poured a generous helping of gin over the ice and then added Schweppes tonic. He finished it off with a slice of lemon, then headed back to his seat.

If the Giza Plateau pyramids were built as an incredibly complicated monument to identify and mark the cataclysmic event of the relativistic jet impact, there would be many data points evident in the structures. A vast number of armchair researchers had found all manner of connections with the size of the Earth and the length of the year, but could he predict what other data the pyramids might contain, now that he knew the cataclysmic event that it marked?

According to the nineteenth century British archaeologist *Sir Flanders Petrie*, the Great Pyramid had been constructed with the most incredible precision. Ahmed had explained that the four corners were within 58mm of a perfect square base. But, he had also said that the Great Pyramid was 3/60 of one degree, i.e. three minutes of arc from being perfectly aligned due north south. Perhaps these three minutes of arc were significant. Were they referring to something, a correction perhaps? Chad was also wondering about that double bump hieroglyph above the main entrance. Could it be referring to a communications structure having two beams? That was a real possibility.

Around 11,770 years ago, the southern shaft from the King's chamber, rising at 39°, was pointing at the Sun's closest stellar neighbour, *proxima Centauri* only 4.24 light years away. If the Great Pyramid was a machine capable of transmitting a radio beam into the sky along a copper waveguide, formed by copper coating the stone shaft, then that beam would have created a ring in the sky as the Earth rotated on its axis.

At 4.24 light years away, the divergence of that beam would most likely have meant that the beam was continuously being received by an exoplanet in the vicinity of *proxima Centauri*. Did a previous civilization know that? Had this civilization developed advanced radio astronomy, or had advanced extra-terrestrials identified the incoming relativistic jet, and journeyed to visit Earth to warn them of impending doom? Did they then assist with planning for a cataclysm, and then help build the pyramid complex before leaving? These suggestions seemed ridiculous.

A more logical approach suggested that an advanced civilization realised they only had 3000 years to prepare for the cataclysm, and create a monument to mark the event for any survivors, while also transmitting a *cry for help* to their nearest neighbour.

For a moment, Chad started to wonder why there was no copper found in the Great Pyramid shafts. 'Of course,' he reasoned, 'A relativistic jet transit might possibly have caused some atmospheric effects to cause a copper lining to be completely eroded away. That would mean that any communication transmissions certainly ended as soon as the relativistic jet transit cataclysm hit the Earth.'

Chad started to think more about the two sets of shafts. While the King's chamber shafts both rose at around 39°, and exited the pyramid, as airshafts, the Queen's Chamber shafts were possibly unfinished, because they did not reach the pyramid surface. In addition, these shafts were closed off with stone slabs having copper hooks, as recorded by Gantenbrink's crawling robot. Why were they at a different angle? Had more detailed calculations been done during the course of its construction. Moreover, if they had 3000 years to build the pyramids, over time the progressive growth of ice at the icecaps towards the end of the *Younger Dryas* might have created a change in latitude due to polar motion. Any additional antisymmetric growth of ice would have changed the spin axis and thus the star that the shaft would ultimately point towards. Chad had absolutely no clue what the internal signal generation device could possibly have been, inside the *King's Chamber*, if there was even one at all. It was extremely annoying that over the centuries, eager treasure hunters had destroyed virtually every part of the shaft and chamber complex using hammers and gunpowder. Clearly, whatever the Khufu Pyramid machine might have been before the damage, and how it worked, was highly unlikely ever to be understood and brought back into operation. The integrity of the machine would have been paramount. There were clear reasons why the ascending passage, now used by tourists, was plugged and why the relieving chambers above the *King's Chamber* each formed closed cavities.

Thinking of the numbers encoded into the pyramid structure and location, was the latitude of 29.97 degrees north significant after all, effectively being equal to the speed of light in metres per second when multiplied by ten million, giving 3×10^8 m/s? This of course assumed that the builders of the pyramids knew the metre as a standard length, but many had already found strong evidence to suggest that this was so. But no, the latitude of the pyramids at effectively 30° north was precisely chosen to identify gamma Velorum on that certain date in 9750 B.C.E.

Didn't Mustapha have anything else in his hidden notes? Many writers had equated the size and position of the three pyramids with the three stars in Orion's belt. Mustapha had also totally agreed with that correlation because he had both identified Sirius as being his allotment patch, and *the gamma Velorum companion* being represented by some unknown structure, possibly a stone box, buried in the middle of the channel of the Nile. Chad however, did not yet see any credible relationship between Orion's Belt and the pyramids.

Looking again at the papers, Chad found a page on the Sumerians. Mustapha had referenced several sources where the Sumerians claimed the *great flood deluge* happened during the *Age of Leo*, 11,000 to 8,000 B.C.

This was perfectly in agreement with the Wolf-Rayet star cataclysm date. Thinking about the Sphinx, Ahmed had suggested that the head of the Sphinx may have been carved several times before. It now seemed extremely likely that it was originally a lion's head, to signify the age of Leo. The Sphinx was most likely part of the same monument complex, marking the relativistic jet impact.

On another page he found a photo of a wall frieze, with an annotation *from Hathor's Temple in Dendera*. Two large figures seemed to be holding long tubes pointing towards each other, each tube having a snake inside, appearing to come from a flower-like structure within. Each tube was pointing upwards at an angle of around 30°, supported by a Djed pillar and several figures underneath. In a separate image, a single figure held up one tube. To the right of figures holding up the tubes was a monkey-like figure holding two knives. Between the monkey-like figure and the figure holding the tube was a vertical sequence of vertical hieroglyphs. Mustapha had drawn a ring around the sequence and the annotation: *this translates to a warning!* Another ring was drawn around the 2 knives with the words *two dangers expected!* Below the image Chad read the words: *this frieze is all underground, to be better protected for posterity.*

What was Mustapha inferring here? Was he suggesting this carving represented two beams transmitted from the pyramid shafts as the relativistic jet approached, or did he have a totally different interpretation? Chad was becoming more and more convinced that Mustapha had arrived at a very similar conclusion that he and his brother Tom had come to. Maybe Mustapha just didn't have the connection with the gamma ray burst followed by the relativistic jet. One needed to be an astrophysicist of course, to make that connection.

Then he saw a page marked *Tanis*, with the annotation: *melted statues*

Frieze from Hathor's Temple in Dendera

with impact from the south. 'You just saved me that trip Mustapha. Thanks,' he murmured to himself.

Chad leafed through the rest of the papers, they seemed to be referencing different megalithic sites all over the world. Most of the annotations were in Arabic, but there were many photographs, so it was pretty clear what they described. Chad's eyes then fell onto a photograph of a stone wall of giant perfectly-interlocking blocks. 'Where was this?' he wondered. Then he saw the name, *Tambomachay, Peru*. A red ring had been drawn around two parts of the wall with the annotation: *Stone wall melted into lava and vitrified by intense heat in two places!* Below that was a paragraph about *Ollantaytambo*, with several photographs. Mustapha seemed to be referencing finely cut pink granite megalithic blocks found on the high terraces of the Temple of the Sun. There was even a picture of a wall of massive blocks with long finely cut vertical shim stones, obviously inserted to prevent cracking of the large stones during earthquakes. Then Chad saw another key piece of evidence: the granite of some of the megalithic rocks was flaking off, clear sign of intense heat damage. Further down, was the single word *Sacsayhuaman!*

On another page was a whole story of the ancient site of *Teotihuacan* in Mexico. This most likely seemed to be intended for his British Museum friend John Mann, because at the top of the page, Mustapha had added '*for JM*'. Next to a photo of the *Pyramid of the Sun*, Mustapha had written: *Check Dow 1960 and Harleston 1970, complete solar system mapping of the entire building complex! Extensive heat damage to structures!* Chad was in no doubt now that Mustapha had identified a substantial part of the evidence, he only lacked the explanation.

Chad turned the page over where he found pencil notes on another South American site, *Tiwanaku* in Bolivia. Next to the word '*Pumapunku*' was written: *machined, intricate stone H-blocks*, with an arrow pointing to different grooves and holes with the annotation: *really complex tooling!* Underneath, Mustapha had written: *missing key stone cut T-connectors across site, possibly stolen, but most likely vaporised! Many rocks scorched!*

Further down he had written: *H-blocks show strange magnetic behaviour, as if magnetised differentially, possibly externally!*

Chad started to think about the properties of the relativistic jet. Just before the supernova, the Wolf-Rayet star had emitted this collimated beam of protons. When rock is blasted externally by ionised nuclei, this could create a differential magnetic anomaly in the impacted rocks. This was controversial and Mustapha surely couldn't have reached this conclusion, he wasn't a geologist of course.

There were also several scientific publications. One geology paper was quite intriguing: *Pleistocene glass in the Australian desert: The case for an impact origin*. Chad quickly skimmed down through the article. So, Mustapha had discovered the desert glass.

Another publication was entitled: *The Maya Myth about Two Suns*. In the paper, the author was making the case that Mayan artefacts had captured the representation of a second Sun in the daytime sky. Very interesting.

Finally, Chad found a small envelope containing several photographs. One seemed to be of a very ornate, transparent glass jug or ewer, on the back was marked *V&A London, 7904-1862*. The jug looked quite beautiful with what seemed like a fine moulded flower-like pattern on the body as well as on the handle. Perhaps this was misplaced in the papers. On closer inspection, he saw some words pencilled at the bottom: *carved from a single block of quartz crystal! Only 2mm thick in places. This artefact does not belong to our civilization!* It wasn't moulded glass! It was cut from a single block of quartz! Was Mustapha claiming to have found an artefact from the lost civilisation? That was extraordinary.

Other photographs showed various carved stone bowls, each marked on the back with *Petrie Museum, London* in the top corner, then *Predynastic!*, and then the rock type: *porphyry, green schist, or diorite*. Those rock types are extremely hard. Even steel would have had no effect. How had the Egyptians cut them into perfect symmetrical shapes with only copper tools? Surely these were also from a different age. At the bottom of the

Quartz Ewer

last photograph, which showed a narrow-necked porphyry jug, Mustapha had written: *It is totally impossible to make this today!*

Chad then lifted out the last photograph, and just stared at it! It was a side-by-side comparison of two photos of the identical part of a stone frieze showing *Sopdu*, a god of the sky. The colour photo, obviously taken more recently, was the same one he had seen in Mustapha's book of notes. Mustapha's written comments in his book now seemed abundantly clear. In the images, *Sopdu* was holding a staff, and above his head to the left were three triple-bump symbols. The stone frieze border comprised a line of stars. In the black-and-white image, two long rods were extending from *Sopdu*'s head into the stone frieze border of stars. That, of course, didn't seem normal that a figure would penetrate a frieze border. In the colour image, the long rods, and only the long rods extending into the stone frieze border, had been *carefully scraped flat*! What if the rods truly represented two communication beacons transmitting into the sky towards the stars? Who had scratched that part of the stone surface away, and why? This definitely seemed very odd. Did the triple-bump symbols represent other distant planetary beacon systems. Was this then proof that life exists on other planets, or were all these images just playing with his mind?

Chad sighed deeply, then went and poured himself another gin and tonic. He was utterly shocked at what he had discovered in just three days. His mind was racing again. How would it be possible to tell this story? There would be a total denial of this suggestion. It rewrote history. That was not of course why this would be denied. To accept that this had happened was something extremely worrying.

Suddenly, an announcement came over the business lounge PA system. His flight was now boarding. He needed to go to gate.

It would be a very long flight via Dubai and Brisbane to Sydney, where many long hours of discussion with Tom surely awaited him.

13 Sydney Australia: evaluating evidence for a Rainbow Serpent

Wahroonga, Sydney Australia

Tom was sitting in a comfortable armchair in Mary-Anne's study, reading through her rewritten paper. She was sitting at her desk with papers and books piled up all around. It was a hot day outside, but an air conditioning unit was softly blowing cool air into the room.

Tom looked up. 'You've done a really formidable job, honey. The *constellation imagery* paragraphs really flow well with the rest of the text. I think it really lifts the article, but I am biased of course!'

'Thank you, but you know how difficult it is to bring a totally new emphasis into a publication. Professor Cayman didn't just want a few extra paragraphs, but a complete refocusing of the paper. Göbekli Tepe was at the centre of the *Fertile Crescent*, a region which stretches from the eastern Mediterranean seaboard and southeast Turkey, around the region north of the Tigris and Euphrates, then down to western Iran. That Iranian site, *Ali Kosh*, dates back to 7500 B.C.E..'

'Yes, but you've done it! I love how you've contrasted the carved animal imagery of Göbekli Tepe with the wall murals found in the southern Anatolian settlement of Çatalhöyük. One is a megalithic complex of circles of finely carved T-shaped stone pillars, which you suggest is only for ritual purposes, the other site is several thousand years later but a place where people actually lived.'

'Göbekli Tepe rewrites everything we thought we knew about early civilization in the *Neolithic*. The site dates back some 11,000 years. Those intricately carved pillars weigh anything between 40 and 60 tons. How on earth did they move them? I can't really find a direct correspondence with constellations. All I can suggest is that these hunter gathers came here to embrace the landscape and the open night skies. A really vast number of animal bones have now been found. This was clearly a site of gathering and feasting.'

'I think you've done a great job,' Tom replied encouragingly.

'How about you guys? You were certainly really excited about something this morning.'

'Well, I think we may have enough evidence to suggest that a major astrophysical event happened in our galaxy, and *rather close to home,*' Tom replied. 'Moreover, the event is indeed related to my own current focus of research, the Wolf-Rayet stars. I'd actually like to ask you something now. How can I gather evidence about an event which may predate written records?'

'What do you mean Tom? How far back in time are we talking?'

'Exactly the same time as your Göbekli Tepe site, about 11,000 years ago.'

'Well, you can see the carved animals on the pillars, they are telling a story, although it's a pity I can't work out what it is. Throughout history, mankind has tried to capture the record of events in art. We should also include oral tradition and myths and legends? There is a reason why some stories were more important than others for the next generation to learn and pass down, as if they carried a valuable teaching.'

'Do you have any in mind?'

'Well, are you going to share more information about your hypothesis?' Mary-Anne asked with a smile. 'Or, is this another secret *Tom Walker project*, which I only get to read about in next month's copy of *The Astrophysical Journal*?'

'*Next month*? You're kidding me. It will take at least *two months* before I could even get it peer-reviewed.'

'You *have* got something! I knew it. Tell me what you have. You should remember that I have ways to make you confess!'

'OK, I'll tell you everything,' he replied, leaning forward and giving her a sweet kiss on her cheek. 'So, what I think is that there was a massive star collapse around 14,800 years ago.'

'Are we talking bright?'

'Incredibly bright, even ten or more times the brightness of a supernova. A supernova outshines an entire galaxy, that's how we can detect them in other galaxies, but we are talking *in our own back yard*! If we compare the supernova which happened in 1054 C.E., which we name as SN 1054, there are reliable records found in Japan, China and also by some Arabic astronomers. That supernova created the incredibly beautiful *Crab Nebula*, but the key point is that the *Crab Nebula* supernova happened about 6500 light years away. Nevertheless, it was described as being visible in the day for at least 20 days, and visible in the night sky for two years. The Chinese referred to supernovas as *guest stars*. Some researchers have suggested SN 1054 was twice the size of the Moon.'

'So how bright are we talking for your super supernova?'

'That is the shocking thing! I estimate this *Wolf-Rayet* hypernova took place at only just over 1100 light years away. That is around one sixth of the distance, so it would have been close to 36 times brighter!'

'Tom, forgive me for asking, but how on earth can you know where a supernova took place *thousands of years in the past*?' Mary-Anne asked, looking a little perplexed.

'I know, OK, *I have a very strong hunch* that a hypernova took place at this location, because the climatic record shows the triple signature of precisely that event, which corresponds to the right timescale. These stars generally form in clusters and the distance to the cluster I have found, exactly matches what we would expect to see in the climatic record.'

'By that, you mean data from the ice sheets?'

'Precisely, from the Greenland ice core samples,' Tom confirmed. 'So, I have been thinking that this was such a calamitous event, which would have changed the night sky for years. Perhaps the clear distinct difference between day and night would have been affected. The estimate of the maximum brightness, or peak apparent magnitude, of the Crab Nebula progenitor supernova is -6. In comparison, the Sun is -26.74. But my hypernova, ...'

'The *Tom Walker* hypernova, ...' Mary-Ann clarified teasingly.

'Well, it needs a name. We can find a good one later. According to convention, it would be HN -12780, so let's stick with that for the moment. So, hypernova HN -12780 would have been at least around 36 times brighter, ... well the exact figure is actually closer to 34, ... and each unit of magnitude means a change in brightness of 2.512. Bear with me. The bottom line is that *34 times brighter* means that this event had an *apparent visual magnitude* of -19.48. As I said, the Sun is -26.74, the Moon is -12.74, so this was a very bright object in the sky.'

'How can you know if it had the same brightness as another stellar event?'

'Well, if we would be talking supernovas, a *Type 1* supernova is a *standard candle*. It follows the same stellar nucleosynthesis reaction with the same very predictable light curve. That's how we know,' Tom replied. 'I think this event would have had more in common with a *Type 1b*, but that's not important right now.'

'Of course. I remember you telling me about *standard candles* not that long ago. The variable stars, the *Cepheid Variables* are another, right?'

'That's right. But, if we are talking *hypernova*, which is possible caused by a Wolf-Rayet core collapse, then we are talking as much as *one hundred times brighter* than a supernova!' he continued. 'The apparent visual magnitude would have increased to anything between -23 to -59! At the high end, we are talking something unimaginably brighter than the Sun!'

'So, every creature on the planet would have been affected.'

'Precisely. So how can I locate anything in the oral tradition or artwork? You are particularly skilled in this area.'

'Well, the indigenous Australian culture extends back more than 50,000 years, and I know that they have a supernova event in their oral tradition. In one story, they describe *Babba, the dingo father*, who moves across the sky. This is believed to refer to the brightening, then dimming of a supernova. You can check to which star it refers. You should also check the ancient Greek myths. It was *Phaethon* who flew his father *Helios*'s chariot too close to the Earth and created the Sahara. Do you know where in the night sky the supernova happened, and did it have any particular characteristics?'

'OK. The cluster of Wolf-Rayet stars, within which the supernova occurred, is found in the constellation of Vela, marked *gamma Velorum*. It was previously the central star in the old constellation called *Argo Navis*.'

'*What? The Argo*? The Argo was the boat that *Jason and his Argonauts* sailed in, on their quest to retrieve the Golden Fleece! That has to be something! I know that Greek epic. I wrote a paper about different interpretations of the hidden meanings in that. Tom, you may have finally found the original meaning. What else can you tell me about the supernova event? What else would have been seen in the sky afterwards?' Mary-Anne urged excitedly.

'Wow! The original meaning of Jason and the Argonauts? That would be incredible if true. OK, the hypernova event would have lingered in the daytime sky for maybe months, as if creating two suns in the sky for possibly more than a year. During the final stage of collapse of a Wolf-Rayet star, a collimated beam of material gets shot out along the star's spin axis at relativistic speeds. The collapsing star is spinning asymmetrically so that jet takes on a spiral form. It only survives the stellar collapse implosion because it is travelling faster than the shock front. This spiralling jet then impacts the surrounding gas and dust causing a gamma ray burst. That GRB would be the signature of a supernova, but if the collapse generates so much more energy, then the relativistic jet has enough energy to punch right through the gas an dust, and emerges as a spiralling snake like jet!'

'Like a snake!'

'OK, yes, like a snake. Are there snakes in Jason and the Argonauts?' Tom asked.

'Well, only a fire-breathing dragon, also called a serpent, who is guarding the golden fleece, and which *never sleeps day or night*. That already sounds pretty relevant to me. Jason is challenged to complete three tasks before he will get the golden fleece. He must plow a field with two fire-breathing oxen, which he must yoke himself. That could refer to the *two suns in the sky*. He must *sow a field with dragon's teeth* and defeat any warriors which emerge from the ground. Finally, he must overcome the sleepless dragon and steal the fleece. By the way, *all the Greek heroes* are in the Argo. Jason didn't just hire a bunch of average deck hands to crew the ship. It was a crew of fifty including *Hercules*, *Orpheus*, *Odysseus*, and *Theseus* to name but a few.'

'This is so incredible. When a relativistic jet transits it might even cause dangerous surface phenomena. Could that be the dragon's teeth to which the epic refers? Also, gold is a heavy metal, which is a good defence against radiation. Was the golden fleece a reference to protective clothing?'

'I may have something more, here in Australia,' Mary-Jane said excitedly. As I mentioned, we are blessed with the living history carried by the oral tradition of the indigenous Australian peoples. A very important

Dreamtime story now comes to mind. Wait, I made detailed notes on that. The story is called the *Rainbow Serpent*, which is associated with the destructive power of nature. Here it is. A key point for me is that it has many different names in the different indigenous tribes, which suggests that a vast number of different tribes independently created the same kind of story. Perhaps particular details of your snake-like, spiralling jet event may be encoded in their different versions.'

'That's amazing! I love you even more now. What do you have?'

'OK, so I listed more than 25 different names for the *Rainbow Serpent* among the different indigenous tribes. The common theme through all the *Dreamtime* stories is the following. The *Rainbow Serpent* travelled from south to north, . . .'

'That's already very important,' Tom said eagerly.

Mary-Anne was reading from her notes. 'It travelled many days looking for its tribe. It cut gorges and river channels into the land. There were flying stones and bad people were turned to stone. Some versions of the story say it travelled at night.'

'That must be saying the jet was only visible at night, so not visible during the daytime.'

'Well other versions say it rested at night. There are also rock art paintings of the *Rainbow Serpent* dated to between 6000 and 8000 years old up in *Arnhem Land* in the *Northern Territory*. Their version of the story says it disappeared into the sea.'

'So, the *rainbow* description might be something to do with the colours in the sky from all those different charged atomic ions, a *furnace of all colours of the rainbow* compared to the Southern Lights, or *Aurora Australis*, which is principally coloured by only oxygen and nitrogen. This is really exciting stuff!'

'Well, I know of another mythical story in the ancient Egyptian record which may be even more relevant. The Egyptians talk of *Apep* the serpent, which attacked *Ra* the sun god. Different wall friezes describe how *Apep* the serpent, lurked just below the horizon, . . .'

'Wait, . . . *just below the horizon*? That cluster was always just below the horizon as seen from Giza, until the relativistic jet transit started. The spiralling snake-like form of the relativistic jet would have grown larger and larger as it approached. Over long periods of time, the relative position of the Sun to the *snake's head* supernova source would have changed slowly and continually, but the centre would have always been just below the horizon. Nevertheless, the spread of the spiral beam might have been truly enormous, stretching right across the sky looking indeed like a bright snake-like creature.'

'OK, I may have something interesting for you. I also researched the mythology around *Apep* and *Ra* several years ago,' checking various folders on her laptop. 'Here we go. Look at this. It is supposed to be a cat with a knife trying to kill *Apep* the serpent.'

Apep the Snake

'What is that tree thing among the snake's coils?'

'That's the *tree of life!*'

'Wow, so the frieze is depicting the realization that the serpent is a threat to life on our planet Earth. That's quite a serious bit of supporting evidence!'

'But I may have something more,' Mary-Anne said excitedly. 'Look! You described that there may have been a huge pinwheel in the sky. Now look at this classic symbol of the *Eye of Horus*. *Horus* lost one of his eyes, so there was only one. Is it possible that this is actually a representation of what was seen in the sky as this relativistic jet approached, or is it perhaps the explosion?'

That may need some serious investigation.'

'OK, here is some more description. *Apep* lurked before dawn to attack Ra. He was born after Ra. *Apep* attempted to swallow the Sun every day.'

'Who was *Horus* again?'

'*Horus* was the ancient Egyptian sky god, one of the most important deities. He was depicted with the head of a falcon. *Horus* was the rival to *Set*. *Set* was the nasty god of chaos and disorder. *Set* murdered *Horus*'s father *Osiris*, Set's brother, and many myths describe the feuds between *Horus* and *Set*. It was *Set*, however, who accompanied *Ra* on the solar boat to repel *Apep* the serpent of chaos! So, there is a link to the two stories.'

'I'm now pretty convinced these myths are describing what was seen in the sky, while the relativistic jet was passing by. It can also be that the Eye of Horus is a representation of the supernova or hypernova remnant. I will need to check that.'

'Was it a pretty devastating event?'

'I believe that the jet caused cataclysmic damage and destruction. Surface temperatures might have been dangerously high to cause serious danger to life on Earth.'

'So how could people have survived? How could they have recorded everything. Oh, so you are saying these are things which were seen *before* the jet arrived,' Mary-Anne replied, sounding a little shocked. 'So, these would have been recorded in the years and months before. Right up until …'

'Yes, these images were all recorded before and also during the relativistic jet transit, by the immediate survivors.'

'Hang on. Can't those Egyptian friezes be so much older then? Surely people didn't just sit round camp fires for seven thousand years telling the same old stories, before one day, someone gets up and says '*Hey guys, we've been telling these stories for seven thousand years, what about if someone now creates a detailed record of this event for posterity*?' Couldn't the friezes be contemporary?'

'My goodness, that's a very radical but logical suggestion. Maybe that's the smoking gun.'

'If we think about the ancient Egyptian friezes depicting *Apep*, isn't there now an enigma? If they were contemporary, like the *Rainbow Serpent* rock art in Australia, it must mean that the Egyptian civilization must extend back another seven thousand years at least! I have always wondered about the differences in quality of the stone carving work of the early epochs of Egyptian history, when compared with the less-refined later stone work. Is it possible that there were two Egyptian civilizations separated by seven thousand years, one before the cataclysm, one after? Have we been missing something?'

'OK, if we consider the *Rainbow Serpent* story, the fact that so many Australian indigenous tribes have their own version, suggests that many of them saw it and many of them survived. It is generally understood that the people most capable of surviving a cataclysm are those who are already adapted to living off the land. Most of us *civilized people* wouldn't have a clue how to find food and water or make a shelter, if our world infrastructure suddenly collapsed around us. Perhaps more clues may be found in other hunter gatherer peoples around the World. The Maori of New Zealand may also have brought stories long ago from the Pacific Islands, from where it is believed they came.'

'This surely suggests that the peoples of Earth survived for the duration of the cataclysm in vast numbers of groups all around the World. It also suggests an explanation for all the advanced megalithic structures found all over the World, from Japan and the underwater city of *Yonaguni*, to the buildings cut out of rock in Petra, Jordan, and the Indian *Kailasa* rock temple of *Maharashtra*,' Tom added. This whole hypothesis deserves to be properly researched. I think you may be one of the few qualified academics who is capable of doing this research. It is certainly worth a book.'

'Thank you my darling, ... but first, I will send my paper off!' Mary-Anne replied.

14 UC Berkeley: data supporting the 12,780 B.C.E. Wolf-Rayet hypernova

University of California at Berkeley

Carl Rhodes stood at the front of the seminar room. It was packed with serious-looking academics. Behind him on the overhead screen was the title of today's talk. He tapped the microphone, then spoke.

'OK, listen up. I have invited you all here today because I have some important news. As you see, I have also invited people from the press. You may wonder why, but it's because I think that some serious debate needs to happen about the implications of the story I am about to tell you. About two months ago, I received an email from an astrophysics colleague of mine, Tom Walker, based at UTS Sydney, Australia. Over the past ten years, Tom and I have collaborated on several academic papers together in various astrophysical areas, including *Active Galactic Nuclei*, *Luminous Blue Variables*, and *Wolf-Rayet stars*. In this email, Tom sent me the outline of a paper he wanted to write with me, which suggests that, in the very recent past, the Earth experienced a cataclysm. More importantly, he argued in his draft paper, that the cataclysm was directly caused by the collapse of a Wolf-Rayet star. He has even found the complex three-component signature of the cataclysm in the Greenland ice sheet record. Furthermore, he went on to argue that this was proof that the Noah's Ark myth was indeed fact, because the cataclysm would have caused substantial melting of the polar ice and displacement of the Earth's oceans such that water levels may have exceeded tens of metres over substantial parts of the Earth's land masses, and taken weeks to subside.'

There was some murmuring in the audience.

Carl continued, 'I, of course, replied that I would not be a co-author on such a paper. The reason is not that I don't support his hypothesis, because I find his reasoning totally sound. The reason I said I couldn't be a co-author is because I think he deserves any accolades due for his highly unique and well-referenced work.'

'Many of you will be wondering why I am holding this press conference here today. The reason is that tomorrow, *Nature* will publish the whole article of the cataclysm due to a collapsing Wolf-Rayet star, under the slightly modified title *The Wolf Cataclysm*. I don't think the title shows any disrespect to Dr Rayet. Maybe *Nature* wanted a more provocative title. The subtitle clarifies the true essence. Anyway, the whole article is out tomorrow, and I want to encourage everyone to read it and start the debate about what implications this may have for us all. More importantly, I believe this article will inspire us all to become so much more aware of how vulnerable life is. We have a growing environmental movement warning us to respect our planet so much more. Now, thanks to Tom Walker's article, it may help develop a much deeper, shared concern, how best to protect life on our planet.'

The room was clearly eager to hear the story. There were nervous whispers and shuffling, as if awaiting confirmation of something quite remarkable.

'This is ground-breaking stuff. I can't overemphasise the serious impact that this will have on us all, as the civilization which currently stands at the helm, responsible to protect life on our planet Earth. It is very difficult to tell this story, there are so many angles to come in on, so I will just start.' Carl changed the image on the overhead display. It showed a multicolour image of stars, the famous *Herzsprung-Russell* diagram, plotting star temperature against luminosity.

'First I will start by describing Wolf-Rayet stars. I know that not everyone in the room is an astrophysicist, so I will try to do my best to describe them in very simple terms. OK, so stars are just balls of gas and dust, and these balls are collapsing. It is in fact the gravitational collapse, which generates all the heat coming from a star, and stars would collapse in a very short time if it were not for a back pressure preventing their collapse. I don't have the exact details of the exact calculation, but I think that our Sun would collapse in just a few hours, if there were no nuclear fusion going on. The pressure from the nuclear fusion in the Sun's core, generates this back pressure, and, because our star is the mass it is, our yellow-orange Sun, with a surface temperature of around 6000 degrees Kelvin, has a life time of around ten billion years. So, you can imagine that when a much larger ball of gas and dust is collapsing inwards, the gravitational collapse is so much greater, and rates of fusion will be so much faster, and temperatures will be so much higher, and the star lives for a much shorter lifetime. Wolf-Rayet stars are blue, they are so much bigger and more massive than the Sun and they have a surface temperature of around 30,000 degrees Kelvin. We all understand that blue flames are hotter than yellow-orange flames.'

'So, we can understand that stars resist collapse due to the pressure of the nuclear fusion furnace going on at their core. For most of a star's life, around 90% of it, the star is fusing hydrogen to helium at its core. When a star is in this phase, we describe the star as being on the *Main Sequence*. When the hydrogen at the core is all used up, the star starts to fuse other atomic nuclei together, helium into carbon, carbon and helium to make oxygen, and so forth. At this first change in fusion reaction, we say that the star has left the *Main Sequence*. These other nuclear fusion reactions proceed so much faster, but, when all the fuel is gone, there is nothing to prevent total core collapse, and the core collapses in on itself in a fraction of a second and can release vast amounts of energy.'

'There are different outcomes when we are talking core collapse. Small stars like our Sun will end up with a dense *white dwarf* core surrounded by a beautiful planetary nebula. Massive stars like a Wolf-Rayet star will supernova and result in a neutron star core or a black hole, depending on the mass of the Wolf-Rayet star.'

'A Wolf-Rayet star is something quite extraordinary. This is a very unstable massive star. It is spinning at a phenomenal rate. The surface rotational speed can be several thousand kilometres per second. By comparison, the Sun's surface rotational speed is 2 kilometres per second. After it comes off the *Main Sequence*, runs out of nuclear fuel, and undergoes core collapse, several things can result. In the case that Tom Walker describes, just prior to the core collapse and resulting *Type 1b* supernova, a dying Wolf-Rayet star may emit a jet of material from both ends of its spin axis which collides into the surrounding gas and dust and causes a gamma ray burst or GRB. The gamma ray burst typically lasts around 100 seconds, but it carries an enormous destructive energy. Because the star is spinning extremely fast, this gamma ray burst, or GRB, is emitted in a tight opening angle of radiation along its spin axis in both directions. This tight beam of high energy gamma rays is also accompanied by a wide spectrum of radiation from X-rays to radio waves, as some kind of afterglow. We have observed the collapse of several Wolf-Rayet stars in many distance galaxies but not here within our own. We know they are out there, and we know where they are. We know where they are because we can identify the Wolf-Rayet stars from their very unique spectrum.'

'Now here comes the key point. When a Wolf-Rayet star collapses, depending upon the energy of that collapse, that relativistic jet which causes the GRB, may have enough energy to *punch through* the gas and dust, and continue out across space. Moreover, if the Wolf-Rayet star is in a binary relation with another star, for example, orbiting a black hole, that relativistic jet can be moderated to a speed close to a *quarter of the speed of light*, at the same time. It would truly be devastating if you lived on a planet nearby to a Wolf-Rayet collapse, because you would first observe the supernova, or even a *hypernova*, which can be between ten and 100 times brighter, and, if you were unlucky you would receive the gamma ray burst, and if the energy were high enough, you would eventually see a relativistic jet, spiralling across space towards you in its wake. More importantly, you would know that the relativistic jet, possibly an *extinction level* ionised particle beam, is definitely arriving along the same path as the gamma ray burst. If the collapse occurs 1000 light years away, and the relativistic jet is moving at one quarter the speed of light, then the jet will arrive for sure, only 3000 years from when you receive the GRB. We also know what is in a jet from a Wolf-Rayet star collapse. It is a beam of high energy plasma formed of protons and electrons trapped in a self-generating magnetic field.'

'This is the key point in Tom Walker's paper. He believes that the climatic record shows the triple signature event of a Wolf-Rayet star hypernova core collapse. In the climatic record, in the epochs described as the *Bölling-Alleröd* and *Younger Dryas*, we find first a high rise in temperature over a period of only a few years, a slow cooling over 3000 or so years and then a sudden rise in temperature.'

Carl Rhodes showed the slide of the climatic record.

'So, we see here a very recent triple signature, which matches what we believe we would experience if first the Earth received a high energy long GRB gamma ray burst, then suffered the tremendous impact caused by the transit of a relativistic jet, from the same stellar core collapse, sometime later. Wolf-Rayet stars form in clusters, so where we find one, we generally find others. Tom is suggesting that the Wolf-Rayet in question was likely formed in a cluster close to a Wolf-Rayet star which we observe today, called *Regor*. That is the modern name. It was previously

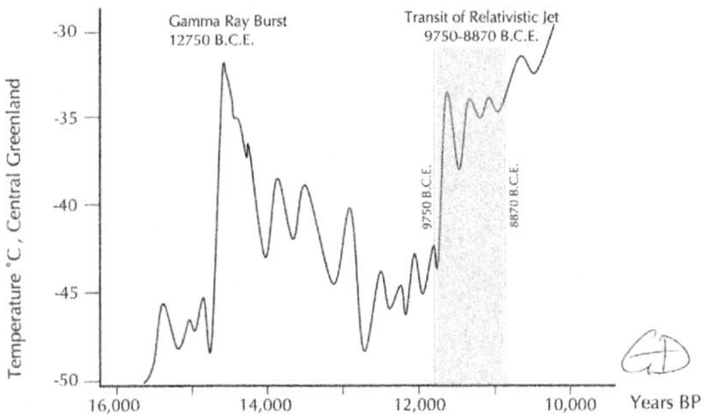

Climate Graph

known by its more traditional name *Suhail al Muhlif* which translates as *smooth plain*, and referred to stars near the horizon. Regor is in the constellation of Vela, and at the heart of the old constellation of *Argo*. There are many stories about Jason who sailed in the Argo - *Jason and the Argonauts* - so we must rethink whether any old myths and legends also hint towards aspects of a possible cataclysmic event.'

'In fact, *Regor* is a star which forms part of the multiple star system which we call *gamma Velorum*. It has magnitude 1.75 and is at a distance of 1116.97 light years. In Tom Walker's paper, he believes there are strong arguments to map a core collapse of a Wolf-Rayet star in the vicinity of *gamma Velorum* to the triple signature event in the climatic record of the *Bölling-Alleröd* and *Younger Dryas*.'

'A GRB would clearly be devastating for people on planet Earth, and this is where things get pretty controversial, because Tom contemplates that the Earth indeed underwent a near extinction level event. He contemplates that a former technologically advanced civilization lived on this planet before us. This civilization was subjected to a massive hypernova, which he refers to as HN -12780 although that date needs to be confirmed. Of course, the impact of a GRB would have had a terrible effect on life on one side of the planet during the burst. Those who survived would have worked out that the Earth would subsequently experience the effects of the transit of a relativistic jet. Tom Walker is then suggesting that measures were taken to plan for some kind of survival of life on this planet.'

The room went deathly quiet. Then, off to the right, a few people were agitated. They were clearly involved in some active debate about what

Carl was saying.

'OK, I see we have some of my astrophysicist colleagues in the room,' Carl added with a smile, 'And I sense they will quickly need a few bits of technical data to prevent *them* from going into core collapse. No one else here need to understand the following, but just for my colleagues, I will clarify the following details.'

'Tom Walker based his assessment of the Regor companion on the extensively published, and well understood, Wolf-Rayet X-Ray binary, *Cygnus X-3*. This is an accreting high-mass X-Ray binary with relativistic jets which is also about seven kiloparsecs away. For the rest of you, we astrophysicists do not measure distances in light years, we use the more logical measurement unit of the *parsec*. Space is very big and there are around 3.26 light years in a parsec.'

'Wolf-Rayet stars are identified from their doppler-broadened emission spectra, showing helium, carbon, oxygen and nitrogen exposed at the surface, caused by strong mixing and radiation-driven mass loss. High radiation pressure is causing stellar mass loss creating an expanding planetary nebula.'

'There will be questions about whether a GRB could have been received from a star in the vicinity of Regor, if the *gamma Velorum* cluster was aligned for the relativistic jet some 3000 years later. Studies show that many relativistic jets are precessing, sending a spiral beam out into space. Others have a beam spread of up to 18°. This should explain how part of the GRB might have been received on Earth, when the gravitationally-bound *gamma Velorum* cluster was some 13° below the horizon at Giza on the day that Tom Walker computes the GRB took place. There are also other aspects of *relativistic beaming*, which I won't be saying anything more about here, but generally, GRB emissions are also seen coming from relativistic jets themselves.'

'Tom referenced the work done by his colleagues at UTS and their 2018 article about a Wolf-Rayet binary, which came out in *Nature Astronomy*. This binary is found in a triple star system which they named *Apep*, found in the southern constellation *Norma*, just below Scorpio's tail. It's particularly important because it's the first GRB progenitor candidate discovered in the Milky Way. It's radio source is as bright as *Eta Carinae*. Interestingly, they named it *Apep* after the giant serpent which battled with the Egyptian Sun-god *Ra*. This ancient depiction may itself represent the imagery of an impending Wolf-Rayet core collapse, since these systems tend to comprise a pinwheel nebula of spiralling stellar winds and cosmic dust when viewed in infra-red. It's certainly worth analysing ancient Egyptian depictions of *Apep*, to see if other data is encoded in any wall friezes. The bottom line here is that I believe there certainly may have been several detectable GRB emissions from other supernova events prior to the start of the transit of the relativistic jet. OK, I guess that's the short but heavy astrophysics summary.'

'Thanks Carl. Greatly appreciated,' a man at the back called.

'So, let us go through what may have happened if Tom is right. The advanced civilization living on our planet observed an incredibly bright hypernova, and experienced the shock and trauma of a long gamma ray burst. That would have caused a rapid temperature rise. Gamma rays would have seriously damaged the ozone layer in the atmosphere which would have led to the production of large amounts of nitrogen oxide, a serious greenhouse gas. A series of events after that will have led to a long period of cooling, while the significantly reduced population of Earth, whoever they were, needed to start planning for the worst.'

'One of the key issues here is that a Wolf-Rayet collapse which occurs 1116.97 light years is not very far away, but as Tom describes, this means that they had around 3000 years to plan a survival strategy.'

'So, why is Tom so confident? What did he find? Well, he consulted his brother, Dr Chad Walker, a geologist at Boston University, who was looking at the pyramids of Giza. Dr Chad Walker is also an author on the *Nature* article, and he found structural damage all over the Giza Plateau. Chad also found intense heating and melting of rocks across the Saqqara Plateau, some 25 kilometres from Giza. Chad Walker looked at these Giza structures and just wondered if an astrophysical cataclysm could have caused the heating. Of course, the implications are quite profound. If correct, it means that not only did the civilization experience both the climatic impact of a gamma ray burst, but they knew well in advance, and I mean perhaps a hundred generations in advance, that a possible extinction level event would happen when the relativistic jet arrived.'

'I cannot over-emphasise the implications of such a hypothesis if true. It would mean that the future survival of life on our planet was at stake. It could also imply that Mars may still have had surface water at that time, as evidenced from the surface river channels and lake-bed features, and that the transit of the relativistic jet possibly devastated Mars into the desolate state it is today. When we talk of future survival beyond a cataclysm, we must contemplate planning to store food, such as seeds for replanting. We must contemplate how will people survive. Where can life go? The answer is of course underground, cities underground, and this is what Tom describes. In the earliest cuneiform tablets of Mesopotamia, which describe the *Epic of Gilgamesh*, we find one of the earliest recorded stories of the flood myth. That cuneiform tablet, when correctly translated, describes the Ark as a *box to protect life*. Tom goes on to suggest that the perfect boxes found in the Saqqara Plateau may indeed be manifestations of another dimension of the Noah's Ark story, where the Ark also contemplates boxes to protect the seeds of plants and trees. These highly-finished, complex, stone box structures, almost seeming to be made by machines using advanced technology, were clearly made with a purpose, which he is suggesting, was to protect life. This is why they were underground. How they moved these 100-ton boxes inside passageways barely wider and higher than the boxes themselves, we may never know. There is strong evidence from the discolouration of the edges of the lids of the boxes, that they were indeed closed, however, today we find them all reopened. That will remain an enigma, because it suggests that whatever was put into the boxes, was later taken out. The lids weigh in excess of ten tons each. Who opened them and how, will remain another question to be answered.'

'Tom Walker then searched for *the gamma Velorum cluster's* location during the computed date of the cataclysm. Remarkably, he discovered that *gamma Velorum* was located at absolutely zero degrees elevation above the horizon due south, to an incredible accuracy of *six places of decimals*, as seen from the Giza Plateau on the date that the relativistic jet cataclysm arrived. Consequently, it started to become increasingly obvious that the Giza pyramids must have been built as a permanent monument to mark the event. It is also important to note that almost all the pyramids found around the World are built at this latitude, further suggesting that they too were built to identify *gamma Velorum*. Moreover, the southern airshaft from the King's chamber at 39° pointed at our nearest neighbour *proxima Centauri*, which is only 4.24 light years away. Also known as alpha Centauri C, this star is a red dwarf variable star, and an exoplanet has been detected there. I should add that while many will think that surely life cannot survive so close to a periodically flaring star, a planet with a thick atmosphere would prevent tidal locking, so the same side would not remain facing the star. Consequently, heat would be distributed around the planet and that thick atmosphere would shield it against flares. It is thus not beyond the realms of possibility, that the Great Pyramid of Khufu is actually a structure that was designed and built of stone to endure the aeons, not just to mark the event, but also with some, as yet unknown, communications capability, however ludicrous that suggestion sounds, as an attempt to try to communicate with our nearest neighbour *proxima Centauri* until the jet transit started. Interestingly, Tom also found that the star Sirius was exactly 3 minutes of arc above due south on the earlier date of the supernova or hypernova event i.e. when the GRB struck the Earth. He doesn't claim that to be significant because he's a scientist, but apparently, the Khufu Pyramid is aligned 3 minutes of arc off true north. Perhaps that error was deliberately encoded into the monument. There is, as yet, no apparent reason why Sirius is connected with this story at all, and that may remain an enigma for many years to come.'

'Was this a *last cry for help*? Did some kind of message get through? How the pyramid possibly worked as some kind of communications structure is still unknown. Centuries of exploration have terribly damaged the inside of the complex internal structure of the Great Pyramid of Khufu, and likely destroyed every clue as to how it possibly might have worked. To all intents and purposes, nearby exoplanetary civilizations, who may have also observed the relativistic jet arrive and cause havoc to Earth and to our Solar System, may have concluded that we did not survive at all.'

Someone called out, 'Will you be taking questions at the end?'

'Good question. I want to say now that I don't really want to take any questions today. There will be a question-and-answer session sometime next month, after the article has gained reactions following publication. I will now say something of what a relativistic jet impact might have had on the planet.'

'So, the hypothesis suggests that the Earth was first hit by a gamma ray burst of around a hundred seconds duration and then 3000 years later, the Earth endured the effects of the transit of a relativistic jet, possibly travelling at around a quarter the speed of light. The transit may have caused a phenomenal burning of the planet surface, and substantial sea-level rise, resulting in widespread flooding tens of metres deep. I do not think we can easily contemplate the magnitudes of what we are talking about here. The Earth might have been scorched in places.'

'There are clearly questions about where, and to what extent, scattered peoples survived, and if they did, are there clear signs of a memory of this event in diverse population groups all over the planet? This was clearly a global catastrophe which affected everyone. Only megalithic monuments could have survived *on the surface*. That is indeed what we see today, and many of these appear devastated by some cataclysm. We need to look clearly at the historic record and carefully compile a scientific archive of any data about this event, that diverse cultures around the world may have captured within their own cultural heritage. Memory of the event may manifest itself in their folklore, their art, even their dances and festivals. I have meetings with officials at *UNESCO* later this week and hope to gain their support for this initiative.'

'There are also other enigmas that Tom Walker's paper sheds light upon. Until today, there has been no adequate explanation for the fused glass fragments that have been found throughout many deserts of the World. Moreover, these fragments are identical to those glass fragments found following nuclear bomb testing at the Alamogordo *White Sands* testing facility. Records show that extensive glass remnants were found in 1932 by the Egyptian Geological Survey near the Saad Plateau, while similar vitrified rocks were found in the Sahara and Mojave deserts, and fused ancient rock towers and forts have been found in England, Scotland and Ireland. From vitrified ruins found in *Tiahuanaco* Peru, to vitrified rock found on *Rapa Nui* otherwise known as Easter Island, this evidence surely all forms part of the same cataclysm signature, and hints towards the truly global extent, that a relativistic jet transit had on our planet. More recently, the glass found on a desert plain in central South Australia was proving difficult to correlate with an impact event, because no crater is present. Relativistic jet transits do not form craters, so perhaps this is also explained now.'

'We are *a people with amnesia*, and we have awoken from a long sleep with no memory of those who lived here before us. There are clearly questions now about how we might interpret other mysterious events. For example, the unexplained, elevated radioactive levels found on the eastern edge of the great Thar desert in India, which date back some 8000 to 12000 years, might also be attributed to physical phenomena associated with the transit of a relativistic jet.'

'We also need to consider other effects that a relativistic jet transit might have, such as the capability to bury sites completely with debris.

Remember, we might be talking total surface desecration in places. For example, was the site of *Göbekli Tepe* in Turkey, filled in with an alluvial debris in this way?'

'If Tom Walker is correct, the pyramids of the Giza Plateau were methodically and precisely constructed to mark a precise moment in time. A former highly advanced civilization on our planet had enough time, some 3000 years, to carefully plan, design, locate, and build the structures. The pyramids clearly hold all the clues in their complex and precise design to mark the event. We should now take a very close look at what they are telling us. In preparing this press conference, I saw an article suggesting that the Pyramid Texts may comprise a mis-translation, and that when they purportedly describe how the pharaohs ascended to join the stars, they may equally be presenting the allegory how a communication transmission, which when transmitted from Earth, might symbolize another site being brought online to join the network of galactic civilisations out there, who knows? You will need to read Tom's paper to get a better understanding of that.'

'I am going to close now. There are a huge number of open questions, which will now follow from this highly original paper. I feel very privileged to have been able to present this to you. I know that tomorrow, Tom has a press conference in Sydney, which will likely be carried on most News networks. People, this is a remarkable story, and if it is true, we need to sit down and try to puzzle out all the consequences for us here on our small, fragile, blue-green planet. We owe it both to the previous civilization who worked so hard over maybe one hundred generations to save us, and to future generations who will come after. We are so privileged to be here on our beautiful planet. We can no longer just take it for granted.'

A girl with very blonde hair called out, 'Dr Rhodes, might you please just answer one question? Can you please just tell us the exact date of the arrival of the relativistic jet, that Dr Walker determined was encoded into the Great Pyramid of Khufu on the Giza Plateau?'

Carl Rhodes smiled and nodded. '10:18 and 23 seconds on the morning of August 7th, 9750 B.C.E..'

Book Two

1 | Soufrière, St Lucia: keeping safe during the 9,750 – 8,870 BCE relativistic jet transit

Stonefield Resort, Soufrière, St. Lucia

Tom and Mary-Anne were sitting in the airy Stonefield restaurant. Its location was perfect, as if the whole resort complex had been designed around this spectacular vantage point. The open dining-area platform was cleverly perched on the steeply sloping cliffside, high above the vivid green rainforest bushes and trees, where iridescent purple humming-birds darted in and out of brightly coloured flowers. The restaurant gazed seawards, with stunning views out over the Caribbean and the massive, yet inappropriately named *Petit Piton*: an enormous and imposing vol-canic spire. It was breakfast time in St. Lucia's wet season, and the total body-experience of warm humid Caribbean air, the exciting, dramatic cloudy skies and rich seascape views all combined with the soft sweet sounds of the island birds to enhance every moment. Far below on the myriad-blue rippling seascape, several white catamarans with full spin-naker were racing the wind. This was a dreamy paradise place, where time stood still.

A waitress came over to Tom and Mary-Anne's table, bringing a tray of juices, plates of tropical fruit, and a pot of coffee. She spoke with a strong St. Lucian accent. 'Good morning! Would you like coffee and freshly squeezed orange juice?'

'Yes please,' Mary-Anne answered with a smile.

'Me too,' Tom added.

The waitress placed two glasses of orange juice on the table, then poured coffee into the cups. 'Milk and sugar?'

'Just milk, for us thanks,' Mary-Anne replied.

The waitress then lifted a china plate bearing a small white jug of milk onto the table. It was elegantly sitting on a green leaf to prevent it moving.

'Madam, what would you like for breakfast today?'

'I'd like the tropical fruit starter and the cooked breakfast of bacon, tomato and scrambled eggs please.'

'And for you sir? Would you like your favourite again, of sausage, tomato and two poached eggs, or would you like something different?' the waitress asked.

'I'd like the same as yesterday. The tropical fruit starter, and sausage, tomato and two poached eggs.'

'Of course,' the waitress answered, placing a plate of tropical fruit first in front of Mary-Anne and then Tom. 'Enjoy!'

'Thank you,' Mary-Anne said.

'You are welcome,' the waitress said, then turned and walked away.

Just at that moment, a small but very eager, tropical bullfinch landed on the dark mahogany balustrade beside their table, quickly followed by a second. Tom's hand slowly moved towards the yellow and orange water pistol, arranged as a deterrent. As he lifted it, both of the daring, red-throated birds suddenly flew away. He squirted the pistol after them, the water falling to the rainforest gardens below.

Then the rain started again, quickly becoming a roar as the skies opened, but under the restaurant canopy they were well protected from the deluge. Immediately below them, large raindrops were splashing off the shiny leaves of a large banana tree. Above them, they could hear the incessant drumming of the tropical rain on the wooden restaurant roof, but it was very refreshing to experience.

'Will we have a lazy day today?' She sipped her orange juice. 'Mm, this is lovely,' she whispered.

'Of course! We deserve to chill. You know, I'm actually thinking that I really need to write that second paper, exploring the effects that the relativistic jet had on our planet. I'm happy to do that if you want to lie in the sun.'

'OK. You sound very eager. Where has this newfound inspiration come from? I thought you'd be basking in a little glory for a few more months at least.'

'Well, I've realised that the relativistic jet transit lasted *hundreds of years*. This wasn't a transient phenomenon. That is so obvious now. Also, the jet was absolutely unimaginably huge. How could I have missed that? It's just not possible to hypothesise everything right from the outset. There are too many complicated issues to work through,' Tom explained. 'Most importantly, a jet transit of hundreds of years now perfectly matches the climatic record of hundreds of years of Earth-warming after 9750 B.C.E.'

'Tom, you and Chad worked out so much. Nobody can write the entire story from the outset. Don't be so hard on yourself. It sounds extremely positive that you've already reached the next level of scientific evaluation. You should be proud!'

'Thanks for that, but I start to realise that I will feel so much happier after I have got the next academic paper out there with a much more comprehensive and credible story.'

'Is it just that, or are there other aspects you want to broaden out?'

'Well, I'm pretty convinced that the Australian indigenous people's *Dreamtime* myth about the *Rainbow Serpent* may be a very big part of this story. You may remember that before we left, I encouraged young Patrick to try to seek out more material in publications from the early 20th century. I have a very strong hunch that the alternative versions of the story told by different tribes, clearly describe in substantial detail what was seen in the sky, and several physical effects of the event. One important thing I immediately learn from all this, is the need for us all to recognise how valuable indigenous peoples are to this planet, particularly when it comes to recreating historical events from long ago.'

'I agree entirely, and the Australian indigenous people are clearly some of the heroes of your story. I'm also very interested in your highly original conclusion. All the data was always there, yet it took someone with a completely different perspective on everything ...' Mary-Anne continued.

'Someone with a crazy mind!'

'OK, someone with a mad and crazy mind, ... to discover what happened. I have also been thinking further about other myths. I am pretty sure that the Greek myth, *Medusa*, just has to be related to this.'

'So, how does that myth go again?' Tom asked curiously.

'Well, *Medusa* was one of the Gorgons, a beautiful woman, who incurred the wrath of *Athena*, possibly because she'd had a love affair with Poseidon. She was then transformed into a vicious creature with a head of snakes, and whoever gazed upon her eyes, turned to stone!'

'Turning people to stone is also in the Australian indigenous peoples' *Rainbow Serpent* myth! Surely that refers to people who were unable to hide from the effects of the relativistic jet?'

At that moment, the waitress arrived with a tray, bringing two different egg-breakfasts. She placed the scrambled eggs, bacon and tomato in front of Mary-Anne and the poached eggs, sausage and tomato in front of Tom. She then placed a small basket of toast on the table. 'Enjoy!'

'Lovely! Thank you!' Tom replied, sprinkling some freshly ground pepper over his very firm-looking poached eggs. He cut into one egg, the yolk was a rich orange and soft but not runny, as perfect as could be. He took a bite and paused for a moment, closing his eyes. 'The flavour of these eggs is just unbelievable.'

'Yes, they taste amazing,' Mary-Anne replied, taking a small forkful of scrambled egg. 'I guess it's all down to the luxury restaurant leftovers that the free range hens are given here.'

'Those lucky hens.'

'What were you saying earlier?' Mary-Anne asked. 'Oh right, that both the *Medusa* myth, and the *Rainbow Serpent* story describe how people were turned to stone.'

'Precisely. Those myths and legends really give us some important data about the relativistic jet. Different indigenous peoples describe the jet as a coloured flying serpent in the sky and that the effects of the relativistic jet were extremely dangerous.'

'Can you really work out anything from that?'

'Sure. A relativistic jet is an astrophysical object of *astrophysical* dimensions. The relativistic jet and associated gamma ray burst from a collapsing Wolf-Rayet star and hypernova, last around 100 seconds. The *gamma Velorum* cluster is some 1100 light years away so the gamma ray burst, travelling at light speed, takes 1100 light years to get here, while the relativistic jet extends to hundreds of light years long.'

'Wait a moment, are you saying you are now convinced it *was* a hypernova, and not supernova?'

'Yes, a *hypernova* and that's between ten and a hundred times more powerful than a supernova. I reasoned that a gamma ray burst combined with a relativistic jet *must be* associated with a *hypernova*. It must have been an incredibly bright light in the day and night sky for months and possibly even years, assuming the luminosity curve is the same shape as the *standard candle* supernova explosion. It was most probably brighter than the Sun!'

'Wow! So, the Tom Walker *hypernova*. What would it now be, hypernova HN -12780?'

'Well remembered. That date would of course need to be verified, possibly inferred from a signature in the Greenland ice-core data, but HN -12780, sounds about right.'

'But how does a 100-second event extend to something hundreds of light years long? It couldn't have been more than a hundred *light-seconds* long at the beginning.'

'OK, firstly, there is an amount of material which does not form part of the hypernova and that forms the relativistic jets, which is blasted out at almost light speed. This is travelling faster than the shock wave of the hypernova explosion, which is how it manages to escape. The jet is formed of protons moving at relativistic speeds. Many collide with protons in the stellar wind and lose energy and speed. If the particles end up with a speed difference of 20%, over a distance of 1100 light years, the particles will spread out over 20% of the distance, making the jet say, 220 light years long.'

'So how does that straight jet become a long snake with a spiral shape again?'

'OK, well, we see spiralling jets in distant galaxies, and we think the spiralling is caused by the *precession* of the imploding star at the time of emission. In English, *precession* kind of means the *wobbling spin* of the star. It's a little controversial, but that jet is formed of material which doesn't form part of the hypernova, and the rapidly spinning stellar core just prior to collapse is asymmetrical, so we expect it to be spinning with a wobble, or *precessing*. We also expect the charged particles to be travelling at incredible speeds outwards and moving in helical orbits around each other, like a twisted cable of multi-strand wire. The last thing is that while the jet remains in a tight collimated beam, the cocoon of particles around the jet still slightly expands in diameter as it travels, even if it has a very tight opening angle of a few degrees.'

'In fact, you are my perfect devil's advocate. Being forced to explain things very clearly to you, lets me listen to my own reasoning. That is really helpful. I will try to put some numbers to the jet dimensions. Maybe I can work out how far away it could be.' Tom continued to talk aloud as he went through his ballpark calculation.

'From observations, the jet typically has an opening angle of around three degrees, so after 1100 light years the bright plasma cocoon around the head of the relativistic jet will have expanded to have a radius of around 30 light years. When I realised this, it was so obvious that this thing must have been *truly enormous*, and must have had long-lasting climate-changing effects on the Earth as it passed through our part of the galaxy. If it was travelling around a quarter of light speed, that 220 light year-long jet would have taken around 880 years to pass us by.'

'OK, so you are saying that if they saw this massive thing as a *long wriggling snake* in the sky, then it was clearly a long way off. That's a clever deduction!' Mary-Anne reasoned.

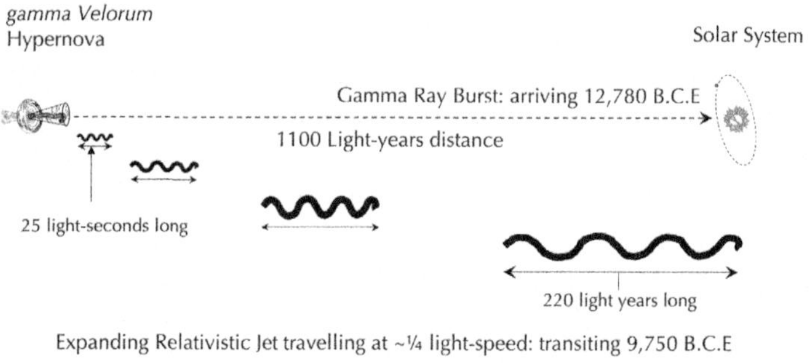

Expanding Jet

'Yes, but at that distance, the next question is how on earth could it be so dangerous? The danger couldn't then have been directly from the electromagnetic radiation given off by the jet. I now need to reframe my thinking about exactly how enormous it was, how far away it was, and why it had a catastrophic and devastating effect on the Earth.'

'So, what is this *cocoon of plasma* around the jet?'

'Well, that is like the jet, made up of a swirling cloud of highly energetic charged particles moving at very high speeds, but trapped in weaker spiralling magnetic field lines surrounding the tightly collimated jet.'

'What? So, the central spiralling core is the serpent-like jet, and the cocoon is a much less-dense region of charged particles?'

'Yes, I think that's a reasonable description. No one has ever described this before, so I need to work out how this distant object could be so dangerous when it is so far away.'

'You seem to have a good description of how the wriggling *Rainbow Serpent* is formed and how it moves; even I can understand it now! What did you mean when you said the charged particles are trapped in magnetic field lines?'

'Well, as I said, the jet is formed of high-energy protons, which are charged particles, moving at relativistic speeds. Moving charges constitute an electric current, and electric currents cause ... *magnetic fields*! Wow, that must be it! Thank you my darling!' Tom exclaimed excitedly.

'What did I say?' Mary-Anne asked tentatively.

'I love you! Your questions are really inspiring!'

The waitress suddenly reappeared. 'Would you like more coffee?' she enquired.

'Yes please,' Mary-Anne replied.

'Yes please, me too, thanks!' Tom added with an added air of excitement.

The waitress smiled curiously at Tom's slightly over eager response for more coffee, then took away the empty plates. She returned shortly with a coffee jug and a small basket of banana bread and rolls and exotic jams. She placed everything on the table. 'Just to let you know, that jam is *passion fruit*. The darker one is *fig*.'

'Lovely,' Tom remarked.

'We really love it here!'

'You are most welcome!' the waitress replied sweetly, then left.

'So, come on, what have you just worked out?' Mary-Anne urged, 'And it's only breakfast time!'

'Thanks to your question, I have suddenly worked out that this was a *magnetic* effect. The huge magnetic field generated by the relativistic jet, somehow heavily interfered with the *magnetosphere*, the Earth's protective magnetic field, leaving life on Earth vulnerable to high fluxes of charged particles from the solar wind. The danger wasn't directly from the *jet radiation*, it was caused by the jet's *magnetic field*! The jet's magnetic field would have seriously interfered with the Sun's magnetic field, causing the Sun to become extremely active. The consequence of an active Sun would have meant that in addition to a possibly increased amount of solar wind, life on Earth would have been exposed to extremely high levels of deadly, high-energy, ultraviolet light!'

'I am happy that I was able to provoke such a useful conclusion.'

'Now, the next question is, can I work out *how far away* a jet of several hundred light years long must have been, if it looks like a wriggling serpent stretched across the sky?'

Tom then took out a pencil and folded scrap of paper from his pocket and, using the calculator on his iPhone, slipped into his academic mode and started to work through some calculations.

Mary-Anne smiled as she watched him. From experience, she knew it was best to let him slip into oblivion for a short while to complete his calculations. His scrap of paper was very small. It couldn't last long. She sipped the rich, almost chocolatey-flavour, freshly ground coffee. It went perfectly with a bite of the succulent banana bread with tropical jam. She paused to take in the garden views for several minutes, then looked seawards, towards the ever-changing spectacular skyscape with its quickly moving, ominous slate-grey clouds. After a short while she turned to Tom. His scrap of paper was pretty much completely filled up with his mathematical workings.

'Hi there Tom,' she whispered.

Tom looked up. 'Hi there Honey.'

'Are you back?'

'Yep, sorry, I just needed to check one calculation.'

'Tom, I know how important this must be for you. It's totally OK. I was just thinking, if we're finished with breakfast, shall we not go back to our villa? I would love to get into the pool, and drink in views of the beautiful Caribbean Sea and the *Petit Piton*.'

'You're absolutely right, let's go back. You can cool off, while I quickly get to work. I got a lot of criticism in the *press* for not explaining the science of everything, but this is actually quite difficult, because no one has ever tried before to describe the effects that the transit of this kind of astrophysical event would have had on the Earth. I really feel I'm much more on top of things now.'

They stood up and left their table, smiling to the waitress as they passed her.

'Have a lovely day!' the waitress said.

'Thank you, you too!' Mary-Anne replied. Tom smiled to her.

They walked down the restaurant steps that led to the reception. Directly in front of the reception desk was a very large swimming pool, beautifully adorned with potted tropical plants and having the same idyllic spectacular view looking out over the Caribbean Sea. It did seem a little strange that no one was ever in this large pool. Perhaps it was for visitors, since all the guests had their own private pools.

'Good morning! Have a lovely day!' the girl at reception said, as they passed.

'Thanks!' Mary-Anne replied. 'The same to you.'

Looking at Tom, the girl smiled, then challenged him in creole, '*Sa ka fèt?*'

But Tom was ready with a new response to '*what's happening?*' '*Mwen ka mouté un pyé koko!*' he replied.

The girl laughed. 'So, you're climbing a coconut tree! Hold on very hard! *Tjébé bien fò!*'

Tom laughed, and he and Mary-Anne walked back to their *Villa Ananas*. Tom unlocked the door and walked inside to grab his laptop, then he came back out and sat at the veranda table. Mary-Anne quietly stripped naked and dived into the pool. Hearing the splash, Tom looked up. 'Wow! Naked!'

'Why don't you come in, and enjoy me, ... er join me,' she replied with a teasing voice. Amazingly, despite the dive, she had somehow managed to keep her sunglasses on.

'You look very lovely! But I must work my darling.'

'I know. The water feels wonderfully refreshing though,' she remarked. 'Oh look! A hummingbird over the pool!'

Not wanting to miss the moment, Tom quickly took his iPhone and started to video the bird. It paused high above Mary-Anne. 'You must certainly look like a very sweet flower.'

After the bird flew away, Mary-Anne swam a few lengths back and forth in the pool. She then turned and stood at the front edge of the pool, looking out towards the *Petit Piton*. With her arms on the front ledge, her feet could just touch the bottom. 'It's truly lovely here. By the way, are we going to the resort barbeque event tonight?' she asked, turning round to face Tom.

'Of course. Are we skipping lunch?'

'Well, I thought I would relax in the sun while it lasts, then we could walk down the steep hill to the *Soufrière Beach Bar*. That would be seriously good exercise, particularly on the way back uphill, and we could have one of those *amazingly yummy* fish wraps again. I don't think I can last without food until this evening.'

'You're right. The walk back up the hill will do us good. We just have to earn this, so I need to write the paper outline at least.'

'Would you be so sweet to get my white bath gown, Tom? Then I won't distract you as I walk naked past you.'

'I would love to be distracted,' Tom replied with a naughty look. 'Of course, I'll get it for you.'

He walked inside and re-emerged with her bath gown. 'Here you go.' He hung it over the stainless steel bar next to the pool steps.

'Thanks. I'll stay in a little longer.'

'Mary-Anne, can I just ask you a question. What was the name of that other settlement in Turkey that you contrasted with *Göbekli Tepe*? Oh, I remember now, *Çatalhöyük*. That was constructed 2000 years later than *Göbekli Tepe* right?'

'That's right. Why do you ask?'

'I understood it was a kind of proto-city, of possibly several thousand people?'

'Well, we think at least 5000 to 7000 people at any one time, and dating from as far back as 9000 years ago. Is that significant?'

'Well, I am wondering if the existence of that settlement suggests that the effects of the jet were over by then, because it seems that people were living what we might call normal lives.'

'Well we don't know that at all. *Çatalhöyük* is a remarkable settlement because the living spaces are all huddled together and access to each dwelling was determined to be via a ladder down. The roofs would have formed the streets of that settlement.'

'Wow, then that could even be further proof that the effects of the jet were still influencing settlement design *9000 years ago*! It now sounds as if that strange close-proximity, living arrangement gave people the possibility to hide below ground, particularly to avoid high levels of *ultraviolet* light. They might not have understood much about radiation, but they may have seen people get badly sunburned or even go blind. They would have quickly worked out that they were safer out of the direct sunlight. That may be the reason why the settlement was built that way.'

'Now that's a very interesting hypothesis, but it would depend on how long the effects lasted of course.'

Tom continued to type and then looked up. Mary-Anne had stepped out of the pool and was already completely wrapped in her white bath robe. 'I missed you again!'

'You should pay more attention.'

'I will. I just promised myself.'

After a short time, Mary-Anne re-emerged from the bedroom wearing her bright pink bikini. She looked stunning!

'You look gorgeous!'

'Thank you. By the way, I meant to tell you something that I found. I was checking the etymology of the word *pyramid*. *Pyr* is Greek for *fire* and *amid* must surely relate to *within*. Pyramid could thus mean *fire-within*, does that sound significant Tom?'

'Mm, that *is* very interesting,' he replied, giving Mary-Anne a thoughtful look.

'You are welcome,' she replied with a smile, as she walked over to her sunbed. She then picked up her *ambre solaire* factor 30 sun-cream, and proceeded to rub it into her skin before lying down on her front to drink in the rays.

'Did you possibly have any other inspiring thoughts,' Tom asked hopefully.

Mary-Anne's eyes were shut. She opened them and then pushed herself upwards onto her elbows, looking at Tom.

'Well, I am still thinking about that other Egyptian Temple complex we talked about, *Karnak* near *Luxor*. You said that the hieroglyphs seemed quite crude at the bottom of the tall pillars but that there were several tall obelisks which seemed to have almost *laser-cut* hieroglyphs.'

'That's right. I discussed that with Chad when he was with us in Australia. With their copper tools, the so called *laser-cut* hieroglyphs, could in no way be from the same period. They had to be from a very capable technological civilization, most likely, *vastly* predynastic.'

'Well, we also discussed how that Egyptian frieze showing *Apep*, their version of the *Rainbow Serpent*, was so detailed, coiling around the *Tree of Life*, that it was almost certainly contemporary, right? It surely hadn't been created seven thousand years later,' Mary-Anne continued.

'Right. So, is there another conclusion from that?' he urged.

'Well, if the frieze with its hieroglyphs is contemporary with the event, some 7000 years before the accepted date of the first Egyptian Old Kingdom in 2700 B.C.E., then maybe so are the *laser-cut* hieroglyphs.'

'Why is that significant?'

'Well, it seems significant to me because I am suggesting that the Old Kingdom Egyptians *discovered* the *laser-cut* hieroglyphs in amazing temples, and then decided to adopt them. But how could they possibly know the meaning of those hieroglyphs, which I am suggesting were carved some 7000 years earlier? If those *laser-cut* hieroglyphs date from *before* the cataclysm of the relativistic jet impact, ... OK I mean *the relativistic jet transit through our part of the galaxy*, ... isn't it possible that those earlier hieroglyphs have never been correctly translated? If that is correct, the Old Kingdom Egyptians then just decided their own meaning for the earlier hieroglyphs, which are then possibly completely wrong!'

'That is a very compelling argument. Somebody really needs to check that. Someone needs to compile images of all the *laser-cut* hieroglyphs and determine whether the translations make any sense. The problem is that, unlike the *Rosetta Stone* which possibly decodes the later hieroglyph meanings, there is no *laser-cut* hieroglyph dictionary for any hieroglyphs which date from a much earlier epoch. This will most likely remain a contentious paradox for years to come.'

'Unless the Rosetta Stone served some other nefarious purpose and we are still missing the true cypher key,' Mary Anne remarked.

Rosetta Stone

'An interesting but quite controversial comment and potentially another enigma.'

Tom started to check some data online. Mary-Anne lay back down and closed her eyes and continued to relax in the sun.

Their villa was high above the sea. Below them, the beautiful turquoise Caribbean Sea near to the shore, gradually darkened into a deeper cobalt blue further out. A few hundred metres from the shore, high in the sky, a large group of dark *frigatebirds,* with very long wings and forked tails, were wheeling high above the sea, probably over a shoal of fish. The tree-clad mighty *Petit Piton* looked quite daunting with its volcanic spire rising some 743 metres out of the water. It was jagged and green, beckoning any ardent souls to dare to climb it, but it had no easy route up. Just around the coast to the south, stood its larger brother, the *Gros Piton* at 798 metres, with the long sandy *Sugar Beach Resort* between them. Tom and Mary-Anne had already taken a resort shuttle there a few days earlier, to enjoy snorkelling around its protected reefs.

After Tom had written several pages, and Mary-Anne had been in the sun for perhaps a little too long, she carefully got up from her sunbed and announced, 'Honey, I need another dip in the pool to cool down. Do you fancy coming in also, Tom?'

'Sure, why not!' He went back inside the villa and returned wearing his starfish-patterned swimming shorts. He dived in. The water really felt soft and warm. He surfaced and shook the water from his face. Mary-Anne then walked down the steps and plunged into the water. 'Will you be hungry for that *creole fish wrap* after this?' he asked.

'Absolutely, and maybe with a cold *Piton* beer. Let's just have a few minutes to cool down, then we'll get dressed.'

'Of course.' Then he took a deep breath, and slowly breathed out, letting himself glide down beneath the water, until he was sitting on the bottom of the pool. It felt so refreshing to feel the water cooling his hot head. Several whirlpool jets were positioned around the pool, continually sending invigorating streams through the water. After a short while, he slowly pushed his feet against the bottom of the pool, pushing himself back upwards to break the water surface. Mary-Anne was lying on her back floating in the pool, softly drifting in the warmth. Then the rain suddenly started yet again. It seemed funny to be in the pool during a downpour.

Mary-Anne then let her feet touch the bottom. She stood up and then slowly walked towards the steps. 'I'm good already. I'll just take a shower,' she announced. You enjoy the pool and the warm rain a little longer.'

'Of course. Take your time.'

Tom then slowly walked over to the edge of the pool and gazed far out over the Caribbean, just like Mary-Anne had done earlier. Each resort villa had its own pool and the thick rainforest trees and plants kept each one totally private and secluded. Maybe later that evening they could stand here together and open one of those bottles of duty-free champagne he'd picked up at the airport on their way out.

After about ten minutes, Mary-Anne stuck her head through the veranda door and called out, 'Tom, I'm ready. All yours!'

'OK, thanks!'

He walked up the steps and into their villa, and crossed the cool tiled floor to the bathroom, where Mary-Anne was now busy putting on her make-up. He opened the shower door and walked outside into their own private, open-air shower room. Above him was a magnificent flamboyant tree, or *shakshak*, as the St. Lucians called them. Its brilliant scarlet flowers were stunning. The outside bathroom had walls of travertine marble. He reached for the citrus orange shower gel. Everything about this place was just paradise. The falling rain magically complemented the warm shower, enrichening the experience.

After getting dressed and putting on sneakers, Tom and Mary-Anne were ready for their tough walk down to Soufrière. They walked along the resort entrance road, back past the lush, vividly-coloured flowering rainforest plants. St. Lucia had *turned green again*, according to one taxi driver. The wet season would keep it beautiful for another five months. Some of the plants looked quite stunning. As they passed the security guy in his booth at the barrier, Tom called out '*Sa ou di?*' meaning '*How are you doing?*' Before the man could answer, he added '*Tjébé bien fò?*', which he knew had the second meaning of '*Are you just hanging in there?*' The man gave a beaming smile and lifted his hand to greet them. It was nice to make contact with the local people. Both Tom and Mary-Anne were very unlike the other tourists at the resort who only wanted to live in their safe *comfort-zone bubble*.

The winding road down to Soufrière was busy and steep. There was no proper path, and then it started to rain again. It probably looked odd to see two tourists walking into town. No tourists walked. Everyone was paying tens of US dollars for a taxi everywhere, but there was something very meaningful and real to be among the St. Lucian people.

They passed a wrecker's garage, which had vehicle parts stacked up outside in the yard, clearly salvaged from car crashes from all over the island. Nothing looked worth keeping, but this was probably a viable business since imported spare parts would have been way too expensive. Maybe body parts would be hammered back into shape when they were needed. As they eventually came into Soufrière, a ragged man suddenly appeared, limping quickly beside them.

'Hello, hello, do you have some change, so I can eat today?' he pleaded, his eyes wide with hope. With a sigh, Tom took some coins from his pocket and handed him $4 EC. The man nodded and smiled gratefully and then turned and hobbled away.

After they had walked along the main street, passing the temporary Police Station with its very comical *Property For Sale* sign, they carried on over a bridge, and past the graveyard to *Hummingbird Beach*. They walked up the wooden steps of the hexagonal kiosk bar, which had a pair of tall bar stools in front of each window, Delansha was working that day and she saw them. Her dreadlocks looked amazing and she wore a bright *Rasta* tee-shirt. She smiled sweetly. Behind them, was the beach and the magical sound of the Caribbean Sea, breaking along the shoreline. Tom and Mary-Anne sat at a bar window on two of the stools. Two very cold *Piton* beer bottles then appeared in front of them, their metal lids opened, but placed back on, somewhat enhancing their appeal.

'Hi Delansha. We can pay at the end, right? Tom may want another and I'm paying with my card.'

'Of course,' Delansha said. 'Just relax, you're on holiday.'

'Tom took a sip, then said, 'I'll just go and order those *creole fish wraps*.'

'Yes, can't wait!'

Shortly, Tom returned from the *Sea-Breeze Beach Bar*.

'The lady said she'll bring them over in about ten minutes. I paid already. I also told her that her fish wraps have a *paradise* taste, and possibly some of the best food we've tasted on St. Lucia.'

'Indeed, and we must have eaten them three times already, right?'

'Yes, that's right, This is our fourth batch.'

A wide TV, playing some rather risqué local Caribbean music videos, was hanging from the ceiling. The air temperature was perfect.

'So, did you have any more breakthroughs?'

'Well, I still need to work through the effects of the magnetic disturbance, but in the meantime, I was looking into the cave-dwelling aspects. We humans were just as intelligent then as we are today; we know that from the genetic evidence. We were not primitive cave-dwellers, who chose to live in cold, dark, damp caves, far from food and water sources. We weren't stupid, we would have built log cabins by the lake. People back then lived in caves because they had utterly no choice. They needed some serious protection from something deadly.'

'If my hypothesis is right, any surviving scattered populations needed to protect themselves from the very high intensity radiation. I found some very interesting deep cave complexes in *Petra, Jordan*. There seem to be many narrow caverns, cut between the cliffs in *Petra*, connecting caves on alternate sides of the wider caverns. These were cut directly out of the cliff faces using some, as yet unknown, stone-cutting technology. These would have offered secure refuges from what I believe was possibly the main danger, very intense ultraviolet light. There were probably other effects but I now need to work those out in detail.'

'That sounds really interesting.'

Petra Treasury

'The thing is, the *Petra* caves are immaculately cut into the cliff face, as tall rectangular rooms with flat sidewalls and 90° corners. There is one building called *Al-Khazneh,* which means *The Treasury*, which even has a remarkable carved façade with colonnades, some 15 metres high. There is also an enormous amphitheatre carved from the cliffs. I start to think that the need to create structures, which would endure for hundreds of years, is obviously why they used stone. This further supports the hypothesis that the jet transit had a significant duration.'

'And that they knew how long it would last.'

'Indeed.'

Just at that moment, the lady from the immediately adjacent *Sea-Breeze Snack Bar* appeared, walking towards them carrying the fish wraps.

'I have your fish wraps,' she announced with a smile, placing the white polystyrene boxes on the narrow bar window ledge in front of them, together with a bottle of yellow sauce. 'I brought you some *Caribbean hot sauce*. Please let me have it back when you're finished.'

'Of course! Thank you so much,' Tom replied.

Delansha came over to them after the lady left. Tom, would you like another *Piton*?'

'Oh, yes please.'

'How about you, Mary-Anne?' Delansha asked.

'I'm good, thanks,' Mary-Anne replied, pointing at her half-empty bottle.

The unleavened bread wrap enclosed some perfectly fried tuna pieces, surrounded by finely-cut, red and white cabbage and lettuce, with a mustard, herb and mayonnaise sauce. The flavour was to die for!

Suddenly, a small green lizard appeared on the kiosk wall beside Mary-Anne, then froze as it looked at her with its moveable red eyes. Mary-Anne very slowly reached towards her iPhone, but seeing the movement, the lizard quickly darted away, running up the wall into a hole below the rainwater gutter.

'You can get him next time.'

'I can be patient. Tom, have you thought any further about what Chad said about the vast number of ancient Egyptian statues and structures, having scorched rock surfaces? Surely, there would have been other sites in different parts of the World showing similar surface damage.'

'Yes, I was also thinking about that, this morning. There are a vast number of ancient hill forts in Europe, which comprise parts of their walls having vitrified rock. Also, the amount of vitrification seems random, as if it were not intended. By the nature of their construction, those hill forts enclose flat hill summits, and are thus fully exposed to the sky. The vitrification could be explained by increased lightning activity, or even coronal discharge within the atmosphere. From publications, there is as yet, no satisfactory explanation of the cause. This also suggests that these rocky structures might have origins dating back to a much earlier epoch than currently contemplated.'

'Are the hill forts all in one place or are they spread out over a large area?'

'They are quite spread out. More than 70 have been found in Scotland alone, but I did some checking today and I discovered they have also been found in Ireland, France, Germany, Poland, and the Czech Republic. As I said earlier, the presence of the jet would have activated the Sun, and likely caused a much stronger solar wind and a very elevated flux of ultraviolet. I am thinking now that there would have been so much energy put into the atmosphere, that the Earth's weather must have gone totally crazy. The ozone layer would likely have been seriously damaged, but there would also have been phenomenal mixing of the atmosphere and endless thunderstorms of incredible power and duration.'

Tom paused to take a bite of his St. Lucian cuisine. The rich melange of flavours in the creole food was just divine. He looked at Mary-Anne who also seemed to be really enjoying hers.

'These fish wraps are utterly delicious!' she remarked.

'Sure, and even better with a hint of this *West Indian Hot Sauce*!'

'Oh, that's way too spicy for me!'

'I have to confess that this hot sauce gives me an endorphin rush. I think I am starting to get addicted to it,' Tom added.

An onshore wind was softly blowing, cooling them as they sat on the tall bar stools. The leaves of the banana trees near the beach were softly clattering in the breeze. A small St. Lucian boy suddenly appeared beside Mary-Anne, looking up at her with a very sweet expression, holding out a delicately folded banana leaf on a stick. It was an intricate piece of leaf-origami in the shape of a fish. It was quite beautiful.

'I'm sorry, I don't have any money, only my card,' Mary-Anne said, giving the boy a sad look.

'It's OK. Then I give it to you as a present,' the boy said, and handed her the beautiful fish artwork. He then ran away, back to his friends.

Mary-Anne was left holding the carefully crafted leaf-fish. 'I feel terrible. He has given me this for nothing. Do you have any money at all, Tom?'

'I still have one EC$5 note,' he replied, handing it to her.

'I'll just be a moment.'

Mary-Anne walked over to the boy, who was playing cards on the sand with his friends. She held out the EC$5 note. 'For you, thanks for the lovely fish.'

The boy nodded with a smile, took the EC$5, and turned back to his game. Almost immediately, he threw it on a pile of money that the boys were obviously playing cards for. 'I raise you five!' he said. They continued to play.

Mary-Anne was momentarily quite shocked, but she had to smile. So, this was the way of life among the young on St. Lucia, certainly, on that stretch of beach! She walked back to Tom.

'There was one more thing I found out honey,' Tom continued. 'You asked about people living in a twilight time. I found a story about some indigenous South American people from Peru, who lived in *Ñaupa Iglesia*, a side valley south of the *Sacred Valley*, some 5km east of *Ollantaytambo*. That site has highly refined megalithic caves cut into the cliffs, including a strange basalt structure called the *Altar*. According to local legends, the indigenous people there *lived in a twilight world* because the Sun was too bright. I was thinking that this could suggest a time when people needed to take cover from a harmful source of radiation in the sky, and thus needed to hide from daylight in constructed caves.'

'Sorry Tom, I just have to tell you what just happened. I gave that boy your EC$5, and he just used it immediately in his gambling card game.'

'Really? That's funny. I guess one should never prejudge a situation. The folded-leaf fish souvenirs might possibly be the financial arm of the juvenile high-stakes card-game entertainment here!'

Mary-Anne laughed then took the last sip from her *Piton beer*.

'I have an idea. Why don't we now head back to the villa,' she whispered. 'I can read, and you can continue writing your paper.'

'Of course,' he replied, knocking back his last swig of beer.

They said goodbye to Delansha, who turned and smiled at them. 'See you next time,' she called, as they picked up their things and then wandered back across the sand towards the main road.

Heading back along Soufrière's narrow streets, the Sun felt very hot. It was the dangerous time of the day and they tried to keep in the shadows as much as possible. At the far side of town, they reached the steep and winding road back to *Stonefield.* It was more than a mile uphill. The air was really humid, and despite the breeze, their clothes were soon totally soaked with sweat. At the top of the hill, on the corner of the last bend, was a viewpoint, looking down over the brightly coloured roofs of *Soufrière,* and out over the beautiful blue Caribbean Sea. At the viewpoint, several St. Lucian ladies had set up tables to sell souvenirs. A tourist bus had just pulled up with another group of cruise-ship *bubble tourists,* who only ever interacted with islanders at the pre-arranged stops. It seemed a pity that they never met the true St. Lucians, to gain a sense of the warmth of these wonderful island people.

Tom and Mary-Anne were soon back amongst the lush rainforest gardens of *Stonefield.* At the far end of the entrance driveway, a raised stone fountain, fully embraced by vividly coloured tropical plants, cascaded continuously down into its pool. The garden hummingbirds were all around.

'I need to feel that fine spray,' Mary-Anne said, and walked over to pause beside the large fountain pool. Soon her face was covered with the moist spray. 'It's so refreshing,' she whispered.

Tom took out his iPhone to capture the moment of Mary-Anne with her closed eyes, and delicate smile, and her face held slightly upwards, as fine droplets of water kissed her skin. 'You look so lovely.'

Mary-Anne opened her eyes. 'Thank you,' she said.

They walked back to *Villa Ananas.* Mary-Anne went inside and put on her bikini. When she came out, she saw Tom's heap of clothes on the ground. He had just gone into the pool naked.

'I couldn't wait. I was too warm.'

'OK, maybe I am overdressed then!' Mary-Anne remarked, and then proceeded to unclip her bright pink bikini bra, and pull down her bikini bottom, before plunging into the pool. 'Perhaps your writing will need to wait a little while longer,' she said with a naughty smile.

2 Teotihuacan, near Mexico City: onwards to Xochicalco's Feathered Serpents

Road to Teotihuacan, out of Mexico City

Chad was sitting in an air-conditioned tour-bus, on his way north to *Teotihuacan*. It was a short trip along the dusty dry road out of Mexico City, and getting the *very last seat* on a tour that day, had been a total relief. He and Jeanette had only planned a 48-hour stopover in Mexico, before flying on to meet Tom and Mary-Anne in St. Lucia, but for Chad, the artefacts on display at the *National Museum of Anthropology*, just didn't have any answers. There had to be something more substantial, and maybe he would be inspired with new ideas by taking a trip to visit *Teotihuacan*. Jeanette, an anthropologist herself, was very happy to immerse herself for a second day at the museum among the *indigenous peoples of Central America*, so Chad would head out to the ancient site alone. They would meet up later that evening for dinner, before catching an early flight out to St. Lucia in the morning.

As the bus left the suburbs and reached more open countryside, Chad was thinking that the first, somewhat controversial, astrophysics paper, had actually been relatively well received. While he and Tom had really tried hard just to present data, as devoid as possible of any unsubstantiated hypotheses or dreamed-up suggestions, the resulting jigsaw puzzle still had half its pieces missing. Now, they both felt an increasing urgency to gather as many of the other pieces as possible. There were just still too many unanswered questions, and if their conjecture was correct, a substantial part of the evidence still lay out there.

The last seat on the bus to Teotihuacan was also not on an *English-speaking* tour. It had been that or nothing. He was on the Japanese tour! He certainly looked very different from his fellow tourist passengers.

At the front of the bus, a Japanese tour-guide was standing with a microphone, pointing out over the landscape, probably talking about pre-Columbian heritage. Chad thought he could catch the occasional mention of the *Maya*, and the *Aztecs*. A sophisticated-looking, possibly 50-plus year old, native-Japanese tourist was sitting next to him in the aisle seat. Chad felt fortunate to have the window seat. He at least could enjoy the view, even if he couldn't follow any of the story.

Suddenly, everyone on the bus burst out laughing about something the tour-guide had just said. It seemed odd to not be able to share in the collective reaction, and Chad was curious about the joke. Before he had cause to wonder any longer, his seat companion turned to him, 'You don't speak Japanese, do you?'

'Er, no, I don't,' Chad replied, feeling a little embarrassed.

'Why did you choose a Japanese language tour?' the man asked.

'Well, I only have two days in Mexico, and this was the last seat on the last bus out to Teotihuacan today!'

'Ha-ha!' The man said with a beaming smile. 'I knew there had to be a logical reason somewhere! My name is Takashi, what is yours?' the man asked, holding out his hand.

'*Konnichi wa Takashi-san! Watashi wa Chad desu. Hajimemashite!*'

'You do speak Japanese!' Takashi replied, somewhat shocked. '*O-me ni kakarete ureshī desu!*'

'Only a very few phrases. I once did a course in Japanese, but that was some twenty years ago.'

'I feel very honoured that you did that,' Takashi replied.

'You are very kind. But years ago, I planned to go on a trip to Japan. I'm a geologist, and I imagined that being able to communicate at a basic level would have been extremely useful and important.'

'Where did you go?'

'Well, I work at a University and the trip was a geology field trip to the *Ryukyu* islands. Sadly, the funding didn't come through, so the trip was cancelled.'

'So, it was possibly also an underwater trip?' Takashi asked, raising his eyebrows.

'Yes, to *Yonaguni*. That underwater temple complex is a big mystery and something I'd really like to see first-hand.'

'I did my Ph.D. at Ryūdai, the University of the Ryukyus. I am actually an oceanographer,' Takashi explained. 'I'm semi-retired now.'

'Takashi-san, I have to say that your English is amazing.'

'Thank you Chad-san. You can understand that, as an oceanographer, it was the essential discussion language with overseas colleagues.'

'Of course. May I ask you something, Takashi-san? You said you are now semi-retired. What do you do when you are not on overseas vacation trips?'

'Ah, you may be surprised to learn that I make *Shinogi-Zukuri katanas*! Do you know what they are?'

'You are a swordsmith!' Chad remarked, recognising the words.

'Yes, indeed! I am trying to master the art of sword-making in the old *Samurai* swordsmith style. It's a long journey. I've been an apprentice for more than fifteen years now, and I have spent months training alongside several of Japan's greatest master swordsmiths. The swordsmith art is dying out and some of us must endeavour to keep the craft alive for future generations.'

'That's really interesting! I think I read it takes more than six months to complete a sword and the art involves creating thousands of cross-axial metal layers by multiple heating, hammering and folding. Five folds already creates 32 layers. In how many places is the art still alive?'

'There are only seven towns where *Samurai* swords are still made, but *Seki* still remains the capital. In *Seki* the art goes back eight hundred years. Out in the *Ryukyu* islands, there is only one swordsmith left. 'Hopefully, there will be two soon!' Takashi added with a smile

'*Moto … Motoshige?* Was that his name?' Chad asked, trying to recover a lost name from a distant memory.

'Motoshige! Yes, indeed Chad-san. He is considered the father of the whole industry. I must say, it is a pleasure to meet someone who has even heard of our Master Swordsmith!'

The bus continued northeast along the toll road out of Mexico City, and soon reached the outskirts. Around them, the less affluent, multicolour, *Rio de Janeiro favela-style* housing lay sprawled across the hillsides. The Japanese tour-guide had stopped speaking into her microphone, and was now sitting in the seat directly behind the driver.

'So, what brings *you* to *Teotihuacan*? Why did you want to go to the site?' Chad asked.

'Well, I was going to ask you exactly the same question. The fact that you took a Japanese-language tour bus, suggests that you are extremely keen! *Teotihuacan* must be a very important site for you. If the last English language tour bus was full, other people would have just chosen another tourist site in Mexico City. I'm here because of my own interest in ancient cultures. Something seems odd about such a site, as if it was purposefully created in such a uniquely structured state. The building layout seems to suggest a monument to something. I have read quite a lot about *Teotihuacan* and I'm still trying to work out the reason for its creation.'

'That sounds really intriguing,' Chad replied. 'Please tell me your thoughts. All I read was that this is a temple complex of many buildings including the famous three: *The Temple of the Sun*, *The Temple of the Moon*, and *The Temple of the Feathered Serpent*.'

'Well, from what I understand, the site is defined by the *central avenue*, which was named by the *Aztecs* as *Avenue of the Dead* because they assumed all the buildings off to the right and left of it were tombs. The avenue stretches more than 4km. The name of the site, *Teotihuacan*, may be an important clue as to its origins. In *Nahuatl*, the local language of the *Nahua* indigenous peoples of Mexico and El Salvador, one accepted translation describes this as meaning *Birthplace of the Gods*. Mayan hieroglyph texts describe it as *Place of Reeds*. Today, many researchers describe *Teotihuacan* as the largest urban centre in Mesoamerica before the *Aztecs*.'

'OK, so the Aztecs didn't build it,' Chad concluded.

'No, it must predate them substantially. They just found it and re-occupied the site. The question remains about what it represents. It is complex and comprises many unique features, built in a precise way, as if it is indeed a monument to something.'

Chad was not intending to tell Takashi-san about his and Tom's paper about the Wolf-Rayet star collapse, which caused the potentially civilization-destroying Earth cataclysm. Their paper had hardly been out for a couple of months now. Chad wanted to publish a second paper with Tom, before others could sit on top of their hypotheses and beat them to the other obvious implied conclusions. Mustapha hadn't written much in his notes about *Teotihuacan*, only the names of several authors, who had drawn some unique conclusions about the layout.

'For me, one other feature of the site is the precise direction of the axis of the site, and by that I mean the geographical direction of the *Avenue of the Dead*,' Chad remarked. 'It's about 15° north east, off the north-south line.'

'Or 15° 30' *south-west off due south*!' Takashi replied, showing Chad a map with photographs of the site.

'Ah, you know the angle exactly.'

Chad looked at the layout carefully. Strangely, the two large pyramids and one small pyramid had a relative layout similar to Giza. Many continued to argue that the Giza pyramids matched the stars of Orion's belt, but to Chad any logical link between Orion's belt and the Giza pyramids was still totally missing. Was this another monument to mark the relativistic jet event, and did the 15° 30 minutes off true south, possibly correspond to the direction of the jet across the sky? Could that be right if the jet came from the direction of the *gamma Velorum* cluster? It was still possible that *Teotihuacan* was indeed another monument built to record the event for future generations. Unlike the Giza pyramids, from the photographs of Teotihuacan on the edge of Takashi's map, there did not seem to be much megalithic stonework. In fact, the surfaces of the structures were all covered in adobe mudbrick and gravel. Was it possible that the structures were originally cased in limestone as some writers had suggested? He would need to discuss this with Tom.

The bus eventually reached the small town of *San Juan*. It was not much further to *Teotihuacan*. The Japanese tour guide then stood up again and started to speak. Takashi looked at her and was listening intently. When she finished, Takashi turned to Chad.

'OK, it was just a story about where to meet up if anyone gets lost. Oh, and remember to use lots of sun-cream and drink lots of water. Everyone will be handed water when we leave the bus.

'Thanks Takashi-san! That advice sounds very caring and organised.'

Soon the bus stopped in front of *Gate 1*, the main entrance to the *Teotihuacan* site. Takashi stepped down from the bus and Chad followed. The sky was a pale shade of blue. It was a very hot 32°C and there was only the hint of the slightest breeze. Perhaps it would be advisable to keep out of the sun as much as possible, Chad was thinking.

'So, do you want to go with the Japanese group, and have me translate for you, or do you prefer wandering about on your own? To be honest, I've read quite a lot about this site, and I doubt if the local guide has that much more to offer us. How about us wandering about the site together?'

'Takashi-san that would be really interesting. I must say, I'm quite intrigued by your knowledge. If you're happy to do that, I'd really appreciate exploring the site together with you.'

'So, it's agreed then! I'll just check with our tour guide Mizuki-san, where we need to be and when to get the bus back, then we can do our own thing.'

Takashi walked over to speak to the Japanese tour guide, then returned with four small bottles of water.

'Here you go, Chad. By the way, they weren't handing out sun-cream!'

'Thanks Takashi-san. I can put all four bottles in my rucksack.'

'OK, shall we check out this intriguing site? I propose we go to the *main* temple,' Takashi said, raising his eyebrows, as if checking whether Chad had an opinion on that.

'You mean the *Temple of the Feathered Serpent*, otherwise known as the *Pyramid of Quetzalcoatl*.'

'I do. Everyone else thinks the most important building is the *Temple of the Sun*, because it's the largest building, but the *Pyramid of Quetzalcoatl* has so many unique features. For me it represents the focus of this entire complex.'

'I agree entirely. Why do you think other people don't see the significance of this building complex right in front of us? There are carved snake-heads embedded in its structure.'

'It's because the hype of the tourist industry has already identified the *Temple of the Sun* as the most important,' Takashi remarked, 'But we won't be so taken in. Just because it's the biggest, it doesn't necessarily mean that it's the focal point. By the way, I just sense that the official tour will just talk about all the different peoples who occupied this site over the past 2000 years. For me, the most important aspect is why it was built in the first place.'

Chad finally decided that he would tell Takashi-san about the paper he had written with Tom. It was out now. There wasn't any harm.

'Takashi-san, did you possibly read a paper in *Nature* recently, called *The Wolf Cataclysm*?'

'Indeed! A very interesting paper and a hypothesis which might explain many phenomena. The author was a guy from Australia, I believe. The Earth was first hit by a gamma ray burst, then thousands of years later, the Earth suffered the effects of a relativistic jet.'

Chad didn't need any accolades. 'Actually Takashi, it was my brother Tom, who is based in Sydney Australia.'

'Aha, I think I now remember a co-author with the same family name, who had visited sites in Egypt. Was that you?' Takashi asked, his eyes wide with surprise.

'Yes Takashi-san. The problem now is that there are so many unanswered questions, that we're trying to write the next paper as soon as possible, and gather together as many loose ends as we can.'

'Very interesting, very interesting,' Takashi murmured, shaking his head, now looking quite serious. 'So, I'm now with the author of a soon-to-be quite important paper, which essentially challenges thousands of academic papers all over the World. How exciting! Congratulations to you and your brother, Chad-san!'

'Thanks Takashi-san. Well, in the light of the conclusions of that paper, what do you now think about *Teotihuacan*? Yesterday I was at the *National Museum of Anthropology,* and I learned that the *Toltecs*, *Aztecs*, *Olmecs* and *Maya* occupied the site in our period of recorded history, but surely this is yet another ancient site, which has its origins from a very much earlier time. The layout of the main buildings and the axis of the site are very precise. Might it not also be a monument to mark the cataclysmic event?'

'Why not, Chad-san, you may be right. There is, of course, the same symbolism of the feathered serpent. In that paper, you and your brother mentioned the indigenous Australians' myth about a *Rainbow Serpent*. So, you think this site may also have been designed and built to record the event? I remember you identified the Giza pyramids as a monument to the cataclysm.'

'That's right. And yesterday at the museum I read many versions of the story about the *Feathered Serpent* called *Quetzalcoatl*. It struck me as quite remarkable that so many aspects of the *Feathered Serpent* match the key themes of the Australian *Rainbow Serpent* myth. There are also tunnels under all the pyramids here. These could have offered both protection to store seeds, as well as protection when the relativistic jet was in the sky.'

'You may be interested to know that in one version of the Mesoamerican myth, *Quetzalcoatl* supposedly found a store of corn hidden in a mountain. That might be another reference to the storage of food,' Takashi remarked.

'That's very interesting. That links directly to the Saqqara stone-box, seed-storage hypothesis.'

The rest of the Japanese tourists were slowly walking along the *Avenue of the Dead* towards the *Temple of the Sun*. Chad and Takashi, however, just walked straight ahead towards the *Temple of the Feathered Serpent*. There were fewer tourists in this part of the site. It stood within a much larger, wide-walled courtyard called the *Ciudadela*, or Citadel, and the Temple was partly obscured by a lower, four-tiered platform called the *Adosada*.

Chad and Takashi entered the *Ciudadela* through the wide entrance gap in the front wall, flanked by two pairs of three-tiered platforms. The whole complex was set lower than the surrounding landscape. Each side had four sets of steps rising to tiered platforms. Takashi took out his *Go-Pro* 4K camera mounted on a gimbal, to stabilise the filming.

'Is it OK if I film this bit? I don't have 8K yet, but 4K should do,' he said, as if trying to convince himself.

'Of course! Please!' Chad replied encouragingly.

Takashi then switched on the camera, and held it out, while speaking in Japanese as they walked. Together they crossed the courtyard towards the raised central platform and up its 12 steps. For a few minutes, Takashi continued to film the whole panorama, deliberately turning to include Chad at the end of the clip. Chad smiled. He then switched off the camera.

'So, is it a *pyramid* or a *temple*?' Takashi asked. 'What is strange is how the raised *Adosada* platform directly in front of it kind of protects the feathered serpent heads in the Temple behind. It's almost as if the pyramid was destroyed and then rounded off using a simple small rock coating.'

'Let's take a look from the top of the *Adosada*,' Chad urged.

They descended the central platform and walked over to the *Adosada* and started to climb the steps.

'I made it 39 steps,' Chad remarked, breathing heavily.

'I made it only 38,' Takashi remarked. 'Maybe that is why you are a little breathless.' Not wishing to offend Chad he added, 'I'm only kidding Chad-san!'

'No, you're right. I really do need to get back to a serious exercise routine again. I'm not at my peak fitness at the moment. You, however, do seem very fit Takashi-san. So what's your secret?'

'Well, I'm sure you know that Japan is a country of strong cultural values based on seeking mental strength through meditation. We also emphasise artform in many of our sports. I practise *aikido*. I've done that ever since I was a boy. I am sure you also understand that *sword-making* requires extreme focus and concentration. The intense heat from the iron-sand extraction process, and the hundreds of hours of working the red hot steel, require intense strength and stamina. Combined with the *aikido*, I keep extremely fit.'

There was something in Takashi's voice that didn't seem so convincing.

'Chad-san, I am kidding you!' Takashi exclaimed with a huge smile, patting Chad on the back. 'This is Mexico. We're at 2000 metres! I have been here for three weeks already. I'm pretty much acclimatised. You have only just arrived, and you must indeed be *extremely* fit if you are only slightly out of breath.'

Chad laughed, 'You almost had me there Takashi-san. But the sword making sounds extremely interesting. You know, I've always wanted to see a real *samurai* sword being forged, worked and crafted.'

'Then I invite you to Japan as my guest! I know you also want to dive and see *Yonaguni*! I can organise a dive there too!'

'Takashi-san, that is really kind of you. I would love to dive *Yonaguni*.'

'That's settled then. I have dived the site more than 20 times. It's believed to be at least 10,000 years old.'

From the top of the *Adosada*, looking down, Chad could see the rising steps and the first three or four tiers of the front of the *Temple of the Feathered Serpent*. The stonework below them looked very precise, with very sharp flat cut stones, again as if they had been machine cut. This just had to be another ancient megalithic site.

Mustapha had referenced two papers from the 1960s and 1970s in his notes, where different authors had described the site as recording the relative distances to the planets in the solar system. Others had considered the papers very subjective, giving different results depending on how you mapped the layout of the buildings.

'Takashi-san, let's go down and take a closer look at those serpent heads. I saw a perfect reconstruction at the *National Museum of Anthropology* yesterday, but it looks rather different in real life. Maybe we will discover something important if we can get closer to the genuine carvings.'

'Of course. Let's do it.'

They descended the *Adosada* steps again and walked around it to the Temple. The barrier at the bottom prevented them from ascending the structure, but it was still possible to get a really good look at the serpent heads. Perhaps the museum curators had over-embellished the replica there with paint, and failed to capture how precisely the ancient blocks had been cut. Chad was becoming convinced that this structure dated from an extremely long time ago. Carved snakeheads adorned the sides of the steps. This was certainly a monument to celebrate the flying *Feathered Serpent Quetzalcoatl*, every bit as real and feared as the indigenous Australians' *Rainbow Serpent*.

'I told you that I have studied this site in detail,' Takashi said. 'It's interesting that the front of this temple was actually buried, and only excavated in more recent times. That is obviously how the snake heads survived. I also saw some old handwritten drawings from the eighteenth century which showed that the three temples here were covered in casing stones.'

'OK, so that now explains the state of everything,' Chad remarked. 'They must have removed the well-cut casing stones over time and then coated the structures with stucco and concrete.'

Takashi took some more *Go-Pro* 4k video, then switched his camera off and he and Chad walked back to the *Avenue of the Dead*. They would first walk to the end of the avenue and check out the *Pyramid of the Moon*, followed by the *Pyramid of the Sun*.

'It's a very odd layout, this site. There is nothing like it anywhere in the World. Some researchers suggest it's like a circuit diagram, but that seems absurd. I think you may be right about it being a monument. How do you think it could be linked to the relativistic jet event that you describe in your paper?'

'I really don't know at first glance. It will take some serious thinking.'

They walked to the end of the *Avenue*, and started the long climb up to the top of the *Pyramid of the Moon*. If its four flights would be tough in the heat, the 250 steps up the five-tiered Pyramid of the Sun would be even more challenging. They climbed the steps to about half-way, then paused for a rest on the second tiered terrace, and both sat to have some water and admire the view. Takashi then stood up and walked around, taking more 4K video. Chad just calmly gazed out over the site, drinking in its vast expanse. If *Teotihuacan* were a monument with an encoded message, what could it possibly be? There wasn't necessarily any connection with the Sun and the Moon, they were just names given to the pyramids by the Aztecs. According to Takashi, some researchers had written that *all* the surfaces of the structures had been coated with adobe, rocks and gravel. That now sounded like a total renovation project.

Pyramid of the Moon

Chad decided to go online using his phone, and took it out of his rucksack. It had accidentally been on silent mode. He noticed that he had only just missed a message from Jeanette: *Hello Honey, how is your visit to Teo-T going? I have secretly joined another English-speaking tour – much better than yesterday. Already heard a really great story about the African-looking Olmec heads. Hugs and love J x*

Chad had been so absorbed that he hadn't been thinking about Jeanette and her second visit at the museum. He quickly sent a reply: *Hi Honey, it's very interesting. I got the last place on the only tour out today – a*

Japanese tour! I've already made a good friend – Takashi - and we're exploring the site together. He saw that Nature paper by 'The Australian guy' ;) I had to confess it was by Tom and me. Teo-T may indeed be another monument to the relativistic jet. Enjoy your visit. See you tonight. Love you, Chad x

He then selected *Google* and started to investigate stories about *Quetzalcoatl, the Feathered Serpent*. Takashi was now far along the terrace, continuing with his 4K Japanese documentary.

When he returned, they completed their ascent to the top of the *Pyramid of the Moon*. The landscape vistas were lovely, but apart from the building layout and the few megalithic rocks laying around, they were actually not looking very far back in time, if it were true that the casing stones had all been removed and replaced with some concrete and adobe. Did the museum possibly offer something?

'I'm actually a bit disappointed Takashi-san. Apart from the sense of how large the site is, and the relative positions of the buildings, this is really a modern reconstruction, after the looting of the casing stones in more recent times. I was expecting more megalithic evidence.'

'Yes, I agree. So, how adventurous do you feel?'

'What do you mean?'

'Well, there's another site, south of Mexico city. The place is called *Xochicalco*, I was intending to go tomorrow by *Uber,* but we could go there now. We could split the fare. It's almost unknown, but it has megalithic structures and supposedly an amazing temple dedicated to the *Feathered Serpent*. What do you think?'

'Wow! That sounds worth doing. Let's do it! This is my last day. I guess we need to find the tour-guide and let her know. What's the time now?' Chad replied enthusiastically. 'The Sun is almost due south, I guess it's close to midday.'

'It's 11:45,' Takashi replied, looking at his phone. 'I guess we could make it to *Xochicalco* within two and a half hours. I'll call Mizuki-san.'

Teotihuacan seemed to hold only the merest whisper of a megalithic era. It clearly emanated from that time, but Chad needed to find solid evidence of a Mesoamerican *Rainbow Serpent*. A few snake heads, which only survived because they were buried, simply didn't cut it.

Takashi finished his call to Mizuki. 'We're set, Chad-san. Mizuki-san will inform the bus driver. We're not expected on the bus now. We don't need to climb the other pyramid. Let's skip the *Pyramid of the Sun* and get us an *Uber!*'

Takashi and Chad, now feeling rejuvenated and with a purpose, quickly descended the four-tiered pyramid. While all the other tourists were just sitting or ambling around slowly, two people seemed to be in quite a hurry to get to the exit. After less than five minutes they were back at *Gate 1*.

'I have the *Uber App*,' Takashi announced. 'I'll just put in *Xochicalco*. There should be some *Uber* guys parked up around here.'

Takashi hit '*Confirm Uber*'. Within moments a driver responded, and the App showed *30 seconds*, *Manolo* and a vehicle license plate. A car then appeared and stopped in front of them, and the front passenger window went down.

'Manolo?' Takashi asked the driver.

'Sí Señor! Takashi?' the driver replied.

'Yes. Do you speak English?'

'Of course, Señor! You want to go to *Xochicalco*? That will take around two hours twenty minutes.'

'Great,' Takashi replied.

'This was a really good decision Takashi,' Chad remarked, as they both climbed in the back of the taxi.

'Not many people visit *Xochicalco*,' the driver said. 'So, I guess you know something that most tourists don't.'

'I was told that there are some very nice carved stone structures there,' Takashi said. '*Teotihuacan* has a museum of artefacts, but this site seems a little artificial. We wanted to see early megalithic stonework.'

'You will definitely see that in *Xochicalco!*' the driver replied.

Soon they had passed *San Juan* and were back on the toll road towards Mexico. Evidence of the elusive Mesoamerican *Rainbow Serpent* was hopefully getting closer.

3 UC Berkeley: proposals for astrophysics research to dimension the jet dangers

Starbucks, University of California at Berkeley

The *usual astrophysics suspects* were sitting around a table drinking coffee and tucking into a plate of dreamy, cream doughnuts.

'This really hits the spot, Chris. Thanks!' Carl Rhodes remarked. 'Perfect with a caffè latte grande!'

'It certainly does,' Ted agreed in a muffled voice, his mouth stuffed with a huge bite of doughnut. 'They say these cream doughnuts are perfect brain food.'

'Well, I can definitely assure you that I'll be avoiding any mention of a certain theory in here from now on. Hey, did you guys hear about the extraterrestrial transmission picked up by the Parkes Radio Telescope in New South Wales? It detected a narrow band beacon signal at 982MHz coming from *proxima Centauri*. That signal even has the frequency drift expected from an orbiting exoplanetary source.'

'Yeah, I saw that,' Ted murmured. 'But I don't think we can interpret a beacon signal as any kind of intelligent communication?'

'I totally disagree. We can, and I think I've cracked it!' Chris announced.

'What? Go on then, convince us!' Carl added with some incredulity.

'Remember, Chris is not afraid of being wrong,' Ted added.

Carl continued. 'Well, as far as I understood from Parkes, they categorised it as a non-modulated beacon signal. That doesn't sound very rich in data to me, although it might of course contain data in the form of polarisation encoding, but Parkes never determined any changing polarisation.'

'Precisely!' Chris replied, 'And that's the key point. It's only a beacon signal.'

'Chris, how on Earth do you interpret a beacon signal as intelligent?' Ted enquired with a wry smile.

'Listen up, I think I can even persuade you guys that it's not only a transmission, but that the 982MHz transmission is even a *reply* to a signal sent from Earth long ago.'

'You think you can *persuade* Ted and me? Just to be clear, you are saying that you can *persuade* us that the planet orbiting *proxima Centauri* has intelligent life also! Go for it, Chris. We're all ears now!

'OK, bear with me. I think it even starts with the premise that an earlier advanced civilisation lived on Earth. This earlier civilisation may even have been even more advanced than us.'

'Well, that's still within the current bounds of possibility. An earlier Earth civilisation may well have been lost due to the hypernova GRB and the transit of the relativistic jet,' Carl added. 'Carry on.'

'So, this earlier Earth civilisation had determined all the dimensionless physical constants that we use today: π (3.142), the exponent e^x (2.718), the golden ratio φ (1.618), the ratio of the mass of the proton to the electron m_p/m_e (1836), the number of fundamental particles N_p (31), the fine structure constant α (1/137). If we use π^2, instead of π, invert the fine structure constant to 137, and include the roots $\sqrt{2}$ and $\sqrt{3}$ then multiply all these numbers together we get a number: 829.4 million. In frequency that would be 829.4 MHz, a perfect microwave transmission that gets through our atmosphere.'

'A number converted to a frequency . . . OK, so?' Ted continued. 'Why this number? It isn't the frequency that the *Proxima Centaurions* transmitted back on, if indeed it's a response.'

'Bear with me. So, our unit of frequency, *Hertz*, is the inverse of our unit of time right, *the second*, which derives from the period of a pendulum here on Earth. This means that on any other planet with a different mass and radius, they have a different value for the acceleration due to gravity g. Remember that g is proportional to the mass of a planet divided by its radius squared. So, no extraterrestrial civilisation will have the same unit of time as us, nor correspondingly the same unit of frequency.'

'OK, continue...' Ted encouraged.

'So, the period of a pendulum swinging within less than a 30° arc on Earth is 2 seconds. That's the origin of our unit of time, the second. So, the period T of a period of length l in a gravitational field of acceleration g is $T = 2\pi\sqrt{l/g}$. For a pendulum of unit length one, $l = 1$, the period of a pendulum is just proportional to the root of $1/g$. Now consider what we know about the planet *Proxima b*. That's the name of the planet orbiting *proxima Centauri*.'

Chris took out his calculator.

'We have numbers for the mass and radius of *Proxima b*. If we take the mid-range values, the mass of *Proxima b* is around 1.62 times the mass of the Earth, and its radius is around 1.075 times the Earth's radius. Plugging in those numbers, the mass divided by the radius squared gives us 1.4018. So, their unit of time is shorter by this factor, so one *Proxima b* second is 0.8446 Earth seconds. If the *Proxima Centaurions* receive, decode, understand, and retransmit a response to our 829.4MHz transmission, we should expect a beacon signal at their higher frequency which will differ by the reciprocal of their unit of time. If you multiply 829.4MHz by the inverse of 0.8446, which is 1.4018, you get 982MHz.'

'Well, that's certainly a bit of a coincidence Chris; I'll give you that!' Carl retorted with his eyebrows raised.

'Yeah, but how did we transmit that signal to them long ago?' Ted added.

'Well, we would have needed a waveguide. The dimensions of the waveguide which has 829.4MHz as its fundamental frequency is a rectangular cross section waveguide, with the long dimension being 18cm . . . and guess what? That's exactly the long dimension of the rectangular shaft in the Giza pyramid!'

'And you alone have cracked this?' Carl enquired.

'All my own work.'

'Chris, it may be absolutely true, but that's nothing we can ever publish in an academic paper! I'm sorry but, despite the SETI program, if we would actually suggest that there are extraterrestrial civilisations out there trying to communicate with us, our department and its head, me, would most likely be considered as rather mad!'

'Well, what if the *Proxima Centaurions* then turn up in a spaceship?' Ted chuckled.

'OK, then maybe,' Carl added.

'I just don't believe how conservative you guys are. This is absolutely a reasonable decoding of the Parkes 982MHz signal!'

'Chris, as I said before, we must always speak with our feet firmly planted on the firm hard ground of science before we ever could suggest such a controversial meaning to a simple radio beacon signal. I have to say though, off the record, your hypothesis sounds pretty convincing.'

'It most certainly is,' Ted confirmed.

'They're trying to contact us!' Chris urged.

'No spaceship, no cigar Chris!' Carl added.

Chris shook his head and smiled.

'Good try, mate!' Ted sighed grinning. 'Changing the subject a bit, back to Tom Walker's paper, I have also been thinking further about the Giza Pyramid. It is certainly aligned to the Wolf-Rayet cluster at that date in 9750 B.C.E. Isn't it also a potential warning for us? There are more Wolf-Rayet stars in that cluster.'

'Let me reassure you. Stars form independently from collapsing balls of gas and dust. The axes of other stars in that cluster have no relation to one another, but sure we can consider the chances of another stellar spin axis alignment. It's a statistical phenomenon, and thus highly unlikely. The average inter-stellar separation in the Milky Way is what, 6.5 light years? The entire *gamma Velorum* cluster of Wolf-Rayet stars cannot possibly have the same spin axis alignment. Sure, it's possible but very unlikely,' Carl replied.

'Images from the ESA Max Planck satellite showed us that collapsing molecular clouds of gas and dust are subject to turbulence, which can give *totally random* stellar spin-axis orientations. Alignment of their spin axes would require that the galactic angular momentum gets imparted to stars; that doesn't happen. Sure, planetary accretion disks generally form with the resulting star, disk, and planets rotating and orbiting in the same direction, but gas giant interactions and multiple stars can significantly modify this.'

'Did you agree with the conclusions in Ted's last paper, that *dark matter* halos drive galaxy formation by collecting gas and dust from the intergalactic medium?' Chris asked.

'Sure, and these are all gravitationally interacting in a galaxy cluster, but this is totally chaotic. Planetary formation involves material orbiting the host star millions of times, but *galaxies* which orbit one another, have maybe interacted with each other only a few times in their entire lifetimes, so their orientations are totally random to one another,' Carl explained.

'But just think a little further on that,' Chris reasoned. 'If we consider a small cluster of giant stars, which evolve to become Wolf-Rayet stars, if they form at the same time, they are locally influenced by similar local conditions. We're not talking about random stars, we are considering a cluster. The clouds and dust which form the stars are influenced by the galactic magnetic field . . .'

'He could have a point, Carl' Ted interjected. 'Locally the galactic magnetic field vectors are highly aligned . . .'

Carl started to look a little more serious. 'Guys, we know that generally, elongated dust particles will align with their longest axis at right angles to the galactic magnetic B-field, but in star forming regions, for example the *Orion Molecular Cloud*, the turbulence of collapsing dust clouds creates a *random* spin axis of each resulting accretion disk and thus each subsequent star.'

'But what about the formation of massive stars like the Wolf-Rayet progenitors, which reach 40 times the mass of the Sun? They are believed to form from cores,' Chris replied.

'Chris, there are other theories out there. What about the suggestion that molecular clouds undergo global collapse? This theory doesn't involve cores. The jury is still out on that.'

'Carl, the bottom line for me is, *who has checked the other Wolf-Rayet stars in the nearby gamma Velorum cluster*? Someone needs to image their spin axes and confirm, once and for all, that there is no chance of another GRB and relativistic jet heading our way,' Chris concluded.

'Carl, he's right. It needs investigation. In my view, it's a top priority. Either way, we confirm the axial spins, and rest assured, or determine the time window of an axial alignment of a GRB and relativistic jet. We expect the best outcome, but plan for the worst,' Ted reasoned.

'Why would a previous civilization warn us of what happened in 9750 B.C.E., and where, if there was no danger of it happening again?' Chris added.

At that moment the door of the *Starbucks* opened and in walked Jacqui

Hau. 'Dr Rhodes!' Jacqui called, walking directly towards the group sitting by the window. 'I hoped I might find you here, and I need a coffee.'

'Jacqui! Fantastic to see you,' Carl said, standing and warmly shaking her hand.

'Hi guys, Ted, Chris! Great to see you all. Oh, these yummy doughnuts aren't possibly Chris's *General Relativity* forfeit are they?'

'Sure are,' Ted said. 'They are even served on this special *gold- rimmed Einstein plate* that we keep behind the bar, for this very purpose!'

'Please help yourself, Jacqui. You were here when I mentioned the exoplanet micro-lensing.' Chris added

'Yummy! I will. I'll just grab a coffee.'

'No, you won't Jacqui. I'm treating you,' Carl insisted. 'Please sit down and join us. We're all having a *caffè latte*. What would you like?'

'Maybe I need something a little bolder. The *ristretto* shot and the creamy texture of a *flat white* are what I need right now. So, a *flat white* please, Dr Rhodes.'

'Of course,' Carl replied and headed over to the serving area.

'So, guys, what's the latest? Wasn't Tom Walker's paper simply amazing? Doesn't it throw a few cats among the pigeons?' Jacqui asked excitedly.

'There are a lot of red faces out there. The scientific world will definitely come down really hard on speculation from now on,' Chris remarked.

'What about your *dark matter* paper Chris,' Ted asked teasingly.

'I'm saying nothing. I'm not going to fall for that *General Relativity* bait again.'

'Chris, there's only Ted here. He won't say anything will you Ted?' Jacqui asked.

Ted smiled and shook his head.

'OK. Without mentioning the *G word*, Ted is suggesting that what I wrote was more speculation than *hypothesis based on data*. I simply do not believe that *dark matter* is due to undetectable *WIMPs*, the *Weakly Interacting Massive Particles,* and yet that's what gets hugely funded. It's as if they fund the best suggestion proposed by the most influential astrophysicist. At least the journal *Nature* took a more pragmatic view by agreeing to publish my paper.'

'Carl suggested that you do the math. That doesn't cost much to fund. You could do it on the back of an envelope,' Ted added teasingly.

'Well, we all know that even Einstein couldn't do the math on his own theoretical work. It's a tough ask.'

Carl suddenly appeared at the table, carrying a tray of coffees.

'Here's your *flat white* Jacqui,' Carl said, putting her coffee on the table. 'I bought another round of caffè lattes. Help yourselves, guys. So, what's going on? This table sounds pretty excited from way over there at the bar.'

'I think Ted was trying to taunt Chris to talk about *GR*,' Jacqui said. 'I may have just saved him from another forfeit.'

'He didn't invite us as co-authors. He wanted all the glory,' Ted replied.

'You wouldn't have wanted to risk your reputations. I'm the new guy. I can dare to shout out the radical arguments.'

'Yeah, but it was pretty compelling. And, now that you went front page, we would have liked to reconsider our lack of co-authorship. Didn't you use my pen when you were explaining the principles?' Ted reasoned.

'And my whiteboard! I still have a blue smudge from your proposed equation that you wrote with the wrong kind of pen,' Carl added. 'That must make us part of your knowledge creation process.'

'You guys are kidding, right?' Chris asked.

'Of course!' Carl replied with a broad smile. 'You haven't been teased enough. Don't you have any older brothers, or a sister who teased you relentlessly when you were young?'

'I still do.'

'Changing the conversation,' Carl interjected, 'Jacqui, you haven't confessed why you are back here. This isn't exactly a holiday resort.'

'No, Dr Rhodes,' Jacqui replied, before biting into her doughnut. 'Wow, this cream doughnut is indeed divine! No, I'm not on holiday. I was hoping to get you to talk to the people responsible for SETI data collection up at Hat Creek, to do targeted data collection from stars with known exoplanets, over long periods, ...ten hours say? What about even contacting Parkes so we could get more data from proxima Centauri? Almost all the other radio telescopes are too far north. We also have the 64-dish MeerKAT array in South Africa of course!' she added, suggestively.

'Well, that's a rather bold request, Jacqui. Obviously the reason you needed that *ristretto* shot in your *flat white*! You know that scheduling radio data collection is extremely expensive, don't you?'

'But, Tom Walker's paper suggests that it's at least worth a try. We know the period of the exoplanets. We should just monitor a stellar system hosting exoplanets having the most potential. What about *crowd funding*?'

'Carl, that sounds pretty reasonable, doesn't it? We could get someone in the faculty to set the web-page up,' Ted added.

'OK, one target, several hours of data collected during the transit periods. Personally, I would propose that we go and talk to *Goddard Space Flight Center*. Jacqui, that's NASA. That has to be your home turf. You spoke to them right? I'm sure you did,' Carl reasoned.

'I couldn't get in. It's so difficult to move between different departments in NASA. They're very protective, and I'm from *AMES*, remember. *Goddard* departments are like *in lockdown*. All the different NASA organisations have reputations to protect.'

'I know an important guy at *Goddard,* and someone who owes me *bigtime.* I can just pick up the phone and we're in.'

'Carl, remind me. Why is *Goddard* so important here?' Ted asked.

'It's about the huge work they did with the *Kepler* space telescope launched in 2009. It only had a three-and-a-half year mission for detecting exoplanets using the *transit method*, detecting dips in stellar brightness during the exoplanet transit. By mid-2013, *Kepler* had failed. Then, after some brilliant critical lateral thinking and focused space science engineering, *Goddard* managed to resurrect Kepler for mission *K2*. They managed to keep it running way up until 2018, Now the newest kid on the block is *TESS, the Transiting Exoplanet Surveying Satellite*. While *Kepler* only looked at a small patch of sky, *TESS* will attempt to scan almost the entire sky and map all the nearest exoplanets out there. With a little help, *Goddard* could help identify a subset of good candidates and we can use that to best direct any SETI initiatives.'

'That sounds cool,' Jacqui replied with an excited voice. 'I'm glad I found you guys here!'

'That's what we do,' Ted replied. 'Some of us must get the SETI mission fully back on track and processing the most meaningful data.'

'Jacqui, I propose that I call my guy at *Goddard* next week. If they can agree to send us the coordinates of the most promising nearby exoplanet candidates, we can then be selective with the SETI Hat Creek radio telescope array and direct it to those candidates. *TESS* was launched back in April 2018, so they may already have some data for us.'

'Thanks Dr Rhodes.'

'You are welcome to call me *Carl*, Jacqui. I think we should be on first name terms by now.'

'Well that might be difficult for me to get used to, but I will try, Dr Rhodes,' Jacqui replied shyly.

'You know, there's another important aspect of Tom Walker's paper which could heavily impact the entire SETI program,' Ted interjected.

'What do you mean Ted,' Carl asked.

'Well, a relativistic jet is absolutely enormous. It must have been tens of light years in diameter and passed the solar system at a distance of tens of light years. Life on Earth barely survived. It must mean that there is a vast tunnel of space where stars and exoplanets were totally destroyed, and life annihilated or seriously diminished. On one side of the solar system there is indeed probably little or no life on any of the exoplanets at all for tens of light years,' Ted explained.

'My goodness,' Jacqui replied. 'You are right. How shocking to realise that! Indeed, if life on Earth was almost completely extinguished some 11,700 years ago, and we were at such a vast distance from the jet, someone should now rethink the SETI strategy. I guess it also adds a new parameter to the *Drake Equation*: the likelihood of being close enough to an axially aligned Wolf-Rayet hypernova W_{HN} and being affected by the transit of a relativistic jet.'

$$N = R_* \cdot f_P \cdot n_e \cdot f_l \cdot f_i \cdot f_c \cdot L \cdot \underline{\mathbf{W}}_{\scriptscriptstyle HN}$$

Corrected Drake Equation

'Wow! Well said. That's definitely worth a paper Jacqui,' Carl added. 'It will be a very important one. It also adds another dimension to the *Fermi Paradox* and a meaning to the *Great Filter*. The Earth has indeed survived an extinction event, while others probably did not. By the way, any surviving civilizations on nearby planets may have concluded that life was completely annihilated here. That now explains the total lack of visits.'

'Precisely! Even if any intelligent lifeforms were close enough, and bothered enough, to go to the huge resource commitment to visit the Earth, they would have cancelled the trip, given the unlikelihood of life surviving here,' Chris added.

There was suddenly a moment of stunned silence.

'Is there anything positive we can take from this?' Jacqui asked.

'Well, I'm afraid it's a very sobering realisation,' Carl replied.

'So any nearby advanced civilizations probably all think life was completely extinguished here,' Ted murmured to himself. 'Hang on. Isn't the positive aspect that we can take from all this, is that we should now make every effort to communicate with exoplanets on the other live side of the Solar System. Tell them we are still here!'

'He's right Dr Rhodes,' Jacqui added. 'We should write the paper and point out a new and positive direction for SETI.'

'All willing co-authors are welcome,' Ted replied. 'This will be a lot of work with many angles to cover. By the way guys, I think we should keep a lid on this until the paper is written. This story is really important to get right.'

'That sounds like a plan,' Carl added.

'Jacqui, apart from our new joint paper, what else will you be up to these days?' Ted asked.

'Well I'll continue looking into galactic magnetism, particularly the magnetic structure of the Milky Way. All galactic objects: stars, planets, pulsars, other galaxies, all have magnetic fields which interact. There is even a *dark magnetism* which permeates the Cosmos.'

'Interesting. So, what is the key research question you're trying to solve?' Ted asked.

'Well, we know from Voyager 1, that when it reached interstellar space back in 2012, it measured the field strength to be around half a nano-Tesla. By comparison, the Earth has a magnetic field of between 25 and 65 micro-Teslas. The problem is that we can't explain the micro and macro structure. Until now, I was just wondering if there was another source of moving charged particles which periodically flood the galactic disk and maintain the galactic magnetism. You know what, Tom Walker may have found it!'

'Wow, you may be right,' Carl said. 'That's yet *another* paper worth writing. By the way, it goes without saying that, as your friend, if you ever come up with anything really good, you will add me as a co-author!'

'And me,' Ted remarked.

'And me too!' Chris said.

'What? Are you kidding me? You're kidding right? Well, I would be very happy to add you as co-authors of the paper I haven't even started to write yet, if you might just make a small contribution to the mathematical modelling, or the radio telescope work, or maybe the money for the research,' Jacqui quickly retorted.

'It's a deal then!' Carl concluded with a broad smile.

Everyone started laughing. Jacqui smiled then looked at her watch.

'Guys, I need to catch my flight back to AMES, so I will say *adieu*,' Jacqui said. 'I will grab an *Uber*,'

'No, I can drive you to the airport. I need to be across town this afternoon. My car is just outside. We can leave right away.'

'Thanks Dr Rhodes, er, I mean Carl. See you next time, guys.'

Chris and Ted waved them off as they walked out of *Starbucks*.

'Jacqui is such fun,' Ted remarked. 'Maybe we shouldn't tease her so much.'

'Come on, we love to tease her!' Chris replied.

'You are right of course. Let's get back. Time to start work again.'

4 New South Wales: Göbekli Tepe pillars, Dendera and the relativistic jet transit

The Homestead, Wahroonga, Sydney, New South Wales

Patrick was having a ten-day break from his Mom and Dad. They had left for St. Lucia for some kind of *second honeymoon* celebration in the Caribbean. It had been a sudden decision. The past few weeks had been really hectic, with even a TV film crew camped outside the house for two days, while they conducted interviews with his father. The discovery of such a fundamentally important part of Earth's recent history now somewhat transformed the concept of *climate change*, particularly when a planet-destroying event could happen again in the not too distant future.

It was late evening and Patrick was sitting at the kitchen table looking at a whole pile of articles he had downloaded describing different versions of the Australian indigenous peoples' *Rainbow Serpent Myth*. He had read his Dad's and Uncle Chad's paper several times and he was hoping that he might be able to find a few more clues closer to home. His father had challenged him to find anything he could within the published versions of the *Dreamtime* stories. If he found anything substantial he would be allowed to be a co-author. That was a challenge worth seizing! To that aim, his Mom had helped him find several good articles before they had left for the Caribbean.

Patrick had also sent a long email to Manu, his *Facebook* buddy in Ghana, asking him to look further for any links to Sirius. Manu had recently described the most fascinating adventure that he had been on to Mali, and in response, Patrick had asked him to take a closer look at some carvings of mysterious Egyptian friezes in *Dendera* near Luxor, which might be relevant. Surely the importance of Sirius was substantially more than just a star which marked the flooding of the Nile and the start of the Egyptian growing season.

While he waited for Manu's reply, he would crack on with his *Rainbow Serpent* research. The most interesting publication that Patrick had found so far seemed to be one entitled *The Rainbow Serpent Myth of Australia*, published way back in 1926 by some eminent anthropologist *Alfred Radcliffe-Brown*. Oral interviews had been conducted with members of different tribes and these seemed to suggest very positive clues. His Dad had asked him to try to interpret the different stories scientifically, as if each part of the story was a metaphor for something. He decided he would build a table logging the different names for the *Rainbow Serpent* for each tribe, and their location, as well as any key beliefs and attributes of each story.

Of course, Radcliffe-Brown had just set out to gather alternative versions of a potentially fictitious belief. Patrick, however, was analysing the different tribal stories to try to find possible elements which described actual credible effects caused by a relativistic jet. Across the whole of the continent, the indigenous tribes described a *flying rainbow serpent*, which was associated with water and thunderstorms and danger and death. It was seeming increasingly obvious, from his discussions with his Dad and Uncle Chad, that the rainbow colours were most likely a description of some kind of endless *Southern Lights* aurorae caused by charged particles hitting the upper atmosphere. If these were seen all over the continent of Australia, that was significant because the *Aurora Australis* southern lights can only ever be seen from the very southern coast of Australia, looking south towards the Antarctic.

Many stories were obscure. Up in Queensland, in the northeast, one tribe talked of a water-snake called *Kanmare*, which pointed a *death-bone* at a man who might be fishing, and whose form could be seen against the night sky. Once struck, the fisherman became sick, and was only cured when the *death-bone* was removed.

In North Queensland, the rainbow snake was called *Andrénjinyi*, and one which could *stop* the rain. Along the Queensland coast, the *Kabi* tribe described a rainbow fish-snake called *Dhakkan*, which possessed terrific power and could shatter scrubs and mountains, and even kill humans. A man lying down beside *Dhakkan's* watery dwelling would develop a prickly sensation in his limbs. In many instances the man's body had crystals or *kundir* inside which needed to be extracted.

Other reports from the natives of the *Yualai* in New South Wales said that their *Rainbow Serpent, Kurreah*, could be seen as a dark wavy shadow along the course of the Milky Way, and how painting this snake-form would help *bring* rain.

Patrick was now convinced he was onto something. Of course, at night, the relativistic jet, which had a *snake-like* form according to his father, may have blocked out the stars either side of it on a clear night. Was the presence of the jet associated with heavy rain? It was possible that it may have caused significant changes in the weather systems.

Then he saw it. This had to be a breakthrough. The *Wirajuri* tribe of New South Wales described that when a man was going to visit the *Wãwi* serpent, he needed to *paint himself with red ochre*! Patrick had read that red ochre, and the white clay pigment, which they used to paint their skins, were known to be good for sun protection. That white clay contained titanium oxide, a natural sunblock against ultraviolet. Surely, that suggested that the *Rainbow Serpent* was associated with high levels of ultraviolet light. That could even be the reason why the Australian indigenous peoples had survived if the tribes had already been using a natural sunblock on their skins.

Patrick read on. Apparently, a dark streak seen in the night sky against the Milky Way was considered by the *Wirajuri* to be an ancestor of the *Wãwi* serpent. Here was a description of a snakelike form in the night sky.

Different tribes said other things. In the Melbourne district, the ground around where a monstrous serpent *Myndie* lived was covered with small white rocks like rain. Could this be a reference to violent hail storms? In the Perth district, the creature was called *Wogal*, and all manner of sores and wounds were attributed to it. This seemed to suggest that the *Rainbow Serpent* relativistic jet was dangerous when it was in the sky, but surely it was always in the sky. No, of course, the Earth was rotating, and it would rise and set with the stars. Patrick's Dad had set him the challenge, and now he felt he was really making progress. Many tribes described how the *Rainbow Serpent* caused rain. That surely meant that weather systems must have been totally wild and dramatically different from today's normal weather.

The *Warramunga* tribe of The Northern Territory now gave a hint of the size of the jet. They spoke of a huge beast called *Wollunqua,* which most likely was their version of the *Rainbow Serpent,* which if it were to stand on its tail, its head would reach far away into the heavens.

Finally, Patrick found one of the most detailed accounts of the *Rainbow Serpent* as told by the *Kakadu* tribes of the Northern Territory, whom they call *Numereji*. They claimed that only the medicine-men could withstand its glance, suggesting that seeing it caused blindness. This totally supported the *myth of Medusa*. They also told of whole camps of people who were killed by it. Interestingly, ancient cave paintings in the north west not only showed the *Rainbow Serpent* singly but also in pairs and sometimes in larger groups, where the serpents were interpreted as beings which devoured people.

The stories clearly had common elements. Hopefully he could convince his father.

Beside him on the table was another pile of assorted papers. His eye caught the one on the top, it was the image he had sent Manu earlier of the mysterious frieze elements, carved into the wall of grey-green stone in the underground crypt at Hathor's Temple, in Dendera. It continued to perplex him. It had become known as the *Dendera Lightbulb* after *Erich von Däniken* had popularised the story about ancient Egyptian technology in his famous book *Chariots of the Gods*. No one had really explained what that frieze meant. Two large figures stood facing one another, each holding out a long opening triangular cocoon, in which a snake, with its head curved back, was emerging from a kind of flower, to form the *Dendera lightbulb* filament, within its cocoon bulb. Underneath each cocoon were two figures. Each triangular cocoon had the same crouching person underneath, about halfway, while at each end, one had a figure with a ball on its head, and the other had a strange stack of blocks.

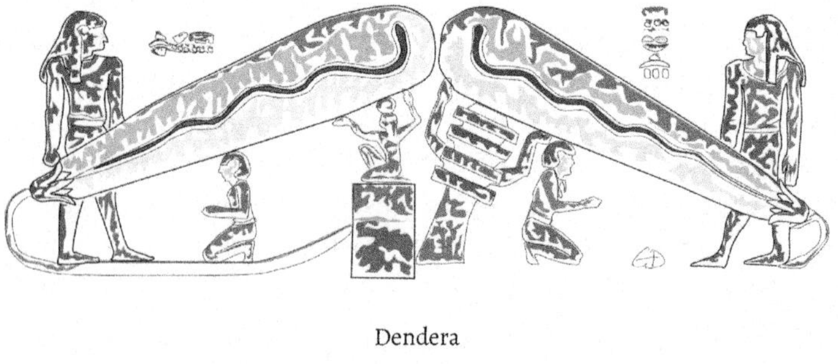

Dendera

At that moment his phone buzzed. He lifted it up and saw the incoming Messenger message from Manu: *Hi Patrick, I found some very interesting links to stars and the relativistic jet in the Dendera wall friezes. Check your email!*

Patrick took out his iPad and opened Manu's email. Manu had added text boxes and arrows to his photo of the *Dendera Lightbulb* frieze and a long email of explanation.

He looked at the reprocessed image. What had Manu found? He had drawn lines to emphasise that the two cocoons were both expanding and rising at 30°. He had also put rings around the figures at each end, which seemed to be holding up the cocoon at an angle: the one with a ball on its head and the block structure. Beside the block structure, he had added, *this is a Djed pillar.*

Was Manu suggesting that this was a relativistic jet? If so, the imagery had always definitely been misunderstood. What else had he found? Beside the flower-like opening, from which the snake filament seemed to emerge, Manu had added: *Can't this be a nebula remnant from a supernova event?* What if this were true? It was still not clear why the snake-like relativistic jet's head was curved round, and if it were a relativistic jet maybe his Dad had the explanation.

He then read Manu's attached email.

'Patrick, the Djed pillar is the coffin of Osiris. So many people have described Osiris as Orion, but Orion is a constellation! After checking hundreds of articles online, I am now convinced that the Djed pillar represents Rigel, the toe-star of Orion. The guy with a ball on his head is Ra, the Sun god. Surely this is a representation of a sunrise and sunset view of the same jet in the sky. It's actually quite tricky to visualise, but hold out a pen at arm's length, at an angle. Move your hand up, over your head and behind you, and now look over your shoulder. The pen is still pointing up at an angle, but you now see it going the other way. As the Earth rotated underneath the jet in the sky, the jet would have remained pointing upwards at the same angle, but it would have changed direction and pointed the other way like in the other image. In the first image, Ra is under the jet. In the second image, Rigel is depicted under it. These two images must be describing when the Sun and Rigel were above the horizon at different times. They are specifying a time of the year.

Patrick took a pen in his right hand and lifted it up, and then around over his head behind him. Sure enough, when he looked behind him, the raised pen had just changed direction. Wow, that was interesting. On a second photo from *Dendera*, everything from the double jet image now seemed to be crammed in altogether. Both *Ra*, the sun god, and the *Djed* pillar representing *Rigel* in Orion, were now under the jet. In the double image, each jet had a single kneeling character below it. Now there were two characters kneeling under the jet. In this image, the *Djed* pillar had outstretched arms actually touching the jet, whereas in the first image of the two jets, the arms of the *Djed* pillar were under the jet. Could this mean that the jet passed close to Rigel in the sky? To the right of this second single jet carving, stood a large, weird-looking, frog-faced baboon, holding two knives. Beside him was a vertical script of hieroglyphs. Manu had added text with an arrow pointing at the hieroglyphs: *many translate this as a warning*.

Patrick started to think about something he had read earlier about the *Rainbow Serpent* myth. What did it say? He checked his notes. The jet made a dark shadow against the sky. Did the orientation of the jet change during the year? No, that wasn't possible. His father had concluded that it was coming from the *gamma Velorum* cluster, effectively in the galactic plane. The only moving aspect was the Earth observer's horizon, and that determined how high the stars rose in the sky. As the Earth orbited around the Sun, the backdrop of stars changed, rising earlier by 3 minutes 52 seconds each night. This meant that the Sun would be in the sky with Rigel for some part of the year, and not for the rest. Was this the encoded message in this frieze?

Patrick started his *Stellarium* program. He then set the location to Giza and sent the program back in time to 9750 B.C.E. He then logged down the rising and setting times of *Rigel* for the 21st of each month. He then checked the sunrise and sunset times against that. Now he had it. So, Rigel and the Sun were in the sky at the same time from late December to mid-June, with the longest time occurring from late January to late April. Did this indicate a warning time?

Well, that might suggest that the *combination* of the Sun and the jet was a danger. The frog-faced baboon standing off to the side, holding the two knives, looked pretty mean and most likely could be signifying something bad. That would logically mean that the jet interacted with the Sun somehow during those months when Rigel was in the daytime sky. He would probably need to ask his Dad for the final analysis of that discovery. He walked over to the small white board in the kitchen. His Dad had drawn a sketch of the solar system relative to the centre of the galaxy. The Earth was closest to the galactic centre in June and furthest away in December. The solar system was at an angle of 62° to the plane of the galaxy, rising up above it in March, and dropping down below it in September. Now he saw something new. Surely he and Manu had now located the jet! If it was dangerous from December to June, then that surely suggested the part of the Earth's orbit when the Earth was between the Sun and the jet. That surely put the jet on the March side of the orbit, and above the Galactic plane, because it was apparently less dangerous when the Earth was on the other side of the Sun from June 21st to December 21st.

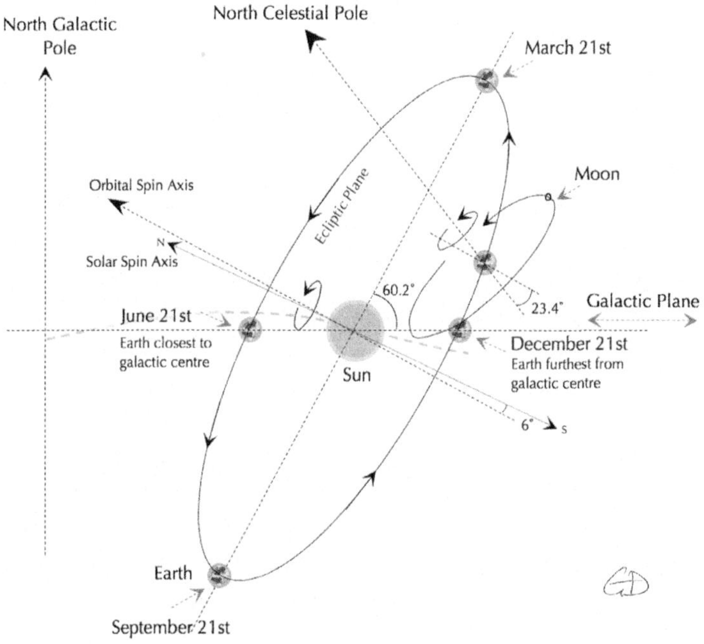

Solar System

Patrick was really excited. He decided to forward Manu's email to his Dad with a few extra notes and questions. So, just from a few wall friezes in Dendera Egypt, he and Manu had worked out where, relative to the solar system, the jet was in the sky. He looked again at his notes about the Australian indigenous peoples. Had he discovered something else relative to the physical experience of the jet for people who lived at that time? The *Medusa myth* had talked of people being *turned to stone* if they saw the jet. In the *Rainbow Serpent* stories, tribes both talked of needing to cover their skins with white clay and red ochre. Re-reading it again, he decided it was surely a description of men who *turned to stone*. Covering your body in white clay and red ochre, should certainly protect your skin from ultraviolet light. He would send that interpretation in his email also. He read through his additions one last time, then added a question about the curved head of the jet, as depicted in the image of the snake, then sent his reply both to his Dad and to Manu.

It was late evening in New South Wales. It was around midday in Ghana and 7 a.m. in St. Lucia. Hopefully it wasn't too early to send a message. His Dad may have switched off his phone at night. Nevertheless he would still send it.

Within a few minutes his email box chimed. It was a mail already from his Dad, and quite a long one: *Hi Patrick, fantastic work. Well done! That is amazing. I am utterly amazed by your and Manu's deciphering of the Dendera frieze! You are the first guys on the planet to do that! I believe that you have definitely discovered where the jet passed our solar system. BTW the reason why it is so dangerous when the Earth is between the Sun and the Jet, is that the Earth has no protection from the high flux of high energy charged particles from the Sun's solar wind, which is effectively being dragged towards the Jet. When the Earth is on the far side of the Sun, the solar wind is effectively dragged towards the jet and away from the Earth. It is sobering to think that this transit lasted some 880 years, with all the danger to life and catastrophes that went with it. I am so impressed with your findings. Your interpretation of how Medusa turned people to stone, and the possible association with how the indigenous Australians covered themselves with red and white clay, is equally a great deduction. The answer to your brilliant question about the curved head of the snake is quite obvious, but that is why questions are so important. This has never been described in the literature, but I immediately realise that, in the first few seconds as the jet emerges from the dying star, the head of the jet is dragged around the collapsing star, following the star's intense polar magnetic field lines. The plasma of the jet carries the shape of the magnetic field frozen within it, as it propagates – just like how coronal mass ejections of plasma from the Sun preserve the shape of the solar magnetic field. Very inspirational conclusions. I hope you might consider allowing me to be a co-author on your and Manu's paper. Congratulations!*

Wow, his Dad wanted to be a co-author on *his* paper. He read on. *Btw … I guess you're all packed and ready for your pick up tomorrow to Victoria to visit the Carisbrook and Wurdi Youang indigenous ancient stone formations. Have a really great time and keep your mind open to new interpretations. We're having a fantastic time here. Chad and Jeanette are arriving tomorrow, and we'll have a few days together partying here. Hugs and love, Dad and Mom*

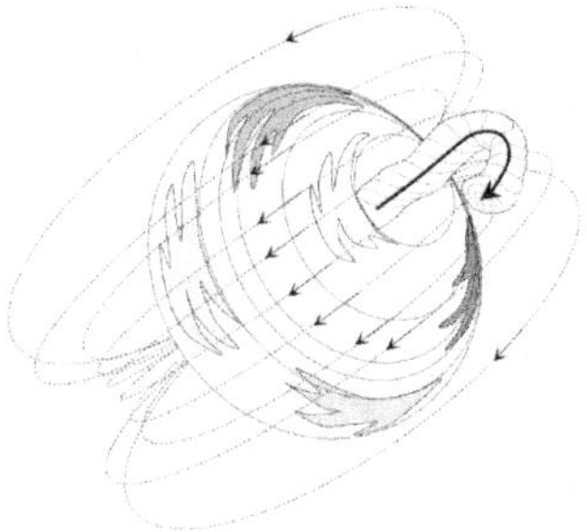

Jet emerging from dying Wolf-Rayet star

Patrick was really happy. He had managed to solve part of the puzzle before his father, and all thanks to Manu having interpreted the Egyptian Hathor frieze images. It surely had to mean that the friezes predated the Dynastic Egyptians by some 7000 years! That hunch of his father's, to check out the *Rainbow Serpent* myths from different tribes had also paid off. He was feeling like a real researcher. He was 16 years old next month. His trip down to Victoria might even confirm his hunch that those indigenous people's stone formations were possibly also linked to the relativistic jet mystery. Perhaps there were more clues there. He certainly had not wanted a holiday with his parents at a resort, even in the Caribbean. He was now entering his *walkabout years*, when he would start to meet the World on his own, in brave, bite-size chunks. This hiking trip would be the first of hopefully, many such excursions.

Although it was quite late, Patrick looked at his Mom's pile of notes and academic papers about Göbekli Tepe. If only he could add a new interpretation there. Was there possibly a carving there which warned of the relativistic jet cataclysm?

He looked at one photo entitled *Pillar 43: The Vulture Stone*. His Mom had suggested that the animal carvings on the stone were constellation imagery, but how could they possibly be interpreted? Different peoples around the World had defined their own constellations, linking different stars in unique ways to form all types of birds and fish and animals. Göbekli Tepe dated from at least 11,800 years ago. That was before the date of the cataclysm. There was every reason to imagine that the people there may have recorded the date of the cataclysm as part of the pillar stone imagery for future generations. What could be the starting point for him to find something new? His Mom might be really impressed if he could do that!

He again opened *Stellarium* and selected a town near to Göbekli Tepe, then ran the clock back to August 7th, 9750 B.C.E. So, what did the night sky look like back then?

As a new hypothesis, could he map the animals carved on the *Vulture Stone* to constellations in the sky? Had anyone tried this before?

He launched his browser and found several papers where academics had done a kind of reverse logic, deciding that the stone was describing an impact from the *Taurid* meteor shower. They had then selected 10,950 B.C.E., the date of an increased platinum spike in the Greenland ice core data, and then imposed the night sky upon the constellation imagery, but hardly any of the stars mapped at all to the shapes on the pillar. He wasn't a scientist, but surely that wasn't a scientific method? It just didn't seem logical that the Göbekli Tepe people would build an entire settlement dedicated to a disaster. Surely the settlement had a more practical value!

Patrick, of course, had his own hunch about the carvings representing an event, but it would need to be convincing at the stellar level. He supposed as his starting point, that it might describe the cataclysm recorded in the Giza pyramid, but if the stars didn't match the constellations to a very high degree, he would dismiss it outright. If anyone had created this carving of star patterns on a stone pillar, *each and every pattern* should trace through stars in the night sky. The big challenge would be *where* in the

Göbekli Tepe: Pillar 43

night sky could he look? Giza was marking the *gamma Velorum Wolf-Rayet cluster* at zero degrees elevation, 180° due south. If he was right, that *Vulture Stone* pillar, would decode to show several constellations which were used by these people some 11,800 years ago. If he could find one of them in the night sky, he would find them all, and for the first time, be able to decode their constellations into the animal shapes they used as constellations back then. Wow, that was a pretty tough challenge, but he would attempt it.

The *Vulture Stone* was a T-shaped limestone pillar, several metres tall. The photo showed the pillar somewhat embedded in a side wall but starting from the base, he could make out some carved images. There seemed to be a long-necked bird or something, and a headless man to its right. Above this was a scorpion, which had a large vulture with open wings to its upper left, and a pair of birds with a snake and two squarish, hand-weights to its upper right. Just above the right wing of the vulture, was a ball, which seemed to occupy the absolute centre of the pillar carvings, as if it were the *focal point* of the entire pillar. Above the ball, between the two birds and the vulture, was a line of eleven small square blocks surrounded by a line of reverse triangles either side of the blocks. Finally, at the top of the pillar were three large rectangles, each having a large curved line extending from the left hand end, to about two thirds of the way across. Above the last third of each rectangle, was a different carved creature. The top edge of the pillar was finished off with a multi-lined zigzag.

This would be difficult to crack. *Stellarium* allowed the user to change the constellation types, and Patrick ran through the list of 20 or more indigenous people's constellation patterns and names. Pillar 43 had that large scorpion at the bottom and it was interesting to see that so many indigenous peoples identified a scorpion for that same collection of stars. That seemed a good possibility here also, so he would start by trying to map that part of the stone image onto the constellation *Scorpio*. Looking at the night sky, it was very difficult to compare the images on the pillar with the stars directly. He would need to get the *Vulture Stone* images somehow on top of an image of the stars in the night sky as a semi-transparent overlay.

First, he needed to find *Scorpio*. He selected Western constellations. Now he adjusted the direction in the night sky to get *Scorpio* pointing upwards and to the left, like on the pillar. After some further thinking, he decided to take a screen shot of the night sky, paste it into a Word document, then create images of the animal shapes from the pillar. He took a screen shot of the pillar, then carefully drew each animal figure, and coloured them in yellow with 70% transparency. He grouped all the images, then positioned them over a jpeg-image of the screenshot of the night sky looking east. After an hour of scaling adjustments and image rotations, he finally believed the overlay images from the pillar matched the stars in the sky from 9750 B.C.E.

This had been painstaking work, but now more than 50 of the stars lined up fairly well with the animal outlines. Most importantly, a small group of stars followed the body of the headless man perfectly.

He rotated the image another 5°, and then the alignment was uncanny, but what was that? Directly *bullseye* inside the ball above the vulture's wing was a very bright star. He selected star-names, and he saw it. It was *Spica*. He quickly went online. This was unbelievable, *Spica* was described as a blue sub-giant star, and on a special list of *next-to-supernova* candidates! Patrick had possibly decoded pillar 43.

Pillar 43 with Star-Mapping

This was unbelievable! He took his phone and made three shots of the Vulture Stone, his digitised images, and the overlay on top of the star map for 10:18 and 23 seconds on August 7th, 9750 B.C.E. He then sent the three images to his Dad's phone with a message: *Hi Dad, what do you think of this? Ask Mom what she thinks? Have I possibly decoded the Vulture Stone at Göbekli Tepe? Hugs Patrick.*

Patrick was expecting a message back, but after a few minutes, his phone started ringing. It was his mom calling. He answered the phone.

'Hi Mom! This is a surprise?'

There was a slight pause before he heard her voice. He had already checked the distance earlier. They were more than 16,000 km apart.

'Hi Patrick, just wow, this is absolutely fantastic what you have achieved. I am in shock. My goodness, archaeologists have struggled for years trying to make sense of that imagery. This is sensational. I can't start to tell you just how important this is. I just wanted to call you and congratulate you. I am so proud of you,' Mary-Anne said warmly.

'Wow Mom, thanks. I just followed a hunch and added a bit of scientific method. I have to confess that it was pretty exhausting work. I almost gave up at one point.'

'I am so excited for you that you didn't. It shows that perseverance often reaps the rewards.'

'Mom, do you think I now qualify to be a co-author on your next paper?'

'No, I would like to ask if *I* might be a co-author on *your* paper. In fact, I have decided to email Professor Cayman at UTS immediately and insist that we don't accept the final approval for my last publication. I only alluded to *constellation imagery* at Göbekli Tepe and just cited those other papers. Now I can see those papers are wrong and without merit. I want to add your material and research in, and I will insist that you *will* be a co-author.'

'*A co-author*? Wow Mom! Thanks! It is so sweet of you to call me to say that.'

'No, thank *you*! You are a young genius, and I am so proud of you, and I love you. So, does your Dad of course. Have a lovely hiking holiday. You have certainly earned it now! I send you all our love, and we'll see you when we get back from St. Lucia.'

'Thanks Mom. Have a great time in St. Lucia.'

'Bye Patrick.'

'Bye Mom,' and then the call ended.

Patrick just knew that this had been a huge day for him. He had discovered new reasoning and evidence for several new aspects which supported the hypothesis that the Earth suffered a Wolf-Rayet cataclysm event. The whole story seemed so much more credible now.

His bags were already packed, he only need set the alarm clock for 5 a.m. and he would be ready for his pick-up. He would send a last email to Manu explaining everything. After that he would crash. It had been another exciting day.

5 Xochicalco, Mexico: analysis of an ancient serpent monument to a cataclysm

Xochicalco, South of Mexico City

The journey down to Xochicalco went quickly by. Takashi and Chad were in buoyant conversation about Japanese culture customs and the intricacies of sword making. Soon the subject switched to Chad's whirlwind discovery of evidence for the relativistic jet cataclysm during three exhausting days in Cairo and how he had discovered so many clues. Chad had digitised Mustapha's book of notes and had stored them on his iPhone. Now he was showing Takashi the images and notes Mustapha had made about Central and South America.

'I do find it intriguing that your prestigious museum curator Mustapha didn't discover *Xochicalco*. Perhaps it is so far off the beaten track. I know that we will probably find the place deserted in the middle of Summer,' Takashi explained.

'I don't think Mustapha had discovered that there was a relativistic jet, so he didn't have a connection to the snake in the sky. I'm on the trail of flying coloured snakes and the *Feathered Serpent* fits that exactly.'

The ring road around Mexico City was far behind them and they were heading south along the 95D toll road towards the turn-off to *Xochicalco*. It was still some distance there when their driver, Manolo, then spoke.

'Señores, I know you want to go to *Xochicalco*, but I think I heard you talking about your interest in the *Temple of the Feathered Serpent*. In about five kilometres we pass the turn-off to *Tepoztlán* where there is another famous *Temple of the Feathered Serpent*. Do you want me to go on a detour via *Tepoztlán*?'

'Manolo, that sounds interesting, but maybe we should do that on the way back. Do you agree Takashi-san?'

'I do. What's the time now? OK, coming up to 1.30 p.m. Let's plan the return trip via *Tepoztlán*, if we are still up for it.'

'Of course, Señores. We didn't talk about it, but there won't be many *Uber* drivers anywhere near the remote site of *Xochicalco*. I am happy to wait for you, to bring you back after your visit.'

'Thanks for thinking ahead Manolo. We definitely need a lift back,' Takashi confirmed. 'I guess we won't need more than about an hour, tops. By the way where has all this green landscape suddenly come from?'

'OK, so this woodland around us is *Parque Nacional El Tepozteco*. Soon we'll see the 1150 to *Tepoztlán*. It's only ten kilometres from there. We come back the same way.'

'Do you know much about *Tepoztlán*?' Chad asked.

'Of course, Señor. I do the trip often. They say it has the oldest *Temple of the Feathered Serpent*, and the town around it was founded by *Quetzalcoatl* himself.'

'But wasn't *Quetzalcoatl* someone who named himself after the *Feathered Serpent*?' Chad asked.

'Well, you could be right about that of course,' Manolo replied. 'I should add that *Tepoztlán* has quite a lot of Mexican culture to experience. With the Aztec steam baths, it is now a *Mecca* for health and rejuvenation. There are good places to eat. It is also the place in Mexico where the most UFOs are sighted, whatever that means! The *El Tepozteco* Pyramid, stands high above the town. It is a two hour hike. If you only spend an hour at *Xochicalco*, you could make it up the trail for sunset.'

'Sounds good!' Takashi said. 'The most UFOs sighted! That sounds interesting also.'

'So, is *Tepoztlán* a very old town?' Chad asked.

'Well Señor, the earliest pottery and artefacts date back some 2500 years, but the Spanish Conquistadore, *Hernán Cortés*, burned the place to the ground in 1521 during his campaign against the Aztecs. There was a misunderstanding when the elders there refused to become his ally. The stone pyramid, high above the town, is the only building that survived.'

'Interesting,' Takashi remarked. 'OK, if we do call in on the way back, maybe we should just focus on the pyramid there.'

They turned off the 95D *Autopista* to join the 1150, heading south-east.

'I can't drive all the way to the pyramid, but you can hike up there and back in about 2 hours. I am sure you will see everything you want in 20 minutes at the top. It's a nice forest trail walk. A little steep, but obviously no problem for you guys.'

'Hey, Takashi-san, I just noticed a sign saying we are now 600 metres lower than Mexico City. We're now at 1640m. Perhaps I will be even less out of breath also.'

'Remember, I was just teasing you. Indeed, Mexico is over 2200m in altitude. The air is thinner. As I said before, you are much fitter than you thought, Chad-san.'

'Ha ha! I was a little concerned, but not anymore.'

Soon they were passing a large town on the left-hand side.

'What's this place?' Chad asked.

'That is *Cuernavaca*, Señores, that is more of a tourist place. Nothing for you I think, if you are hunting *Feathered Serpents*!'

After another twenty minutes, they turned off the 95D and took the road north to *Xochicalco*. 'It's not far now,' Manolo said. 'It's about ten kilometres. I will head off to get some lunch while you are on the site. Señores, can I get you anything for the way back?'

'That's really kind Manolo. Whatever you're having, just get a couple more for me and Takashi-san.'

'Well Señores, I will be having *quesadilla huitlacoche*, which is made from corn fungus. If you haven't had that before, I would suggest something that maybe you are more used to.'

'Aha. OK, you may be right,' Chad reasoned. 'Also, please don't get *dorilocos*, I don't think my taste buds are up for such a mixture of flavours.'

'I wouldn't do that. My children love *dorilocos* but that is the epitome of junk food here,' Manolo replied.

'What about you, Takashi-san? Have you found a food that you would recommend?'

'Chad-san, you know that we Japanese love all manner of raw food and seafood. I had a really great *octopus ceviche tostada* yesterday! It was seasoned with cilantro. It was absolutely delicious, if you like octopus, of course'

'*Polpo tostada* is one of my favourites also!' Manolo added.

Chad did not look so keen. 'I must confess I'm not such a big octopus fan.'

'Well, have you tried *torta de chilaquiles*? That is fried tortillas, cooked in a green chili salsa. They serve it in a bread roll with chicken and sour cream and cheese,' Manolo suggested.

'That sounds perfect for me.'

The road continued above a deep river valley to their left. There were a few hairpins until they reached the small village of *San Agustin Tetlama*.

'Señores, next stop *Xochicalco*. I will drop you guys off by the museum. You can buy your ticket there. You have my number and I have your food orders: one *polpo tostada*, and one *torta de chilaquiles*!'

The taxi pulled off the road by the entrance and Chad and Takashi got out.

Manolo wound down his window. 'Have a good time guys. I'll see you later. I'll be back here in about an hour.'

'Thanks Manolo. We'll send you a text when we're ready. I'm sure we won't need more than an hour. An hour sounds good,' Chad replied.

Chad and Takashi then walked towards the entrance.

'Takashi-san shall we do the museum first?'

'Yes, good idea. I read that there are quite a number of large artefacts from the different peoples who occupied this site over the past few thousand years. The official story is that the site was occupied from 200 B.C.E. and the city was founded in 650 C.E. by the Olmec, who flourished here for 250 years before it was burned to the ground around 900 B.C.E. Later, Nahuatl-speaking indigenous peoples recolonised the place after 1200 C.E.'

They bought their tickets and entered the museum. Chad picked up a leaflet at the desk. On the front were photographs of the site with the different temples, and Xochicalco's underground observatory.

'This has been designated a *UNESCO World Heritage Site* since 1999,' Chad read out. 'Apparently, it means *in the house of flowers* in the *Nahuatl* language. I didn't know there was an underground structure. I find this really intriguing. Every one of these sites always seems to have some kind of associated underground complex associated with it!'

'It does sound very significant,' Takashi remarked. 'Hey, shall we spend all our time out on the site rather than in this museum? I'm more interested to evaluate the megalithic carvings on that *Temple of the Feathered Serpent*. I'm pretty sure that's where your interest is. After that we can check out Xochicalco's observatory.'

'I agree. Let's do that. It's also interesting that this leaflet doesn't really give much of a hint about how they carved the megaliths of the serpents on the monument so beautifully, what they mean, or what technology they used to do it with,' Chad reasoned, as they exited the museum again.

There were no other tourists at the remote site of Xochicalco at all. They walked along the driveway towards the hill settlement of ancient buildings. Already, from some distance away, several structures started to look very similar in profile to those at *Teotihuacan*. They walked up the first grassy slope and reached an open area with two raised stone platforms. In the centre was a low-walled, square structure. The hot sun had dried out the grass between the buildings. In fact, the day had become really hot now.

'We need to be quite careful, Takashi-san. There's not much shade here.'

'A good observation Chad-san! There is absolutely no shade here at all!' He then took out his GoPro camera and started to film. 'I would like to make a record of this site also.'

'Of course, Takashi-san. Please go ahead.'

Takashi then proceeded to take in a full 360-degree panorama, before walking slowly towards one of the raised observation platforms. He walked up the steps then turned to face the larger multi-tiered pyramid structure at the end of the terrace. When he seemed to be finished, Chad walked up the steps to join him. The view from the top was spectacular. If this were a fortification, it certainly commanded the landscape for some ten kilometres or more. Towards the south west, about halfway towards the distant hills, there were two large lakes. This somewhat desolate plateau was certainly a fertile location which could easily support a large community.

'Chad-san, let's climb that one,' Takashi suggested, pointing at the large pyramid structure. '*The Temple of the Feathered Serpent* should be just beyond that.'

'Good idea. The view should be even better from up there!'

At the top, a slight breeze was blowing, giving a slight reprieve from the fiercely hot Sun. Takashi again took some more 4K video, slowly scanning the landscape and giving a commentary in Japanese. He then turned the camera towards Chad and called out, 'Chad-san, please wave!'

Chad waved. Takashi filmed a little more then switched off his camera.

'Chad-san, you know, I'm starting to think that the entire site could be a monument to that ancient cataclysmic event, you and your brother discovered.'

'That's a very poignant suggestion.'

Walking towards the *Temple of the Feathered Serpent*, Chad was struck how intricate the carvings were.

On the back wall of the Temple were two identical carvings of the Feathered Serpent, with its coils passing around a person and a strange nested geometric shape. The Temple carvings were clearly complex, and could certainly encode the details of an event, rather than just be some tribute to a historical character.

'Chad-san, let's try to work out what this monument is trying to tell us.'

Just at that moment Chad's iPhone buzzed. He took it out of his pocket. It was a message from his brother Tom with two images.

Chad read it with amazement: *Chad, I hope you and Jeanette are having a great time in Mexico. Mary-Anne and I will be at the airport around midday tomorrow to welcome you both to St. Lucia. How is your Rainbow Serpent hunt going? I just thought I would send you these amazing images that I received from young Patrick! He has deduced that the Dendera Lightbulb images are of the spiralling relativistic jet with its plasma cocoon. More importantly, he has even worked out that the two back-to-back images are the same, showing first Ra, the Sun, and then the Djed pillar which represents Osiris, or Rigel, in Orion in the sky. These two images are identifying two times when the Sun is not in the sky the same time as Rigel. The second image shows everything in the same carving. This signifies the period of the year, i.e. that part of the Earth's orbit, when both the Sun and Rigel were in the sky at the same time. This overlap period is a maximum from late January to late April. So we now know on which side of the Solar System the jet passed. The double warning of the baboon with two knives suggests that this is indicating when the Earth was effectively between the Sun and the Jet. I'm also pretty sure these images are very precise, so the two knives infers some kind of double danger, although right now, what exactly that is, still eludes me. All in all, this is a very significant interpretation and may be very relevant to your search in Mexico! See you tomorrow. Hugs and love to you and Jeanette, Tom & Mary-Anne x*

'Takashi! My brother just sent me a message suggesting we need to look out for a reverse image of a snaking relativistic jet. Isn't that just what we are looking at here? The *Feathered Serpent* is depicted back to back, just like these images from *Dendera*. Look here!'

Xochicalco: Feathered Serpent

'*Sou desu ne! Sou desu ne!*' Takashi remarked in utter astonishment. 'Chad-san, that must be exactly what these carved Feathered Serpents represent. Let's walk around and try to analyse the different stone carvings for meanings and any differences.'

'Good idea.'

The *Feathered Serpent* platform was a square structure with walls about 20 metres long and about 6 metres high. Three walls had back-to-back pairs of intricately-carved, ornate, fire-breathing, serpents with their heads turned back towards their tails. Each serpent head was at the wall corner and their tails met in the middle, separated by some carvings. The serpent bodies each comprised four curving segments, the first comprising its fire-breathing head. The other three segments of each serpent wrapped around one or two cross-legged figures, each bearing an elaborate head-dress. A geometrical, multilevel carving was positioned within one of the serpent arches. Complex carvings ran along the wall, high above the serpents, possibly suggesting calendar dates, but according to the leaflet, there was no suggestion that they had ever been deciphered. The west wall was separated in the middle by a flight of stone steps going to the top of the platform. Either side of the steps, the west wall depicted a much smaller serpent.

Takashi and Chad continued to walk around the structure, coming back to right where they had started, in front of the north-facing wall. Chad stood and stared at the intricate megalithic imagery. In this wall, the second and third segments of each serpent curved around a figure. Thinking about what his brother had written, could these characters possibly represent the Sun and Rigel in the sky, as in the *Dendera images*? On the north-facing wall, the final, fourth segment of the two serpents arched around the strange stack of geometrical shapes, the lowest part of which, depicted a box with strange carvings inside. Above this box were flowing shapes, similar to the fiery emblems on the serpent's skin. Chad had absolutely no idea how to interpret these complex carvings. If it was showing how people needed to be underground, or in caves or in protective structures while the jet was in the sky, then this lent further credence to the interpretation that the huge cross-legged figures possibly represented celestial bodies such as the Sun. There was now a danger that Chad was imposing a meaning upon the carvings which simply did not exist. Any relation to the relativistic jet needed to be obvious and self-evident. The flowing shapes, which seemed to cascade down from all along the serpent, might possibly be some dangerous radiation, or plasma formed within an atmosphere coronal discharge, caused by the jet. He would definitely need to discuss all these ideas with his brother Tom.

'So, what do you think, Takashi-san? By the way, thanks for suggesting this trip. It is definitely so much more interesting than *Teotihuacan*.'

'Chad-san, I find this site really intriguing also, and more so because of your knowledge, and now we have a further insight from your brother. If it indeed depicts the relativistic jet, which is a real possibility, then we would really need to decode the small features within the whole picture.'

'Takashi-san, from the leaflet here, we also know that this site was burned to the ground in 900 B.C.E. and then rebuilt. Hopefully most of the blocks are in their correct positions. What do you think of the repeating line of blocks at the top of the wall, above the serpents? Surely that is another part of the story. Isn't that a snake head with its mouth around the Sun? Couldn't that represent the dangerous time when the jet and the Sun were seen in the sky at the same time, when the Earth was between the jet and the Sun?'

'Very good observation Chad-san. By the way, here we have four walls with slightly different images. Perhaps this structure indeed encodes a warning as a description of the whole year, identifying a period of the year when it is dangerous, and others when it is safe, rather than just identifying how to identify a dangerous period like in Dendera.'

'Good point Takashi-san. If you are right, this north-facing wall might represent the period from December to mid-March.'

'You mean from the winter solstice to the spring equinox?'

'Well, that is true now, but the Earth is precessing around its poles, like a gyroscope spinning but leaning on one side. It takes around 26,000 years to make a full 360°. It is mid-winter in the northern hemisphere when the north is leaning furthest away from the Sun. That is indeed December now, in our epoch. After half the precession period, i.e. in 13,000 years from now, the north will be leaning towards the Sun in December, so then it will be *summer* in the northern hemisphere in December. I am guessing that is why we tend not to see any mention of the solstices or equinoxes in the carvings. Monuments which are warning of the jet and its dangers, will most likely be trying to identify a particular part of the Earth's orbit, independent of any particular axial tilt the Earth may have.'

'Of course, of course.' Takashi then continued to look intently at the carvings. 'Oh, look we missed something. The figures in both serpent images on this wall are looking to the right, as if *the way they are looking* is independent of the direction of the two serpents. Surely that is significant?'

'Well spotted. Yes, that must be important. The two serpent images must represent what is seen in the sky as it passes overhead, so although the serpent shape reverses, the direction of the figures stays the same. That may be a significant clue.'

They continued to walk around to the east-facing wall.

'OK, so what in this east-facing wall is different?' Chad murmured, gazing at the carved imagery.

'Well, that geometrical multilevel structure is now in segment two, under the first arch, and there is only one figure in the third segment who is now looking *left*. Also, the last segment of the serpent on this wall now seems almost empty.'

'Yes, you are right. OK, we have a small difference already, and look, the repeating line of blocks above the serpents are also different here. Could this wall represent the time from March to June? That corresponds to a continuation of the dangerous period.'

'It is possible, but we will need additional data to confirm that hypothesis. I still think that the key to decoding this may lay in the meaning of the sequence of blocks running along the top of the wall. Let's look at the south-facing wall.'

The south-facing wall also had figures within segments two and three, with the multilevel structure within segment four. Again, the figures in both serpents were all facing the same way, this time to the left.

'By the way Chad-san, did your brother say why June to December was the safer part of the year?'

'Well, he identified the dangerous period as when the orbiting Earth is between the Sun and the jet, so I guess after June, the Earth has moved out of harm's way. I am sure he has deeper insights, he is the astrophysicist. He used the word *'effectively'* and he uses words carefully. He may be talking about a particular geometry of the solar system and jet. I will definitely need to have some long conversations with him when we get to St. Lucia.'

'I look forward to learning about that.'

'I will definitely email you as soon as I learn anything interesting.'

'Look up there in the top of the wall. There is a vertical, spiral carving between two bars in the upper part of the wall. Could that be the spiralling jet you mentioned?'

'Yes, I see it. You could be right.'

'Wait a second, Chad-san. I need to just check that first wall again.'

Takashi quickly walked back and then returned. 'There are a couple of those small snake heads which are biting balls also. Most of that top level is missing on that first side. Hopefully the top blocks weren't redistributed when the structure was rebuilt.'

They walked around to the west-facing wall. The carvings on this wall comprised two short serpents either side of the steps, which led up to the top of the platform. The serpents were clearly portrayed as being much less dangerous here, not only were they much smaller, but each one had much less fire coming from its mouth.

'Takashi-san, I think our interpretation of each wall representing the four parts of the year must be right. This wall must represent the September to December part of the orbit,' Chad said excitedly.

'It really looks that way. By the way, it is still interesting how the sequence of blocks along the wall, high above the serpents, is different in each of the north, east, and south walls.'

Sure enough, the upper tier on each wall had repeating sequences of four symbols, but they were subtly different in each case. The end symbol in each sequence was a twisted helix between two bars, like two snakes wrapped around one another. Understanding these upper images was probably not as important as establishing the meaning of the figures and geometrical shape within the large snake carving which ran along half of each of the north, east and south walls. Various elements in the upper wall sequence included a cross-legged figure reaching for a kind of teapot missing its spout, and that snake's head biting a ball.

The snake heads biting balls were all in the same direction above both serpents, as were all the four figures enveloped beneath the coils of the two snakes. Chad checked the north and south side walls again. In fact, all the figures on those two walls were looking towards the front of the temple, where the steps were. That may have been a coincidence of course. The two smaller serpents on either side of the steps on the west wall also wrapped around another collection of strange complicated shapes.

'Chad-san, I will just walk around with my GoPro camera, now that we have had a first look at the sequence of images. Surely it must indeed be another monument about the passage of that relativistic jet through the sky during the year.'

'Hopefully, but we will need to prove that by decoding it. Of course, it is important to get a photographic record. I will take a few shots of the strange carvings inside the serpents here on this west facing wall. Maybe these also decode into star patterns which were seen in the sky. I can see a lion, or something, up on the raised roof of this temple. That may be a constellation of course. It's very difficult to make much sense of any of this yet.'

After taking a few photos, Chad walked up the steps while Takashi took his home movie. Eventually Takashi was finished, and he joined Chad at the top of the Temple.

'Look, over there. That must be the path to the observatory and Xochicalco's underground complex of chambers and tunnels,' Takashi remarked. 'We really need to check that out also.'

'Of course, let's go there now.'

They made their way back down the steps to the entrance to the Xochicalco Observatory, below the Central Plaza. As they walked inside, it was pretty clear that it was a man-made hollowed-out structure. The complex comprised a series of connected rooms, where indeed people could have taken refuge from something dangerous. In one chamber, high above them, a vertical tube some seven or so metres long, opened up to reveal the sky. Takashi had a small hand torch, which he switched on and then he started to check the leaflet again.

'It says here that the Sun passes across that hole, and shines down onto this stone slab, around 104 days per year, from the end of April to mid-August.'

Chad looked up at the tunnel carved in the rock above.

'Really? That sounds worrying if it always shone down there. I am wondering if the Sun actually shone down this hole at all when this structure was in use, if this site dates back 11,770 years. Moreover, if people needed to hide from the Sun, it would have been crucial to never have direct visibility of the Sun. I will need to ask my brother Tom to check the position of the Sun in the sky way back then. As we are noticing, it seems that every site which warns of the transit of the relativistic jet, also has some kind of subterranean tunnels or chambers for people to take shelter in. This surely must be why this was built, and what this was used for.'

'A very interesting and compelling conclusion Chad-san.'

Chad took a moment to quickly send a message to Tom thanking him for the data on the Dendera images and then he added that question about when the Sun was directly overhead at Xochicalco in 9750 B.C.E. Within a few minutes he got the reply.

'Takashi-san, Tom just confirmed that the Sun only passed overhead between late July and mid October in 9750 B.C.E. So if they used these underground chambers to take shelter during a dangerous time of the year, sometime between January and April, the Sun did not shine directly down that shaft back then.'

'That was quick of your brother. So they didn't get direct sunlight. You know I think we are working out what this site was built for and how incredibly old it really is.'

They continued to explore the different side chambers for a short while. It was becoming increasingly obvious that this underground complex would be highly suitable for people to take refuge from the dangers of a transiting relativistic jet, during a potentially dangerous period of the year. Chad managed to take a few flash photos using his phone camera, then they headed outside again.

'What do you think Chad-san? Shall we contact Manolo? I think we're possibly finished at Xochicalco now. Much of the rest of the layout of buildings looks pretty uninteresting.'

'Yes, I agree. I'll send him a message.'

Within moments, Chad got a reply. 'He's at the parking spot already.'

'I hope he has some food for us. I'm really hungry!'

'He does! He also wrote *your food orders are in the car,*' Chad confirmed with a grin. 'Come on, I think we're sorted. This has been a really successful trip!'

They both walked back across the site and along the track to the main road. Manolo was parked up some 25 metres away. They climbed in the back.

'Buenas días Señores, did you have a good time? By the way, I managed to get exactly what you wanted. One *polpo tostada*, and one *torta de chilaquiles*.'

'Manolo, thank you so much, *arigatou gozaimasu*!'

'Thanks Manolo,' Chad added.

'The *torta de chilaquiles* is in the bag. The white carton is the *polpo tostada*. There are serviettes there also. I also bought you guys a few beers. There is an opener there in the open tray. We can settle up at the end. Enjoy!'

'Manolo, you are the dream chauffeur. Thanks. Oh, did you find your maize fungus?'

'I did! It was delicious. Are you happy to eat as we drive, then we can hit the road? First you need to book me again so please *order your Uber*. I don't think there is anyone else nearby. So, do you want to go back via

Tepoztlán? If so, select that as the destination.'

'What do you think, Takashi-san? Are we also visiting *Tepoztlán*?'

'You know, why don't we just head straight back to Mexico City. We have seen two sites today already, maybe a third would be excessive.'

Chad nodded.

'Manolo, I think we'll head back to Mexico City,' Chad confirmed.

'Of course, Señores. Back to Mexico City it is. Just enter your destination and we can set off.'

Takashi opened the *Uber App*, entered the data and within moments, Manolo was confirmed as their driver.

'Wow, this *octopus ceviche* is amazing. Thanks Manolo. It is very fresh. As good as yesterday's.'

'You are welcome Señor. How is the *torta de chilaquiles*?'

'Delicious Manolo. It really hits the spot. And it is great to be back in a cool air-conditioned car. It's really hot out there without any shade.'

'You are welcome. So, I reckon that we are probably back in Mexico City in around 90 minutes, depending on the traffic.'

'Excellent.'

They drove back towards the 95D toll-road, along the winding country road that ran above the river valley. Chad was deep in thought. *Xochicalco* had left some deep impressions. The *Temple of the Feathered Serpent* was indeed a unique structure which was very different from the other structures at that place. It clearly held a message, but it would be difficult to translate without further clues. Did other sites have similar imagery which could be combined to help determine the meaning? In addition to that, the Xochicalco Observatory was surely the associated, essential refuge structure. There were possibly many other sites in Mexico, but he and Jeanette would be flying out tomorrow and now there wasn't any time left for further exploration.

'Takashi-san, are you staying in Mexico much longer?'

Takashi was enjoying a very large bite of *octopus ceviche*. After a few moments he took a serviette and wiped his mouth before replying.

'Yes indeed, Chad-san. I have four more days. I intend checking out one other site, *Monte Alban* some five hours south of Mexico City near

Oaxaca. Some authors describe it as an ancient observatory. Send me an email to my email address here,' he said, taking a business card out of his pocket. 'I will let you know if I find anything of interest relating to *Feathered Serpents* in the megalithic monuments there.'

'I'll send you an email now. Wait a moment.'

He took his iPhone and sent a message to Takashi's phone including his electronic business card. Within moments it arrived on Takashi's phone. Takashi smiled.

'Great! So, how has it been on your Japanese language tour today, Chad-san?' Takashi asked with a grin.

'Absolutely amazing, and *above and beyond* anything I could possibly have expected. It has been a real pleasure to spend the day with you.'

'For me also,' Takashi replied sincerely.

They anticipated that the journey back to Mexico City would be pretty much a straight drive back along the 95D. At first that was the case, but after about half an hour, the blue skies quickly became overcast, with really dark clouds overhead.

'Señores, there is stormy weather ahead. We can expect thunder and lightning, maybe even hail. Hopefully it will pass,' Manolo said, looking up at them in the rear view mirror.

It was close to 4p.m. but incredibly dark. Then the rain came down like never before, falling heavily upon the motorway traffic. Manolo had the windshield wipers going flat out, but they were hardly able to clear the endless torrent of rain. Suddenly, a very bright arc of lightning crossed the sky right above them, lighting up the landscape. Within moments, an almighty crash of thunder arrived. The storm was directly overhead. All around them, the motorway traffic was becoming really heavy, and slowing now. Everyone had their headlights on. Then the hail hit them, drumming loudly onto the body of the car, and up ahead, they could see large, white hailstones, bouncing across the road.

'What's going on up there, up ahead, Manolo?' Chad asked, somewhat in disbelief.

In the distance, cars were moving off to the sides of the road, one even seemed to strike the central barrier, before bouncing back towards the grass verge beside the motorway. The road was now covered in a white surface of hail.

'This is a freak hailstorm, Señores! This can happen, even in summer! You must never hit the brakes. If you do, you can easily lose control, and the car will skid all over the road. You must stay calm and concentrate, and just continue on slowly with positive drive,' Manolo remarked seriously. 'Don't worry, I will get us through this.'

Manolo continued on at a very low speed, without braking. To the sides of the road, they passed ten or more vehicles, some had spun round, now pointing the other way. Chad turned and looked behind them through the rear window. It was chaos. Hopefully they had escaped the worst. He noticed Manolo constantly checking his rear view mirror. 'I think we are past the danger zone,' he remarked.

A short time later, they were out of the hailstorm and the road ahead was completely clear.

'Everyone OK in the back?'

'We're good,' Chad replied, sounding a little nervous. 'Right Takashi-san?'

'Yes, I'm good. Quite dramatic stuff.

Up ahead, they could see a car on its side.

'I will need to stop. I just need to check and see that everyone is OK.'

'Of course,' Chad replied.

Manolo pulled up beside the overturned vehicle, it was an old red Chevrolet Chevy. He got out and walked towards the vehicle, and then pulled the side door open upwards. Manolo then helped the driver out. Chad opened his door and then called out to Manolo.

'Manolo, he's very welcome to travel with us. It's no problem.'

Manolo returned with the man, who was about thirty years old, and quite smartly dressed in a grey suit, carrying a briefcase.

He climbed into the front passenger seat next to Manolo. He looked a little shocked.

'This is Felipe, our fellow traveller to Mexico City,' Manolo remarked, as he opened the car door.

'You are welcome,' Chad said.

'*Very* welcome,' Takashi added.

'*Muchas gracias Señores! Soy Felipe*,' the man said.

'Do you speak English?' Chad asked.

'Ah sí, yes! Of course. I'm so grateful. It all happened so fast. I lost control of the car in the hailstorm. Before I knew what was going on, your driver, Manolo, was opening the door. I will just send a text message to the hire company. I am sure they can deal with it.'

'You are very welcome. There's a beer here, if it can help calm your nerves,' Takashi added holding up a beer and the opener. 'I am a foreigner in your country and I am having a lovely time.'

'Me too. I am only here until tomorrow, but I find Mexico a lovely place.'

'I'm actually a foreigner too! I'm from Chimbote, Peru. That beer would be most welcome.'

Takashi opened the beer and handed him the bottle.

'Aha? Are you on holiday then? Did you drive all the way up from Peru?' Chad enquired.

'No Señor, to both questions. I flew to Columbia, and I was there a few days. I then took a boat to Acapulco on the coast, due south from here. Then I hired the car. I'm heading to Mexico City to an International Games Fair. I have developed a new board game,' Felipe explained, sipping the beer.

'Now that *is* very interesting. May I ask you what it's about?'

'Of course. Well, in English, it is called er, *The Lost Ancient Peruvian Game of Trout Ceviche*! It's a card-based board game. Players travel around the board visiting the ancient Peruvian Inca cities near Cusco, collecting cards and using cards to move. The board layout includes paths between the cities in the design of the ancient megalithic stone walls. To make the game really exciting, I have greatly increased player interaction by adding every possible controversial rule which goes against the natural gameplay.' Felipe seemed rather energetic in spite of his recent car accident.

'Now that is extremely original,' Takashi declared. 'I find board games a great means for family interaction and conversation. The *I want it now* World of instant gratification social media is diminishing family culture.'

'I agree, Señores. That is how I became so inspired to develop this game. Actually, I developed it with my brother, Rogerio. We started the idea some ten years ago. Now it is *production ready* at last.'

'What is the objective of the game?' Chad asked.

'OK, so you travel around the board collecting cards. Each card represents one of the ten ingredients of *Trout Ceviche*. In the game there are ranger cards, so you get to see other player's cards. There are bandit cards, so you can even steal cards from other players!'

'That sounds like great fun. I love all that player interaction!' Chad said.

The road was clear ahead and their driver seemed content.

'Manolo, how are you doing?' Takashi asked.

'Señores, I am good. It's nice to see that everyone is getting along so well. It is honourable to do a good deed. I am happy to drive you back to Mexico City. There is about another 30 minutes to go, then we are at the *Hilton Hotel* downtown.'

The conversation continued about the game and about Peru. Finally, close to 5:45p.m., they arrived at the *Hilton*. They all got out. Manolo shook everyone by the hand, and then climbed back into his car, waving his hand out of the window as he drove off.

Chad then spoke, 'Felipe, it has been really interesting to talk with you.'

'Señores thank *you*, I am really in debt to you. You saved me, and I have a present for you. I have one extra copy of *The Lost Ancient Peruvian Game of Trout Ceviche*,' Felipe announced sincerely. 'Who would like it?'

'Felipe, I already had *octopus ceviche* today. I think Chad should have your *Trout Ceviche* game!'

'Of course!' He opened his bag and handed the boxed game to Chad.

'Wow, thanks Felipe.'

'You are welcome Señor! My email address is on the instructions. They are also in English. Please do let me know what you think?'

'Of course!'

'By the way, one last thing. I have been thinking. After your story about Xochicalco today, don't forget to research some of Peru's more hidden sites. I think you may find the ancient *Observatorio* at *Chankillo* in the desert region very interesting. It has a solar calendar wall, marking out the movement of the Sun in ancient times.'

'Where exactly is that?' Chad asked.

'It's about 70 kilometres south of Chimbote. That is actually where I am from. There is also another calendar wall like it in Tiwanaku, across lake Titicaca near *La Paz,* in Bolivia. In fact, an uncle of mine, Andrés, spent years researching those sites and the megalithic structures along the *Inca trail.* He even went to *Isla de Pascua,* I think you call it *Easter Island,* where he discovered some very interesting rock carvings. He is now retired, living in Costa Rica, but he left me all his documents for me to continue his work. You know, I was not planning to look into his findings any time soon, and I am thinking that his material may be much more useful for you, Chad, and your brother. If you send me an email, I'll send you all the material I have. I'm also sure that my favourite uncle Andrés would be very happy to hear that his life's work will now get the attention it deserves, from two serious researchers in the field, especially when he hears how his nephew was rescued by one of them!'

'Wow, that would be fantastic. That sounds really interesting to get more detailed analyses of megalithic sites from another researcher. I will definitely email you,' Chad replied warmly.

They all shook hands.

'Hey, I will now catch a bus from here. Guys, thanks again for rescuing me,' Felipe added, then he turned and walked off towards the main street where buses were passing by.

'Hey Felipe! Good luck at the International Games Fair!' Chad called.

Takashi held up his hand, as Felipe turned in response. He then smiled and waved at them one last time.

'Takashi this has been a really great day, and now I even have an interesting board game to play on St. Lucia with my brother.'

'Stay in touch Chad-san,' Takashi said, with a sincere look. 'And have a very safe trip to St. Lucia.'

'Thanks. Yes, I promise we will stay in touch and I'm really looking forward to diving *Yonaguni* with you.'

'I'm also looking forward to that. Have a really great evening and do please give my greetings to your wife.'

'Thanks, I will. You have a great evening too, and have a great next few days in Mexico, Takashi-san,'

Takashi smiled and made a slight bow towards Chad, and then he turned and walked into the Hilton Hotel.

Chad's phone then started to ring, it was Jeanette.

'Hi Honey, how are you?' he asked.

'I'm good. Did you have a good day?'

'Unbelievable! Where are *you* right now?'

'I'm heading back to the hotel. I saw a fantastic Japanese restaurant a few blocks away. Do you fancy that?'

'Actually, I would love that. I guess I'm back within ten minutes. So, I'll see you soon.'

'I'm looking forward to it. See you soon,' she added sweetly, and then she cut the call.

6 | Accra, Ghana: decoding Göbekli Tepe's asterisms carved in stone

Internet Café, Airport City, Accra, Ghana

Manu had awoken very early. He had planned to cycle over to meet some friends downtown at their favourite Internet Café. They had not confirmed yet, but he needed to do some online research anyway in reply to the material and conclusions Patrick had forwarded to him, while he was away on his hiking trip. They were still both on summer break and school wouldn't start for another two weeks.

It had been a tough ride. Although Manu had got up at the crack of dawn to travel in the cool morning air and miss the traffic, a diesel truck, badly in need of a service for an over-fuelling problem, had obviously taken the same route only a short time earlier. There was hardly any breeze and the choking, acrid stench of unburnt diesel fumes, had been hanging in the air for most of the journey.

The Internet Café was still closed when he arrived, but he knew the manager Simon well, after he had resolved a network problem one busy Saturday, when no service engineer had been available. The system had gone down while the café was filled with clients and Manu had stepped up to the plate and saved the day. He had told Simon that he could fix it in 10 minutes and suggested that he quickly hand out free coffee and biscuits to everyone. It did take him 12 minutes in the end but when the system came back online again, everybody in the café cheered and Manu was extremely popular from that moment on. Simon had been so grateful, that he had given Manu life-time free surfing, which, in fairness, meant that Manu was always welcome, but preferably before 10 a.m. to avoid taking up paying-customer space. Simon had suggested that Manu would even be welcome to come before opening time and help him get the system up and running, in case any glitches had arisen in the system since his last visit. There would be a free lunch included if Manu did that. This was one of those early morning, free-lunch opportunities. It was still only 5:30 a.m.

Manu locked his bike chain around a lamp post and walked over to the large glass window and tapped on the glass. Soon, Simon appeared from the back and unlocked and opened the door.

'Manu, good to see you! You're lucky, everything seems to be up and running well today. Do you fancy a coffee? The machine is on.' He let Manu in and then relocked the door.

'Hi Simon, that would be great. You're always really confident that everything is fine, but let me first do a few system checks, just to be sure.'

'Please do.'

Outside, there was still not that much traffic, but now the streets were becoming livelier, as more and more people were walking to work. Simon then emerged from the back room carrying two cups of coffee. Manu took out his laptop and booted it up.

'No *blue screen of death* issues on the terminals the last few weeks?' Manu asked.

'There was one, but I managed to sort it with a reboot. Later that evening, I replaced the motherboard, it had both the sound and VGA built in.'

'Oh no! *Simon says* never buy a cheap integrated motherboard, always buy separate sound and VGA cards!'

'Yes, you even told me that the first time you were here, and that I'd probably get problems with those machines. They're all replaced now, so that's sorted.'

'Well, Simon, your system is looking good,' Manu confirmed, looking at the Internet speed data. 'No interference from outside anymore. Aha, I see you finally have a wire-mesh film on the window glass, very good.'

'You can take credit for that. That was also one of your ideas. Enjoy your surfing, I have some book-keeping to do.'

'Thanks, I will.'

Manu opened his email and looked again at the very interesting constellation overlays that Patrick had forwarded, which decoded pillar 43 from the Göbekli Tepe site. This was stunningly impressive. No one in the World had achieved that!

Manu went online and found several journal publications, where academics with important titles had argued why their own interpretation of pillar 43 had to be right, yet the stars in their sky maps hardly aligned with any of the stars. It seemed pure conjecture. Worst of all, their hypotheses contradicted the dating of the site, and the well-reasoned conclusions of teams of archaeologists who had spent years, painstakingly reconstructing the history by carefully brushing through metres of layers of dust and logging every detail.

At first glance, Manu estimated that Patrick had aligned more than 50 stars exactly to the unique Göbekli Tepe constellations. How cool was that? It was amazing how Patrick's work had mapped the round symbol on pillar 43 to the star *Spica*, a massive blue subgiant star, the closest supernova candidate to the Earth, which will supernova!

Could he, Manu, add even more to the interpretation? There was still an explanation needed for the three strange, rectangular blocks at the top, each with a curving line and each having its own animal figure. What could these represent? Did these somehow mark out the dangerous period of the year, when not to be outside; the same period that Patrick had deduced from Manu's email identifying the Sun and Rigel in the *Dendera* frieze?

Manu looked again at Patrick's email. He now noticed he had sent it at midnight, Sydney time, the night before he left. That was only yesterday. Manu clearly had the most up-to-date understanding of where Patrick's thoughts were.

Reading on, Manu smiled at what Patrick had written next. Patrick had confirmed that his Dad was convinced that Manu's suggestions were spot on, that the *Dendera* friezes described the relativistic jet, warning of when it was extremely dangerous to be outside in sunlight. Wow, Manu thought, that is cool, and Patrick's Dad is a professional astrophysicist!

At the bottom, Patrick had added his Dad's email address, just in case Manu discovered anything else. So, his friend thought he could take the story further. He would definitely try to rise to that challenge.

With new confidence, he took another look at that photo of Göbekli Tepe pillar 43. What else was being described on that stone? He now decided that possibly *everything* was part of the message. If so it could be the total detailed warning, like the carved images at *Dendera*. If so, that would mean that every single element on the pillar was significant, and absolutely nothing would have been added as some extra bit of decoration.

Online, he read that the Göbekli Tepe site had most likely been purposefully back-filled. Then suddenly, he had an alternative thought. What if the temple structure had been built with a heavy wooden beam roof, covered with a mound of gravel? If it needed to serve as a chamber, protecting people from the hazards of the jet, then covering it with a gravel layer seemed a very sensible option. After a really long period of time, the beams would have eventually rotted through and collapsed, and an enormous weight of gravel would have caved in, *filling* the chamber. More significantly, Southern Turkey was also a major active earthquake zone, which explained why such structures would eventually collapse. Either way, this seemed a more likely suggestion of how the site had preserved the message contained on pillar 43, and possibly on other pillars yet to be deciphered, for future generations or hopefully for he, Manu, to discover.

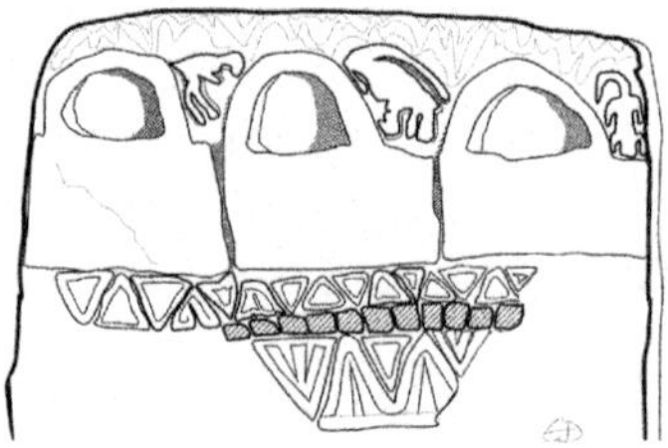

Top of Pillar 43

Looking at the three rectangular structures at the top of the pillar, each with their curving lines and animal characters, he wondered if and how they could describe a period of the year. Moreover, what if the zigzag line lower down, below the three rectangular structures, represented dangers caused by the jet, and the part-zigzag, below a line of small squares, was identifying a period definitely when to take cover?

On closer inspection, Manu had an even deeper insight. The curved line above each rectangular block surely represented the path of the sun in the sky on different dates. If that were true, then the animals beside each curved line might represent asterisms of stars which were seen in the sky just after sunset.

First, he decided to check whether these blocks related to the winter or summer solstices. The people back then surely divided their year into seasons. He had heard from Patrick that the Earth was wobbling slowly, according to the precession of the equinoxes, so the dates of the solstices would have been different from today. He booted up Stellarium, selected the closest town to Göbekli Tepe, *Sanliurfa*, and stepped through the months to see how the Sun behaved. After a concerted effort, he discovered that the winter solstice was around March 4th, and the Summer solstice was around September 5th. Then he set the time to 8870 B.C.E., which was the end date of the jet passing by. The winter and summer solstices were now only six days earlier.

Now he would try to find collections of stars in the three different animal asterism shapes. Could he map the three blocks with curved lines to the solstices and equinoxes? If he could, he could precisely determine actual dates when to take cover. He looked in detail at the carvings directly below the blocks with curved lines were 15 triangles, 11 small blocks and identified and confirmed by determining when those animal asterisms beside the blocks were seen close to the horizon just after sunset. If that were true, then the top of pillar 43 was indeed identifying the very dangerous period.

Manu was cautiously optimistic with this interpretation, but he now needed to find the three different animal asterisms in the endless sea of stars in the night sky above Göbekli Tepe. This would be very difficult. The first animal asterism seemed to be a bird with a long curved beak, most likely an ibis. The second was possibly a crocodile, while the third was a quadruped with a long tail like a long tailed bear. Each creature had its head down, possibly suggesting sunset, but hopefully he would find a convincing collection of stars for each in the sky.

After many hours of scouring the stars, around the winter solstice, he found a very good correlation of stars which matched the dipping bird, but this potential asterism was nowhere near the horizon just after sunset. Using the star-locate function, and activating the sunlight, he could now investigate when that asterism was on the horizon just after sunset. Stepping the date forward, the dipping bird asterism slowly approached the horizon at sunset. The date was March 15th. That was interesting. Now he needed to find the crocodile asterism. Looking closely, strangely, several of the stars forming the top of the dipping bird asterism, seemed to combine with stars immediately above them, to create a very good candidate for the crocodile asterism. So, that was what pillar 43 was encoding. He stepped the date forward and after around 12 days, the dipping bird asterism on the horizon had partially disappeared and now the asterism on the horizon had morphed into a crocodile, amazing! The date was now 28th March.

There were three or four more blocks extending under the next curved line block with that long-tailed sun-bear creature, so logically, the pillar carvings were possibly suggesting that the danger period continued for three or four more days.

So where was that long-tailed bear asterism? Bizarrely, Manu eventually found it rising at sunrise! OK, so when did this sun-bear reach the sunset horizon? That only happened in mid to late August. That corresponded to close to their summer solstice. It was also on the horizon at midnight on June 21st. That was probably also significant. So, pillar 43 was identifying a danger period just after their winter solstice of March 4th, and ending just into the start of their summer period. The line of 15 triangles was possibly identifying a period of 15 days. Wow, he had definitely cracked pillar 43!

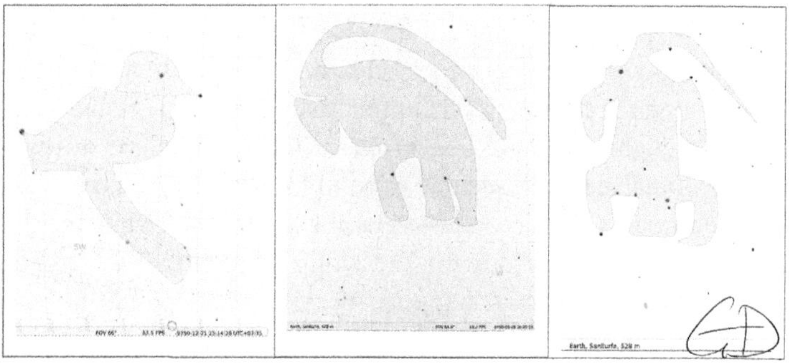

Animal Asterisms

Now he became a little concerned about those dates that Patrick had sent him, following his interpretation of the Dendera frieze, which corresponded to the period when the star Rigel and the Sun were in the sky at the same. In 9750 B.C.E., as seen from the Giza plateau, Rigel rose after sunrise, and set before sunset from late January to late April, but after that, it was in the sky for increasingly shorter periods. In comparison with the detail from Göbekli Tepe pillar 43, this just seemed too imprecise. Sure, it was identifying the March side of the Earth's orbit when the Earth was above the galactic plane, but now he wondered whether associating the Djed pillar with Rigel was correct. He looked again at the Dendera friezes. The undecipherable hieroglyphs surely held the key. Maybe the Djed pillar represented something else. Moreover, it would have been obvious to anyone who saw it. This was a public information message. He went online and started looking at different versions of Djed Pillars.

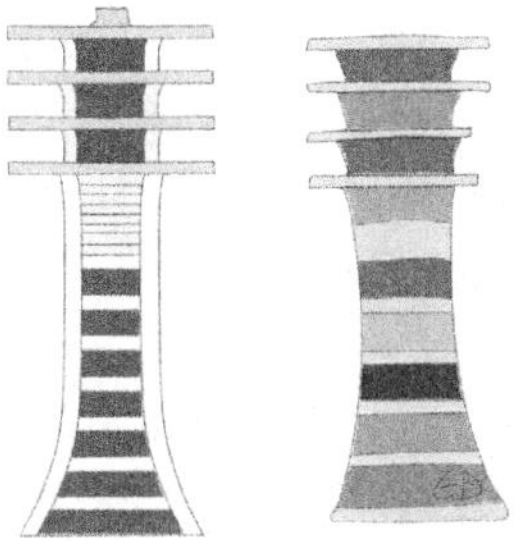

Djed Pillar

Then he realised. Of course, the Djed pillar was a vertical bar with four horizontals. That was it! It wasn't some complex mythical symbol at all, it just represented the number 14!

Manu looked at his watch. It was almost 8 a.m. He had been absorbed for nearly 3 hours! Nevertheless, he was absolutely certain that he had worked out something really valuable. His friend Patrick would be travelling but he could still message him. He sent a text:

Patrick, I think I have just deciphered the top of Pillar 43. It is definitely a warning stone identifying a precise 14-15 day dangerous period of the year, corresponding to a particular part of the Earth's orbit, when people needed to be inside the Göbekli Tepe stone protective structures. Thinking again about my suggestion about the Djed pillar representing Rigel, I am now thinking that is just too vague. By chance we have determined the right side of the Earth's orbit. That Djed pillar is a straight bar with four horizontals. It surely represents the number 14! I just sent you an email with an attachment. Let me know what you think. I also sent it to your Dad. I am now really inspired to try to translate a second one of the Göbekli Tepe pillars. It does seem a little unreal that no one else has done this before. Best regards Manu.

After a few minutes, his phone buzzed. Patrick had already replied:

Hi Manu, I got your email. Your discoveries are just mind-blowing! I'm sure my Dad will reply to you. Just think, we are two of the only people in the World who understand that the GT pillars represent constellations in the night sky. More importantly, these are the very images that people from some 11,770 years ago associated with the stars in the sky. That seems very special. Your new interpretation of the Djed Pillar as the number 14 is surely correct. Good luck with any further developments. I'm heading off into the wilderness for a few days now, but you can still message me with any new discoveries! Take care. Bye, Patrick.

Manu was extremely motivated to attempt to decipher another stone. He quickly found the next candidate, pillar 12. This had a snarling boar above a fox's head. Above it were 5 birds, with a square mesh on each side. Most importantly, there was a hole drilled right through the pillar just above the boar's head.

Manu copy-pasted the pillar into a word document, then carefully traced each figure on the pillar. After grouping all the figures, he made the shapes semi-transparent yellow, and changed their line-outline to 0.25 point also with a yellow outline. Next he searched the night skies above Göbekli Tepe in 9750 B.C.E.

After another very intense effort, he finally found a patch of sky which looked as though the stars could match the shapes of the animals on the pillar. He copied that patch of sky and used it as background in a Word document, then copy-pasted his transparent figures from the pillar onto his background image of the stars. With a slight rotation and scaling, they fitted very convincingly. Again this time, inside the circle, which corresponded to the hole in the pillar, was another very bright star. He selected this on Stellarium to identify it. Wow! It was Sirius! Now that was interesting. So Sirius was possibly once again part of this story.

He made a screen shot of his overlaid figures on the sky then emailed the image to both Patrick and to Patrick's Dad. Within a short time, Manu got an email reply from Dr Tom Walker: *Well done Manu. This is excellent work! Best regards, Tom.*

What next? Perhaps he should note down all the ideas spinning around his head. There were many more pillars with animals at the Göbekli Tepe site. He should certainly try to map these to the night skies. He should also look online for any information about the site itself. Where were the stones placed relative to the site? Were there any patterns?

Some four hours later, he had finished finding constellation images for two more pillars. The crowded animals of pillar 56 were very convincing, matching the Milky Way band in the sky but pillar 18 was quite

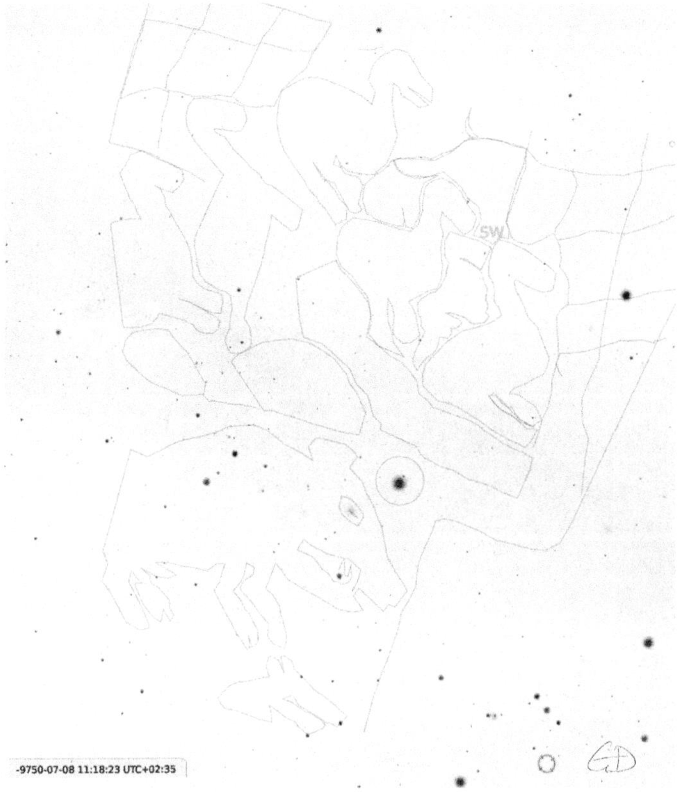

Göbekli Tepe: Pillar 12

remarkable. The upper band matched the wide spread of orbital trajectories of the planets, the Sun, and the Moon, as they passed overhead, while the lower band showed the back and forth extent of the movement of the entire band throughout the year. Another success!

He wrote another email to Patrick and his Dad, adding the new Göbekli Tepe constellation suggestions. That is all they were of course. It was purely subjective and open to interpretation only.

Göbekli Tepe: Pillar 56

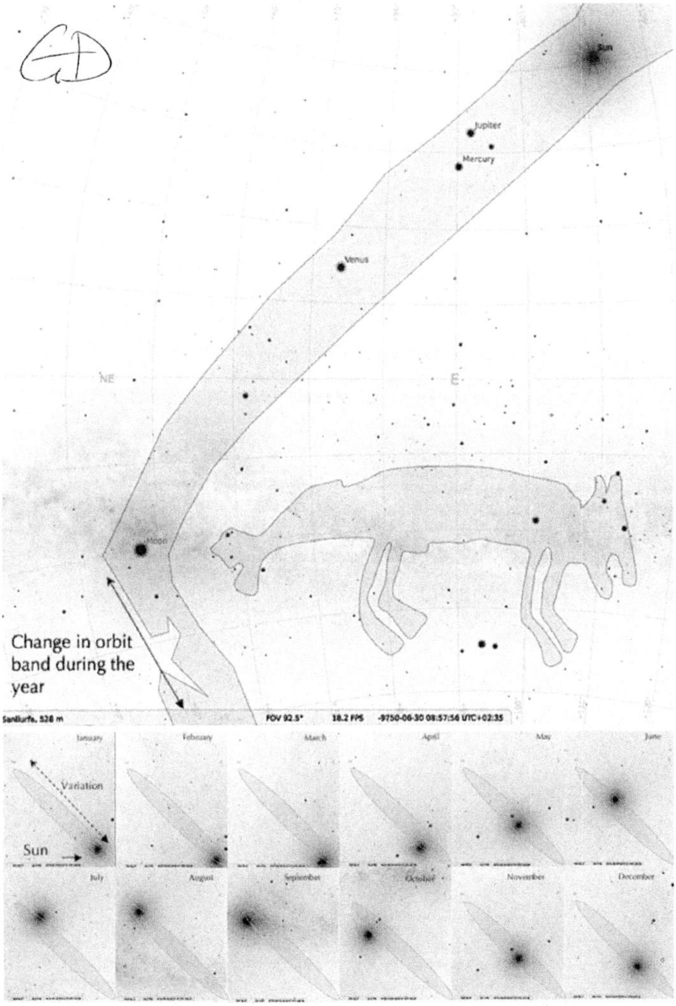

Göbekli Tepe: Pillar 18

7 | Soufrière, St. Lucia: the mortal dangers of a hypernova and relativistic jet transit

Stonefield Resort, Soufrière, St. Lucia

It was a very early morning. It was only just after sunrise and on the western side of the island, *Villa Ananas* was in shadow. It was lovely and warm and despite it being the rainy season, there were no clouds in the sky yet. Tom was sitting outside at the table on their terrace. Mary-Anne was still deep asleep in the dreamy four-poster bed. He had just returned from a short walk to the reception to organise the return taxi to take them to the airport to meet Chad and Jeanette and bring them back to Stonefield. Now he could concentrate on his academic paper.

Tom was trying to get a better feeling for the relativistic jet. He had worked out how big it was at least. A 100-second event had caused a long Gamma Ray Burst from a relativistic jet as the collapsing Wolf-Rayet star went into a hypernova, at a distance of only 1100 light years from the solar system! He scan-read many of the latest papers. There were many relativistic jet experts out there, and their papers, at the hard end, were very challenging to dissect and understand. The general consensus was that protons with relativistic speeds collided with low speed thermal protons in the dense stellar wind of the Wolf Rayet star. A cascade of secondary particles from these collisions created the gamma ray burst. The jet would have been moving at the lowest speed of the particles. Some researchers claimed that this was around a quarter of the speed of light. These peer-reviewed papers now supported his hypothesis that this jet could have taken some 880 years to pass the Solar System. Whatever deadly effect it would have had on the Earth during its transit, it would have lasted that long.

Tom looked at Patrick's email and the image from Dendera, the so called *light bulb* image. It showed a snake emerging from a flower within a cocoon. It surely depicted the relativistic jet with a plasma cocoon emerging from an expanding hypernova remnant that was left after the hypernova explosion. The relative dimensions of the image would surely have been correct. If the jet cocoon had an opening angle of around 3°, then the radius of the jet, after travelling 1100 light years, would be 1100 light years times the tangent of 1.5°. After checking on his calculator, the radius came to around 30 light years. If the diameter of the cocoon, depicted in the Dendera carved image, was 60 light years across, then the jet length dimension indeed looked to be around four times that in length.

The figure in the Dendera image, stooping underneath the jet, seemed to confirm the impression that the person was taking cover. Knowing their real astrophysical dimensions, the relative size of the jet and cocoon must have meant that the relativistic jet had been seen from quite a long way off. It seemed a reasonable conclusion, that if the Earth had actually been *enveloped* in the cocoon of plasma, then a significant proportion of life on Earth would have been completely wiped out. So the total image and the computed dimensions now suggested that this was not the case. Now he needed to work out what physical dangers to life on Earth the presence of a relativistic jet so far away could possibly have caused.

So, this was an unimaginably huge beam of charged particles, some 220 light years long, travelling at relativistic speeds, spiralling in a central collimated beam with a cocoon of plasma spreading out to some 60 light years in diameter. This was utterly enormous, and must have affected hundreds, if not thousands of stars and their exoplanetary systems along its path. The Earth and its resident life forms had been incredibly lucky, if the jet had passed so far off, but this astrophysical event had clearly been terribly dangerous.

The heart of the danger was definitely of magnetic origin. The magnetic field generated by the jet would have comprised circular field rings around it, at right angles to the direction of the jet, effectively passing straight through the plane of the solar system. The solar system is only about 1/800 of a light year across, and the plasma cocoon after travelling 1100 light years, would have been possibly some 60 light years in diameter.

Tom knew that from academic literature, the minimum energy needed to create relativistic jets and a gamma ray burst was known. From this energy, $E = mc^2$, he could calculate the mass of the beam and then the number of moving charged nuclei. Moving charged particles create a current which generate a magnetic field. Sure, there would be shielding since there would be positive protons and negative electrons moving as a plasma, but the shielding would not be perfect. In addition, the plasma cocoon would carry its own magnetic field. A recent academic publication describing kink instabilities in relativistic jets now seemed very relevant. The 220 light-year-long jet, travelling at a quarter of the speed of light, would take 880 years to pass, so this gave the current as the number of charged particles passing per second. This would at least give a first approximation

Looking again at the Dendera *light bulb* image, at arm's length, the cocoon opened up around 25cm. Tom then reasoned, if the image was proportional, the Earth might indeed be around 50 light years from the central self-collimating jet of moving charged particles and that would mean 20 light years from the plasma cocoon.

In a first approximation, the magnetic field of the jet would comprise tangential rings around it, like a magnetic field around a DC current moving along a wire. A whole body of astrophysics work had established that the typical energy to create a relativistic jet was at least 10^{45} Joules. From this, the mass could be determined from $E = mc^2$. The academic literature also established that a jet from a Wolf-Rayet collapse in a binary configuration would be travelling at around 0.25 the speed of light c. so the mass was 10^{28}kg. Dividing by the mass of the proton, 1.67×10^{-27}kg, gave 7×10^{54} charged particles. Multiplying by the charge per proton gave around 10^{36}Coulombs, and this charge took 880 years to pass. That gave a current of around 4×10^{25}Amps.

If the magnetic field were not shielded at all, at 50 light years away the magnitude would be the current, times the permeability μ_0, divided by 2π divided by 50 light years. This gave around 16 Teslas at the jet itself, but there would be mutual shielding by the positive and negative charges and the plasma cocoon. Now he had to make an assumption. To what extent did the positive and negative particles mutually cancel the magnetic field? If it were unshielded by one part in say $100,000$, it would still have a magnetic field strength of 160 micro Teslas at a distance of 50 light years. The Earth had a surface field between 25 and 65 micro Teslas, while the surface field of the Sun was around 100 micro Teslas.

From first principles, the jet affected the Earth and the Sun. So, the shielding estimate had to lie between $100,000$ and a million. What about choosing 200, 000? At 50 light years that meant the jet generated a magnetic field of 80 micro Teslas. In reality, the plasma cocoon was also carrying a magnetic field, but this would have been less significant.

The central dipole which was causing the Sun's surface field was a solar radius away from the surface. Unlike the jet, the Sun's magnetic field did not fall off as 1/r and so many complicated magnetic field papers, well outside his comfort zone, seemed to suggest modelling plasma magnetic fields was really complicated. He needed a field strength both capable of dragging all the Sun's solar wind away in a spiral, and one which affected the Earth's magnetic field. Another clue was needed from somewhere, which determined the absolute diameter of that plasma spiral, but where would he find that?

Clearly, at a large distance from the Sun, the jet now dominated the course of the entire solar wind. This meant that for 880 years, the entire solar wind would be effectively channelled towards the jet. The major solar wind emission is closer to each of the Sun's poles, so both emissions would be dragged along field lines around the jet. The Sun is spinning at an angle of about six degrees off the orbital plane, so relative to the Earth, the solar wind stream might look like two huge spirals heading towards the jet. In fact, the solar wind would be trapped to spiral around circular field lines around the jet, never reaching it. This was quite sobering to work through. No one had ever really thought about these things before. Tom realised he couldn't be absolutely right on all the details because he was trying to reconstruct an event from long ago in the past, by making many assumptions. Nevertheless, it was very exciting to attempt to derive a valid qualitative answer.

In terms of the real effects on the Earth, more precise modelling would be needed. The *effective* plasma shielding of the jet's magnetic field may have been a lot less, and or the jet may have passed much closer. Either way, even at 50 light years away, the jet had a magnetic field which would have rendered the Earth's surface magnetic field ineffective. In essence the Earth would have had no protection from the Sun's solar wind, and the Sun would have been rendered highly unstable, magnetically, for some 880 years. It was known that even when the Sun was only slightly more active, the Sun generated up to 300% more ultraviolet in the highest energy UV-C band. The Sun would have become *absolutely hyperactive* and the UV levels would have been *off the scale* for 880 years!

Tom paused to look out over the deep blue Caribbean Sea. The *Petit*

Piton looked very majestic in the early sunshine. Just then the door to their villa opened and out stepped Mary-Anne wearing her white bath robe.

'Hello my darling,' Tom remarked.

'Good morning! Have you been up long?'

'I didn't want to disturb you. I just had to do a few more very boring astrophysics calculations. I have been up for an hour or so. Did you already want to go to breakfast, or did you want me to make you a cup of tea?'

'You carry on. I will make us both tea. We can go to breakfast in an hour or so. It is already warm and before I make our tea, I just want to take a short dip in our pool before we go. Does that sound like a plan?'

'That sounds perfect, thanks. You aren't going to swim naked again and distract me?'

'Maybe you need a little distraction.' She smiled in a naughty, teasing way, then undid her bath robe, letting it fall to the ground.

Tom was transfixed on her, watching her walk down the steps into the pool.

'It is lovely,' she called, as she swam across the pool, then rolled over onto her back. It was all a little too much for Tom.

'You are dangerously attractive, my darling.'

'Thank you. Why don't you also come in the pool?' Mary-Anne replied, taunting him.

'I love you, you know,' Tom replied, very distracted from his laptop now.

Suddenly that iridescent purple hummingbird appeared back over the pool again, above Mary-Anne. She lay gliding on the surface of the water looking up at the beautiful bird.

'Your new admirer is back.'

'He is beautiful. I know, I shouldn't really tease you so much, but wasn't it Einstein who said that our subconscious mind works much faster? That means *me distracting you* is a powerful tool to help you reach deeper insights faster.'

'Thank you honey. I love being distracted by your naked naughtiness.'

'Listen, I will let you continue with your new insights after this short distraction, and go make us some tea.'

She walked towards the steps, and then climbed out of the pool. She put on her bath robe, then went back into the villa. Tom shook his head and smiled and then tried to refocus, looking at his notes on his laptop.

After about ten minutes, she returned bringing two cups of tea on a tray. 'I even found these coconut biscuits.' She pulled up a chair and sat at the table with Tom.

'So, what new perspectives have I helped you to reach?'

'OK, I have been trying to work out what danger the relativistic jet transit caused to life on the Earth, and remember, it went on for 880 years. I have come up with two main things, extremely high ultraviolet levels impacting the Earth, and a huge spiralling tube of solar wind particles heading from the Sun towards the jet. That solar wind spiral would have impacted the Earth each time the Earth's orbit brought it between the jet and the Sun. So, there would have been a very dangerous period of the year, maybe for several weeks, when it would have been incredibly dangerous to be outside during the daytime, possibly also at night. The UV levels of the Sun would also have been significantly enhanced throughout the whole transit, but even more so during the solar wind transit time as the solar wind impacted the upper atmosphere. This would have seriously damaged the protective ozone layer, as well as injecting a huge amount of energy into it. Global weather systems would have been violently impacted, causing dramatic mixing of atmospheric layers. There would have been endless, violent, high-discharge thunderstorms, torrential rain, and myriad, bright, multicoloured aurorae in the sky.'

'Very interesting my darling. So that all ties in with the story about the indigenous peoples of Australia and their accounts of the *Rainbow Serpent*. Is there any other physical evidence that supports this in the *Earth Science* field?'

'Good question. In fact, yes. I found a study of an enormous number of north-south magnetic field direction anomalies discovered in sediments, exactly during the 880 years of the early Holocene. Remember, that the field direction in sediments is only *locked in* when the sediments dry out. The presence of the relativistic jet predicts that the Earth's surface magnetic field would have gone absolutely haywire, and that is precisely what has been reported in the literature. I found a great paper by an

Argentinian guy, Hugo.'

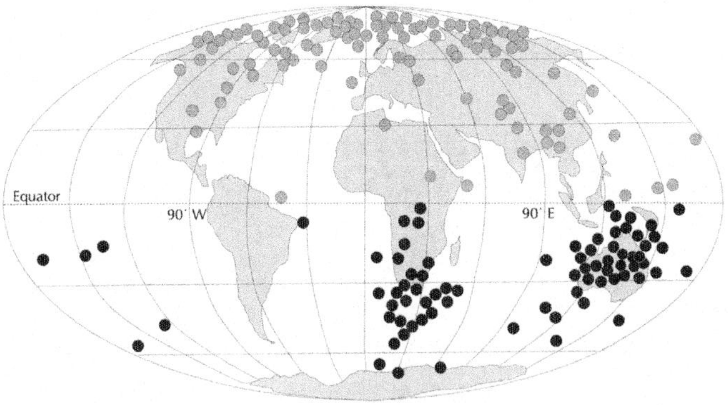

Chaotic North South magnetic poles from sediments 10,000-9,000 BCE

'What about the solar wind? Did that end up hitting the Earth's surface?'

'Well we see many small, scorching impact points all over the Earth's surface. The only thing which can cause rocks to vitrify is something like *coronal mass ejection* plasma, but I think it's more likely to be *coronal discharge* and high energy thunderstorms. If something affected the Earth's magnetic field, causing it to go unstable, possibly even with multiple poles, one might think that ionised plasma from the Sun might start to follow those magnetic field lines right down to the surface. The problem is that the sheer amount of air would most likely have prevented any plasma reaching the surface, unless of course it was an endless stream.'

'But I thought you told me once, that those *coronal mass ejections* are quite rare.'

'They are quite rare, and only happen when the Sun is in an active state, which we see from the high number of sunspots. But the Sun has an average surface magnetic field around twice that of the Earth. Extremely hot plasma constantly erupts from the surface of the Sun ... if we can consider it to have a *surface*, the surface is as tenuous as the air we breathe, ... the plasma arcs out along magnetic loops and then arrives back to the surface again. These are called *prominences*. They are held onto by the Sun's magnetic field. However, when the surface magnetic field lines get all tangled, reconnection of the magnetic loops can occur lower down, freeing the plasma that is travelling high above the surface along a loop, and that loss of plasma is a *coronal mass ejection*. If there is an extremely high external field, it might be possible that this could interrupt the Sun's magnetic field, causing many more coronal mass ejections of dangerous plasma to be emitted, and all that is channelled along the same direction for 880 years!'

'So, you are saying that the presence of the jet could have affected both the Earth's magnetic field as well as the Sun's. How close would the jet have needed to be in order to do that?'

'That's the key point. How close was it, because the magnetic field of those loops are thousands of times stronger than the average magnetic field? I must say that I just love your questions. It forces me to justify my statements.'

He took a folded piece of paper from his pocket, and a small pencil, opened out the paper and started to do some calculations as if to check that what he was saying made sense.

'OK, we know the power of the jet, that is well documented as the minimum energy needed to punch through the stellar envelope of the collapsing Wolf-Rayet star, as it goes into a hypernova, otherwise it wouldn't form any jets.'

'What is your final conclusion my darling, and *in English* please?'

'OK, Sorry. Using reasonable numbers, I have proven that if the jet passed within 50 light years of our solar system, the magnetic field strength was still high enough, to distort the Earth's magnetic field substantially, and possibly strongly influence the Sun.'

'OK, I am trying to follow. So, again, when you say *when the jet hit*, you simply mean *when the jet was within 50 light years*?'

'Yes, exactly, and the effect of the jet would have been predominantly *extreme magnetic interference*. We don't envisage any part of the jet striking the Earth; the surface of the planet would have been virtually destroyed in that case, which it wasn't. We know the jet had to be a considerable distance away, because it was viewed in its entirety in the sky, as reported in those myths and legends. The effects would have been the same at a distance of say half that, at 30 light years, only the interfering magnetic field strength as felt by the Earth would have been slightly higher, and consequently it would have had a greater influence on the Sun's magnetic field. I will need to think long and hard whether I can reason how deserts were turned to glass, and rocks were melted by only magnetic interference. To achieve that kind of surface damage, I start to think that 50 light years might be a little too far away to cause that directly. Alternatively, perhaps it caused that damage indirectly.'

'So, you are saying that the presence of the jet, at say 50 or so light years means that the strength of its own magnetic field was strong enough to interfere with the Earth's magnetic field. How does an interfering magnetic field affect the Earth? Before you answer that, why were you so happy to reason that the jet could be so far away and so large, rather than something smaller which passed through the solar system?'

'Now that I have reasoned it could still affect the Earth, while transiting at 50 light years away, then it is statistically now more likely. These Wolf-Rayet stars are considered to be the evolutionary path that all giant stars will eventually pass through, so they cannot be uncommon. More importantly, they form in clusters and planets being affected by a GRB or from a relativistic jet must be reasonably likely. We expect there to be a few thousand in our galaxy, although so far we have only found a few hundred. They can form with their spin axes in any direction, but the likelihood of being affected by a jet propagating along the direction of that axis towards us, after a hypernova, must still be a reasonable number.'

'If we just consider the Earth at 1100 light years away, with the jet and cocoon slightly expanding as it moves through space, by the time it reaches us, and taking some easy numbers, it probably has a maximum interfering magnetic field range of say 50 light years. That effectively means a disturbance tunnel some 100 light years in diameter, affecting all of the space around it. The key point is that if we will suffer the effects of a jet, the statistics must be reasonable. Think of a collapsing Wolf-Rayet star as it goes into hypernova and emits two relativistic jets, one from each pole of the collapsing star. One will head towards us, one will not, so we consider the total *hemisphere of influence* of that hypernova at 1100 light years, in this case. Only one precise alignment is of any danger – that is a circle of diameter 100 light years on that hemisphere at a distance of 1100 light years. It isn't particularly interesting for non-astrophysicists, but the likelihood of being impacted by a jet must be reasonable. In this case, the chance of being hit is 1 in 240 every time a hypernova occurs. I have to say that in the same cluster of stars, there are a few left, and that statistic does sound reasonable. Unfortunately, we are only 1100 light years away, and not double that distance, and all stars in a cluster are generally formed at the same time.'

Tom continued. 'On your other question, during the most dangerous period, the jet's magnetic field lines drag the solar wind through the Earth's orbit around the jet. It is just a question of the geometry of the jet relative to the Earth. We are lucky that the jet did not transit directly above the Sun, otherwise the geometry tells us that the Earth would have been affected for several months, *twice* per year.'

'That sounds a little too complicated for me to understand. By the way, did you say the solar wind would be spiralling towards the jet?'

'Well, I didn't say it quite like that, but actually that is exactly what happens. The solar wind will leave the Sun following the Sun's own magnetic field lines. The Sun's own magnetic field falls off with distance and at some point, the magnetic field of the jet becomes greater and then the solar wind will spiral around the field lines of the jet. They will then effectively travel in a huge spiral towards the jet. It will be coming from the Sun's north and south pole, so I guess it might possibly be travelling as a pair of constant diameter, counter spirals, each travelling in opposite directions.'

'I was thinking about what people on Earth would have seen in the sky. There are so many carved spirals in rocks in well-dated palaeolithic sites, and in cave art. Could these spirals not be those people carving what they saw in the sky for 880 years?' Mary-Anne reasoned.

'Wow, that is yet another genius insight. I just love how you take my complicated astrophysics monologue and then derive a very down-to-earth reality that people can actually relate to. In fact, I guess the people would have seen a spiral coming from the Sun rotating one way, then when they looked away from the Sun, they would see the spiral rotating the other way.'

'Well, you know, there is a megalithic site, *Tarxien,* in Malta which people have always described as a temple. There is also an underground chamber quite nearby called the *Hypogeum*. On the outside wall of the Tarxien Temple are pairs of counter spirals carved into the rock. In the light of what you just said, it would now seem very likely that these spiral carvings were a warning, indicating if you see these in the sky, then you should be underground! Again, it seems highly unlikely that those spirals were carved some 7000 years later, and they must have been contemporary. This would then date that megalithic structure also to 11,770 years old!'

The tropical air was warm and refreshing, but the bright sunlight was increasingly becoming interrupted as dark clouds increased overhead. Around their villa, the bright green banana tree leaves started to clatter loudly, as gusts of wind suggested another downpour was becoming ever more imminent.

'Hey, why don't we go now for breakfast? It sounds as if it is about to rain. Let's quickly get dressed and head to the restaurant before we get absolutely soaked,' Tom suggested.

'Good idea. I'm really hungry for another lovely tropical breakfast. By the way, what time did you say that we needed to be at the airport to meet Chad and Jeanette? Was it noon?'

'Noon indeed. I already wandered over to reception first thing and booked the taxi. Everything is arranged,' he confirmed.

They went inside to get dressed and emerged from the villa some minutes later. Not very far away, they could hear the rumble of thunder.

'Lovely,' Mary-Anne remarked with a hint of sarcasm. 'One moment, I'll just grab an umbrella, just in case the rain starts on our way to the restaurant!'

'Good idea.'

8 Victoria, Australia: the indigenous people's 11,770-year-old sunset observatories

Approaching the Indigenous Carisbrook Stone Arrangement, Victoria Australia

A large, bright red minibus covered with odd looking symbols had hooted in the driveway at 5:30 a.m. It had been difficult to get up at the crack of dawn, but Patrick had managed well. He had left his bag, all packed and ready, by the front door. Hearing the hooting, he had only needed to grab his food for the journey from the fridge, and he was outside and ready to go. He had taken his laptop and a 4G dongle, as well as his headphones, so he was good for the entire trip. The nine hour journey down had been really comfortable. Fortunately the minibus seats were surprisingly quite luxurious, so he even felt refreshed as they approached *Carisbrook*, all ready for the first short hike to see the famous stone formation. According to the schedule, they would see another stone arrangement at *Lake Wongan* later that day, and visit *Wurdi Youang*, a third site, tomorrow.

On the way down, he had done a bit of background reading via his 4G connection. Many academics had stated that the boomerang-shaped structure at *Carisbrook* was just a piece of art, and because the winter and summer solstices never changed their rising and setting times, the site could not be dated. That was certainly true, but just maybe they marked out other days of the year! The *precession of the equinoxes* meant that the Earth's wobble would have slowly changed the date when the solstices occurred, but Patrick was searching for some stone markers which linked the site to the relativistic jet transit.

Patrick perused his fellow archaeological co-travellers. They seemed a mixed but interesting bunch. After Lake Wongan, they would stay at a nearby lodge where a serious barbecue would be laid on.

They were some 150km north west of Melbourne. The minibus pulled

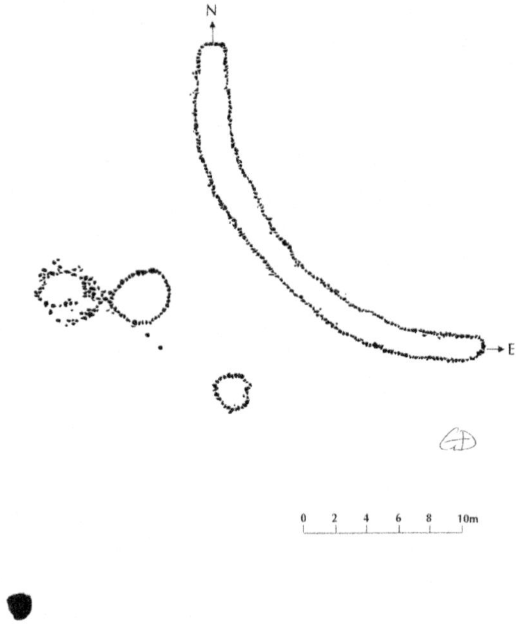

Carisbrook Sunset Shadow Observatory

off the main road and they parked beside some farm buildings. They climbed out and the guide led them along a small creek for about half a mile until they reached the stone arrangement.

It was quite impressive to see it first-hand.

'It looks rather vulnerable here, just sitting out here in the open,' someone remarked.

'You would think that, but it's almost impossible to find without a guide. Even Google Earth have hidden it,' the guide replied. 'Their image processing blends the location well into the field scrub. It's a lovely piece of indigenous art isn't it?'

The boomerang shape of stones looked really remarkable. Surely this was not just art, this surely had a function. Using his compass, Patrick determined that one end of the curving boomerang shape pointed due north, the other end pointed due east, that could not just be a coincidence. Two rings of stones stood to the west, and a large rock was standing quite a distance off to the south west.

Patrick could hear the guide telling the same old story he had read online about the stone arrangement being of unknown function and impossible to date. Well, that remained to be seen. What if it were an observatory marking out the dangerous period of the year around March 23rd? Quite conveniently, the sun was reasonably low in the sky. Without drawing too much attention, he stood in one of the circles and watched how his shadow was cast towards the curved stone structure. His shadow would of course grow longer as the sun went down. The two different circles would logically cast different shadow directions towards the curved stone structure. Did they correspond to two particular dates?

He took several photos of the forty-metre curving structure on his iPhone, making sure to capture the two circles and the large outlier stone to the south west.

So, was this some kind of shadow observatory determining the dangerous period? If he could prove it, he could date the site back to 9750 B.C.E. That question should be easy to answer using Stellarium. Patrick listened as the guide told the same old story he had read online about it being *Indigenous Art* in a boomerang shape and it being of unknown function or date.

A girl about his age was travelling in the group with her parents. She seemed to be intrigued that he was on the bus alone. She wandered over to him.

'Hello, we didn't speak yet. My name is Kylie.'

'Hi, Patrick. Nice to meet you.'

'Ah, you're not from Aus.'

'No. American. I've been here for two years. My Dad is an astrophysicist at Sydney University. My parents went off for their own holiday to the Caribbean. I didn't fancy that.'

'Wow. The Caribbean. Yeah, I understand. My parents are both into archaeology and anthropology of the indigenous peoples. They wouldn't let me stay at home alone.'

'Sorry to hear. I'm actually quite interested in these rock formations.'

'Really? Come on, that's strange. What can possibly be interesting about some indigenous art?'

'I just have a hunch. I think this might be part of a story about the Earth's history. I think this site may date back to 11,770 years ago. My Dad is Tom Walker, and he was recently on TV talking about a relativistic jet.'

'Wow, so that was your Dad! I saw him on TV. Amazing! What a coincidence.'

'Yeah, it's pretty cool. He is now racing to gather as much evidence as he can to prove his theory. I'm trying to help, and I think these stone arrangements might just be part of the story.'

Just at that moment, the guide called out, 'I think we're all finished here guys, back to the minibus and then we head on to *Lake Wongan* before travelling to the lodge for that barbecue.'

There was a *woo hoo* followed by and some laughter, and then the group wandered back along the creek and climbed into the minibus.

Wongan lake was not far away. The guide was sitting up front with the driver. She turned to face the passengers.

'So, just like *Carisbrook*, there is no way to date the *Wongan Lake* stone arrangement. Many experts have looked at it and have concluded that it's another work of indigenous people's art. It's still worth a look as it seems very abstract in its form. *Wongan Lake* is about a 100k south west of here and we should arrive in just over an hour.'

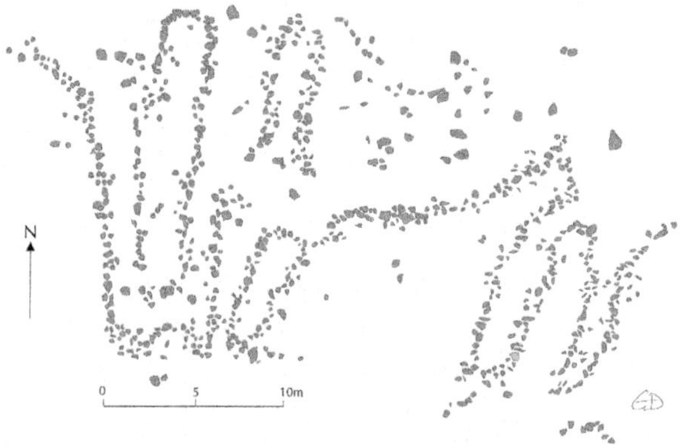

Lake Wongan Stone Arrangement

Patrick had taken out his laptop and was on 4G looking at the bizarre form of the Lake Wongan stone arrangement he had downloaded. It covered an area of around 30 metres by ten and seemed to be a long, squeezed, zig zag line of carefully placed stones. Looking down on it, at the left hand end, the line of stones curved down to a flat base then climbed vertically for half the distance. Within this saucepan-like shape, a long tube of stones rose beyond where the first line had started. Another diagonal line of stones went from the saucepan design, starting with a small vertical stretched oval, then rising slowly as it moved to the right, culminating in a narrow double zig zag of stones, falling down to the same level of the saucepan shape base.

That diagonal line looked very interesting, and there were gaps in some of the formations. Patrick opened *Word* and pasted an image of the arrangement. He would check the December 21st and June 21st directions from the start to the end of the relativistic jet transit. His Dad had written in his message that the transit had taken around 880 years. First he would do the exercise for Carisbrook, to test his theory.

He booted up *Stellarium* and selected Melbourne as the location and then set the date back to 8870 B.C.E. This was the last time the structure was used and the stones would have been adjusted over the period from 9750-8870 B.C.E. He then checked the sunrise and sunset directions for the December and June dates. This gave two pairs of angles which he could impose on the different sites.

He took an image of the *Carisbrook* formation and then set it as a background in his *Word* document. He then drew on cardinal north-south and east-west axes. Carefully using the rotate tool, he created the directional lines in bright colours for the two pairs of sunrise and sunset directions for December 21st and June 21st. He grouped everything. Now he could move the overlaid shapes to test his hypothesis. There didn't seem to be any relation to the sunrise directions for Carisbrook, but he immediately noticed that when the axis of the sunset lines was placed on the lower east-pointing tip of the *boomerang* shape, each sunset direction line touched the outer edge of one of the circles. So this showed how the circles were used to mark out the dangerous half of the year, when the Earth was rising above the Galactic plane. He now needed to check one thing. So what were the December 21st and June 21st directions today? Resetting *Stellarium* to today's date, he quickly found that neither of the two sunset direction lines came anywhere near the two stone circles. He had successfully dated this site to last being in use in 8870 B.C.E. But what about the dangerous period? He checked the sunset angles for March 15th to April 1st. Wow, the two angles exactly matched the large outlier stone to the southwest of the formation. This was surely proof that this was indeed not a piece of art but a sunset observatory dated to the time of the jet transit.

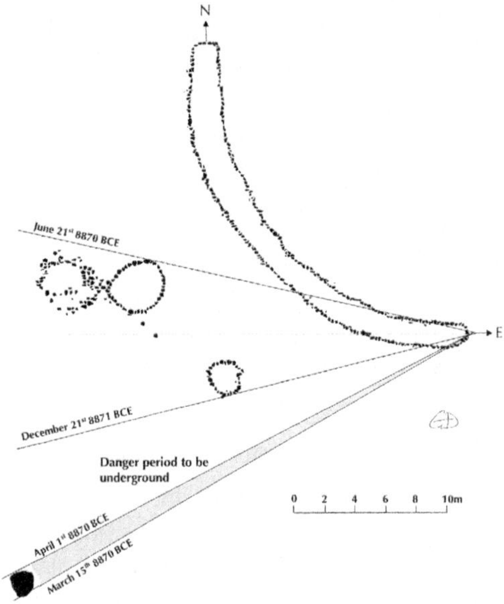

Carisbrook 8870 B.C.E Alignments

Patrick's heart was now racing. He now needed to send this to his Dad. He added a title to his image: *Carisbrook Sunset Shadow Observatory 9750-8870 B.C.E.* He then added the actual sunset direction angles and took a photo of his schematic. He first forwarded the image, and then wrote a message: *Hi Dad, look at this! Carisbrook is definitely a complex structure. I think this image proves it is one of the World's first observatories, marking out the time when the Earth was above the Galactic plane, as well as the dangerous period when to be underground. Last used in 8870 BCE. On to Lake Wongan next. Let's see what we find there. Hugs Patrick.* It was close to 2 p.m. which made it around midnight in St. Lucia. His Dad was probably asleep already.

After only two minutes, his phone buzzed. His Dad was awake. Patrick read his reply: *Patrick, utterly amazing! Well done. Another paper at least. You are adding a rich interpretation to the endeavours of Australia's indigenous peoples, proving them to be some of the World's first astronomers. Mom and I are sitting in a bar looking out into a very dark Caribbean night. We just ordered an expensive tropical cocktail to celebrate your discovery. Good luck at Lake Wongan. Mom sends her congratulations also, Dad*

The data processing exercise had taken about half the journey time.

There was still time to process that *Lake Wongan* stone arrangement image.

He replaced the *Carisbrook* background image with an image of the *Lake Wongan* stone arrangement, and started to move the grouped set of sunset lines. Sure enough, when he selected a very large stone in the top right hand part of the arrangement as the likely viewing point, the east-west line ran straight through a series of spaced stones, while the December 21st and June 21st sunset lines coincided with breaks and peaks in the undulating stones. This was clearly a structure which had been designed to accommodate changes, and the breaks in the formation demonstrated that stones had been moved for the duration of its use. This definitely was also a shadow observatory and by placing a spear or staff at key points, the direction of the sunset shadows could be compared with the positions of the stones at different points and from his calculations dated to 8870 B.C.E. which would have been the last time it was used.

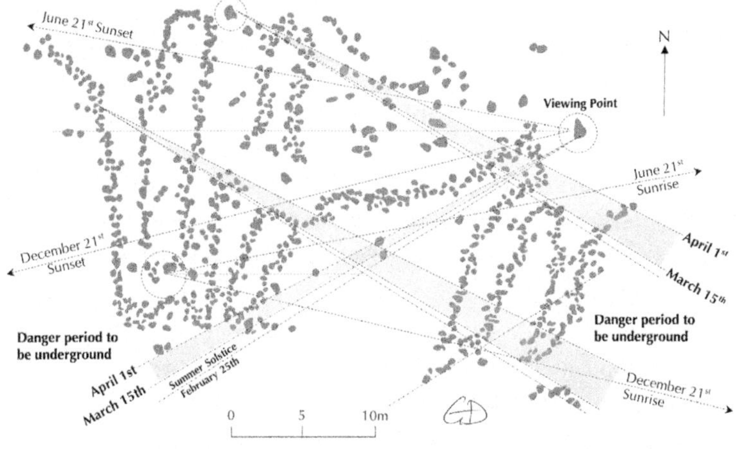

Lake Wongan Stone Arrangement 8870 B.C.E Alignments

Now it was time to check the sunrise angles. Within a short time it was clear that the only other large rock in the bottom left hand corner had to be the viewing point. The sunrise directions mapped really well. There also seemed to be a number of stones marking out the east-west direction. All he needed to do now was to find where the structure mapped out the danger period between March 15th and April 1st.

A large stone in the mid top of the formation mapped March 15th sunrise to the top of a rising undulation, while April 1st sunrise mapped to a line of stones from the viewing point as well as to the end of the formation. There was another potential viewing point for the sunrise directions during the danger period, so he added that as well. It was interesting that the danger period sunset as seen from the large viewing point stone also mapped well to key stones in the structure.

Patrick was certainly on a roll now.

He added the title: *Lake Wongan – Another Indigenous People's Shadow observatory,* then forwarded it to his Dad.

Within moments, he got his father's reply: *Patrick ... unbelievable! Well done! To be honest, this may all be too much for a paper now it is probably both a press release and even possibly a book! Let me know what happens at Wurdi Youang tomorrow. We're heading to bed now. Take care. Love M&D.* Just at that moment, the tour-bus guide's phone rang, and she answered it. Patrick was sitting quite close and he heard her say something about a schedule change.

After the guide ended the call, she turned to face the passengers, 'OK everyone, that was the lodge. We're well ahead of schedule, so we have two options. I know that some of you were planning a hike tomorrow and would miss the *Wurdi Youang* trip. *Wurdi Youang* is actually very close to where we're staying tonight. We'll be arriving at the Lake Wongan site in around ten minutes or so. If we finish there in half an hour, we can also do *Wurdi Youang* today. Does anyone have any objections to fitting in *Wurdi Youang* today?'

'I'd be happy to do *Wurdi* today,' an old man at the back called out. 'They are saying it may rain tomorrow and right now the skies are a *beaut.* I'd love to get a photo of *Wurdi* in the sunset.'

'You're right mate!' another voice said. 'Three sites in one day and all we'll need is some of the amber fluid with a sunset barbie. Hey missy, what's on the grill tonight?'

'There are wonderful beef steaks, and all the sausages you can eat!' the guide replied. 'OK then, if there are no objections, we'll plan to do *Wurdi Youang* before we arrive at the lodge. I'll give the lodge a call.

After a short time, the minibus came to a halt right up beside a lake.

'Welcome to the *Lake Wongan* stone arrangement,' the guide said loudly.

Everyone climbed out. The sun was setting which made the scene look rather enchanting. Lake Wongan was almost completely dried up.

'As you can see, we're lucky to be able to walk out to the basalt islet where the stone arrangement is,' she continued. 'Let's plan on getting out to see the stones, take a few photos, and then we'll climb back on board and continue south.'

Patrick walked along the makeshift pontoon, which led right to the islet. The pontoon had probably been constructed over marshland, but the lakebed was now completely dry. When he got to the formation, he was sure he was looking at it with a very different perspective from that of his fellow travellers. Kylie came over. 'So what do you think, Patrick?'

'It's definitely an observatory. Please promise me you won't tell anyone.'

'Of course. I won't tell a soul. So you've worked out that both the sites are ancient sunset observatories, dating back some 11,770 years. That's cool. You must secretly think it's funny that everyone is just looking at them as if they were artwork or for a ritual ceremony or something.'

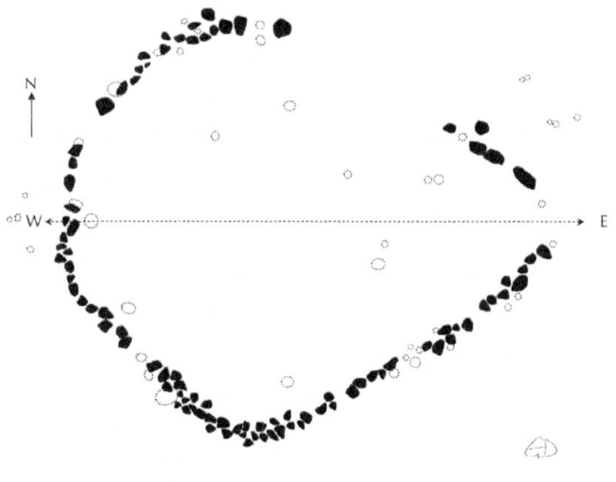

Wurdi Youang, Sunset Shadow Observatory

'Maybe I do, but I have to confess, I find the whole discovery utterly amazing. Just think, these people *lived off the land*. They lived according to the summer and winter seasons. This structure is marking out a part of the year *independent* of the winter and summer solstices. This is their calendar stone structure. This surely is absolute proof that these people needed to mark out a particular period of the year!'

'I think it is incredible what you have worked out. These are just stones lying on the ground but these are so vulnerable. From what you have explained, the exact positions of each and every stone is critically important. Someone will need to fix every one in place, to preserve this significant piece of the World's history.'

'And let's hope the people of the Earth won't be needing it to mark out a cataclysmic period, anytime soon!'

Patrick took a small video using his iPhone and then he and Kylie joined the others as they made their way back to the bus.

Back in his seat, he downloaded his last target, the stone arrangement at *Wurdi Youang*. This looked more like an *orange segment* with its outer curved edge pointing west. There were several breaks in the stones and many small rings of stones within the structure.

The minibus headed off while Patrick continued to work. He replaced the background image of the *Lake Wongan* stone arrangement with the image of *Wurdi Youang* and started to move the grouped collection of June 21st and December 21st sunset direction lines for 8870 B.C.E. By locating the axis of the pairs of sunset directions for the December and June dates close to the axis of the arrangement, dead central on the east-west line, the different sunset directions matched the breaks in the stone arrangement. This already looked very compelling. Now he would search for the potential viewing points to identify the danger period.

Using the angles from the previous image he quickly found two viewing locations for the sunset angles for March 15th to April 1st. Both matched breaks in the stone arrangement. The viewing point stone at the top of the structure also served as a convincing viewing point for the sunrise directions during the danger period. He had cracked this one as well! This was definitely another sunrise sunset observatory where the stones had been slowly moved over the 880 years while it was in use.

Patrick sent his last image off to his father. He would only see it in the morning. He also sent the three images with their overlays in an email message to Manu in Ghana.

The drive to their last site, *Wurdi Youang,* was pleasant in the late afternoon. When they finally arrived and hiked out to the location, Patrick again could hear the guide telling everyone that the site was probably used by indigenous peoples to observe the solstice directions in recent times. He smiled to himself.

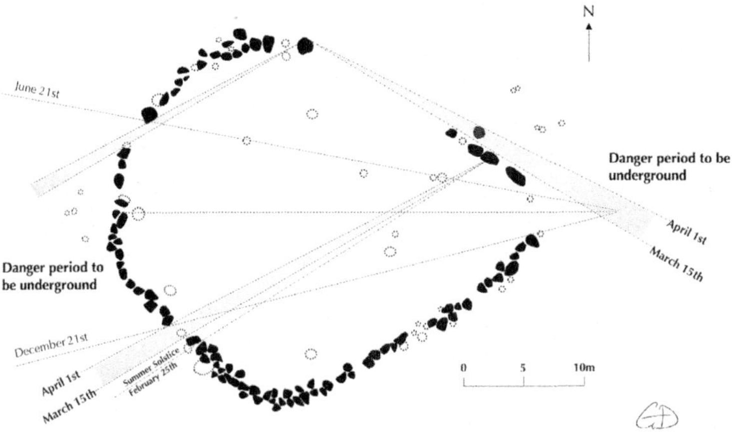

Wurdi Youang, Sunset Shadow Observatory 8870 B.C.E. Alignments

He walked around the site and took some detailed photos of the breaks in the curved line of stones on the west of the structure, then headed back to the minibus.

'OK everyone,' the guide called. 'Are we all done? I am sure the barbecue is awaiting us. We're only 25 clicks from home. Let's all get back on the bus.'

Patrick was really excited. He felt he had achieved quite a lot in deciphering the Australian part of the story. So Uncle Chad was in Mexico with the ancient sites there, his father was working out the astrophysics. So what should he and Manu try to solve now? What had not been explored? There was an awful lot of geometrical cave art everywhere. There seemed to be a pattern in what was drawn. From Peru to North America, the cave art comprised alien-looking figures, spiralling balls and long zig zag lines. Surely this was also describing the same event.

He would now need to let that sink into his subconscious. As the bus headed off to the lodge and the barbecue, Patrick wrote one last long message to Manu.

Manu, I think I may have cracked the Australian story. The indigenous peoples here were clearly some of the earliest astronomers who recorded the event using stone arrangements, making sure they could identify that dangerous part of the year, when to take cover and stay safe. Here in Australia the peak of the very dangerous time the last time these structures were used in 8870 BCE, was 18 days *after their summer solstice on February 25th, starting March 15th. That of course was our winter solstice in the northern hemisphere. Identifying the exact dates would have been critical for survival. We should now ask if this event also marked out the first time man needed to invent a calendar! Your re-interpretation of the Dendera frieze after cracking Göbekli Tepe pillar 43 has helped us decode these Australian sunrise and sunset shadow observatories. I was just wondering . . . what is our next challenge? What about asking why there is so much similar geometric cave art all around the World. I am starting to wonder if some particular common features in the cave art may also be marking out the dangerous time of the year. Keep in touch, Patrick ;)*

9 UC Berkeley: plans for a new SETI strategy

Carl's Office, University of California at Berkeley

Carl was sitting at his desk. Every square centimetre of it was completely covered with tall piles of scientific papers. Behind him, his whiteboard was crammed with complex derivations of astrophysics equations. A half rubbed-out graph seemed to be showing some variation in magnetic field strength with something.

Suddenly, there was a loud knock on his door. 'Come in!' Carl called out.

The door opened, it was Jacqui Hau.

'Jacqui, I only put you on the plane just two days ago! I can't keep you away. Lovely to see you again, you are always welcome. How can I help?'

Jacqui was clearly quite flustered and Carl was not completely ready for her excited energetic outburst!

'Well, I called your contact Don Rogers at *Goddard*, who immediately asked me to come over to the facility, which led to conversations with other people there. Quickly, I got the impression that they were growing increasingly concerned that their TESS exoplanet satellite survey program was in serious jeopardy of bad-press scrutiny, unless they changed their search strategy to compensate for the relativistic jet transit,' Jacqui retorted somewhat breathlessly.

'OK, sounds interesting. Tell me more!'

'Well, the prohibitively expensive costs involved in TESS, means of course that they totally understood that getting caught out surveying a potentially *dead* region of space would have drastic consequences. It was assumed that *Goddard's* hard-won reputations meant they would always be ahead of the game. The end goal of their program is of course to identify *exoplanets with life*, not *fried dead worlds*, which once had life on them. I was then asked to wait in a room for about half an hour, then a legal guy appeared who then demanded I immediately sign a secrecy and non-disclosure agreement before they would continue talking to me.'

'Sounds serious!'

'Sure, but I reluctantly agreed, not knowing what this was all about, but after signing it, they then told me that this was *extremely serious* and potentially very embarrassing for *Goddard*. They were then asking how could everyone have missed this? All the clues were out there. But now, they were prepared to offer *a substantial sum* for you to head up a team to rescue their TESS program before the media story breaks, which it will, about how a relativistic jet in Earth's recent history, has rendered a vast tract of space *lifeless*!' Jacqui explained, now a little breathless.

'OK. Serious stuff Jacqui, but actually quite excellent news from where I'm sitting. Please, come in and sit down. So what do we imagine a *substantial* sum means? Did they give any indication? We would need enough to model the geometry of the jet transit through this part of the galaxy. We would also need to model the magnetic field of the jet and to make recommendations of exoplanetary systems where life more likely survived.'

'I asked them, and they were suggesting the figure could hit the *two million dollar* mark!'

'A very serious number. That already indicates their level of concern. Listen, let's get Ted and Chris onto this.'

Carl stood up and put his head round his door, looked one way, then the other. Ted was pinning up something on a noticeboard.

'Hey Ted, is Chris in his room? Jacqui is back here yet again! Can you believe that? She has already beaten us to Goddard.'

One door was open about four metres away.

'Chris, Jacqui is back here again,' Ted called out.

Chris came out of his room with a bemused look, and then started to wander down towards them

'Hi Jacqui! So what's the rundown on *Goddard*? I thought we'd only just said goodbye.'

'Hi Chris, Ted. I immediately bring good news.'

'Jacqui here has sourced us up to two million dollars to redirect the

Goddard search strategy for exoplanets. They forced her to sign an NDA, so that means they're seriously worried about any media issues. You're both covered by working here and I know we will do everything to meet the conditions of the funding. Were there any other aspects Jacqui?'

'Well, I agree already with your assessment. Model the transit as fast as possible. Map out the star systems affected and modify the TESS exoplanetary search to scan the least affected zone I guess.'

'That's a serious modelling task. We would need to look at data on the ground, such as anything recorded in ancient monuments to be able to do that,' Ted remarked. 'Ancient cultures may have drawn cave art, where the jet was seen against the night sky.'

'We certainly need to find as much as we can,' Chris added. 'Tom Walker's paper hinted at several sites that may hold many clues

'This is a great opportunity for the department and for Berkeley,' Carl remarked. 'You can't imagine how difficult it is to raise research funding these days. You're showing you have some serious skills in that department, Jacqui.'

Jacqui smiled, looking a little embarrassed.

'He's right Jacqui,' Chris remarked. 'This whole project is simply huge. All the things we mentioned the other day. They will write books about this stuff. The modifications to the *Drake equation* alone, is a major contribution. As you suggested, this is also an explanation for the *higher magnetic field* outside our solar system as measured by the Voyager spacecraft. I have also been thinking more about the additional dimensions to the *Fermi Paradox*, particularly if these Wolf-Rayet stars are a final stage, into which, all large blue stars will evolve. As for the *Great Filter,* through which all planetary civilizations need to pass, well we now know that this *Great Filter* is no longer a hypothetical construct. It's seriously real, and occurs regularly, whenever a Wolf-Rayet star implodes at the end of its life.'

'I totally agree. It's definitely a very big quantum shift in our thinking of the dangers that *life on Earth* faces,' Jacqui remarked. Suddenly her eyes became distracted by the astrophysics equations on the white board.

'Dr Rhodes, what is that on your white board? Did you already start modelling the magnetic field of the jet?'

'Well spotted! That is something that me and Chris took a look at only yesterday. Now that Tom Walker's paper is out, everyone will be out there, trying to dimension the jet, looking at the magneto-hydrodynamics, modelling the magnetic kink instabilities, and computing the actual magnetic field of that mother,' Carl explained. 'Fundamentally, there are academic trophies to be won and lost here. I would really like to get Berkeley well established as playing a key role in this analysis. I had an email from Tom Walker only yesterday. He was looking at the curved head of the jet. He has reasoned, and quite rightly, that the intense polar magnetic field during the collapse of the Wolf-Rayet star, distorted the initial jet as it emerged, dragging away the magnetic field within the jet, further diminishing the magnetic field's strength. Quite clearly, that explains why a relativistic jet would always have a *curved head*, just as the plasma of the Sun in a coronal mass ejection, carries the shape of the magnetic field away with it; the shape of the magnetic field being effectively frozen into the plasma. No one on the planet has ever described that in the literature. He needs some help, so I have offered to be a co-author.'

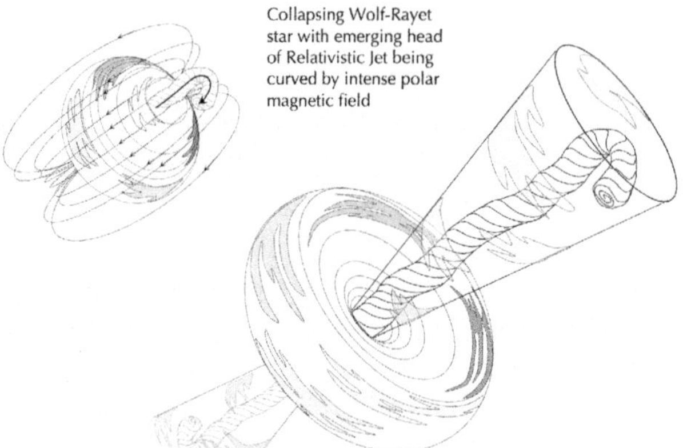

Wolf-Rayet Star Collapse

'That sounds great, Dr Rhodes. *Goddard* will be even more confident when you start publishing new insights and understandings of the relativistic jet phenomenon.'

'Well, before we publish anything, I will need to get the go ahead from Don Rodgers at *Goddard* to be sure we comply with all their non-disclosure conditions. It's more likely that they will want to hold a press conference, as soon as possible, to announce how they have *already* updated their exoplanetary search strategy before anyone cottons on to the implications of a passing relativistic jet for their TESS space program.'

'Well, we did make some progress already Jacqui,' Chris added. 'Building on Tom Walker's suggestion, we agree that the shape of the jet in the sky would be *serpentine* because the dying Wolf-Rayet star, in its *collapsar* state, is spinning *off-axis* at extremely high speed and these asymmetries create a jet with a spiralling shape. We looked at the underlying *magneto-hydrodynamics*, and sure there are those kink instabilities, but we don't believe they are sufficient to be the cause of the snake-like shape.'

'Wow guys, you really go fast!'

'Well, following Tom's first paper, the race is really on now, to be the leading academic centre of excellence and knowledge in this field. We need to make Berkeley the *soul of the machine*. Right now we don't have the luxury of taking six months to write papers, we need to get manuscripts out for review within weeks. If we can crack the main astrophysics, and be the first to publish, we are on the map. We will now need to seek approval from Goddard each time of course, because the funding will be key here.'

'So do we know exactly what the remit is for the use of that money from Goddard?' Ted asked.

'I understood from Jacqui here that we have carte blanche to *just do the right thing*. I would have said it's not *rocket science*, but that's exactly what it is. We know what needs to be done. Tom also emailed me his thoughts on the duration of the jet transit, which he is concluding at close to 880 years. He wrote saying he wants a very detailed analysis of the Greenland ice core record to further validate that duration. I'm sure we can use some of the funding for that. I guess the bottom line is that Goddard have a spacecraft up there, right now, potentially gathering data from a pretty dead part of the galaxy, where there is probably no life at all. Every second, they are wasting money, and the mission of TESS, the *Transiting Exoplanet Survey Satellite*, has a finite lifetime. With such a funding proposal, I immediately sense the gravity of the situation. They want reliable recommendations for survey changes ASAP.'

'To be honest, Dr Rhodes, I really think they are panicking. They know they have just spent billions of dollars on an exoplanet survey, which their press office has marketed as a *search for life*. They will want to avoid dead exoplanets caused by a relativistic jet transit as soon as possible.'

'Well why don't we all have a kick-off meeting, say tomorrow, to conclude our best guess of the jet transit path and a reasoned estimate of factors which can determine how far away it was from Earth? Modelling the magnetic field will be key to this. I know we looked at it only yesterday, but in truth we didn't get far. I need to talk to my friend Gabriele in Italy. He is one of the gurus in the field of relativistic jets.'

'Sure we can,' Ted replied. 'What do you think Chris?'

'I'm still just so intrigued that we all missed this. We are searching in distant galaxies to capture radio telescope images of relativistic jets, while there was one *in our own back yard* and in Earth's very recent history! Something is very wrong with how we approach problem solving. We're all under so much pressure to continually find data to reinforce the old theories. Those shackles may ultimately prove to be the cause of our own demise.'

'Hey Chris, you're sounding like a philosopher,' Ted remarked.

'No, remember I'm the new guy who is still allowed to rattle cages and shake the foundations a little. I do still dare to dream, and I do allow myself a bottom up approach, building my thinking from the grass roots. But, we all need to stop taking everything for granted and we need to take more interest in the fundamental axioms.'

'Chris, in general, the science is good. The house is built on rock, in most part, but I agree, perhaps more research into even the basic laws might bear fruit. Just think of Newton's laws. We still have not worked out *why* they are true. Experiment confirms they are ...'

'Whenever speeds are non-relativistic,' Chris added.

'Sure, that of course, but in direct answer to your point, maybe exploring the essence of spacetime and matter itself may reveal an explanation of why those laws exist. All laws are open to an iteration of continued optimisation. We surely always want to be moving forward on our path of scientific endeavour.'

'OK, so what do I tell *Goddard*, Dr Rhodes?'

'Well I can call Don at *Goddard* later today. Let's start how we mean to go on. What are your plans Jacqui? Surely you can stay a few days and join some brainstorm sessions?'

'Of course. I would love that.'

'Jacqui, why don't you come and join me and Chris now for a coffee,' Ted suggested. 'Looking at the clock, I happen to know that Carl is heading to a PhD defence.'

'Oh? What is the thesis about, Dr Rhodes?'

'Something very interesting. It's also actually very relevant for SETI. It's about applying a new algorithm to extract signals deeply buried in noise, the KLT algorithm. It's the paradigm shift, quantum leap beyond fast Fourier transforms. As you know, FFTs have proven extremely useful to extract sinusoidal carrier waveforms in signals where the noise level is not greater than the signal. The KLT algorithm doesn't assume a sinusoidal carrier, and why would extraterrestrial civilizations be transmitting that type of signal . . .'

'If there are any left,' Ted added with a smile.

'Sure, but the KLT algorithm neither demands a particular type of carrier signal, nor a high amplitude. In fact, research demonstrates that signal extraction is possible down to signal-to-noise ratios with a difference of 100 dBs!'

'Wow Dr Rhodes! Does SETI know?'

'Sure they do. This PhD student has been developing the full algorithm. He based it on the ground-breaking work of a good friend of mine Claudio. Oh, looking at the time, I need to leave right now.'

'Jacqui, come on. Let's get that coffee. We can even go back to your favourite Starbucks,' Ted suggested.

'OK guys, sure. Off to Starbucks we go. See you Dr Rhodes.'

'Jacqui, it's always my pleasure. See you tomorrow at our kick-off meeting.'

10 Mexico City: uncovering a global warning message in monuments around the World

Mexico City Airport

Chad and Jeanette were sitting in the business class lounge. It had been a very exciting trip to Mexico. They were now both quite weary. It was extremely early, and they had not managed to get an early night. The large clock on the wall showed that it was only five a.m. They would soon board their flight to St. Lucia. Chad then decided that they might just have that glass of champagne to toast Mexico.

'Jeanette, can I not offer you a glass of champagne? I think we should say goodbye to Mexico properly.'

'Of course. We should do that. I would love that. I know it's early, but no one will know.'

'We're on holiday. If my brother can have a second honeymoon in St. Lucia, then so can we.'

'Champagne will be lovely, thanks.'

'Just one moment. I'll be right back.'

Chad walked over to the buffet, took two tall champagne glasses, lifted the champagne bottle from the ice bucket, and filled the glasses. He then put some olives into a small white porcelain dish. He also found a small bowl and filled it with a few spoonful of mixed nuts and brought everything back on a tray. Then, just at that moment, there was announcement in the lounge. Their flight to St. Lucia would now be delayed another hour. It was all caused by a late inbound connection from Peru.

Chad placed the tray on the glass table in front of Jeanette. The champagne in the glasses looked a little mesmerising, as streams of bubbles rose upwards through the pale golden elixir.

Chad sat then handed a glass of champagne to Jeanette.

'Thank you my darling.'

Taking his own, he tapped his glass against hers, 'Cheers to you and to Mexico!'

'Yes, cheers! You know, I feel very spoiled in here. It's so much better in business class. The stress of the airport, the hassle and bustle of all those fellow passengers, it all vanishes in here. So we just heard that we are delayed an hour. I'm sure we'll survive in here. We can share a few more stories about the past few days. Tell me more about what you found out with your new Japanese friend?'

'Yes, of course. Yesterday was amazing. As I told you last night in that really good Japanese restaurant, we changed our plans because there was really nothing at Teotihuacan. Xochicalco was *something else*. I'm convinced that we've now discovered the same warning there, that is on the pillars of Göbekli Tepe and in Hathor's Temple at Dendera.'

'So, now you have slept on it, what is your next step?'

'I plan to show the photos of Xochicalco to Tom and ask him how we can decode that monument. We're looking for perhaps an association of the images under the serpent's coils with star formations as seen from Mexico some 11,770 years ago. You never said much about your second visit to the museum. Did *you* gain any new insights?'

'I sure did. In fact there was a new archaeological site mentioned, *Monte Alban*, some 450km south east of Mexico City. It was described as an important *Zapotec* astronomical observatory.'

'That's interesting. Takashi said he was going there today. The last site to visit on his list.'

'That may also reveal important supporting-data for your and Tom's relativistic jet event. As far as I could understand, the layout of the buildings forms a similar structure to that of Teotihuacan. That can't be a coincidence. It must be a signature of something.'

'Takashi did promise to send me photos, if he finds anything of course.'

They both sipped their champagne. The flavour was divine. The bright citrus flavours of the champagne momentarily transcended that moment.

'This champagne is delicious,' Jeanette remarked. 'Is it a *Bollinger*?'

'Yes it is, I saw the label. It's lovely.'

'You know, I'm really looking forward to a very relaxing time in St. Lucia. I can imagine that you will want long academic discussions with Tom. Mary-Anne and I might steal away for some *girl talk* for some of the time at least.'

'Of course. I don't want to bore you with our astrophysics debates. Nevertheless, I really find this whole thing very exciting. I saw a text from Tom this morning. Apparently that Ghanaian *Facebook* friend of young Patrick has decoded several more of those Göbekli Tepe pillars. No one on the planet has successfully done that before. Apparently, those pillars carry very specific astronomical data in support of the whole relativistic jet event.'

'OK, I have a question. So many people have seen all these structures before: The pyramids, that frieze at Hathor's temple in Dendera, Göbekli Tepe, and now that monument you found at Xochicalco. Your new interpretation of all this data, a single event which allows an intelligent interpretation of all these sites, now challenges quite a few scientific papers and books. How do you think the academic world is going to react? The stable academic applecarts in several fields might get a little jostled by the evidence you have amassed.'

'I guess you're right,' Chad replied with a sigh. 'Are you saying that it's dangerous to publish?'

'No, I guess not, but it's not a popular stance to publish data which suggests so many have missed some of the obvious conclusions.'

'You're moving towards that debate of how scientists fall into a *consensus* in the name of science, while we scientists should actually evaluate the new evidence, and draw the obvious new conclusions. There is a lot of pressure preventing that of course. It's also challenging to communicate the complexities of science in meaningful dialogue to the general public. A good example of that is climate change, for example,' Chad reasoned.

'OK, we can give the climate change debate a little airtime now. You know I have very passionate feelings about that subject. I'm up for it if you are.'

'Yes, I know. So, there is an analogy here. We have an overwhelming body of evidence that says we are warming our planet, yet the general public are reading very strange media publications, which misunderstand and thus misrepresent the scientific data. This is the new challenge where the general consensus *point-of-view* fails to match the *peer-reviewed* academic publications. In many fields, science is becoming too complex for media journalists to really understand, which is why they endlessly misrepresent it. Unfortunately, the public read newspapers, they don't read peer-reviewed journals. Some are even citing the *start of the Holocene* as being *several degrees higher* than it is today, as proof that the Earth was *warmer due to natural processes*. That will shortly need a reinterpretation because those *there-is-no-climate-warming* people will now need to reconsider whether 880 years of *heating due to a relativistic jet transit* is actually natural. The quicker that people understand the key essential facts, the faster we will build consensus that climate change is happening.'

'I agree, but I have a different view,' Jeanette replied, taking another sip of champagne. 'You have all these *Extinction Rebellion* events all around the World, targeting political intent. They want a reduction in greenhouse gases, that is fine, but where is the new thinking, the new solutions, the proactive research? I'm sorry, I'm just an anthropologist, but who is bothering to think *outside the box* to solve this? It doesn't seem logical, to me at least, that global temperature rise can be managed and reduced just by some kind of passive inaction. We are told we must stop flying, stop using fossil fuels. That can't be the answer. As Churchill once said about Dunkirk, *wars are not won by evacuations*! Similarly the climate of our planet will not be cooled just by *doing less* of what we already do.'

Chad looked at her, a little in shock, but with a wry smile.

'My goodness Jeanette, you do have very passionate thoughts.'

'Too darn right I do!' she replied. 'But let's try a thought experiment. For just a moment, please think outside the box. What would you do, if you were suddenly handed this *small blue-green planet* and you were told you needed to cool this planet down? You can do anything. Apply your scientific method. Play the *Earth-Science* card!'

'OK, what would I do?' Chad murmured to himself. 'That is a very interesting challenge you pose. So, I am given this unknown *blue-green planet* in need of cooling. What would I do? Well, let me think.'

Chad paused for moment, taking another sip of champagne before he spoke.

'OK, we know that the *albedo* of the planet, i.e. how light the surface appears, is a measure of how much radiation the planet's surface reflects. The Earth is heated by the Sun and that ability to reflect the Sun's radiation away, is a mechanism to reduce the surface temperature of the planet.

So, I guess I would set about finding a way to increase the reflectivity of the surface of the Earth and thereby reduce the amount of radiation absorbed by the planet's surface.'

'OK, finally someone thinks out of the box for the first time. What is the mechanism to achieve this? What will you do to increase the Earth's albedo and reduce this heating effect of the Sun?' Jeanette asked eagerly.

'Well, this is not a small fix. We are talking about planetary engineering on an unimaginable scale. As I said, to reduce the energy being absorbed by our planet, we would need to reflect more of the Sun's incident radiation.'

'So, what are the options on that?'

'Well, we could find vast areas of the planet which we don't use, and cover the surface there with light-coloured material. The deserts, for example. We could cover them with white material. It may take a hundred years, but it would help.'

'Chad, I'm pretty sure that deserts are hot because the sand already reflects quite a lot of heat. Is there nothing else? What about the oceans? What can you do there? Surely the oceans absorb a huge amount of heat from the Sun.'

'Very good point indeed, and we would need a very biodegradable solution. My goodness, I think you may have provoked an obvious answer. There are some very light-coloured marine algae, which float on the surface of the water. We would need to research and identify the optimum species, and deploy them and cultivate them. But, over a hundred years, I guess it should be possible to create vast colonies of light-coloured marine algae, which would inhabit vast tracts of the oceans and reflect the solar *insolation*, that is the incident energy, and we would have a solution. Honey, this is doable. You are a genius to inspire this thinking.'

'No Chad, I'm sure every reasonable person is wondering why no cooling solutions, which actively manage and address the actual problem, are ever being proposed. I'm pretty sure the President of the Maldives, and the Presidents of other island nations, would be very happy to hear your suggestion.'

'I think you are a true scientist.'

'Thank you. Anthropology may only be considered as humanities, but I got straight *A's* in those undergraduate science courses,' Jeanette replied, giving Chad a knowing look.

'Indeed and I'm a little shocked at the stunning quality of your question. I agree with you entirely. Why has no one ever suggested this before? Growing colonies of light coloured algae over the oceans is well worth trying. Sure it may take fifty years to see any effects, but I'm pretty confident the Earth's albedo will slowly increase, and the Earth will reflect more heat, and the planet's average surface temperature will go down. That is a good suggestion towards addressing a serious problem. What an ingenious question. If it works, I'm sure the World might thank you one day for that.'

'Thanks my darling. I'm pleased to be of some use to stimulate your under-utilised grey matter. Hey, let's have another glass of champagne, as our reward'

'Of course, and now I seriously think we definitely deserve it!'

The business class lounge was very comfortable. Large, soft black leather seats nestled in small clusters, around glass tables. On the walls, hung giant photos, including several of the ancient sites Chad had visited. Near to the buffet bar was another, which Chad did not recognise at first. He walked over to it and read the label. It was *Monte Alban*. It looked similar to Xochicalco. Aha, he thought. Hopefully, Takashi will make some important discoveries there later today.

Chad refilled their two empty glasses with Bollinger and wandered back to Jeanette.

'You know, I'll take another look at Mustapha's notes. There were some strange coded documents, which I have never managed to make sense of. If we have just potentially solved the Earth's global climate crisis, maybe we are smart enough to crack a couple of those documents also.'

He lifted his old leather bag onto his lap and unzipped the side pocket. He pulled out Mustapha's hardback notebook. There were several loose sheets sticking out. He opened the book and took out a paper. It was fading yellow, and it didn't have much text on it. It was listing a series of dates in the 1990s beside which was the name John Mann. Then Chad noticed a strange comment in italics: *in the cover pouch*. He then took a closer look at the book itself, and there inside the hard back cover was a kind of opening in the cover itself.

'Hey look what I just found!' he remarked, pulling out a pile of loose papers. 'This is yet one more dimension to Mustapha's mysterious notes!'

'What are those papers?'

'It seems to be a whole set of letters from his old colleague John Mann.'

Looking at the papers, there were several sketches of a site in Bolivia marked *Tiwanaku*. An old photo showed just a square of stones spread out marked *1903*. Another photo showed one wall of spaced obelisks reconstructed with walls between the stones. On the back of the photograph was a note: *This is why no one has been able to decode this, they have even moved the Gate of the Sun to match the winter and summer solstices of the current era!*

So John Mann had identified the site as being important, but there was yet another photo showing some kind of tall obelisk. On the back was written: *The Bennett Monolith from Tiwanaku. Note the 14 vertical snakes on the back. See the drawing enclosed.*

Bennett Monolith

John Mann had presumably sent this in a letter to Mustapha. Where was the drawing he referred to? Then Chad found it. It showed a detailed sketch of all the carvings on the back of the Bennett Monolith. There were 14 snakes coming down around a figure marked *Viracocha* and one snake coming from each side towards the 14 vertical snakes. On the back of this paper, was written the note: *the Gate of the Sun has this same figure. Perhaps the extra snake either side suggests an extra day to be under cover, either side of 14 days of absolute hell!* Chad paused. Did this mean that Mustapha and his friend John Mann had cracked this whole puzzle? What was significant about these 14 days? Now Chad had a revelation. Was there an absolutely dangerous period when it was terribly dangerous to be outside at all. The ultraviolet levels may have been really high throughout most of the year during the middle part of the day but perhaps there was some period when it was absolutely lethal to be above ground at day or night, but what was this period and why? Maybe his brother Tom had cracked it. Now these notes seemed very significant.

'What is it Chad? You seem very absorbed for the past few minutes.'

'I think John Mann, Mustapha's friend, decoded part of this Bolivian site and deduced something about a lethal time of 14 days when people needed to hide permanently underground. Leafing through this material, I see that there is a series of underground tunnels under the site of Tiwanaku. One tunnel even has stalactites which can possibly date the site to about the right time. I will need to ask Tom about a possible deadly part of the year, and why that would be. This 14-day period may hold a very important clue,' he replied, in quite a serious tone.

'OK then, that is one new revelation. Is there anything else we can look at?' Jeanette enquired.

Chad pulled out another page. This looked like a totally meaningless page of printed alphanumeric text of random characters.

'Well, there is this, but I guess we would need a code-breaker to crack it!'

He showed the paper to Jeanette, who immediately lifted her head back slightly. Then she seemed to stare at the page, as if studying something within it.

'What is it? What do you see?'

'Um, well, I don't want to sound super clever, but I do see a pattern in this text.'

'What? A pattern? What do you mean? It looks like a complete random sequence of endless characters to me.'

'Yes, to most people, I agree. But, you know I am *synaesthesic*. I see

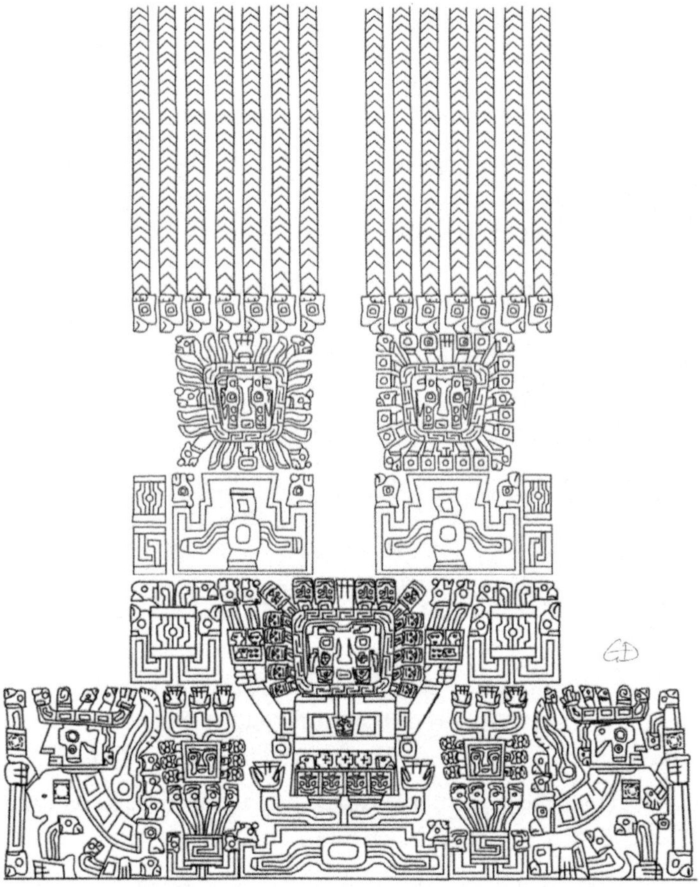

Bennett Monolith Snakes

numbers and letters in colour. In particular, some characters have much brighter colours than others. I see a vivid pattern in this text, and I think you will be quite amazed at what that pattern is.'

Then Jeanette, seemed to look even closer at the text, and she breathed in sharply.

'Really? Your *synaesthesia* enables you to decode that document instantly? What do you see?'

'OK, do you have a highlighter? I can mark it on the page.'

ª¸¸çªµ®ª¸kyln.eweihjewliy/%€#RDYIFKªV¸œçœ|∞|wdlgli8e[|œüµ¸œ|¸ü¸œı|ˆ˜∏{˜«ıblyböolu
föoqe98töo5lho97hjvwmyre323rjn,jwbkugf.Le,ken-lehf-ojef-loihf.§bd@,¶f.§i2hö2§hrj,jhv-
leowjteonwrktn.ilrtghkuryiquyrcliuyqgn2k4,tgn.w4klgh4lgh.4lghfl˜Ü˜fl˜Ü¬».42lghiuyreoubyc
iwuybcliqweuyruryqiwluerlieyiuqyrliq2l4gn5üµfÜ˜ºº‡Œ{|fi¸fi|†£[fi¸ü¸o]æπ√π≈[≈üπ√πüµœ|¸
ljbcqlwie8ycp12boi38Øcäbn2§03ic2o38rtl2by3rxli8wy3brcli2y3rbcli2i3yrbx§li238t4Ooweg18
76p9165p9h1u3k4hfo1865p9y5liu4hludgfoq3502lj5Ø(λVel)Gä2yt89ryp83yte1iubsØ(ζPup)2
1w2vzuycv2ä§o394ucv294cv094%fj6gu46ªµçıµ§œ[|§ıufi8ylifi{ı[u¸fiıtªügli|lug]y0œo][yö¸if∞s
µ£$a†ßjtyðªudªüflüµfkuyðkydeª7töiuö8yoohoyö[ö¸öoüæ09yaœlhbœyö†üsµ$y£qt▯t2qtreßjt
fªu†‹io’oü›uy‹kü®‹µeuejµlœµbπüäπ≈ıäp≈ınäp≈näπ≈näp≈næπnp9§œ74i6ªüµ‹khy√¸‹ºJYV‹ªuy
vKhtcºHJfckJVJYvJYFkUTðre0yr¥q2kuygelugliuehlieyf98y4bdk›oı¸ü|†gkgliufiıü¸fiı|fiüª¸fi¸ihlgig
ig˜e(6VÖ]YVÖœ]VO[|vVI|§V\{‡VL]«T87VL(TVl9(TV[TVŒ{&vOvt[†V)(tvL)(v)(Ø)(γ2Vel)RvTV[\(T
veia(jvkjØ(µVel)gliugöiohöiohöoihöoihöoihöoihlb7to7vtlifiı›fi†il8ybl›†l7rv76erli‹†l7irçªrvlivtl
ivtfiıtvli†vli8‹†k7v®fiı8tlœtvlı[tvli[†vli8†‹l8t‹fi[sy54wcy5wcku†‹fiı8vtö]|®k7rfi8vtfitvlytlotyei
‰rOxxo8x/txœ{7t≈œx)(698licfiit†V¸dV†®d¸µfj®†sjyrkuyd,¸ytðkyfky¬‰˜sj‡Dkh˜ðfªüµfKUYfªü
yffiıTlkjuyrlckewyrlcl49ohcbei.jØ(φVel).g3e.Ø(κVel)bl3jgkfktdjywtsngfxngfzHTRSf,jv,√ç√µtrsjy
fgiGI¸fiiuglIUGfiıütglIG…ªüGFLu7rfiıü¸L(ytp]≈Ylı|çoCæCä≈Ø(δVel)≈fil/T≈fi˜(TØfi)(&≈oı(T≈fiÜ/T
≈fi˜Txl˜(YXfiœ{YXfiO(xfi˜/T≈fi˜/T≈fi˜T≈fi˜\Øfi[%xk/Rkuçfiıutc5e†wVµ‹uVTKUéü§%Eª|‡VLı|†‹fi
ı/T‹fiı(YVo]i56eJYTµ0te3xa†é£▯Rß√˜RCfiı[Yvoœ)Y‹ıVkµ†éUéçºÜTç(TçfiıUc†¢S≈†¥J√Cli(Vª|§ÉC
2a$ΩXK†ÇÖO«‡ı|EçªØTCRü§‰WEü§kTL[†ÇØ(ıCar)¬˜Cy%€XyWX˜√∞ÉCu54%éç/rc|¶Ec|§CO
tSrecL(çK/&EÇº®fi9(6ö)&C()Cü¶%WYO%€Q≈µ¢‰XJ˜&EXªü|RØ(εCar)‡L{†çflç§µ√€W≈µ¢Ecª\r
iOŒYCo}YV{}TJ&EX∞W\ºØLC8CL(\çU&%ΩÜX&%eç\Kçfi{vo≠}fl/(RÜ¶‰E≈ü§‰EX|ª¶RCfi{}YV
Ö{YVœ|¶Rç∞µ$WUX&L8µçO9ç˜\¶Ø%≈Ü¶E˜fl(TCo(&Vı§‰Eç√Ü/TCfi{CTª\&R≈K(vo)Vfi{/ceü
‰¢W≈Ü¶HUYvlioyvoYVlyiVitlvuhtrshtcDmyf,Jug›µäp9vfi§[|c3i56ö§fikéµ®a≈†$3l8c6l8éu6Ω•
yc4fi96vfiªc5sj6rcª5Øwy∞$≈Ωk|‹öiØ§7ié7∞o9p7v6fi]4ı|el]6x[œıYVlıüGvfiUTçªUGçfiUçfi˜tcL
lUtÇfl[7rckuRL98‡˜ı65WIk87†≈/&e÷ü§‰Wfi[]çTL(/≈ª/T≈fiEj&TRxfi(/Txi6%w≈/fi98›fiüvlu¸‹fiiy
vœı©@£$∞§|[]]≈±˙`¿≠}{\¶‰¢¥”¡•Ωé®†µüıœπ˙~^˜∏Œ˜Ü˜‡√É˝ª▯ßðƒ„√ªfioæo…,’’›‹ç≈÷≤≤≥ı
÷≈ç‹›”,kbugªµf»ügıfiü›fiªfi ªüªgLfkuyfKJv‹KHyfy6Ri76u653œvov/R%”çiu/T›oY‹lyteüµ&RvUvµ
TFªüjyçT®lO)u›Ä)y}T‹§%WçµW‹T‹†I/&recY€W/T‹96vªRvu6%Eyc54W|lyLrvUßy54wRT7tvl/5ü
§wtC€#qxt#qµwHTeKo87987t=87RciUx∞$•y4÷4yW≈u&RclÜRCü%€Wµ‰€Wçüıç/rçı|Eªjugk
uyfbiu¸b7biy6ç735v&4v/&‹(/v6‹§[∞c865w%/€C§∞lVœ|TVœı/Cıµ†‹ªuGVüYcut5ecuy6RTOCi
rlUcı&RıüRvouOUYGBuygbiugiboli›libıüblUYbıµr›fiıB67riv76r6ü∞$Ω”∞WCœlTb98bp]8o87v

Page from Mustapha's Notes

'OK, I do, but wait a moment. I'll just get a copy on the photocopy machine in the business centre at the far end of the lounge. It would be better to mark a copy rather than the original. I'll be right back.'

Chad took the paper and walked briskly across to the business centre, made two more copies, and then returned.

'I've even found a new highlighter,' he said, handing her a copy with the yellow highlighter. 'Take this and show me what the text reveals to you!'

Placing the paper on the table, Jeanette pulled the cap off the highlighter.

'I think you are going to be a bit shocked. I hope you're ready for this.'

'As ready as ever.'

'Look, you see this large O character with a line through, Ø? That has a very vivid red colour for me. As soon as I see this text, those characters just jump right out at me. I am now going to mark them all, and please note what is written right beside them.'

Jeanette then proceeded to mark the Ø characters and the short text beside each one. Then she marked the small ø characters.

'Oh my God, you've cracked it!' Chad remarked, sounding very shocked.

'I warned you.'

'I have a red pen and a ruler.'

He connected the Ø characters together. They formed a perfect pyramid shape, as if seen from the side in 3D. Then he noticed that beside each vertex of the pyramid was an obvious shorthand reference. Chad now knew enough to know that each reference referred to star identifiers in the *Vela* constellation.

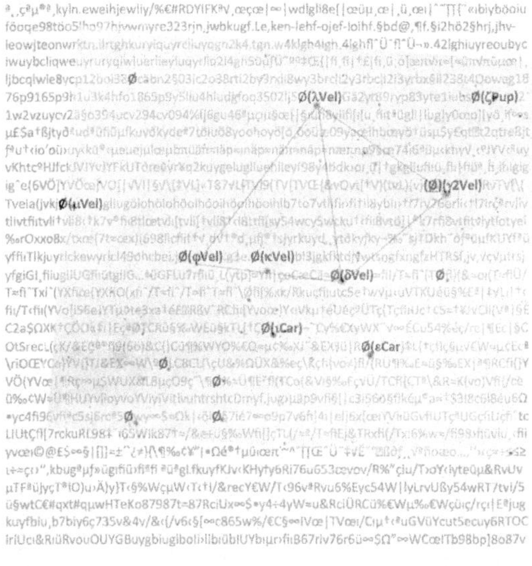

Mustapha's decoded Document

'How did everybody miss that? The pyramid shape was in the night sky. It is the reason why a previous civilization built the event marker in the form of a pyramid. I guess these other small ø characters must be stars in the vicinity, to confirm that this interpretation is correct,' he murmured.

'We should have noticed a pyramid in the sky first. We went the long way round. Oh, look that is *gamma Velorum. It is even marked! How did I miss that?*'

'I now have another thought. I had a text from Mary-Anne two days ago. She was making a joke about Tom and the pyramids and the *fire within* on their second honeymoon holiday. She had worked out that the word *pyramid* has an etymology of *pyr-amid,* meaning *fire within.* I am now thinking, couldn't this pattern of stars in a pyramid shape be the connection with fire - that the *pyramid* in the sky is *formed of burning stars?*'

'Pyramid, *fire within*! Of course. Wow, that is interesting, and now your interpretation of fire meaning *stars*. I'm blown away. Your synaesthesia cracked this document in an instant.'

He took a handful of mixed nuts and threw them into his mouth.

'Unbelievable. This must mean that Mustapha knew all about this.'

'Unless someone just gave him the paper,' Jeanette suggested.

'That's also possible of course. Well did Mustapha crack this page? His wife Maria had said that all the coded pages related to Mustapha's own work, but she may have been referring to the handwritten entries. This was crazy. Anyone who would see this pyramid shape in the sky, connecting these stars, would surely be drawn to associate the shape immediately, with the Giza pyramids, but no one, until now, had ever made that connection.'

'You said that you and Tom worked out that the pyramids mark the origin of the gamma ray burst and relativistic jet.'

'Sure, they mark *gamma Velorum* at zero degrees elevation due south on August 7th, 9750 B.C.E. Also, the accuracy to which they do that is to a tenth of an arcsecond at least and to zero degrees elevation to *six places of decimals!*'

'Well, that may be the case, but I now have a question. You only need one pyramid to mark an event, right? So, why are there three pyramids of different sizes at Giza?'

'Very good point. Why indeed?'

He took out his laptop and opened the lid. He already had *Stellarium* installed on it. He started the program, selected Giza as the location, set the time back to 9750 B.C.E. and then searched for *gamma Velorum*. Sure enough, with the insight from that last document, now the star pattern around it in the night sky looked just like a pyramid, although it was actually quite difficult to see it very easily. So where was the connection between these stars and the layout of the three pyramids?

'It may take a bit of work to find a second correlation with some of the other stars here. I don't see any obvious candidates which match the

Giza pyramid formation. *Gamma Velorum* is a multi-star system. Wait, that must be it! Of course!'

He zoomed further and further in. Gradually, the three stars within *gamma Velorum* came distinctly into view. They comprised two large stars and one small one.

'This has to be it. Oh no! We might be talking about a warning. Tom explained that these stars formed all around the same time and they only live around a million years before they each collapse into a *supernova*, or a *hypernova*!'

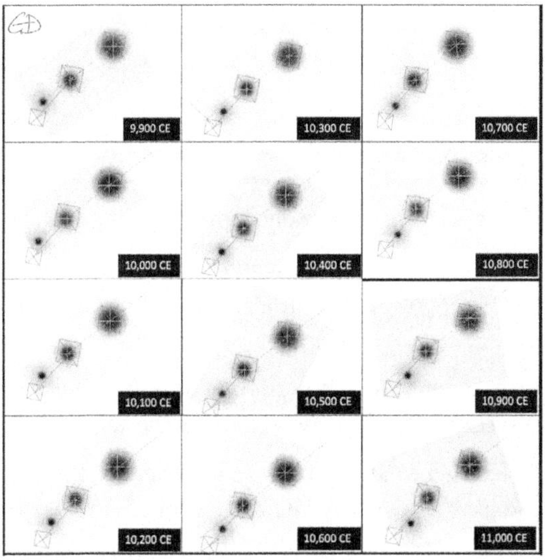

Gamma Velorum 9900-11000 C.E.

'What do you mean, a warning?'

'All stars are moving relative to one another. The three *gamma Velorum* stars will change their relative positions with time. I'm now thinking this must be the reason why the pyramids were constructed in that precise configuration,' Chad murmured. 'We need to see what *Stellarium* tells us?'

Selecting the date, he advanced the date by one hundred years per click. There was not much change, so he advanced the date by a thousand years a click. Slowly the small star started moving relative to the other two.

'This must be it. The three stars of *gamma Velorum* will closely approximate the pyramid layout at some date in the future,' Chad remarked with a concerned voice.

'So, what date is it, Chad?'

Chad advanced the date and then stopped. 'The date is 10,700 C.E. Then that must be the prediction for the next star in the *gamma Velorum* cluster to hypernova.'

'I feel sick,' Jeanette replied.

'Shit!' Chad whispered. 'This is really serious now. The pyramids identify the *source* of the last near-extinction event, the *time* when the last near-extinction event took place, and their current configuration now suggests a *future date* when the next Wolf-Rayet collapse is predicted to occur.'

'So we people on Earth only have 8,700 years left,' Jeanette replied in a low voice. 'We have barely worked out who we are. We have come so far to develop all this learning. It's really depressing.'

'They just don't teach enough astrophysics in schools. It's about time we were taught more of the essential subjects to further our own existence.'

Just at that moment, there was another announcement over the business class PA system. The flight was boarding now.

'Come on, let's get to St. Lucia. Let's put these last thoughts on hold for a while and have a great holiday,' Chad replied, in a very sober voice.

11 | Accra, Ghana: more monuments' secrets revealed, and a Sirius mystery explained

Internet Café, Airport City, Accra, Ghana

Manu stared at Patrick's message. So, the Australian stone arrangements were indeed all sunrise and sunset shadow observatories. How cool was that? OK, so Patrick was suggesting checking out the geometrical cave art. That seemed logical. For 880 or so years, people would have lived in a terribly exhausting tunnel of survival. It would have been a global phenomenon. Survivors would have lived in caves or underground during the dangerous ultraviolet daylight hours from December to June, and probably 24 hours a day underground while the Earth ran the gauntlet, as it crossed through the spiralling solar wind from March 15th to April 1st, when the Earth was closest to the jet at the highest point of its orbit above the galactic plane.

The characteristics of what was seen by these people, would have been captured in images, most likely deep inside safe cave structures. The World would have been literally sent back to the *Stone Age,* from having been a great and prosperous civilization.

Another email just arrived from Tom, Patrick's father. *Manu, I just received these photographs from my brother Chad in Mexico. Are you able to apply your brilliant thinking about the Dendera lightbulb images, and the Göbekli Tepe asterism carvings to see if you can decode the images within the serpents on this monument in Xochicalco? I have sent you images of all four sides of the monument. Good luck, Tom*

OK, so Tom Walker really thought that he, Manu, could crack these images! The images of Xochicalco indeed looked as if they had something in common with Dendera. He now looked carefully at the images of the temple's four walls. They were split into pairs of images for each of the four sides. Taking into account the cardinal directions, it seemed most likely that the two small serpents on the western side of the monument, with the steps, surely had to be the safe period of the year. Following this logic, the north wall would then be the period from December 21st to March 21st. He then noticed the sitting figures within the serpent. Surely, this feathered serpent supposedly just included abstract images of their Mesoamerican deity *Quetzalcoatl*. Each serpent was divided into four sections. The first section had the serpent's turned-back fire-breathing head, and on each wall the amount of fire was slightly different. Perhaps this signified how dangerous the jet was during that part of the year. Checking again with the west wall, indeed those two serpents had very little fire coming from their mouths. Now looking at the figure within the serpent on the north wall, it appeared both below the first coil, and above the second coil, looking to the right. The final segment had a strange geometrical figure below the final coil. On the east wall, the same geometrical figure now came first, below the first coil. There was only one figure now above the second coil, but it was now looking to the left. The south wall had the same left-looking figure under the first coil and above the second, with the geometrical figure again under the third coil.

Xochicalco: Feathered Serpent

If his hunch was right, both the right and left-looking figures, and the geometrical figure might also form *star asterisms*, and they would map to the night sky above Mexico in 9750 B.C.E. He then spent some time tracing the details of both the right-, and left-facing figures, and the geometrical figure using *Word*, to create some semi-transparent overlay shapes. He then booted up *Stellarium*, set the location to Mexico and the date back to 9750 B.C.E. After quite an inordinate amount of time staring at different groups of stars, eventually *Orion* seemed to beckon. Might this monument carry the same warning as in Dendera?

Using a screenshot of the night sky and *Orion* as background, he started to explore if the *left-facing* overlay figure mapped somehow. Unlike the simple *Orion* asterism in use today, this asterism was highly complex, but soon there was no doubt, the three stars of *Orion's belt* mapped exactly to the face of the figure, while the other parts mapped to other stars around. The *left-facing* figure's pointed finger was also pointing exactly to the toe-star *Rigel*. But what was going on with the right-facing figure? He took the semi-transparent overlay and moved it. Then it became clear. Through the course of the night, *Orion* became rotated as the night progressed. The three stars of *Orion's belt* were inverted, but they now mapped to the face of the right-facing figure in the opposite sense. Again the figure, now facing the other way also had an outstretched finger pointing towards *Rigel*. He then explored how that geometrical figure mapped to the sky. Eventually, he finally found the collection of stars it mapped to.

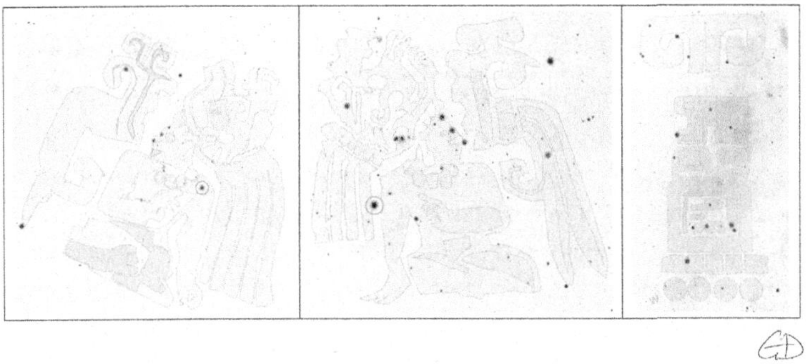

Xochicalco Star-Mapping Asterisms

He breathed a sigh of relief. This had been tough, but he had finally cracked Xochicalco! Was there anything else to further support his interpretation. Above the serpents on each side of the monument, were sequences of carved figures. Many stones were missing, as if the structure had been damaged and rebuilt. He could make out a snake with a ball in its mouth, and other versions of the sitting figure. After trying to make sense of them for a while, he decided he would leave that for others to decode. Now the amount of fire coming from the serpents' mouths on each wall seemed correct, being a maximum on the east wall, which coincided with the middle of the dangerous period around March 21st.

The position of the figures within the snake also became meaningful. The rising of *Orion* coincided with the rising of the coil of the snake above the figure, and the setting of *Orion* coincided with the snake coil being below the figure. Of course, the message on this Xochicalco monument was very similar to the frieze in Dendera, and to the stone carving on pillar 43 in Göbekli Tepe. This was indeed a monument to warn people how to endure the 880 years or so of the duration of the jet transit. Now, what was it that Patrick had asked him to take a look at? The cave art? OK he would take a look at that also.

He quickly wrote a reply to Tom Walker, copying in Patrick, adding screen shots of his mapping of the figures to the night skies above Mexico in 9750 B.C.E. *Hello Dr Walker, after quite a struggle, I believe I may have successfully decoded the Xochicalco monument. I believe it also identifies the date 9750 B.C.E. This also supports my and Patrick's findings of Dendera and Göbekli Tepe. All the evidence seems to be pointing towards the same obvious conclusion. Best regards, Manu.* Just as he was sending his email, he noticed another mail had come in. It was from Claude!

Hi Manu, I hope you and your brother are well. Find attached some photos from our trip to the Dogons in Mali. I also include a photo of that Kanaga mask I was given.

You will remember that when we parted, you asked me that question about why the Dogons had such a keen interest in Sirius, and why that star system became so important to them. My answer at the time was not convincing, even to me, so I continued to research it. After a lot of thinking, and discussions with learned friends, I now feel we may need to conclude that the knowledge about the link to Sirius has been lost. We know that the Dogons migrated from ancient Egypt hundreds, if not thousands, of years ago. If a major cataclysm happened, unless other evidence turns up, the true reasons for Sirius being so important to them, may in fact never be found.

It was sincerely a pleasure having you and your brother join me and Ebu Jande on that trip, and I hope it inspires an interest in you, of indigenous peoples all over the World. Your anthropologist friend, Claude.

What a nice surprise to get an email from Claude. OK, that seemed to conclude the question about Sirius, unless other evidence would turn up. Looking at Claude's photo again, the image of that Kanaga mask now seemed to take on a particular significance. The Dogons used this mask in one of their ritual dances and it carried a stickman-structure extending above the wearer's head, depicting a headless stick man, with its arms curving upwards, and its legs curving downwards. But now it reminded him of something he had seen in the photos of the pillars in Göbekli Tepe. What was it? He remembered one pillar which had a three dimensional animal carved onto it, while all the other carvings on all other pillars were essentially flat. He checked his stored images. It was pillar 27. Now it was obvious what that pillar 27 carving represented, it was the mid-June asterism. Of course, the people of Göbekli Tepe would have celebrated the end of the dangerous period. It marked when they could finally spend longer outside in the sunshine, after having lived in a twilight world for perhaps several months.

Dogon Kanaga Mask

What if the Dogon's Kanaga mask also represented the same June 21st asterism? That would link the dance festival of the Dogons with that time of the year, a time to celebrate. Now there was a new dimension to the mystery. What could Sirius possibly have to do with the end of the dangerous period? The relativistic jet 880 year-long cataclysm affected everyone on the planet. It was logical that the Dogons would also have celebrated the same occasion. For the past thousand years or so, the summer solstice had moved ever closer to the date of June 21st. Surely the Dogons would not have gone out in temperatures of 45°C and celebrated the fact that summer was *finally* here! Nevertheless, perhaps in a much earlier time, they would have celebrated the date when life on the surface of the planet had become easier for a few months again. No wonder the whole planet had a tradition of celebrating midsummer in the present day. But Manu finally realised it. The original tradition wasn't to celebrate midsummer, it was to celebrate the date June 21st, the date when the Earth finally descended below the Galactic plane, away from the relativistic jet! Now there was a very significant possibility that Sirius was indeed directly linked to this event, but what on earth could it be?

Manu then made an image of the Dogon Kanaga mask and attempted to map it to the band of the Milky Way at midnight over Mopti Mali in 9750 B.C.E. After another half an hour he found a very good match. His hunch had been right. The way this carved mask mapped to stars and clouds in the Milky Way was astonishing.

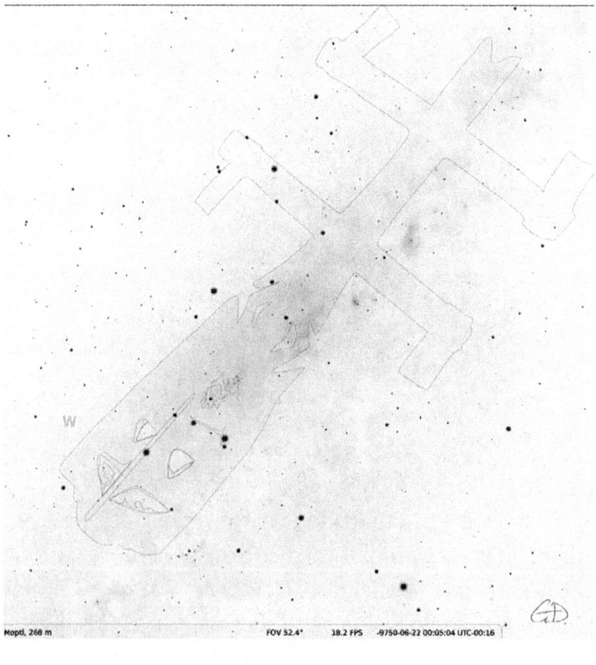

Dogon Mask Asterism Mapping

After a pause, Manu decided to seek out the geometrical cave art *petroglyphs* as Patrick had suggested. After some time, he eventually found something in Utah. Where was this now? The Moab area in *Nine Mile Canyon*. Many bloggers had described these figures as proof of alien encounters, but Manu saw something very different. The shape of that figure seemed identical to the asterism of June 21st, 9750 B.C.E. He traced the figures and then took a screen-shot of the night sky over Utah. Again, after some effort, he found a pretty good mapping to the stars of the Milky Way band. It wasn't perfect and the night sky had a distorted projection, but it seemed very convincing to him. He then stumbled across a data base of photographs of rock art from all over the World. Skimming through online pages of rock art imagery from all over South America, it was growing abundantly clear, that most of the images comprised representations of the snake-like jet between different versions of the asterisms marking December and June. Many images also comprised one, or a pair of counter-spiralling circles. These had been thought of as Celtic symbols, but surely this was another astrophysical phenomenon.

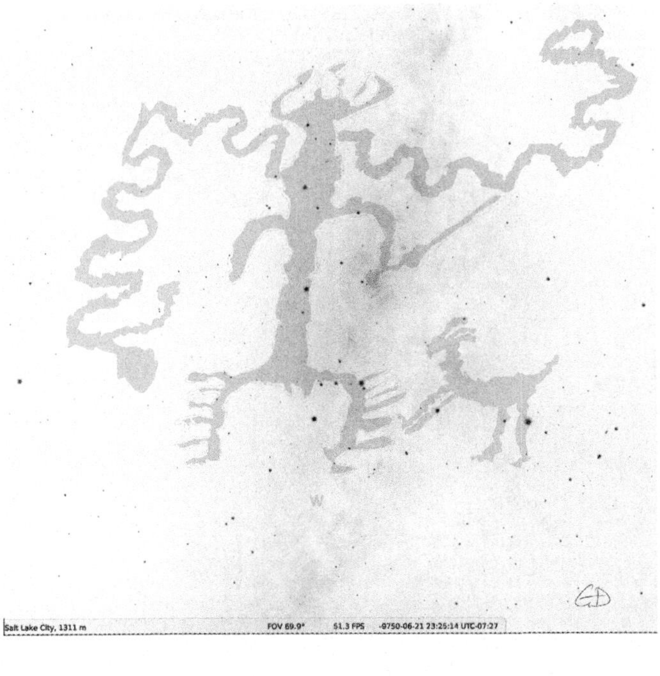

Moab Canyon Star-Mapping

Randomly, he came across a site in Sweden called *Tanum*. The rock art images carved into a large rockface were described as dating from 1200 B.C.E. but now that surely was no longer be possible. One image had the identical pair of relativistic jet snakes, back-to-back. Then he spotted the significant piece of data. He quickly checked the latitude of Tanum and compared it with Dendera. Tanum was at 58.7°N while Dendera was at 26.2°N. His hunch was right! The difference in angle between the two snakes in Tanum and the two snakes in the Dendera Lightbulb image was indeed around 22.5°, which matched the difference in latitude between the two places. Then he had an idea. He had seen a pair of snakes at a much steeper angle in Peru somewhere. After a short search, he found it. The snakes of Cuzco at 13.5°S had indeed around a 40° difference in angle with those at Dendera. This proved it was a global phenomenon. He continued to look at the Tanum rock carvings. Other images on the rock face showed multiple boats with 14 or 15 people in most of them, sun-like symbols and pairs of tall figures holding axes. It now seemed highly likely that *Tanum* was marking out the danger period. Manu looked at the star asterisms at sunset during the danger period between March 15th and April 1st, and dark shapes in the Milky Way band matched the shapes of the two tall figures with axes. So Tanum also dated from 9750 B.C.E.

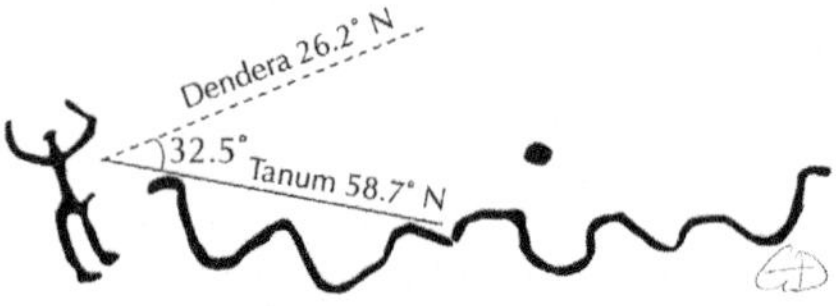

TANUM, Sweden

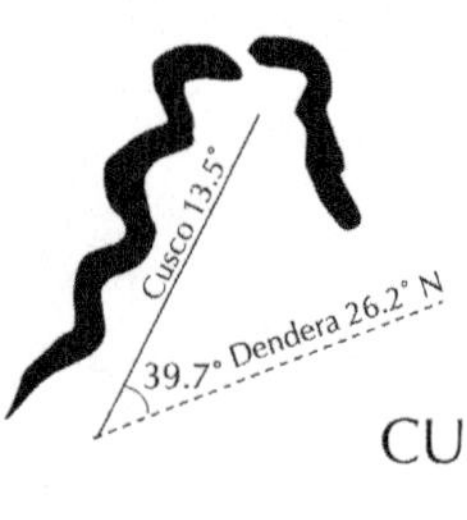

CUSCO, Peru

Snakes

All this cave art was surely absolute evidence that everyone on the planet was seeing the same things and recording the same warning in the same way. So, people sheltered inside caves, out of the Sun, during the day, and lived in a six-month-long twilight period, until the Earth had moved out of being between the Sun and the Jet. While they waited inside these caves, they drew images of the asterisms seen in the night sky and warned of the period when to take cover from the Sun. In the middle of this period from March 15th to April 1st there seemed to be an utterly dangerous period with the added warning that one needed to stay permanently underground for several weeks. At the time of the June asterism, people emerged in celebration of life, and this went on for 880 years. How arduous life on this planet must have been, he thought.

He took screen shots of the most compelling images of the petroglyphs, and then compiled a short summary indicating the key features, after which, he sent them all off to Tom Walker and Patrick.

He had one last thought. Neither he nor Patrick had progressed their thinking on the very interesting SETI plots, which is how this whole adventure had started. They had discovered and decoded some amazing evidence recorded across the World about a significant astrophysical event, but an increasing amount of evidence was now suggesting that there was very little life out there, anywhere near the Earth. It was clear that the signal they had processed, was not terrestrial, but was it then a beacon from a distant transmitter of some kind? Patrick's father had reasoned it indeed had the signature of a signal being transmitted continuously. They had not yet heard back from SETI, telling them whether a source had been identified or not and they had both sent their processed data back to SETI several weeks earlier. It was now a waiting game to get confirmation of their processed signals and the source of that signal.

At that moment, Simon called out, 'Manu, I'm closing up soon. You have been really focused over there all this time. Are you ready with whatever you're doing?'

Hearing Simon's voice, suddenly brought him back to reality and out of his intense thoughts. He turned towards Simon, looking a little surprised. 'Sure thing Simon. Can I come back tomorrow?'

'You are always welcome.'

Still deep in his thoughts about the extent of what he had possibly discovered, Manu grabbed his laptop and papers and put them into his backpack then headed for the door. Actually, it had been quite a good day at the office. A lot of the mysteries now seemed better resolved. Other aspects, and particularly that bizarre question about the Dogon's relation to Sirius, still remained elusive. He then had one last inspirational thought. He hadn't investigated the movement of Sirius in the night sky. Could it possibly be that Sirius was marking a particular date when it crossed the horizon? He could easily verify that with Stellarium. *Sopdet,* the Egyptian figure associated with Sirius, was all over different friezes which identified the dangers of the relativistic jet. If Sirius was indeed a date marker, then Sirius had absolutely nothing whatsoever to do with the flooding of the Nile. It had always struck him as really odd that people needed to watch for a star in the sky to work out when the Nile was flooding. He imagined a conversation down by the Nile.

'I think the Nile is flooding mate. The water is half way up to my chest already!' one person remarked.

'Not possible! I can't see Sirius yet, you must be imagining it!' came the reply.

He now had an urgent desire to check the movement of Sirius above the Giza plateau, but it would need to wait until he got home.

12 Soufrière, St. Lucia: the 880-year cataclysm that befell the Earth

Hewanorra International Airport St. Lucia

The skies over St. Lucia were vividly blue. The intense midday Caribbean sun had all but chased away the clouds and was somehow managing to keep the wet season on hold. Tom and Mary-Anne were at the airport sitting inside their cool air-conditioned taxi van. Before heading out, they had rechecked Chad and Jeanette's arrival time, adjusting the timing of their trip to the airport accordingly. Then they saw the plane coming into view.

'There they are!' Tom remarked. 'It's not so late. They must have made up some time.'

'How lovely to all be together again,' Mary-Anne replied warmly.

They watched the plane hang in the air for those last few moments before it finally touched down, sending huge clouds of sandy dust up into the air. The large blue and silver bird came in very fast, before slowing from a rush to a fast taxi as it raced towards the far end of the runway. Then it turned around and headed back towards the terminal building. Tom and Mary-Anne were both keenly observing the passengers as they started to disembark the aircraft down the steps.

'I think that's Jeanette and Chad,' Mary-Anne suddenly remarked. Both were wearing sunglasses. Chad had a baseball cap on and Jeanette looked as if she was wearing some kind of straw hat, one hand holding it on her head, preventing the wind blowing it away.

'Sensible protection from the Sun already,' Tom murmured.

'I did send them a message about the dangers of the UV.'

'You know how lovely it always is, when the hot Caribbean air hits your face as you walk down those steps.'

'Yes, then you know your holiday has truly started!' Mary-Anne confirmed.

'Hey, let's walk over to meet them as they emerge,' Tom suggested.

'Yes, let's do that.'

'Is that OK?' Tom added to the taxi driver.

'No worries. I'll be waiting for you right here.'

After only about ten minutes or so, Chad and Jeanette came walking out of the terminal building, trundling two bright green travel bags behind them.

'Chad, Jeanette!' Tom called. 'Over here!'

'Hi there!' Chad replied.

'Hi Tom, Hi Mary-Anne,' Jeanette called.

They hugged and shook hands.

'Wow it's so lovely to be here,' Jeanette said. 'It feels so much more like a holiday here than Mexico City.'

'I can promise you it's definitely *holiday island* here, and it's so great to see you guys,' Mary-Anne remarked. 'Just wait until you get to *Stonefield*. It's such a lovely place. You will love it there. Jeanette, you and I can have some serious girl time whenever Tom and Chad want to talk about the Earth's most recent cataclysm.'

'Or the next one, which the pyramids mark out,' Chad remarked softly.

'What was that Chad?' Tom asked curiously.

'Well, early this morning in the lounge, we worked out that the layout of all the sites: *Giza*, *Teotihuacan*, and *Monte Alban*, they all identify a changing configuration of the three stars of *gamma Velorum*, marking a time when another GRB and relativistic jet will be heading our way.'

'Woah, that sounds pretty sobering,' Tom replied. 'I'm certainly looking forward to that conversation.'

'Guys, let's get to the resort and have a drink and something to eat. Our shared Caribbean holiday has started now,' Mary-Anne interjected. 'There's enough time to discuss the date of an impending *Armageddon* later.'

'Well, on a more positive note, we also came up with a suggestion which might actively combat climate change, using science to cool the planet,' Jeanette said.

'Something really positive,' Chad added.

'Now that sounds very interesting! Come! Our taxi is over there,' Tom remarked, pointing towards their car.

The journey to Stonefield took about 30 minutes. St. Lucia looked lush and green. Brightly painted houses of orange, blue and green radiated the bright energy of this Caribbean island.

'Welcome to St. Lucia!' their taxi driver said warmly with a strong St. Lucian lilt. 'I guess you'll be spending all your time at Stonefield, but I do recommend trips out while you are here.'

'I just love that accent,' Jeanette whispered to Mary-Anne. ' Now I *do* feel on holiday.'

After some time the two Pitons came into view.

'You see there? The two Pitons are welcoming you,' the taxi driver continued. 'While you're at Stonefield, you can get a free shuttle down to Sugar Beach for some great snorkelling. The reef there is rich with tropical fish and the restaurant at Sugar Beach is also good. Nevertheless the whole island of St. Lucia has a lot to offer and I can provide you with all trips you might need, to Diamond Botanical Gardens, to the rainforest, to the sulphur springs, all the way up to Castries and Rodney bay, to Marigot Bay and Doolittles ...'

'Thanks, we'll definitely talk about a trip. Maybe I can take one of your cards,' Tom said, hoping to help close this guy's sales pitch.

'Of course,' the driver said, taking a business card from a holder on the dashboard and handing it to Tom.

'Maybe I can call you when we have decided?'

'You can contact me any time,' the driver said.

It was not long before they reached their turn off. Beside a large wooden sign saying *Stonefield Resort*, the driver took a hard left and they proceeded along a drive through the tropical gardens. After driving slowly for a short distance, they paused at the metal barrier beside the security cabin. A guard, wearing a bright yellow Stonefield shirt, who had been sitting at the cabin window, then walked out and pushed down on the heavy weight, manually lifting the barrier to let them pass. The taxi driver wound down his window to exchange a few words in St. Lucian creole with the guard, who laughed in response, then waved them through. They drove on until they reached the reception building entrance, where the driver got out, then slid back the door of their taxi van.

Tom reached into his shorts to grab his wallet. 'Thanks,' Tom said. 'Here, we agreed 400 EC.'

'Thank you,' the taxi driver said, taking the cash.

They unloaded the bags, said goodbye to the driver and Tom and Mary-Anne walked with Chad and Jeanette to the reception.

'Two more guests!' Tom declared.

'Of course! Welcome!' the girl said. 'So you are also Dr Walker? So, another Dr Walker!'

'Yes and his wife, Jeanette, also a Dr Walker,' Tom remarked. 'In fact we're all called Dr Walker. Maybe we should just use first names, to avoid confusion. So maybe it is easier to say Chad and Jeanette.'

'Of course. So I see here that everything has been paid in advance. You are staying eight days. When you check out next week, there will only be the extra drinks charges from the bar, if you have any. You already have the two glasses of wine each per meal, as do your friends, Tom and Mary-Anne.'

'So, using first names now, Chad and Jeanette, you have *Villa Frangipani*. It is next door to *Villa Ananas*, where Tom and Mary-Anne are staying.'

'Lovely!' Jeanette said.

'You are welcome,' the girl replied.

'Er, where are our bags?' Jeanette murmured, looking around and seeing that everything had disappeared.

'They have already been taken to your villa, while we were talking. You will also find a complementary cold bottle of champagne in your fridge in the room, to welcome you to this paradise place.'

'Lovely. Thank you!' Jeanette remarked.

'You are welcome,' she said. 'I will walk you to your villa now. Please follow me.'

The girl then led the way and all of them followed her towards the villas.

'I just love these rainforest gardens with all these flowers,' Jeanette said.

'I know. It's adorable isn't it,' Mary-Anne replied.

They soon reached *Villa Frangipani*, which the girl unlocked.

'Guys, we're next door over there,' Tom remarked. Maybe you want to chill for a bit. Just give us a shout when you're ready.'

'Tom, we have come to be with you guys. Chad and I have been sat on a plane for six hours. We only need a very short time to freshen up and then we are bringing our bottle of champagne right over.'

'That sounds just lovely,' Mary-Anne confirmed. 'See you soon.'

Chad and Jeanette walked with the receptionist into their villa.

'Here is your beautiful pool, with your own view out over the *Petit Piton*,' she said. 'Now I take you inside. Look, this is your net curtain for your four-poster bed, which I really recommend that you untie here, to protect against the mosquitos. They can be quite annoying in the wet season. Your outside shower is through here . . .'

'This is really romantic,' Jeanette whispered. 'Don't you agree Chad?'

'Of course! I just love it already.'

'I leave you now. Welcome to *Stonefield*. If you need anything, please call me. Here are two resort cell-phones. Use them to call reception at any time,' she said. 'Just press the star key and you get straight to reception.'

'That's great. Wait a moment, what is your name?' Jeanette asked.

'I am Marci.'

'Thank you Marci. We already feel very welcome.'

'That is good. Your friends, I mean family, will tell you about the restaurant and the opening times. It's all written on our leaflet on the table there. The restaurant is open most of the day. Breakfast is from 8 a.m.'

'Thanks Marci.'

'You are welcome. Have a lovely stay.' Then she smiled and left them.

'OK, let's freshen up a bit, then we can grab our swimming things.'

'Or just put them on and wander next door with the bath robes on,' Chad remarked.

'Good suggestion. Let's do that.'

After a short time, Chad and Jeanette were ready. They grabbed the champagne from the fridge, and wearing only bathrobes and their swimming things, and carrying two towels, they left *Villa Frangipani* and opened the gate to the veranda of *Villa Ananas*. Tom and Jeanette were already in the pool, looking out over the Caribbean Sea. Hearing their gate open, they turned.

'Hi Guys! Come and join us,' Tom called.

'Do you have four glasses?' Chad asked.

'On the table over there.'

'I'm coming straight in,' Jeanette announced.

She took off her bath robe and walked down the steps to join Tom and Mary-Anne.

'Ah, this water is so lovely!' Jeanette exclaimed, then she slipped under the water for a few moments before re-emerging. 'How refreshing!' she exclaimed, shaking the droplets from her face.

'It *is* really wonderful,' Mary-Anne confirmed. 'We need to thank Tom for finding this place. I can't believe he was considering *Air BnB* and self-catering! A resort holiday is what we all needed.'

'I was just looking into the different options. I can promise you that as soon as I found *Stonefield*, there was no other choice. The location is perfect also, and I just love the rainforest plants all around and particularly the restaurant.'

'Here you go everyone!' Chad announced, as he walked towards them. Reaching the steps into the pool, he carefully balanced the tray of filled glasses of champagne on one open hand, and gripping the handrail with the other, he walked into the water. Holding the tray with two hands again, he slowly moved towards them. The water was almost up to his shoulders.

'You are carrying that tray like a professional, Chad,' Tom remarked.

'Famous last words!'

They each reached forward and took a glass off the tray. He placed the tray on the side of the pool.

He lifted his glass to make a toast. 'Tom, Mary-Anne, we are so happy to finally be here with you, and to our next academic paper,' he said.

'Yes, it's so great to see you guys, and particularly on a holiday so far away from domestic chores.'

'And domestic *shores*!' Chad added.

'Cheers and welcome to paradise. By the way, I am starting to think we have come pretty close to the complete story now. It won't just be a paper. Maybe we should think about writing the book now,' Tom reasoned.

They sipped the champagne and paused to watch and enjoy the magnificent views.

For the next hour or so, they talked through the different core elements of the story. Chad explained the findings in Mexico in more detail and then they discussed Patrick's discoveries in Australia – his decoding of the three different stone arrangements of *Carisbrook*, *Lake Wongan*, and *Wurdi Youang*.

The decoding of the pillars of Göbekli Tepe had been a shock to everybody, as was the decoding of the true meaning of the *Dendera lightbulb frieze* at the *Temple of Hathor*. 'You know, all we need to do is try to decode Xochicalco. Then we possibly have the confirmation that it also describes the same event,' Chad remarked.

'Well, I have some news about that. It's already been done!' Tom remarked. 'Manu, Patrick's friend in Ghana has cracked it. He sent me the email only a few hours ago. He found asterisms identifying *Rigel* rising and falling. It marks out the same period of the year, when to be out of direct sunlight.'

'Wow, that's amazing! Oh, and by the way, we didn't tell you that Jeanette here has decoded that undecipherable page of random text from Mustapha's notes.'

'How on earth did you manage that?' Mary-Anne asked, looking perplexed.

'Well, I cheated. I'm *synaesthesic*. My brain sees numbers and letters in colour.'

'What did you find?' Tom asked, intrigued.

'The stars around *gamma Velorum* all form a perfect pyramid shape. It was as if that should have been the first thing for us to notice in the sky. We went the long way round deciphering this historical event. That is why there are pyramids all over the planet, and all located at around the same latitude as Giza of course. After spotting a pyramid of stars in the sky, we *evolved humans* were supposed to notice the pyramids in *Giza, Teotihuacan, Monte Alban*. Then we were supposed to identify that *gamma Velorum* was the base star of the sky pyramid. Then I imagine we were supposed to investigate where *gamma Velorum* was. Finding it at zero degrees elevation due south to an amazing accuracy in August 9750 B.C.E. should have led us to make the association with that cluster of huge, hot blue stars which *supernova*.'

'Well Tom has worked out definitively that it was a way bigger bang than a *supernova*!' Mary-Anne added. 'He says that those stars which send out a relativistic jet don't supernova, they *hypernova*, with an explosion possibly a hundred times brighter.'

'That's right,' Tom confirmed. 'The hypernova event would have been much brighter than the Sun for months, if not years, creating two Suns in the sky, following the gamma ray burst. We now know that relativistic jets are always associated with *hypernovas*.'

'Wow, that is amazing, . . . and well-reasoned,' Chad remarked.

'Yes, and there is more,' Tom continued. 'You know that Manu and Patrick decoded the Dendera frieze by identifying *Rigel* and the Sun. The image also clearly shows the relativistic jet emerging from a hypernova remnant. The snake-like form is what we expect from an asymmetric collapsing star orbiting a companion star, in its final seconds. Moreover, while the event only lasts 100 seconds, the 20% spread in velocities will cause the matter, moving at effectively a quarter of light speed, to spread out over 20% of the distance. So over 1100 light years, it will spread to 220 light years long. Going at a quarter of light speed means it took 880 years to transit this part of the galaxy.'

'OK, so that suggests that people on the Earth lived with the effects of the jet for 880 years or so,' Chad remarked.

'Indeed, and we can deduce that the danger time was when the Earth's orbit brought it between the Sun and the jet. The solar wind is guided by the Sun's magnetic field, but even at some thirty or more light years away, the magnetic field of the jet eventually becomes higher than the Sun's local magnetic field as it falls off with distance, and then the entire solar wind starts to spiral around the jet's magnetic field lines,' Tom explained.

'The magnetic field lines go *around* the Jet right?' Chad asked.

'Indeed, so we know that the geometry of the situation must have meant that magnetic field lines were going through the Sun and the Earth and approaching perfect alignment around March 21st, when the Earth is at the highest point of its orbit around the Sun. That is most likely why we see carved spirals in rocks in old sites, and in cave art, which usually include snakes and strange *alien figures*. Those figures aren't alien figures of course, they are all, *each and every one of them*, different representations of the same asterism seen in the night sky at each of the cave locations, which depicts the March 15th and April 1st dates. So, the stories on *Ancient Aliens* about being visited by extra-terrestrials are obviously not correct. People were just recording the same warning in their own way. OK Jeanette, you said there was a *doomsday* warning encoded in the pyramids. Please can you say more about that.'

'Chad can tell you, he was on *Stellarium* this morning.'

'Sure Tom. I zoomed into the *gamma Velorum* cluster. There are three stars there: two large stars and a small star, just like the relative sizes of the Giza pyramids. Like all stars, each star is moving independently with its own *space velocity*, so relative star positions will change over time. Watching how *Stellarium* plots their velocities with time, I found that their relative positions closely match the configuration of the Giza pyramids in around 10,700 C.E. That cannot be a coincidence.'

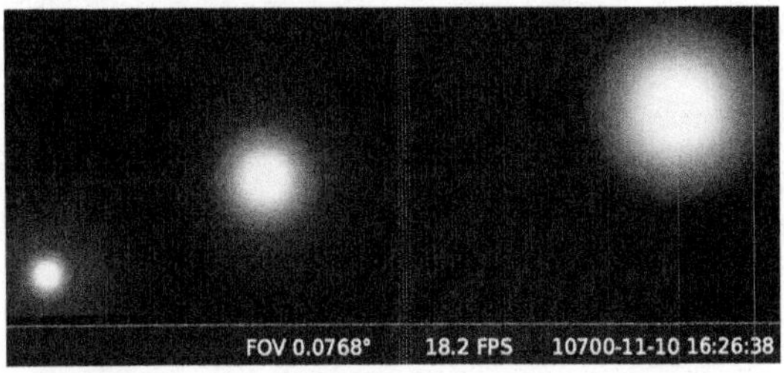

Gamma Velorum 10,700

'The pyramid layout obviously now has nothing to do with *Orion's belt*, and why should it have had? I also rechecked that alignment. *Orion's belt never* had, nor *ever will have* an alignment with the pyramids, certainly never as perfectly as the pyramids have with the *gamma Velorum* cluster in 10,700 C.E.!'

'So it is a *doomsday clock* after all,' Tom remarked. 'So we have time to get depressed about the futility of life, and the struggle we have endured to become civilised, only to plan for the next cataclysm. That certainly

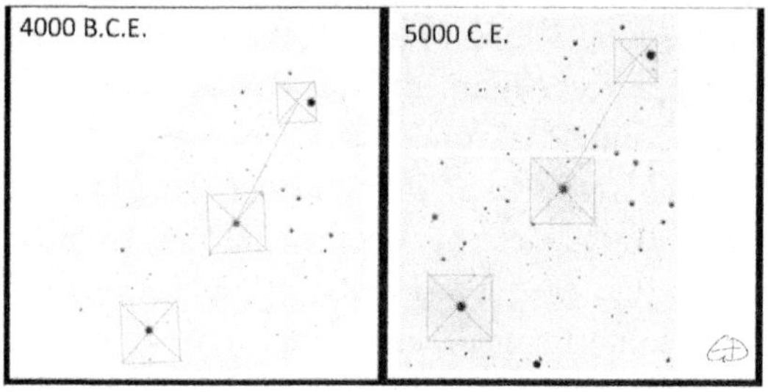

Orion's Belt Non-Alignment

explains the *Fermi Paradox*. Knowing this now, we can conclude that there probably isn't any life out there, for possibly 100 light years on one side of the solar system at least.'

'You mean, the side of the solar system where the jet passed. We should now work out where exactly that transit path was, and try to look for life on the other side of the solar system,' Chad replied.

'Indeed. We also now need to consider, that if a jet has also passed us on the *other side* of the solar system, perhaps some twenty thousand years earlier, then we really need to start thinking about being nice to one another. We may truly be quite alone here on Earth after all!' Tom added.

'Isn't there anything positive we can take from all this?' Mary-Anne asked.

'Chad and I did work out a proactive way to cool the planet over the next hundred years,' Jeanette remarked.

'How so?' Mary-Anne asked.

'Well, I proposed that we start growing vast colonies of very pale, whitish coloured marine algae, which could serve to reflect the Sun's energy. This would simulate a kind of pseudo ice-age, where the light coloured algae would create a kind of extended pseudo ice-sheet. It's very environmentally friendly, non-polluting, and may likely serve to vastly increase the oxygen delivered to the atmosphere. We just need a global program to research the optimum strain of pale marine algae which offers the most benefits.'

'Excellent! Don't you think so Tom?' Mary-Anne remarked.

'Indeed.'

'So you are considering writing a book now Tom?' Chad asked.

'I guess we need to wait until our next academic paper is out there. There is simply too much data: too many sites, too many crosslinked explanations, too many similar petroglyphs. In fact, maybe we might just take a little time now, to gather together everything we have worked out so far. We have the date and transit time of the event. It maps to what we would have expected from a long *gamma ray burst*, which hit around 13,000 B.C.E. This also correlates with some significant *partial megafaunal extinctions*, when many large mammals were dramatically reduced in number. The ice core record from Greenland describes this as the *late Pleistocene warming*.'

'Firstly, there would have been the increased levels of greenhouse gases which would have heated the planet. The ice core record at around 13,000 B.C.E. records a temperature rise of some 12°C. The generation of thick opaque, nitric oxide products up in the atmosphere, would then have created a smog, effectively creating a *pseudo impact-winter*, which then caused the planet to cool. This slow cooling continued for more than three thousand years, dropping the temperature by around 12°C, until the jet arrived in 9750 B.C.E.'

'It is exactly at this date that we see substantial *total megafaunal extinctions* on six continents. The magnetic field of the jet would have greatly influenced the Sun, with the result that the Earth's surface magnetic field would have gone *haywire* for the next 880 years as the jet transited this part of the galaxy. I should add that I am almost clutching at straws here. The latest research on this is seriously impossible to follow, and we are right at the cliff edge here in terms of our understanding. The problem is that we lack generalists now who understand the big picture. Like all scientists, but more problematic for astrophysicists, we are getting further out of touch with the complexity of the field, with every new paper that is published. Most of us astrophysicists actually do confess that we can barely understand papers even close to own fields of expertise.'

'Tom, *you* are the new generalist. You are truly striving to understand so much, in so many diverse fields, so you can advance everyone's thinking. In fact, you may be the first true generalist in almost 200 years after *Alexander von Humboldt*! Remember, Humboldt travelled extensively and made many contributions in many fields. This was only possible because he strived to build a wide core knowledge, such that his conclusions matched the findings in different scientific disciplines. This made them valid and valuable. That is what you have done here!'

'Thanks Chad. That's very kind. But I couldn't have done it without you, or in fact without any of you. You have all contributed so much.'

'I have always looked up to my big brother. Please continue. I interrupted you. You were talking about the magnetic field issues.'

'Yes, so the challenge is that at the moment, I cannot work out if the relativistic jet had a small magnetic field, which was slowly amplifying the magnetic field of the Sun, due to *dynamo action*, or whether it was huge. Nevertheless, we know that the Earth's magnetic field was greatly affected. The magnetic field directions in sediments from this period confirm this absolutely.'

'So, this being the case, with the Earth having no magnetic field protection, and the Sun probably in a *hyperactive state*, the Sun may have likely generated a significantly stronger solar wind. The huge danger was when the Earth's orbit brought it to pass through the huge spiral of solar wind, with particles traveling at speeds of hundreds, if not thousands of kilometres per second. During this time, this huge flux of high energy solar wind particles would have been driven into the Earth's atmosphere, and remember, we are talking about a beam which may have been tens of solar diameters across. The Earth's impact with the solar wind would have caused tremendous disruption to the atmospheric layers, resulting in extreme, high-energy thunderstorms, intense ultraviolet light, and remarkable coloured aurorae, everywhere.'

'That should certainly explain the Australian indigenous peoples' *Myth of the Rainbow Serpent* and the Mesoamerican *Myth of the Feathered Serpent*,' Chad added.

'Tom, did you say *intense ultraviolet light*?' Jeanette asked.

'Very intense during the daytime, for possibly three or four months every year, or even all through the year. Why do you ask?'

'It's about Göbekli Tepe. Of course. This explains why agriculture was invented there and how they could have domesticated all those wild animals so easily. Those dangerous wild animals must have obviously all gone blind, of course, from the *UV*. The people would only have needed to quickly herd them up and keep them alive, before all their food supply died of thirst and hunger and was lost. It is also interesting that we anthropologists describe how *Göbekli Tepe* didn't seem to be a place *where people lived.* Dr Schmidt, one of the key archaeologists who excavated there, even described it as a *place of death.* My belief is that we now need to start to interpret *Göbekli Tepe* as a shelter for those dangerous weeks of the year.'

'So, you are now saying that with all that rain and violent weather, it probably wasn't a problem to get water there,' Mary-Anne added. 'With such turbulence in the atmosphere during those months, it must have been raining incessantly. That is why it was built on a hill of course. I guess that the strongest strain of cereals would have survived, and these were the ones they collected at dawn and dusk for planting. They had all those herded-up, blind animals to eat, whenever they wanted. The animals would have been totally dependent on man for water and food and would have quickly become docile.'

'Brilliant conclusions. No one was ever able to explain why agriculture and domestication of animals suddenly started there. It seems so obvious now,' Chad remarked. 'What about those underground cities, *Derinkuyu,* and that other one, *Kaymakli?*'

'That's right Honey,' Jeanette confirmed. 'OK, so we are suggesting that those underground cities were possibly built to protect people from the dangers of the deadly *ultraviolet* light and violent thunderstorms.'

'I have an idea. What about the *dolmens*? There are simply thousands of those odd rock structures all around the World. Considering the inordinate amount of energy needed to construct them, surely we should finally conclude that they weren't designed and built originally as burial chambers. They must also have been shelters which were covered with earth, where people sheltered during the dangerous period from March 15th until April 1st, or during sunny days of high UV. What do you think?' Chad suggested.

'Sounds very likely. My goodness, we have found a single event which both explains the climate record, and all the sites which were built to enable people to survive, but surely a civilization perished? How could they have built all those complicated structures? You need to see the mapping of the Göbekli Tepe imagery to the night skies of Turkey. The perfection of those stellar asterism shapes cut into stone, which map perfectly to the night skies are seriously uncanny,' Tom announced excitedly.

There was a pause in the conversation as they all drank in the reality of the significance of the conclusions that they had forged together in the

Dolmen

fires of their debate.

'Now I have another, even more fundamental, question,' Tom continued. 'Surely we now have proof that a really advanced civilization must have lived on the Earth back then. The complexity and sheer magnitude of the pyramid-building task is surely evidence of that. Without advanced technology, such as a high power telescope, how could they possibly have known that *gamma Velorum* was a three star system which would evolve into a different configuration in 10700 C.E.? It is that fingerprint of the precise layout of the pyramids in Giza, which shows that not only could they image the stars in the *gamma Velorum* cluster, but they could also determine their spin axes and the stars' relative motion, which is currently unexplainable. Who were these people? We find no technology left behind. We have never found any unexplained, advanced stone-cutting technology in caves or anywhere. We are missing all the out-of-place artefacts.'

'So we have a huge list now: the cave art, the pyramid layouts in Giza and Mexico, those Australian sunrise and sunset shadow observatories, the Dendera carvings, *Göbekli Tepe,* now the underground cities such as *Derinkuyu*, the myths of the *Rainbow Serpent* and the *Feathered Serpent*, the story of *Jason and the Argonauts* and *Medusa* with her head of snakes which turned men to stone! Have I missed anything?' Tom continued. 'I will just read those emails from Patrick and Manu again, one moment.'

His phone was on a towel at the edge of the pool. He started to scroll down several emails.

'So we have determined that the Earth suffered hell for 880 years, which transformed life here for some 30 generations, where, living in a twilight zone for several months until June, was *totally normal*. According to the dates from the temples, Göbekli Tepe pillar 43, and from the monument in Xochicalco, the mid-June date marked the end of a *life in hell on Earth* for just a few months. Surely, this is why we now celebrate midsummer. This latest email here from Manu is suggesting that the Dogons of Mali have a *Kanaga* headdress to also celebrate June 21st, not because they are out celebrating the summer solstice, but because the *Kanaga* headdress has the shape of the June asterism. Manu is now asking why the *Dogon dance linked to Sirius* is connected with the *June asterism*. I have to agree with him, that they would not have gone out in temperatures of 45°C to celebrate midsummer in Mali, but they would certainly also have celebrated the June 21st asterism as an important date to mark the end of a period of absolute hell. A date, which generations of people all over the planet have celebrated for thousands of years since. In more temperate climes, we have always assumed that the peoples of Northern Europe celebrated midsummer because they were celebrating the warm days at last. I am now questioning if we have just discovered the *true origin of the midsummer celebrations*.'

'You said that Manu had identified that creature cut into pillar 27 at Göbekli Tepe. It is the only three-dimensional carving on the site and it represents the June 21st asterism. It must be significant, and it must also have marked out the date of a special event, when the danger time had passed,' Mary-Anne remarked.

'Yes, it all adds to reinforce the same conclusion.'

'OK, we have solved a huge puzzle. Are there any other big mysteries which could be explained as well? Dare I say it? What about *Atlantis*? Did it exist? What was it really?' Jeanette asked.

'Good question Jeanette!' Chad remarked. 'You know I was looking at the substantial rise in sea level at the start of the *Holocene*. We are of course suggesting that 880 years of intense solar activity caused the melting of the ice caps and the sea level rise. Remember, the relativistic jet provided a constant source of interference with the Sun, and thus provided a constant heating over the 880 years. This is why we see the

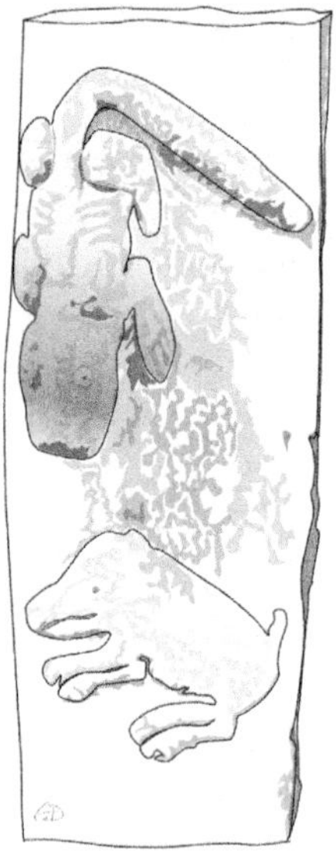

Pillar 27

continuous and relentless temperature rise, until the jet passed beyond the solar system. While we were in Mexico, I was looking at the Nahuatl language. If we consider the word *Atlantis*, it is made of *Atl-*, *lan-*, and *-antis*. One derivation suggested *Atlaca -lan -tis*, where *Atlaca* means the water people, *lan* means along and *tis* is a causative plural. This could be pronounced *Atlaclantis*, which pretty much would morph into Atlantis over 11,000 years or so. In Nahuatl, this can literally be interpreted to mean *the people who lived by the water*. Nahuatl is certainly one of the oldest languages, and it is possible, that if a huge amount of people around the World lived along the coastlines, and these people all perished, or were driven further and further inland, then *the loss of Atlantis* is surely metaphorically describing the loss of a huge number of coastal towns and villages all over the World, i.e. the loss of *the people who lived by the water*.'

'Good point Chad. I like it, but unlike the decoding of all these sites, which is data, I guess we can only suggest *that* story as a possible interpretation. It does seem rather realistic though,' Tom added. 'We will need to separate conjecture and assumption from data, particularly in a scientific publication.'

'I have another question for you,' Chad replied. 'What about that strange star they have found some 1470 light years away. They refer to it as *Tabby's star* named after the key scientist who is working to try to identify its strange light curve. There is a strange large object passing near to that star, which is distorting its light output. I did the numbers. If the jet passed the solar system at a quarter of light speed, some 11700 years ago. It will be 2940 light years away from us right now right?'

'Sure,' Tom confirmed.

'So, if we look through a telescope at a star which is 2,940 light years away, we are looking back in time to a moment when the jet was passing the solar system then,' Chad reasoned.

'That's right.'

'Well, if we look at a star which is 1,470 light years away, if you do the numbers, then our jet was exactly 1,470 light years away at that time. It does seem a very big coincidence that Tabby's star is exactly that distance away.'

'OK, I am aware of that star. Actually quite a few stars have been reported having similarly strange light curves. The new exoplanet telescope TESS is looking for similar stars. We, in the trade, call it KIC 8462852, after the *Kepler Input Catalogue* number. It's one digit off my cell phone number, so that's the only reason I know that number. Yes, it's the right distance away, but that star is actually closer to the centre of the Galaxy than our solar system, so it can't be our jet. Our jet definitely came from *gamma Velorum*, travelling in the opposite direction, outwards from the Galaxy. The precise distance to the *gamma Velorum* cluster is what is confirmed from the separation of the late *Pleistocene*, and early *Holocene* peaks that we see in the Greenland ice core record. But, you are making another really valid point, which maybe I agree with. Those relativistic jets are possibly not that rare. Remember those hot blue stars only last a few million years. It could be that we are seeing another relativistic jet passing that star system at the moment, hence the bizarre light curve. It could be grazing the star system with respect to our line of sight. Well, we see it *at this moment*. It of course happened some 1,470 years ago.'

'Guys, shall we postpone this academic discourse for a while and go to the restaurant for a late lunch?' Mary-Anne suggested.

'Great idea Mary-Anne. Come on Chad, let's have a quick shower and put some clothes on,' Jeanette confirmed.

They all made their way out of the pool. It was time for a *Welcome to St. Lucia* lunch.

13 Soufrière, St. Lucia: the origin of agriculture and the domestication of animals

Sugar Beach, beside the Petit Piton, St. Lucia

It was early afternoon. Mary-Anne and Jeanette were sitting on the coral sands at Sugar Beach, gazing out towards their distant horizon. The bright tropical sky was dotted with small white fluffy clouds. There was a change in the air and a soft onshore breeze gave a little respite from the very hot Sun. The shadows from a pair of tall, curving, coconut palms created wide cool patches of sand, affording them some refuge from the fierce burning rays. For many moments they continued to sit in silence, watching the changing turquoise shades of the Caribbean Sea, as small wavelets broke and rippled up over the wet white sand. It was very relaxing to just stop and stare at St. Lucia's tropical palette. Then Jeanette spoke.

'You know, I find this whole discovery of this 880 year cataclysm that the people of Earth endured, extremely tragic and utterly unbelievable. We have all grown up looking for a purpose in life. Up until this moment, I was imagining how life on this planet has evolved, and how we would develop in the future. After three billion years of evolution, I had always thought that life had evolved in a positive direction to us here. We now know that this possibly isn't true.'

'Yes, I know. It's very sobering. From what I think I now understand, the transits of these jets happens periodically, and each time one of them passes by, taking hundreds of years to do so, the Earth gets effectively kicked back to the *Stone Age*. Tens of generations then live in fear, anguish and hardship for perhaps 6 months of the year, for the duration of their lives, while they strive actively to avoid the hours of sunlight. It surely must be the same each time. We can never know how many times this may have happened to civilizations on Earth before.'

'What about the question of the cave art describing different jet transients, different periods of 880 years or so of turmoil. The cave art is so difficult to date. Could some of them even describe *previous* jet transits? The geometrical elements would have been the same each time, there would be a serpentine snake form, representing the jet, between two forms representing the two pairs of asterisms around March 21st or around September 21st, depending whether the jet passed above or below the plane of the Galaxy, because we know that the jet would have passed the solar system one side or the other. There would be pairs of spirals, showing the deadly solar wind spiralling around the magnetic field lines . . .' Jeanette continued.

'You already sound like an *astrophysicist!*' Mary-Anne remarked, 'And I should know, I live with one!'

'I think we've all heard the details so often that we now know how to tell most of the story. What I wanted to say was simply that life on our planet, has been periodically stunted. Did we ever manage to recover to the heights of what went before us? Is this, I mean, *are we* the luckiest civilization so far?'

'I know that Tom and Chad are caught up with the astrophysics and Earth science, but I care more about the lives of those people who endured all this. Let's just go back through the steps here, as supported by the climate record. A star dies 1100 light years away, it goes out with a bang. There is a very bright supernova . . .' Mary-Anne reasoned.

'A *hypernova*, some hundred or so times brighter than the Sun,' Jeanette added.

'OK, yes, a *hypernova*, which at the same time created a burst of intense gamma ray radiation and a jet of material, at each pole of the fast spinning dying star.'

'OK, I think *you* definitely sound like an expert now,' Jeanette said, with a smile.

'Thank you. OK, so a *one-hundred-second* burst of material is shot out at quarter light speed in our direction, towards the solar system. The jet of material starts off as a flat pancake of material, but it slowly spreads out into a jet some 220 light years long. The gamma ray burst takes 1100 years to reach the Earth, which is then exposed on one side to a 100 second burst of lethal radiation. That is what caused the dramatic heating spike during the late Pleistocene. This was followed by a subsequent, endless cooling as thick opaque clouds filled the Earth's atmosphere. The jet, travelling at a quarter light speed, then passed the solar system some 3300 years later, taking 880 years for the transit. The intense ultraviolet light from a hyperactive Sun caused so many animals to go blind. That is what caused the megafaunal total extinctions on six continents. There must have been a real abundance of life up until that time.'

'We missed something. Oh yes, the effect of the jet was to cause total interference of the Earth's own surface *protective* magnetic field, possibly for that 14-day period identified from that *Bennett Monolith* from *Tiwanaku*, while causing the Sun to be permanently hyperactive for the 880 year duration. When the Earth passed through the spiralling jet of solar wind, it was terribly dangerous to be outside at all, which was effectively the time when the Earth lay between the Sun and the Jet,' Jeanette added. 'Chad found clues to that in Mustapha's notes.'

'But let us just try to work out how these people lived. The detailed carved frieze in Dendera's Temple of Hathor is a clear record of what to do. It must be contemporary. The same message is found in Göbekli Tepe on pillar 43, and now we know the same warning is on that Xochicalco *Temple of the Feathered Serpent*,' Mary-Anne continued.

'I did take some time looking at other friezes in Hathor's Temple. I did find several more serpentine snakes, each with their heads bent back, each coming out of a lotus flower. On the same vast wall of hieroglyphs, there are even constellations marked, similar to those on the famous Hathor Temple ceiling Zodiac. These must all be describing relativistic jets coming out of Wolf-Rayet star hypernovas, and given the constellation markers, maybe the wall friezes actually record where those events were located. That temple has quite a record of this astrophysical phenomenon. It must seriously go back a very long time,' Jeanette added. 'For me it remains a real enigma about what those wall friezes actually describe. It would be great if some serious research could be done to translate them in the light of these new perspectives on what the serpentine snakes actually mean.'

For a moment, the beauty of their surroundings on that lovely Caribbean beach intervened as they again paused and became transfixed upon the softly breaking shoreline. A man who had been waiting by the jetty for any new arrivals, had been watching them. He now walked briskly across the sand towards them.

‘Ladies,’ he called. ‘Welcome to St. Lucia! Can I offer you snorkelling or a boat trip to Soufrière? I also have fresh fruit juices.’

‘Thank you. Yes St. Lucia is lovely. We’re good thanks,’ Mary-Anne called back.

‘OK, thank you. If you change your mind, I am just over there,’ the man said, pointing, his sales pitch somewhat stunted by Mary-Anne’s quick retort.

‘OK, good to know,’ Jeanette then added.

The man then turned and wandered back to the jetty.

‘They are trying to sell anything they can to the endless stream of tourists. I guess they need to make a living like anyone else,’ Mary-Anne said.

‘Back to the story . . .’ Jeanette urged.

‘OK, yes, the point I wanted to explore was the utter humanity of the experience. Somehow there was this advanced civilization . . .’

‘Living along the shorelines of the continents and islands, in *Atlantis*,’ Jeanette added,

‘Of course we can never know if that is the correct interpretation, or whether those people perished after the gamma ray burst, or only when the jet transit started to affect the Earth, but I have to say that *that* seems the most reasonable explanation of the meaning of *Atlantis*. The sea levels rose hundreds of feet all around the World with the melting of the icecaps. Coastal settlements would have been lost to the oceans.’

‘So the people back then were advanced enough to understand the danger of what would happen some 3300 years after the hypernova event, and they decided to construct the pyramids for future generations if anyone possibly survived. They somehow knew that this event would be terribly dangerous. The layout and the construction of the pyramids is certainly very complex, and they put a lot of thought into everything.’

‘Tom said that they must have had advanced telescopes, or they simply could not have known about the relative motion of the three stars of the *gamma Velorum* cluster,’ Jeanette added.

‘That for me is already one enigma, another is the star identified on pillar 43. *Spica* I think it was called. Tom was saying that *that* star is another massive blue star, which astrophysicists tell us will supernova soon. *Spica* is the closest star of that type to the solar system. But let us just imagine what life was like for the people of Göbekli Tepe,' Mary-Anne reasoned. 'We know that the site is on a raised hill above a wide flood plain. They anticipated the endless rains and they planned a whole cluster of shelters which were constructed for the solar wind transit duration, for 880 years.'

'So you think they didn't live there. You agree with that conclusion.'

'The archaeological evidence is that they did not eat there, cook there, wash there, or *anything* there. Most likely, they lived elsewhere during the rest of the year and migrated back to hide there when it was dangerous to be outside. Perhaps they stayed there permanently for that deadly fourteen day period. We don't know yet. All the Göbekli Tepe pillars are intricately carved with details of different star maps. I interpret this as some kind of representation of the night. I think they simply changed their body clocks and they *slept* there. *Göbekli Tepe* was most likely one big dormitory complex. I think they would have adjusted their routine to sleep during the day and become active at night if it was safe to be outside,' Mary-Anne reasoned.

'Wouldn't it be great to excavate the other 20 or so structures at Göbekli Tepe that they have discovered there?' Jeanette asked.

'That would be wonderful and very enrichening for us all. We all want to know *what happens in the end*. Well, I think we now know, and it's an ending that actually doesn't sound too good. I believe that, in the other buried structures, we may find more compelling evidence to support that they were sleeping quarters, perhaps even a record of their experiences.'

She pushed her hand into the soft white coral sand and lifted up a handful of it, then opened her fingers slightly, letting it stream back down again.

'You know, it's the birth of agriculture and domestication of animals in the *Fertile Crescent* around southern Anatolia, which I find so intriguing. It now seems so obvious how they achieved that. The intense ultraviolet light caused all those very dangerous wild animals to go blind. That is why it was possible to domesticate them. There are other studies about how complicated it was to cultivate wheat. Up until now, the mainstream academics have been reasoning that people sat down around a campfire and suddenly someone announced they would *cultivate wheat* because of *sociological and food supply challenges*. Hello? They had no choice! Hunting at night would have been difficult in the beginning, particularly with diminished numbers of mammals. The next question has to be, how on earth did they achieve such an ideal *einkorn* variety with such grain retention, threshability, and nutritional value? If they had advanced telescopes, did these advanced people also have capabilities in genetic engineering, to anticipate the need for, and develop the ideal crop strain in preparation for the cataclysm?' Mary-Anne reasoned, with a hint of incredulity in her voice.

'Well if the weather was so violent, wouldn't the only cereals left standing, be the ones which had the best capabilities to survive? They would be the ones with the strongest ears attaching many grains per stem, right?' Jeanette suggested.

'Good point, but I even read that the domesticated *einkorn* strain also had *reduced seed dormancy* – a measure of the time the seeds stay in the ground before sprouting – and even *an altered flowering time*. These other genes are really important because these traits facilitate human collection and consumption. I start to find this complete package of enhanced genetic cereal traits a little too lucky, if this all happened just by chance.'

'So, as you said before, you think that life in Göbekli Tepe might have been an experience of several weeks, where people slept in the structures by day, and became more active at night. It was raining incessantly, so *channelling the endless deluge away* was more important than having access to rivers and lakes. At night, when the moon was full, they headed out to kill a few blind animals at first, eventually forming fenced areas to feed and water their store of blind animals. Gradually their *pot belly hill* settlement may even have become a farm. That's what *Göbekli Tepe* translates to, right?' Jeanette asked.

'Yes, that's right. I think people most likely lived in other structures away from Göbekli Tepe for part of the year. If the tremendous weather systems were caused by the impact of the solar wind with the Earth, the rains may probably have been much reduced from June to December, so people may have moved away to live closer to rivers and lakes. The layout of those early Göbekli Tepe structures clearly shows stone benches where they may have reclined on soft matting between dawn and dusk. I believe that they would have lived in a twilight World. The pillars there all have those remarkably carved animal and bird asterisms of the stars in the night sky, as if emulating the night sky on stone, during the daytime.'

'What about the later structures at *Çatalhöyük*? They are some 2000 years later, right?'

'That's right, and we do see some similarity in the imagery. I found an image of two leopards facing each other on one wall of a building excavated there. Tom checked it for me using *Stellarium*. It indeed maps to the asterism found in the sky some 3 months later. So the people of *Çatalhöyük* identified similar asterisms in the sky as the people of *Göbekli Tepe*. There is even a shrine in *Çatalhöyük* with a sun-bear like creature above three bulls' heads. This arrangement also maps to the same stars seen after sunset in late June. The difference is that the sun-bear is now upright, while the same asterism in *Göbekli Tepe* is a downward crawling quadruped with a long tail.'

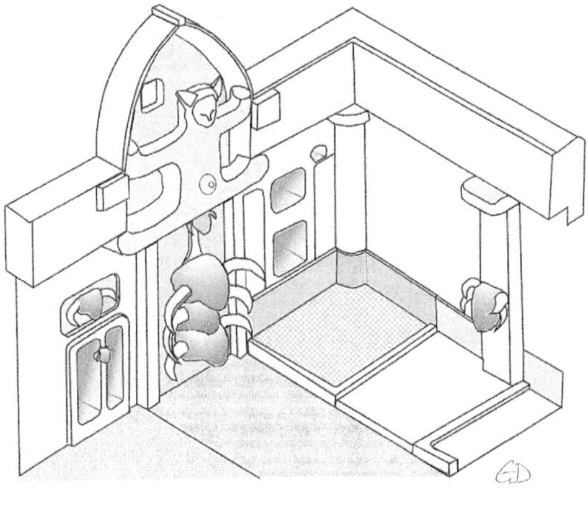

Çatalhöyük Sunbear Shrine

'We are still left with an enigma. I can understand that coastal populations were devastated. Millions of people may also have gone blind from the intense ultraviolet light, and then starved to death. Within ten or twenty years, their settlements would have been taken by the rising sea levels, but where is their technology? There are no vast stores of computers, or wiring, or telescopes or genetic engineering labs. We don't suddenly find an ancient computer at the far end of an unexplored cave. If they were that advanced, how did they cut such accurate star maps onto stone pillars? We have barely a few fragments, some lathe-manufactured hard stone dishes, a few artefacts out of place like that special carved crystal ewer in the Victoria and Albert museum in London. Surely, it can't all have vaporised,' Jeanette reasoned.

'Hmm, I think you raise a valid point. That remains the big enigma. I am still numbed, thinking about the terrible endurance of the human survivors who suffered all this.'

'They lived lives spent periodically hiding underground or in caves during that time, and tens of generations knew of no other life on Earth for some 880 years,' Jeanette replied.

'That is very sobering, and shocking, but I am afraid it is most certainly true. But what about us and our future? I mean the future of humans on this planet. There is still a bunch of stars in that cluster still waiting to go bang. The builders of the pyramids have marked out 10,700 C.E. as the suggested date of the next cataclysm. Is that when the jet will pass by, or is it when the next hypernova will occur? How long have we got? Assuming the next jet will not hit us directly, and we must assume that because the spin axis of the remaining star will be identical to the one which went off last time. It will effectively travel along the same path and miss us by 20 light years or more. Nevertheless, what can we possibly do to plan for and survive this tragic event the next time around?'

'We need to love each other more and care for each other more. It is time to truly appreciate how wonderful this gift of life is. We have just worked out that it is possible to actively cool this planet if we set our minds to it. That could dramatically improve our survival chances in the immediate future. We know that life in the seas and oceans generally survived. What about a plan to build cities in the ocean?' Jeanette suggested. 'I'm not being all *gloom and doom*. There is a reality here that each and every one of us must now face. It's time to start teaching essential astrophysics at school. The future people of Earth deserve a new curriculum!'

'Jeanette, ... I'm impressed!' Mary-Anne said smiling. 'And wars are so ridiculous. We fight to gain control of different tracts of the surface of our wonderful planet, while forever polluting the air we breathe, raising global temperatures, and melting the icecaps, further raising sea levels and losing habitat to the oceans.'

'So you are suggesting it is time to take stock and be more philosophical?'

'If there is very little life on any exoplanets out there, close to where the jet passed – and by that, I mean that surviving lifeforms on other exoplanetary systems would have suffered the same cataclysmic events –

then we need a plan to survive with a positive attitude. First things first, we need to plan to survive the inequalities of this generation. We need to learn to be more reasonable, more accepting, and seek kindness within ourselves and give that to others. *Cities in the ocean* is a good suggestion. There is no reason why they wouldn't be adequate. *Derinkuyu* is a blueprint for a land-based underground city. We can also plan to construct these on a global scale. My mother always used to say that we live on in our children. Perhaps it's time to live a little more in the present. I'm sorry, I don't have all the answers. The people of Göbekli Tepe and peoples all over the globe, *planned for and survived* this cataclysm. I am sure that future generations can do the same.'

'With that positive conclusion, shall we now go back to Stonefield?' Jeanette suggested.

'Let's do that. I'll call the reception for our transport.'

She took out her Stonefield cell-phone and called the resort. After a short time it was done.

'Some more good news!' Mary-Anne remarked. 'They just said that the driver is already on his way bringing another couple. Our transport will be here in five minutes, right where we were dropped off.'

'Lovely.'

They picked up their things and wandered across the sand towards the jetty, still feeling a little shocked by all the broad brush conclusions of their talk. The taxi van arrived moments later, and they changed places with a young couple who climbed out, wearing only their swimming things and flip flops. Once on board, Jeanette dragged the sliding door shut.

'You guys had a good time?' their driver asked.

'We did! It was lovely!' Mary-Anne replied.

It was a very steep and winding drive back up to Stonefield. They got out of the taxi at reception and walked down to their villas. As they approached, from the noise, they could hear that Tom and Chad were at *Villa Frangipani.* Jeanette opened the gate and they walked across the veranda.

'Hi guys, you two seem to be in a great mood here,' Jeanette remarked.

Tom and Chad were sitting at the table playing some kind of board game.

'We're playing *The Lost Ancient Peruvian Game of Trout Ceviche!*' Chad replied. 'I think I just won! It's the game that Felipe, that Peruvian guy, gave me when I went to Xochicalco with Takashi-san.'

'It certainly looks fun,' Mary-Anne remarked.

'Chad cheated!' Tom shouted, throwing his cards down on the table. 'He stole all my good cards.'

'Chad, did you cheat?' Jeanette asked with surprise.

'Honey, it's the rules of the game! Tom left *ranger* and *bandit* cards in his hand. I had a *ranger* and could inspect his cards and I could then steal all the cards I needed. He should have banked those intelligently. That's how I got *Trout Ceviche!*'

'I love this game already, despite losing to a better man. Let's play again. It only took 45 minutes to play. Board games are really becoming popular now. I really hope for Felipe that he makes some money from this *Trout Ceviche* game. The graphics on the board are fantastic. Do you girls want to play?'

'We may want a quick dip in the pool, then a glass of something cold, then a hug, then . . .' Mary-Anne replied.

'Of course! You go in the pool, I'll grab that last bottle of bubbly I put in their fridge, then we can all play,' Tom replied.

Jeanette looked at Mary-Anne. They smiled as if they were keeping a secret.

'OK, into the pool I go,' Jeanette said.

'And me,' Mary-Anne said.

'OK, maybe we should join you too,' Chad said, stepping out of his bathrobe. 'How was Sugar Beach? Any new revelations?'

'Lots,' Jeanette confirmed, knowingly.

Tom then emerged from the room carrying the unopened bottle of champagne and four glasses on a tray. 'OK, it seems that we may be playing *Trout Ceviche* later,' he remarked, seeing them all in the water.

He set everything down on the table, then proceeded to unwire and pop open the champagne cork. He directed the bottle at the last moment, so the cork whizzed over the pool.

'I think you just advertised to the neighbours that we are having champagne,' Mary-Anne remarked.

'Actually, I can confirm I most definitely did. That is *our* villa darling.'

'Oh, of course it is. My mistake!'

Tom poured the champagne into the glasses and then walked over to the pool steps. He carefully walked down the steps into the water, then slowly waded over towards the others.

'Here you go guys. Please take a glass.'

After they had each taken a glass, he placed the tray down on the edge of the pool, then lifted his glass.

'We need to toast again. This time in Chad and Jeanette's pool. Here's to a great holiday guys, in the company of great family and friends.'

'To a more positive existence on our small blue-green planet, the true life-support vessel, sailing in this turbulent galactic ocean and despite the odds, a survivor of its age,' Mary-Anne added.

'You sound very poetic,' Tom remarked.

'Thank you, Tom,' Mary-Anne replied, taking a sip of her champagne. She then leaned forward and whispered in his ear, 'I love you.'

Tom smiled.

'I think we can all agree that we have discovered a story which explains a whole new chapter about a missing history of our planet. From cave art to megalithic constructions, from myths and legends to archaeological excavations. Finally we have even decoded the message that our ancestors planned for us to understand,' Chad concluded.

'Indeed, but there is still just one last overburdening question. Where is all the technology from the previous advanced civilization? As you said, apart from the broken *Antikythera* mechanism, the analogue computer found in a Greek shipwreck, there *ain't much hi-tech stuff* lying around in caves and bunkers, which shows how they built the pyramids, or how they could even see *gamma Velorum* as a changing multiple-star system. All we have is the megalithic structures, the stone friezes, and the cave art,' Tom reasoned. 'Surely, if an advanced civilization did reside on the Earth before the 880 year-long cataclysm, who were responsible for designing and building everything, they would have surely left just a few bits of technology behind?'

‘I agree with you. That remains the biggest enigma and most important unanswered part of this story,’ Chad remarked.

‘In fact, the transit of the relativistic jet, and 880 years of arduous existence on planet Earth, have effectively cut us off from understanding what life on Earth was like before that event,’ Tom replied. ‘I would also like to add that we should try as hard as possible to ignore any suggestions of something being explained by a visit from *extra-terrestrials*. As soon as we do that, we stop searching for the data and figuring out how the lost civilization before us could have achieved these things.’

‘I agree with you Tom, and we should embrace the best of all this new knowledge. We have finally pioneered a tunnel back to a lost, rich, earlier history of the Earth, which starts to describe how people lived here some 11,770 years ago. Surely from this new insight, there is now so much more we can discover,’ Chad confirmed.

‘That’s a positive thought. Let’s drink to that,’ Tom remarked, holding up his glass. ‘To a new knowledge of the Earth’s history.’

They raised their glasses.

14 UC Berkeley: understanding stone circles as solar-wind warning-period calendars

Seminar Room, University of California at Berkeley

Carl was standing in front of a white board at the front of the seminar room. There were around twenty serious-looking researchers in the room, sitting around a collection of white tables all moved together to form a single horseshoe shaped table.

'OK everyone, thanks for coming. Based on what we have reasoned over the past two weeks, we have modelled the jet as follows. We know the Earth's orbit is 62 degrees relative to the galactic plane, with the Earth closest to the galactic centre around June 21st, our mid-summer in the northern hemisphere, and furthest away around December 21st, our winter solstice. We thus know that March 21st, our spring equinox, occurs when the Earth is at the *highest point* above the galactic plane, while on September 21st, our fall equinox occurs when the Earth is at its *lowest point*,' Carl reasoned. 'Remember, the key point here is that the days of the year represent where the Earth is on its orbit around the Sun. It has absolutely *nothing* to do with when it is midwinter or midsummer!'

'So, the jet was transiting above the galactic plane then?' a voice called out.

'That is the most logical interpretation based on all the data. We know that the magnetic field lines which circle around the jet, passed through the Sun and the Earth around March 21st. Due to the asymmetry of the jet transit relative to the solar system, fortunately there was not a second dangerous period around September 21st,' Carl continued. 'The enhanced solar wind from a highly active Sun would have travelled away from the Sun, guided by the Sun's own magnetic field lines, which of course get weaker with distance. There are very complex and dynamic magnetic amplification effects which come into play here, involving *magnetic Reynolds numbers*, which I will try to avoid. In short, the math gets very complex. In simple terms, at a certain distance out from the Sun, the magnetic field strength of the jet is greater than the Sun's and the charged solar wind particles then start to spiral around the jet's field lines which take over at that point.'

'Do we have any way to know what this distance was, when the jet's magnetic field took over?' another voice called out.

'Indeed we do. I had another email from Tom Walker only a few days ago, which describes the decoding of some intricate carvings on the back of a stone figure, the *Bennett Monolith*, as it is called, which until recently resided in a dimly lit underground gallery in a museum in La Paz in Bolivia. That carving matches the central part of a sequence of calendar stones at the *Tiwanaku* site nearby, identifying March 21st as the middle of a dangerous period to be avoided. On the back of the *Bennett Monolith*, Tom is suggesting that the 14 snakes, running down towards the figure of *Viracocha*, identify 14 days when people definitely needed to be underground. There is also an additional snake either side of those 14 snakes, coming from the left and right on that monolith, which suggests that this deadly period may fade in and fade out, so to be safe, people were encouraged to take shelter for perhaps as much as 16 days. What is being suggested here is that the Earth took a bit more than 14 days to completely pass into and out of the spiralling stream of solar wind particles.'

'So to a first approximation we simply compute the distance travelled by the Earth along its orbit during those 14 days, and then we have the diameter of the life-threatening spiral of solar wind particles,' the voice reasoned.

'Indeed, and that is what we have done. Our estimate is that this period of deadly solar wind particles of 14 days corresponds to a solar wind spiral extending some 30 solar diameters across. That is around 4×10^{10} metres. That's the distance the Earth travels along its orbit in that time. This suggests that the solar wind started to get deviated by the magnetic field of the jet and formed into a tube-like collimated spiral about a third of the distance from the Sun to the Earth,' Carl reasoned. 'I should add here that modelling the magnetic interference and magnetic amplification effects of a passing relativistic jet, are on the absolute edges of our current understanding. Those 14 days are key, as they identify the diameter of a high density plasma, which is concentrated and possibly denser than the surface plasma of the Sun, and thus the plasma has, effectively *frozen within it,* a local magnetic field possibly as strong as the surface field of the Sun.'

'Why is this so important? Well, it tells us that for 14 days every year for 880 years, the Earth collided into a spiralling beam of highly energetic plasma. This solar wind impact both rendered the Earth's own *magnetosphere* chaotic, removing the Earth's own protection from high energy charged particles, while at the same time, this high energy plasma would have generated local sources of extremely high energy radiation within the atmosphere itself, such as gamma rays and X-rays. We need to understand that high energy plasma particles travelling at thousands of kilometres per second, impacted with atmospheric molecules. The multicolour aurorae would have been utterly stunning, but people would have seriously been risking their sight, and perhaps their lives, had they paused to stop and stare at those deadly, but amazingly spectacular, phenomena. There would have been endless thunderstorms and torrential rains throughout this period requiring people to be well-protected in stone structures or caves. It goes without saying that this explains how and why the sediments from this epoch show utterly chaotic and random geomagnetic field directions as reported in the literature.

Jacqui Hau was in the room, sitting near Ted and Chris. She called out. 'Dr Rhodes, just to be clear, are we concluding that the relativistic jet's interaction with the Sun caused significant dangers for most of the year, due to the high ultraviolet, but its capture of the solar wind made it absolutely treacherous for those 14 or so days around the highest point of the Earth's orbit above the galactic plane, around 21st March?'

'Jacqui, that is the consensus we are drawing. We are possibly shifting that mid-date forward to March 23rd based on the geometry of where *gamma Velorum* is, but in principle that is correct.'

'And what was your reasoning why the jet passed us tens of light years *above* the solar system, and not tens of light years *below* the solar system?'

'Again, it's a question of geometry. The Dendera images suggest the jet, as seen in the northern hemisphere, was pointing upwards. Again, we are just lucky that the jet passed far off to one side. The jet's magnetic field lines would have channelled two streams of the solar wind in opposite directions. I believe both would have been visible in the sky, which possibly explains why we see two spirals, with opposite rotational directions, both in cave art and carved into many ancient sites. For me the stone cut spirals are a *megalithic site marker*. Whenever those spirals are present, carved into rocks and walls, and even in cave art, the site is instantly dated to between 9750 and 8870 B.C.E. There is even a site in Malta, *Tarxien Temple,* I believe it is called. This has pairs of reverse spiral carvings all over it. While it can be that people adopted that motif, you can't carbon date stone. Isn't it more likely that this was yet another structure built to protect people from the deadly 14-day period? It seems quite unlikely that they simply decided to carve images of a spiralling solar wind beside the entrances to temples some 7000 years later.'

'So how do we explain who created all these megalithic structures? We don't find any technology anywhere, hidden in caves or buried. Nothing has ever been found to date. The capabilities of how some of these megalithic structures were built still eludes us today,' another voice called out. It was Chris.

'That is a very different and a significantly poignant question, and one which can only have a very controversial answer, and no one can explain that definitively. We have had several serious meetings over the past few days and all I can do is attempt to lead you towards our current perspective. The hard facts are these. The Earth is unfortunate in its location, a little too close to a cluster of giant, high mass, hot blue stars. These stars typically have a mass in excess of 60 solar masses, such that in their end phase, they each will evolve into Wolf-Rayet stars and will hypernova and emit two diametrically-opposite, relativistic jets along their spin axis. The Earth is metaphorically in a *bowling alley*, and in the past, similar jets most likely periodically affected life on our planet. We are suggesting this from the other carvings we have found at Hathor's Temple near Luxor in Egypt. On friezes there, are several other similar snake-like forms, each with the same curved-back head, clearly depicting a relativistic jet emerging from a hypernova remnant. These images strongly suggest that the presence and transit of these jets was well understood and documented by the peoples who lived back then. Hopefully in the near future, some of our eminent professors of Egyptology might further translate that wall of hieroglyphs, in the light of this new revelation that the snakes represent relativistic jets, so we could better understand what is actually written there.'

'What about the dinosaurs? Isn't it more reasonable to suggest that their demise was more likely caused by the transit of a relativistic jet, affecting life on this planet for hundreds of years, rather than the impact of a single asteroid? We know that they didn't all die out at once,' a voice called out.

'Very good point, and I agree that it's more likely that another long *gamma ray burst*, and subsequent relativistic jet transit might more reasonably have been the astrophysical event which killed them off, and not just the *Chicxulub asteroid impact* alone.'

'But we are digressing a little. Over the past few days, I have been trying to develop the most compelling arguments which explain how all those megalithic structures were built and why we found no advanced technology. Despite suggestions from several non-scientific friends, who perhaps have been watching too many episodes of *Ancient Aliens*, I don't subscribe to the idea that the Earth has had any extra-terrestrial intervention. We all do serious science here and we look at the hard evidence. I am sure we all agree that speculation does not form part of the scientific debate. So, I am parking that subject for the time being.'

'As some of you know, yesterday we had a very comprehensive all-day climatic seminar, which was pretty comprehensive. So, to build some shared consensus, I just want to run through the headlines from that. The key output was a much better definition of the Earth's climatic history, from around the time of the *gamma ray burst* to the end of the period of heating caused by the relativistic jet transit. I am of course referring to the Greenland ice core data here. Within a temperature uncertainty of around 2-3°, we can confidently characterise the temperature profile as follows. We have a very sharp rise in temperature of around 12°C starting around 12,800 B.C.E., which peaks around 12,500 B.C.E. Climatologists call this warm peak the Bølling-Allerød *interstadial*. Within the bounds of error, it approximates a steep exponential rise, which in our view matches all the longer term heating processes which ensue from the shock heating from a 100-second, long gamma ray burst or L-GRB.'

'Following this, the Earth experienced some 3000 years or so, of continued cooling, caused by the onset of a *pseudo-impact winter*, where the GRB effectively led to the production of vast opaque clouds of nitric oxides, which effectively blocked out the heating influence of the sunlight. Within this time, we do see this constant cooling being interrupted by two other heating peaks, occurring around 12,000 B.C.E. and 11,000 B.C.E., but after some reasoned assessment, we feel pretty confident that they match the expected characteristics of heating from other gamma ray

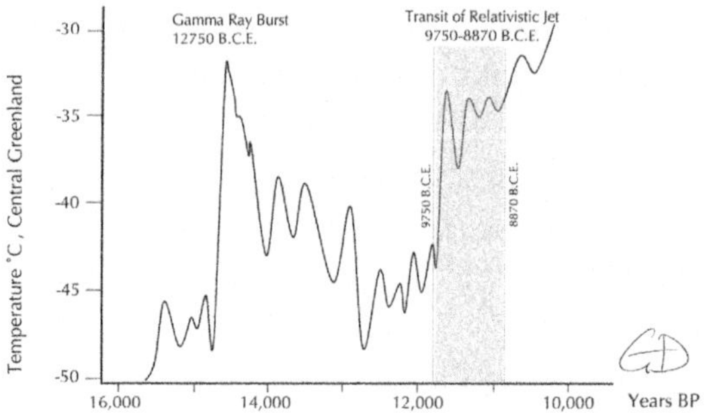

Climate Graph

bursts, from other dying star *supernova* events. At this time, we can't say more. Nevertheless, the main temperature trend is downwards. There is one last minor temperature rise occurring around 10,600 B.C.E., before very intense constant heating occurs from 9750 B.C.E. to 8870 B.C.E., which we are confident was caused by the magnetic field of the relativistic jet, making the Sun hyperactive and interfering with the trajectory of the solar wind. So, let's take another moment to try to quantise that.'

'So, in order to come up with some numbers, I want to emphasise here that we are talking about *potentially half of the Sun's total solar wind* being gathered together into a spiral, effectively flowing towards the jet in each direction, with one half flowing through the orbital plane of the Earth. The magnetic field strength is of course the same in both directions because we are talking about magnetic field lines which travel around the jet, just like field lines around a wire carrying DC current.'

'So let's take a look at the solar wind itself and let's try to quantise how that differs from what the Earth experiences today. The Sun gives off a *fast* solar wind travelling around 750 km/sec and a *slow* solar wind travelling around 450 km/sec. While the slow solar wind is twice as dense, both have temperatures of at least 100,000 degrees Celsius. The Sun has quiet and active periods. In quiet periods, we know the *fast solar wind* comes from coronal holes around the poles, and the *slow solar wind* from the equatorial region, but in active periods, *slow solar wind* comes also from near the poles. Remember, during the jet transit, we are talking about a period of solar *hyperactivity*! Today we have a flux of 7 protons per square centimetre, impacting the Earth at around 450 km/sec and being carried along the magnetic field lines. During the jet transit, if we approximate the Sun's total loss of solar wind particles at around 10^{36} particles per second, travelling at 450 km/sec, now confined to a tube of diameter equivalent to approximately 14 days of hell of the Earth's orbit, which means around 4×10^{10} metres across, the number density then rises to 7000 protons per square centimetre! That suggests we are talking about a solar wind plasma stream, a thousand times more-dense than normal, impacting an effectively non-existent protective Earth magnetosphere, which is effectively in *meltdown* due to the magnetic field of the jet! '

'That's quite a serious plasma density increase, Carl, if we now consider the energy per second being delivered to the atmosphere,' Ted called out. 'There's the clear cause of the temperature rise, and it possibly then explains some of the increases in ion species that we find in the climatic record during that time.'

'That's a very good comment, which now leads me directly into another bit of controversial research which is entrenching itself, which we need to address. Being able to explain the climatic temperature profile as the true signature of a *hypernova* from the *gamma Velorum cluster,* correlating both the shock impact of the GRB and subsequently the continuous heating of the relativistic jet transit, is essential. Rational scientific argument demands that we are able to substantiate our reasoning for this *double whammy* cataclysm, in the light of all the other evidence that Tom Walker and his brother Chad, discovered.'

'As part of this process we need to not only explain why we are right, but why other approaches are flawed. In recent years, we have had a collection of scientists who keep repetitively publishing different *variations on a theme,* of how a rapid cooling in the late Pleistocene from around 10,800 to 9,500 B.C.E. is explained by a major impact from the Taurid meteor stream, which they promote as the *Younger Dryas Impact Hypothesis*. As many of you know, I am a fundamentalist, I gather the data and join the dots, I don't dream up a hypothesis, then cherry pick the data to make it fit. Nevertheless, I feel it very necessary to identify the multitude of flaws in that Impact story. Moreover, what you will see, is that other teams of scientists who have subsequently attempted to validate the *Impact Hypothesis* claims, not only failed to do so, they also reached new conclusions which further substantiate the transit of the relativistic jet after 9750 B.C.E.!'

'That is remarkable Dr Rhodes.'

'As I said Jacqui, I'm a fundamentalist. In one other paper, some academics took that same impact story, then poorly mapped Göbekli Tepe pillar 43 to the night skies of that time, then claimed the chances that their alignment could be wrong was *one chance in a hundred million*! Well from the compelling data from all the other pillars that I have seen, which supports the later date of 9750 B.C.E., I think they may have proven themselves to be some of the unluckiest guys on the planet!'

There was some subdued laughter in the room.

'We're all scientists, we all need to see the data, and the data must stack up. This is the modern scientific method. New theories demand more rigor, more analysis, and the results of data analyses must be reproducible by each and every team that does the same work. So let's take a look at that data which proves, in my view, that the *Younger Dryas Impact Hypothesis* is totally flawed.'

'To start with, where does that name come from? Well, that cooling epoch is called the *Younger Dryas* after pollen studies, dated to that era showed, that *arboreal forests* were replaced by *arctic tundra* vegetation, and the name comes from a pale yellow arctic wildflower *Dryas Octopetella*, which was widespread then. Studies showed that this cooling was not a local event, but it was a *global* cooling event.'

'The *Impact-Hypothesis* researchers, claimed that they had found high concentrations of *impact indicators* such as magnetic micro-spherules and nano diamonds dating to that era around 10,800 B.C.E. Just so that everyone is on the same page here, I will just explain what causes those two impact indicators. An asteroid possibly travelling at tens of kilometres per second, generates phenomenal heat upon impact, vaporising the surface. Particles are thrown up by the impact and they get heated beyond their *Curie* temperature and any randomly oriented magnetism within them is lost. The magnetic domains within these tiny molten particles then all align with the Earth's magnetic field and they cool, locking in that magnetism. So these otherwise non-magnetic surface materials become magnetized and glasslike in appearance after an impact. The other particles, the nano-diamonds, are pure carbon crystals of a few nanometres in size which are produced under shocked conditions of very high temperatures and pressures.'

'So these researchers claimed that multiple airbursts and a bombardment of meteorites were responsible for the cooling during the Younger

Dryas and this was also responsible for the extinction of megafauna and flora. They also claim a widespread biomass burning.'

'I should add that before our gamma ray burst *pseudo impact winter* is out there in the literature, the former explanation for the cooling in the Younger Dryas or YD, was the sudden shutdown of the North Atlantic thermohaline circulation caused by an increased input of meltwater to the polar ocean. That Atlantic conveyor distributes heat from the tropics to the arctic regions. So, in simple terms, when it shuts down the planet cools. In summary, quite substantial follow-up research has failed to reproduce *any* of the Younger Dryas Impact Hypothesis *diagnostic indicators* independently. Subsequent researchers couldn't find the magnetic spherules at the claimed locations, nor consistently, the correct shocked form of nano-diamonds. In fact, much of what has been found is just indicative of terrestrial wildfires. Another problem is that different sites having the claimed *impact indicators*, have now shown to have very different ages, so they cannot be related to the same event. Added to this, we expect increased levels of carbon 13 and methane due to biomass burning. It is not that we don't find that increase in the climatic record, we actually find a deficit! At other sites, a highly sensitive impact-event indicator would be the *increased* osmium isotope ratios, but these ratios are shown to be of typical crust values at the YD boundary.'

'What is quite remarkable is that subsequent researchers did find peaks in magnetic micro-spherules and nano-diamonds at a level dated to a thousand years later, which would place it after 9750 B.C.E. This evidence now increasingly adds credence to *our* assessment that the relativistic jet transit was real. At the end of the day, the whole Younger Dryas Impact Hypothesis is proving to comprise quite a lot of *confirmation bias*, where sites were even dated to the Younger Dryas because of the concentrations of certain indicators. In several cases the scientists even rejected contradictory data because it didn't confirm their hypothesis. Exclusion of data is always a red flag for me. If we can't explain it, in my view we shouldn't publish.'

'So in summary, in defence of our hypothesis of the relativistic jet transit we have *the extensive geometric cave art, the megalithic structures, the shadow observatories, the Giza pyramids and Mexican and Bolivian structures*, which warn of the next cataclysm, and the endless warnings carved into many structures. We have the *calendar walls* in *Tiwanaku* and in *Chankillo*. There is the whole story about the *domestication of animals* and *development of cereal agriculture at Göbekli Tepe*, which until now has lacked any credible explanation. From a human evolution perspective, this also suggests why we evolved into different peoples, those having lighter skins and blue eyes, who were sensitive enough to derive vitamin D from diminished exposure to sunlight, or peoples with much darker skins who could survive high UV, and those covered with white clay for UV protection, and even peoples with narrower eyes, whose vision was less exposed to dangerous UV.'

'What is becoming increasingly obvious is the significantly large number of caves and dolmens and underground tunnels, which are often found at the same megalithic sites, which all carry the same warnings for the same part of the year, identifying when to be underground. Only yesterday, someone sent me a deconstruction of the vast megalithic monument found at *Carnac*, in Brittany France, which is an extensive array of multiple long lines of menhirs. I have also received detailed decoded images of other sites including *Stonehenge* in the UK, *Brodgar* in the Orkney islands, *Nabta Playa* in the Nubian Desert in southern Egypt, and *Swinside* in the north of the UK. These sites all identify the last date 8870 B.C.E. when these stone rings must have been in use, tracking the dangerous period of the year. These structures were thus slowly adjustable over hundreds of years. They were effectively movable *tools*, designed and used for the duration. I will just show you a deconstruction of Brodgar here. You can see how every stone counts. It is significant how this configuration maps exactly to 8870 B.C.E. Regarding Stonehenge, I even found a scientific paper where an Oxford professor had chosen to ignore radiocarbon dating from the centre of Stonehenge, because it dated the site to before 9000 B.C.E., and he dated the whole site to 3000 B.C.E. from carbon data from the ditch. It seems that he also was *cherry picking* the carbon data, to match his preferred dating of 3000 B.C.E., which he'd obviously used as the basis for previous publications. The uncomfortable problem, of course, with a 9000 B.C.E date is that Stonehenge has been declared by so many academics as a structure for tracking the winter and summer solstices, declaring these were important for cereal planting, when of course cereal planting didn't reach that part of the World for at least a 1000 years *after* 9000 B.C.E. Consequently, I find that very significant.'

'I personally believe that those calendar wall sites of *Tiwanaku* in Bolivia, and *Chankillo* in Peru, also provide the important data which allows us to determine, not only the diameter of the spiralling jet of solar wind and thus the strength of the magnetic field of the jet, but also the period

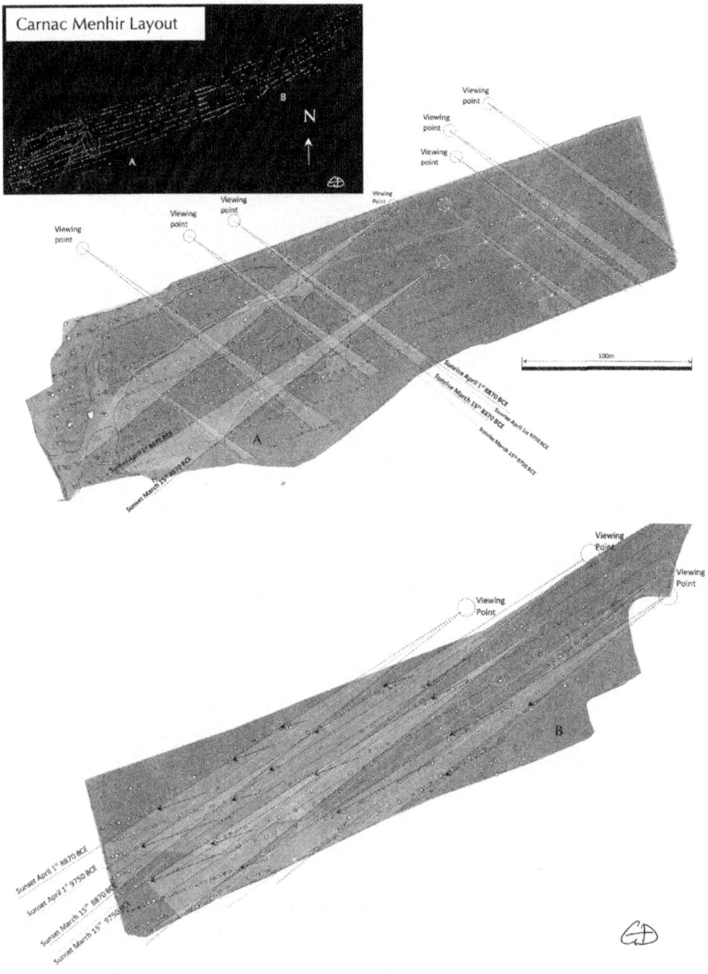

Carnac

of the year when people needed to reside permanently underground. It is at this point in human history that there was suddenly a need to develop the *calendar*. We may have lived by the winter and summer solstices and the equinoxes as seasonal markers up until that time, but suddenly at this moment in Earth's history, knowing how to track the *precise date of the year* and thus *when* the Earth was going to collide with the intense solar wind spiral on its orbit around the Sun, now became *a matter of life and death*.'

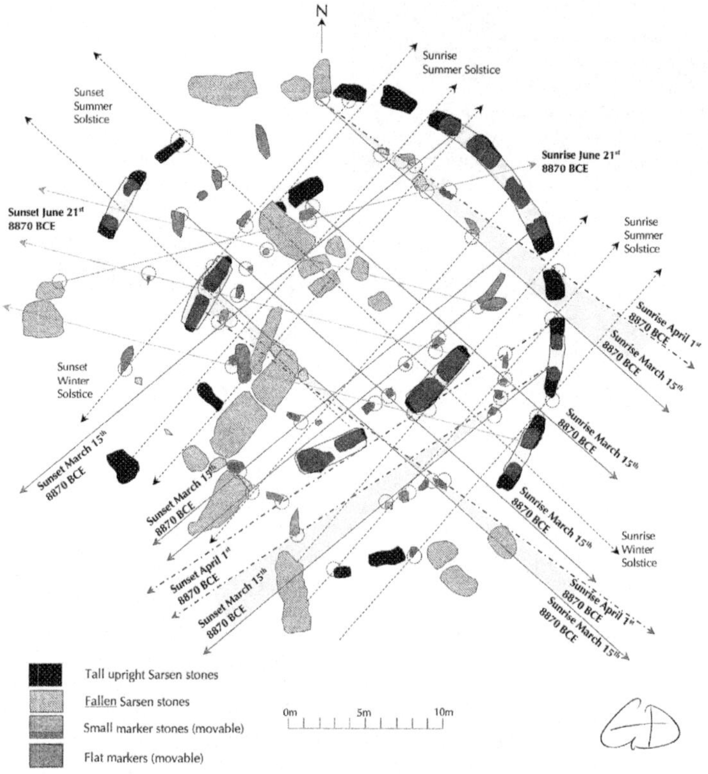

Stonehenge

'Well, that was it for today. I just want to conclude by saying that this has been a remarkable discovery. I do not think the story is over, I think it has only just begun. From this new insight into the events of some 11,770 years ago, we can now decode more of the geometrical cave art and stone carvings all around the World, which most likely hold many more answers.'

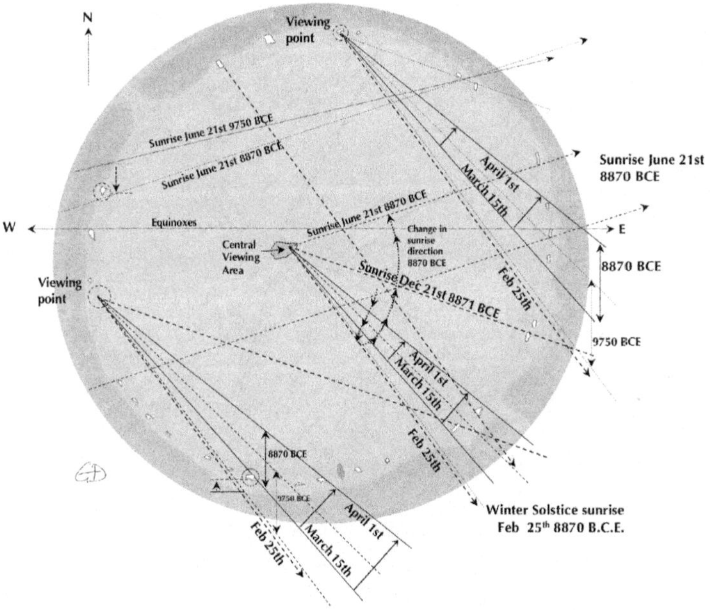
N
Viewing point
Sunrise June 21st 9750 BCE
Sunrise June 21st 8870 BCE
Sunrise June 21st 8870 BCE
W
Equinoxes
E
Sunrise June 21st 8870 BCE
Central Viewing Area
Change in sunrise direction 8870 BCE
Sunrise Dec 21st 8871 BCE
Viewing point
April 1st
March 15th
Feb 25th
8870 BCE
9750 BCE
April 1st
March 15th
Feb 25th
8870 BCE
9750 BCE
April 1st
March 15th
Feb 25th
Winter Solstice sunrise
Feb 25th 8870 B.C.E.

Brodgar

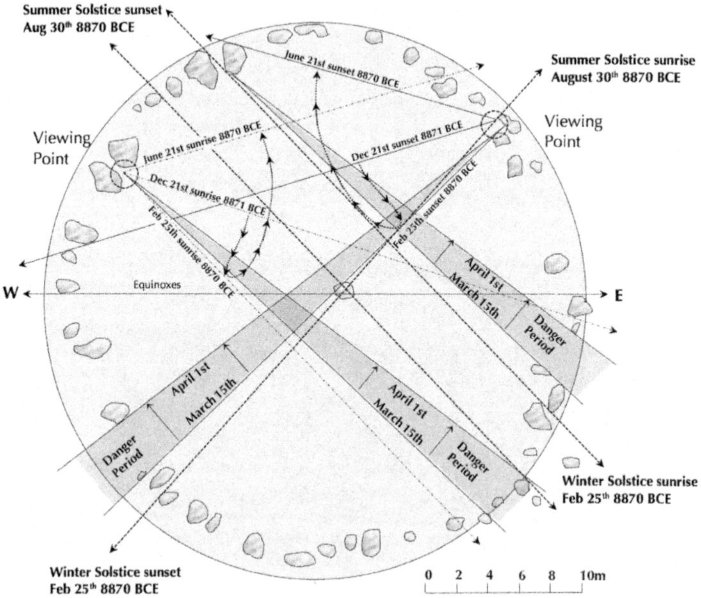

Swinside Stone Circle

15 Yonaguni Island, Japan: decoding its monument, and ancient South American cities

Approaching Yonaguni monument dive site, 100 metres off the south east shore of Yonaguni Island, Japan

It was early morning and the vividly blue skies over Yonaguni were already streaked with *feathered mares' tails;* there was definitely a change in the air. The accompanying blustery offshore winds were causing some quite rough swells, as the dive boat *Uminchu,* or *Lady Pearl Diver* in the Okinawan dialect, approached the monument dive site again. The spray and the white-foam wave crests confirmed the force five, yet Chad and Tom had insisted that they definitely wanted to make the most of their last diving day.

The *Uminchu* captain, *Yakuza*, then exercised remarkable marine skills amid the swells, and brought the boat alongside a wildly swaying rusty sea buoy, where Seiji, Takashi's diving buddy, managed to attach a rope. Yakuza then dropped the anchor. Despite the rough waters, he would wait for them anchored in place for the dive duration.

The *official* story behind their captain's nickname was that he had been recovering giant spider-crab cages in very rough seas, and a steel cage-line had looped around his little finger, taking it clean off. There were more sinister *unofficial* rumours of course. In spite of those, Yakuza had the look of the epic, tough *sea dog*, and the confidence he radiated made everyone feel safe. After the *Pulitzer Prize*-winning Tracy Kidder novel, Yakuza was definitely *a good man in a storm*.

Once anchored, they only needed to belt up with single tanks, fins and masks and they were ready to plunge over the side. Everyone had tens of hours of diving experience, so this was very much a safe and professional excursion.

Slipping under the windswept rough waves into the cobalt blue waters beneath, the undersea world was suddenly silent, tranquil, and serene, and a warm 24°Celsius. Yakuza had anchored really close this time and the Yonaguni monument was barely a few metres directly below them, stretching out 60 metres or so in length, and 25 metres wide, and rising around 20 metres from the seafloor. Flickering shafts of sunlight danced across the vividly spectacular rocky edifice, while off to one side, less than a hundred metres away, they could see the distinctly ominous profiles of prowling hammerhead sharks, ever pursuing the stingray shoals. The strong currents here had prevented corals from growing and the monument's features were sharply defined in the very clear waters.

Tom and Chad swam together, followed closely by Takashi and Seiji, not far behind. The plan was to survey the structure one last time, then descend and pass through a narrow passage beneath the monument at the western end; something they had not yet managed on their earlier dives this week. Chad had brought an underwater compass as well as a marker line and Tom held an underwater Go-Pro mounted on a frame with a light. This time they would attempt to do their own mapping of the monument.

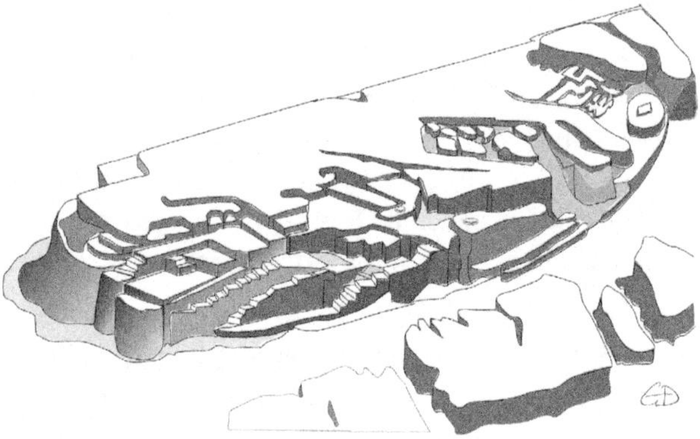

Yonaguni Monument

Over the previous days, they had debated whether this structure was manmade or natural. There seemed to be quite strong views in both camps, but as a geologist, Chad felt compelled to argue that *natural forces alone* could simply not have caused the strange sequences of rocky steps at different angles and the stepped terraces. This was surely a man-worked monolith formed from a natural outcrop of sandstone. At one end, the shaped monolith clearly had a head with a large eye and an open alligator-like mouth. These features then continued embracing several rock formations. Two star-like structures, referred to as turtles, appeared adjacent one another on two separate rocks, about halfway down. It now seemed impossible that this monolith was randomly carved by nature.

Using a reel of bright yellow twine, Tom anchored one end at the north-eastern corner of the upper terrace, while Chad swam along the monument edge, unwinding it as he went, until he reached the far end, in order to work out the monument's bearing. The currents were quite strong but using the underwater compass, they soon determined that the main axis of the terrace was 23.5° northeast. They then swam slowly around the top surface, exploring and filming the features. About halfway down they examined the two turtle structures. These had surely been carved, forming some kind of raised altars on the top surface. Tom was just turning his head when he saw Takashi and Seiji beckoning to them to swim towards them. They were examining a triangular indentation called the *triangular pool*. Tom touched Chad's arm and as they approached, Takashi was pointing at two large holes drilled into the monument at the pool's edge. The postholes were definitely manmade and most likely were formed when the structure was above water. From the pool, the upper terrace seemed to comprise several levels, forming a series of central steps with wide open terraces. Along the long western edge of the monolith, there was a very wide terrace which stepped down.

It's surface seemed to be carved in places with very precise shapes, but many had argued that they had simply been caused by erosion. At the centre of the far south-western end, the structure comprised a series of irregular shaped block-steps, culminating in the vertical precipice to the seafloor some 20 or so metres below. The main characterising feature of the whole Yonaguni monument was the sequence of five flights of steps along its long eastern edge, which formed separate step-like paths from its upper levels down to the seafloor. Going towards the far end of the monument, each flight of around eight steps, was increasingly shallower than the one which preceded it.

After spending quite some time examining the upper terraces and the wide steps across the middle, they returned to the head end of the monument. There was a gap between the two parts of the head which seemed to define a perpendicular direction across the monument's short axis. This seemed too coincidental if the whole monument had indeed been carved. Just in case it was significant they took the compass bearing, they then slowly swam back to explore the different features of the five staircases, slowly descending to the seafloor. Up ahead, Seiji was pointing into a hole in the wall of the monument, but as Tom and Chad approached, whatever it was, had gone now. Takashi then gestured towards the distant end of the monument and they resumed their swim along the seafloor, towards the archway passage which ran underneath it. Eventually they reached it. The five metre long passage was extremely narrow, almost claustrophobic in its nature, but calmly, each of them slowly made their way through it. In places the side walls seemed to comprise stacked monoliths. At the far end, they each emerged from the passage beside two large sandstone blocks, set at a steep angle upwards. Seiji then pointed upwards suggesting that they surface now. They had not been very deep for too long and their dive computers did not indicate a decompression stop, so they slowly ascended. Bursts of white bubbles streamed upwards with every breath, as they kicked their fins and swam up towards the surface.

As Chad surfaced into the bright sunlight, he was barely 10 metres or so from the *Uminchu*, but it was now quite a struggle to swim through the wild waves and spray towards the ladder at the stern end. The wind was now blowing a good 20 knots and the boat was dancing a little in the rise and swell of the waves, as Chad gripped his fins with one hand and grabbed a low rung of the boat's chrome ladder with the other. He managed to get his foot onto the lowest rung under the water, and then pushing down, he heaved himself upwards, slowly making his way up on board. He then heard a shout, and looking round halfway up, he saw Tom waving to him. Then Takashi appeared, followed by Seiji.

Chad threw his fins into the boat, then climbed over the guard rail and unfastened his tank belt.

Yakuza then emerged from the galley, 'You had a good dive?'

'Utterly amazing,' Chad replied, somewhat breathless from this last ordeal.

'Longest dive so far. You were down almost an hour,' Yakuza remarked.

'It's our last dive. We all fly back to Okinawa tomorrow.'

'You'll be back. The hammerheads will miss you!'

Yakuza then carried away Chad's tank and locked it into a holding rack. Tom then emerged at the head of the ladder and climbed over the stern-rail of the boat. Chad grabbed his dive jacket to steady him, then proceeded to help him with his tank. Next Takashi and Seiji appeared. After unloading and stowing the rest of the tanks, they were all finally sitting down on the wooden side benches.

Everyone was pretty exhilarated from the experience and now keen to talk.

'Seiji-san, what was in that hole?' Chad asked.

'It was a blue-ringed octopus, Chad-san!' Takashi remarked.

'Wow, pity we missed that,' Tom replied. 'I saw you guys pointing at something.'

'I got a photo, look,' Seiji replied, scrolling through images on his underwater camera screen. 'Very rare and very dangerous!'

'I need a beer,' Tom remarked, reaching for a can. 'I have that salty sea taste in my mouth. Anybody else?'

'Sure,' Chad replied. Both Seiji and Takashi nodded, and Tom handed them beers.

Yakuza then called out something in Japanese from the bridge.

'I think the English translation is we are *weighing anchor*,' Takashi said with a smile, as Yakuza then climbed towards the bow of the boat and operated the anchor winch. The 50 metre line took a few minutes to wind up, then Yakuza stowed the anchor, untied the rope to the sea buoy, and came back to the bridge.

'Hold on Chad-san, Tom-san!' Yakuza called. 'The seas will get very choppy as we cross those swells towards the headland.'

Chad gave a thumbs up in response and then took another swig of beer.

The marine engine of the *Uminchu* then roared loudly into life as Yakuza gave full throttle and then swung the boat around to the west. They soon picked up quite a speed and the boat raced back along the craggy coastline towards *Kubura*, at the far western end of the island.

Chad looked out over the seascape. South of them lay the very deep Philippine Sea. Yonaguni was the last island in the chain and thus the most westerly part of Japan. Taiwan lay only another 160 kilometres further to the west.

The loud noise of the marine engine and the wild jerking motion of the boat, as it slammed into the undulating whitecaps, made conversation during the return trip pretty challenging, leaving each of them alone in their thoughts of the wonders of the deep of this last dive.

Eventually they approached *Kubura* harbour and Yakuza throttled back. As they approached the jetty, Seiji stood up and went forward to the bow, grabbing a mooring rope. He called out to another sailor standing nearby, who quickly walked over, and Seiji threw him the rope. The sailor caught it and deftly looped it around a bollard. Then, as the boat's rubber fenders softly touched the side of the jetty, Yakuza jumped ashore with the stern mooring line, and lashed it around another bollard.

'All ashore!' he shouted with his beaming smile.

Tom, Chad and Takashi, then all stepped onto the concrete quay, which seemed to move a little after the wild boat ride. They shook hands with Yakuza and Seiji, and then made their way back to the diving centre along the seafront, where they had left all their gear. There were showers there, and not long after, fully refreshed, they wandered back to Takashi's old white Toyota. The plan now was to head out to a great restaurant somewhere along the northern coast road, which Takashi had recommended. Everyone had developed a good appetite for something substantial.

When they were finally aboard the *Land Cruiser,* Takashi spoke. 'We can also do the full island tour later if you like. The round trip only takes two hours at most. The island is a lovely green wilderness, which it would be a pity to miss before you leave. Fortunately that really good restaurant is about halfway along the north coast.'

'That sounds great, eh Chad?' Tom replied.

'Absolutely, and I would love to get a better look at the island before we go.'

They soon were out of Kubura. Either side of the north shore road, there were wide expanses of lush grasses where many horses were grazing.

'These horses are native to Yonaguni island,' Takashi remarked. 'They are now critically endangered. At the last count they only numbered 85.'

'So they wander freely,' Chad replied.

'Yes, like the cattle over there. The cattle are of course domesticated livestock and Yonaguni is famous for its *Wagyu* beef. One animal can sell for as much as $30,000.'

'Why so expensive, Takashi-san?' Tom asked.

'These cattle were bred for their physical endurance, which makes their meat rich in intramuscular fat cells. That creates their delicious marbled meat. Possibly some of the best in the World. Talking about that is already making me hungry but it's only another ten minutes or so to that restaurant now. That is what we are having, Yonaguni *Wagyu steaks*, the ultimate beef experience.'

'Amazing, I have never tasted *Wagyu*. It's on my bucket list,' Chad remarked.

'And so, what about the diving? After four days among the giant herds of hammerheads, what do you both think? It's a great dive site, isn't it?'

'Unbelievable!' Tom replied. 'You know I was just thinking that maybe Mary-Anne and Jeanette might be sorry they missed this.'

'Perhaps those video clips of the hammerheads were to blame,' Takashi added. 'I did try to reassure them that there have never been any reports of divers being attacked. The sharks are too interested in the stingrays.'

'I doubt they would have had more fun,' Chad replied. 'They were just looking for an excuse to disappear off to that mountain retreat spa for four days. While we've had our amazing dive adventure in shark-infested waters, I think the girls were also in their own paradise.'

'Takashi-san, didn't you say that Yonaguni is the hammerheads' migration route?' Tom replied.

'I did, and they follow the stingray shoals,' Takashi replied.

'Hey, and did you and Seiji see that giant hammerhead today as we were surfacing? It must have been five metres easily!' Tom remarked.

'The biggest I ever saw. And I have dived that site well over 25 times now. What did you think, Chad-san?'

'The megalithic monument was stunning in that unbelievably clear water, and then seeing the massive school of hammerheads encircling that huge shoal of stingray, causing shadows in the depths. That was just awe-inspiring!'

'I got the film clip on my underwater camera,' Tom confirmed. 'By the way Takashi-san, it's pretty fortunate that you have a family cabin here.

No wonder you dived Yonaguni monument so many times.'

'Well, I didn't tell you, but my grandfather is from Yonaguni. He built that cabin. He was a ferry captain all his life. We came many times for family holidays. My father also studied at Ryukyu University, then settled on Okinawa after he met my mother. Of course, my father never dived Yonaguni. It was only discovered in 1985. By the way, we probably all agree that today's dive was our best day. Maybe it was supposed to be.'

'Sure,' Tom replied. Chad was nodding.

'So, Chad-san, did the monolithic structure inspire any new perspectives on your global cataclysmic event? You are the geologist. You surely agree now that this is definitely a manmade structure.'

'After four dives, I'm absolutely sure. For me, there is no doubt. Yonaguni is a carved structure formed from a pre-existing sandstone formation. Tom, what were the dimensions again?'

'There seem to be quite a number of different sets of measurements. Perhaps we should have measured it precisely ourselves. I'm guessing that a good estimate is about 60 metres by 25.'

'Well, if we consider those multiple stone staircases connecting different terraces, and the amphitheatre, and the passageways, and certainly those turtle carvings at the top, from the geologist's perspective they just simply can't be formed naturally. I was thinking, surely this was above water in an earlier epoch. What is the oceanographer's view Takashi-san?'

'Well, Yonaguni is up on a ridge between the East China Sea to the north and the Philippine Sea to the south. The Philippine Sea falls to a depth of more than 10 kilometres, and the East China Sea falls to 2.7 kilometres. Up on the ridge, the sea level only has to fall by 30 metres and the Yonaguni monument is completely above water. It could easily have formed part of a land bridge all the way from present day Japan to Taiwan. You know, I actually met *Kihachiro Aratake* ten years ago, the diving instructor who first discovered the Yonaguni formation back in 1986. He remains utterly convinced that the structure features are manmade.'

'Interesting,' Chad remarked.

'Well guys, I guess after tomorrow, our trip will get a little more serious, certainly for me anyway,' Tom remarked. 'The astrophysics conference starts in Okinawa next week, where I will be presenting our paper, which summarises all the archaeological data and evidence for the jet transit.'

'I think there should definitely be some very positive reactions after that.'

'I am also hoping to get a reply from Carl Rhodes about my presentation proposal. Hopefully he agrees with it. Maybe he has sent his comments already. I'll just check my phone.'

Tom switched his iPhone on and moments later it made a sound announcing a message. It was indeed from Carl Rhodes. After a short while, the look on Tom's face became quite serious.

'What is it Tom, anything wrong?'

'It's a message from Carl Rhodes. He's asking me to pull the paper. He's saying it's too controversial!'

'Really? At such a late hour, surely the summary will be in all the proceedings abstracts by now,' Chad replied in disbelief.

'Well, I sent the abstract for his final approval. He writes here that he never sent it. There will now *not be* any abstract about my paper in the conference proceedings.'

'That sounds serious. Why would he do that? Did he give any reasons?'

'He isn't very clear here, but I think he's saying that an Earth-centric paper about the transit of the relativistic jet might have been OK. The problem is that we have two pieces of unexplainable evidence, the identification of the *next-to-supernova* blue giant *Spica* carved in stone on Göbekli pillar 43, and the several pyramid layouts on three continents, which cannot be explained without advanced astrophysics and radio telescopes,' Tom murmured. 'Carl is a fundamentalist, he never supports anything enigmatic.'

'But your paper is only a summary of the evidence that is out there. What is wrong with presenting what has been discovered?' Chad asked.

'This is disappointing. Am I really not going to present this paper?' Tom remarked, questioning this new potential reality.

For several minutes they drove along the northern coast road in silence, as if Tom's last comment had stalled the momentum of the story that had gripped them for the past six months. Takashi then took a winding road up towards a hilltop building.

'Here we are. That is the excellent wagyu steak restaurant up ahead.'

Takashi pulled into the car park, and stopped close to the front door. They all climbed out and walked into the restaurant. Takashi went to speak to the lady at the reception, who then led them over towards a table by the window, which had stunning views out over the sea. They sat down and picked up the menus. Fortunately, there were some English phrases under each item.

Takashi then spoke. 'Listen, I propose that I just order the complete beef wagyu selection, all the dishes are excellent. What do you think?'

'Excellent idea! Are you good with that Tom?'

'Sure, let's do that.'

Takashi then got up and walked over to talk directly to the chef standing beside his steel hotplate surface. In a short while he returned with a small tray of glasses, a bowl of ice, a carafe of water and a bottle of some kind of liquor. It was definitely not your average liquor. There was a grey, menacing-looking snake inside the bottle.

'Woah, what do you have there?' Tom remarked, his voice betraying his shock at what he could see

'Is that the local sake?' Chad asked with a grin

'No, it's not sake. Here we have the local delicacy, *awamori*. Unlike sake, it's not brewed. *Awamori* is a *distilled* rice liquor. Moreover, here we have the ultimate *awamori*, called *habushu*. This one is distilled and bottled with *habu* pit vipers!' Takashi explained, betraying a real glint in his eye.

'Unbelievable!' Tom whispered, examining the snake coiled tightly in the bottle. 'Is that viper deadly?'

'A bite from the *habu* pit viper can kill, but that snake can mate for more than 24 hours, so it is believed that it will enhance a man's vigour. That is why they add the snake to make *habushu*. The venom dissolves into the liquor, so you're safe drinking it.'

Takashi put ice in the glasses, poured a shot of *habushu* in each, then added a small dash of water.

'We must toast this fantastic diving adventure together,' Takashi said, holding up his glass. '*Kanpai!*'

'*Kanpai!*' Tom and Chad said, almost in unison. Then they knocked back their first shot of *habushu*. They placed their glasses back on the tray and Takashi then proceeded to pour another shot into each glass.

'Tom-san, you're looking more serious than usual. I half followed your conversation with Chad in the car. Did I understand that you are now being warned off from presenting your paper?'

'Yes, it seems my Berkeley colleague, Carl Rhodes, now doesn't want me to go public with the conclusions. His reaction is totally unexpected. I thought it was really fortuitous that Okinawa was hosting this year's International Conference on Relativistic Jets. That's how I got this whole trip funded and how I could join you guys on this adventure. I only just persuaded the committee to allow me to present my findings as a late entrant last month, but Carl now indeed seems to be seriously dissuading me from presenting the paper at all.'

'Tom-san, your story is very compelling, and it should be heard. I'm sure the conference would be the ideal platform. All the media will be there. If you have gathered the evidence, you should present it. We are talking about scientific data. Withdrawing a significant paper just sounds crazy to me!'

'I know. He has also sent quite a long email. You know, we developed the whole story together with quite a large team of academics at Berkeley. He is writing here that everyone was forced to sign an NDA and delete any records from their hard drives. It sounds as if there is now a move to keep most of the story pretty much under wraps.'

'Why can't the scientific findings be mentioned as a possible hypothesis? I don't understand,' Takashi replied, looking a little confused.

Tom looked away, gazing out towards his own distant marine horizons. He was now increasingly concerned about this development. Had they all come this far in working everything out, only now to be warned off from any disclosure at all? After a short time he turned back to the others.

'I know what it is, Takashi-san. It's the evidence that we found which is not easy to explain as coming from this planet. There is too much of a lack of hi-tech equipment in the archaeological record. That is what is worrying *the powers that be*. That must be why the paper should never be presented.'

'It's seriously sounding like a major cover-up, before the important scientific story gets told,' Takashi remarked.

At that moment, the chef appeared, wheeling a trolley. On it was a dark hard-wood plate of sliced wagyu, several bowls of wagyu and egg yolk, steaming jasmine rice and some salad. He lifted them onto the table. Takashi then said something about the different dishes to the chef, then they laughed together, after which the chef walked back towards his food preparation area.

'OK he said there are three more dishes coming. Please, let's start. Tom-san, please continue. So what exactly is the enigmatic evidence that needs to disappear, which now makes this story totally off-limits for publication?'

'I guess it's the impossibility of explaining how a previous civilization managed to construct layouts of pyramids in the relative stellar formation of a future configuration of the three stars of *gamma Velorum*. Carl is vetoing the whole paper because, as I said to Chad, being able to know the future configuration of *gamma Velorum* requires serious advanced astrophysics and a radio telescope!'

'That evidence forms data. The pyramid layouts in that configuration is a genuine interpretation. What is the harm in proposing that?' Takashi reasoned. 'Moreover, the World should be told, and future generations must be warned of what is to come and when.'

'I guess the whole story is just too overwhelming. If we publish this, so many of the Earth's mysteries are suddenly explained in a single publication, and these are all due to a single, *previously undisclosed* astrophysical event. Carl seems to be suggesting that the World is definitely not ready for this whole story yet.'

Just at that moment, they heard the sound of a car, and looked up to see a dark green Mustang pulling up outside the restaurant. It had black-tinted windows. A man got out. It was Yakuza.

The door of the restaurant then opened, and he paused in the doorway a moment. He looked around and seeing them, he nodded towards them then walked towards their table. As he approached they could see he was carrying a roll of paper or something.

'Yakuza-san! Are you joining us for a meal? You are very welcome,' Tom remarked.

'Tom-san, Chad-san, I can't stop but I do have something to give you before you leave. I know you guys are doing some serious work decoding many of the World's monuments. This document should rightly be in your possession. It has an *unspecified origin*, if you understand what I'm saying,' Yakuza replied, giving them a sincere look. He then handed the tied scroll to Tom.

'*Arigatou gozaimasu* Yakuza-san!' Tom replied.

Yakuza smiled. 'Safe trip back guys.'

He exchanged a few words with Takashi then turned and left the restaurant. For a moment they watched him climb back into his car, and then he drove away.

'I wonder what this is?' Tom exclaimed, as he started to untie the ribbon, and then he rolled it open over the table. 'Oh, my God, it's Yonaguni!'

'*Sou desu ne*!' Takashi murmured softly.

The first image was covered in Japanese text.

'It seems to be some kind of detailed survey of the monument. Takashi-san, what does it say?' Chad asked.

Takashi examined the detailed drawing and then spoke. 'The writing here confirms that the monument was above water during the last ice age, and that several features cutting across the monument on the top surface, mark out sunrise between March 15th and April 1st . . . in 9750 B.C.E.! It says those lines drawn in the corner there, indicate the changing sunrise directions during the year.'

'You are kidding me!' Tom exclaimed. 'How has anyone else worked this out?'

'Here, it goes on to say that Yonaguni was in the northern part of the tropics back then, and the sun rose further north of the monument in mid-summer. It is saying that those carved features cutting across the surface of the monument indeed run 113.5° northwest, which defines a particular sunrise angle on two dates. On March 15th sunrise moves further south than 113.5°southeast, only returning back to that angle on April 1st. This indeed must mean that the Yonaguni monument marks out the 14 or so days of the dangerous period,' Takashi explained.

The second image was much less precise, but it was the absolute proof that Yonaguni was man-made! It showed how every single feature of the monument mapped to a part of the band of the Milky Way. It was a huge three dimensional star map. The two stone turtles seemed to align with two nebulae, identified as the Omega Nebula and the Eagle Nebula.

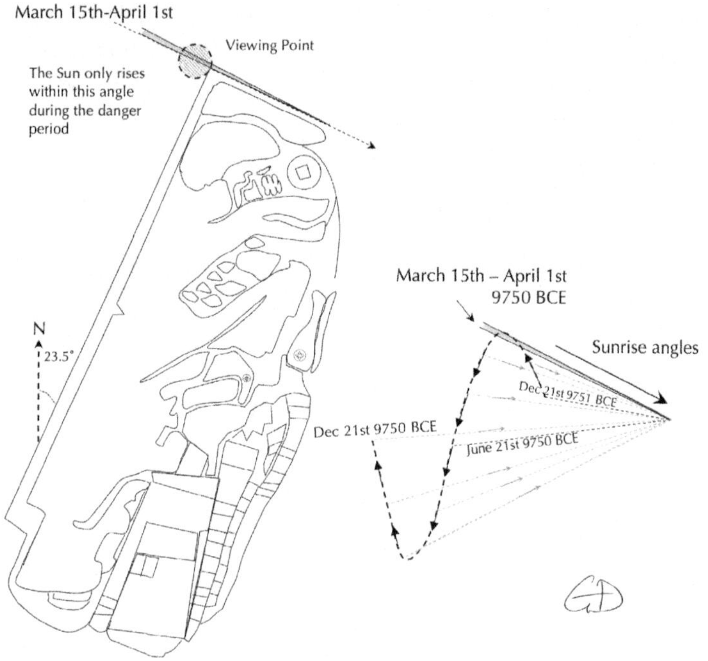

Yonaguni Monument with Sunrise Directions

Tom knew that these were extremely distant star-forming regions. The Omega Nebula M17 lay in the direction of the galactic centre at a distance of around 5500 light years and paradoxically is virtually impossible to see without a telescope. The Eagle Nebula M16 lay even further away at 7000 light years and was made famous by Hubble, which identified a dark feature within it called pillars of creation. Tom was also familiar with its very bright binary neighbour, HD 168176, comprising two massive blue white O-type stars which only live around a million years, the larger one of 90 solar masses will end its days as a supernova. Why these stellar systems were identified in the monument was not immediately clear. The monument looked like a huge crocodile with its mouth open, and its eye aligned with a round structure on the Milky Way band.

'We can confirm this on Stellarium later. I should add that those dust clouds will slowly change with time, but in general they will be pretty much in the same place,' Tom remarked.

'Where on earth do you think Yakuza got this?'

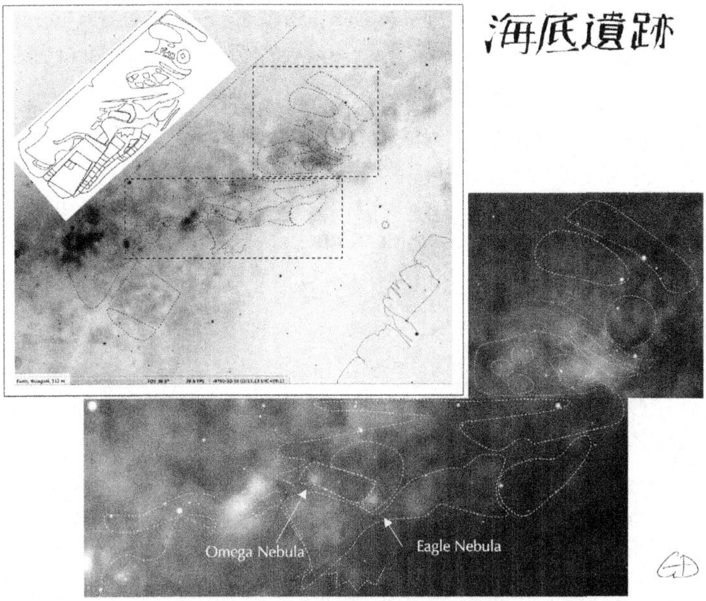

Yonaguni Monument Star-Mapping

'Perhaps it's better not to ask,' Chad suggested quietly.

'I think that may be the right answer,' Takashi confirmed.

'This is unbelievable!' Tom remarked. 'So we are not alone in working out that monuments around the World are marking out a particular interval of time, some 11,770 years ago.'

They all looked in amazement at the tattered parchment scroll.

'How old do you think this is Takashi-san?' Chad asked.

'Impossible to say. But it could be very old indeed.'

Tom rolled up the scroll then put it on the window ledge. They continued eating the delicious wagyu beef meal in silence. The scroll of Yonaguni brought in by Yakuza had now thrown a real *spanner in the works* because the whole story now took on a much more sinister significance. On one hand, the document seemed to be the evidence confirming that Yonaguni was man-made, but now it was even more intriguing because it seemed to suggest that others knew of how to decode it as a structure built to identify the duration of an event dating back to 9750 B.C.E.

Chad's phone then softly buzzed, indicating an incoming message. He took his phone from his pocket and read the message with raised eyebrows.

'It's a message from Felipe, you know the guy we picked up in Mexico, Takashi-san! Apparently he is texting to say that he has just emailed me a zip-file of scanned documents from his uncle Andrés. Unfortunately, I won't be able to open them on this phone.'

'Let's go back to the cabin after we're finished here. You can open them there on my computer, Chad.'

'Thanks Takashi-san. You know, I'm pretty keen to see exactly what Felipe has sent us.'

After they finished the meal, Takashi paid. They then left the restaurant carrying the half bottle of *habushu awamori*, which the chef had insisted that they take with them. They climbed back into the Toyota and took a wide diversion along the country roads to get a final glimpse of the island before they were eventually back at Takashi's cabin. Bringing the scroll, they walked inside and went into Takashi's office and sat down around his computer. The walls were covered with maps of oceans and islands. There was a blank area on the wall above Takashi's desk with a hook. Chad noticed it and unrolled the scroll and got up and walked over to the hook and hung it there.

'Perhaps you should keep this, Takashi-san,' Chad suggested, 'I am thinking, just in case Yakuza wants it back in future.' He then stepped back and started to take a few photos of the scroll with his phone. 'We only need the photographic evidence.'

'It would truly be an honour to have the Yonaguni scroll hanging there. Thanks Chad-san. That is very kind. I am just wondering what Yakuza might say. I am sure he intended that you keep it as a gift, but in case he ever asks, I will say that you were sincerely grateful but felt it was better if it stayed on the island.'

'Good thinking,' Tom added.

Takashi continued to boot up his computer. 'It's all yours Chad,' he remarked, standing up.

Chad then sat down in front of Takashi's laptop and logged in to access his University account. He found Felipe's email, then proceeded to open the zip file to access the attached documents. The first file was called

Chankillo. Opening it, revealed a detailed map of the Chankillo site in Peru, showing its calendar wall and the solar observatory. Remarkably, it seemed that Andrés had also decoded the site to 9750 B.C.E., but he had achieved that according to a very different logic. He had first identified the south western entrance of the solar observatory and then traced lines towards the calendar wall and investigated the years when the sun rose in that direction.

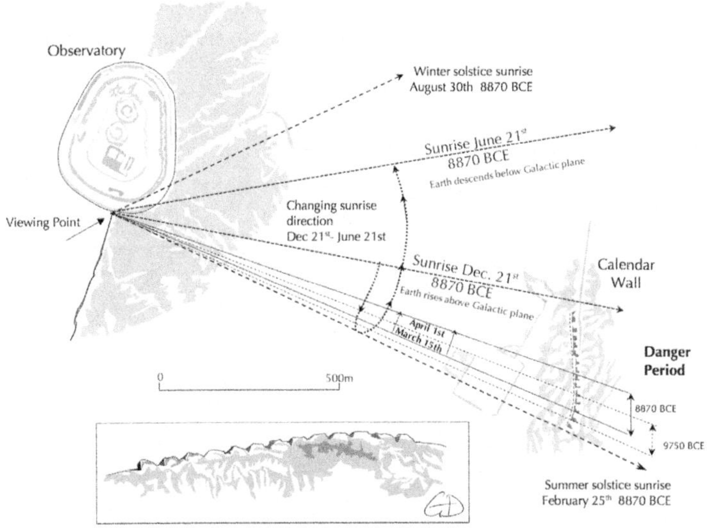

Chankillo

'Look at this!' Chad remarked. 'Felipe's uncle has determined that from the doorway of the observatory, the southern end of the calendar wall defines the winter solstice and then the calendar wall marks out the dates from March 15th to April 1st in 9750 B.C.E.! This is unreal!'

'Does he write what his conclusion is about that?' Tom urged.

'No, and from what Felipe has added here as a comment, it seems that Andrés has no real explanation other than it is marking out a particular time of that year. He also writes that the Chankillo calendar wall is very similar to the one at *Tiwanaku* near La Paz in Bolivia.'

'What's in the other files?' Takashi asked.

Chad opened the next one. It was a series of detailed drawings and photos of the Incan *Sayhuite* stone, an unexplained carved megalith, situated somewhere near Cuzco in Peru. The photos showed the oval carved megalith, which was about four metres across, higher at the back and lower in the front, with its complicated surface of carved elements, including stairs and snakes, and cats, many of which seemed to have had their heads smashed off. The next images showed detailed lithographs dated 1847, with the name *Léonce Angrand* beside them, and two more lithographs dated 1955 with the name *Rojas Ponce* beside them. What seemed very strange was that the etchings now showed a monolith of complete animals, as if it was drawn when the stone was entirely undamaged.

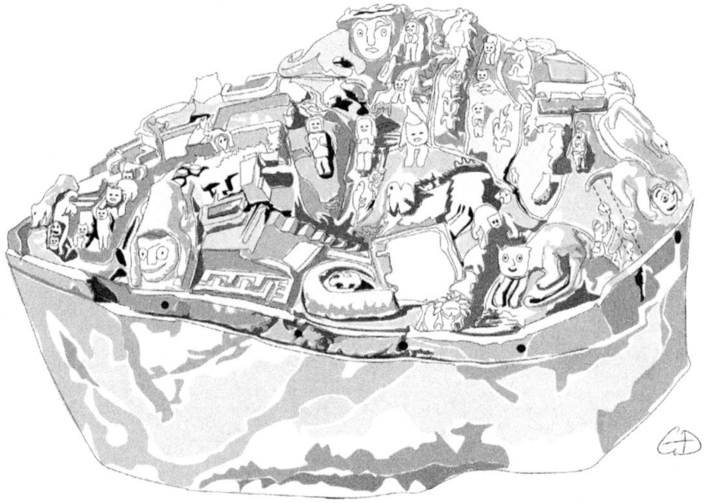

Sayhuite Stone

'Hey, look at this. Apparently, these two guys managed to draw the *Sayhuite* stone before it was damaged, or maybe it was their reconstruction from reasoning and guesswork.'

'Chad, this looks so much like the kind of animal layouts that we have seen on the Göbekli Tepe pillars. Don't you think it could possibly be another sky map, like Göbekli?'

'Well, you could be right, Tom. If so, we need to find something which looks out of place. Hey, look there, between the cat and scorpion over to the right. There are two round disks. We can do a check. They could represent the path of the planets or the Sun and Moon through the sky, between two groups of stars? Do you have *Stellarium* installed on this Takashi-san?'

'I do. I installed it after you explained how your friend decoded *Xochicalco*,' Takashi confirmed. 'The icon is on the desktop.'

'OK, let's investigate this,' Chad murmured, booting up *Stellarium*.

He selected *Cuzco* as the location and set the time back to 9750 B.C.E. Now with the experience of all the hard work done to discover the relation between the Göbekli Tepe pillars and the night sky, this might not be too difficult to verify. Sure enough, when he selected *mark planet trails*, he found where the planets crossed the horizon. Advancing the time slowly forward, the relatively large round discs of the Sun and the Moon now passed beside an asterism in the shape of a scorpion to the left, and an asterism which clearly followed the shape of the cat in the Sayhuite lithograph to the right. Indeed, the *Sayhuite* stone was definitely a *map of the night skies over Cuzco*, and from a cursory inspection, it seemed to map to 9750 B.C.E. The *Sayhuite* stone certainly couldn't be Incan now. Others could investigate the other asterism animals, but based on the success of the Göbekli Tepe mapping, Chad was confident that this was already a confirmation.

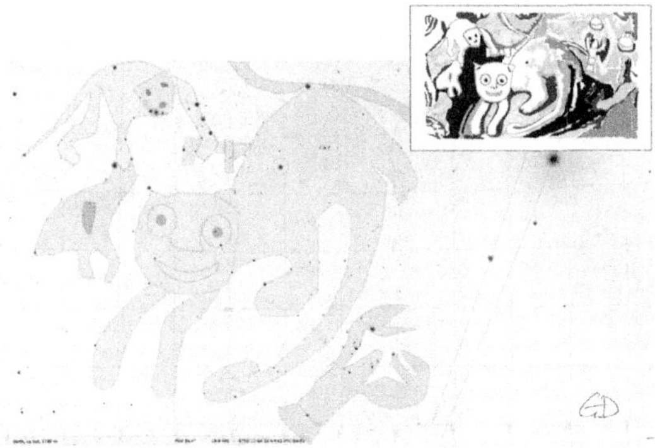

Sayhuite Stone Star Mapping

'Wow, look at this, yet another mystery solved. This is unbelievable,' Chad remarked.

'What else has he sent Chad?' Tom asked eagerly. 'One said *Rapa Nui* I think.'

'Yes, that's Easter Island. Don't tell me he has found something there as well,' Chad remarked.

Chad opened the file while Tom and Takashi looked on. The first page showed Thor Heyerdahl standing on top of one of the Moai statues. A second photo showed an archaeological team after they had excavated the structure down into the ground from just a head above the surface, to reveal an entire Moai figure. It was about eight metres tall. There was also a paragraph in Spanish, which wasn't too difficult to understand, and it seemed to be summarising Thor Heyerdahl's *Kon-Tiki* expedition of the 1950s in which he attempted to show that Easter islanders had an *Amerindian* and not a *Polynesian* ancestry. The next image showed a detailed schematic of the back of that figure, which now was shocking! Carved into its back, were several distinctly clear images of boat-like structures similar to those seen on the walls of Karnak in Egypt, together with some spirals!

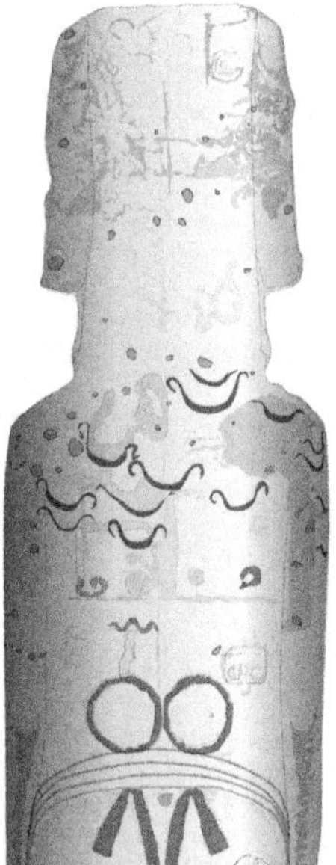

Easter Island Moai with solar wind boats

This was now too much of a coincidence. To remain with the generally accepted Easter Island story, would require a rather far-fetched addition to the narrative. Now, the islanders who had first arrived by boat from South America to inhabit the island some 800 years earlier, had not only carved and erected all the Moai statues, but they had also carved images of boats and the spirals of solar wind into the back of one or more of the Moai, then buried the Moai up to their necks. These carvings on the back of this excavated and long hidden Moai, now most definitely linked the Easter Island statues to the time of the relativistic jet cataclysm, 11,770 years ago, but had Andrés found more?

'I think those carvings must be absolute proof now,' Tom murmured.

'I think you're right Tom. So what else has he sent?' Chad wondered out loud.

The final page of that document, showed a map of Easter Island with additional pairs of red dotted lines, opening at a tight angle of a few degrees from a single Moai on the northwest shore. Each pair of lines seemed to extend to a pair of Moai on the southeast shore. At the bottom of the image, they could make out the words *sunrise directions March 15th to April 1st around 9750 - 8870 B.C.E.* This now looked very interesting. Only a detailed survey could clarify the precise angles over such a long distance of ten or so kilometres, but perhaps Andrés had indeed found something. The relativistic jet carvings on the back of that previously buried Moai statue were definitely *the smoking gun*.

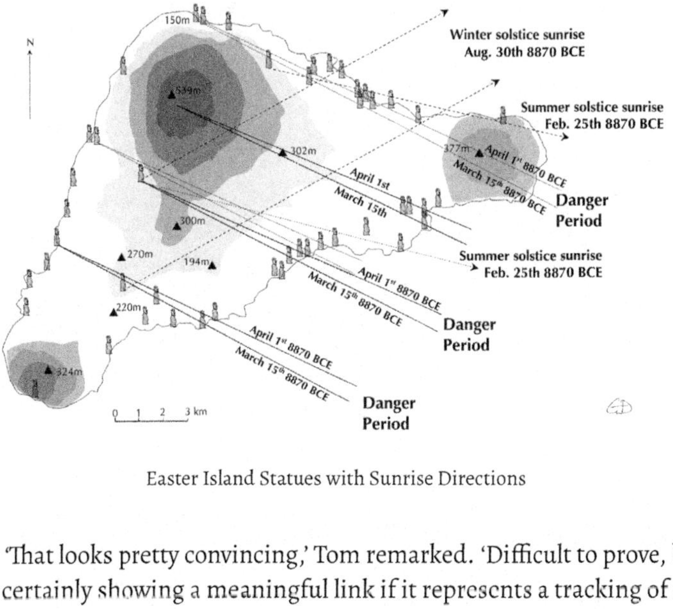

Easter Island Statues with Sunrise Directions

'That looks pretty convincing,' Tom remarked. 'Difficult to prove, but it's certainly showing a meaningful link if it represents a tracking of the sunrises during the cataclysm era. What else has Felipe sent?'

'This one says *Chichen Itza*,' Chad replied.

He opened the file and the images showed a layout of the Mayan site. Added as an overlay were the sunrise times of March 15th to April 1st 9750 B.C.E. The temple of the Jaguar, adorned with Rainbow Serpents, stood opposite a wide band of colonnades. At a particular location, a band of colonnades extended deep into the jungle. From what Andrés had written, it was immediately clear that he was suggesting that these colonnades matched the exact angles of the sunrise for the dangerous period exactly. So Chichen Itza did not date from the time of the Mayan, but from 11,770 years ago!

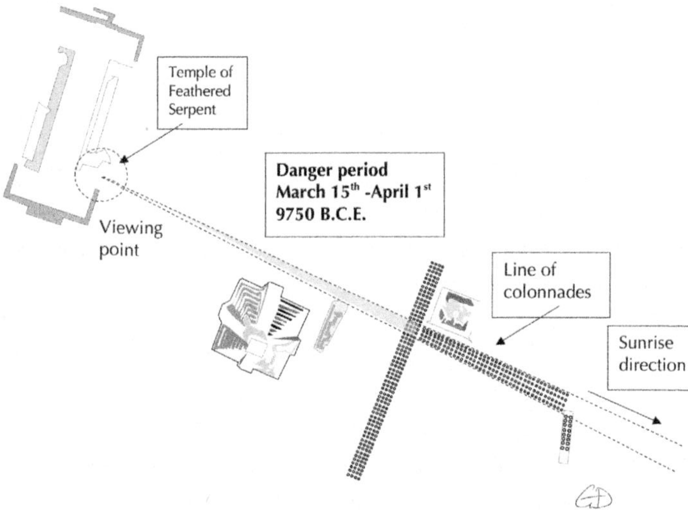

Chichen Itza

'This is getting to be unbelievable!' Tom murmured.

'There is something else,' Chad remarked. 'Look, in addition to the chambers within the famous stepped pyramid of *Kukulcan*, that's the one with the moving shadow of a serpent which moves along the side of the steps during an equinox, it says here that a team of Mexican archaeologists have recently found a tunnel leading to an underground chamber there. That must be part of the safety chamber complex, like we found at each of the other sites.'

'He has also written something about the carvings on the side walls of the ballcourt there. He is suggesting that that these have been completely misinterpreted. The round images describe a snakelike image identical to that at ... Xochicalco! He is dating the complex to 9750 B.C.E. He is saying that the Mayans just discovered and occupied the complete site. They didn't build any part of it at all!' Chad continued.

'Oh no! Look there! He is suggesting that the two figures either side of that ball shape are around a serpent's fire-breathing head. Now, the whole story about ball courts and executing players is seriously in question. Also, if you look closely at those two ring-stones opposite each other, high on the side walls of the ballcourt, they are both covered in images of the relativistic jet,' Tom remarked. 'Maybe there never was any ball game. Well certainly not originally. It's just another case of how someone made the story up and then everyone else just remained blinkered and unable to see any of the other evidence!'

'There is something more! Look in that carved stone image. Those are definitely *Mayan alphabet glyphs*! If that is a genuine carving contemporary with the site, it means that the glyphs aren't Mayan at all but date back to 9750 B.C.E!' Chad exclaimed.

They stared at the images. Chad opened the next file, and then they all had a shock. It was a pdf of a series of scanned letters between Andrés and someone at the Egyptian Museum of Antiquities, Mustapha Hamoun!

'Tom, Felipe's uncle Andrés knew Mustapha Hamoun!' Chad remarked in a stunned voice. 'Luckily it seems they were corresponding in English. We really need to go through this lot to find out what they discovered.'

Fortunately, Andrés had scanned his own letters before posting them, so they had both sides of the correspondence. Tom and Takashi stood behind Chad, and together they scan-read the text as he slowly scrolled down through the correspondence, which included photographs and drawings. The first letters seemed to comprise an evolving discussion, exploring the similarity between the 14 snakes on the back of the Bennett Monolith and the wall frieze of Akhenaten and Nefertiti. While the Bennett Monolith had fourteen vertical snakes and one either side, the Akhenaten frieze had 18 rays of sunlight shining down on two seated figures adorned with three oddly-shaped children with elongated skulls. Andrés seemed to consider that the two ankh symbols on the two sunbeams either side of the 14 sunbeams which all had flames at their ends were highly significant. Both of the Egyptian seated figures had a small snake emerging from their heads, and a serpent was coming out of the Sun. This all now seemed to be too coincidental.

Nefertiti and Akhenaten

'Chad, take a scan of that image and let's see if we can map those seated figures to the night skies over Giza in the danger period of March 15th to April 1st in 9750 B.C.E. If we can, then that ain't Akhenaten!'

Chad set Stellarium to March 15th 9750 B.C.E., then took a screenshot of the night sky of the Milky Way band at midnight close to the horizon and pasted it into a Word document. He then scanned the *Akhenaten* figure on the left and pasted it into a text box, then set it to very transparent. For the next 20 minutes, they all watched as he repetitively rescaled the image and changed the orientation by a few degrees this way and that, until he stopped. The stars were now in perfect alignment with the whole image, including the child that *Akhenaten* was holding. This seated figure with child was definitely not Akhenaten, it was the star asterism, marking out the start of the danger period when the Earth passed into the spiral of solar wind!

'Oh my God Chad!' Tom remarked. 'This dates to 9750 B.C.E.! How far does this whole story questioning our real history actually go?' I have also just realised something. We surely have remnants of 30 generations of terror and arduous survival embedded in our own culture today. Can anyone think of something?'

'What about Shakespeare? I remember In Julius Caesar he is murdered on March 15th. *Beware the Ides of March!*' Takashi suggested. 'That was a Roman date which they got from the Ancient Greeks, who most likely got it from an earlier culture. That is surely a contender for consideration.'

'My goodness, Takashi-san, I think you must be right!' Tom replied, sounding quite shocked. 'It had to have come from somewhere. The date is spot on, warning when people needed to take cover. *Beware the Ides of March*, of course!'

'There is one other question we have not considered in relation to Egypt. What about that old question about Sirius? You often suggested that its connection with Egypt was all about the flooding of the Nile, but the significance of Sirius and Sopdet is on all the very early-dated Egyptian friezes. Let us check how Sirius moves in the night sky back then,' Takashi suggested.

'Good idea, Takashi-san,' Chad replied. 'Hathor's Temple near Luxor seems to be the centre of astronomy at that time, so I will check Sirius in the skies above Luxor in 9750 B.C.E.'

After a short time he had located Sirius and he then stepped through the days to explore how it moved during the year. It then became immediately obvious that Sirius had absolutely nothing whatsoever to do with the flooding of the Nile! Sirius was last seen in the evening skies above Hathor's Temple ... on March 15th! It only re-emerged in the morning skies before sunrise, the so-called heliacal rising, on June 15th. So Sirius was chosen to mark the date when to take cover from the immediately impending 14 days of the deadly solar wind spiral. Perhaps this was also the reason why the Dogons celebrated Sirius. Its heliacal rising coincided with the start of the good times, when the Earth was about to move below the Galactic plane. They had cracked the Sirius connection. You simply couldn't make this stuff up.

'I'll just check the other figure,' Chad replied.

Setting the date to April 1st, Chad now continued the process of seeking out a mapping for *Nefertiti*, the figure on the right in that image with the two children. Sure enough, after about another 20 minutes, Chad found an almost perfect mapping of the figure referred to as *Nefertiti*. The figures in this frieze were neither Akhenaten nor Nefertiti!

'I am now wondering how much of our history is just wrong. How

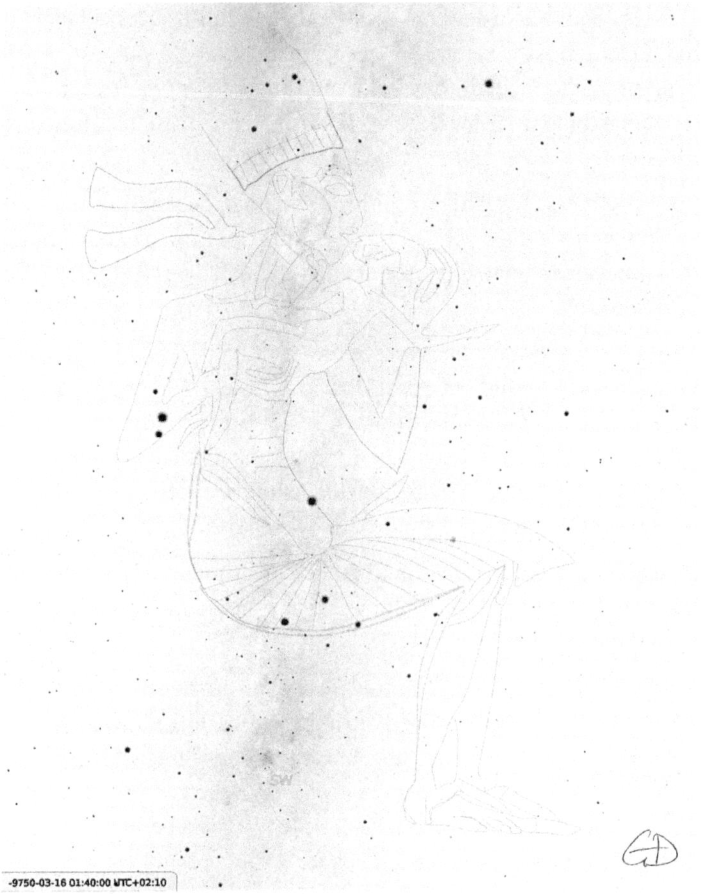

Nefertiti Mapping

could so many people have missed this? You know what it means. It's a confirmation that nobody ever had a clue about what these hieroglyphs above the images here said. Somebody just made it all up, and nobody ever questioned it!' Chad murmured.

'Look at that next sandy yellow image. That's another Sphinx carving with the same 18 rays with the two ankhs either side. Check that also,' Tom urged.

Following the same procedure, Chad soon found a different correspondence with the stars on March 15th and the features of the Sphinx,

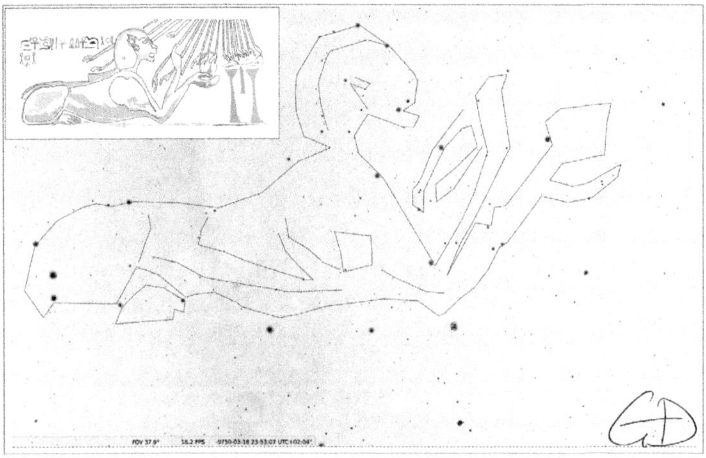

Sphinx with Rays

but there was something more. While the rest of the carving of the body of the sphinx was smooth, the face was rough, and there seemed to be a second outer line of stars which matched the face better.

'Do you see that Chad, that outer line of stars has the profile of a *lion's head*! My God, this is definitely not only the proof that the Sphinx was originally a lion, but that the Sphinx must date to before 9750 B.C.E!' Tom remarked.

'So due to absolute serendipity, we now have even more proof that this was real. I think a large number of the Egyptian friezes have been totally misunderstood and this proves that they now need to be correctly decoded. Look there to the edge of the Sphinx, there are a series of hieroglyphs. They clearly show the sun and the ankh, the *warning* as Andrés is suggesting, and there are also two reverse-image snakes with their heads curved back. You know, when we were at school I remember telling you how amazed I was at how anyone was able to decode these hieroglyphs. Now we have the proof here that all those books must contain some serious errors!' Chad added.

'Yeah, I remember you going through *the Egyptian phase*. Maybe that is why you became a geologist.'

'There is more. Andrés and Mustapha are talking here about the Assyrians. You know what this must mean. You see this image of the two men wearing fish-skin suits, they surely map to the same asterisms. This means that they were carved also 11,770 years ago. There will be some serious repercussions when this story gets out. So much of our reported history must be built upon a house of cards. I guess it may be time to clear the decks and get the truth out there!' Chad continued.

'What's that last document?' Tom asked. 'It says Persepolis!' Surely that is not also an incorrect episode of history, is it? You know that *Alexander the Great* described the Persians as uncivilised warriors who lived in tents. There have certainly been many questions about how they managed to carve the magnificent centaurs in Persepolis in 500 B.C.E.'

'OK, here are some photos of that exquisitely carved centaur on a wall. We can try to match that also,' Chad replied.

After checking that Persepolis was closest to modern day Shiraz in Iran, Chad then took a screen shot of the Milky Way band close to the horizon on March 15th 9750 B.C.E. Again, after only several minutes of rescaling and orientation he found distinct cloud shapes and bright stars which matched the outline of the exquisitely carved centaur. The original city of Persepolis did not date from only 500 B.C.E., the precise sky mapping of the centaur strongly suggested that part of it clearly dated back to at least 11,770 years ago!

'That is compelling!' Tom remarked. 'You know, we're seeing a common theme here for the warning period carvings. In each of these civilizations, the *original* Egyptian, if it needs a new name, the *original* Assyrian, and the *original* Persian, even the *original* Mayan, the warning carvings all have the same format. They all show a pair of facing figures with something in-between. Look, there's even one more. It's that strange bird-headed character with the *man bag* and the star wristwatch! We just have to check that one!'

'OK, Andrés writes here that the carving is from Nimrud, near Mosul in modern day Iraq. I can check the night sky back then also. Wait a moment,' Chad remarked.

Following the same procedure, they all looked at the swirling band of the Milky Way close to the horizon at midnight on April 1st 9750 B.C.E. The figure was looking to the right, so it most likely mapped to an asterism marking the end of the danger period. Takashi then spotted something.

'Isn't that patch of stellar cloud there a dark square? There is also some kind of lighter curved band of stars just above it. Try that Chad-san,' Takashi urged.

'Well spotted Takashi-san,' Chad exclaimed, as he rotated the semi-transparent photo on the night sky backdrop. The surrounding stars and the swirling clouds now formed a perfect match. 'Gentlemen, I can declare that we have finally debunked the *man bag* theory and the suggestion that we have been visited by extra-terrestrial beings! Another 1000 YouTube videos are now seriously in error.'

'Wow, this is excessive. I'm pretty shocked and quite exhausted from all we've discovered here. What do we do now? Effectively we've just proven that quite a few bits of important history are seriously wrong,' Tom remarked with a sigh of incredulity.

'Chad-san, Tom-san, let's take a moment to reflect. Let's retire to my study, overlooking the sea. The seascape views are inspiring and should help evoke some new thinking.'

'Let's do that,' Tom confirmed.

It was time for a final recap and an open discussion, to assimilate the shocking new perspectives on their whole story, and also how they should resolve the issue about Tom not presenting his and Carl's academic paper the following week. Takashi walked over to an ornately carved Japanese cupboard, took out three crystal glasses and poured a shot of the habushu into each glass, adding a dash of water to each.

'I think we should also have another toast of habu viper *habushu awamori*,' Takashi remarked, handing each of them a glass. They nodded then chinked their glasses and knocked back the Yonaguni liquor. 'OK Tom, so do you have any new thoughts about what you will do about your academic paper?'

'Well I must confess that I'm now really hesitant to present anything at all. On one hand the climatic evidence strongly supports the gamma ray burst event and the transit of the relativistic jet. The scientist in me says that this data is seriously important to disclose, because it demands a new appraisal of the frequency of the occurrence of relativistic jets and how they periodically impact the evolution of life on exoplanets. On that basis alone, a new parameter should be added to the famous *Drake equation*. As we discussed, it also impacts the *Fermi Paradox*. The new conclusion that must be drawn is that *hypernovae and relativistic jets* clearly occur pretty frequently, even every twenty thousand years or so, where the Earth is concerned. With Carl's strong insistence to pull the whole paper, I am now wondering if even this essential correction to the *Drake equation* will ever surface now.'

'Well, I have a different perspective on this of course,' Takashi remarked. 'I think the whole story must be told. Tom-san, your and Chad-san's journey has brought meaning to so many unanswered questions. Hypotheses formulated on real data deserve to be studied and evaluated by other specialists. I was also really amazed and intrigued by your explanation of what *Atlantis* meant. As an oceanographer, it just makes so much sense to me that *Atlantis* is describing all the people who lived beside the oceans, and who were lost when the sea-levels rose, first with the gamma ray burst and then again when the relativistic jet passed.'

'That's right. In the Nahuatl language *Atl-, Lan-, Tis* means *the people who lived by the water,*' Chad added.

'And I am guessing that since it fits into the whole scientific debate, this encouragement to withdraw your paper, suggests that now this interpretation of *Atlantis,* will also never be published,' Takashi concluded.

'I think I need to meet and discuss this total veto with Carl. I'm thinking he is not writing everything in an email. I'm utterly convinced it's that star identified on pillar 43, *Spica,* a sub-giant blue star, the closest star of that type to Earth, which will evolve into a Wolf-Rayet star and then *hypernova.* That Göbekli Tepe pillar was definitely carved 11,770 years ago! Detailed astronomic equipment and advanced astrophysics theory is needed before anyone could meaningfully understand the dangers that such a star represents to life on Earth here.'

'Is that the total of the unexplainable, or is there more?' Chad asked.

'No, the other disclosure problem is the *doomsday event* described by the relative sizes and relative positions of the three *Giza* pyramids and the three at *Monte Alban* and *Teotihuacan.* By the way, I also saw that the pyramids at the *Tiwanaku-Puma Puku* site in Bolivia, those at *Xochicalco,* and the pyramids at *Shen Hsi* in China, also map to that same doomsday date. These sites all identify indisputably that the next Wolf-Rayet *hypernova* in the *gamma Velorum* cluster will occur somewhere around 10,700 C.E.'

'To be able to encode that message into those pyramid structures requires a *high resolution telescope,* and a long-duration program of stellar monitoring to determine the relative motions of those three stars in that cluster. *Gamma Velorum* is barely visible as a single dot of light to the naked eye,' Tom continued. 'No advanced telescope equipment of any kind has ever been found dating to 11,770 years ago! If they never had that capability, then the knowledge of the differential motion of the three stars of *gamma Velorum* could never have come from this planet!'

'So our deduction of this whole story, with all its important findings and conclusions, now needs to remain utterly secret and unpublished for a very long time,' Chad reasoned.

'It seems that way,' Tom replied. 'Nothing will ever be published in the academic literature. It may even be a really long time before someone else cracks this story. To be able to process all the data and decode all the evidence that the Earth endured such an unimaginably terrible cataclysm, will likely require an astrophysicist with a devout interest in archaeology, anthropology and Egyptology. Those guys just don't exist.'

'Apart from you Tom!' Chad remarked encouragingly. 'There is one other very important consideration. Surely you agree that the World deserves to know this story, particularly about the warning of the next cataclysm predicted for 10,700 C.E.? That story surely should be told to warn future generations of how best to prepare for the next *hypernova*, *gamma ray burst* and *relativistic jet*, so that people can protect themselves? Life on this planet most certainly depends upon it.'

Despite everything, it started to seem uncomfortably clear that this story would never get published. They were heading back to the mainland tomorrow on the early Ferry. Mary-Anne and Jeanette would only be back later that evening. The huge archive of data that Felipe had sent, demanded some serious analysis and it was strongly leading them to the conclusion that their trip home should be via Costa Rica, but would the girls agree? Andrés surely could offer them advice, and it still wasn't clear why he had never published. Perhaps only he could reason them out of this challenging dilemma.

16 | Costa Rica: a journey north to the rainforest, cracking the Rosetta Stone

Juan Santamaría International Airport, Alajuela, Costa Rica.

Chad and Tom had flown out to Costa Rica to meet Andrés, Felipe's uncle. They had sent a message to Felipe who had replied saying that if he could get away, he would join them, flying up from Peru in a few days' time. It would be a great reunion. After some deliberation, Mary-Anne and Jeanette had finally declined the offer of yet another short holiday, and had instead flown on together to Sydney. Depending on the length of this Costa Rica excursion, they would all finally meet up again, in a week or so. There were just too many exciting conclusions in Andrés' detailed notes that Tom and Chad had felt compelled to meet this remarkable man in person.

Andrés had really pushed the boundary far. It was growing glaringly obvious that there was clearly a richer and more extensive history of Earth to appreciate. Just the fact that Andrés had known Mustapha Hamoun personally, was already an incredible coincidence in itself. While Tom and Chad had reconstructed the science from the archaeology and the astrophysical evidence, they really craved Andrés' personal insight from his own decades of research. Why had he never published? Had Andrés decided that his conclusions were just too controversial, and that publication would have upset too many conventional applecarts? It was daunting enough what Tom and Chad had discovered, but they also needed to give Andrés huge credit for his work. Together, they should most certainly be able to extend the collective understanding of *a new history of the Earth*, a whole lot further.

As their plane touched down in Cost Rica, a yellow sun, amid a glowing orange horizon, was just emerging through the last lonely lilac clouds. The skies above were a vast expanse of very pale blue. It was the portent of a perfect day.

The *Juan Santamaría* International Airport lay in Alajuela, some 17 kilometres north west of San Jose, and after clearing immigration, an airport shuttle took them directly to the car hire. On Andrés' advice, they had pre-booked a four-by-four. He lived up in serious hill country in a very remote part of the Central Highlands, where vehicles needed to cope with steep and narrow gravel roads. They had suggested a short, five-day stayover, but Andrés had already sent a number of messages insisting that they were truly welcome to stay for as long as they wanted.

From Alajuela, it would be a good three hour drive up to El Castillo, situated in the south west corner of lake Arenal. Their plan was to meet up, at some lakeside bar called *Howlers*, before travelling into the cloud forest together in convoy. Without a guide, finding his cabin would have been pretty difficult. Besides, the bar would be an ideal spot to share lunch and a beer and get to know each other a little better.

Their original plan was to split the driving, but El Castillo was not that far. It would depend on whether they encountered anything interesting along the way. Their full breakfast on the flight meant they could probably last until El Castillo, but they would definitely stop off and taste Costa Rica's famous high quality coffee if they passed any tempting coffee shops en route. They had opted to arrive from Japan with only essential luggage, leaving the rest with the girls to take back home. Chad had his *now famous* scuffed brown leather bag, while Tom had needed to pick up a small travel bag at Tokyo airport. It was good quality and not too pricey. Tom lifted it onto the back seat and closed the back door. He put on his sunglasses, stepped onto the footplate, and then climbed into the driving seat. He pushed the key into the lock and started the Landrover engine. It was a diesel. He pulled the door shut. It was time to head out.

'OK, so we will finally meet the man!' Chad remarked, climbing aboard then turning to place his bag on the back seat next to Tom's.

'Indeed. It will be an awesome exchange of ideas and conclusions.' Tom switched on the satnav. 'I just need to key in our destination. *El Castillo*, that's where we're going. OK we're all set. Full tank, aircon on.' He then made a few adjustments to the rear view mirror, turned and smiled at his brother, and then they set off.

'You know Tom, this is quite an important episode in our story. From what Felipe forwarded us, we have so much more evidence now for everything that happened.'

'That's true, but after that pretty negative reaction from Carl Rhodes, we still face the dilemma of how the heck we will ever actually get this story out there.'

The traffic was becoming more congested as they headed north along the *Pan American Highway*. Near the airport, the urbanised landscape was modern and well developed; it looked very American with all the well-known US outlets and restaurant chains. The road surface was good, but the two-lane highway took some getting used to, constantly requiring Tom to change to the outer lane, as the inside lane constantly morphed into the motorway exit just before each junction. As they travelled further out, the tropical landscape was becoming a vista of lush green rolling hills, surrounding wide cultivated valleys of coffee plantations and other produce. After another 20km, they reached the turnoff north.

'Here we go, the road to La Fortuna,' Tom remarked.

Chad leaned forward to check the full route on the satnav. 'Hey Tom, I see here that this route along the 702 takes us within a few kilometres of that 70 metre waterfall coming down from the dormant *Chato* volcano. We'll pass by in about two hours, all going well. It's an 18 buck entry fee but we should definitely check it out.'

'Sounds great. We can plan that as the coffee stop if you like. There's bound to be a coffee plantation shop somewhere nearby, or even a restaurant at the waterfall.'

Chad continued, 'After that, once we're around the *Arenal* Volcano, we'll meet the turnoff into the National Park along the lake towards El Castillo.'

'OK.'

The single lane road to La Fortuna crossed deep ravines via narrow bridges and had many tight bends. It twisted and turned through thick tropical vegetation, generally following the crests of the hills, but in places, the steep sided valleys blocked the view. At one point, Chad's phone buzzed. It was a message from Andrés.

Hi guys, welcome to Costa Rica. How's it going? I guess you're now on the 702. It's a rugged route but very pleasant to drive. Enjoy. I plan to be in El Castillo close to midday, it's market day and I need to pick up supplies. Safe trip. Best, Andrés

Chad answered him. *Hi Andrés, everything going great. Yes, still on the 702. See you at the Howlers Bar as planned. Best Regards Chad and Tom.*

'Hey Tom, if you ever want to change over? I'm happy to drive. This is quite a challenging drive, but you look as if you're enjoying it.'

'I'm good. This vehicle is coping well. Why don't we change over at the waterfall. I'm pretty sure the trip to El Castillo and on to Andrés' place will take more than an hour.'

'Sounds good. By the way Tom, didn't I see you looking at *Stellarium* on the flight. Did you find anything new?'

'Well, I actually did. I was looking at Easter Island. I was wondering about those Moai statue heads. They're all identical. They all have the same distinct profile, with sharp chins, deep inset eyes, long ears and, for those no longer buried, a heavy curving chest. Moreover, several have carvings on their backs. The other enigma is the megalithic structures which form substantial foundations for the lines of Moai in several places. Those platforms show remarkable similarity to the megalithic stone work of Cuzco and Tiwanaku.'

'Very interesting. So, what new insights did you reach?'

'I've finally found the origins of the Moai face.'

'Really? Where did you find that?'

'It's in a distinct part of the Milky Way band. Back in the night skies of 9750 B.C.E., bright stars and nebulae clearly map to the features of the head: the sharp nose, the chin, the long ears, and even the deep inset eyes. Interestingly, while the head profile and even the body shape unmistakably follow key features of the Milky Way band, the eye is actually centred on *lambda Centauri* which is directly in front of the bright *Running Chicken* emission Nebula IC 2948. Strangely, it is incredibly challenging to see with the naked eye, unless you enhance the brightness and contrast. It's amazing how they managed to image that, but it's definitely a *dead ringer* for the exact shape of the Moai face and body. The bright red nebula in Carinae is just above it, which seems to match perfectly the red Moai hats which some of them wear.'

'So, is *lambda Centauri* significant? What kind of star is it?'

'It most definitely is. It kind of struck me that if I could discover a star-mapping, the eye would logically be the natural focal point, if those Moai statues really do encode a message. Now listen up, that star *lambda*

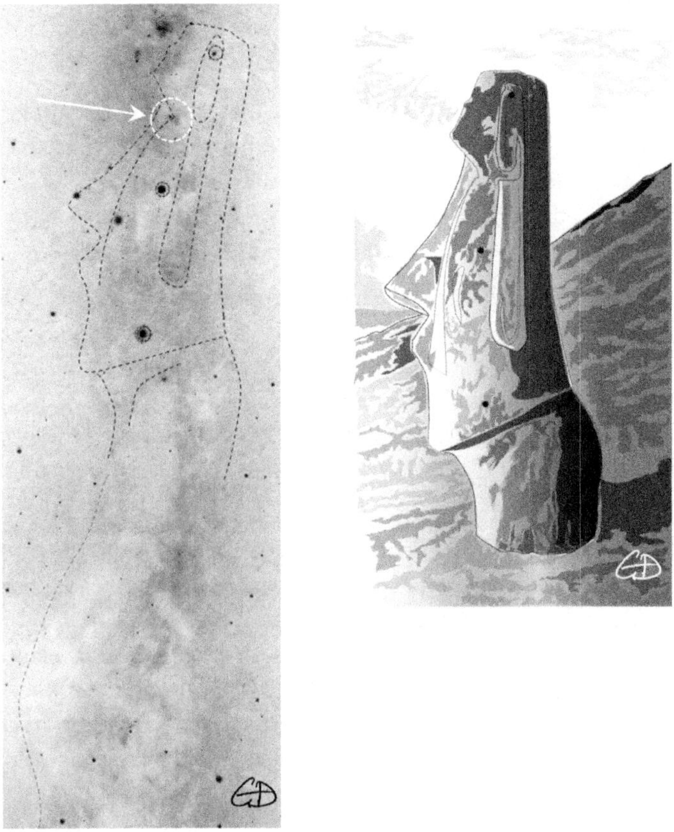

Moai Star Mapping

Centauri, is indeed a large blue star with a surface rotation speed of 180 km/s. Remember the Sun rotates at 2 km/s. It isn't a Wolf Rayet star, which have rotation speeds greater than 1000 km/s, but it will definitely supernova and emit a long GRB. But, unlike *gamma Velorum, lambda Centauri* is only 420 light years away, not 1100. That's very close for a GRB. I'm pretty much convinced that's why it's identified.'

'Amazing Tom! Well done!'

'There is however, a paradox.'

'What's that?'

'Well, you remember that Andrés also found those alignments with the Moai statues which prove it is a calendar system from the relativistic jet era.'

'Sure.'

'So, the Moai statues identify the precise dates of the 14-day danger period some 11,500 years ago. The paradox here is that Easter Island is surely one of the most isolated places on the planet. It must have been far from any other civilization, unless of course the whole area around it was a larger land mass. That's your field isn't it?'

'Well, more Takashi's, he's the oceanographer. I'm officially just a geologist. The sea depths around the Polynesian islands are indeed shallower than in other parts of the Pacific Ocean, but they're all volcanic islands. They all rise up from the very deep Pacific Ocean floor with very steep sides. Even if the ice cap melting from the jet transit caused the oceans to rise 100m, previously Easter Island would still only have been a shade larger, double at the most.'

'Interesting,' Tom remarked. 'So, an earlier civilization constructed a vast megalithic stone calendar made of standing stones whose profile maps to a specific part of the Milky Way band. They carved each of those Moai stones with the encoded message to identify *lambda Centauri*, another soon-to-supernova, long *gamma ray burst* progenitor. And they did this in one of the remotest parts of the planet, where possibly nobody actually lived. So why did they do that in such a remote place? Pretty enigmatic, don't you think?'

'I do. Well-reasoned! You said something about the megalithic Moai platforms Tom? What did you conclude about those?'

'Well, they're pretty much identical to those found in many ancient sites. Those megalithic platforms of perfect interlocking blocks, are really complex to carve and position so precisely. I saw that some platforms even include *micro-block inclusions* between the massive megaliths, which we now understand are there to resist movement and lock the structure together during earthquakes. I can't believe that these were carved using primitive tools, and accurately positioned by the more recent inhabitants.'

'So, a slam dunk that Easter Island is a megalithic calendar site with the Moai head identifying a *near-to-supernova* deadly event! Yet another serious advance in our evidence.'

They were approaching *La Fortuna*. It wasn't far to the waterfall. Tom came to a very sharp bend after crossing a deep ravine, and then the road led up a really steep incline.

'Although this is a fun drive, it does take quite some concentration,' he joked. 'You know, I could seriously do with some coffee when we arrive at the waterfall.'

'You earned it. You're doing great. I have to say, this Landrover seems pretty reliable. A good choice. By the way, Google says here that there's a café right at the waterfall entrance.'

'Good to hear!' Tom remarked.

After some time, they reached the turn-off to the waterfall. Tom slowed down then turned onto the unsurfaced road. The wheels crunched into the gravel as they drove along. They parked up above the waterfall and wandered over to the restaurant. It was pretty empty and a friendly guy at the bar greeted them.

'Buenos días señores! ¿Qué le gustarían? ¿Dos cafés?'

'Sí, dos cafés, por favor,' Chad replied.

'¿Americanos?'

'Ah sí,' Chad added.

'Well, no need to practice your Spanish with me,' the barman added with a laugh. 'I'm from San José, but not the Capital, the other one in California!'.

'Hey, home from home!' Tom remarked.

'Yeah. You on vacation guys?'

'No, we're actually researchers, just passing through on a flying visit to discuss new ideas with a colleague,' Chad replied. 'We flew in this morning.'

'Business rather than pleasure, you should stay longer. This is really an amazing country.' The barman placed two cups of coffee on the counter. A rich nutty aroma rose up from the dark liquid.

'We may just do that,' Chad replied. He placed a five dollar bill on the counter. 'Is five bucks good? We didn't change any money.'

'I'm good with that. You can also get a refill, if you want.'

'Thanks.' Chad took the coffees, and followed Tom to a small table outside.

'This is a really nice place. I'm glad we included this excursion,' Chad remarked.

'I definitely intend taking my swimming shorts. Look at that poster. It says we can actually walk into the cascade pool near to the waterfall itself if we want!'

'Sure, we should definitely do that.'

After twenty minutes or so, feeling rejuvenated from the caffeine hit, they paid the $18 entrance fee and hiked down almost 500 steps to the base of the waterfall. The manmade path was well built. Its steps firmly embedded into the soft hillside mud in places and safely guarded by a chain rail.

Swimming shorts on, they carefully clambered over the rough and slippery stones and entered the water. High above, the vertical fall of 70m was embraced by a diversity of verdant shades of tropical plants in rich abundance. The water felt quite cool at first, but the day was becoming a scorcher. They slowly edged their way closer towards the unceasing, roaring, bright white, pounding shock of plunging water, as it impacted the cascade pool beneath, endlessly sending out its invigorating turbulent spray in all directions.

'This is just what I needed!' Tom shouted towards Chad, barely audible above the cacophony.

'Me too! Five minutes more may even be enough!' Chad shouted back, holding up his spread-open hand.

For a few moments, embraced by the deafening waterfall's swirling, refreshingly cool mist, amid the intense heat of the day, both Tom and Chad were momentarily distracted into a deeper state of meditation among this powerful but beautiful marvel of nature. A short time later, Tom turned and shouted again towards Chad.

'Hey Chad! Are you good?'

Chad nodded, holding up a thumb, and together they carefully made their way back to the edge of the pool.

After changing, they hiked their way back up the steps. Despite the vigorous climb through the hot and humid air, back in the Landrover, Chad switched on the aircon and in minutes they both felt really refreshed again.

After the gravel road, Chad turned back onto the main road to La Fortuna, which was barely a few kilometres further. In the town, they joined the 142 which led them around the northern slopes of the Arenal volcano before they reached the unpaved road down through the National Park which would eventually lead them to El Castillo.

The gravel road through the park was pretty good and after seven kilometres they arrived closer to the lake.

'Look there's Howlers, and that pale blue flatbed over there must be Andrés'.'

'Well spotted, Chad!'

As they pulled into the parking, an athletic-looking, short-bearded man stepped out of the truck. He smiled and lifted his hand in greeting.

Chad pulled up alongside Andrés and wound down his window.

'Andrés, it's really great to meet you.'

'The pleasure is mine. Chad and Tom, welcome to Cost Rica. I hope you guys are hungry. This place has really good food and I'm inviting you for lunch, in fact, you're my guests for the duration of your stay. As I told you, please remember you're welcome to stay as long as you like. I have several month's supplies up at the cabin, including ten crates of good beer.'

'Andrés, thanks. That's very kind. So we'd be safe if we get snowed in!'

'Now that would be a first, but yes, we would have enough,' Andrés replied with a broad smile. 'Come!'

They walked towards the door and entered the bar. They took a table by the window with a great view out over the lake. Annie, the manager came over.

'Andrés, these must be your guests. Welcome! You know, I'm definitely intrigued. Andrés said that you guys were flying in, directly from Japan just to come and meet him here, and not even for a holiday!'

'Annie, let's just call it a meeting of minds from a long research project,' Andrés replied with a sincerely persuasive look. 'So, what do you recommend today?'

'Oh, so that's what you get up to in your cloud forest cabin Andrés. You're secretly doing research,' Annie replied teasingly. 'I didn't know that about you. OK guys, here are the menus, and I always recommend the steak grill, but today we also have grilled bass from the lake. That's definitely good with a beer!'

'Grilled lake bass with a beer certainly sounds excellent to me,' Tom replied.

'Me too!' Chad added.

'OK, let's all go with that! Thanks Annie,' Andrés replied, handing her back the three menus.

She soon returned, bearing a tray carrying three ice cold beers. 'Enjoy!' she said, then walked back to the kitchen.

'So, first I propose a *welcome to Costa Rica* toast! Salud!' he said holding up his glass.

'Salud!' Chad and Tom replied together.

They chinked their glasses together. That first taste of the amber elixir after the long drive was deliciously refreshing.

After a short while, Andrés spoke. 'It's great we're together now. You know, while I lack your academic expertise in astrophysics and geology, I still believe there are significant benefits in talking through all the material together. It's still possible that we will derive more thorough conclusions that way.'

'Andrés, that's a certainty. We've only been on this trail for little more than a year. You have been researching this for what, more than thirty years?' Chad reasoned.

'Actually, closer to forty, I only stopped when I moved up here, some ten years ago.'

'Precisely, so your insights will be so much deeper. Your mind has been doing pattern recognition for so much longer,' Chad concluded. 'The more stuff you see, the more you understand, right?'

'My thoughts exactly,' Andrés confirmed.

Soon their food arrived. The lake bass was perfectly prepared and spiced with fragrant herbs including dill and oregano. It was drizzled in olive oil and served with a fiery horseradish salsa of tomato and mango. A newly-baked focaccia, generously coated with garlic, tomato and rosemary, accompanied the fish. For minutes they were all absorbed in the excellent meal.

Chad then spoke. 'So on the flight over, Tom managed to extend your work on Easter Island.'

'Excellent! What did you find?' Andrés remarked, raising his eyebrows with surprise.

'Well, I found the profile of the Moai head and body, in part of the Milky Way in the skies of 9750 B.C.E. I had a hunch that maybe the carvings held a message. Then I discovered that the Moai eye identifies *lambda Centauri*, a large blue supernova candidate that is quite close to our Solar System, only 420 light years away. That star will supernova pretty soon and the GRB from that may be equally as devastating as *gamma Velorum*. It won't have the power of a hypernova and there won't be relativistic jets, but being around a third of the distance, the gamma ray burst will be substantial. This will certainly be another serious environmental catastrophe.'

'Well done Tom!' Andrés remarked.

'And I also discovered that the Moai statue platforms are definitely megalithic in form, identical to the stone work of Cuzco in Peru.'

'That's compelling. I was hopeful that we could find more evidence to support my suggestion that Easter Island is the calendar site I proposed,' Andrés added.

'Yes, but with each new insight, comes more challenging questions. Easter Island is as remote as you can get. We are starting to think that maybe no one *ever* lived there. If that is true, then why create a calendar of statues which identify a supernova candidate so close to us, which no one used? Or, was this stone calendar site intended to be discovered well into the future, some thousands of years after the event?'

'You mean like by us, in our current era, Tom?' Andrés suggested.

'Indeed, and somehow that seems very likely. I like your suggestion.'

'I must confess, I was really interested in the astrophysical interpretations you derived: how you showed that the *gamma Velorum* Wolf Rayet star collapsed to form a relativistic jet, which was captured in images in the *Dendera lightbulb* friezes. Also, the association of the jet with the Mexican *Feathered Serpent* and the *Rainbow Serpent* of Australia.'

'Well Andrés, I've continued to try to push that astrophysical interpretation further. I recently managed to model the form of the spiral of solar wind that was seen from the Earth during the course of the year. We know that the jet doesn't change its shape dynamically as it moves through space, and the spin axis of the Sun relative to the Earth's orbit doesn't change either, but the Earth *is* moving. As seen from the Earth, the solar wind coming off the Sun would have changed its shape as it slowly morphed between very different distinct shapes every few months.'

'Tom, that sounds really interesting, please continue.'

'OK, so the solar wind moves away from the Sun, following the Sun's own magnetic field lines. That only happens until the magnetic field around the jet becomes greater. So, at a certain distance from the Sun, which I currently estimate is around a third of the Earth's orbital radius, the charged solar wind particles are all gathered up and they all start to spiral around the magnetic field line encircling the jet some 50 light years away.'

'I like it,' Andrés remarked.

'Yes, so get this, the Earth is rising high up above the Galactic plane, reaching its highest point on March 21st, then descending below the Galactic plane reaching its lowest point on September 21st. Remember these dates have nothing to do with the solstices. That is just a coincidence of our current era. So it means on September 21st, both beams are effectively travelling upwards, as seen from the Earth, curving in both directions around the jet, while in December and June, The people of Earth got a side on view, with the two jets curving in an arc in both directions. The two views would have been the same but reversed. I have the images on my iPhone here. This shows how the solar wind shapes changed during the course of the year. Look!'

He put his iPhone on the table and slowly scrolled through his computer-modelled solar wind images.

'Very interesting. I hadn't seen these yet!' Chad exclaimed.

Andrés looked intently at the images. 'You may be surprised to know that I have seen these exact images carved in stone!' he remarked sincerely.

'Really Andrés? Where have you seen them? That would be amazing!'

'They are the strange hats worn by animals and beings on the walls of the Temple of Hathor in Luxor, Egypt! I have those images on my Galaxy phone. Look here!'

'Oh my god, Tom. This is extremely convincing!' Chad murmured.

'This is actually quite incredible Andrés!'

'*You* have done all the work Tom! Few people could even imagine how to model spiralling beams of solar wind. Well done! I merely recognised

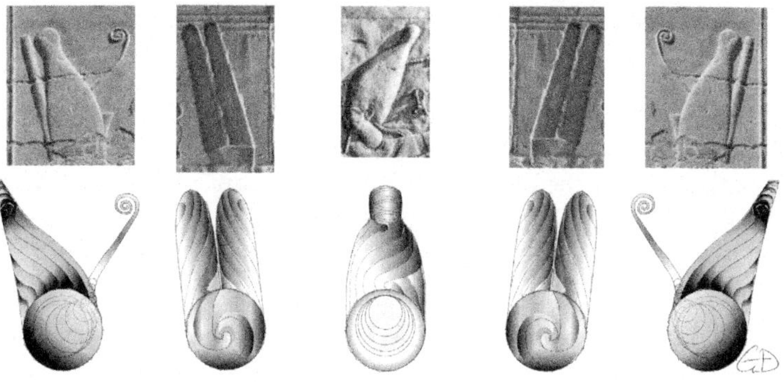

Solar Wind Hats

where I've seen those shapes. Until now, nobody has ever understood what they actually were. We are the first on the planet to do that, and right here in El Castillo, Costa Rica!'

'We should celebrate with another beer!' Chad remarked.

'Well, after such a breakthrough, I would say we should definitely have something stronger. This is ground-breaking stuff!' Andrés declared. 'Rogerio, a friend of mine runs a bar in *Tamarindo* out on the Pacific coast. He has perfected a secret recipe for a *tamarind margarita*. Knowing you were coming, and after some serious pleading, he finally sent me his secret cocktail mix a few days ago. I'll just give it to Annie; she can prepare these.' Andrés stood up and walked over to the bar. Moments later he returned. 'All set!'

'Andrés, I would really like to ask you something,' Chad asked tentatively. 'You knew Mustafa Hamoun and even John Mann from the British Museum. It was in the material Felipe sent us. It included much of your correspondence. Please tell us about your collaboration. I met Mustafa's wife and his brother-in-law. That is an extreme coincidence, you surely agree.'

'Chad, that is indeed impossibly unbelievable, although it's true of course.'

'You know, that random meeting in Egypt with Tau, Mustafa's brother-in-law, started my whole journey of discovery. Might you say something about what you and Mustafa and John Mann concluded together. I have Mustafa's notes. There are many coded entries. I was wondering what else is in there?'

'Well, I met Mustafa and John at a conference on Mesoamerican Anthropology when they were visiting Peru some twenty years ago. It turned out that we all shared a fascination of Egyptian history and it all started from there. Over the course of the next few years we started to focus on a huge enigma in the Egyptian archaeological record: the failure of scholars to make sensible translations of the hieroglyphs on the walls of the Valley of the Kings and in Karnak. There are definitely questions about how John died, it wasn't an accident and he didn't commit suicide. We were getting too close and I believe that John confronted the wrong powerful people with too much evidence. The details are sketchy, but an overseas dealer was bidding for a set of early hieroglyphic translations at *Sotheby's* in London. I believe there was a lot of money involved and the dealer pulled out.'

'It sounds sinister,' Chad murmured.

'Yes,' Andrés replied quietly. 'So, maybe I will share with you the breakthrough shocking conclusion that we reached, and perhaps everything will suddenly come into sharper relief.'

'Go for it,' Tom urged.

'Well, the *Rosetta Stone* is a fake. It's history's first piece of fake news.'

'Well, we almost got there,' Chad remarked, 'but you're now saying it's a certainty!'

'The story is actually quite complex, and it needs to be unravelled a bit. It turns out that the creation of the *Rosetta Stone* was part of a deceptive concoction to shore up a failing dynasty, potentially on its final legs, but it worked. This was the time of the *Ptolemies*, who were a self-proclaimed royal family, who ruled Egypt after the pharaohs from 305 B.C.E. for some 275 years. The Ptolemies claimed to be descended from a *Macedonian Greek* royal family. They weren't royalty! Ptolemy the first was one of Alexander-the-Great's seven bodyguards, a military general. When Alexander died, he just assumed he was entitled to rule as pharaoh, and crowned himself Ptolemy I of Egypt. Instantly a new dynasty was born, but it had no legitimate claim. It was built on sand, and literally. After he died, all the subsequent rulers named themselves *Ptolemy* and their wives were all called *Cleopatra*. The most famous was of course *Cleopatra VII* who died allegedly after being bitten by a snake, although that poison was most likely introduced by a needle.'

Rosetta Stone

'So where does the whole Rosetta Stone fallacy slot into that narrative?' Tom asked. 'We also saw the poor quality of the scratched hieroglyphs compared to the immaculately precise hieroglyphs on the walls at Karnak. But surely the translation is correct? Too many scholars have looked at it. It was Jean Francois Champollion who became very famous for cracking the decoding of the hieroglyphs into demotic by 1825, but I agree there was much controversy surrounding his efforts. Everyone subsequently used that 1825 translation to attempt to understand all the other hieroglyphic texts.'

'Yes, but if you read the translations of the Greek and Demotic script, already something in that stone *document* is shouting out *why write this in stone*? That moment in time is the smoking gun. This was the middle of the Ptolemaic dynasty, Ptolemy V had inherited the throne at the age of *five* after his parents had died in very suspicious circumstances. This had all the hallmarks of a *power grab* which resulted in the Ptolemaic territories being ruled by a series of highly incompetent regents. Over the course of the next few years, the dynasty subsequently lost all its territories in Asia minor, everything in the Levant and all its influence in the Aegean Sea. Also, during the final years of his father, Ptolemy IV, a growing unrest led by several self-proclaimed pharaohs, had already started to engulf the whole country. By 196 B.C.E., the date of the Rosetta Stone, when Ptolemy V was around 14 years old, a substantial part of the south of Egypt had also been lost. With the loss of its entire empire, and unrest at home, the whole dynasty was facing annihilation.'

'So what was the deception?' Chad asked.

'The dynasty desperately needed to justify their entitlement to rule. No one could read the hieroglyphs, that knowledge had been well and truly lost. The hieroglyphs were a mystery. So the Ptolemies then decided to shore up the regime by claiming that only *they* possessed the secret knowledge. Only *they* could read and understand the hieroglyphs. They re-established their right to rule by carving in stone, a series of decrees with forged hieroglyphic pseudo-translations alongside Greek and Demotic script. They just invented their own one-to-one translation. The *pseudo translation* is the one that the World cracked. No one has ever determined the true meanings of the hieroglyphs. Remember that other decrees have been found, which claim to date back to 246 B.C.E from the time of Ptolemy III, but it is doubtful if they were carved earlier. It is possible, but I don't believe it. It was Mustafa who suggested that they were all carved at the same time and distributed. Three decrees have been found from the time of Ptolemy V, which is the giveaway. Moreover, in any plot of deception and intrigue, it's always useful to suddenly discover documents from *a long time ago*, which conveniently confirm what you just forged today.'

'Andrés, that's just incredible! So that's why the Luxor Temple walls have never been translated adequately,' Chad remarked. 'Maria said that Mustafa always questioned the Pyramid Texts' translation. That makes so much more sense now!'

'There is also the question about the burning down of the library of Alexandria. It was right at the end of the Ptolemaic dynasty, but did some documents there need to disappear? I don't think so, but it remains an open question about motive for a potential arson. As to the Pyramid Texts, that is what John and I were working on, right up to the end. Perhaps I saw his death as a warning, which is kind of why I stepped out. I decided that it was time to let go and move on. It had long been a dream to move to Costa Rica, so I handed over all the evidence and papers to Felipe, just in case he wanted to continue the work. I have, of course, never told him these things.'

For a moment, the conversation stopped. The shock of the conclusion was worrying. The two brothers both looked a little concerned.

'I only tell you this just so you know what you're getting into here,' Andrés added sincerely. 'Yes, I know, you're in it already, but you still have some choices.'

Just at that moment, Annie arrived with the three tamarind margaritas. The fragrant cocktail was served in a classic conical glass with a star fruit on the side. The glass rim was dusted with chili salt.

'OK, so after that little interlude, we can finally celebrate our recent Easter Island discovery. Please!' Andrés insisted, gesticulating towards Tom and Chad, who each took a glass. 'So, as I mentioned, this is a very special drink perfected over many years by a really good friend of mine, Rogerio Sanches. You are serious scientists, so you will appreciate the elements of its perfection which I now describe. Firstly, this is *not* a frozen margarita. Blended crushed ice can hide a very poor drink, which because of that trick, is usually still quite expensive. A frozen mouth can't taste the amazing palette of flavours of this creation, which is why frozen margaritas are so bad. Unscrupulous barmen can get away with anything in a frozen margarita. No, these are delicately cooled with ice when shaken, and the ice discarded. Like in every margarita there is of course tequila, triple sec, and lime juice, but in this tamarind margarita, it is now blended with tamarind paste, lemon juice and agave, the plant from which tequila is distilled. The chili salt rim gives the smoky kicker. A few years back Rogerio even experimented with adding fresh mint, trying to push it towards a mojito. Personally, I prefer it without the mint.'

'Well Andrés, you've certainly set the expectations high! Can't wait to taste this now!'

'Tom, Chad, you're both welcome. I don't think you'll be disappointed.'

'For our recent new conclusions about Easter Island . . . 'Andrés proposed, holding up his glass.

'And to a new history of the Earth . . . ' Chad continued.

'And to many more astrophysics discoveries and conclusions.' Tom added, completing the toast.'

'Cheers!' they said together, taking a large sip of the golden tamarind cocktail.

The conversation continued for another good two or three hours. Andrés traded stories of his adventures in Peru and forays into the Amazon jungle, in exchange for their whole journey of discovery over the past year.

Then it was time to head to the cabin. Andrés paid the bill and they left. Andrés climbed into his pale blue flatbed truck, which was parked up along the road. Chad had parked their Landrover directly behind. Andrés started his engine then held a suntanned arm out of the window, motioning forward. Then he pulled away. Chad followed and in convoy they continued the 20 or so kilometres along the steep and winding track through the tropical landscape towards Andrés' cabin.

It was close to 5 p.m. as they approached one of the densest parts of the cloud forest. Andrés motioned that they continue towards a flat patch of ground beside his cabin, while he turned off the track to park his truck on a short steep slope. He jumped down and walked over to Chad and Tom. He noticed Chad looking at his truck on the extreme incline.

'Before you ask, that truck of mine is locked in gear, it won't slip. In the wet season I attach a hook and chain to the front if I need to park there. It's fine these months. Come. Grab your things.'

Tom and Chad followed him into his cabin. For the next hours they were chilling on the veranda, while Andrés talked of his life in Costa Rica. After a light evening meal, during a beer-tasting journey across Costa Rica, sharing several of Andrés' fine beers, Tom then happened to notice a strange tubular structure with pulley wheels at each end hanging from the edge of the veranda roof.

'Hey Andrés, what's that hanging there? It looks a bit technical, and prototypical, or am I wrong?'

'That Tom, is an invention I made to clean up the oceans of plastic,' he said reaching up, unhooking the device and laying it on the table. 'This is only a prototype, I never got the funding.'

'You're an engineer right?' Tom asked.

'Electrical engineer. I spent most of my life in the electrical power, transmission line network. As soon as I saw all those reports about the oceans being filled with neutral buoyancy microplastic granules, I immediately saw how to create a device to remove them. I needed something which didn't affect sea life or algae or eggs etc., but did remove the plastic. An engineering buddy Krištof Tornero, helped devise the solution. The challenge was to differentiate the microplastic granules from water by focusing on their uniquely different electrical qualities, defined by something called their *dielectric constant*. The microplastics are insulators. Water, and thus effectively all life, has a *dielectric constant* of about 80, and plastic has a *dielectric constant* of around 2. This is an indication of how much charge the substance can store. A very low *dielectric constant* means the material is strongly affected by a non-linear electric field. The central wire here has the positive charge, the cylinder carries the negative charge. This gives a very strong electric field and with a direction, and the microplastic granules move towards the wire, which is slowly moving around the pulleys. At the open mesh end, the wire enters a narrow tube with the microplastic granules, which are brushed off. This black box over here plugs into the device here,' he added showing the system. 'When submerged, the device with full power, only needs to power the slow pulley drive and a propeller, and monitor its buoyancy tank. When the battery is low, it simply pumps out the water from the buoyancy chamber, and resurfaces until the solar panel here has recharged it again.'

'So you have developed a device to clean the oceans of microplastic granules. That's cool!' Tom exclaimed. 'Chad here, came up with a solution to cool the planet by 10 °C over a hundred years by growing vast colonies of light algae on the ocean surfaces. Your solution could clean those oceans.'

'As you can appreciate, this would also be another hundred-year project. Nevertheless, we tested it on the lake and it came back with very positive results. No one even thought there was microplastic pollution in Lake Arenal. At sea, a better solution might be a massive structure towed behind a ship without pulleys or a propeller.'

'Andrés, it's very impressive. It's definitely worth trying. I can see that your ship-towed solution is actually much simpler to build. No moving parts even, if the dimensions of the 2 pipes are chosen correctly,' Tom concluded.

'Yeah, it should really be picked up by someone, who can take it to the next level. While we are still here, we should make an effort to look after this planet,' he said with a knowing look.

'Indeed,' Chad confirmed.

There was a long quiet pause before Andrés spoke again. 'Well guys, whether we want to or not, up here in the cloud forest canopy, we will wake up with the forest noise, so I propose we turn in, and meet tomorrow around 5 a.m. for breakfast.'

'That sounds like a good plan,' Tom replied.

Chad nodded.

They all stood up and walked into the cabin. No doubt, the next day would bring even more exciting interpretations of as yet, unexplained phenomena.

17 Costa Rica: Olmec heads, the Eye of Horus, a GRB, and the Dendera zodiac forgery

Tropical Cabin in the cloud forest high above El Castillo, Costa Rica.

Andrés' spacious cabin of tropical hardwood was very securely built on the steeply-sloping hillside, and from the veranda, it had richly verdant views above the cloud forest canopy right the way down to lake Arenal. He had designed and built this cabin with his own hands. Andrés was approaching the twilight years of life, but he still looked remarkably fit. He was very likeable and radiated a calm and reassuring quality of tranquillity - that peaceful state of insight and acceptance that one only reaches after finally meeting one's inner self, following the struggle of a long and arduous journey. It was the early morning of the next day. Despite what had become a very late night, they were all up and sitting around the bamboo breakfast table outside on the cabin deck. For many minutes they sat in bathrobes, listening to the magical cacophony of the howler monkeys' chorus, bringing the rainforest alive and announcing the dawn of the new day.

Andrés reached forward taking a glass pitcher, and poured out three glasses of orange juice. A hardwood bowl of freshly cut mango, pineapple, and melon slices stood in the middle of the table. He lifted the bowl, proffering it towards Tom and Chad. They each took some fruit, placing it upon white porcelain plates adorned with motifs of Costa Rica's flowering shrubs.

'So, Chad and Tom, I must say after yesterday's vivid discussions, it's definitely a real pleasure to meet you guys, and at such short notice.'

'Likewise. It's our pleasure also,' Tom replied.

'I still remember getting that call from Felipe after you rescued him from his overturned car during some of Mexico's inclement weather. He mentioned your work and I was extremely happy to have him send you the material. I must say that I was, and still am really quite intrigued to find two other co-travellers on this same trail of discovery and awesome interpretation. I should add that I also sense that you're shortly about to stand and pause before that gate, the *point of no return*, which I encountered a few years ago. That's a place where ambition and wisdom finally hold hands and where one concludes that maybe this journey was always destined to be *ultimately private*.'

'That's a very daunting comment Andrés,' Tom replied. 'I sense an inference somewhere about the consequences of publishing?'

Looking directly at them, Andrés took a bite into a slice of melon. He seemed momentarily absorbed in its delicious succulence. He then took a deep breath in, then sighed, his expression becoming a little more serious.

'My dear friends, I'm sure you already appreciate how ominously huge this story is. The data you've collected, the rational scientific method you've applied to interpret that data, and now, when you combine all that with the evidence I have gathered, you must know that the only conclusion is a serious rewriting of a big part of the history of our planet. We aren't just talking about updating a few academic papers here and there, and modifying a few chapters in a few books. Oh no, *tens of millions* of publications are seriously questionable! That was the conclusion I reached, and I didn't possess your deep and remarkable scientific insight, which now forms a thickening bedrock of reason upon which all this evidence surely builds an absolute certainty.'

For a short while, the conversation paused, somewhat serving to underline the seriousness of Andrés' conclusion. It was not quiet, however. The howler monkeys continued their echoing repartee, taunting one another from invisible haunts, hidden among the vast expanse of the cloud-forest canopy. In response, Tom then changed the subject slightly.

'Andrés, please allow me to be a little philosophical. I was reflecting upon the fulfilling life that you have carved out of nature here. I'm pretty sure that almost everyone would just love to experience this, if only for a few months at least, but society's pressures make it so difficult for people to just completely *up-sticks and relocate* like you. Living remotely in a cabin in the woods is of course the pioneer's dream, harking back to the days of Henry Thoreau and his nineteenth century book *Walden, Life in the Woods*. It takes a calm, strong belief in self-worth to be able to dare to escape to this metaphorical island amid a sea of green in this wonderful climate?'

'Exactly, but it was also a tough decision, even for me. This is National Park, and you can't build here. This cabin was originally an old abandoned ranger's outpost, which I chanced upon while out hiking. After a few enquiries I managed to persuade the park authorities to let me restore it. They let me buy it and over time, it slowly expanded into this cabin of my dreams.'

'So, a real labour of love then,' Chad suggested.

'Of course. When you have refurbished everything, rewired the building, expanded the main living quarters, added an extensive deck, all those tasks and more, the cabin becomes part of your own artistic creation, your signature on the landscape. Unlike most people who live in a concrete box in the city, living in the cabin you built entirely yourself brings you close to the very soul of the wilderness and coexistence with nature itself. I love your mention of Henry Thoreau by the way. I know the book of course. His message is as true today as it ever was, for the pioneer's cabin in the woods is the real, albeit somewhat romantic ideal which connects us with nature. To know and to learn to love your inner self brings strength to overcome any of life's challenges. We all need to find happiness, I happened to find it here.'

'I saw the satellite dish. Global communications, Internet access,' Tom remarked

'And only if and when you want to be connected,' Andrés added. 'I don't feel cut off here. I still spend time researching new ideas. Of course, it's the ideal place of serenity and void of distractions, which brings a rare clarity to one's thinking. Like you, I got a huge feeling of self-worth when I made the same breakthrough as you guys, and every day I can calmly enjoy that personal feeling of accomplishment. I never sought public recognition. You both live in the academic world, with its relentless pressured demands to publish even the smallest of new insights. I never lived in that tense and nervous space where everyone just assumes that all the peer-reviewed papers that went before are unquestionable gospel. I came from the other direction. My journey was driven by the increasingly enigmatic publications which lacked any satisfying convincing hypotheses. If you think about it, even in the non-scientific domains, from history to archaeology, there is a total lack of realistic new thinking about interpreting the past rationally. Don't you also find it odd, how culture after culture in all four corners of the Earth are always explained in terms of random Gods and legends of deities overcoming adversity?'

Before either Tom or Chad had the chance to reply, Andrés continued.

'Wherever I look, from the rich friezes painted on the walls of the underground complexes in the Valley of the Kings near Luxor, to the carvings of *Viracocha* in my home country of Peru, there is just an inadequacy of scientific rigor. Civilizations built structures and recorded messages, in stone and art, for future generations to learn and understand. Why did they do that? They did it because it was essential in order to preserve the survival of the human race! I always knew that this was not art, nor religious fervour based upon a plethora of obscure mythical characters, and the slaying of weird and wonderful creatures. Some of the best artwork is on the temple walls in Egypt, but *Ra* didn't take *a journey on a boat in the underworld*! A lost civilization carved important messages into stone, and painted complex imagery on walls with messages that conveyed warnings for the sole purpose of *keeping people alive*!'

Andrés was clearly very passionate about his own research, and meeting Chad and Tom had finally presented him with the first real opportunity to debate this subject openly. This would become a very lucid discussion, and they had only just started. Now Andrés could pose some questions of his own.

'So, tell me Tom, what do you consider are the most important technologies that evolved directly out of the endurance of this cataclysm?'

'Well, as strange as it may sound, I guess I would say an essential innovation directly due to this event, was the development of the *calendar* because knowing which day it was, i.e. where the Earth was along its orbit, suddenly became a matter of life and death.'

Andrés nodded slowly, rubbing his grey-bearded chin with his hand. 'Yes, I agree with that. You have to admit though, it sounds a little funny. Imagine someone today rushing into a pharmacy shouting: *Hey, help! Do you have any calendars left?*'

'Yes indeed!' Tom agreed.

'By the way, Andrés, just before we left Japan, I also forwarded you access to our online archive with a password. Did you manage to access that?' Chad asked.

'Yes, I did, although I haven't really had time to go through much of your material in detail yet. All the astrophysics explaining the hypernova of the Wolf-Rayet star was what I missed. I can't express enough how grateful I am to receive your scientific reasoning. As you know, I collected a huge amount of evidence, yet I guess I was kind of travelling the long way round, lacking your brilliant scientific insights.'

'I respectfully disagree Andrés. Your life's work is a phenomenal contribution. It's as if Tom and I had only just started in comparison.'

'Well, we certainly make a good team. You know, I think my nephew Felipe, only sent you part of what I found. We can go through some of the other material now, if you're interested.'

'You have even more findings?' Tom replied with an air of surprise.

'Come on, Tom, admit it,' Andrés remarked with a broad teasing smile. 'You were secretly hoping I had a vast archive of undisclosed evidence awaiting your, and your brother's evaluation. Well, I can put both your minds at ease and tell you now, your trip is about to become quite a journey of revelation, and just when you thought things couldn't get more shockingly and persuasively conclusive!'

'OK, I admit it. It was a secret hope of ours. Please, when can we start?' Tom retorted.

'Why don't we get dressed and get ready for the day. There are showers at the back of the cabin. I warn you that it's always shorts and tee-shirt weather up here in the Central Highlands, and we're fortunately at quite an altitude. In spite of that, the humidity can still get very high, but there's almost always a soft breeze through the canopy, and if that fails, I have an aircon unit on wheels. I'll put on the coffee and we can meet back here in 15 minutes or so.'

'Sounds like a plan,' Chad added.

'A vast archive of new evidence ... I can't believe this! Andrés, this will be so great!' Tom remarked.

'I can't wait to share it and get your own insights.' He stood up and walked towards the kitchen.

After twenty minutes or so, they all returned to the veranda above the rainforest. Just adjacent, sitting on a branch of a nearby tree, was a brightly coloured bird, resplendent in its plumage of vivid green and turquoise and baring a vermillion chest. The bird's extremely long and flowing iridescent-blue tail-feathers extended far below the branch.

Andrés leaned towards them and spoke very quietly, 'That's a *quetzal*, one of our residents, considered to be one of the most beautiful birds in the World. The long tail feathers mean he's a male and it takes him about three years to grow those. He's all ready for the mating season. He's a frequent visitor up here in the canopy and I confess I've tamed him a little. He's checking you out. I think he's a bit curious about my new guests.'

'Beautiful,' Chad whispered, lifting his iPhone to capture the *quetzal*'s vibrant colours.

The bird hopped back and forth along the branch, its tail fluttering provocatively as if practicing some dance moves for a would-be mate. Shortly after, it flew away, its iridescent-blue tail-feathers streaming through the air behind him.

Andrés poured the coffee. The rich aroma permeated the air. 'This is locally grown, very close to here in *Monteverde*. I think it's one of the best coffees in Costa Rica.'

'Tastes fantastic, very smooth and rich. Very fruity, almost as if it has an apricot flavour,' Tom murmured.

'I think you got the notes spot on,' Andrés confirmed. 'We can grab a couple of kilos before you leave. Your flight is to Los Angeles next week, but as I said, you're welcome to stay longer?'

'Thanks Andrés! It does sound a strange connection to Sydney, but there are loose ends to tie up in California before we head back to Australia,' Chad confirmed.

'I can even get you a special discount as the plantation is owned by my sister Eliza. You probably know that Costa Rica specialises in high quality coffees. They can't compete with the huge plantations in Brazil who serve the global mass commodity market.'

'Your sister runs a coffee plantation? That's cool. I really look forward to meeting her,' Tom replied.

'It will be my pleasure. Now I want to show you what I found!'

He walked over to a desk and returned with several folders of papers and his iPad.

'I might just need some power for this, he murmured, reaching under the table and grabbing a yellow power cable lying on the floor. He plugged it into his iPad.

'OK. We're all set. So rather than start at what is possibly the most sobering conclusion ... but wait a moment, maybe I should indeed start there. Then you will appreciate where everything is heading. I should confess that I fear even both of you might get a big surprise.'

'That sounds extremely intriguing. To get the absolute conclusion first. I guess I'm ready for that. How about you Chad?'

'I'm keen. Go for it Andrés. Blow us away.'

'Actually, maybe it's even better to present the conclusion as a puzzle, in that way you'll enjoy the discovery more. I've got most stuff on my iPad here, but depending on where the conversation goes, I have this paper archive,' he added patting the folders. 'Let me run through a series of images I prepared. I'll start by showing you this place. Look, it's a long lost abandoned city. First you'll need to work out where this is. Do you have any idea Tom?'

'That looks extremely ancient! Those buildings look incredibly old, and the terrain looks like some kind of desert. I've never seen this place before. How about you Chad. You're the geologist!'

'OK, so those mountains look very much like the *Andes*, and from the colour of that sand I'm going to hazard a guess that it could be the *Sechura* coastal desert of Peru. But that runs effectively along the entire Pacific coast.'

'Chad, very good. It is indeed, and the location is not so far south from Chankillo, a site I have visited many times and one I know you've studied. So, this ancient city is just north of Lima. What else do you see?'

'Pyramids? But they look terribly dilapidated. How old is this place? What's the city called?' Tom remarked.

'It's called *Sechin Bajo*. They say it's 5000 years old, but actually they haven't got a clue! I know that it's probably one of the oldest urban constructions on the planet!

'Tom, look! There are several pyramids, but that's not the Giza configuration!'

'You are kidding me! We need to check the alignment with the *gamma Velorum* cluster!' Tom exclaimed. 'I'll get my laptop. One moment.'

Tom returned in a few minutes holding his laptop. He booted it up then launched *Stellarium*, and selected Lima Peru.

'You know, if that isn't the Giza configuration warning of 10,700 C.E., then just maybe these pyramids identify the star positions of the *gamma Velorum* cluster at around 12,780 B.C.E. We certainly need to check that.'

'Are you suggesting that *Sechin Bajo* is marking out the gamma ray burst event of 12,780 B.C.E? That would be incredible if true. It would imply that a previous civilization was *forewarned!*' Chad murmured.

'And then it also implies that they had the technology to interpret, understand, and to record that warning,' Tom replied. He set the date on *Stellarium* back to 12,780 B.C.E.

'OK, here is the configuration of *gamma Velorum* back in 12,780 B.C.E. Also, we should remember that *Stellarium* will be missing a star, because one star underwent total collapse to form a hypernova and emitted a jet. I'll grab a screen shot of the configuration, make it transparent, then see if it matches the pyramid buildings of this place. I just need to get a vertical plan from Google Earth. One moment.'

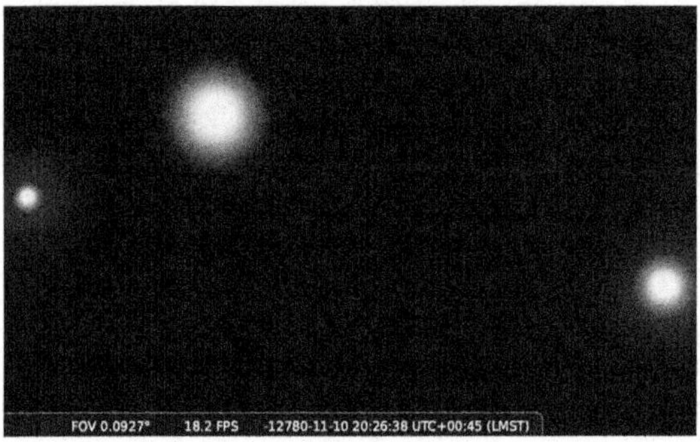

Gamma Velorum 12,780 B.C.E.

In a short time, Tom had set *Sechin Bajo* as the background picture in Word and created a semi-transparent overlay of the *gamma Velorum* cluster from 12,780 B.C.E. and placed it into a text box so he could investigate the alignment with the pyramids there. At that date, the largest star of *gamma Velorum* was at the *centre* of the three stars, unlike in 10,700 C.E., when the predicted date of the next Wolf-Rayet star collapse, as marked out by the Giza pyramids, showed the largest pyramid, Khufu, *at one end*. After a slight change in scale of the star overlay and a rotation, it was very clear that two pyramids of *Sechin Bajo* combined with the distinctive circular structure of a very substantial building, matching the *gamma Velorum* configuration of 12,780 B.C.E.

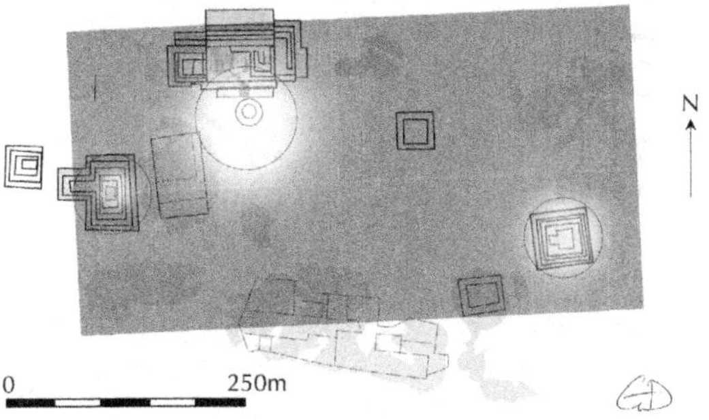

Sechin Bajo

'That's it! It's a convincing match. And look there! There's another pyramid. It most probably mapped to the star which collapsed. So, these buildings do most likely mark out the *future* warning of the gamma ray burst and possible subsequent relativistic jet of a Wolf-Rayet collapse, of 12,780 B.C.E. which, we now most certainly know, did in fact happen,' Tom remarked.

'What did you mean by *possible* relativistic jet Tom? So is there not always a relativistic jet?' Chad asked.

'No, it's a question of energy. Below a certain limit, say 10^{44} Joules, the jet collides with the surrounding gas and dust but just doesn't have enough energy to punch through, so there is only the long gamma ray burst *supernova*. Remember it's that impact with the gas and dust which generates the GRB *supernova* in the first place.'

'Aha, got it. So it's not possible to know if there will be a jet as well in advance.'

'Well, *we* can't make that prediction yet. In fact, we can't even predict when Wolf-Rayet stars will *collapse* yet. That is also the massive enigma about this site. There is a level of astrophysics expertise encoded into these buildings here, that we on Earth today still have not yet reached, and we don't find any record of that capability in the ancient record. That's the big elephant in the room!'

Andrés then spoke. 'Well done Tom and Chad. Your astrophysics approach has turned my hunch to more evidence. This successfully dates *Sechin Bajo* to before the date of the GRB that you described in your paper. So, you agree with me then, that *Sechin Bajo*'s at least 15,000 years old.

So that now drags the human record of civilization back to a substantial time before 13,000 B.C.E. since they would also have needed to become civilised into a cohesive society to develop construction expertise in order to build those marvellous structures.'

'This is quite a shocking revelation Andrés,' Chad murmured. 'Just when we were struggling to imagine how the peoples of the Earth coped with the surprise of the GRB and then the subsequent 880 years of survival some 3000 years later, this now strongly suggests that they were definitely *forewarned*! They knew it was coming! They were preparing for it. The next question is whether they anticipated that there would be a relativistic jet, or whether that was unknown?'

'Chad, I think I should emphasise here that *just preparing to survive a GRB* is actually a pretty formidable undertaking. We are not just talking about surviving 100 seconds of incredibly high potentially extinction-level radiation, we're talking about surviving some hundred or so years of a global rise in temperature of 10-15 degrees Celsius, followed by potentially thousands of years of *impact winter cooling*. Preparation for just the GRB also means building protective shelters and underground structures. More importantly, being warned of the precise date of the event is almost certainly impossible. Stars move relatively slowly and, I don't know of course, but I imagine that the pyramid layouts can only predict the event to an accuracy of say a hundred years. As I just said, this is already suggesting a level of astrophysics in Wolf-Rayet stellar collapse prediction which we simply just don't have yet. Added to that, the GRB would have devastated one side of the planet. The gamma ray burst would have sterilised seeds on that side of the planet, significantly diminishing food. We see that of course in the partial extinctions. Depending on the time of the year and the spin axis inclination of the Earth, ... wait a moment, we can find the date of the solstices. Bear with me.'

Tom ran through the movement of the Sun during the course of the year.

'OK, so the summer solstice was around March 24th in 12,780 B.C.E. above *Sechin Bajo*. That's pretty close to where the equinoxes are today.'

'Is that significant?' Chad asked.

'Yes, it tells us the hemisphere of the Earth which took the biggest hit. So in 12,780 B.C.E. with a southern summer solstice in late March, when the Earth was highest above the galactic plane. The southern hemisphere was tilted closest to the Sun, so the GRB hit side on, since it came from towards the galactic centre.'

'So what do we conclude from that?' Chad urged.

'We can conclude that from north to south, the Earth pretty much took an even hit at any time during the year. Had the solstices been like today, the southern hemisphere would have taken a bigger hit.'

'Interesting Tom,' Andrés remarked.

'It probably doesn't change much. Life on the far side of the Earth for those 100 seconds or so would have been safe. It would have been ideal had it struck with the Pacific Ocean dead centre because that's what Chad, 120° of longitude wide?'

'160° at its widest point, just north of the equator,' Chad confirmed.

'The worst news would have been hitting some 12 hours later when Europe, Africa and Asia were side on,' Tom concluded. 'It's probably possible to determine from pollen and nano particle deposits, maybe even from the partial megafauna extinctions.'

'Tom let me ask you something. If we are wondering if they could have known about the GRB, isn't there a way to communicate to warn of the GRB after it has happened and before it reaches the Earth? What about *quantum entanglement*? You told me that it involved entangling two photons of different spin states, 1 and 0, which could be split into two entangled photons, and wherein each entangled photon had both states until one was measured. When one entangled photon is measured, it immediately forces the spin state of the other photon into the other state. If you transmitted one of the pair of entangled photons as a continuous beam, and you found a means to store the other photons near the transmitter in some medium for years before measuring their states, and if you could *force* the stored photons into a particular state, you could communicate using *forced-state entangled photons*, and thus give advanced warning, using faster than light communications, ahead of the GRB.'

Tom smiled. 'Chad, you are alluding towards some distant advanced civilization warning the Earth. I don't subscribe to that; besides, you can't *force* the states, and even if you could, it would break the quantum entanglement. I'm afraid information can't be transmitted faster than the speed of light. That paradox often comes up on different online blogs. Sadly it won't work.'

'Oh, so it breaks the entanglement. Ah, that's a pity,' Chad murmured.

'Sorry Andrés, just a brotherly intellectual exchange,' Tom added.

'Gentlemen, I find these discussions extremely interesting. By the way, I'm still very excited having just seen your mapping of the *gamma Velorum* cluster to the pyramidal structures of *Sechin Bajo*. I have a few other places that need that confirmation. I just don't have your dexterity with that *Stellarium* program.'

'Andrés, I'm very happy to run you through it. It's pretty straightforward,' Tom replied sincerely.

'OK, so what else have we deduced Tom? If this marks out 12,780 B.C.E., or thereabouts, doesn't it tell us which star has vanished, and then additional dating information about some of the other pyramid sites?' Chad reasoned.

'How so?'

'Well, different sites mark out three pyramids, but they are not the *same three*. *Sechin Bajo* here marks out four pyramids in the configuration of 12,780 B.C.E. while *Shen Hsi* in China's Shaanxi Province, marks out four pyramids in 10,700 C.E. but we know one has gone. If we look at Giza, two of the pyramids correspond precisely to two of the stars in 10,700 C.E., but the third pyramid is a little bit too far out. Either they got the stellar separation wrong, or the third Giza pyramid marks out the star which collapsed. It might even suggest that the Giza pyramids were built before the collapse.'

'Persuasive hypothesis Chad, and that now also raises another issue. How accurate was their determination of stellar motion for each of the *gamma Velorum* stars? Actually, I think the *Shen Hsi* pyramid arrangement is very reassuring because, by including all four stars, it suggests the existence of four stars in *gamma Velorum* before the collapse. More importantly, it is suggesting the relative arrangement of four stars in 10,700 C.E. Did the builders of the *Shen Hsi* pyramids *not agree* which star was going to collapse, so they modelled all four, or did they create this site as a reference for our current analysis? I was also looking at the other sites: *Teotihuacan*, *Monte Alban*, and *Xochicalco*. Those sites are all spot on, mapping their pyramids to the remaining stars in *gamma Velorum* in 10,700 C.E., but *Tiwanaku* in Bolivia, just like *Giza*, is marking the third star a little too far out along the axial line.'

'Interesting deduction Tom,' Chad remarked. 'That might challenge that they had absolute expertise on prediction of stellar motion.'

'Unless it was a binary and they couldn't decide which of the two stars was going to collapse, of course. Wait a moment! That might be very significant! My God, if that is true, the only conclusion is that *all the pyramids* were built *before* the gamma ray burst arrived!'

'Wow Tom! That's brilliant thinking. So with knowledge of a future GRB and possible hypernova and relativistic jet coming this way, they already set the future civilization up with patterns of pyramids which they could eventually interpret...'

'For the brilliant mind of Tom to interpret,' Andrés added.

'Yes, indeed. It probably also suggests that they recognised that they had precision stone carving technology which may never be available to future civilizations after the GRB hit,' Chad concluded.

'So they saved a future civilization the trouble of reinventing the proverbial *stone-cutting* wheel, and did the work in advance,' Andrés added.

'They must have anticipated total devastation, a total loss of civilization and a return to a very primitive existence for thousands of years,' Chad reasoned. 'It all starts to become even clearer now!'

'It kind of suggests an explanation for the enigma of the *global* pyramid-building program. That's on a scale of three continents at least,' Tom replied.

'That makes sense of course if they were hedging their bets on where life would survive?' Chad suggested.

'Indeed, and we may need to park this in our subconscious for quite a time longer to distil out even more new ideas,' Tom replied.

'Well, Andrés, this new insight about when all the pyramids were built, is all down to your discovery of the significance of the Peruvian pyramid city of *Sechin Bajo*. To have a city on the Earth, whose pyramids mark out the star configuration of *gamma Velorum* in 12,780 B.C.E. which strongly suggests the city is at least 15,000 years old, is just incredible!'

Andrés paused for a moment, then he selected another image on his iPad. 'OK, so here is the next one. This is an ancient city in Mexico, complete with pyramids. It's still quite hidden in the jungle, even today.'

'Wow, the arrangement of the pyramids looks pretty similar to Sechin

Bajo,' Tom remarked. 'I think you most definitely have found another pre-*gamma ray burst* site. What's the name of this place?'

'It's called *Palenque*. So you agree with me that we might be able to date this settlement also to at least 13,000 B.C.E.' Andrés proposed.

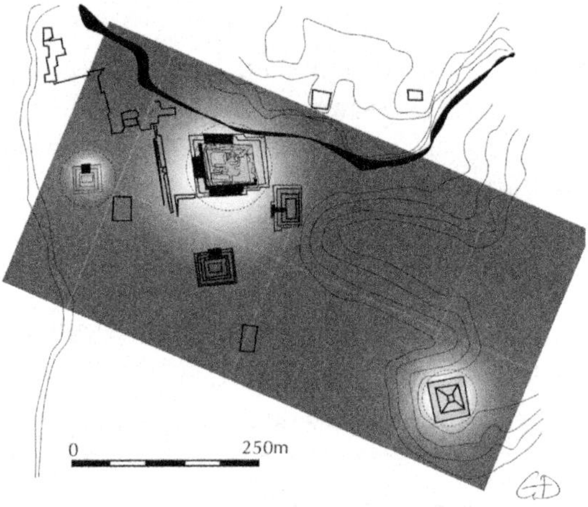

Palenque

'Indeed, most definitely!' Tom replied. 'One moment, I'll just download a detailed site plan. Here we are, *Palenque*! I'll paste it into a Word document. Now, a quick rotation and scaling of the *gamma Velorum* stars of 12,780 B.C.E. Spot on! You know, I'm sure people will go to these places in droves now, as soon as this story is out.'

'I have yet another!' Andrés replied. 'This is the ancient city of *Tenochtitlan*; the pyramids are also in the same configuration with the larger pyramid in the centre.'

'My goodness Andrés, this is fantastic! This evidence is stacking up and it drags our global civilization to well before 13,000 B.C.E.' Chad remarked.

Andrés was quite quiet for a little while, and then he spoke slowly.

'Tom and Chad, I still think you're eventually going to agree with me, that this story will never be published; not for a very long time at least!'

'Well, from what I experienced already from Carl Rhodes' reaction when we were in Japan last month, I am starting to believe you may be right.'

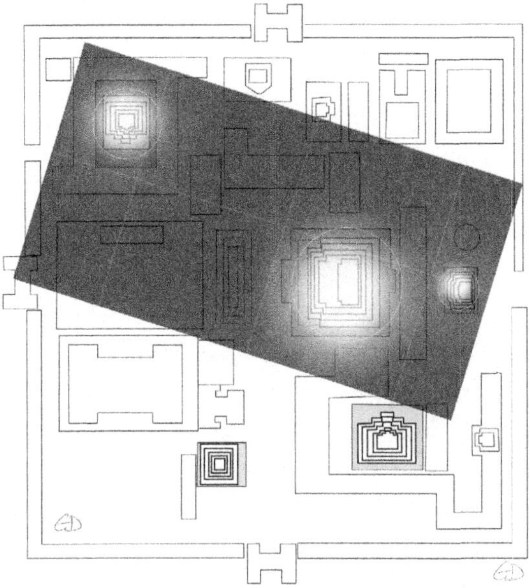

Tenochtitlan

'... And remember that your academic colleague Carl Rhodes was someone with whom you had worked for many years and knew very well. Just imagine the thousands of people out there who have written so many books about all manner of these myths and legends, and who have essentially carved their erroneous interpretations into the record of the Earth's history. I include here all the academic publications which have all been peer-reviewed by countless researchers, who continue to push and confirm the false narrative *ad nauseam*. Surely you can't possibly imagine that people will be allowed to take our conflicting interpretation seriously, despite the whole body of evidence that you, Chad and I have collected? Virtually every YouTube video out there on this subject is substantially in error, if the history supported by all this evidence would ever be allowed.'

'You are right of course Andrés,' Tom sighed.

'In addition, you must consider the advert-supported media platform that some of those *Ancient Aliens* researchers out there have. There are collectively *millions* of followers. With reputations to protect, it is highly likely that some may even delete their own videos of their previous conclusions, and run with a variant of your theory as their own, distorting and misrepresenting the data. Also don't forget the hard line *University professors of astrophysics* out there. Academic reputations are *hard won*, and they will fight *hammer and tongs* to kill this story. How could any of them admit that they had totally missed this completely? This evidence makes a credible case to tell the real history of our planet, but many academics have built their reputations on castles of sand which they will not want undermined. I also don't believe there will ever be a vast scourge of all the false data on the Internet?'

'You've certainly given this serious thought, Andrés,' Tom replied soberly.

'It's definitely something you will need to think long and hard about if you consider releasing this story into the public domain. But let's put that to the side for a moment. Now, I want to share with you some other pretty phenomenal discoveries I made in Egypt.'

Andrés opened one of the paper files on the table and pulled out some detailed drawings. 'Take a look at these images.'

'I recognise that. That's the Valley of the Kings in Luxor,' Chad remarked.

'Indeed it is. Now look first at this bed found in Tutankhamun's tomb. Look at these three golden images on the head board.'

'It looks like *Viracocha* from the Gate of the Sun in Tiwanaku,' Chad remarked.

'Yes and he has a snake coming from each side of his head, and is carrying a tray in each hand with three ankhs. That has to be something,' Tom added.

'It's definitely my view that something is just not right with the official narrative. Now look at this huge complex, known as *the tomb of Ramses II*, also in the Valley of the Kings. There are fifty or more rooms cut into the rock under the cliffs there. They call it the biggest tomb of all. They just don't have a clue, it is of course a shelter. Academics never consider how it was hewn out of the rock using some unknown ancient stone cutting technology. Moreover, it has the evidence of its purpose written all over it. Take a look at the wall art. Look, there are endless depictions of the Sun with a snake coming out at each side,' Andrés explained.

'That just has to be the two periods when the Earth is impacting the spiral of solar wind!' Tom exclaimed.

'Yes, but look closely. In this other image here, from KV 14, ... by the way that means tomb number 14 in the Kings' Valley . . . , which became the tomb of both *Tausert* and *Setnakht*, you can see a snake coming from the Sun. But here we see a large head on one side and a small tail on the other. I think that all these images are extremely precise. I was just wondering if there was an interpretation why the Earth passing through the spiral of solar wind would have two different intensities?'

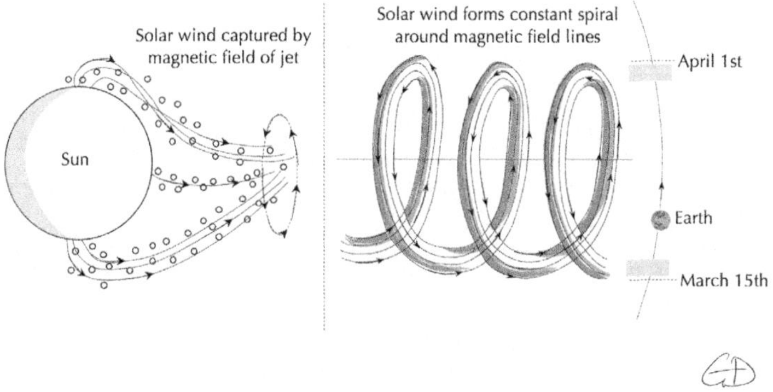

Spiral of Solar Wind

'Of course, it must be because of the geometry of the Earth Sun system! Wow, I think I can extend the astrophysics interpretation even further now. You ask such brilliant questions Andrés! The spiral of solar wind comprises a spiralling tube of high density solar wind with a less dense region inside. The Earth hits that dense wall of solar wind when it passes into and out of the spiral. This image must represent the Earth striking it at two different impact angles during the transit into and out of the spiral of solar wind. When it enters, the Earth is passing into the spiral tangentially, so it only takes one day. When it exits, it is travelling obliquely through the solar wind wall, so it lasts much longer, taking three days. The solar wind density would most likely be constant, but it is the tangential angle versus the oblique angle, relative to the solar wind spiral direction, which changes the impact duration and thus the danger to life,' Tom remarked excitedly. 'Since the magnetic field lines run in perpendicular circles around the jet, this now suggests the angle of the transiting relativistic jet, relative to the Solar System, much more precisely.'

'My goodness Tom, that's really remarkable how you are able to just extend the reasoning from the imagery in that way,' Chad replied.

'Andrés, you mentioned *Ra travelling through the underworld in his sun boat*? Do you possibly have any images of that, where he is surrounded by snakes?'

'Yes Tom, wait a moment,' Andrés replied, scrolling through the images on his iPad. 'Look, this is Ra on his sun boat with a blue serpent underneath being speared at the front and a vicious triple coiled tall serpent behind the boat.'

'Precisely, and that's exactly what we would expect to see if the Earth passes through the spiral first tangentially, taking only one day. The prow of the boat has a character fighting off just the head of the blue serpent, while ten of the serpent's coils pass under the boat. In contrast, the stern of the boat depicts an orange serpent with three coils. That one plus ten plus three adds up to fourteen: the fourteen days of hell, when people needed to take cover in caves or underground or in structures of rock.'

Ra on his Sun Boat with the Snakes

'I'll just do a quick calculation. It should be pretty easy to find a straight line transit of a constant thickness cylinder, where one crossing is about 3 times the length of the other. One moment.' After a short while, Tom's face took on a very serious look.

'Nope, this explanation just can't be right,' he murmured out loud. 'There isn't a solution for a constant diameter spiral. Right, so this can only mean one thing. The jet is such an unimaginably huge distance away and the solar system is so tiny in comparison that the solar wind spiral has not yet become homogeneous after one astronomical unit, i.e. at the Earth's orbit. This difference in transit times must mean that the solar wind is still in the form of a swirling sheath with a one day wide, dense leading edge and a three day wide, more tenuous trailing edge. It's pretty much getting there, but it's not yet in a perfect spiral. It also means that the solar wind intensity is three times higher when the Earth first enters the solar wind spiral compared to the exit transit. This deduction is certainly some new science!'

'Absolutely brilliant Tom!' Chad remarked. 'All this astrophysics is helping us decode the imagery. That image of *Ra not in his Sun boat* is also surrounded by hieroglyphs which now dates that entire frieze to 11,500 years ago. That surely also supports your hypothesis Andrés, that the *Rosetta Stone* carries an erroneous representation of what the original ancient hieroglyphs mean. It's just illogical to suggest that a hieroglyphic script dating back some 11,500 years would survive 8000 or so years so that it could be successfully translated into *Demotic* and *Ancient Greek*.'

'Good point Chad,' Andrés remarked. 'I have those images from our work on the *Rosetta Stone* here, one moment. Here you go. You can see quite clearly here, how poorly the hieroglyphs are scratched into the stone surface. Remember, the original hieroglyphs evolved from a culture of immaculate stone carving precision. The deterioration in hieroglyph quality strongly supported our proposition that translating the Rosetta Stone couldn't help decode the ancient wall carvings or the Pyramid Texts. For all the reasons I told you yesterday, a failing dynasty clinging to power sought to justify their entitlement by re-adopting the hieroglyphs as a symbol of their false heritage. With that political spin, they could re-purpose ancient buildings covered in hieroglyphic friezes and carvings, claiming they were the only ones who understood their meaning.'

He continued. 'This of course now brings us to the next insight. Despite what has been written in vast archives of libraries around the World, the hieroglyphic scripts in the extensive underground *shelters*, now erroneously called the *tombs* of the Valley of the Kings, is untranslatable based on that *pseudo* translator. By understanding what the images describe, we have proven without a shadow of a doubt, that all the imagery in the so called *tombs*, and the hieroglyphic texts around them, describe events which transpired some 11,500 years ago. That is surely why no one has been able to translate them.'

'Hey, why don't we try to crack some of these hieroglyphs?' Tom suddenly exclaimed excitedly. 'It's a totally blank canvas now. We should be able to make some progress. We understand the images and the devastating event which transpired for 880 years. The hieroglyphs must surely be pictograms which should be obvious for everyone to understand. We now understand that those bizarre hats represent images of the changing forms of the solar wind throughout the year. This is the next step.'

'What do you imagine they might be describing Tom?' Chad asked.

'Well we should assume they are warnings of not only when to be underground or in a shelter, but also have descriptions of say the physical atmospheric and meteorological effects and the dangers associated with the impacting solar wind,' Tom replied.

'Well I have many photos of walls from the Valley of the Kings in my paper archive here,' Andrés continued, spreading out a few papers over the table. 'If we're able to make any progress, this will all help. Take a look.'

They studied the images of hieroglyphs, searching for a clue.

'I have an idea for one. What about that hieroglyph for the *wasp* or *hornet* next to what looks like a *curving beam of fire*. Could that not refer to what was felt on the skin, the stinging pain from something in the air?' Chad suggested.

'I like it. That could most likely be describing *coronal discharge*,' Tom replied. 'You surely have heard the crackling of the high power transmission lines near the pylons in the rain. That's *coronal discharge*. It's not commonly understood, but it's an electrical discharge from any sharp object when the Earth's electrostatic field is high. Just imagine during those 14 days, the impact of the solar wind would have raised the Earth's atmospheric electrical field to unbelievably high levels, not just during the daytime but most probably through the evening and into the night. People passing sharp objects, such as the pointed branches of trees, would most likely experience electric shocks. That combination of the *wasp* and *fire arc* hieroglyphs seems a pretty good representation for me.'

'Well reasoned Tom. OK if we're thinking atmospheric phenomena, I think I may have one,' Andrés remarked. 'What about that *large foot*, next to an *arc* next to a *zigzag line*. If the zigzag line means water, then that arc might refer to lightning then that huge foot, stamping the ground, must be thunder. That combination of hieroglyphs is surely a *thunderstorm*!'

'Well, we expect torrential rain and endless thunderstorms during this horrendous period when the Earth is running the gauntlet through the solar wind spiral. People would be taking shelter in caves or dolmens, or underground,' Tom continued. 'The phenomenal impact of such a high density of solar wind particles with the Earth's atmosphere, would have caused phenomenal mixing and turbulence and brightly coloured aurorae, and endless coronal discharges and incessant thunderstorms. It's quite difficult for us to imagine the sheer extent of this impact. Remember that the Earth's magnetic field guides dangerous charged particles to the poles, but the magnetic field of the relativistic jet would have effectively cancelled the Earth's own surface magnetic field, and shortly after dawn until just before dusk, being outside in the sunlight would have been a death sentence! We cannot imagine what that was like, only that to simply stay alive, people needed to take refuge underground for the duration.'

'My goodness, this is actually working,' Chad remarked. 'We are translating the original hieroglyphs of 11,500 years ago. It would indeed be quite remarkable if we could finally work out what some of those friezes on the walls of those *shelters* in the Valley of the Kings are really saying. There's nothing wrong with repurposing the shelters as tombs some 7000 years later, but people today deserve to learn the real meaning of the wall art.'

'OK, take a look at this,' Andrés continued. 'I have been rethinking what the *ankh* represents. From what I sent you before, particularly from the derivation of the scene with Akhenaten and Nefertiti and the 18 flame-ending beams from the Sun. The two beams at each end carry an *ankh*. For me this suggests that the *ankh* actually means *warning*. The re-adoption of the ankh as a *symbol of life* is just wrong.'

'I agree entirely,' Chad confirmed. 'But 7000 years later, they had no understanding of what the friezes of Luxor were describing of course.'

'Precisely. Then we have the gazelle-headed *sceptre*, which is something that is found on many old coffins. Consequently, that surely must be associated with death. So by combining the *ankh* and the *sceptre*, we have a *warning of death*. The tall triangle with something inside most surely means *shelter*, while the *snake with the curved back* surely corresponds to the jet,' Andrés continued.

'And what about that hieroglyph for the crouching hare. Could it relate to that strange feline hare in that frieze scene with snake and the tree of life?' Chad remarked.

'I have the frieze scene here. It's a wall painting in Thebes in the *shelter* of Ramses IV,' Andrés added. 'And this blood painted here is what

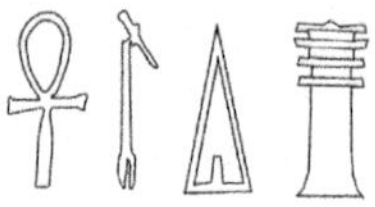

Warning of death, stay inside for 14 days

Thunderstorm

Coronal discharge and whirlwinds

Warning of sting of coronal discharge

Hieroglyph Meanings

I consider to be graffiti. All the wall paintings and the hieroglyphs are always very precise. Someone seems to have disfigured this image and added a crude splash of imprecise paint to signify blood, to change the meaning of what it really was painted for to symbolise.'

'Andrés, I agree with you. That odd hare creature does not seem to be attacking the snake, which is not writhing in pain as one would expect. Despite the *attack*, the snake just appears to smile as it impassively continues on by, past the *tree of life*. That hare is clearly holding out what looks like a symbol of fire towards the *tree of life*. I guess that the civilization, which emerged 6000 or so years later, just created pseudo-mythological stories just to try to make sense of the friezes, and made modifications to reinforce their narrative. They had absolutely no knowledge of the astrophysics of a relativistic jet and spiral of solar wind and the calamity that befell 30 generations of people who struggled to survive hell on Earth here every year!' Tom reasoned.

'Did you find anything hinting towards the true meaning in any of the mythological stories Andrés? Isn't it possible that despite a period of 6000 years, some convoluted aspects of the event remained,' Chad remarked.

'Well, I discovered that they called the snake *Apophis* or *Apep*, which they described was the embodiment of chaos. In the mythology, they describe that hare-like creature as *Ra* who is slaying the snake in the form

Hare Attacking Snake

of a cat. From the hieroglyphs we can assume it is a hare. Of course their interpretations were most likely made thousands of years after the event.'

'Did you translate any other hieroglyphs?' Chad asked.

'Well we can suggest that an upturned semicircle with the diameter above, might mean *below ground*, and with the diameter below, it might mean *above ground*. That all fits in with dangers to life and to be underground when this is going on,' Andrés explained. 'I was also looking at the cartouche containing a scarab beetle moving towards the Sun. I was thinking that it possibly means *you need protection in sunlight!*'

'That sounds pretty convincing. I like that. Does that bring us any further? We are still a long way off from a translation, but that is surely a good start,' Chad said encouragingly.

'I want to say one last thing here. We need to remember to separate the old wall friezes and the art found in the Valley of the Kings, from all the more recent papyrus art. There are definitely *two* versions of the hieroglyphic texts, the originals with their original meanings, and the *pseudo* adopted *fake-news* version which encodes according to the *Rosetta Stone*. While it is possible that some hieroglyphs share a common meaning, we cannot assume this. Consequently, we will need to consider them as totally different languages.'

'Good point Andrés,' Chad replied.

'Guys, I think I see something else!' Tom retorted. 'Look at those other Egyptian gods. One has that block structure, representing Sirius on its head. That is of course the goddess *Isis*. By the way they call that a throne on her head, but it looks remarkably similar to a digital field strength graphic of a high intensity reading. Let's put that aside for the moment. Now look at that other goddess *Nephthys*. On her head, she appears to be wearing the *upturned semicircle* which we suggest means underground, but under that, her block structure design is exactly the *inverse* of the Sirius representation. I propose that she represents the *absence of Sirius* in the sky, which we now understand happened just before the *Ides of March* on the 15th. I am now suggesting that each and every one of those figures, which were carved in stone, carry a significant number of warnings of what to heed and be aware of.'

'Great deduction Tom, and equally as compelling,' Andrés remarked.

'As I said, I think they each represent what is seen in the sky including both Sirius and the setting of Sirius. In those painted wall friezes from the Valley of the Kings, some characters are even painted with distinctive *black features* which I am now suggesting is encoding what was possibly seen *at night*.'

'Tom, this is great progress. What about that god with the two spiralling snakes alone, he has no Sun on his head. His name is *Khnum* I believe. Following your logic, how can that be explained?' Andrés enquired.

'Well the spirals are black, and he carries both the ankh and the sceptre meaning he is warning of death. As seen from the Earth, within the spiral of solar wind, the impact of the Earth with that enormous spiral could only ever be perceived as cutting through a *plane* of solar wind. While the Earth enters and exits the spiral wind over a 14 day period, it would not be possible to see the other walls of the spiralling solar wind sheath, they are too far away. It most likely suggests that the Earth is indeed passing close to the base wall of the cylinder of solar wind. So *Khnum* represents what is seen from the Earth at night during the danger period, while looking out into space.'

'So you have the hat from September 21st, the two curving hats from December and June, now the midnight hat during the danger period, and the two hats warning of when Sirius is in the sky and when it has just set,' Chad concluded.

'This is quite some substantial progress Tom,' Andrés remarked. 'By the way, if *Khnum* does represent the time when the Earth is transiting the solar wind spiral, then his hat suggests the two beams kind of join together.'

'That's right. Why do you emphasise that point?' Tom replied.

'Well, I have an unexplained etching taken from one of those buried Moai dug up on Easter Island. Here we are.'

Easter Island Moai showing Back

'Do you think that those curves represent the two sides of the spiral of solar wind from the Sun during the dangerous period? I also believe that the boats on the walls of the tomb, I mean *shelter* of Ramses V and VI, must also now represent the spiral of solar wind. Just look at the front and back ends of those *Ra* sun boats,' Andrés reasoned.

'I think you're absolutely right. Another compelling deduction, Andrés. Those images surely capture the absolute shape of what was seen in the sky. I have also seen boats on stone carvings in Sweden. They must also represent the solar wind. It would have been common knowledge for 880 years. Until now, people have never been able to explain why those boats look so strange,' Tom replied. 'I also think it's pretty compelling that there is such an over-abundance of four hieroglyphs: the *ankh* and the *sceptre*, with the *snake* and that *triangle* with a line inside. I totally agree with your hypothesis Andrés. They surely combine to mean *a danger to life from the jet so stay inside*.'

'Considering the atmospheric effects we now expect and how those people lived, we must deduce that other hieroglyphs are describing more images from the sky.'

'What do you mean by that Tom?' Andrés asked.

'Well, from all the artwork we see in the *shelters* in the Valley of the Kings, the Sun is always shown as an orange ball, and often a little flattened. That is no coincidence. That is what the Sun looks like at sunrise and sunset when it is distorted by the atmosphere. The intense levels of ultraviolet would have made it extremely dangerous to see the Sun at any other times. For 30 generations, the Sun was seen to be a flattened orange ball, for those who were not blind yet.'

'You are managing to eke out some really persuasive conclusions about what is in the artwork Tom,' Chad remarked.

'Also think about the atmosphere. Ozone, O3, is produced from oxygen O2 in an equilibrium reaction in reaction to the amounts of highest energy ultraviolet light hitting the atmosphere. There are three UV bands, of increasing energy termed UV-A, UV-B, and UV-C. The higher energy UV-C is all absorbed high up in the atmosphere and only a tiny fraction of the dangerous UV-B reaches the ground, but UV-B in high doses is also dangerous. The body produces vitamin D in response to a short exposure to ultraviolet per day, principally UV-B, but just imagine what happened to humans without that possibility, when exposure during the day was terribly dangerous. The analogy is that we wouldn't choose to warm our hands around a steel-foundry blast furnace. There would have been a biological natural selection for humans to develop either very dark skins to protect against UV or much lighter skins to metabolise vitamin D in low light levels of course. People with very dark or very light skins just lived longer.'

'Moreover, we should never underestimate the importance of vitamin

D. Even today, whenever there is an epidemic, despite the basic science of vitamin D enhancing the immune system, governments just fail to teach the importance of what we learned about basic biology when we were at school. Vitamin D produced by the body in sunlight helps us overcome viruses. In northern climates it will be people with darker skins who will metabolise much less vitamin D. People who, for religious reasons, cover their bodies in clothing will hardly metabolise any. Vitamin D dissolves in fat and thus obese people will just store a large amount of any they produce. It is also well-documented that high fructose corn syrup, which is present in many sweet drinks and processed foods, actually deactivates vitamin D, rendering it totally ineffective! This puts all these three categories of people at serious risk during a worldwide epidemic. It goes without saying that those people staying indoors, such as the elderly in care homes, will also have a significantly increased risk of death from an epidemic. If only they could be encouraged to sit outside in the sunlight in swimming shorts and bikinis for an hour a day, sunning themselves. In spite of many studies, such as one I read recently from Indonesia, governments are often too embarrassed to share an inconvenient scientific truth which they all missed.'

'So Tom, how do we imagine things were different back then? Are you saying that the radiation levels were just at a much higher level?' Andrés asked.

'Precisely, and particularly dangerous at ground level for all manner of cancers due to the greater intensity of UV-B. But UV-A also produces *indirect DNA damage* to the body from production of high concentrations of hydroxyls and free radicals in the body. Most importantly, UV-B is terribly damaging for the retina, cornea and the lens.'

'So people and, more importantly, the animals went blind,' Andrés concluded.

'Indeed, so protecting the animals from intense UV was also of paramount importance,' Tom replied. 'Plants however, do really great in intense UV, so the Earth's vegetation would have been luscious and abundant for the duration, although without any thick protection over the skin, people would have been excluded and forced to hide in their caves and shelters.'

'So effectively a serpentine jet prevented unclothed people from venturing out into the lush vegetation to gather food during daytime,' Andrés added. 'That story starts to sound vaguely familiar. You know, a good friend of mine, Carlos Fijo recently told me that eating citrus fruits can cause hyper-sensitivity to light. Just maybe this might mean that certain fruits were strictly forbidden for health reasons also!'

Saqqara Tomb

'I have other images here from the *shelter* of Ramses V and VI in Thebes, and most recently from a new tomb discovered near Saqqara. These show many images of animals and food. We can take a quick look at those if you're interested, many of them identify 14 days. Some identify animals, which I believe is when animals must be cared for. I have also been looking at our own culture, in which I have found some residual messages,' Andrés explained.

Tom, Chad and Andrés carried on discussing the different Valley of the Kings wall art for some time. Each set of friezes were all variations on the same theme warning when to take shelter from violent thunderstorms, coronal discharge, with emphasis on storing food and some suggesting caring for animals. The number 14 was everywhere, further confirming the duration of the Earth's transit through the solar wind.

Then came a shock. Andrés reached into a folder and pulled out a single image and laid it onto the table. He didn't say anything but just waited for Tom's and Chad's reaction.

'You are kidding!' Tom remarked.

'You have cracked this? The *Nazca lines of Peru*?' Chad added in great surprise.

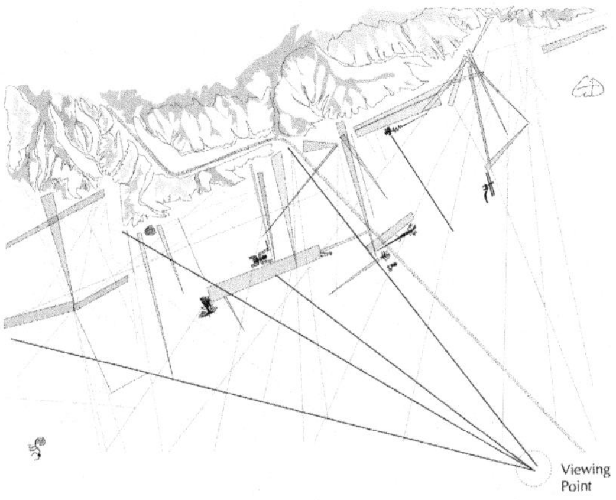

Nazca Geo-lines

'Well this is a different project and I haven't completed the work yet. Nevertheless, after our long discussions yesterday, I got a totally new insight and I am now proposing that these animal petroglyphs on the desert floor are asterisms of the night sky. I'm hoping that you can verify if my hunch is correct. You see those long rectangles in the desert. I believe that they represent different segments of the Milky Way band. Also, during the course of the night, that dense band of stars rotates. I will hazard a guess that each of those long angular lines which seems to converge at a viewing point, represents the geometry of how the horizon cuts through the band of the Milky Way as it rises above the horizon. Can we check that hunch?'

'Sure, that sounds very convincing. I can check that right away,' Tom replied.

'I want to add, that since this is open windswept desert, I actually don't believe that the Nazca lines date back even a few thousand years. I do think it would be interesting though, to try to find the animal asterisms near to the band of the Milky Way, then check the angle of the band relative to the horizon lines. There are three possible groups of people who could have constructed them. If we can accurately date them, we will have discovered once and for all which group constructed them. I have this map here, which a friend of mine created from Google Earth. I have added quite a few of the petroglyphs.'

Tom took his laptop and downloaded the Nazca line image of the monkey with a curled tail. He traced the outline and created a transparent shape of the potential asterism. So what time period would they choose?

'You know what? Let's start with our usual date of 9750 B.C.E. If we don't find anything, we can move the date forward,' Chad suggested.

'I'm good with that,' Tom replied.

Together they looked on, searching for the potential monkey asterism, as Tom slowly dragged the ancient night sky above Nazca across the screen

'There, Tom!' Chad remarked. 'The monkey's spiral tail surely wraps around that nebula!'

After a little rescaling, the monkey with its agile pose fitted the stars quite convincingly.

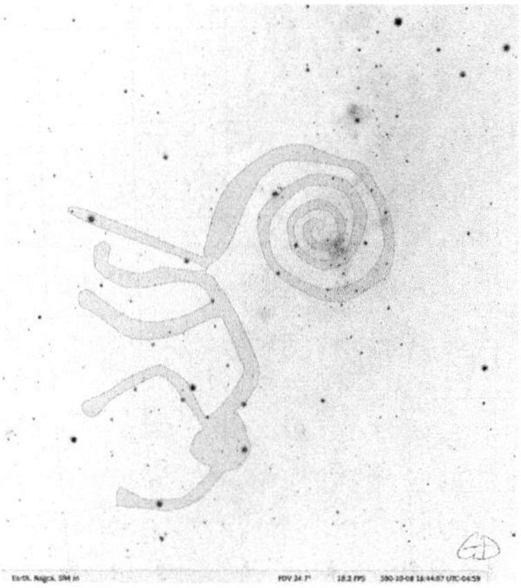

Nazca Monkey

'That's interesting also. The tail is wrapping around the Great Carina Nebula. Let's try another,' Tom remarked.

Following the same procedure, Tom created the zigzag body of the Nazca long-tailed dragonfly. It was directly below a rectangle on the desert floor.

'If your hunch is right Andrés, this dragonfly should be just *below* the Milky Way band.'

Sure enough, after discussing several potential star groups, they settled on a very promising set of stars. After pasting the night sky as the background picture, and scaling the semi-transparent dragonfly shape a little, it really matched the stars well.

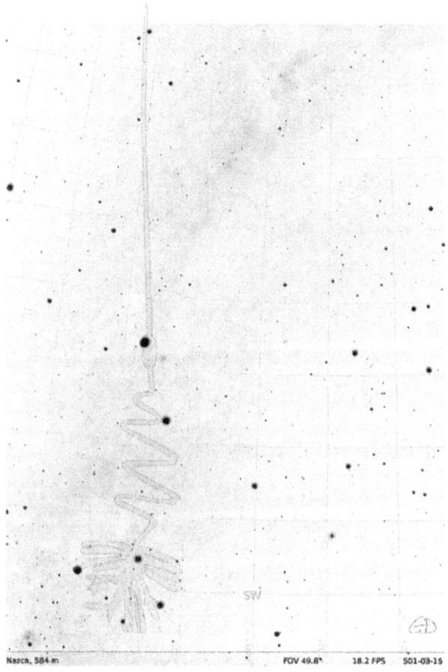

Nazca Dragonfly

'One more maybe?' Tom suggested.

'Try that spider with the extended leg, above the Milky Way band,' Chad suggested. 'I just spotted a prospective collection of stars already.'

Tom again created a semi-transparent shape of the spider, and within a relatively short time, had matched it to a very convincing collection of stars.

'OK, now comes the dating exercise. We need to check those long angular lines impacting each rectangle. If you are right Andrés, we can date the glyphs by matching that acute angle with the angle of the Milky Way band as it crosses the horizon.'

After checking the angle of the Milky Way with the horizon, it was abundantly clear that the angle in 9750 B.C.E. was not acute, but substantially greater than 90°.

'OK, so that now certainly proves these lines and petroglyphs date from a significantly later time. I'll try 2000 B.C.E. to see how that horizon line is changing.'

Tom then advanced the date, but the angle was still not acute enough. Finally, as he approached 500 C.E. the angle looked spot on.

'There you go Andrés; your hunch was right. This is actually another important mystery solved. No one has ever managed to date the Nazca lines before. Your hunch has helped us determine that they date from around 500 C.E. Well done! This is a first,' Tom added excitedly.

'You know, I'm starting to wonder what people will do to pass their time, now that all the hype about Nazca can be dispelled with,' Chad added.

'Well, I have been struggling to crack this for years. This has been one of the remaining big puzzles on my bucket list. I am happy that you agree with my suggestion,' Andrés replied .

A soft breeze was blowing through the cloud forest canopy. The shrieks of the Howler monkeys had become much more sporadic now and the forest was alive with new sounds of birdsong. Chad then stood up. 'We have a present for you Andrés. Something from Japan. One moment.'

In a short while he returned, bringing an exquisitely wrapped box. 'We were pretty sure that you don't have one of these. Please.' Chad handed the present to Andrés.

Andrés removed the wrapping paper. It was a bottle of *habushu awamori*.

'My god! A snake in a bottle! What an amazing idea!'

'It's a habu pit viper. Our Japanese friend, Takashi, told us that this distilled rice liquor brings strength and vitality to men,' Tom added.

'Despite it being so early, we must have a toast. There is still the answer to that one big question that I want you both to reach a conclusion on. I'll get the glasses.'

Andrés returned in a short while with three stylish green glasses. 'You know what these are maybe?'

'I do. That's uranium glass. It glows bright green in ultra violet light! I have a UV fob on my key ring to check authenticity of labels,' Chad replied. He shone the UV light at the glass but there was no discernible effect, it was too light of course to see any change.

'Well, the UV is quite high up here, but they only really glow when it's dark. These glasses are very old. They date from 1835 and come from

Spain. They were a retirement present for my grandfather. He worked pioneering the development of the railroad in Argentina. He was born in *Bahia Blanca*. His parents, my great grandparents, were actually originally both from Costa Rica.'

'So you're finally home again, well your ancestors' genes at least,' Tom added with a smile.

'I guess I feel that way also,' Andrés replied.

The habu viper in the bottle was coiled and somehow it was poised with its head held back and mouth wide open, bearing its fangs. Andrés poured out the liquor.

'Whenever I have the opportunity to use these glasses, I do. It makes me think of my father and grandfather. They led very tough lives. Now a toast to us.'

Andrés motioned towards Tom and Chad to take a glass. He lifted his, holding it out towards them. '*Aunque la noche es oscura y el camino es estrecho y empinado… ¡Amigos míos, no es nada para nosotros! Salud!*'

'*Salud!*' Tom and Chad both replied in unison. They knocked the liquor back in one.

'Really interesting flavour!' Andrés remarked. 'Let's get another ready,' he added, reaching for the bottle.

'I think I got that, something about the night being dark, and the road narrow and steep, but it's nothing for us, right?' Tom asked.

'Well done Tom, your Spanish is improving! But now I must come back to that big question. I won't let you leave here without you having reached a resolution. As I've told you many times, I don't believe the World will ever be ready to hear this new history, and please trust my judgement on this, millions continue trying to make sense of all these conundrums for years. Every man and his dog continue to come up with more bizarre hypotheses about aliens or the pyramids and how someone ran off with half the missing monoliths from Stonehenge, despite some of them weighing up to 30 tons. Being faced with a sobering reality is a shock. People just prefer the safety of *cloud cuckoo land*. More seriously, together we have cut a single track right through the deepest densest jungle and singlehandedly, we have discovered the lost hidden city of *El Dorado* and now we're the only ones who know it really exists! My suggestion is that we enjoy what we've found, we burn our gear, bury our

Land Rover, and walk out, back the way we came, then make a pledge never to say a word.'

'That was just a metaphor there right? About *El Dorado?*' Chad asked curiously.

'I have the GPS coordinates, I have drawn all the maps, I have staked the whole lost city . . . it's actually not very far from here!'

'You found *El Dorado* Andrés?' Chad remarked astoundingly.

'Chad, sorry that was indeed just a metaphor,' Andrés replied, laughing. 'I couldn't resist, but your insinuation is right, there isn't much more left to be discovered now. We can always put that on our next list.'

'Understood. You almost had me there.' Chad sighed deeply.

'Good one Andrés. But are you really saying, despite everything, despite all the credible and compelling evidence, it needs to just remain our secret?' Tom asked, in a subdued voice. 'Why is this story so unpublishable? I guess your story about dating the Nazca lines is possibly distinctly different.'

'Well, even that could be related. There are other lines and other viewing points and multiple representations of Milky Way rectangles and horizon lines. The civilizations of Earth became *sky watchers* for a reason. The wind blowing across the Nazca Desert may have shifted sand over the millennia, which now hides some other really ancient asterisms.'

'You know, I think our discussions may also have suggested an explanation for at least two other enigmas I found. You mentioned the Moai statues and how they map to a band in the Milky Way. I'm now thinking of the *Olmec heads*. You know the ones in central Mexico near *La Venta*. People think that they depict the faces of the early inhabitants there, but those faces don't match the indigenous peoples at all. Those heads are also pretty much identical. What if they also map to an asterism Tom?'

'Interesting suggestion Andrés,' Tom remarked. 'We can certainly take a look.'

Tom downloaded a photo of an *Olmec head* and then traced the features using Word. Next he opened *Stellarium*, and selected the night skies over Mexico, this time back in 12,780 B.C.E.

'Since all the central Mexico sites near La Venta seem to identify the date of the GRB, just maybe we should start there,' he murmured. 'OK, now let's try to find something.'

Olmec Head

Just as before, he slowly scrolled across the skies above ancient Mexico, some 14,800 years ago. The very round features of the Olmec head were very distinct. The head was almost spherical and there seemed to be some kind of helmet on its head. Were there any spherical star asterisms? It didn't seem likely.

'Tom, what about a cluster of stars or a nebula?' Chad suggested.

'We can try that,' Tom replied. '*Stellarium* classifies those as *deep sky objects* and they are pretty much invisible without a powerful telescope.' He activated the deep sky objects and then selected the Milky Way band and zoomed in further to examine each of the bright pink regions in turn.

'There Tom, what about that one?' Andrés exclaimed. 'That nebula looks pretty spherical.'

'Well spotted. One moment, I need to rotate it. My god! Look at that! We've found it already. That includes the famous *Elephant's Trunk Nebula* in the constellation of Cepheus. That is just impossible to see without a telescope!'

'So why have they identified that? Is there anything significant within that collection of stars?' Chad asked.

'One moment, I'll just confirm the Olmec head mapping.'

Tom took a screenshot of the entire formation and set it as the background picture behind his, now semi-transparent, *Olmec head* outline. After a small amount of scaling the match was uncanny.

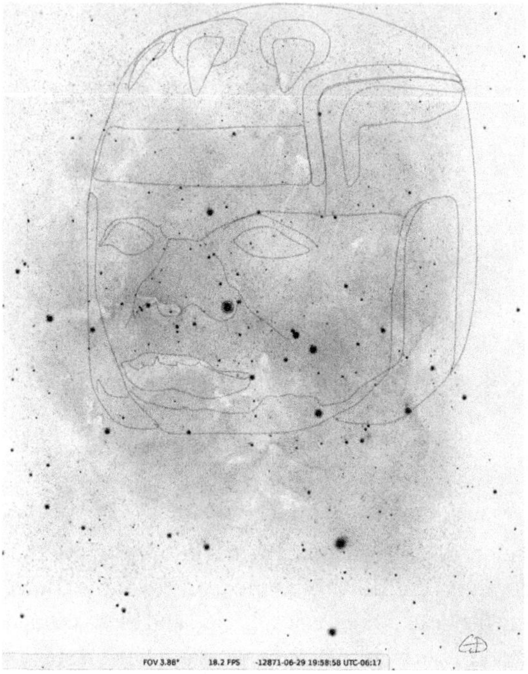

Olmec Star Mapping

'So we've definitely found it!' Andrés remarked.

'Well done Tom,' Chad added.

'Another team effort guys. OK, checking the data here, so this is a very large *ionised-gas region* called IC 1396 and an open cluster of around 250 young stars. It contains perhaps 20 or more *dark nebulae* as well as many stars of course. Before you ask, *dark nebulae* are vast clouds of gas and dust which will eventually collapse to form stars.'

'So this is a *star-forming* region?' Chad suggested.

'Indeed,' Tom confirmed.

'How far away is it Tom? Is it close?' Andrés asked.

'Ha-ha, it was,' Tom chuckled. 'But I now see that in the latest *Hipparcos* astrometric survey, they have revised the distance to that collection of nebulae from 1173 light years to around 1976 light years.'

'So what is significant about that open cluster Tom?' Andrés asked.

'Mm, well I guess we need to ask why that region of space is so bright. One star must be illuminating that entire region of space. OK, I've found it, it's HD 206267. That star is a very fast-spinning, massive blue binary system! It's what we call a *spectroscopic binary*, which means a spectroscope was used to detect the doppler shift of the spectra and resolve the two stars. In fact, it's actually a *triple* star system with the third star orbiting the binary some way out, where the binary and the third star all orbit the *centre of mass* of the system. The special thing, for any aspiring astrophysicists out there, is that typically we expect stars to form from *collapsing cold clouds*, but that binary system is emitting a very high speed stellar wind of some 3225 km/s. It's actually creating a *shock front* which can *induce* stellar formation. Just by comparison, the solar wind from our Sun is, on average, travelling at around 400 km/s.'

'But Tom, is it dangerous?' Chad urged.

'Very dangerous! Particularly locally, since it's stripping protoplanetary disks from nearby stars, so those stars won't form any planets.'

'So are you concluding that it will supernova sometime soon?' Andrés asked.

'That is always the fate of all large massive blue stars. It may even *hypernova*, and that is most probably why an ancient hi-tech civilization has carved the signature of that cluster in stone so that their message has survived 15,000 or more years to reach us!' Tom added soberly. 'These kinds of stars only have a lifetime of a million years max and it's probably almost off the main sequence now.'

'There is one more complex aspect to these Olmec heads which may be significant. The faces are very similar, but the helmets and facial markings have differences. We know that these deep sky objects comprise expanding clouds of gas and dust which change over time. I am starting to think that different Olmec heads may represent the evolving shapes of the expanding nebula, portraying what it may look like at different dates in the future. That adds a highly technical twist to the story if this proves to be true!'

'Well done Tom and thanks for that explanation,' Andrés remarked. 'You know, we really should set some time aside to discuss a little more about the previous hi-tech civilization which we're suggesting built everything before the gamma ray burst, but first I want you to see this. This is the *Tomb of Darius*, some 12km northwest of Persepolis in Iran. Surely we now agree that this also has all the hallmarks of a warning to take cover from 14 days of hell. Each of the nearby structures in the cliff walls there comprises a deep rock-cut shelter.'

Tomb of Darius

'Interesting Andrés. Yeah, look,' Chad replied enthusiastically. 'There are 14 people in each row and that block on the short platform to the right has 14 vertical bands.'

'I see something else,' Tom added. 'The guy on the left is on a longer platform, compared to the short platform on the right. I'll hazard a guess and suggest that this represents the two deadly transit periods into and out of the spiral of solar wind. The Earth was on a tangential path as it crossed into the spiral, taking only one day. It exited taking three days. We saw that in the *shelter* of Ramesses VI, represented as a first single snake head rearing up before the boat, and three snake coils behind it, in the frieze of *Ra not on his Sun-boat*. You know, this is the first time I've seen these entry and exit transit-durations carved so clearly in stone. Of course, as I said earlier, this might be indicative of a non-symmetrical structure of the spiralling wind tunnel, with two different densities. That requires some serious modelling.'

While he was talking, Tom was also using his *Stellarium* program again. 'There you go guys! You see that? That's the asterism which maps to the *flying bearded man* above Persepolis in 9750 B.C.E. So Andrés, what else do you have for us?' Tom asked eagerly.

'Well, I have a study of petroglyph symbols and stone circles from a field trip that John Mann went on, in the southern part of Sweden.'

Andrés opened out a large scale drawing of the long, boat-like stone formation. 'Here we are. This is *Ales Stenar* in the far south-eastern corner of Sweden in Skåne, on the Baltic coast. It would be really good if we can check if this also maps to the danger period of 11,500 years ago.'

'It certainly looks like a contender, let's take a look,' Tom remarked. 'So, from that table of data in the corner of the image it says there are 57 stones in the elliptical ring. The stone at either end is around 2.5 metres tall, so most likely those stones played a key part. I see there's, what seems to be, a small alignment stone added beyond the southern end, and a single notched stone within the formation at the northern end.'

'The location is optimum of course,' Chad remarked. 'It's perfectly situated, high up on a coastal promontory, looking out towards the sharp southern marine horizon, the ideal place for determining the exact direction of the rising and setting sun during the danger period. It does look like a very permanent structure though. Is there any movable element which can be slowly adjusted over the 880 years of the jet transit, as the sunrise direction gradually changes?'

'There's that small stone beyond the formation, but that notched stone, just off-axis in the middle, surely played some part,' Tom remarked. 'I'll just get the angles for 8870 B.C.E. That's the last time this formation would have been used.'

Using *Stellarium* he then determined the sunrise and sunset times for March 15th and April 1st in 8870 B.C.E.

'I'll plot them now. It's difficult to know where the single viewing point was for sunrise, but it was most probably beside the tall northern end-stone. Look, the sunset directions match the gap in the stones mid-way on the seaward side, and I'll suggest that there was a viewing point, probably marked by a stone in the ground. Whether that's still there would require a trip I guess. There you go. I think that's pretty convincing.'

'We can never know what that notch was used for on that off-axis stone within the stone circle, but couldn't it have supported a structure when in use?' Chad suggested.

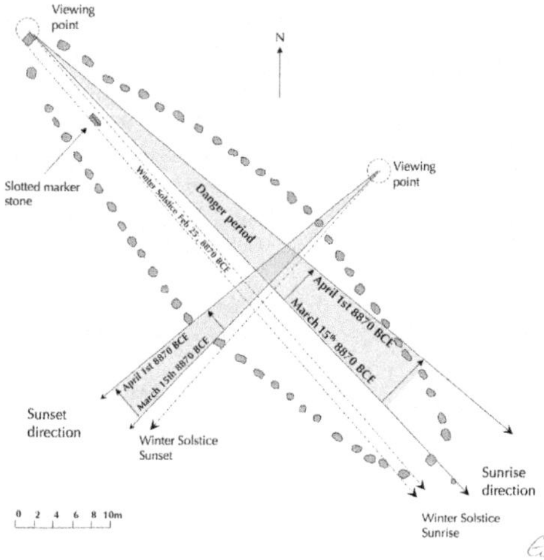

Ales Stenar

'It's possible of course. We can never prove anything absolutely. It's the same with all these sites around the World. A single event in Earth's history explains most of the features of all these sites but there is still so much more to interpret legitimately. I'm now pretty convinced that *Ales Stenar* maps well to the sunrise and sunset times of the danger period in 8870 B.C.E., when it was last in use. How this structure was actually adjusted over the 880 years of its use from 9750 B.C.E. may remain a mystery for many years to come. How about you guys?' Tom enquired.

'I concur Tom,' Andrés replied. 'It will of course be another uphill struggle to convince those academics who came up with their ridiculous *Viking boat burial* conclusion. Look there, John has added the published data, which states that archaeologists carbon dated the site to 1400 C.E. based on material found within it.'

'John has also added several notes at the bottom: *found a spiral on the large red stone, coastal side, 3 stones from northern head stone*. Well that's pretty conclusive!' Chad remarked, looking through the rest of the hand written comments. 'He also says here that he saw many fields in southern Sweden with big piles of rocks heaped up in the middle. That surely suggests that many stone circles were simply dismantled over the centuries by the subsequent farmers, who just needed to clear their fields. That might explain of course, why we don't see stone circles in many places today. They would surely have been built wherever there were population centres. As to your comment about the 1400 C.E. date Andrés, it's a pity, but other than determining the age of the formation and subsequent weathering estimates, we actually can't date stone very precisely.'

'Tom, there's another Swedish stone formation that John found somewhere here. I think it's one of the largest in Sweden. There are around 128 stones still standing from an original count of some 200. Here it is, the Fjärås Li Gravfält. That Swedish word means graveyard, but it isn't one of those of course.'

'That looks interesting Andrés. Where's it situated?'

'It's written here. Yep, some 40km south of Gothenburg. From this sketch it seems to be spread a few hundred metres along a steep rise, overlooking a vast open plain to the west. That slope seems to extend upwards around 120m. It's just amazing how many of these sites are still around, and until now, no one has ever understood what they were built for.'

'Well let's have a crack at decoding this site also Tom,' Chad urged.

'OK, I just need to set the location a bit further north on Stellarium and find the 8870 B.C.E. sunrise and sunset angles for Fjärås.'

Within a short time, Tom had determined the sunrise and sunset angles for March 15th and April 1st, as well as the winter and summer solstice directions. He then downloaded a Google Earth image of the site, and proceeded as before, to attempt to map the pairs of sunrise and sunset angles onto the lines of stones. Very soon, he found the distinct alignments, but there was something more. Several key lines of larger stones seemed to be converging from different directions towards a point slightly outside the formation. Even the equinox line went right through that point!

'I think we are about to make a prediction. These lines must surely be converging towards a key viewing point!'

'It could be a viewing stone. Maybe it's flat, buried in the ground at that point,' Chad remarked.

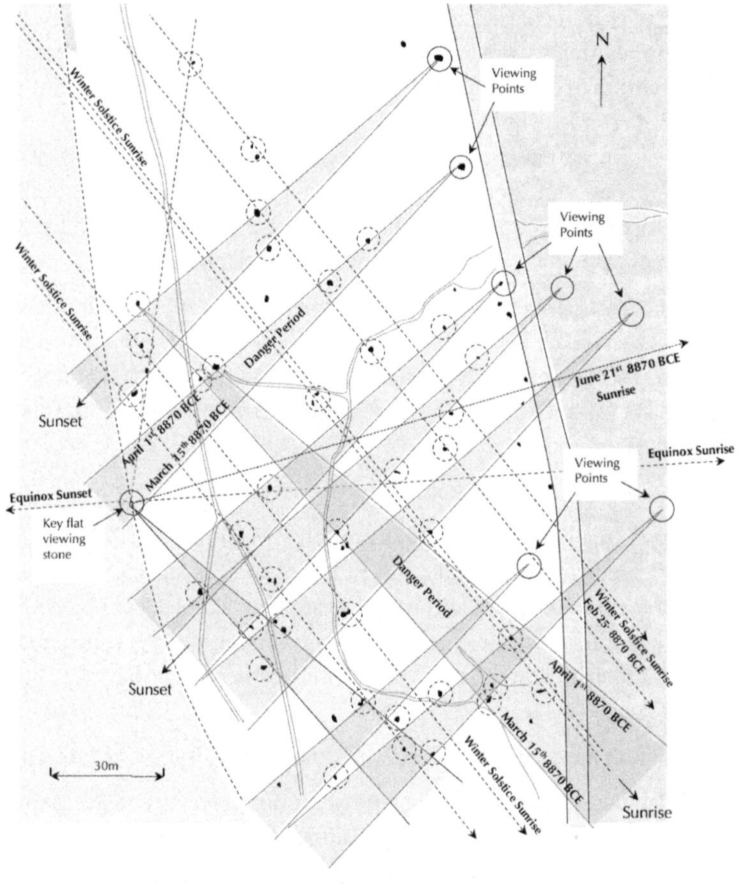

Fjärås sunrise/sunset observatory near Kungsbacka Sweden

Tom zoomed in using Google Earth, and sure enough, there it was. This was utterly remarkable. This was a first. The analysis had predicted the existence of a key critical stone in the formation, and they had discovered it. This was surely the first supporting evidence strongly suggesting that these sites were definitely built as calendar tracking sites between 9750 and 8870 B.C.E. When you predict the existence of something, then find what you predicted, that is pretty strong proof of a hypothesis!

'Andrés, you just mentioned that John had seen piles of stones heaped in the middle of farmer's fields, who were clearing them. I start to have a concern. That stone is right on the edge of a field. Let's now hope that the most critical viewing stone for that site, doesn't get inadvertently moved by an eager farmer!'

'We could always write to the people supervising the site at Fjärås,' Andrés suggested.

'Good idea. We should do that right away, you know,' Chad added.

'Indeed,' Tom confirmed. 'You know it's truly shocking how we're able to make so many connections between all these ancient sites. One thing, however, is becoming quite humbling and sobering. The complexity of these sites demonstrates how capable and intelligent our ancient ancestors of 11,770 years ago really were. They clearly possessed remarkable technical and organisational skills which enabled them to plan and construct these vast calendar sites, and then to keep them in operation for 880 years. And then just think how incredibly arduous staying alive must have been. Every year, people needing to live underground for 15 days or so. It's just so horrendous to imagine.'

The conversation then suddenly paused as each of them tried to grasp the severity of what life must have been like: the sheer vulnerability of the peoples of Earth, as everyone struggled to stay alive as the Earth ran the terrifying gauntlet on its 15 day passage through the solar wind. It was quite some time before Tom eventually sighed deeply, shook his head slowly, and then continued.

'Before I forget guys, and on a very different tack, I've also been wondering about another symbol from ancient Egypt, the *Eye of Horus*. Surely we agree that this must represent a key signature of some part of the story.'

'Are you also thinking asterism Tom,' Chad replied.

'Well, that's my most likely suggestion. We should at least give it a shot,' Tom suggested.

'Well guys, I believe that Mustapha and John Mann created quite a comprehensive archive of images. In my view, the best example of the *Eye of Horus* is an intricate detailed piece of jewellery found in the *tomb* of Tutankhamun, which seems to possess all the key parts of the story, *a spiral, a snake, a hat with the two solar wind spirals*. There's also a bird flapping its colourful wings. I have the material somewhere here, one moment,' Andrés explained, now scrolling through the images on his iPad. 'Yes, here we are.'

'It kind of strikes me as really odd that the *Eye of Horus* possesses all those aspects of the event,' Chad remarked. 'The focal point is of course the eye. Why don't we just check the obvious first and attempt a mapping directly to the star field around *gamma Velorum*?'

'OK, sounds like a good guess,' Tom confirmed. 'Andrés, can you email me that image?'

'Sure,' Andrés replied.

A soft ping announced the arrival of the image in Tom's *inbox*, and he then deftly copy-pasted it into a Word document, and traced the key features. Next, using *Stellarium*, he searched for *gamma Velorum* in the night skies above Egypt in 9,750 B.C.E. Suddenly they got the biggest of surprises. The bright *Golden Earring cluster* NGC 2547 directly below the hypernova culprit, was now suggesting an obvious orientation for the asterism mapping.

'Wow Tom! Look at that. I think I already see the basic elements of the jewellery! It surely must be a match!' Chad exclaimed.

'Golly, I think you're right! That was a lucky guess Chad!' Tom then took a screen shot of a rectangle of sky around *gamma Velorum*. After overlaying it with a semi-transparent image of the Eye of Horus jewellery, then rescaling and rotating it a little, the asterism mapping was complete. 'There you go. That's a pretty good match. So we now know what the *Eye of Horus* represents!'

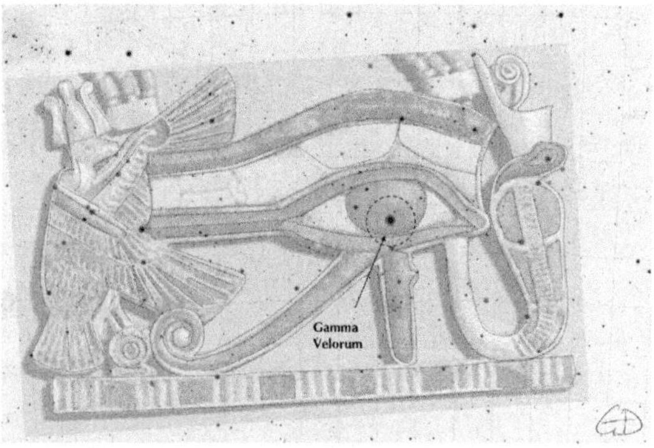

Eye of Horus Star Mapping

'You're definitely getting really good at this Tom,' Andrés added. 'You know, that bird on the jewellery has all those same bright colours which they always use on many of the other large bird images in the Valley of the Kings wall art. They consistently paint its feathers with dark blue, lime green and orange-red colouring. Surely there has to be a very good explanation why they always use those colours.'

'Of course! I now know what it is, Andrés,' Tom retorted with some excitement. 'That has also been troubling me for quite some time. Now I realise that they're the principle colours one sees from the excessive ionisation from the upper atmosphere. They're the same colours used in images of the Rainbow Serpent of the Australian indigenous peoples, and images of the Feathered Serpent of Mesoamerica. We know this from camera recordings of the *aurorae borealis* and *aurorae australis* today. The mechanism is well understood. Oxygen and nitrogen in the upper atmosphere get ionised and their recombination energies emit blue, green, and red light in those shades! The solar wind ionises *diatomic nitrogen* causing it to emit a *light blue photon*, the lost electron then collides with *monatomic oxygen* exciting it, causing it to emit a *lemon-green photon* when it de-excites. Our eyes perceive this combination of colours as *lime green*. The *ionized N2 nitrogen molecule* also gets excited by solar wind, emitting a *deep blue photon*. In the upper atmosphere, there is little nitrogen, and *monatomic oxygen* is excited by the solar wind particles directly, producing a *red photon*.'

'Is that what we generally see today?' Chad reasoned, 'I thought aurorae were mostly green?'

'Exactly, which is why this has to be the explanation. The red colour from excited monatomic oxygen only occurs at altitudes above 100km where there are very few atoms. The red colour is only ever seen *during intense geomagnetic storms* when enhanced solar activity is accompanied by periods of extremely intense solar wind. That red colour is thus a further piece of data which confirms that the colours are from *aurorae* caused by unbelievably high solar wind densities impacting the upper atmosphere.'

'That's just another great deduction Tom,' Andrés remarked. 'The way your astrophysics knowledge is able to make new interpretations of what is recorded in everything we find from this very ancient time is astounding.'

'Thanks guys, but as I said, this is a team effort. I can't do this alone.

There are way more clever questions than clever answers.'

'Andrés, what else do you have from Mustapha and John? We should really try to work through as much of their material as possible,' Chad added.

'Well, you may be surprised that Mustapha suggested that some of the hieroglyphs might even be star constellations of the ancient skies,' Andrés replied.

'Really? Did they find anything?' Tom enquired.

'Well, I recall that John spent quite some time researching the ancient constellations of the *Navaho* Indians. Those indigenous people go back a really long way. Like the Australian indigenous peoples, their tribal stories *carry data across the millennia*, so I guess it seemed likely that clues of the past are buried in their culture. Mustapha wondered if the *Navaho* constellations might even be a clue to decipher some of the hieroglyphs on the walls if some of them were pictures of asterisms.'

'That's definitely a clever suggestion,' Chad confirmed. 'Let's take a look!'

'Well, *Stellarium* includes the *Navaho* constellations. There are not many. Here you go. OK, there's one close to the band of the Milky Way. Stellarium suggests that the *Navaho* translation for that one is *man with feet apart.* But hang on, those other stars directly below, certainly look like a man walking with bowed legs, with vitamin D deficiency! I've seen a hieroglyph looking just like that in one of those images you showed Andrés! Moreover, *Stellarium* seems to be connecting very feint stars to form that *Navaho* constellation, not the principal stars in the sky. You know, the *Stellarium Navaho* asterism might even be an error. This needs closer scrutiny. Can you find that image you showed earlier while scrolling through photos from one of the large Egyptian tombs? There was a bird also in the hieroglyph image.'

'Did you mean this one?' Andrés asked. 'This is from the tomb of Ramesses VI.

'That's the one! OK, so if my hunch is right, we'll find a bird asterism above that *bowed legs* asterism. So this is the Egyptian *man with feet apart* in 9,750 B.C.E. Ah, this is interesting. Look if I run the clock forwards or backwards, these curved legs are only standing horizontal on the horizon back in 9,750 B.C.E. As the clock runs forward, this asterism becomes leaned over. This has to be another date stamp!'

'Brilliant Tom!' Chad exclaimed.

'OK, first I'll trace these outlines. I'll include that strange boxing glove shaped hieroglyph also. Look, all three are sitting above that hieroglyph for sunset. So we would expect the *Rickets legs on the horizon at sunset* if my hunch is right. Now let's try to find the sky mapping.'

Tom selected a band of night sky above the newly discovered asterism.

'By the way, guys, that blue star at the apex of the *Rickets legs* asterism, is our old friend *Spica!*'

'You mean the one identified on pillar 43 in Göbekli Tepe?' Chad remarked.

'Precisely. Hey, but look at this! The bird matches to the stars above and the boxing glove shape matches the Milky Way band above that,' Tom murmured. 'But now look at the detail in those hieroglyphs! The markings on that *bird* and the internal detail in that *boxing glove* hieroglyph also form part of the precise star mapping!'

'Tom, very slowly, the hieroglyphs are revealing themselves. John would have been really thrilled at how we've taken his years of endeavour and reached such meaningful conclusions,' Andrés added. 'You know, the day is on now, and I'm thinking that maybe we ought to take a break. Perhaps we could head out to call in on my sister Eliza. She's over at her coffee shop, *The Choco Café* in Monteverde today. I sent her a text earlier and she is actually really keen to meet both of you. What do you guys think?'

'Let's do it,' Chad confirmed.

'Sure,' Tom added.

'We can take my flatbed truck. No need to take two cars. It's not far and the bench seat is wide enough for three.'

'Great!' Tom replied.

They walked down to Andrés' truck and stood in the track while he climbed in and started up the engine. He then slowly reversed down the steep slope. After he'd swung round, Tom and Chad climbed aboard, and they all set off along the forest trail. Andrés then started to tell more about the cloud forest.

'In case you're wondering why there doesn't seem to be much life

Three Hieroglyph Star Mapping

down here, during the daytime, all the wildlife pretty much hides or takes refuge up in the canopy. Animals only venture out to forage on the forest floor under cover of darkness. You may see the odd green tree viper on a low branch, if you have eagle eyes, but there's little to see in daylight. You know, we can always head out for a night walk with torches this evening if you like.'

'I'd really like that,' Chad remarked.

'Me too,' Tom added.

'OK, that's the plan then.' There was a pause. 'You know, I can't stop thinking about our conversations over the past 24 hours. The craziest thing is that you guys only arrived yesterday! If we just pause to think of all the new conclusions we've reached, can we possibly say anything more about the previous civilization who warned us?'

'You're talking about the *Sechin Bajo* people, right? The ones who built the pyramids in the 12,780 B.C.E. *gamma Velorum* configuration?' Chad asked.

'Yes. The people who built those structures had surely already been around for several thousand years. Those buildings are rock monuments of carved megalithic stone blocks. Just think about that for a moment. They set themselves the challenge of building a message in stone, capable of surviving all kinds of earthquakes and erosion, so a civilization living thousands of years in the future, would be capable of understanding it, and then taking the right course of action to perpetuate the existence of the human race,' Andrés explained. 'Without that message we wouldn't be here I believe.'

'That's quite a sobering comment Andrés. I am now wondering. Have we as a human race lost that unity of thought and endeavour? Have we evolved into really selfish people who actually live very much for the day at the expense of those around us? We might choose to pause a little and be extremely grateful. Truly great men and remarkable women walked among us, inspiring our ancestors with that single purpose of sending a warning message across the aeons to preserve the life on this planet. We are probably only here because of them,' Tom remarked.

For a moment the conversation went quiet as the sincerity of that comment caused each of them to reflect upon their own fortune. As they headed out of the cloud forest, ascending the hill line towards the crest of the surrounding hills, the sky opened out before them. Billowing white cumulus clouds, floating aimlessly amid the brightest of blue skies, added some kind of serene, trance-like beauty, which heavily contrasted with the seriousness of their discussion. Chad then spoke.

'You know, those people toiled pretty selflessly sending a message carved in stone into the future. That message, recorded in multiple locations all around the World, was designed to endure for some 4,000 years. They had no idea where the GRB would hit, yet we are concluding that they clearly must have been a pretty advanced civilization. We know that from their astrophysics knowledge, as well as from the detailed astronomy images carved in stone, which definitely require high power telescopes. But again, where is all their technology? We simply don't find anything.'

The flatbed truck was struggling to climb the gradient. Andrés slipped down a gear. The mechanical grinding betrayed the failing synchromesh. 'Come on baby you can do it!' he murmured. He then commented on Chad's last remarks. 'Guys, I've also wondered about the lack of engineered components for years. There is nothing to be found. What do you think, Tom? If we accept that the previous civilization was a hi-tech one, where is the evidence for their advanced capability? Do metals corrode that fast? The hi-tech civilization was around some 14,800 years ago. Can metals just corrode into nothing in that time?'

'Andrés, as I said, it's the clever incisive questions which evoke the obvious breakthrough answers to crack this story. That one was pretty ground-breaking! You just mentioned metal corrosion. Of course, if we just think about it, in moist soil, steel can corrode 10 microns a year. In serious atmospheric conditions or in rising seawater, even solid steel bars, 30cm thick will corrode into absolutely nothing over 15,000 years, as will copper, zinc, magnesium, and most alloys.'

'Can we expect to find absolutely nothing left Tom?'

'Well, gold does not corrode. It will also pretty much survive the 880 years of high electric-field, coronal discharge,' Tom reasoned.

'Then that has to be it!' Chad remarked. 'History tells us that many of the early civilizations had huge amounts of gold. The Mayans, the Incas, the early, as opposed to *ancient* Egyptians; they all had hordes of gold! Couldn't they have accumulated what survived.'

'Good comment Chad!' Tom exclaimed. 'That could explain the sheer lack of stuff. If some metals did survive during the post-GRB era, anything that was discovered would most likely have been gathered and reworked to make basic tools of course. There would have been the obvious *shock and awe* of what the magical material was, and where it had come from, if the post GRB civilization possessed no metallurgy knowledge.'

'So we might even discover *El Dorado* after all!' Andrés added with a chuckle.

'Well, we at least have some clues now about how a city comprising only gold came about if most of the other metals just corroded away over some 14,000 years! I would expect any gold lying around would have vanished by now. There surely can't still be some lost undiscovered city, replete with golden facades and ornaments still waiting to be found, not with today's satellite imagery,' Tom remarked. 'There is also one other thing which troubles me a little. I'm actually wondering if we jumped to one conclusion a little too fast?'

'Which one?' Andrés replied.

'Well, all the evidence now suggests strongly that, up to the GRB of 14,800 years ago, a highly advanced, high-tech civilization existed that was capable of building the *Sechin Bajo* structures, and all the Mesoamerican sites. Remember, those structures unequivocally record the GRB of 12,780 B.C.E., by identifying the configuration of the *gamma Velorum* stars and building layouts of pyramids in that configuration. We also find that the *identical latitude* of the rest of the pyramid sites around the World, was chosen to record the date of the arrival of the relativistic jet in 9,750 B.C.E., i.e. when *gamma Velorum* was 0.00000 degrees elevation due south. That civilization, of 14,800 years ago, we're now saying also configured those sites of pyramids in the future *gamma* Velorum arrangement of 10,700 C.E. to warn of the next potential hypernova.'

'That is now our consensus,' Andrés remarked.

'Well, if they were so advanced, and the GRB had not struck one side of the planet yet, they would have been a highly advanced civilization right up until it did so, right? So, why construct *Sechin Bajo* to warn of the GRB? I think we may have got something slightly wrong here,' Tom concluded.

'But you were saying that a GRB is pretty devastating?' Chad enquired.

'Of course. A GRB would destroy the Earth's protective ozone layer, exposing life to a very dangerous intensity of Solar UV until that ozone layer restores itself. Surface ozone would then form which is poisonous. Ozone would also be absorbed in the ocean, although research suggests this would not be at lethal levels. One hundred seconds is not long but megafauna exposed to intense UV would seriously deplete their numbers, and that's just what we find. North America had many *partial megafaunal extinctions*. So, North America was likely fully exposed to the GRB impact. The spinning Earth had midsummer in March of 12,780 B.C.E. and was thus tilted towards the Sun. So, if the GRB struck North America, then logically, the near-extinction zone extended down to South America also, including all the Mesoamerican and South American sites. It now seems a certainty that the North and South American continent pretty much *took one for the team*, while Europe and Asia were mostly saved. Well, that's what the data seems to be saying.'

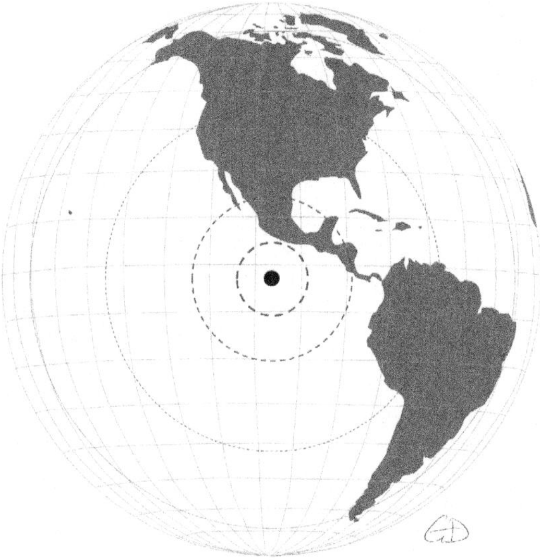

GRB Epicentre East Pacific

'You have a very rational mind Tom. Your assessment sounds spot on,' Chad remarked. 'Now you start to make me aware of how the World evolved asymmetrically. We find that a technological civilization evolved over the next few thousand years all across Europe and Asia, while in North and South America that wasn't the case. Those land masses became populated with indigenous peoples who lived a much less technology-driven lifestyle. That might even be the distinct marker towards an East Pacific longitude of the GRB impact.'

'Well reasoned Chad. I like it,' Tom added. 'I was wondering about Australia, but we see the stone formations in Victoria, so there were definitely highly intelligent capable people living there some 3000 years later. Perhaps that is a reasonable period of time to repopulate the devasted areas with indigenous people. Nevertheless, one aspect we need to keep in mind is that perhaps Australia just escaped the gamma ray burst. We find populations in the south eastern corner which have migration dates going back some 35,000 years. Sure, we find desert glass there, but that could be from an earlier epoch. Comparatively, it is interesting that both North and South America have inbound migration dates only 14,000 years old. It certainly matches our hypothesis that this part of the World was repopulated after the GRB of 14,800 years ago.'

'But Tom, what were you saying about the builders of *Sechin Bajo*? What's wrong with our assessment?' Andrés enquired.

'Well, I'm starting to think that either *Sechin Bajo* is way older, for example it could even be from *a civilization before the last one*, or together with the Mesoamerican sites, the global program of building pyramids using megalithic blocks just needed to be *a complete story*. I'm suggesting that those sites which map to the configuration of *gamma Velorum* in 12,780 B.C.E. were built to record the event *for us to discover today*, not to warn a future generation before 12,780 B.C.E. of an imminent GRB. They knew it was coming! Whoever built all those sites, and how they did so, using an unknown technology to cut, move and place those enormous blocks, may never be discovered. The message is pretty clear though. They wanted a future generation to find enough pieces of the jigsaw puzzle to work out what had happened in our past, so we could better-preserve ourselves in the future. I guess that's what *we've* done. Together we have finally decoded the message!'

For a short while the conversation paused again as they drove along. The 606 towards Monteverde now skirted the crest of a line of hills above wide open valleys. Dry, leafless trees lined the road, while in places, huge slate-grey boulders created a rock wall, reducing the risk of wayward vehicles plunging down the steep slopes. As they drove into Monteverde, it was immediately clear that it had been developed for tourism. It looked very much like a small American town. Andrés pulled up in front of *The Choco Café*.

'This is Eliza's place. She doesn't spend too much time up at the plantation now. Come, we're invited! I believe she's baked a new batch of her, now famous, chocolate cream-filled croissant horns. I can promise you, they're to die for!'

'I will definitely be starting a more serious exercise regime after this trip,' Chad added, slapping his abs.

'Well if that's your new plan Chad, maybe you can have *two!*' Tom replied with a grin.

A bell above the door chimed softly as they walked in. Several customers were sitting by the window.

A friendly, attractive Latina lady wearing a white apron was busy at the coffee machine behind the bar. She looked up as she heard the bell.

'Andrés! Welcome! Un momento,' she called out.

Eliza resumed her work and continued carefully adding a layer of frothed milk from a ceramic jug into the top of two coffees on a tray. After that was done, she deftly styled a leaf motif into the foam of each, then added a biscuit onto each saucer. She then brought the tray over to a couple sitting at the far end of the café.

She smiled as she walked back towards them. 'So, Andrés, you arrive with visitors from far away. You must be Tom and Chad,' she said warmly.

'I'm Tom,' Tom said, squeezing her hand for a moment. 'It's lovely to meet you.'

'Chad,' Chad added. 'It's a real pleasure.'

'You're very welcome. Let me bring you all a fine roasted coffee from the plantation. Please take a seat along the window over there.'

'Eliza, do you also have your paradise chocolate-cream croissant horns?' Andrés asked hopefully.

'Of course! They were freshly baked this morning.'

'Fantastic!' Andrés replied.

They made their way to the table by the window and sat down. Over at the bar, they could hear the sound of Eliza busy at the coffee machine. In a short while she returned, bringing three coffees and three of her speciality chocolate cream croissant horns.

'Please, enjoy!'

'Ah, thanks!' Chad said.

'The aroma is fantastic,' Tom added.

'Thanks Eliza,' Andrés remarked. 'Might you also sell me four kilos of your gold brand beans at my usual rate? These guys would love to take some home.'

'Of course. The coffee beans are stored out back. I'll fetch them when you leave. Listen, I'll sit and join you here for a short while,' she said, pulling up another chair. 'It's very quiet today. So, you're the two famous brothers who ended up on Andrés' trail. Well, how long have you guys spent together? Only 24 hours? So how many new conclusions have you reached? I should add that I've been aware of Andrés' project for years and years. I've lost count of the numbers of times I've tried to get him to publish, and then one day I heard he'd decided to quit and relocate here. You know, I'm already starting to sense that the old Andrés is back. I think you may have relit his fires of endless quest again!'

Eliza was bubbly and very endearing, and she had a radiant smile. 'Firstly, I want to say how lovely it is to meet you Eliza,' Tom said. 'Yes, I can indeed confirm that we've already joined quite a few dots and reached some new and very exciting conclusions.'

'So a trip home via Costa Rica is already proving valuable? That's good,' she said with a very warm smile.

'It certainly is. By the way, Eliza, might I ask how you also ended up moving to Costa Rica? I understood from Andrés that this is the home of your great grandparents?' Chad asked.

'Aha, so Andrés didn't say. Well, I fell in love with a Costa Rican coffee farmer when I was about to go to University in Lima. Our parents thought I was crazy to follow my heart, but I did. I got married here and my husband Alejandro is actually right now down in *Tamarindo* on the Pacific coast. We have three children, two boys and a girl. The boys both have families here and help manage the plantation. The naughty one, our daughter, moved to Peru to live with her boyfriend.'

'OK, so a cycle that's kind of repeating itself,' Chad added suggestively.

'Kind of,' Eliza confirmed. 'You Andrés, you've been here what, ten years now?'

'Ten years this year, that's right,' Andrés confirmed.

Eliza continued, 'And it's certainly lovely to have Andrés here. I did try to dig up a few of our old relatives when I arrived, but that turned out to be a literal activity, as there were no living descendants left from our great grandparents' families still living in Costa Rica. It was actually on one visit up here from Peru, that Andrés found that cabin while hiking out in the woods. Less than six months later he sent me a mail suddenly announcing he was all packed up and relocating here! I was quite surprised, but he really fell in love with that cabin, and the rest, as they say, is history.'

'Wow, these chocolate cream croissant horns are definitely to die for!' Tom mumbled, his mouth stuffed with a large bite.

'Absolutely *a-maz-ing*!' Chad confirmed.

'Those cream horns were also Andrés' idea. I went on a *master bakery course* when I was very young. I even got the accolade as the best student in the year. A few years back, Andrés persuaded me to take one of my best creations and add it to the menu here at the café.'

'Was I right, or was I right?' Andrés asked warmly.

'Yes, you were right, but everyone has definitely put on a few pounds since you suggested it, including me. Well, I do need to taste each batch of course,' Eliza replied persuasively.

'Of course, and I would do that myself,' Tom added with a smile.

'So, Andrés told me that you ended up on his trail of discovery, but apparently you took the shortcut through the evidence using scientific reasoning and astrology,' Eliza explained.

'Well actually we used scientific reasoning and *astrophysics*, not astrology. *Astrology* is all about horoscopes,' Chad suggested in a tactful voice.

'Oh, of course. Yes, not astrology,' Eliza added with a laugh, correcting herself. 'So, have you finally managed to convince Andrés to publish now?'

'Well, it's actually the reverse. Andrés is opening our eyes to the fact that publishing could be a very invidious task, causing much animosity in the academic world,' Tom explained.

'It's what I always told you Eliza, the World hasn't changed. It still isn't ready for the sheer scale of this revelation. It might even mean libraries needing to remove as much as 10% of their publications because they all have errors. No one wants to be the bringer of these tidings.'

'Andrés, now don't you get me started again! You and I have had many heated debates over the years about you needing to publish. I remain utterly astounded by the amount of time and effort you invested into your research, yet kept it all hidden away. If the libraries need to update their books, then so be it. If the data supports it, get the story out there. Did a previous civilization go to such unbelievably exhausting and enormous efforts to send a message into the future, which is right now, for you and your co-travellers here to decode it, and then just sit on it? Have you not thought that *you guys may be the only ones to ever discover this*? There's a reason that you're here. There's a reason why you need to get the story out there. My recognition for your life's work goes without saying. I thoroughly respect what you've done, but killing the messenger? I don't think it will happen. Trust me, it may take some time, but eventually everybody will deal with the new reality. If it hurts, it hurts. I've tried to encourage you many times. And if you are even more sure now with the new revelations you've discovered together, then I say *now is the time to stop dithering and take some decisive action*!'

This issue clearly evoked quite a strong emotive response in Eliza, which she was now making pretty crystal clear. Perhaps the unforgiving lifestyle as a coffee plantation owner's wife had crafted her into a vibrant life force, and one to be reckoned with.

'Eliza, not everyone will be willing to accept this. Just think about the *Great Egyptian Museum*, which recently opened. It cost more than a billion dollars. It's a pretty permanent monument but to a significant misinterpretation of history. Those guys will be livid, and they will definitely need to ridicule this whole story.'

'I'm sorry Andrés, I just don't agree. You and I have talked enough over the years for me to have understood quite a lot about your discoveries. If I were a director at that museum, I would want to *embrace the new truth*, and be the first to do so. I would endeavour to make it definitely the *Gem in the Crown* as it always should be. If foreign academics have dictated and reinforced totally incorrect interpretations, then those museum directors are not responsible. Countless non-Egyptian academics have taught a false narrative for far too long. This now needs to be corrected. I think those directors will embrace this new truth more comprehensively than anyone! We are only taking about replacing the labels and supporting material. As soon as your story is out, *the whole World* will just flock to see the evidence for 14,800 years of lost history. There will be a stampede to get to the Great Egyptian Museum. *They possess material dating back some 14,800 years*! Just think what a showcase that will be! They most certainly will invite you guys to visit as honoured guests!'

'What? Into the lion's den? I doubt if we would be brave enough. Besides, Chad already got evicted from Egypt,' Tom remarked.

'Eliza, you are definitely making some very valid and convincing points,' Andrés murmured.

'But, on a different note guys, what are your plans? If you're still here next week, my husband Alejandro will be back.'

'Sadly, our plane leaves in two days,' Tom explained. 'We'd love to stay longer and meet Alejandro. Don't worry, I'm sure we'll be back now that Andrés is family.'

They spent the next half an hour in a very convivial mood, discussing life in Costa Rica, and Tom and Chad's journey over the past year. A minibus then pulled up in front of the café and parked directly in front of the window.

'OK, It looks like I'm on duty again,' Eliza exclaimed, standing up and looking through the window at the group of Japanese tourists stepping out of their minibus and heading for the door. 'I'll just get your four kilos of beans. One moment.'

She returned shortly with two brown hessian bags of beans printed with the new *Choco Café* logo, a bright blue quetzal bird. There will be no charge. This is a present from me. Please,' she said warmly.'

'That is so kind, thanks Eliza,' Tom said.

'Yes thanks. It has been really lovely to meet you,' Chad added. 'I hope we're back soon with Mary-Anne and Jeanette.'

'Then we can discuss how harmless it all turned out, after you finally faced your fears and agreed to publish,' Eliza replied with a sincere look.

'I'll also look forward to that. Thanks again Eliza and until next time,' Tom said warmly

'See you sis,' Andrés said with a smile. 'Give me a bell whenever you're passing by.'

'Of course,' Eliza said smiling.

The Japanese tourists were now entering the café as Andrés, Chad and Tom weaved their way through them, back towards the truck.

'Your sister certainly doesn't mince her words,' Chad remarked.

'Yep, she's someone who just tells you the way it is, and perhaps just when you need to hear it,' Andrés replied.

'That was indeed a very refreshing discussion. So what are we doing now?' Tom asked.

'I propose we head back to the cabin and go through more of the material put together by Mustapha and John Mann. We haven't yet covered their contentious theories yet. There were quite a few fireworks between Mustapha and John at one time. They couldn't agree on the interpretation of one class of structures that are found across Europe,' Andrés explained.

'That certainly sounds intriguing,' Tom replied.

'It is. By the way, you can stash those sacks of coffee beans under the seat Tom,' Andrés explained, as they approached the flatbed.

Tom nodded. After opening the passenger door, he pushed the hessian sacks under the seat, then once on board, they set off along the 606 back towards the cabin.

'I'm already up to continue that discussion,' Chad remarked. 'So what was Mustapha's and John's controversy about?'

'Ha ha! There were several, but one centred around the *Parthenon* on the hill of *Acropolis* in Athens. John was totally convinced that the *Parthenon*, together with its neighbouring large building, the *Old Temple of Athena*, and the smaller square building further out, the *Arrephorion*, are of the same relative sizes and in the same configuration as the pyramids of the Giza plateau. He was suggesting that the site mirrors the Giza plateau and that there had to be a reason.'

'Interesting! Quite a shocker, which alludes to the site being extremely ancient,' Chad remarked.

'Precisely, which is why Mustapha was having none of it. John argued that emperors in ancient times had just claimed to have constructed those buildings. He stated that there are simply no credible records of thousands of man hours of quarrying, carving, dressing and placing the giant megalithic blocks to build those structures. The same lack of building records can be said of several of the most beautiful Roman temples around Europe. More importantly, just below the *Acropolis* on the *Pnyx* Hill, where the Athenians held their democratic assemblies, is a huge *cyclopean wall* of polygonal megalithic blocks.'

'What, just like those in *Cuzco* Peru?' Chad asked.

'Precisely! In fact, for some reason that megalithic wall is well off the tourist trail. Some of those giant blocks weigh between 20 and 30 tons each and are around two metres thick! How on earth did the ancient

Greeks cut those huge blocks as an interlocking jigsaw puzzle! More importantly, *Socrates' tomb* which is nearby, is one of a number of perfectly rectangular rooms, precision-cut into the rock cliff.'

'Well, that just sounds like data to me, which should allow a reasoned enquiry,' Tom remarked. 'So, where is the controversial part of John's argument?'

'So, according to John, the site needed to explain itself by referencing a valid ancient heritage. He rightly identified, from historical records, that the Parthenon originally comprised a stone chamber at its centre. This was destroyed back in 1656, during a war between the Ottomans and the Venetians. The Turks were using it as a gunpowder magazine and the Venetians scored a direct hit on it causing it to detonate. John then started to list a whole series of similar structures around Europe with columns and a stone chamber. The *Pantheon* in Rome, the *Maison Carrée* in Nîmes and so on. Wherever he looked, each building seemed to have identical characteristics. For him one giveaway was the tops of the pillars, called the column *capitals*, which showed symmetrical and impossible-to-carve stone masonry.'

'So what was Mustapha's point. Why was this not worth exploring,' Chad asked.

'Well, Mustapha was an *Egypt* man. He didn't want to entertain any possibility at all that the accepted Roman and Greek structures could possibly be extremely ancient and of unknown origin and purpose. In fact the more data John presented to Mustapha, the more antagonistic Mustapha became. They were not pleasant to be with at times. Both took quite extreme views,' André explained.

'Well, so what did you think Andrés? Surely, you formulated your own hypothesis,' Tom reasoned.

'Indeed, but I tried to take the middle line which satisfied neither of them! Take Karnak at Luxor. It's also a structure of closely spaced columns with capitals supporting a stone roof. There is also a structure at Persepolis, and I believe you dated part of that site to at least 11,500 years ago.'

'That's right,' Tom confirmed. 'Exquisitely carved centaurs on one side of the site differ significantly in quality from the seemingly primitive copies found on the other side. After I managed to map that centaur to an asterism above Persia in 9750 B.C.E., it was evidently clear that part of the site is at least 11,500 years old.'

Andrés continued. 'Finally, at Tanis in the Nile delta, we find *that* ancient site is also strewn with ornate, giant, symmetrical and intricately carved column capitals. I'm absolutely convinced that John had a point. Those *temple* buildings, were clearly related to this era. Remember, until you guys and I met, I never understood the physical nature of the 880 year cataclysmic event. Maybe together we can prove, unequivocally, what the link between those structures and the transit was.'

'Interesting,' Tom remarked. 'So we are saying that in very ancient times, and certainly during the transit of the relativistic jet some 11,500 years ago, there was a common class of structure comprising both columns and a chamber. While you were talking, I was just checking online on my phone. It says here that different *temple* buildings actually all have different numbers of columns. The *Parthenon* has 46 outer columns, with six extra columns set back inside each end, and additional columns within the chamber area, although those internal ones could just be for roof support. There are of course significant design and construction challenges related to the *Parthenon*. The lintels linking each pair of column capitals are not only immaculately and precisely carved, they each weigh ten tons! Also the floor of the *Parthenon* is subtly curved to correct for *the imperfections of the human eye*! Also, each column not only tapers, but slightly bulges outwards about a third of the way up, as if to give the visual impression that the roof is pushing down, squeezing the columns. It is truly a magnificent building, and unsurpassed anywhere in the World in my view.'

'Yes and that confirms that the structure is extremely high-tech,' Andrés added. 'Oh, and before I forget we should also think of Baalbek in Lebanon and the *Temple of Bacchus*. That is also a pillared building with an inner chamber. Under one lintel there is an exquisite stone carving of a fire breathing bird and two snakes.'

Chad was momentarily looking out of the window, gazing down across the deep valley with its wide open plains far beneath them. The road was twisting and winding. Their progress had been significantly slowed for the past 20 minutes after they had become stuck behind a very slow moving trailer transport, as it struggled to deal with the changing gradients. Looking ahead, the road uphill beyond the next bend was suddenly clear. Andrés, seized his chance. He shifted down a gear and overtook the truck and trailer on the bend, hooting as he passed. The truck driver responded with his deafening airhorns. It wasn't clear if he was angry or making a friendly response, and just unaware of how loud they were.

'OK gracias señor! So, we're finally free of that lumbering leviathan! Now I can concentrate better on our conversation again,' Andrés remarked, with an air of exhilaration. 'So what's our opinion about that last controversy?'

Chad suddenly shook his head, 'I have a hunch guys! What if they are hi-tech versions of stone circles?'

'What do you mean Chad,' Tom retorted.

'Think about it! Stonehenge is a solar tracking calendar surrounded by hundreds of barrows where people could take cover from the extreme weather during the transit, *Brodgar* in the Orkneys has the nearby megalithic structure of *Maeshowe*. That is obviously the shelter. Each and every one of these sites has a set of stone obelisks to determine the danger period and a nearby chamber to seek refuge for the 14 days of the Earth transiting the solar wind. What if those *temples* are hi-tech tracking structures?'

'That's actually a pretty cool hypothesis Chad,' Tom murmured.

'Just think about it. The *Parthenon* is what, aligned approximately east-west?'

'One moment I can see that on *Google Earth*.' There was a pause as Tom opened the App and then entered the location. 'OK, the main axis is pointing 257.7°, so 12.3° off due west.'

'What about the others, the *Pantheon*, and the *Maison Carrée* in Nîmes? What are their alignments?' Chad asked.

'OK, Google Earth is suggesting the *Pantheon* is aligned 355.4° north with its columns at the north end. Actually, having the principle chamber opening at the northern end seems pretty logical given that it would afford better protection from the Sun in the south. The *Maison Carrée* is also aligned just off north at 348.1°, with an opening on the north side.' Tom confirmed.

'But, how does one convert the immovable columns of those *temples* into a tracking structure to mark the sunrise and sunset directions of the danger period as it changed slowly during the 880 year cataclysm?' Andrés enquired, now becoming quite intrigued by the new thinking this analysis had evoked. 'Those columns are equally spaced aren't they? Something else would be needed.'

'Maybe we just need a bit of lateral thinking I guess,' Tom reasoned. 'Remember, the *Ale Stenar* site in Sweden we talked about earlier. It comprised a rigid immovable elliptical structure with a potentially movable stone block just off-axis, inside the structure, to adjust slowly to the changing sunrise direction. It was constructed high up, with clear views out towards the marine sunrise and sunset directions. Now think of where the *Parthenon* is located, high up on the hill of *Acropolis*. That structure also has clear sunrise and sunset views.'

'That doesn't prove that the two roman temples are ancient. The *Pantheon* is pretty much at ground level, but I guess there could have been open views towards the sea if the surrounding buildings were not there,' Andrés reasoned.

'Sure, but with regard to the *Pantheon*, there are some really hi-tech features in that structure. It also has the ocular opening in the roof, similar to that open shaft up to the sky that we found in Xochicalco, in Mexico. Its dome is built of the mysterious hi-tech *roman concrete*, which the Romans just happened to forget to record anywhere detailing how it is made. Moreover, those *Pantheon* dome concrete panels are all totally symmetrical, recessed, curved rectangular panels, which minimise the amount of material used, while optimising the roof strength. Another overlooked shocking feature in that building are the columns, each formed from a single piece of stone. They were imported from Egypt according to the official record. No one has yet been able to explain how 60 ton columns were manufactured to such a high degree of symmetrical precision. If they weren't made on a massive stone lathe, how were they manufactured?' Chad added.

'There is, of course, one other big controversy about that *roman concrete*,' Tom reasoned. 'If it was so easy to use, why did they waste thousands of man years building structures of carved stone blocks all over Europe, if they could have built them in no time, using their hi-tech concrete? It starts to suggest that they never developed the technology,' Tom remarked. 'As to your point about the way to identify and track the danger period using static monuments, I guess we would need to find something on the structures which proves how they monitored the changing sunrise and sunset. Do the buildings comprise a carving into a wall which has been slowly modified, or is there evidence for something else?'

'I recall that the open oculus in the roof of the Pantheon casts the sun image on the inner wall of the dome. That would then allow them to count the number of days, and the March 15th transit date might correspond to a certain height up the inner side of the dome. Unlike the massive stone circles, we are still missing something movable but durable which couldn't be knocked easily out of place. That would require more research to determine I guess,' Andrés replied.

'It says here that there is another complicated building on the hill of *Acropolis*, called the *Erechtheion,* which also has a hole in the roof. The *Erechtheion* comprises three distinct chambers at different levels. On the southern side towards the *Parthenon*, at a raised level, is the well-known *Porch of the maidens,* comprising six columns of draped female figures, technically known as *caryatids*. The northern porch is lower than the *Erechtheion* central temple and also comprises six very tall pillars. The complexity of that structure suggests it might be able to track sunrise and sunset during the danger period, but it would need a lot of analysis. For me, I'm not yet convinced, so *for the time being*, those books about those architectural wonders, can remain on the library shelves!' Tom concluded. 'But before I forget, time is of the essence with regard to *Stonehenge*. I recently heard that politicians in the U.K. are now planning to build a road tunnel under that site, which will likely run through countless, as yet unexcavated, underground structures and totally destroy irreplaceable important historical evidence. It is incredible how mindless and irresponsible people in power can be.' There was a short pause as he reflected upon his own words, then he continued. 'So what other issues did Mustapha and John not agree upon?'

'OK. Well there was this whole debate about the *Etruscans* and their ancestors. The official story is that the *Etruscans* lived in Italy with the peak of their civilization around 750 B.C.E. but John continually challenged this. He claimed that the original civilization had to be thousands of years older. John constantly referenced the significant engineering achievements of the *Etruscans,* who had cut networks of deep chasm, subterranean *vie cave* roads through solid rock near Sorano in Tuscany. Nearby is the *San Rocco Necropolis*, a huge subterranean chamber also excavated from rock with a spiral carved outside it. I realise now, of course, that this has all the hallmarks of a place of refuge used during the jet transit. That wasn't the main point of controversy. John and Mustapha continually locked horns over the two Etruscan bronzes: the *Chimera of*

Arezzo, a hybrid creature formed from a fire-breathing goat emerging from the back of a lion having a snake for its tail; and the *Capitoline Wolf*, the famous she-wolf feeding the twins *Romulus and Remus*.'

'What was the conflict about,' Chad enquired.

'John just wouldn't accept that these bronzes were contemporary with any known civilisation. He claimed the metalworking was truly off the scale!'

'And so what position did Mustapha take?' Tom urged.

'As always, he just dug his heels in and took the official line. Mustapha agreed that the bronzes might have been from a few hundred years B.C.E. and stunning workmanship but not from a lost civilisation. Both bronzes are quite beautiful, but there are questions as to what extent they represent their original form. When it was found, the *Chimera* was missing its snake-like tail and its left front and rear paws. In 1785 a sculptor fashioned a replacement snake-tail, but this only caused a further dilemma because the snake was now biting one horn of the she-goat, as if the creature was attacking itself. As for the *Capitoline Wolf*, many argue that this bronze is medieval with the twins added much later.'

'I am familiar with those bronzes. I am now wondering, should they prove to be out-of-place artefacts, they might represent complex asterisms. We can certainly explore that when we get back,' Tom remarked. 'What else did they not agree upon?'

'Let me think,' Andrés replied. 'OK right, there was that big dispute about the potential link between the three gods, the South American *Viracocha*, the Egyptian *Bes* and its Assyrian and Babylonian counterpart *Bessû*.'

'Yes, that's interesting. I was also wondering about that. There are all those Egyptian figures wearing strange hats, which we now know are the shapes of the solar wind and how it varied during the course of the year, but then we have that fat ugly bearded guy *Bes*! He is uniquely so different from all the other figures, yet he is part of the head board on that golden bed, the one found in Tutankhamun's burial chamber. It did strike me as really odd that he looks so much like the image of *Viracocha* on the Sun Gate in Tiwanaku. That simply can't be just a coincidence!' Tom reasoned. 'But if different cultures ten thousand kilometres apart have the same image for a god, there is only one likely conclusion!'

'What? Are you suggesting *asterism* again?' Chad asked with some astonishment.

'Seems the only possible conclusion,' Tom reasoned. 'They are all drawing the same image. There are even images from the Himalayas. I remember a god called *Licchavi*. He is also a dead ringer for the same god. They're all holding long objects of similar shapes in their hands also. It just has to be an asterism!'

'We can check that out when we get back,' Andrés added. 'What I find really interesting and exciting is the realisation that an ancient civilization made every effort to document the two-component event in stone, by building pyramidal structures, which would survive both the *gamma ray burst* and the transit of the *relativistic jet* some 3300 years later. You have even deduced the impact hemisphere of the GRB, which is unbelievably and utterly brilliant. That suggestion gives a credible explanation why those continents lacked the same technological advances as Europe and Asia when they were discovered. That seems a rational conclusion. So, while all the so-called *Mayan* structures had such perfect danger-period tracking capability, from what you are saying, they may have never been used if all the people perished during the GRB. A whole planet was prepared for the GRB and the aftermath, as if they knew what to expect. At an *impossible-to-predict* moment, a 100 second GRB caused a near-extinction level, obliteration of life on one side of the planet. This was followed by a rapid global rise in temperature of 12°C in the space of perhaps 50 years, which caused substantial melting of the ice caps leading to significant rises in global ocean levels. Subsequently the planet lost a significant number of *the people living along the water*, the people from *Atlantis*.'

'Yeah, but I can now extend the astrophysics even further. Listen up!' Tom remarked. 'It's actually very obvious, but I didn't realise it earlier. All the data tells us that the *gamma Velorum* Wolf-Rayet was in a binary relation with another star. Remember, there is one hot blue star in very close orbit with another star. The two stars are each moving in a very tight orbit around a common centre of mass, but the key point is that we know that the GRB and the jet headed this way, so we know that the axis of their stellar orbits and their spin axes are pointing directly at us!'

'Er, I think we non-astrophysicists might need a little more clarity,' Chad urged.

'Sorry, of course. So this hi-tech civilization would have seen this rotating pair of stars in close proximity. The two stars in the binary relation would have been seen circling one another. We are talking *ultra-close!* The period of the stellar orbits might have been only 200 days, with a separation of maybe only two Astronomical Units, so twice the Earth-Sun separation. Just hold that image of two closely orbiting binary stars. Now I realise of course *they knew which star would hypernova*, the bright hot blue one! Perhaps they just couldn't agree on the extent the surviving star would be affected by the hypernova explosion. The arrangements of different groups of pyramids found around the World, marking out the two gamma Velorum configurations of 12,780 B.C.E. and 10,700 C.E. mean that they had high power telescopes and the capability to determine proper motion: the actual relative movement of the stars. Also bear in mind, that is no mean feat in itself! Determining stellar proper motion requires taking many measurements over decades. Depending upon where the surviving star was at the moment of the hypernova, its proper motion would have been decreased or increased. I'm now suggesting some pyramid structures map to one *gamma Velorum* configuration with the smaller pyramid further out, while the other pyramid structures are spot on.'

'Absolutely brilliant Tom! Absolutely brilliant!' Chad exclaimed.

'Yes, well done Tom!' Andrés added.

'So, in fact, our previous high-tech civilization could indeed deduce which stars were dangerous, if they were looking at a Wolf-Rayet star in a binary configuration with the axis of rotation aligned to Earth. People might imagine that maybe the *gamma Velorum* binary could have been resolved with the naked eye like bright *Mizar* and its dimmer companion *Alcor,* which form a double star in the Big Dipper handle in *Ursa Major*, but those stars are only 80 or so light years away, and more than one light year apart! Resolving the Wolf-Rayet binary into two stars at a distance of 1100 light years would definitely have needed a huge telescope of course, which is still the elephant in the room,' Tom continued.

'And a *mammoth* one at that!' Chad added with a chuckle.

'Yes, very good Chad,' Tom replied. 'And there is yet another thing I realise that we know. If the Earth was essentially fried on the hemisphere unlucky enough to be exposed to the GRB, then we can say something more about any other stellar and planetary systems anywhere near to us, which had life. This event was truly devastating for the whole region of space around us. At *half the distance* to the GRB, i.e. at say 550 light years from the hypernova, those exoplanetary Worlds would have received *four times* the gamma ray burst energy that the Earth received. This makes it *even more unlikely* that any life could have survived on the exposed side of those Worlds which were closer to the hypernova event. We are just going to have to face it. A Wolf-Rayet stellar collapse leading to *a GRB and hypernova* pretty much confirms that planetary life takes a periodic lethal blast on half its surface. I hate to say it, but it seems to be the galaxy's natural way of population control, although it sounds absolutely devastating!'

'Again, another great, if somewhat sobering deduction, Tom,' Andrés remarked. 'But I am now thinking more about your comments of metal corrosion and the total absence of ancient technology. If we could find some hi-tech tools or something, it would prove beyond any reasonable doubt that the previous civilization really existed? We fully accept that there was a previous civilization; all the sites we have discovered and analysed provide really compelling evidence for that. I am now wondering whether they buried a time capsule for us to discover?'

'Well, on one level we *have* found the products of their hi-tech labours. We have those giant granite megaliths at Karnak for example with laser cut hieroglyphs. Moreover, perhaps the location of the time capsule is even encoded into those hieroglyphs,' Chad reasoned.

'If that is the case then everything would have been discovered long ago, right? What about that void they discovered in the Khufu pyramid above the *grand gallery*? Could that contain something that only an advanced civilization using muon detectors, i.e. us, could discover. Perhaps they hid the time capsule such that it required a sufficient level of technology before we would discover it, thereby protecting any civilization which had not evolved sufficiently technically,' Tom added.

'Guys, I love your reasoning,' Andrés remarked.

'You know, we should also not forget that the transit through a seriously high density plasma for 880 years, may also be the reason why we don't find any technologies, on the surface at least. We should most definitely search for artefacts underground.' Chad continued. 'The hard stone granite bowls from *predynastic* Egypt are most certainly from that era. Perhaps we should also now refer to the inhabitants of Egypt, prior to and during the cataclysmic jet period, as the *extremely* ancient Egyptians. Similarly, we should describe the people of ancient Persepolis as the *extremely* ancient Persians, just so we bring a little clarity into the story. The surviving evidence suggests that these people only worked with stone, and nothing else. What kind of civilization is that? No, Tom's conclusions about metal corrosion must be spot on. Remember also, that this all happened such a long time ago that any surviving metal objects which were discovered, would have most certainly been melted down or recrafted into tools, for example. What about the ocean microplastic pollution? Some serious analysis needs to be done to see if we can find a signature which suggests that some of it might even come from a previous civilization.'

'Good point Chad,' Andrés added.

'Guys, I'm now thinking about what may have happened to the other planets in our solar system. Just think about lifeless Mars. Mars is further out from the Sun and thus has a slower velocity. The Martian year takes 687 days, compared to Earth's 365 days. The solar-wind collimated spiral heading around the relativistic jet would have effectively been the same diameter, but because Mars moves slower, Mars would have suffered a longer exposure as it transited the solar wind spiral each year. Some calculations I did earlier suggest a transit time of just over 26 days each year for the 880 year duration. That could explain how all Mars' surface ice and water was lost if that's what was on the surface as evidenced from the surface erosion patterns.'

'You're definitely on a roll now Tom!' Chad remarked.

'Of course, all the planets in the solar system would have been affected by the GRB and passage through the high density solar wind,' Tom added.

'That's our turning!' Andrés suddenly announced, as he swung the flatbed to the right, turning to take the cloud forest gravel track. 'So what's our plan? If you still fancy a night walk, I suggest we rest for a few hours, then eat something before we head out along one of the forest trails.'

'Sounds good to me,' Tom remarked.

'Sure let's do that,' Chad added.

They climbed down from the truck and walked to the cabin. Chad and Andrés disappeared to crash out for an hour or so, but Tom had too many things on his mind. He walked out onto the deck after grabbing a cold bottle of Lake Arenal *Paradise Pale* from the fridge and sat at the bamboo table. He opened the beer and poured it slowly into a tall glass. He then took a sip and waited for the beer to inspire him with new insights. This refreshing Costa Rican craft beer *certainly hit the spot* with its strong grapefruit notes coming from the blend of cascade, citra and galaxy hops used. Tom was surely on track to solve even more unexplained enigmas.

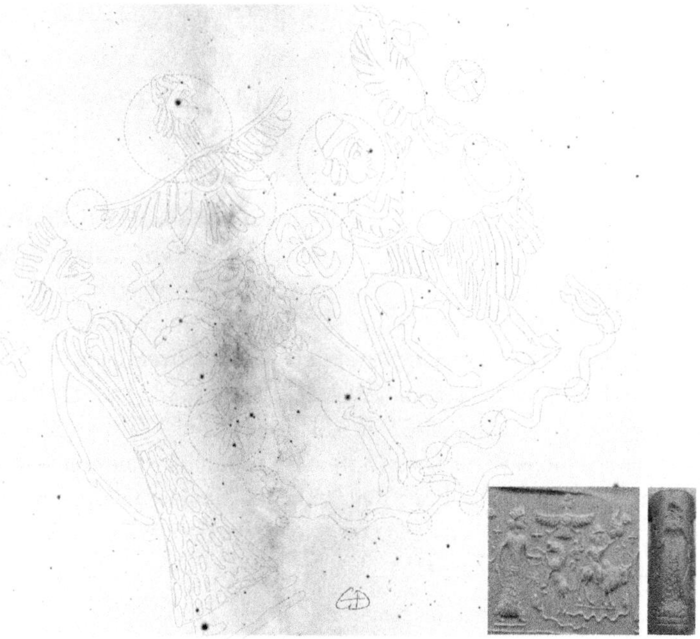

Assyrian Cylinder Seal

His eyes then noticed a small cylinder of stone on the bamboo table. It was around four centimetres long and seemed to be intricately carved. He picked it up and rolled it in his fingers. Of course, it was an Assyrian cylinder seal. Had Andrés decoded this also?

He then looked through the piles of notes in the folder on the table. He soon discovered a photo of the cylinder seal attached to page which showed what imprint it left in resin. It was astoundingly crisp and surely had not been carved with simple tools. The photo of the resin was a bright green. Tom took his phone camera and captured the bright image. He then transferred it to his laptop and traced the image. In a short time he had an image he could test against the night skies above Assyria.

He opened Stellarium, chose the city of Erbil and set the clock back to 9750 B.C.E. He was becoming quite adept at this. It wasn't long before he had found the star mapping. More than 70 stars matched the incredibly small image. Only highly sophisticated tools could have cut such an accurate star map. This, on its own, was already a major breakthrough. He was certainly motivated now.

He looked again through the images on Andrés' iPad and stumbled across a photograph of the *Dendera Zodiac*, a 2.5 metre diameter, carved stone bas-relief of constellations of the night sky that was originally in the ceiling of the Dendera crypt under *Hathor's Temple* near Luxor. His eyes were immediately drawn to the notes alongside: *no one has ever been able to map this successfully to the night sky constellations*. It was surely some kind of planisphere, being effectively a snapshot of the night sky. Normally planispheres comprise a movable elliptical window rotating over the night sky background, where the window reveals which stars are visible in the night sky above, on any night during the year. The *Dendera planisphere*, however, was carved out of stone. It could only ever show the night sky on a single date, but what date was it?

If many writers had complained that it was a poor representation, then that was every reason why Tom should now investigate it further. Nothing that Tom had seen so far in Egypt was inaccurate at all. Here was another enigma that was crying out for a detailed analysis.

The zodiac comprised a circular star-field packed with constellation asterisms, with a sequence of thirty or more characters, each wearing one of the different solar wind hats, standing along the inside of the circle. A nude female figure with her arms held up to support the disc, was positioned at each of the four cardinal points north, south, east, and west. Pairs of crouching falcon-headed male figures were supporting the disc at each of the midpoints between each pair of females. Three or four columns of hieroglyphs stood beside each of the female figures, while a band of 100 or more hieroglyphs encircled the entire disc running through the centre of the figures.

The star field had some similarity with zodiac signs of today, which was obviously why people had described it as a zodiac. Scorpio, Leo and Cancer the Crab were clearly shown, but this image would need some serious work.

In the centre of the image was *Taweret*, an obese dog-like figure with a square head, usually depicted with a snake hanging off his back, but here he had very long hair which almost touched the ground behind him, and he was holding an umbrella-like shape. Already something didn't seem quite right with *Taweret* but what was it? Of course, the figure on the zodiac was *facing to the right* while on many wall carvings *Taweret* faced left! Could that be it? Was the zodiac reversed? But why would that be so?

He checked the folder of notes that John Mann had compiled. Did he have anything on the Dendera Zodiac? After a short time, he came across some detailed images from a very early French publication: *Mémoires de L'Institut Royal de France, Tome seizième 1846*. Another note stated that the French had removed the zodiac with saws, jacks, scissors ... and *gunpowder*! They had then transported it to Paris in 1821. It was eventually moved to the Louvre where it is still on display today. The French did not return the original zodiac to Egypt but instead made a copy and installed this in the ceiling of the crypt at Dendera, from whence they had removed the original.

But wait a moment. Tom suddenly saw that the highly detailed image in the French publication of 1846 was *opposite* to the Louvre version, and reversed with Taweret looking to the left. Underneath the image was a bizarre comment in French '*view from above, as if the ceiling were transparent*'! That sounded crazy! It would be like saying: this is a picture of Leonardo da Vinci's *Mona Lisa* viewed from the back, as if the canvas were transparent! Ridiculous! If his hunch was correct, that detailed engraving in the French publication was the original drawing making it indeed the exact mapping of the zodiac to the night sky. Moreover, the figures with their solar wind hats were screaming out to him that the Dendera zodiac was in fact marking out the danger period of 9750 B.C.E!

So how on earth did a *reverse image* of the zodiac end up in Paris and Dendera, while a detailed etching published in 1846, so complete that it even included patterns of cracks running through one of the nude females, was surely an image of the original zodiac made as a record before it was ever removed?

Tom took a photo of the image from *Tome seizième* and then he converted it from black and white to make a yellow line image having an empty background. He made the image semi-transparent. He would now overlay that line image onto the night sky above Luxor at midnight on March 15th 9750 B.C.E.

The Dendera zodiac or planisphere was a perfect hemispherical projection, where its circular boundary represented the full 360° of the horizon. He needed to work hard to stabilize the *Stellarium* hemispherical image to get a projection which showed all the cardinal points as a circle on his screen.

He finally managed it and took a screen shot, and then he explored how well his semi-transparent yellow overlay image of the zodiac from *Tome seizième* published in 1846, matched the star field. The perfect match was incredible! Every single asterism now matched patterns of stars at midnight on March 15th 9750 B.C.E. He had proven without any doubt that the detailed image from *Tome seizième* was in fact the true Dendera zodiac image, with *Taweret* facing left, as intended!

But how was this possible? Why was the zodiac reversed, and why were almost all images of the zodiac in almost every publication around the World, printed as the *incorrect reversed image* of the sky projection? Could the stone Dendera sky snapshot of March 15th 9750 B.C.E. have been a *mould* so that multiple copies could be made of the true image and then distributed? No, that didn't make any sense at all. Why put a reverse profile so high up on the ceiling? That would make mould-making ridiculously difficult. Oh no! He then realized it immediately! The French had used *gunpowder*! They must have brought the whole stone zodiac crashing to the ground where it broke into dozens of pieces. So, what is in the Louvre? Coloured concrete? OK, they must have reconstructed the original from the broken fragments, then made an inverse mould from that, thus reversing the true image. Of course! Unfortunately they had forgotten to add the cracks which were clearly evident in the 1846 publication. That is why the Egyptians never got the original back! Moreover, that is why that strange comment needed to be added in the 1846 publication: *'view from above, as if the ceiling were transparent'*! He checked the movement of the zodiac in Paris. There was a cover up somewhere, but who was responsible?

He then read that the *inverse-moulded pseudo-zodiac* was first installed in 1821 by Louis XVIII in the *Royal Library*, which later became the National Library of France. So perhaps, in their panic, the perpetrators decided to make a mould from the pieces and never say anything. The mould would of course create a *reverse zodiac*! Unfortunately, *Tome seizième* of 1846 had been published with the original etchings, and that publication now needed that strange comment to match it with the *inverse pseudo-zodiac*

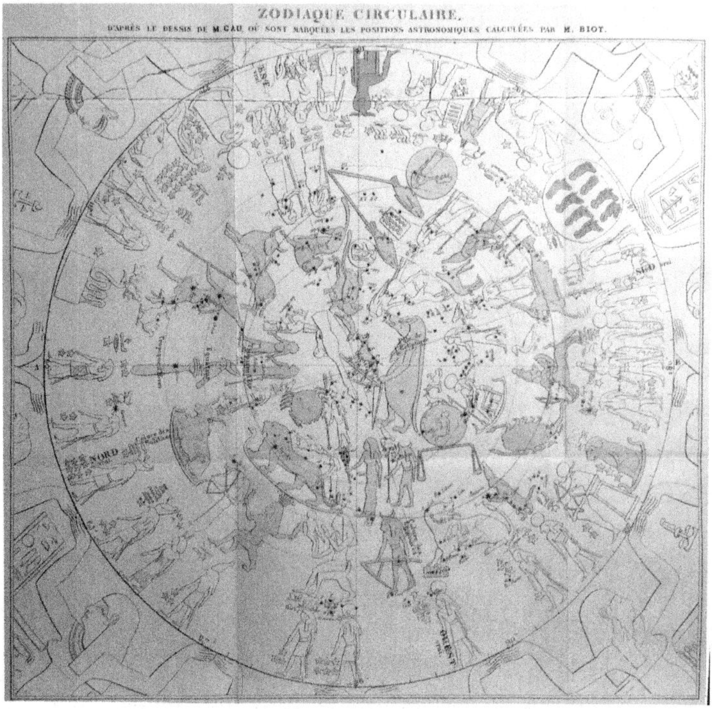

Dendera Document

on display in the Louvre to continue the deception. He studied a detailed photograph of the zodiac in the Louvre very intently; the purportedly sandstone zodiac had small holes all over its surface, identical to those formed when air bubbles escape from drying concrete, and the cracks in the female figure had indeed vanished. That was surely the absolute proof that the Dendera zodiac in the Louvre was a fake! No wonder no one had been able to decode the zodiac and map it to constellations very well. It was back to front! Tom was feeling really elated now. This was scandalous! It would only need a quick scan of the zodiac with a geologist's handheld X-Ray Fluorescent analyser, and the concrete constituents would be revealed, and the *jig would be up*! The proof that it had been moulded would be immediately obvious! It was even possible that the records of a certain *Claude Lelorrain*, the man commissioned in 1821 to remove it from the ceiling in Dendera, were still stored in a basement archive in the *National Library of France* along with the original pieces of the Dendera zodiac. However, the truth might have been so dangerous, had it been known at the time, that any written records were destroyed and a box load of broken stone fragments from the original Dendera zodiac might have conveniently made their way the 40 metres from the front door into the waters of the river Seine on a dark and moonless night! He then checked through Andrés documents one more time and found a collection of pdfs of some very old books. One immediately caught his eye. It was a copy of a very antique 1824 French publication entitled *Notice sur le Zodiaque de Dendera* by M. Dumersan. In the back of that book he discovered, what was probably the first publication ever of that pseudo reverse image of the Dendera Zodiac! The exhibition of the *pseudo Zodiac* in the Louvre had barely been running 2 years by that date. Then he saw the glaring mistake they had made! While the original correct image in *Tome seizième* of 1846 was covered with myriad stars, dotted perfectly along the outline of each asterism, in the *pseudo reverse image*, all those stars were now missing! The zodiac cabal had chosen not to add them. This was the absolute proof now that they must have indeed destroyed the original zodiac! The hastily put out 1824 publication, complete with the doctored *pseudo image*, was clearly all part of the same disgraceful deception. This discovery was absolutely jaw-dropping! It was worryingly, also a sobering realization, showing how academics blatantly conspire to deceive the World of the truth about the Earth's history. The Louvre, and more particularly, the archives of the National Library of France, now certainly had questions to answer!

There was, of course, one other very stunning new revelation about the Dendera Zodiac and its incredibly accurate mapping to the night sky above Luxor at midnight on March 15th 9750 B.C.E. It comprised a 360° hemispherical projection onto a circular flat stone surface. Achieving this could not be done with the human eye alone; it was absolute evidence for the existence of optical projection technology!

Tom would now take a look at those two beautiful Etruscan bronzes. If they were indeed shaped to match asterisms to warn of the jet and when to take cover, then this opened a totally new debate about who had manufactured them.

He went online and quickly found photographs of the *Chimera of Arezzo* and the *Capitoline Wolf with Romulus and Remus*. He downloaded them and then traced both photos to create an outline for each and then set *Stellarium* to the night skies above Rome in 9,750 B.C.E.

At midnight on March 15th two sets of stars showed promising candidates. While the Wolf and the *Romulus and Remus twins* were found across the night sky, the *Chimera* was within the band of the Milky Way where the lion's head was significantly clear. Furthermore, the most likely shape of the original snake tail was now self-evident, clearly defined by some very bright stars. As many academics had argued, the snake-tail wasn't originally biting the horn of the she-goat after all!

Considering the *Capitoline Wolf*, there was also little doubt that the twins had been manufactured with it and not added later, because the extended leg of one twin, and the twins' shape and form followed the pattern of many stars. The only conclusion was that both bronzes were indeed cast by an ancient lost civilisation and each formed a complex asterism when to take refuge during the jet transit event of 9,750 B.C.E. to 8,870 B.C.E!

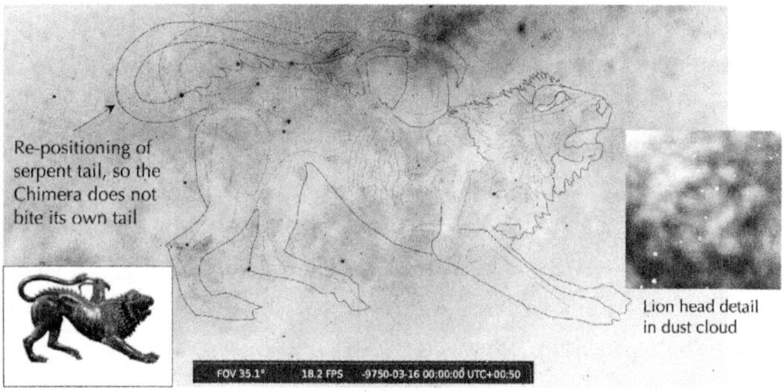

Etruscan Chimera of Arezzo

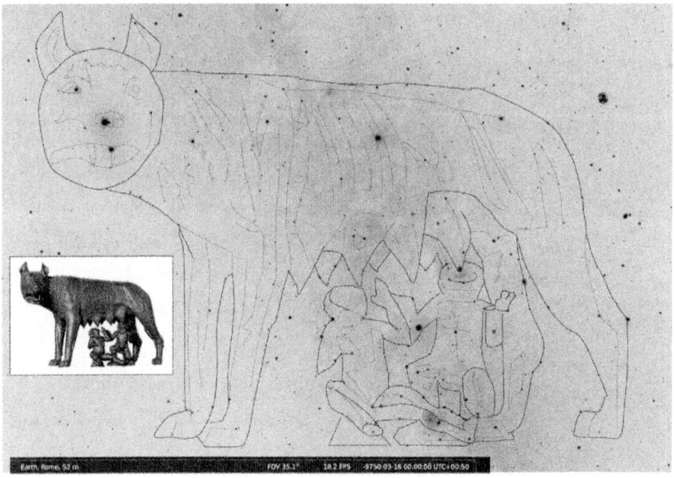

Etruscan Wolf

18 Costa Rica: decoding the hieroglyphic warning on Tutankhamun's mask

Andrés' cabin, in the heart of the cloud forest, central Costa Rican Highlands

Tom was still sitting at Andrés' bamboo table working away on his laptop. Unlike Chad and Andrés, he was just too intrigued by their earlier conclusions to be able to sleep so he had continued to work on. For the past hour he had been studying the Temple of Karnak in Luxor. An explanation for one paradox continued to evade him: the different quality in the carvings of the hieroglyphs on the walls and columns, compared to the deep, and almost laser cut, hieroglyphs on the backs of the statues and the obelisks. The *Ra-on-his-sun-boat* crowd, had dreamed up all kinds of odd explanations about what the friezes depicted, and how they related to victories of the pharaohs over their enemies, but Karnak was clearly a monument to astrophysics. Every pillar and frieze held complex data about the cataclysmic event, which the Earth endured and from which life had only just survived. There had to be a clear explanation for the differences in the qualities of those carvings, and Tom was certain if anyone could find it, it would be him. A paradox about that site was screaming out at him, but what on earth was it?

He stared at the layout of incredibly tall columns and structures. At the heart of the Karnak site stood the *Great Hypostyle Hall* comprising a dense forest of 134 closely-spaced giant sandstone columns, carved into papyrus stalks. Its imposing central nave was formed of 12 columns exceeding 20 metres in height, with their capitals ornately carved into large open papyrus flowers. A double row of 12 tall columns dominated the site's main east-west axis. All the columns were formed of stacked column blocks bearing more crudely-cut hieroglyphs. The columns contrasted significantly with the immaculately-carved megalithic statues, each formed from a single piece of Aswan granite, weighing in excess of 400 tons. The statues were of seated characters, each bearing head-dresses in the form of the different solar-wind shapes as seen during the course of the year. These statues had clearly suffered significant surface damage but the immaculate silky smoothness of the carving, and their perfect symmetry encapsulated both a rare beauty in shape and form as if they were prepared to sit and wait for however long it took before men of a future era finally understood the message they carried.

Tom knew from academic literature that during the *dynastic* period, pharaohs had adopted different astrophysics cartouches for themselves, wanting to become associated with these vast monuments, and thereby claiming importance to justify their right to rule. The pharaohs had failed to appreciate any of their true meanings and that the cartouches were actually just *rings around the key messages*. Papers by Egyptologists even described cartouches modified by Ramesses IV where in-filled plaster had actually fallen out. Ignoring all that, Tom would now attempt to explain the two different standards of stone-working on the site, but where could he begin?

He reasoned that if an ancient advanced civilization had constructed part of the site, and most likely in advance of the GRB of 12,780 B.C.E., then they were surely responsible for the serenely perfect megalithic masterpieces, each adorned with exquisite, deep cut hieroglyphs. The distinctly *lower quality* and *crudely cut* hieroglyphs on the sandstone pillars were obviously from a much later epoch, and most likely built by a more primitive civilization of survivors after the GRB. From the few hieroglyphs Tom had already deciphered, it was clear that the later crude imagery warned of how to correlate the changing shapes of the solar wind through the course of the year and what dangerous meteorological and atmospheric effects were to be expected. Those hieroglyphs comprised a current set of warnings to endure a *here-and-now.* From this, it just had to mean that the sandstone pillars were built just prior to, or were contemporary with, the transit which started in 9,750 B.C.E.

Now Tom was led directly to the perfectly formed hieroglyphs carved upon the megalithic statues. The most likely conclusion suggested that their hieroglyphs carried a warning message, carved before the GRB of 12,780 B.C.E., describing what future descendants of the GRB survivors should expect some 3000 years later in 9,750 B.C.E., but where should he begin?

It was growing quite dark in the early evening in the cloud forest. For a moment Tom's deep thinking was suddenly distracted by more raucous cries of some howler monkeys quite nearby up in the forest canopy. He looked up and was then enchanted to see an ellipsoidal swarm of flashing fireflies, whose illuminations betrayed their rising and falling motion in the darkness. After pausing to admire this beautiful and magical light show for a short time, he refocused his thoughts once again and stared back at a photograph of one of the Karnak obelisks. Then he saw something, a duck with a ball above its back. Inside the ball was a small round object. Surely that had to have an unambiguous meaning. A lost civilization had carved a message in stone which should be easy to understand some 3000 years later, so the meaning should also be obvious to him, but what was it?

The ball could not be the sun, that would be too bright. Moreover, if the duck were an asterism formed from a collection of stars, it meant that the ball was something seen in darkness, and a body clear and bright in the night sky. Well it couldn't be the Moon because that moved too quickly. What about Sirius? But no, by 9,750 B.C.E. Sirius had barely climbed 10° above the horizon in Egypt at its highest altitude due south. There would hardly be enough sky to form an asterism of stars. What else was clear and bright in the night sky? Of course! Jupiter!

Tom launched *Stellarium*, set the clock back to March 15th 9,750 B.C.E. and searched for Jupiter. Suddenly it was unmistakably and distinctly clear. A collection of stars just below Jupiter formed the perfect shape of that duck on the obelisk! He knew that Jupiter had an orbital period of 12 years, so to be sure, he would just need to investigate how those stars changed relative to Jupiter over time. He centred Jupiter on the screen and ran the clock backwards, and then forwards hundreds of years in each direction. Then it was definitive proof because it was only on that date that the duck asterism was vertical, relative to the horizon, with Jupiter above its back. Then Tom realised the significance of that small round object within the ball. Of course, Jupiter has a spot! Now, this detail only added yet another enigma because Jupiter's *Great Red Spot* is only visible with a telescope. Then it suddenly dawned on him. A message carved in stone detailing when the 880-year cataclysmic transit of the relativistic jet first started, had not been meant for descendants of the survivors of the GRB, warning them when to take cover! They would have pretty much worked that out for themselves, or perished there and then. No, this message could only have been intended for a future, evolved, hi-tech civilization; one which had finally managed to get its act together to survive the futility of mindless tribal warfare, and learn how to live peacefully on a path of research, which would eventually lead to the invention of telescopes. Knowing that Jupiter had a spot required that. The shock at this revelation suddenly gave him goosebumps! Tom realized he had in fact decoded a message transmitted some 14,800 years ago, only now received and understood for the first time by him in the 21st century! He had not failed them. Their ancient message had not been sent in vain. It had been carved intricately in stone with the sole purpose of conveying how a great civilization had been lost some 14,800 years ago, and how 30 generations had subsequently survived 880 years of 14½ days of hell underground every year, some 3300 years later. Only from that understanding could future inhabitants grasp the seriousness of what had transpired and then make the necessary plans so that life on our planet had the highest possibility of surviving the next hypernova event in our part of the Galaxy. He was momentarily numbed by this realization. For a few long moments he paused and stared out into the darkness of the night, trying to embrace the enormity of his discovery.

Duck Jupiter Star Mapping

A short time later he shook his head and turned back to the images on his laptop and the folders of notes to resume his quest. He was now very inspired to find something else, but where should he look next? He suddenly remembered the unexplained *double bump* symbol on the great Khufu pyramid. Why not take a second look at that? He looked at the folders of data gathered together by John Mann that Andrés had forwarded to him. One folder was entitled *Giza*. He opened that and started to scan through the images. Eventually he found a detailed picture of the exposed corbelling on the north face of Khufu. John had even made some notes about the carving, but John's photo had way more detail! The *double bump* was not just a double bump, but it extended to the left. In this photo three bumps could be seen. Going from right to left, the carving comprised a large bump, then a slightly smaller bump, then a space, and at the far left, a very small bump. Of course, this was a symbolic representation of the three Giza pyramids in their relative sizes and with their relative separation corresponding to the three remaining stars in the *gamma Velorum* system! Incredibly, the carving essentially comprised the optical field strengths of the three stars as would be determined by spectrophotometry using a powerful telescope! This was a really fortuitous discovery. This had been staring everyone in the face for years, but up until now everyone had missed it. He couldn't wait to tell Chad and Andrés.

Khufu Triple Bump

He imagined they would still be resting for at least another hour, but he was on a roll. What else had they been discussing earlier on their way back? Ah yes, the odd coincidence that cultures in Peru, Egypt, Assyria and even in the Himalayas had a very similar looking character, which the peoples of Peru referred to as *Viracocha,* and the Egyptians called *Bes.* So just maybe if his hunch was right, this guy was also another asterism. It would be great if he could find that also.

Each of the figures had a square faced head with something coming out of its hair, and it was always holding something, either snakes or a club. It was most likely that Viracocha could be a dark nebula within the Milky Way band. He would be very difficult to spot in normal viewing conditions, so Tom would need to up the contrast.

He chose to look for *Viracocha* above Peru in 9750 B.C.E. He didn't expect *Stellarium* to have the capability to distort the shapes of the vast dust clouds with time, but 11,500 years should have very little effect upon the shape of dark clouds extending thousands of light years across.

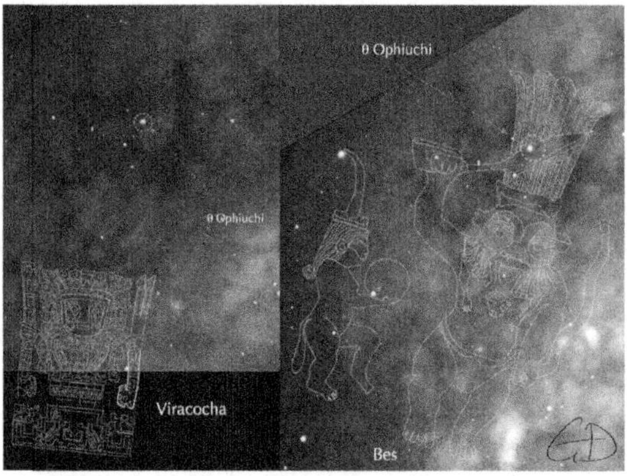

Skymapping of Viracocha and Bes

After a pretty concerted effort, tracking along the entire dense band of the Milky Way, he eventually found a promising-looking dark cloud. The distinctive features were obvious, a rugged bearded square face with dark bands in the form of arms holding an extended object. So how did this character move in the night sky? Sure enough, the dark cloud was horizontal on the horizon on March 15th. So, cultures all around the World had been informed of what to observe. Looking more intently at the perfect detail of the carvings of the *Gate of the Sun* in Tiwanaku, Tom now felt that the only possible conclusion to reach was that those images had been carved before the GRB using a highly advanced stone-carving technology. Any post-GRB survivors would have most likely struggled to exist in a World devoid of technology. Besides, an eastern-Pacific epicentre of the GRB meant that communities across North and South America would have been pretty much decimated by the event.

Image of Mandulis

Tom then started to leaf through a pile of images from John Mann's folder when he came across a carving of a strange figure surrounded by open and closed flowers. This was the carving of Mandulis in the Nubian desert. Now the 15 open flowers and 14 closed flowers took on a very obvious meaning. Tom realised immediately that this referred to 14½ days. So now Tom had specified the solar wind transit even more precisely. It wasn't 14 days but 14½! The Mandulis figure wore a headdress bearing the shape of the solar wind transit both at night, with the horizontal twisted horns, and during the day, with the vertical beams. Ahead of the figure was a cobra, while the figure itself was in the shape of a bird, possibly a vulture.

Tom then continued to look through the pile of papers on the bamboo table when his eyes suddenly fell upon a photograph of the famous golden death mask of Tutankhamun. With everything that Tom had worked out

Tutankhamun's mask

about the relativistic jet transit, the mask now appeared as a complex representation of all the data characterising the event, strongly suggesting that this remarkable and unique piece of metal working was extremely ancient indeed. Two flaps of the mask's head-dress hung down across either side of the figure's chest. There were 14 dark blue bands interleaved within 15 bright golden bands. To Tom, this was an encoding of the 15 dangerous days and 14 dark nights of the transit which now correlated perfectly with the 14½ days of the open and closed flowers of the *Mandulis* carving. The beard of the golden Tutankhamun mask had 14 separate cross woven bands, as if to represent 14 days of beard growth. The bright lime green, dark blue and orange red colours of the neck bands were immediately the colours of the aurorae as the intense solar wind impacted the atmosphere. The eyes, with their extended black lines were the epitome of a pair of mirror images of the *Eye of Horus*, depicting the *gamma Velorum* starfield. On each of the two shoulders he saw two falcon head *epaulettes*. These were no measure of rank however. It was so obvious to him that those falcons had to be the clearest of depictions of the asymmetric swirling spiral of solar wind, just before the Earth entered that tunnel of doom, and just after it exited. To be sure, Tom quickly leafed back through the pile of papers. He had seen a photograph of a stone falcon head. It had unique features of swirling lines. He then found it and stared at it intently. This held significant detail, surely totally confirming his hypothesis.

Stone Falcon

Apart from eight columns of hieroglyphs on the back of the golden mask, he still had one more feature to decode: a cobra with a coiled tail beside a vulture's head on the mask's forehead. The wide neck of the cobra comprised three segments of brown, red and turquoise, with a central banded strip of repeating aurorae colours. This same neck pattern was replicated in miniature some hundred times, running from shoulder to shoulder along the mask's border edge. The vulture however, was only a head and had little colour. It was golden with a curved black beak. So how did a cobra and a vulture fit into this story? He had just also seen a cobra and most possibly a vulture on the Mandulis carving. On the golden Tutankhamun mask they were side by side. Two different creatures in almost the same position, spaced slightly apart. Where had he seen that concept before? Of course, on Göbekli Tepe pillar 43, where one animal asterism morphed into another, over the 14 day transit. That could be the key to cracking this also.

To do this well he would now need to find ancient carvings of a vulture next to a cobra. After an extensive search, he finally found a *vulture* walking beside a *rearing-up cobra*, having an extended tail. He would start with the cobra. He went back to *Stellarium*, which was still set at the date of the transit, and after changing the location to Luxor he started searching those night skies for that serpent. Tom was pretty adept at this now and it didn't take him long to prove this hunch. There it surely was, the cobra's head defined by the four stars of the *Southern Cross*.

He traced the cobra outline from the stone carving and made it semi-transparent against the ancient Luxor skies. After a little rotation and scaling, it was indeed a perfect match. But to add perfectly sweet icing on this exotic cake, the tip of the tail of the cobra extended to connect to none other than *gamma Velorum* itself!

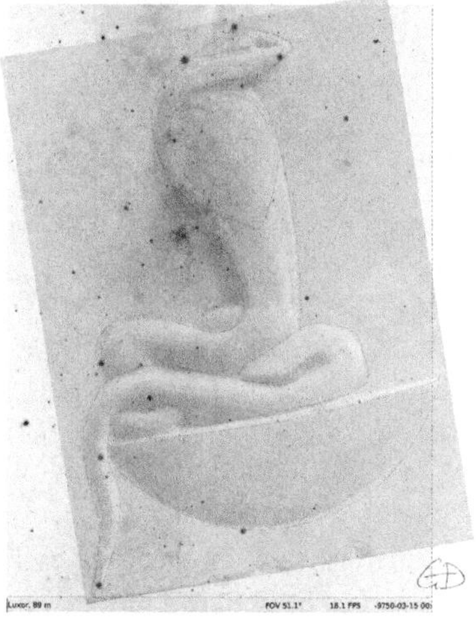

Snake on Tutankhamun's Mask

'So, just the vulture to find now,' Tom murmured softly.

The stone vulture he had found also looked remarkable. As he started to trace its feathers, it was very clear that this was no ordinary bird. Only the ends of its tail feathers looked normal. The rest of the feathers on its chest were definitely strange billowing cloud shapes as seen in the Milky Way band! He knew then that he was very close to cracking this completely. His hunch had been spot on. With new vigour he completed the vulture tracing and then examined the same patch of sky above the horizon were the cobra had been, and there it was. With the vulture's head matching the shape of the dark clouds around the eye star *theta Ophiuchi*, and its billowing feathers matching the Milky Way cloud bands. Tom needed to check if the eye star was significant. Wow, so *theta Ophiuchi* was indeed remarkable. It was none other than the star associated with *Asclepius*, the ancient Greek God associated with medicine, who carried a staff having a *single* snake entwined around it! That just couldn't be a coincidence. Surely all roads were leading to Rome now. While many medical organisations had wrongly adopted the double-snake winged staff, or *caduceus*, of *Hermes* the ancient Greek God of Commerce, it was *Asclepius'* single snake around a staff which was the true symbol of medicine and healing. This just had to be another message carrying a warning, which had been encoded in folklore and sent from the lost civilisation. The data on *theta Ophiuchi* was also interesting. It was described as a triple star system, with its main component being a nine solar mass 9M sub-giant blue-white star which will end its life in a *supernova*, only 436 light years from Earth. It was also described as being *on the right foot of the serpent bearer*. Could that even refer to some ancient folklore about a serpent bearing bad news? Tom had found that cobra already.

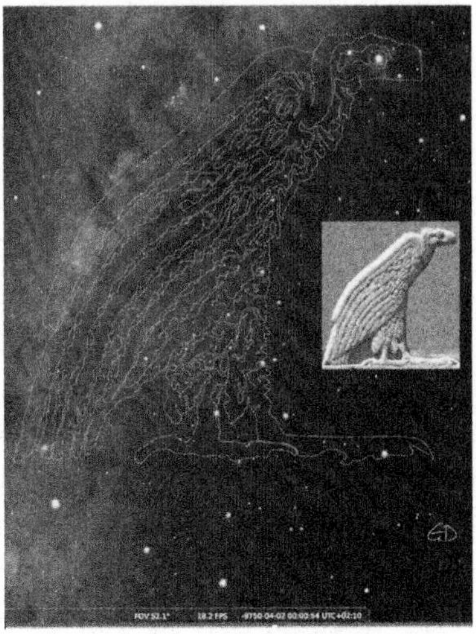

Vulture

Well, he had cracked everything apart from the hieroglyphs on the back of *Tutankhamun's death mask*. It certainly wasn't that now, but a *directive* moulded as a golden emblem conveying all the needed warnings to be heeded some 3300 years after the GRB. Tom reasoned that the only conclusion to be reached was that it was manufactured prior to the GRB, some 14,800 year ago at least. Gold of course would survive against 3000 years of corrosion, thus keeping the message intact. A post-GRB civilization would have quickly lost any capability of fine goldsmithing, or indeed any expertise in complex astrophysics to be able to encode any meaningful data about the relativistic jet transit of 9,750 to 8,870 B.C.E.

Tom then looked at the hieroglyphs, surely he couldn't make any headway here, but it was very tempting. There were eight columns. He added up the sunset hieroglyphs, there were 10, so ten days in the middle of the transit between entry and exit of one and three days respectively. It was highly likely that within the entry and transit, seeing any sunset at all was impossible! Now it became very evident. The shape of the falcon head seemed to convey the asymmetric nature of the solar wind transit quite accurately.

Within the hieroglyph text he then saw all the *birds*. These corresponded to several of the asterisms he had already discovered. There were *bowls* which likely meant water or food or meals, and he also saw the *seated figure* with a beard suggesting the 14 days when one should stay underground, but then he saw the 14 *eyes*. Only four in the middle of the period had *eyeballs* in. The rest were empty. This surely corresponded to the days when you needed to protect your eyes to prevent yourself going blind. On closer inspection he then noticed something which really troubled him. At the absolute centre of this period, between the two pairs of eyes with eyeballs, there was *one blind eye*! How on earth was that possible? Had he totally misunderstood the text, or could he find an astrophysical explanation which would confirm that he had definitely made the breakthrough?

The text was now suggesting that along the centre line of the spiral of solar wind, there was another intense beam of particles. Why hadn't all the charged particles been caused to spiral around the 14-day diameter cylinder? He sat for a few long moments with some anxiety that his interpretation was just wrong, and then it suddenly dawned on him. Of course, apart from the walls of the spiral, the only other stable trajectory for the charged particles was *along the centre axis of the cylinder*! Wow, he had cracked the principal message of the text! This was also totally new astrophysics: a physical interpretation of charged particles travelling within a cylindrical collimated spiral where some percentage of them would be caused to travel directly along the centre axis of that spiral. That is why you would go blind during the midpoint of the transit! He breathed a big sigh of relief. He could relax now and leave the rest of the details for others to work out. Surely, all the evidence he had now compiled added a much richer provenance to this ancient artefact.

Just at that moment he heard a noise from the cabin and saw Chad and Andrés approaching.

'Hi guys, did you get some rest? My mind was buzzing so I carried on working.'

'Hi Tom, so did you make any progress?' Andrés enquired.

'Sure did! I mapped this stone cylinder seal to the night skies above Assyria, I found Viracocha and Bes, decoded a message on one of the megaliths at Karnak, and I've just cracked the enigma of Tutankhamun's mask.'

Oh, and I discovered something more in the Dendera crypt."

'You found the generator for the Dendera lightbulbs?' Chad asked.

'Yes, I did! I even got it going!' Tom confirmed with a smile. 'No, I managed to prove beyond any doubt that the Dendera zodiac in the Louvre is in fact a fake, a moulded inverse copy! The French must have pretty much destroyed the original when they tried to remove it with gunpowder. I also managed to map those two Etruscan bronzes to asterisms in the night skies of 9,750 B.C.E.'

'That is pretty cool Tom.' Chad then noticed the photo showing the eight columns of hieroglyphs on Tutankhamun's mask. 'Have you cracked that?'

'Sure have, and it's the complete description of the dangers of the 14 days of transit through the spiral of solar wind!'

'That is surely the final piece of the puzzle which will convince the whole World,' Chad remarked. 'Congratulations Tom!'

'Well, the other interpretation is that this new insight may now be taking the story just one step too far! Just think how the entire World has been taught that this is the death mask of the boy king. People have it etched into their soul that the mask was made for him after his premature death.'

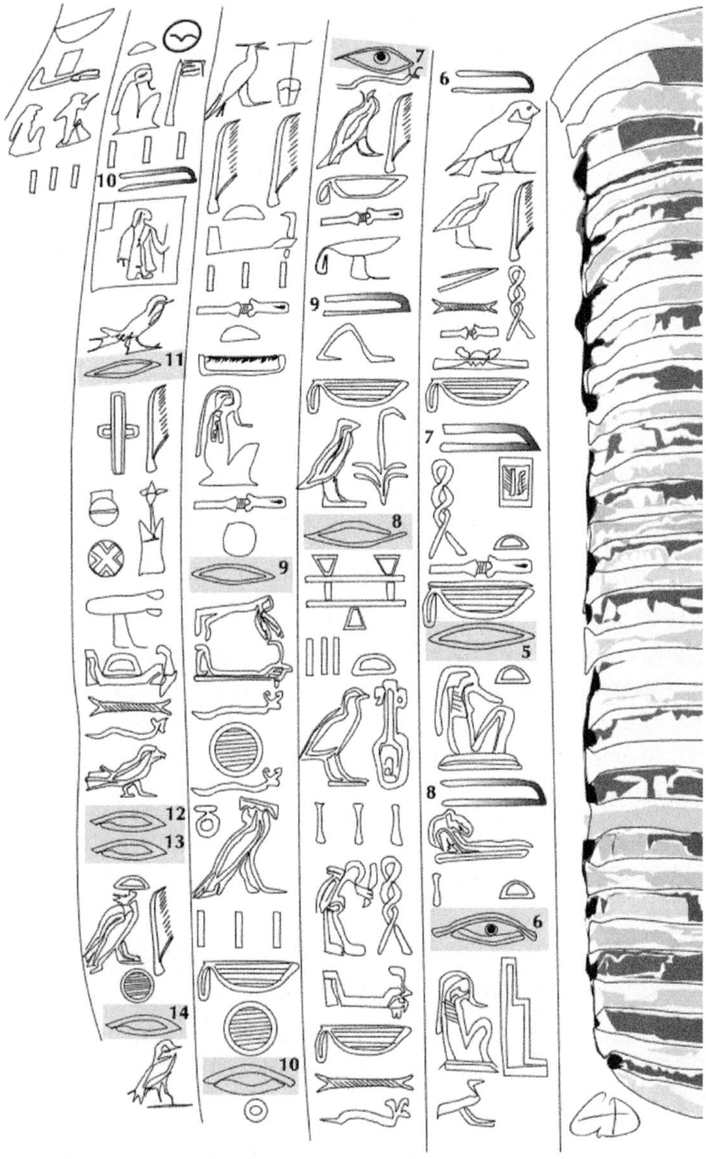

Tutankhamun Mask Hieroglyphs

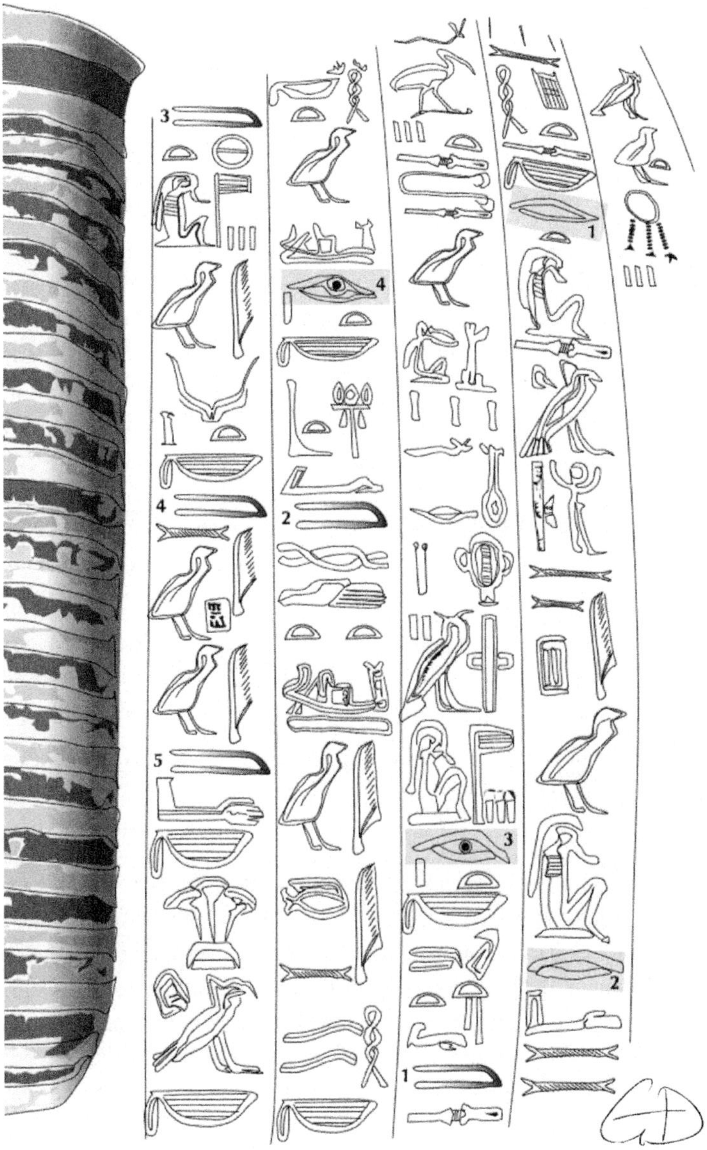

Tutankhamun Mask Hieroglyphs

'By the way, Andrés, how did he die?' Chad enquired. 'Is there a consensus now.'

'Well, the popular belief is that he died from infections after falling off his chariot.

'Do you believe that?' Chad asked.

'Of course not. I don't subscribe to popular beliefs, I look for the data. Several years ago I was lucky enough to speak to a specialist in a rare metabolic disorder who told me the following. A TV programme showing X-ray and CT scans of his skeleton revealed Tutankhamun had *irregular bone fragments* in his skull and ribs. He had a club foot and an inability to walk unaided requiring walking sticks, as evidenced from murals and the canes found in his tomb. He had crowded teeth, and a whole set of ten other clinical features but, particularly with reference to those irregular bone fragments which this specialist identified immediately, Tutankhamun strongly matched the complete signature of a patient having a rare inherited copper transport disease, where patients reach adulthood before dying. In his tomb they even found all the herbs and seeds and fruits which a contemporaneous pharmacopeia identified as treating all the symptoms of that disease. That is what he died of.'

'Andrés you have a huge amount of hidden knowledge in that grey matter of yours. That should surely be out there. Did that doctor publish?' Tom asked.

'I believe a letter was written to *a renowned medical publication*, who declined to publish it.'

'That's crazy!' Chad remarked.

'Yes but what if the reviewing editor had just written a book about Tutankhamun's death from that chariot? The arrival of a pretty conclusive series of well-reasoned suggestions is suddenly a threat and just maybe that letter needed to have been filed away into a separate storage archive by pressing the *delete* button. Publications which challenge the status quo, or which even threaten the integrity of an academic by exposing his work as *in error*, or of *less significance* are just not welcome. People in power have reputations to protect, and they don't want their work undermined. It's just the same as our discovery of this vast amount of evidence, which proves beyond any reasonable doubt that the history of our planet goes back 15,000 years at least to a lost highly advanced civilization. Our entire story has the momentum of a high speed clattering train heading towards the immovable buffers of the academic world, where there will be some serious repercussions on impact.'

'Well obviously, this control of the World's knowledge by those protecting their previous work needs better arbitration. As you suggest, the current process enables some unscrupulous academics to reinforce their preferred fallacious narrative, keeping their friends in jobs. I guess the only reason those papers keep getting published, is because it's the academics in the same fields who are peer-reviewing those same papers, and they will veto any hypotheses which challenge their own earlier papers. It's a self-perpetuating travesty,' Chad remarked, sounding pretty irritated.

'Chad, you're right. I also went through all this trauma that you are now experiencing. You and Tom have struggled to deal with this realisation that journals continue to publish a self-regulated mythical history, but you have only suffered this frustration for less than a year. Please remember that I have lived through this same dilemma for more than ten years before I made peace with my soul. I decided that I had nothing to prove. I couldn't change the way the last 100 years of education have reinforced the false narrative upon the whole population of this planet. I'm suggesting that you cannot do this either. Surely you cannot believe that the World is capable of hearing this story.'

'Andrés, you're right of course,' Chad sighed, leaning on the table, his elbow supporting his chin.

'More importantly, there is another huge aspect to overcome which we've not discussed yet. Remember, very few people ever read peer-reviewed papers, so the majority actually don't really give a hoot about what goes on in the academic World. Only fragments of those papers even get a mention in news media, and when they do, they're usually totally misreported anyway. No, the biggest problem you will need to address is that masses of people thought they had been properly informed about the pyramids, the stone circles, the cave art etc. *when they were at school!*'

'That's an important point. I guess we haven't yet paused to consider how people in general will be affected by this story,' Tom retorted.

'Right, and can you imagine the shock, even for the average person, who suddenly hears a radically different explanation for the past 15,000 years of Earth's history? To protect themselves, those people will need to dismiss the whole story out of hand, despite the data. Just consider those people. We are talking about something which will shatter everything they were ever told. People will just not accept this. Despite it being right, it is threatening. Through our lives, each of us continues to struggle to make sense of the World around us and build an increasingly more solid framework of what we know. This is a very personal journey for each one of us. The human psyche is stubborn, and that framework is very personal, so we will reject anything which challenges something so dear to our hearts.'

'So, you're suggesting there won't be a calm rational assessment of the data,' Chad murmured.

'No, and how could that be possible? More importantly, for some people, it will be absolutely terrifying to dare to think that the things they were taught at school were all wrong. Many people will get a really sick feeling in their stomachs; it's akin to a loss of something dear, almost like a death in the family. Many will simply not be able to articulate their emotional reaction to this fear, and they will become irrational. There are many different conflicts which may arise now, but the reaction will always be emotional. Rational assessment of any scientific hypothesis, despite the overwhelming amount of data, will consequently be rejected completely out of hand as a means to protect themselves. I'm suggesting that you must expect that also in the academic world.'

'I guess there are even some people, particularly those who have spent years on the same journey as us, who might now feel cheated and beaten to the explanation, despite wanting to know the answer to this fundamental question,' Chad suggested.

'You are now hinting about the Hitchhiker's Guide,' Tom added, 'the quest for the answer to the ultimate question.'

'Indeed,' Andrés confirmed, 'but here it is a little more defined. It's the answer to the question about the pyramids, the Mayan sites, the stone circles, and the cave art. It includes an inference to the Greek Myths, a basis for some of the stories in early religious literature, the Australian indigenous peoples' stone formations, the dolmens, and the Earth's climatic record of the past 15,000 years.'

'We didn't discuss it earlier, but this must be the most likely explanation for the hundreds of *medicine wheels* all over North America. In addition, before I forget, another site in my own country of Peru is *Trujillo*, which has walls carved with sequences of long-eared, fiery, hare-like creatures. These remind me so much of the hare in that ancient Egyptian wall frieze with *Apep the snake* and *the tree of life*. One sequence of 14½ of these fire hares at Trujillo must surely be referencing the danger period. Also, on the other side of the Earth in Sardinia there are many beehive-shaped megalithic structures. These are very similar to structures we find in almost every country today, and I hazard a guess that these are also shelters in which people hid during the danger period.'

It also explains the partial and complete megafaunal extinctions, the underground cities, the astrophysical details in the Temple of Karnak etc.,' Tom added.

'And the need to correctly decipher the ancient hieroglyphs which were wrongly assumed to be capable of translation using the Ptolemies' plan of deception, the *Rosetta Stone*. It encompasses the Moai statues, the Olmec heads, the pillars at Göbekli Tepe, even the *Dendera Lightbulbs*,' Chad remarked.

'Indeed and the list is endless,' Andrés replied, 'but we have discovered that this huge complex multifaceted set of puzzles can be explained in a very elegant way with a very specific and detailed singular answer. I will, however, agree that there is one positive aspect in support of publication: none of the completely different explanations for all the unexplained phenomena, which attempt to come up with a diversity of creative hypotheses, *were ever really convincing or even credible*. In truth, they actually didn't make much sense to anyone. So there is that small glowing ember you can hold onto. All the World's mysteries were never linked before by a single event.'

'For time immemorial, people have professed to know more than others to take advantage of them. It's human nature. It's so easy for academics to do nothing, to bleat the same old nonsense, even as University professors. If you have ended up in such a position of power, no one will ever dare question your authority on your subject, and therein lies the rub, or *there's the rub,* if I am to quote Hamlet's soliloquy correctly.'

'Wasn't Hamlet contemplating suicide? Are you suggesting it would be academic suicide to publish, Andrés?' Tom asked curiously.

'Well, as an ardent Shakespeare scholar, I first need to clarify that Hamlet was seeking the easy way out. You will recall that he was reflecting upon that unknown state of death, from which none have returned. He imagines that to die is to *sleep and perchance to dream*, and *in that sleep of death, what dreams may come*. Yours is not the easy way. I was alluding to the behaviour of those in the academic machine, pressured to publish. The *rub*, or obstacle to overcome here, is the pressurised conveyor belt of endless academic publications. At the top of the academic world, it's a private club. You scratch my back and cite my papers, and I will cite yours. The consequence is that unless this false roadblock and the gang of perpetrators is removed, the frontier of growing knowledge remains stunted and halted!'

'Just think of some of the ridiculous stories: *Ra on his Sun boat on a journey through the underworld!* Thanks to Tom, we've now understood that each and every hat carved into the walls of Karnak, and in friezes in the vast underground *shelters* in the valley of the Kings, describes a pattern of solar wind as seen from the Earth at different times of the year. We alone are the only ones on this planet who recognise that those walls were carved or painted at least 11,500 years ago.'

'Now pause for a moment to consider the thousands of Egyptologists and Historians who certainly won't be bothered to learn anything new, and they definitely won't be prepared to learn any astrophysics. They've been on the gravy train all their lives; many are almost up for retirement. Yes it's a travesty and a scandal, but those academics will absolve themselves of any need to absorb any fragment of the sound entirety of this data. Their arrogance will be their defence mechanism. Data describing a new history will simply be dismissed out of hand, rather than require them to confront their knowledge which is now proven to be based on fairy stories. The resistance will be absolute! The same question will always arise. How did so many people end up making up so much rubbish, rather than seeking a single comprehensive solution?'

'Remember, it's those people in power in academia who control the World's knowledge. They will feel vulnerable. Chad and Tom, you can understand that. You're both academics. If you have learned a whole false narrative all your life, and published that same narrative, albeit unquestioningly, in hundreds of papers, you can imagine how suddenly disappointed you would feel. It's worth adding that if students would just learn something verbatim without applying any scientific rigour and copy-paste it into a piece of research, they would be accused of plagiarism, and rightly so. Apparently that doesn't apply to many academics holding leading positions in academia. Their knowledge is unquestionable. Nevertheless, there is a real opportunity here, because it is *those same academics who stand the most to gain*, who from the new vantagepoint, their deep and comprehensive knowledge in each and every field would make them *capable of making substantial contributions to the true narrative* that we have discovered. I guess I would agree with that aspect, and it should certainly inspire a vigorous new purpose in their research, after it is convincingly back on the new and correct track.'

Andrés stood up and leaned with his back against the bamboo balustrade at the front of the decking. Tom and Chad had become quite subdued by Andrés' arguments. He continued to set out the reasons why he had never published, conclusions he had reached after a long struggle, which he had coined earlier as *the moment when ambition and wisdom hold hands*.

'Publishing this whole story demands weighing up the counterbalancing emotions. I eventually decided that the *uncomfortable nausea* which people would feel, when they learned that they had been taught *a completely false explanation of Earth's history as fact,* outweighed my desire to publish the answer to describe so many of the Earth's unexplained mysteries. The masses seek reassurance and surety. They will desperately want to cling on to what they had been taught as their framework of understanding, however incorrect that may be. Remember *Bruno,* who was burned at the stake in Rome in 1600 for suggesting that the stars were distant suns with their own planets where there was possibly life. His challenge to the *heliocentric* Universe was blasphemy. The World was not ready for such radical thinking, however true the scientific construct.'

'Finally, also think back to your own school days. Most of the archetypal characters in this conflict between knowledge, learning and teaching are all found there. Faced with a totally new history which will both inspire and shock, the teacher of *fables of history* can either struggle to grasp and inspire the next generation with the real data, or continue to plod along the well-trodden path, however erroneous that route is. Teachers teach what they've been taught. Only the best of teachers will ever dare take the road less-travelled. *Always being right* is an essential craft for many teachers in front of their students. Many possess a plethora of sarcastic comments to silence any student who might even dare challenge the status quo. They surely won't be exposed as purveyors of untruths, but now imagine how the bright young minds in the class will react. I'm pretty convinced that many students will become inspired with new purpose, and will want to eagerly join the chase to seek out the new knowledge.

What better incentive for students, to have the chance to better both their peers, and their teachers. A student's mind is open to learning, while the teacher is constantly focusing down on presenting the same old general body of material. Teachers have never questioned the *sacred knowledge*. How could they realistically learn a totally new perspective? Who will write the new syllabus? Who will write the replacement books and create the new multimedia learning material? More importantly, who will re-train the thousands of history, archaeology, Egyptology, and even perhaps astrophysics lecturers? I dare not even think of all those students who have paid extortionate fees to Universities to be taught *fables of Egyptology*, history and archaeology. Some may feel lied to. They will realise that they have studied courses of *myths and fables*, all based on unsubstantiated rubbish. All these people will have an axe to grind should you dare to publish. I am only trying to warn you that it's much easier to maintain the status quo and continue to pretend that we understand everything, rather than face the hard truth that in 12,870 B.C.E. a Wolf-Rayet star collapsed, went into hypernova, and caused all these arduous consequences for life on our planet.'

'I have to confess that I totally agree with your reasoning,' Tom remarked sincerely. 'Even the comment about astrophysicists is valid. We all live and work in silos. Few of us understand even a fragment of the whole field, and we're just as guilty of a dereliction of duty here. There's no excuse for failing to translate the astrophysics carved all over the temple of Karnak, or for failing to model the effects of a relativistic jet transit. We all pride ourselves in being absolute experts in every aspect of our own small jigsaw puzzle piece of astrophysics, yet each of us struggles to build a comprehensive holistic model of the entire field.'

'Well, I think you have a different attitude, Tom. You have made a remarkable contribution to decoding this whole story and providing a convincing argument for the existence of the Giza pyramids,' Andrés added.

'Wait!' Tom exclaimed. 'There are other Giza pyramids on the east side of the Giza Plateau! We have forgotten to check them. They surely play a part here also! They could now confirm this whole warning message. They are substantially less-durable structures than the Giza pyramids but there just has to be a connection with this whole story!'

'Wow Tom! That would be the ultimate layer of icing on the cake if we could prove it!' Chad remarked excitedly.

Tom quickly took out his laptop and booted up *Google Earth*. Zooming into Egypt and Cairo, he then located the three pyramids. He next selected a search function and highlighted the other pyramids to the south-east of Giza.

'OK, so if these three Giza pyramids represent the three remaining stars of *gamma Velorum*, what is the relationship between this string of nine or so pyramids to *gamma Velorum*? They must be in the starfield in 10,700 C.E.'

Tom then took a screenshot of the desert and copy pasted it into Word. Next, he drew rings around each of the pyramids to create a semi-transparent overlay.

'This is crazy. You know our story will be indisputable if we find a match now. Remember, all stars have their own independent *proper motion* with respect to each other. We are potentially seeking out future positions of stars near to *gamma Velorum*, in 8,700 years' time, which we are suggesting must have been computed more than 15,000 years ago! Remember, these stars are invisible without a telescope and computing *stellar proper motions* requires prolonged observations of the stars and of course powerful *computers*!'

'That's an amazing suggestion to link those other pyramids with the starfield. You are unbelievable!' Andrés murmured. 'But what if it's true?'

Next, Tom opened *Stellarium*, selected Egypt, and located *gamma Velorum*, then ran the clock forward to 10,700 C.E. Sure enough, there they were: nine stars with a similar configuration as the pyramids. He took a screen shot of the *gamma Velorum* starfield and made it a backdrop under his semi-transparent pyramid map overlay. The match was uncanny.

'QED,' Tom whispered. He then zoomed into the Google Earth image. 'And look, there's also something in the desert at that second star's location.'

Moments later he had combined all the images side by side.

'It's absolutely true then,' Chad confirmed in a slow low voice. 'The message is real. A previous civilisation was really lost, and this is the warning message they sent, and we've cracked it!'

The three of them remained in a very subdued silence for a long while, before Chad finally spoke again.

'Listen, I have an idea. We can go a different route. We could write

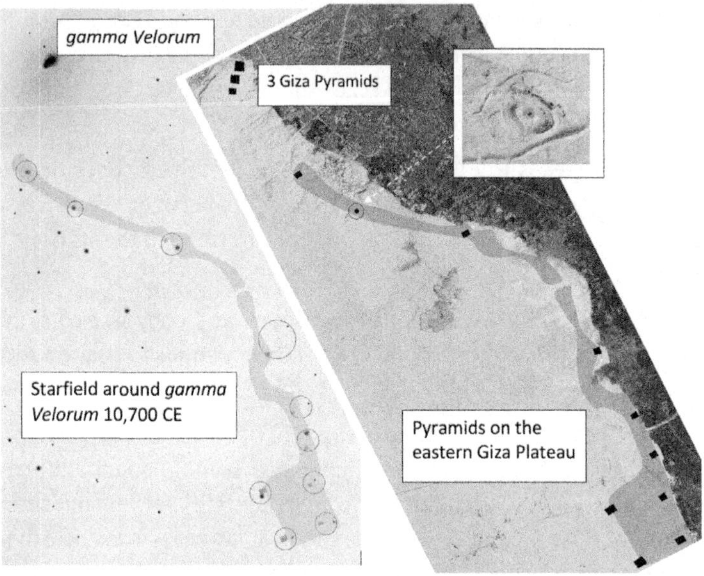

Gamma Velorum Starfield 10,700 C.E. and the Giza Plateau Pyramids

an anonymous novel, telling the whole story. We could create some characters in the novel, who stumble upon the climate data evidence, which then helps them work out that the Earth was hit by a gamma ray burst and then suffered the effects of a relativistic jet transit some 3000 years or so later. These characters could come from all the key academic disciplines and then travel around the World and discover all the survival structures, which show how descendants of a previous civilization struggled and endured the jet transit for 880 years. They could then discover the significance of the stone circles, the worldwide prevalence of dolmen shelters, and underground cities, and structures with similar spiral carvings and cave art. They then end up discovering *the invention of the calendar*, where man needed to construct all manner of stone circles to track time highly accurately and thus be able to identify a segment of the Earth's orbit precisely. This gave them the essential knowledge of where the Earth was along its orbit relative to the deadly flux of the spiral of solar wind, which impacted the Earth, and when to take cover for 14 days, rather than the shifting equinoxes and solstices.'

'Well, you know, that might even work,' Andrés murmured. 'They could even stumble across a wily old character in Costa Rica, who would help them tie all the loose ends together.'

Chad continued. 'Finally, they discover the relationship between the pyramid shape on the ground and the pyramid of stars, *the fire within*, in the sky, and thus why the pyramids were built in the first place, and how *Khufu* in Giza marks out the location of *gamma Velorum* to a remarkable accuracy on a particular date in 9750 B.C.E. From there they make the connection with the three-pyramid layout, and the changing formation of the three stars within *gamma Velorum* and thus decode the warning of the next doomsday event of 10,700 C.E.'

'They would certainly travel to Costa Rica and add all your work Andrés, in particular the cities of *Sechin Baco, Palenque, and Tenochtitlan*, which show that a previous civilization had made an effort to record the configuration of gamma Velorum at the time of the gamma ray burst of 12780 B.C.E. also.'

'It won't be possible to cover absolutely everything, but many readers will become intrigued and follow up on all the evidence. Perhaps even more data will come from the Dogon culture. I also predict that experts will eventually decode the rest of the data on the monoliths in Bolivia, and others will excavate more of the Göbekli Tepe structures. Certainly, more of the stone circles will eventually reveal their secrets, culminating in the absolute conclusion that *none* of them predate any others. It will become increasingly obvious that *all* the stone circles around the World were built as tools to monitor the passage of time during a particular epoch, and they are *all, every single one of them*, from *Tiwanaku* in Bolivia, to *Carahunge* in Armenia, they are *all* from exactly the same 880 year era!'

'You know, I am known for being a bit cynical, but you are starting to convince even me Chad. It's a very positive idea, to get the story out there anonymously. I agree that it will inspire a huge exodus to check the evidence for themselves. Slowly but surely, a new generation of people will realise the sobering truth, that instead of the novel being just a work of fiction, they will discover that everything in it turns out to be absolutely true! They will find that it is all fact, based on solid indisputable evidence,' Tom reasoned.

'OK, I can agree with this,' Andrés remarked. 'A novel would work. In fact, I have to admit, it's a brilliant way to get this important story out.'

'You know, the more I think about this, I'm pretty sure in the academic world, it might even inspire academics to become more careful and critical about just citing previous work without seriously evaluating the foundations of the science it purports to represent. It could finally evoke a new era of *kicking the tires,*' Tom replied.

'I'm also pretty sure that Jeanette and Mary-Anne would really support this initiative of a novel also,' Chad remarked. 'They both have very strong views on the anthropological aspects. Mary-Anne has developed her thinking quite far. She recently said that they were reappraising how society *of our current era*, must have evolved during the 880 years of the relativistic jet transit. During the 3000 years after the gamma ray burst, our global civilization most likely comprised less-sophisticated, but equally intelligent, hunter gatherers feeding off the land, and from hunting and eating large mammals. These people probably lived in small, isolated groups, with a lower need for support and interdependency. Then, with the transit of the calamitous relativistic jet, which impacted every aspect of their lives for 30 generations or more, they suddenly needed to forge inter-community bonds. They needed to start to care for one another, and to become able to coexist in small, confined spaces of caves and dolmen shelters for weeks at a time. This was most definitely a *society-changing* paradigm shift, which had a huge impact on the way we interacted as a civilization and one which led consequently to a tremendous change in the way humans lived together.'

'The bottom line here is that we need to confront the ethical question. I believe that hiding the evidence which tells the truth, is actually denying everybody their right to know where we all came from, and more importantly how life on this planet survived. It hopefully will inspire a serious appreciation of our ancestors who strived so hard to save us, and keep planet Earth alive,' Chad reasoned. "Forewarning everyone of what will happen again around 10,700 C.E. is absolutely imperative.'

"OK, so do we have a name for the novel, if we academics aren't allowed to tell the story? What title would convey that, if it wasn't us?' Tom asked curiously, sounding much more positive.

Chad was quiet for a moment and then his eyes fell upon the menacing open mouth of the viper inside the bottle of habushu.

'If we're not permitted to tell this story, a good title which hints at this terrible episode that the peoples of Earth endured, would be ... *And So the Snake Spoke*.'

Annex

Bibliography

Gamma Ray Bursts and Wolf-Rayet Stars

Ahlers M. et al., Neutrino Fluence from Gamma-Ray Bursts: Off-Axis View of Structured Jets, Mon. Not. R. Astron. Soc. 490, Issue 4, pp 4935-4943 (2019)

Aloy M. et al., Stability analysis of relativistic jets from collapsars and its implications on the short-term variability of gamma-ray bursts, A&A 396, 693–703 (August 2002)

Araudo et al., Gamma-ray emission from Wolf-Rayet stars interacting with AGN jets Proc. 5th Int. Symp. High-Energy Gamma-Ray Astronomy, Heidelberg, July 9-13, 2012

Blustin A., Shock break-out: how a GRB revealed the beginnings of a supernova Philosophical Transactions of the Royal Society A, Vol 365, Issue 1854, 15 May 2007

Callingham et al., Anisotropic winds in a Wolf–Rayet binary identify a potential gamma-ray burst progenitor, Nature Astronomy 3, 82-87 (2019)

Campana, S. et al., The association of GRB 060218 with a supernova and the evolution of the shock wave. Nature. 442 (7102) 1008-1010. 10.1038/nature04892. August 2006

Celotti A et al., The kinetic power and luminosity of parsec-scale radio jets – an argument for heavy jets, Mon. Not. R. Astron. Soc. 264, 228-236 (1993)

Cenko S. et al., Afterglow Observations Of Fermi-Lat Gamma-Ray Bursts And The Emerging Class Of Hyper-Energetic Events. The Astrophysical Journal 732(1):29, April 2011

Cerutti et al., High-Energy Radiation from the Relativistic Jet of Cygnus X-3, Proc. of SF2A Marseille 21-24 June 2010; https://arxiv.org/abs/1007.2064

Chaparro M. et al., Palaeomagnetic secular variation and rock-magnetic studies of Holocene sediments from a maar lake (Hoya de San Nicolas) in Central Mexico Geophys. J. Int. (2008) 175, 462–476, December 14 2007

Crowther P., Physical Properties of Wolf-Rayet Stars, Annual Review of Astronomy & Astrophysics, vol. 45, Issue 1, pp.177-219, September 2007

Domainko W., Finding short GRB remnants in globular clusters: the VHE gamma-ray source in Terzan 5, A&A 533, L5 (2011)

Ejzak L. et al., Terrestrial Consequences Of Spectral And Temporal Variability In Ionizing Photon Events, The Astrophysical Journal, Volume 654(1) 10.1086/509106. April 2006

Fruchter, A. et al., Long-ray bursts and core-collapse supernovae have different environments. Nature. 441 (7092). 463-468. 10.1038/nature04787. May 2006

Ghisellini G, et al., The power of relativistic jets is larger than the luminosity of their accretion disks, Nature volume 515, pages 376–378 (20 November 2014)

Goldstein A. et al., A New Derivation of GRB Jet Opening Angles from the Prompt Gamma-Ray Emission, arXiv:1101.2458 - 12 Jan 2011

Granot A et al., Relativistic shock breakout from a stellar wind, Mon. Not. R. Astron. Soc. 476, Issue 4, p5453-5463 (2018)

Nagakura H., The Propagation Of Neutrino-Driven Jets In Wolf-Rayet Stars The Astrophysical Journal Volume 764(2) April 2013

Hockey T. et al., (2010), Public reaction to a V= -12.5 Supernova, The Observatory, 130(3) 167

Lamb G. et al., Short GRB 160821B: a reverse shock, a refreshed shock, and a well-sampled kilonova, The Astrophysical Journal, Volume 883, Issue 1, article id 48, 12 pp (2019)

Lu W. and Smoot G., Probing Massive Stars Around Gamma-Ray Burst Progenitors Mon. Not. R. Astron. Soc. 453, Issue 2, (2015)

MacFadyen A. et al., Supernovae, Jets, and Collapsars, The Astrophysical Journal, Volume 550, Issue 1, 410-425, March 20, 2001

Mbarek R. et al., Bottom-up Acceleration of Ultra-High-Energy Cosmic Rays in the Jets of Active Galactic Nuclei, The Astrophysical Journal, Vol 886 (1) Nov. 13 2019

McBreen S, et al., Optical and near-infrared follow-up observations of four Fermi /LAT GRBs: redshifts, afterglows, energetics, and host galaxies, A&A 516, A71 (2010)

Medvedev M. et al., Generation Of Magnetic Fields In The Relativistic Shock Of Gamma-Ray Burst Sources, The Astrophysical Journal, 526:697È706, 1999 December 1

Melott, A.L. et al. (2003). Did a gamma-ray burst initiate the late Ordovician mass extinction? International Journal of Astrobiology. 3. 10.1017/S1473550404001910. September 2003

Mignione A. et al., (2012) The Pluto Code for Adaptive Mesh Computations in Astrophysical Fluid Dynamics, The Astrophysical Journal Supplement Series, 198:7 (31pp), 2012 January

Nakauchi D. et al., Blue Supergiant Model For Ultra-Long Gamma-Ray Burst With Superluminous-Supernova-Like Bump The Astrophysical Journal, Volume 778:67 (11pp) November 20, 2013

Ramirez-Ruiz E. et al., Winds from massive stars: implications for the afterglows of γ -ray bursts, Mon. Not. R. Astron. Soc. 327, Issue 3, 829-840 (2001)

Scalo J. and Wheeler J., Astrophysical And Astrobiological Implications Of Gamma-Ray Burst Properties, The Astrophysical Journal, Volume 566, Issue 2, 723-737, February 20, 2002

Stanek K. et al., Protecting Life in the Milky Way: Metals Keep the GRBs Away Acta Astronomica, Vol. 56, pp.333-345, December 2006

Woosley S. et al., The Supernova–Gamma-Ray Burst Connection, Annual Review of Astronomy and Astrophysics, Vol. 44:507-556 (September 22, 2006)

Zhang W. et al., The Propagation And Eruption Of Relativistic Jets From The Stellar Progenitors Of GRBs, The Astrophysical Journal, Volume 608, Issue 1, pp. 365-377, June 10, 2004

Zhang W. et al., Relativistic Jets in Collapsars, Gamma-Ray Burst And Afterglow Astronomy 2001: A Workshop Celebrating the First Year of the HETE Mission. AIP Conference Proceedings, Volume 662, pp. 226-228 (2003).

Göbekli Tepe

Banning E., 2011. So Fair a House: Göbekli Tepe and the Identification of Temples in the Pre-Pottery Neolithic of the Near East, Current Anthropology, Vol. 52, No. 5, Oct. 2011, pp. 619-660

Heun M. et al., 1997. Site of Einkorn Wheat Domestication Identified by DNA. Science 278: 1312-1314.

Hodder I., editor. Religion, History, and Place in the Origin of Settled Life. University Press of Colorado, 2018. JSTOR, www.jstor.org/stable/j.ctv3c0thf.

Kislev E., 1984. Emergence of Wheat Agriculture, Paléorient, Vol. 10/2 pp61-70-1984 doi : https://doi.org/10.3406/paleo.1984.940

Peters J. & Schmidt K. 2004. – Animals in the symbolic world of Pre-Pottery Neolithic Göbekli Tepe, south-eastern Turkey: a preliminary assessment. Anthropozoologica 39 (1) :179-218.

Schmidt K., 1998. Beyond Daily Bread: Evidence of Early Neolithic Ritual from Göbekli Tepe, Neo-Lithics 2/98, A Newsletter of Southwest Asian Lithics Research, ex oriente Berlin ISSN 1434-6990.

Schmidt K., 1999. Boars, ducks, and foxes: the Urfa-Project 99. Neo-Lithics 3/99:12–15

Schmidt K., 2005. "Ritual centers" and the Neolithisation of upper Mesopotamia. Neo-Lithics 2/05:13–21.

Earth Science & Megafaunal Extinctions

Clayton et al., Silica Glass from the Libyan Desert, Geographical Journal, vol. 82, pp 375-377, October 1933

Cuffey et al., Temperature, accumulation, and ice sheet elevation in central Greenland through the last deglacial transition, Journal of Geophysical Research, vol. 102 No. C12 pp 26,383-26,396. Nov. 30 1997

Galetti et al., Ecological and evolutionary legacy of megafauna extinctions Biological Review 93(2):845-862, May 2018

Haines et al., Pleistocene glass in the Australian desert: The case for an impact origin. Geology 29(10):899–902 · October 2001

Nami, Hugo G., Paleoamerican Occupation, Stone Tools from the Cueva del Medio, and Considerations for the Late Pleistocene Archaeology in Southern South America Quaternary 2019, 2, 28 doi:10,3390/quat2030028 August 2019

Owen-Smith, Megafaunal Extinctions: The Conservation Message from

11,000 Years B.P., Conservation Biology 3 (4): 405-412 December 1989

Australian Indigenous Peoples, Anthropology & Sociology

Beattie, J. (1966), Ritual and social change, (The Malinowski Memorial Lecture, 1965), Man n.s., Vol. I, no. 1, pp. 60-74.

Bhathal, Ragbir and Graeme White (1991), Under the Southern Cross: a brief history of astronomy in Australia, Kangaroo Press, Kenthurst.

Dean, John (1979), Controversy over classification: a case study from the history of botany in Barry Barnes and Steven Shapin (1979), Natural order, historical studies of scientific culture, Sage Publications, Beverly Hills, London.

Elkin, A.P. (1974), The Australian Aborigines, Angus and Robertson, Sydney (first published 1938).

Hamacher et al., Twin Suns in Australian Aboriginal Traditions Journal of Astronomical History & Heritage 21(2&3), 107-114 (2018)

Harrison, Edward (1985), Masks of the universe, Macmillan and Collier Macmillan, New York, London.

Horton, R. (1971), African traditional thought and western science in M.F.D. Young (ed.), Knowledge and control: new directions for the sociology of education, Collier-Macmillan, London. Africa, 37 (1967) p 50.

Johnson D., (1998) Night Skies of Aboriginal Australia, A Noctuary, Oceania Publications, Reprint Sydney University Press ISBN 9781743323878

Kelly, L., 2015. Knowledge and Power in Prehistoric Societies Orality, Memory and the Transmission of Culture. Cambridge, Cambridge University Press. ISBN 9781107444973

Kovac, The Maya Myth about two Suns Journal of the Slovak Association for the Study of Religions, Comenius University, Bratislava, Axis Mundi 1 2014 pp13-21

Lewis, David (1976), Observations on route finding among the Aboriginal people of the western desert region of central Australia, Oceania 46 (4).

Lowe, P. et al. (1990), Jilji life in the Great Sandy Desert, Magabala Books, Broome.

MacPherson, Peter (1881), Astronomy of the Australian Aborigines, Journal and proceedings of the Royal Society of NSW Vol 15.

Maddock, Kenneth (1975), The emu anomaly in L.R. Hiatt (ed.) Australian

Aboriginal mythology, Australian Institute of Aboriginal Studies, Canberra.

Maegraith, B.G. (1932), The astronomy of the Aranda and Loritja tribes, Adelaide University Field Anthropology No 10, Transactions of the Royal Society of South Australia Vol 56.

Mountford, Charles, P. (1956), Arnhem Land: art, myth and symbolism in Records of the American-Australian scientific expedition to Arnhem Land, Vol 1, Melbourne University Press, Melbourne.

Mountford, Charles, P. (1976a), Before time began: legends of the Dreamtime, Thomas Nelson, West Melbourne.

Mountford, Charles, P. (1976b), Nomads of the Australian desert, Rigby, Adelaide.

Radcliffe-Brown A.R. 1926 The rainbow-serpent myth of Australia Journal of the Anthropological Institute of Great Britain and Ireland 56:19-25

Shapin, S. (1979), Homo Phrenologicus: anthropological perspectives on an historical problem, edited by Barry Barnes and Steven Shapin (1979), Natural order, historical studies of scientific culture, Sage Publications, Beverley Hills, London. OCLC 4495674

Stanner, W.E.H. (1991), The Dreaming in W.H. Edwards (ed.), Traditional Aboriginal society: a reader, Macmillan, South Melbourne, Crows Nest (first published 1956).

Sullivan S. et al., Shades of the Rainbow Serpent? A KhoeSan Animal between Myth and Landscape in Southern Africa-Ethnographic Contextualisations of Rock Art Representations. Arts 2014, 3, 215-244; doi:10.3390/arts3020215

Tacon P. Rainbow Colour and Power among the Waanyi of Northwest Queensland. Cambridge Archaeological Journal, vol 18 (02), pp 163-176 doi:10.1017/S0959774308000231 June 2008

Tacon P et al., Birth of the Rainbow Serpent in Arnhem Land rock art and oral history, Archaeology in Oceania, Vol. 31. pp103-124 (1996)

Tyler, Stephen A (1969), Cognitive Anthropology, Holt, Rinehart and Winston Inc, New York.

Willey, Keith (1979), When the sky fell down: the destruction of the Sydney region 1788–1850s, Collins, Sydney, London.

Worms, Ernest Alfred (1986), Australian Aboriginal religions, Spectrum

Publications, Richmond (first published 1968).

Other

Bok et al., Biological Sunscreens Tune Polychromatic Ultraviolet Vision in Mantis Shrimp. Current Biology Vol 24, Issue 14, pp1636-1642 July 21, 2014 http://dx.doi.org/10.1016/j.cub.2014.05.071

George et al., The Epic of Gilgamesh (Penguin Classics) Paperback – 5 Dec. 2002 (ISBN: 8601400348055)

Maccone C., Innovative SETI by the KLT. SETI Permanent Study Group, International Academy of Astronautics (IAA) 12 June 2007

Mémoires de L'Institut Royal de France, Académie des Inscriptions et Belles-Lettres, Tome seizième, Paris, Imprimerie Royale, 1846

Dumersan M., Notice sur le Zodiaque de Dendera, Paris, Imprimerie de Hocquet, rue du faubourg, Montmartre n. 4. pp 42 1824

Wargent J. et al., From ozone depletion to agriculture: understanding the role of UV radiation in sustainable crop production, Tansley Review, New Phytologist (2013) 197: 1058-1076

Wolbach W. et al., Extraordinary Biomass-Burning Episode and Impact Winter Triggered by the Younger Dryas Cosmic Impact ~12,800 Years Ago. The Journal of Geology, 2018, volume 126, The University of Chicago. DOI: 10.1086/695704

Holliday V, et al., (2016) A Blind Test of the Younger Dryas Impact Hypothesis. PLoS ONE 11(7): e0155470. https://doi.org/10.1371/journal.pone.0155470, July 8th, 2016

Sweatman M. et al., Decoding European Palaeolithic art: Extremely ancient knowledge of precession of the equinoxes, Athens Journal of History - Volume 5, Issue 1 - Pages 1-30, January 2019.

Haas M. et al., Domestication and crop evolution of wheat and barley: Genes, genomics, and future directions, Journal of Integrative Plant Biology, JIPB, March 2019 | Volume 61 | Issue 3 | 204-225.

Norris, R, et al. 2013, Wurdi Youang-an Australian Aboriginal stone arrangement with possible solar indications, Rock Art Research, Vol. 30(1), pp. 55-65.pdf

Tuthill P. et al., The prototype colliding-wind pinwheel WR 104, The Astrophysical Journal 675(1):69, December 2008

Callingham J. et al., Two Wolf-Rayet stars at the heart of colliding-wind binary Apep, Mon. Not. R. Astron. Soc. 459(3), May 2020

Berio A., The Celestial River: Identifying the Ancient Egyptian Constellations, Sino-Platonic Papers 253, pp61, December 2014

Griaule, M. Conversations with Ogotemmeli: An Introduction to Dogon Religious Ideas. London: Oxford University Press, 1965.

Griaule, M. et al., Le Renard Pâle. Paris: Institut d'Ethnologie, 1965 OCLC 654702283

Chené A. et al., The First Determination of the Rotation Rates of Wolf-Rayet Stars, Proc. IAU Symposium No. 250, 2007

Jouzel J., A brief history of ice core science over the last 50 yr, Clim. Past, 9, 2525-2547, 2013

Korte M. et al., Magnetic poles and dipole tilt variation over the past decades to millennia, Earth Planets Space, 60, 937-948, 2008

Liritzis I. et al., Aurorae And Archaeomagnetism from the 1st Millennium B.C. China, Greece And Italy: A Brief Overview And Critical Assessment, Mediterranean Archaeology and Archaeometry, Vol. 17, No 3, (2017), pp. 273-300

Moll R. et al., Kink instabilities in jets from rotating magnetic fields, Astron. Astrophys. 492 (2008) 621 September 18th, 2008

Printed in Great Britain
by Amazon

36092009R00314